n-Michel Guenassia was born in Algeria, 1950. His novel,
Incorrigible Optimists Club, won the prestigious Prix Goncourt
Lycéens. He is a prolific screenwriter and lives in France.

The
Incorrigible Optimists
Club

JEAN-MICHEL GUENASSIA

Translated from the French
by Euan Cameron

ATLANTIC BOOKS
London

First published in France as *Le Club des Incorrigibles Optimistes* in 2011
by Editions Albin Michel.

First published in Great Britain in 2014 by Atlantic Books,
an imprint of Atlantic Books Ltd.

10 9 8 7 6 5 4 3 2 1

A CIP catalogue record for this book is available from the British Library.

Trade Paperback ISBN: 978 1 84887 541 8
E-book ISBN: 978 1 78239 404 4

Printed by ScandBook AB, Sweden

Atlantic Books
An Imprint of Atlantic Books Ltd
Ormond House
26–27 Boswell Street
London
WC1N 3JZ

www.atlantic-books.co.uk

For Dominique and for Andrée

Translator's note

Some readers may be puzzled by the term 'baby-foot', a *faux anglicisme* for the football game played so remorselessly yet so effectively by Michel and many of his contemporaries in this novel. Known variously in different parts of the world as 'table football', 'kicker' or 'foosball', in France 'baby-foot' has its own federation, tournaments and rules. In the Paris of the 1960s the game became a craze and no self-respecting café could be without a 'baby-foot' table or two.

I should like to express my particular gratitude to Sara Holloway for her sensitive editing of my text. My thanks, too, to various friends who have offered suggestions or advice on specialized terms used in the translation: Irina Brown, Mark Eisenthal, Ben Faccini, Hélène Fiamma, Jeremy James, Agnès Liebaert, Nelly Munthe, Joséphine Séblon. I should also like to thank Adélaïde Fabre, Julie Etienne and their colleagues at the Villa Gillet in Lyon for their kindness and hospitality during the month I spent there working on this translation.

Club: *Klub*/noun; a place at which one meets for social, political, athletic or other ends. [Middle English]

I prefer to live as an optimist and be wrong, than live as a pessimist and be always right.

ANONYMOUS

APRIL 1980

A writer is being buried today. It's like a final demonstration: an unexpected crowd – silent, respectful and anarchic – is blocking the streets and the boulevards around the Montparnasse cemetery. How many are there? Thirty thousand? Fifty thousand? Fewer? More? Whatever they say, it's important to have a lot of people at one's funeral. If anybody had told him that there would be such a multitude, he wouldn't have believed them. It would have made him laugh. It's not a question that can have concerned him much. He expected to be buried hastily, with twelve faithful mourners, not with the honours of a Hugo or a Tolstoy. Never in the past half-century have so many people paid tribute to an intellectual. Anyone would think he was indispensable or had had unanimous support. Why are they here, all of them? Given what they know about him, they ought not to have come. How absurd to pay homage to a man who was wrong about almost everything, was constantly misled, and who put his talents into defending the indefensible with conviction. They would have done better to attend the funerals of those who were right, whom he had despised and poured scorn on. No one went out of their way for them.

And yet, behind these failures, there was something else, something admirable about this little man, about his passionate desire to force the hand of destiny with his mind, to press on in the face of all logic, not to give up in spite of certain defeat, to accept the contradictions of a just cause and a battle that was lost beforehand, of an eternal struggle, constantly repeated and without resolution. It's impossible to get inside the cemetery, where they are trampling over graves, climbing on top of monuments and knocking over tombstones in order to get closer and see the coffin. You would think it was the burial of a pop star or a saint. But it's not just a man they are interring: an old idea is being entombed with him. Nothing will change and we know that. There will not be a better society.

You either accept it or you don't. We have one foot in the grave here, what with our beliefs and our vanished illusions. This is the multitude as absolution for wrongs committed out of idealism. For the victims, nothing is changed. For them there will be neither apologies, nor reparation, nor a first-class burial. What could be worse than to do harm when you intended to do good? It is a bygone era that is being taken to the grave. It's not easy to live in a world without hope.

At this moment, no one is settling scores. No one is taking stock. We are all equally to blame and we are all wrong. I've not come because of the thinker. I've never understood his philosophy, his plays are heavy going and, as for his novels, I've forgotten them. I've come for the sake of old memories. But the throng has reminded me who he was. You can't mourn a hero who supported the oppressors. I make an about-turn. I shall bury him in a corner of my mind.

There are disreputable districts that take you back to your past and where it's best not to loiter. You think you've forgotten it because you don't think about it, but all it wants is to come back. I avoided Montparnasse. There were ghosts there I didn't know what to do with. I saw one of them straight ahead of me in the side road that runs beside boulevard Raspail. I recognized his inimitable pale-striped overcoat, Humphrey Bogart 1950s-style. There are some men you can spot from the way they walk. Pavel Cibulka, orthodox, partisan, king of the great ideological divide and two-a-penny jokes, haughty and proud in his bearing, was striding along unhurriedly. I overtook him. He had grown stouter and could no longer button up his overcoat. His tousled white hair made him look like an artist.

'Pavel.'

He stopped, looked me up and down. He searched his memory for where he had seen this face. Surely I conjured up a vague recollection. He shook his head. I did not remind him of anything.

'It's me… Michel. Do you remember?'

He gazed at me, incredulous, still suspicious.

'Michel?… Little Michel?'

4

'Enough of that, I'm taller than you.'

'Little Michel!... How long has it been?'

'The last time we saw each other was here, for Sacha. That's fifteen years ago.'

We stood there in silence, confused by our memories. We fell into one another's arms. He clasped me tightly.

'I wouldn't have recognized you.'

'You haven't changed.'

'Don't make fun of me. I've put on a hundred kilos. Due to dieting.'

'I'm glad to see you again. Aren't the others with you? Did you come on your own?'

'I'm off to work. I'm not retired.'

His Bohemian drawl had become even more pronounced. We went to the Select, a brasserie where everyone behaved as though they knew him. Hardly had we sat down than the waiter, without his having asked for anything, brought him a strong coffee with a jug of cold milk then took my order. Pavel leant over to grab hold of the basket full of croissants from the next table and gleefully wolfed down three of them, talking with immense elegance and with his mouth full. Pavel had fled Czechoslovakia almost thirty years ago and lived in France in precarious circumstances. He had escaped in the nick of time from the purge that had removed Slansky, the former Secretary-General of the Communist Party, and Clementis, his Minister for Foreign Affairs, with whom he had worked closely. A former ambassador to Bulgaria and author of a reference work, *The Treaty of Brest-Litovsk: Diplomacy and Revolution*, which no Paris publisher wanted, Pavel was the nightwatchman in a hotel in Saint-Germain-des-Prés, where he lived in a small room on the top floor. He hoped to find his elder brother, who had made his way to the United States at the end of the war, and he was waiting for an American visa, which was refused him on account of his past.

'They're not going to give me my visa. I won't see my brother again.'

'I know an attaché at the embassy. I can talk to him about it.'

'Don't bother. I've got a folder that's as plump as I am. Apparently, I'm one of the founders of the Czechoslovak Communist Party.'

5

'Is it true?'

He shrugged his shoulders resignedly.

'When you were a student in Prague in the thirties, the alternative was clear. You were either for the exploiters, or for the exploited. I didn't choose sides. I was born into one. I was young, convinced that we were right and that there was no other solution for our country. It's true: I was one of the leaders of the party. I had a law degree. I believed that electricity and the education of the masses were going to give birth to a new man. We couldn't imagine that Communism was going to crush us. Capitalism would, we were sure of that. During the war, it was clear-cut. You either supported the Communists, or the Fascists. For those who had no opinion, it was their bad luck. We made enthusiastic progress. I never questioned myself. After the liberation, nothing happened as we had hoped. Today, they couldn't give a damn that my friends were hanged, or that my family was harassed until they disowned me. They're not interested in an old Commie, and I've decided to be a bloody nuisance. Every year, I submit a request for a visa. They refuse. It doesn't matter, I continue doing it.'

'Tell me, Pavel, are you no longer a Communist?'

'Still am and always will be!'

'It's a total disaster. It's collapsing everywhere.'

'Communism is a beautiful idea, Michel. The word comrade has a meaning. It's the men who are no good. If they had been given time, Dubcek and Svoboda would have got there. Mind you, my luck's beginning to change.'

'Why?'

'Well, believe it or not, I've written to Cyrus Vance, Jimmy Carter's Secretary of State. He's replied to me. Can you believe it?'

From out of his wallet, he carefully extracted a letter that was in its original envelope and handed it to me to read. Cyrus Vance was replying to his letter of 11 January 1979, telling him that he would forward it to the appropriate department.

'What do you reckon?' he asked.

'It's a standard reply. He's not exactly committing himself.'

6

'In twenty-five years, it's the first time they've done anything. It's an omen. Cyrus Vance is not a Republican, he's a Democrat.'

'Didn't you get a reply before?'

'I was an ass, I wrote to the President of the United States. He doesn't have time to reply to those who write to him. It was Imré who advised me to write to the Secretary of State.'

'You may well have knocked at the right door. If they refuse again, what are you going to do?'

'I'm no longer Czech. I'm not French. I'm stateless. It's the worst scenario. One doesn't exist. I do have a glimmer of hope of seeing my brother again. He's American. We phone once a year to wish each other a happy New Year. He's a foreman in the building trade. He has a family. He lives well. But he can't afford to come to Europe. I'll put in another request next year. And the following one.'

The brasserie had gradually filled up with a crowd of people who had come to take a break after the funeral. One group made its way over to our table. A woman tried to invade our bench.

'May I?'

'It's taken!'

The woman drew back, surprised by his aggressive tone. The little group moved away.

'God, it's like a bad dream! Did you see the bunch of idiots who have turned up for the old bugger? Are they screwed up or what?'

'He was a symbol.'

'I'd go and piss on his grave. He deserves nothing less. He's got nothing to be proud of.'

'He couldn't retract.'

'He knew. Ever since Gide and Rousset. I told him about Slansky and Clementis. He said nothing. He knew about Kravchenko. He condemned Kravchenko. How do you explain that? Howling with the pack. Despising the martyrs. Denying the truth. Isn't that being party to it? He was a shit.'

He remained pensive, his head bowed, his face tense.

'I'm in no position to preach; I shouldn't have said that.'

'I don't follow.'

7

'It's the least you can do, not to bite the hand that feeds you. We survived on the cash they handed out to us. Without them, we wouldn't have got by.'

'Who did hand out cash to you?'

Pavel gave me a sidelong glance as though I were playing the fool. He saw that I was being genuine.

'Both of them. Kessel and Sartre. They used their connections to get us translations, to get small jobs. They knew lots of people. They recommended us to magazines, to newspaper editors. We wrote stuff. If we were broke, they paid the landlord or the bailiffs. How would we have got by? We didn't have a bean. We'd lost everything. If they hadn't helped us, we would have ended up being homeless. It was harder when he became blind and he no longer left his home. Two years ago, they helped out Vladimir, do you remember him?'

'As though it were yesterday.'

'He had some problems.'

He was itching to tell me. In my mind's eye I could see Vladimir Gorenko in the rear room of the Balto, passing his food around.

'What became of Vladimir?'

'Before coming to the West, he was in charge of the oil wells in Odessa. When he arrived, he was given political refugee status. He didn't find work. No oil company wanted him. Even the people he knew and who had done business with him. Nobody lifted a finger to help him. Do you know why? They were frightened of Moscow. If they took him on, it would mean getting on the wrong side of them. They harped on about the Commies and they did business with them. Marcusot, the owner of the café, do you remember, he was a decent man, and he found him an attic room above a delicatessen in rue Daguerre. Vladimir looked after his accounts.

'He paid him in kind with sausages and cooked meals. Well, paying him is overstating it a bit, Vladimir complained because he gave him the leftovers he would otherwise have thrown away.

'We did well out of it. Vladimir shared everything with us. Other shopkeepers asked him to look after them. Gradually, he built up a clientele.

8

It was going well. It didn't please the accountants in the area, who complained. Vladimir has loads of good qualities except that he's a know-it-all. He's always right. He's not a diplomat, if you see what I mean. When the cops arrived, instead of playing dumb and keeping a low profile, he got annoyed and was high-handed with them: "I wasn't afraid of the KGB and I came out of Stalingrad alive, so I'm not scared of you. I work, I pay my taxes, so fuck you!" He wouldn't listen. He carried on in spite of the warnings. You won't believe me, but they put him in jail. For illegally practising the profession of chartered accountant. He argued with the examining magistrate. He was remanded in custody for four months. Can you believe it? A guy who speaks six or seven languages. They closed down his office. He went bankrupt. Who do you reckon helped him out? Kessel went to see the judge and Sartre paid the fine.'

'And what's he doing now?'

'He's working for the accountant who informed on him and he's got his customers back. He's not allowed to take his degree.'

'Sacha mentioned him once or twice. I hadn't realized they were helping you.'

'I didn't know you were a friend of Sacha's. I thought you were a friend of Igor's. No one liked Sacha. He was…'

Pavel stopped when he saw the way I was looking at him. We sat there in silence, amidst the hubbub, with the memories that had come back to haunt us.

'I was friends with both of them.'

'You couldn't be friends with both of them. It was impossible.'

'For me, it was possible. Sacha told me one day that Kessel had paid the rent on his attic room. He was late again and he didn't dare ask him.'

'Kessel had a kind heart. Right up to the end, until last year, he helped us out. You see, I can behave like a little shit, too. You shouldn't expect anything from anyone. You do the right thing and they spit in your face. I can't help it, I'm unable to forget what Sartre said, what he allowed to be said and, above all, what he didn't say. That's why we didn't much care for him. He was an arsehole, an armchair revolutionary. He was generous, but money doesn't make up for things.'

9

'I never noticed anything, throughout all those years. I was young. I had the impression that he liked you.'

'I used to tell him jokes. They made him laugh. He had such a good memory, and yet he never remembered them, and he would ask me to repeat them again.'

'I remember Leonid and his joke about Stalin and the sun.'

'Go on, tell it to me, I'd love to hear it again.'

'Wait, I'm trying to remember. One morning Stalin gets out of bed. It's a fine day. He speaks to the sun: "Sun, tell me who is the handsomest, the most intelligent, the strongest one of all?" The sun doesn't hesitate for a second: "It is you, O Stalin, light of the universe!" At midday, Stalin asks again: "Tell me Sun, who is the most brilliant, the greatest, the most outstanding man of all time?" The sun confirms: "It is you, O great Stalin." Before dinner, Stalin can't resist the pleasure of asking the sun once more who is the best Communist in the world. The sun replies: "You're just a nutcase, Stalin, a psychopath, a raging lunatic, so fuck you, I've now gone over to the West!"'

Pavel burst out laughing as though he were hearing it for the first time.

'You're no good at telling jokes. The French don't know how to tell them. When Leonid told it, it went on for an hour.'

'It's true. It was extraordinary. Do you really think he told it to Stalin?'

'That's what he said to me. Leonid's not the type to brag. You tell me — you were close to him, if I remember correctly?'

'Very close. I'd love to see him again.'

'And yet he loathed Sacha.'

'They had long-standing squabbles that no longer interest people. These days, they're not very important any more.'

He hesitated, said nothing, and shrugged his shoulders. He took another croissant.

'Are you paying?'

'By the way, your book on the treaty of Brest-Litovsk, was it ever published?'

'You're joking! I retranslated it, I rewrote it, I altered it, I shortened it. There was always a good reason. I had some interest from a young publisher. I'd reached 965 pages. He wanted me to cut 250 of them. I decided to drop it.'

'Tell me another joke, Pavel.'

'Do you know the difference between a rouble and a dollar?'

I had already heard this pointless joke. It may even have been he who told it to me fifteen years ago. I racked my brain.

'No, I don't know.'

'One dollar!'

He was delighted and burst out laughing.

'What happened, Michel? We used to hear about you for a while, and then you disappeared.'

'After Sacha died, I went on seeing Igor and Werner. Do you still see the others?'

'You're the only one we don't see any more.'

OCTOBER 1959—DECEMBER 1960

1

It was the only time in my life that I had seen both my families reunited – well, a good number of them anyway, and there were already twenty or so people there. It was my birthday and I'd had a bad premonition. I had sensed danger, without being able to pinpoint it. Later on, I worked out certain signs that should have been obvious to me, but engrossed in the feasting and the presents, I was too young to understand them. My friends seemed to have just one family each; I had two, and they were quite different. They did not get on with one another. The Marinis and the Delaunays. My father's family and my mother's. That was the day I discovered that they loathed each other. My father, who was always cheerful, was the only one who ventured from one to the other with his tray of fruit juices, mimicking the voices of famous actors such as Jean Gabin or Louis Jouvet.

'A little orange juice? It won't do you any harm, it's made of fruit.'

The Marinis collapsed with laughter. The Delaunays rolled their eyes.

'Paul, do stop, it's not funny!' said my mother, who hated imitations.

She remained seated, talking to her brother Maurice, whom she had not seen since he settled in Algeria after the war. My father did not care for him. I liked him because he never stopped making jokes. He used to call me Callaghan. I don't know why. As soon as he set eyes on me, he would adopt a mock-English accent and say: 'How do you do, Callaghan?' and I was supposed to reply: 'Very good!' When we parted, I was entitled to a 'Bye-bye Callaghan!' accompanied by a feigned punch to the chin. Maurice came to Paris once a year for an American business seminar. He made it a point of principle to be the first to benefit from the latest innovations. This was called management. He peppered his vocabulary with Americanized expressions. Nobody knew what they meant, but everyone pretended they did. He was thrilled by the seminar 'How to become a Winner?' He explained the basic principles to my mother, who lapped up his words. My father, who was convinced that it was all humbug, did not miss his opportunity: 'You should have let me know,' he joked, putting on General de Gaulle's voice, 'we would have sent the generals from the French army on this course.'

He burst out laughing, and so, too, did the Marinis. It did not help ease the tension. Maurice took no notice and continued trying to encourage my mother to enrol on the course. When he retired, grandfather Philippe had handed over the reins to his daughter. He was determined she should improve herself, even though she had been working with him for ten years now. On Maurice's recommendation, he had sent her on an American-style course called 'How to become a modern manager'. She had travelled to Brussels for two weeks of intensive training. She had returned with a collection of thick volumes that had pride of place on the bookshelf. She was very proud of them, for they were a proof of and testimony to her skills. They ranged from 'Winning over difficult customers' to 'Building up a network of effective relationships' or 'Developing your potential for decision making'. Every year, she attended a three-day seminar at a luxurious office block on avenue Hoche, and a new book would be added to the red leather-bound collection. The previous year, she had gone with him to the seminar 'How to win friends?', which had transformed her. Ever since, she had worn a fixed smile, the key to her present and future successes. Her movement was relaxed, a sign of her inner tranquillity, her voice soft and calm, evidence of her personal strength and, according to Dale Carnegie, whose ideas the seminars were promoting, they were supposed to change her life. My father did not believe in them. For him, they were a waste of time and money.

'In any case, you'll never make a thoroughbred out of a carthorse,' he proclaimed, with a little smile directed at Maurice.

One week beforehand, I had asked my mother to invite the Marinis.

'We don't normally invite them. We celebrate birthdays in the family.'

I had persisted. Her new smile had deserted her. I, on the other hand, had not given up. If they did not come, there would be no party. She had looked at me with a mournful expression. My mother did not change her mind. I was resigned to the fact. When my father informed me with a conniving smile that the Marinis had been invited, I had been over the moon, convinced that, thanks to me, the reconciliation would take place. I should not have forced her. She took no notice of them. The only outsiders at the gathering were Nicolas Meyer, my one friend, who got bored to death waiting for the cake, Maria, the Spanish maid, who went round from group to group with her tray of orangeade and mulled wine, and Néron, my brown tabby cat who followed her around like a dog. For a long time I thought that having two families was an advantage, for a long time I made the most of it. But, although those who have no family at all will think that I'm a spoilt brat who doesn't know how lucky he is, having two families is actually worse than having none at all.

The Marinis, in their corner of the room, were gathered around Grandfather Enzo. They were waiting. Franck, my brother, had made up his mind which side he was on. He was talking in a hushed voice to Uncle Baptiste and Grandmother Jeanne. My father appeared, carrying an enormous cake with chocolate icing, and began singing 'Happy birthday, Michel'. The Marinis joined in the chorus. This was a custom with them: as soon as they were together, they sang. Each of them had his or her own favourite repertoire and, when they were all together, they formed a chorus. My mother smiled at me tenderly. She did not sing. I blew out my twelve candles in two puffs. Philippe, my mother's father, clapped. He did not sing, nor did Maurice, nor did any of the Delaunays. They clapped, and the Marinis sang: 'Happy birthday, Michel, happy birthday to you'... And the more the Marinis sang, the more the Delaunays clapped. Juliette, my little sister, clapped, Franck sang. Nicolas too. It was at that precise moment that an unpleasant sensation came over me. I gazed at them uncomprehendingly, my awkwardness concealed by the din. This may be where my phobia for family gatherings stems from.

I received three presents. The Delaunays gave me a two-speed Teppaz record player: it played 33s and 45s, with a special loader for the 45s. It was a significant present and Philippe emphasized the delicacy of the pick-up arm and how carefully one had to follow the operating instructions.

'Your mother didn't want you to squabble with your brother any more.'

Enzo Marini gave me a large book: *The Treasures of the Louvre*. He had retired from the rail company and came to Paris once a month with Grandmother Jeanne, courtesy of his discount railcard. She used the opportunity to call on Baptiste, my father's elder brother, who had brought up his two children on his own ever since his wife had been killed in a road accident. A railcar driver on the Paris-Meaux line, Baptiste had apparently once been talkative and outgoing. Whenever they spoke about him, my parents gave one another equivocal glances. When I questioned them, they avoided replying and their silence was even more oppressive than his.

I used to go to the Louvre with Enzo. In Lens, where he lived, there was nothing interesting to see. I don't know where he acquired his knowledge. All he had was his school certificate. He knew the paintings and the artists, and had a preference for the Italian Renaissance. We spent hours pacing up and down the vast corridors until closing time. I loved those days when we were on our own. He didn't talk to me as though he were addressing his grandson, but as if to a friend. I often used to ask him questions about his youth, but he did not like talking about it. His father had left Fontanellato, near Parma, driven by poverty. He had emigrated with his two younger brothers. The three of them had handed on the family farm to their elder brother. He found his way to Northern France where he worked in a mine. Enzo was the first to be born in France. His father, who had always wanted to become French and had forbidden Italian to be spoken at home, had cut all ties with his native land and had lost touch with the rest of the family. Enzo married a girl from Picardy. He was French and proud of it. When some idiot, out to upset him, referred to him as an Eyetie or Macaroni, he replied with a smile, 'Pleased to meet you – I'm Lieutenant Vincenzo Marini, from Lens in the Pas-de-Calais.'

My father told me that he had sometimes had to resort to his fists in order to gain respect. For him, Italy was a foreign land in which he had never set foot. We were astonished when Enzo told us, that same day, that he had begun to have Italian lessons.

The Louvre gave me an education I hadn't expected. Enzo taught me how to recognize artists, to distinguish styles and periods. He pretended to believe that my attraction to statues of naked women was entirely due to the perfect lines of Canova or Bartolini, then he teased me about it. My father had not said a word when Philippe had given me the record player, but he went into raptures over the book, making admiring comments about the quality of the reproductions. He turned the pages with 'oh's and 'ah's of admiration, in his usual slightly exaggerated way. He paused at Leonardo's *St John the Baptist*, with its raised finger and curly hair, unsettled by the mystery of that very irreverent smile.

'You wouldn't think he was a saint.'

'Why don't you come with us to the Louvre?' Enzo asked.

'Oh, you know, me and museums…'

My father always knew how to create a sense of the dramatic. He placed a cube-shaped packet on the table, wrapped in dark blue glossy paper and tied with a red ribbon. Before opening it, I had to guess what was inside it. No, it was not a book. It would not have occurred to my father to buy one. A toy?

'You're past the age to be given one.'

It was not a parlour game either. Everybody began guessing except my mother, who smiled. It was not a lorry you had to assemble, nor an aeroplane, nor a boat, nor a train, nor a model car set, it was not a microscope, nor a watch, nor binoculars, nor a tie or scent, nor was it a set of lead soldiers, or a fountain pen. It wasn't something you could eat or drink, nor was it a hamster or a small rabbit.

'How could you think I'd put a live animal in a box? No, it's not stuffed.'

We found our imagination sorely lacking. I stood rooted to the spot, convinced I'd lost my chance of getting the present.

'Do we have to open it for you?' my father said.

I tore off the wrapping paper in a flash. I thrilled with delight when I discovered the clear plastic box. A Kodak Brownie! I would not have thought my father capable of giving me such a present. Two weeks earlier, passing a photographic shop in the Rue Soufflot, I had stopped to admire it and I had explained the new features of the camera to him. He had been surprised that I was so well informed about photography. In actual fact, I was pretending, he just knew even less about it than I did. I threw my arms around him and thanked him again and again for making me so happy.

'Save some thanks for your mother too, she's the one who went to get it.'

In a few frantic seconds, I managed to feed the film onto the reel. I assembled the family in a compact group, facing the window, directing operations as I had seen the school photographer do for our annual class photo.

'Smile, Papa. Uncle Maurice, stand behind Mama. Smile, for goodness sake, smile!'

The flash went off. I took another one just to be sure. Vocations are all to do with the luck of the draw. Later on, I made up my mind: I would be a photographer. This struck me as a glamorous and worthwhile aim. My father went further: 'It's true, dear Michel, it must be fun being a photographer, and it pays well.'

If I had my father's blessing to boot, great possibilities were opening up before me. Franck, as usual, managed to dampen my enthusiasm: 'If you want to be a photographer, you'll have to improve your maths.'

What did he know about it? Because of him, the discussion took a dangerous turn between those who maintained that photography was an art and that maths was unnecessary, and those who asserted that one had to know all about perspective, optics, emulsion, and masses of other technical stuff. This made me feel uncomfortable. They tried to convince themselves with lots of arguments that nobody listened to. I didn't realize that two people could both be right. As for Franck, he must have been jealous. He had not been given such a fine present when he was my age. Taking photographs is actually not a science, it's a matter of luck. This historic photo of the whole family gathered together, the only one of its kind, stood on the sideboard for three years. It disappeared, for reasons that have nothing to do with its artistic merits.

For a long time, I lived in complete and utter ignorance of my family's history. Everything was pretty perfect in my world. People never tell children about what went on before they came along. To begin with, we're too young to understand, later on we're too grown up to listen, then we haven't got time, and afterwards it's too late. That's the thing about family life. We live cheek by jowl with people as though we knew one another, but we know nothing about anybody. We hope for miracles from our close relationships: for impossible harmony, for total trust, for intimate bonds. We satisfy ourselves with the reassuring lie of our kinship. Perhaps I expected too much. What I know comes from Franck. It was he who revealed the truth to me, following the events that shattered our family on the day of the shop's opening.

There is a gap of seven years between Franck and me. He was born in 1940. His story is the story of our family with its ups and downs and its imponderables. Without him, I would not be here. Our fate hinged on the early months of the war. At that time, my mother's father Philippe was running his plumbing and zinc-roofing business. Before the war, it had branched out into selling kitchen and bathroom equipment. He had never touched a zinc pipe or a blowtorch in his life. He was happy to let others do the work and, to judge by his comments, it was tough. He had inherited the business from his father and he managed it efficiently. The start of his problems can be dated precisely to 3 February 1936 when he took on Paul Marini as an apprentice. My father was seventeen and had no wish to follow in the family tradition of working for the railways from one generation to the next. He wanted to live in Paris. On the day he was hired, he impressed Grandfather Delaunay by soldering some pewter perfectly and in record time. For the next three years my grandfather congratulated himself on having recruited my father, who charmed everybody with his smile, his kindness, his willingness and his ability. Without realizing it, he had let the wolf into the fold. His daughter Hélène fell madly in love with this handsome lad with his velvety good looks, wavy hair and slight dimple, who danced the waltz tirelessly and made her laugh with his imitations of Maurice Chevalier and Raimu. These must have been the most wonderful years for my parents. They were seventeen or eighteen; they used to see one another in secret and no one would have had any idea that they were going steady. In those days, a boss's daughter was not allowed to consort with a worker, especially the son of an Italian

21

immigrant. It was unheard of. Everyone had to keep to his or her place. In time, things would probably have reverted to normal. But war was drawing closer, and there is nothing worse for lovers than being separated by armed forces. I can easily imagine the pain of their separation and what they must have been through, what with my father being called up, and the phoney war in the depths of the Ardennes, and then the disaster. For six months, my mother hid the fact that she was pregnant from her parents. She had felt unwell but the family doctor had diagnosed a fatty tumour. Then they discovered her condition. She refused to say who the father was of the child whom she christened Franck. My father was held prisoner for four years in a prisoner of war camp in Pomerania, without receiving any news. Convinced that she had forgotten him, he discovered the truth on his return to France. The young girl, so carefree and light-hearted before the war, had become a woman. They had changed and scarcely recognized one another.

Had it not been for Franck, they would not have seen each other or got together again. They would have gone their separate ways and their affair would have been merely a youthful memory, known only to them, and soon forgotten. Had it not been for Franck, my parents would not have married and I would not be here today. Franck was five years old. They had to sort out the situation. They shouldered their responsibilities. They were married hurriedly in the town hall of the fifth arrondissement. On the morning of the ceremony, the future spouses rushed off to the Delaunays' lawyer and signed, without reading it, a marriage settlement. Paul Marini may have got the girl, but not the money. Grandmother Alice had a convenient ailment that morning and, since Philippe did not want to leave her, neither of them attended their daughter's wedding. Had my father perhaps been more tactful, he might have succeeded in sorting out the situation, but he rejected a religious wedding on the ridiculous pretext that he did not believe in God. This refusal had worsened his standing among the Delaunay family, which had had its own reserved pew at Saint-Etienne-du-Mont for ages. In a black and white photo taken on the steps of the town hall, the young couple can be seen surrounded by just the Marini family. They are not holding hands, and little Franck stands between them. My parents' wedding day was not a good one. In the late afternoon, they learned that Daniel Delaunay had been killed in Strasbourg. The modest repast planned by the Marinis was cancelled. They went into mourning for an entire year. Alice forgot all about her ailment and declared that she had not been able to attend her daughter's wedding because of the heroic death of her son in the war. In the Delaunay family, the day has always been commemorated as the one on which Daniel died. My parents have never celebrated their wedding anniversary.

2

School did not interest me. I preferred to hang around the Luxembourg, the Place de la Contrescarpe or the Quartier Latin. I spent that part of my life slipping through the net. I did just enough to move up to the next class. My getting into the first year at Lycée Henri-IV had been a close-run thing. Grandfather Delaunay had felt reluctantly obliged to call on the headmaster, who knew the family. Franck had been a pupil there. Despite its old-fashioned etiquette and its musty smell, Henri-IV did have a few advantages. The pupils were reasonably free, and could come and go without supervision. I was fortunate in that Nicolas was the best in the class. I didn't simply copy out his maths homework line by line. I embellished it. I digressed, or allowed deliberate minor errors to creep in. Occasionally, I got better marks than him, when all I had done was to paraphrase him. Then I moved on from minor idiotic cheating, with the book on my lap during essay writing, to the ingenious planning of undetectable crib-sheets. I spent more time preparing these than I would have needed to learn them. I never got caught. In history and geography, I had no need of them. I read the lesson once and it was imprinted in my mind. This enabled me to return the favour for Nicolas as this was his area of weakness. We monopolized the top places. For years, I was reckoned to be a good student and I didn't do a thing. I went to great lengths to appear older than my age. I succeeded effortlessly. I made the most of being almost six feet tall so people believed I was in my fifth year when I was actually beginning my third. For this reason, I had no friends of my own age, apart from Nicolas. I went around with Franck's friends whom I met in the cafés in the Maubert district, where they spent their time discussing things and setting the world to rights.

It was an exciting time. After a long period in the political wilderness, De Gaulle was back in power in order to save French Algeria, which was threatened by Algerian terrorists. People started to use words whose meaning was not very clear to me: decolonization, loss of empire, Algerian war, Cuba, non-aligned and Cold War. I wasn't interested in these political innovations. Since Franck's friends spoke of nothing else, I listened without saying anything, pretending I understood. I livened up when the conversation moved to the subject of 'rock'n'roll'. We had come across this music inadvertently a few months earlier. Usually we listened to the wireless without paying much attention. I read, slumped in a chair. Franck swotted. Then sounds we had never heard before came from the radio. We both looked up at the same time, staring at one another in amazement. We moved closer to the radio, Franck turned up the volume. Bill Haley had just changed our lives. From one day to the next, it became our kind of music and it dumped accordion music and all it evoked into the forgotten past. Adults loathed it, apart from Papa who loved jazz. It was feral music that was going to make us deaf and more stupid than we were already. We didn't understand any of it, but we didn't mind. Franck and his pals discovered loads of American singers: Elvis, Buddy Holly, Little Richard, Chuck Berry and Jerry Lee Lewis became our inseparable companions.

It wasn't just the period that was lively, the Quartier Latin was as well. The name of the Poujadist deputy for the fifth arrondissement was Jean-Marie Le Pen. Elected by small shopkeepers and landladies, he came to blows with 'the reds', that is, those who did not share his views. Around the Sorbonne and boulevard Saint-Michel there were real pitched battles between the students on either side. The traditional left-right divide was swept away by the Algerian war, which added to its chapters of horrific deeds by the day. From now on, you were either for or against French Algeria. Many socialists were for it, many on the right were against it, and many people switched sides, in both directions.

Franck was for independence. A member of the young communists, he had just joined the party proper and was a hardliner. Being close to Enzo and Baptiste, he accompanied them to every *fête de l'Huma*.* That made him a Marini. Grandfather Delaunay never missed an opportunity to make fun of him and to register his disapproval. This simmering war

* The annual festival organized by the Communist daily newspaper, *L'Humanité*. Tr.

explained why Franck was waiting impatiently for his economics studies to be over so that he could leave home. Papa had a foot in both camps. If he had declared himself a communist, Philippe would have thrown him out at once, but my father knew how far he could go. They put up with him because he said he was a socialist, of a radical tendency. For him, it was more important to claim independence from his own family. He did everything to smooth corners with his father-in-law and to make himself acceptable to him. But he wasn't actually a socialist, except in words. In his day-to-day life, it wasn't obvious. Franck, at least, tried to make his life fit in with his ideas. Sunday lunches were livelier than they are in most families. My mother refused to allow current affairs to be discussed at the table, but it was not easy to avoid the topic. As Franck would say, all subjects were political.

For the Delaunays, Algeria was France. But this was not the real reason it was untouchable. Algeria was sacred because Maurice had settled there after the war, when he married Louise Chevallier, a pure pied noir.* Her extremely wealthy family owned dozens of apartment blocks in Algiers and Oran. Maurice looked after his wife's assets and continued to increase their fortune every year by buying more buildings. The word 'independence' was therefore both impossible and inappropriate. Philippe and my mother had stood firmly with Maurice, and De Gaulle's arrival at the helm reassured them. Thanks to our great national figure, Algeria would remain French. No bunch of scruffy terrorists was going to get the better of the third largest army in the world. These *fellaghas* were a gang of bloodthirsty and ungrateful degenerates manipulated by the Americans. Even if the Delaunays admitted that the 'natives' might get forgotten in this impasse, they pledged boundless hatred for those Frenchmen who were betraying their country and their fellow citizens, and were supporting the rebellion. Between Franck and Maurice, there was more than animosity. Each of them stood his ground and made it a point of honour to proclaim his opinion, provoke his opponent and let him know how deeply he despised him. We avoided having them in the same room.

* A person born in North Africa of French descent. Tr.

When they were together, my mother forbade them to bring up the subject. The words: Algeria, war, assassination attempts, self-determination, referendum, generals, colonels, Africa, legionnaires, army, as well as: honour, concern, future, bastard, torture, arsehole, freedom, commie, oil, bad for business, were banned from conversation from the apéritif to the end of the meal. This limited the field of discussion but it allowed the leg of lamb with beans to be consumed without insults flying.

Because of Franck, and to prevent me from following in his footsteps, Philippe and my mother created a sort of cordon sanitaire that stopped me from associating with my father's family. They forbade me to accompany them to the *fête de l'Huma,* and from the way they spoke about it, with an air of purse-lipped complicity, I believed for a long time that secret and unmentionable horrors took place there. My mother was not able to stop me from going to the Louvre once a month with Enzo. He made no attempt to sway me or to bring me over to his side. He was a fatalist before he was a communist. They probably amount to the same thing. If you were born a worker, you were a communist; if you were born into the bourgeoisie, you were on the right. There could be no mingling of the two. For him, it was only the Socialists who compromised. He was annoyed with my father for going over to the enemy's side and he resented him for having betrayed the working class. You were not allowed to change social classes. The world was a simple place; since I was the son of a member of the bourgeoisie, I would become a member of the bourgeoisie myself. In actual fact, I could not care less about their stories, their political persuasions or their rows. I was neither on one side nor the other. Their certainties bored me and were alien to me. Their squabbles did not concern me. What interested me in life were rock'n'roll, literature, photography and baby-foot.

3

Nicolas and I were one of the best teams at baby-foot. He in defence, I in offence. We were hard to beat. When we wanted to play quietly, we went to place de la Contrescarpe. Our opponents were students from the neighbourhood, or those from the nearby Ecole Polytechnique, who were brainy fellows and useless at the game. We could not care less about winding them up. Some of them were annoyed that kids ten years younger than them could thrash them. We behaved in the same way we saw Samy do. We ridiculed them without taking any notice of them.

'Next.'

To begin with, we were over the moon. We made it obvious how thrilled we were. Later on, we relished our victories in silence. We ignored them. We concentrated on the baby-foot, on the white ball and the little red and blue footballers. The students knew what awaited them before they started, and knew they could not beat us. Being ignored was worse than disdain. In order to merit a glance, they had to put us in a dangerous position, score ahead of us or be tied at match point. There were quite a lot of keen players, and when you lost you had to hang around for a long time before playing again. As the number of teams increased, people eventually grew tired and as soon as they lost their concentration they were thrown out, with a little sideways smirk to mark the transfer of power. There were the good players, those who managed at least five or six consecutive games, and those who just about got by.

When we felt on top form, ready to take on the whole world and happy to get thrashed, we went along to the Balto, the large bistro on place Denfert-Rochereau. At the Balto there were two baby-foot tables. We played with the grown-ups and we were respected. It would never have occurred to us to play on the small table next to the pinball machines, even when it was free or when other players suggested a game to us. We conserved our energy for the big shots, those who came from the southern suburbs. Samy was the best. He played on his own against two opponents and won easily. He stopped when he had had enough or when it was time for him to go to work. He had a night job with a sales agent at Les Halles, carting around tons of fruit and vegetables. He was a real rocker with a quiff and sideburns, a huge fellow, built like the side of a house, with enormous biceps and two leather bracelets on each wrist, not the sort of guy you failed to respect. He played at a speed that left us stunned, and he struck each ball incredibly violently. You could count on the fingers of one hand the players who had managed to defeat him. I was one of them. It had happened just three times, and then only narrowly, whereas he had smashed me on dozens of occasions. Samy had no time for students or bourgeois types. He had just one word for us: we were morons, and he regarded us contemptuously from his imposing height. He only spoke to his own kind and to a small number of others, one of whom was Jacky, the barman at the Balto, a mate of his, who came from the same suburb as he did. Rumours were rife about Samy and they were discussed in a hushed voice, behind his back. He was variously either a small-time crook or a major one. Nobody knew whether it was his shady appearance or his black leather jacket that had earned him this reputation or whether it was justified. He had had a soft spot for me ever since I had played 'Come on Everybody' on the Balto juke-box, an enormous Wurlitzer that glistened between the two pinball machines. This had earned me a friendly pat on the back and a nod of approval from him. From time to time, when a pair of good players turned up whom he knew he could not beat single-handed, he took me on to play at the back. I made it a point of honour to be worthy of his choice and I always scored two or three goals thanks to a killer shot, which I was one of the few who knew how to do. Apart from these rare displays of friendship, I was treated as contemptuously as the others, and given the nickname 'complete moron'; I found his constantly changing attitude bewildering. When I had a bit of money, I put on a rock record, and as soon as the guitars started strumming, he gave a sigh of relief and motioned to me with a nod of his head to join him and play at the back. Together, we never lost a single match.

The Balto was run by a family from the Auvergne. The Marcusots had come from the Cantal after the war and had spent their lives in this café. They worked there as a family seven days a week, from six in the morning until midnight. The father, Albert, ran his business masterfully and proclaimed his social success by flaunting his English bow ties, which he collected and which he was forever adjusting in the mirror to obtain a perfect balance. When the takings had been good, he drummed his fingers in satisfaction over his prominent belly.

'The dosh is all there and no one's going to take it away from me.'

The phrase 'bon vivant' could have been invented for old Marcusot. He spoke about returning to the country, and starting up a nice little business in Aurillac or Saint-Flour. His wife, the voluminous Madeleine, had no desire to go back since their three children had all settled in the Paris area.

'It'll be bad enough to be bored stiff once we're in the graveyard, there's no point burying ourselves there during our lifetime. The holidays are quite enough.'

Almost everything the Marcusots made came from the Cantal. Their *truffade* was as famous as it was vast, with Quercy sausages that filled you up for at least two days, and people came from afar to sample their *entrecôte de Salers*. Old mother Marcusot was a fine cook. She used to prepare a home-made dish of the day. The enticing aroma greeted you on arrival and it had earned her three rave reviews that hung inside a gold frame alongside the menu. People used to make many unkind remarks about the stinginess of Auvergnats. But these particular ones were generous and they paid no heed either to the portions or to the bills, which they allowed to mount up over the course of the month, but which had to be settled without any discussion by the beginning of the following month if you wished to be served again. Woe betide anyone who forgot and imagined that he could simply change restaurants, for the Auvergne phone network was quick to remind bad debtors of their obligations.

Behind the bar was the Marcusots' domain. The dining hall and the terrace belonged to Jacky. He dashed around from morn till night: he took orders, and as he tore past threw them at old father Marcusot, who would get them ready; he piled up his tray with a jumble of plates, glasses and bottles, he served without spilling a drop, he worked out the sums in his head from memory without making any mistakes, and all with a smile and attentiveness that earned him generous tips. Jacky had only one passion in life: football. A dedicated supporter of Stade de Reims, he vowed undying hatred for Racing Club de Paris, which was a 'queers' club', the ultimate insult. The world was arranged around this confrontation. You were either for one side or the other. And it did not do to talk lightly about his heroes: Fontaine, Piantoni, and Kopa, whom he did not easily forgive for his 'treachery' in leaving for Real Madrid. When they lost against Racing or Real Madrid, it was a day of mourning, and no one could revive him, not even the Racing supporters, who were the most numerous. Samy shared this passion for Stade de Reims with his pal Jacky. It was in honour of their strip that he played with the red team at baby-foot. When he won comfortably, he never said a word to the loser; he merely picked up the twenty centimes piece placed in the ashtray by those who were awaiting their turn and inserted it disdainfully in the slot to bring back the balls. When he had been hard pressed, and obliged to make an effort to win, he marked his victory with a cry of 'Reims has screwed you!'

The Balto was a vast establishment on the corner of two boulevards. On avenue Denfert-Rochereau, the side with the bar and tobacco counter, there were the baby-foot tables, the pinball machines and the juke-box, and on the boulevard Raspail side there was a restaurant that seated sixty customers. Between the furthest tables, I had noticed a door behind a green velvet curtain. Men of a certain age would disappear through this doorway, but I didn't see anyone come out again. This intrigued me. I often wondered what was behind it. It never occurred to me to go and look. None of my baby-foot chums knew. It didn't interest them. For a long time I didn't bother about it. When it was crowded and I had to wait a long time, I took a book and, without buying a drink, I would sit at a table outside in the sun. Jacky left me alone. He had seen my disappointment when Reims had been beaten in the final by Real. Ever since then, he no longer thought of me as a customer.

The Balto, in those days, with the Marcusots, Nicolas, Samy, Jacky and the regulars, was like a second family. I spent an incredible amount of time there, but I had to be home before my mother returned from work. Every evening I got back just before seven o'clock, and spread out my textbooks and exercise books on my desk. When she returned home with my father, she found me working. Woe betide me if she should get back first and not find me there. When it happened, I managed to reassure her by swearing that I had been working at Nicolas's home. I lied with an audacity that delighted me.

I carried my Brownie around with me and practised taking photographs. The results were poor. People were lost in the background or stood there like dummies. You could not see their faces. My photographs didn't portray anything. I drew closer to the subjects. Occasionally, I succeeded in capturing an expression or a feeling. How to take photos without being seen? I had to cope with an unexpected enemy: Juliette, my little sister, who was three years younger than me. She didn't have to choose which side she was on. She was a Delaunay to her fingertips. She was very much aware of her looks, and her cupboards were stuffed with clothes, though she maintained that she had nothing to wear and she spent her time asking what she should put on when she went out. With her ingenuous air, she obtained whatever she wanted from my parents. But her innocent, artless countenance was merely a façade. My mother, who had complete trust in her, would often ask her whether I had come home at six o'clock as I said I had. Juliette had not the slightest qualm in betraying me with a shake of the head.

She was an unbelievable chatterbox too, capable of rambling on for hours without anyone remembering what it was she was talking about. She monopolized the conversation. It was impossible to have any sort of discussion with her. She never let you get a word in. You just gave up and let yourself be carried along by the flow of words that streamed from her lips without anyone being able to interrupt her. Everybody made fun of her. Grandfather Philippe, who praised her to the skies, called her 'my pretty little windbag' and didn't hesitate to forbid her to speak in his presence. She wearied him. Enzo used to say that she had a little old lady inside her belly.

'You're a *chiacchierona* like my cousin Lea, who still lives in Parma.'

This nickname stuck with her. She loathed it. When anyone wanted to annoy her, they called her a *chiacchierona*. That made her shut up. Sometimes, she would start talking at the beginning of the meal and continue her monologue throughout, unstoppable. Our father would thump the table.

'Stop, Juliette, you're making us feel giddy! The girl's such a chatterbox!'

She protested vociferously: 'I'm not a chatterbox! No one listens to me.'

4

I hated wasting my time. The only thing that seemed worthwhile to me was reading. At home, nobody really read. My mother took all year to read the 'Book of the Year', which enabled her to talk about it and to pass for a great reader. My father did not read at all and was proud of the fact.

Franck had some political books in his bedroom. The only writer Grandfather Philippe respected was Paul Bourget, whose novels he had adored when he was young.

'They can say what they want, but literature was a damn sight better before the war.'

Grandfather bought sets of books from the shops in rue de l'Odéon. He had a bookcase built for them, but he did not read them. But I made up for the rest of the family. I was a compulsive reader. In the morning, when I switched on the light, I picked up my latest and never put it down. It annoyed my mother to see me with my nose in a book.

'Have you nothing else to do?'

She could not bear me not to be listening to her when she was speaking. On several occasions she snatched the book out of my hands to force me to reply. She had given up calling me for dinner and she had discovered an effective solution. From the kitchen, she switched off the electricity in my bedroom. I was then obliged to join them. I read at the table, which exasperated my father. I read when I cleaned my teeth, and in the lavatory. They hammered on the door for me to let them have their turn. I read while I walked. It took me fifteen minutes to reach the lycée, but reading stretched it out to half an hour or more. I took account of this additional time and left home earlier. But I would often arrive late, especially when some thrilling passage brought me to a standstill on the pavement for an unspecified period of time, and I picked up masses of detentions for being unpunctual three times without a valid excuse. I had given up trying to explain to the idiots who were supposed to be educating us that this lack of punctuality was justified and unavoidable. My guardian angel protected me and guided me. I never bumped into a lamppost, nor did I get run over by a car when I crossed the road with my nose stuck in my book. On several occasions, I missed my turn at a pedestrian crossing and the hoot of a car's horn brought me back to reality. I avoided the piles of dog shit that spattered the Paris pavements. I heard nothing. I saw nothing. I walked on automatic pilot and reached school safe and sound. Throughout most of the lessons, I continued my reading with the book propped open on my lap. I was never caught by a teacher.

In due course, I came to classify writers into two categories: those who enabled you to arrive on time and those who caused you to be late. The Russian authors earned me a whole string of detentions. When it started to rain, I would stand in a doorway in order to carry on undisturbed. The Tolstoy period had been a bad month. The Battle of Borodino led to three hours of detention. A few days later, when I explained to the school porter, a student who was supervising us, that Anna Karenina's suicide was the cause of my being late, he thought I was making fun of him. I made my position worse by admitting that I had not understood her motive for committing suicide. I had been obliged to turn back in case I had missed the reason why. He gave me two Thursday detentions: one for being late for the umpteenth time, the other because Anna was a bloody bore who did not deserve such attention. I bore no grudge against him. It allowed me to finish *Madame Bovary*.

When I was drawn to certain authors, I read every word they wrote, even though some books were difficult to get hold of. In the town hall library, opposite the Panthéon, the librarians looked sceptical when I brought back the five books that I was permitted so soon after having taken them out. I couldn't give a damn and continued to persevere with my author of the moment, resolutely tackling everything on the shelf. I devoured classics that had commentaries explaining the links between the work and the life. The more heroic or illustrious the life, the better the novels; when the fellow was vile or a nonentity, I was reluctant to take the plunge. For a long time, Saint-Exupéry, Zola and Lermontov were my favourite authors, and not merely on account of their books.

I loved Rimbaud for his dazzling life, and Kafka for his quiet, anonymous life. How were you supposed to feel when you adored the novels of Jules Verne, Maupassant, Dostoevsky, Flaubert, Simenon and loads of others who then turned out to be complete bastards? Should I forget them, ignore them, and not read them any more? Pretend they did not exist even though their novels were tempting me? How could they have written outstanding books when they were such appalling human beings? When I put the question to my classmates, they looked at me as if I were an Iroquois Indian. Nicolas maintained that there were enough writers who deserved to be read that you didn't have to waste your time with those who had failed to live up to their books. That was wrong. There were repulsive skeletons in every cupboard. When I put the question to my French literature teacher, he told me that all the writers mentioned in the encyclopedia of French writers deserved my consideration; he explained that if you were going to apply these criteria of morality and public spiritedness, you would have to purge and eliminate at least 90 per cent of the authors who featured in the book. Only the most extreme cases had been excluded from the anthology, and only these were unworthy of being studied and should be shunned.

Grandfather Enzo's advice clinched it. One Sunday when we were strolling around the Louvre, I told him about my concern. I had just discovered that Jules Verne was a hysterical anti-Communard and a fanatical anti-Semite. He shrugged his shoulders and pointed to the canvases that surrounded us. What did I know about the artists whose work we admired? If I really knew Botticelli, El Greco, Ingres or Degas, I would close my eyes so as not to see their paintings any more. Ought I to block my ears so as not to hear the music of most of the composers or those rock singers I liked so much? I would be condemned to live in a world above reproof in which I would die of boredom. For him, and I could never suspect him of complacency, the question did not arise, the works were always what was most important. I should take men for what they did, not for what they were. Since I appeared unconvinced, he gave me a little smile and said: 'Reading and loving a novel written by a bastard is not to absolve him in any way, to share his convictions or connive with him, it's to recognize his talent, not his morals or his ideals. I have no wish to shake Hergé's hand, but I love Tintin. And after all, are you yourself above reproof?'

5

We also played baby-foot at the Narval, a bistro in the Maubert district. We went there after school. Nicolas lived nearby. Denfert was a long way away from him. The standard was not so high, but there was more atmosphere, thanks to the students from the Sorbonne or Louis-le-Grand. They feared us. We broke all endurance records, clinging to the handles for hours on end. Certain spectators did not play, but instead placed bets on us and paid for our round. The Narval was the haunt of Franck and his mates. As soon as he set eyes on me, he would tell me to go home and get on with my work. For a long time, I complied, but shortly after my twelfth birthday, I told him to get lost. I wonder how I had the courage to stand up to him. We had just started our game. We were playing with the blue team. On this baby-foot table it was a slight handicap as the front rod was stiff. I managed a shot that rebounded and went in, which prompted a roar of congratulation from the spectators. One of them could think of nothing better to say than yell out to Franck, who was sitting in the café area with his friends.

'Hey, your brother's getting along brilliantly.'

I knew that he was going to come over, put his hand on the edge of the table, and shout at me in front of all the other players. I continued knocking in goals without looking up. There he was, glaring at me. I could see him drumming his fingers irritably. I was playing unusually well. I was slamming in the goals and the experts had fallen silent. I ended on a whirl from the inside left that left them speechless. I was on the point of picking up the coin left by the players who were due to play next when he grabbed me by the hand.

'Michel, go home!'

I saw them all there, with their mocking grins, convinced that the kid would obey his big brother and return to the fold as usual. All of a sudden, I yelled out: 'Never!'

He was surprised by my reaction: 'Did you hear me? At once!'

I heard myself yell out: 'Are you going to hit me? Are you going to squeal on me?'

Franck was not expecting this. He gazed at me in astonishment. He could sense that I was not going to be pushed around. He shrugged his shoulders and went back to his friends. I glanced over at him furtively. He ignored me. We had been kicked out by a pack of idiots who thought they were the champions. Nicolas, who had inserted the first coin, wanted to have his turn again. But I was flat broke. He set off home grumbling. I went and sat down on the bench beside Franck. He continued talking as if I were not there. I was about to go home when he asked me in the most natural way: 'What are you having?'

I was not expecting this. I wondered where the trap lay.

'I've got no money.'

Sitting opposite him, Pierre Vermont intervened: 'It's my round, you little bugger. Have what you want.'

I ordered a really weak lemonade shandy and raised my glass to Pierre, who was celebrating his departure for Algeria. His call-up deferment had just been revoked. He was relieved to have passed his medical as he had feared he might be declared unfit for service. He was a student supervisor for the older pupils at Henri-IV. Built like a house, he played prop for the PUC rugby team. He addressed the pupils as 'silly bugger' almost automatically. It was his way of speaking. To begin with, it slightly took you aback. During the two months before he was called up, we saw one another every day. We became friends. I was surprised, given our age difference, that he should consider me worth spending time with, but I suppose I was the only one who paid attention to him. I have always liked listening to other people. After Sciences Po, he had failed the Ecole Nationale d'Administration entrance examination on two occasions. He had got through the written exam twice, but he had also failed the important oral exam on two occasions. He was, apparently, the only one to do so. He did not conceal his radical views and had decided to devote his life to the revolution. Looking at him with his long hair, his moth-eaten beard and his eternal black velvet suit worn over a thick white woollen pullover, it was hard to imagine how Beynette, the principal of Henri-IV could have accepted him as a supervisor, when he was so fussy about how the pupils dressed. Pierre had just given up the idea of becoming a senior civil servant. It was a clever old system and it had rejected him. He had a deep-seated resentment of all organized structure and, even more so, of the family, state education, trade unions, political parties, the press, banks, the army, the police and colonialism. For him, the bastards should all be killed. And he didn't use the word 'killed' lightly. It meant eliminate them, actually get rid of them. This meant a vast number of people had to be slaughtered. This did not frighten him. His hatred of religion and of priests was boundless.

'We pay them too much respect, bowing and scraping at all their antics. You might as well talk to a wall. What is sacred to them is just an invention of their own uneasy minds. Priests and religion have to be done away with. Don't tell me they do good deeds. We don't need a commandment from Jesus to justify moral behaviour.'

What he loathed most of all, saw as mankind's absolute worst enemy, were feelings. And, worse still, flaunting them.

'If you show your feelings, you've had it. People shouldn't know what you're feeling.'

Once he got going, there was no way of stopping him. No one could interrupt him and argue against him. He spoke quickly, switched subjects all of a sudden, set off in one direction without anyone having any idea of where he was heading, launched into unexpected digressions, and landed on his feet again. Some said he liked the sound of his own voice, but he had a very good sense of humour and never took anyone or anything seriously, least of all himself. Except the Tour de France, that is, which he loathed. I never understood that.

He was Franck's best friend in spite of their being fierce political opponents. They spent their whole time squabbling, splitting hairs, having rows and making up. They tore into one another with unbelievable verbal violence and you thought that this time they had fallen out with one another for good, but then, a moment later, they were laughing together. I did not understand the reasons why the Communists hated the Trotskyites who loathed them in turn, even though they were standing up for the same people. Pierre asserted that he was no longer a Trotskyite and that he abominated them just as much as Franck did. From now on he was a free and unattached revolutionary. I listened to their dialogues of the deaf without daring to join in, embarrassed that they should confront one another with such hatred. I had a long way to go. I spent hours listening to Pierre. I was sufficiently in agreement with him about the necessity of destroying this rotten society in order to rebuild it on sound foundations, even though many details of the destruction and reconstruction remained obscure. And I enjoyed listening to him. He was clear and convincing. But when I interrupted him with a question, for instance: 'Why is this war cold?'

He replied impatiently: 'Oh, it would take too long to explain, little bugger,' leaving me none the wiser.

His chief hatred was reserved for monogamy.

'This aberration that has to be got rid of, because it's bound to become extinct.'

He had decided in quite an arbitrary fashion that no loving relationship should last for more than a month or two, maximum three, except in 'special cases'. I was brave enough to ask him to explain this to me.

'It depends on the girl. One day, you'll understand. Never let it go on for more than three months. After that, you'll be the one who gets fucked up.'

He dumped his girlfriends for the sake of their future happiness.

'It's unhealthy, don't you see? We're making a prison for ourselves.'

Pierre was always surrounded by two or three girls who followed him and listened to him as though he were the messiah. It took me a while to realize that they were his exes. Perhaps they hoped that he would change his mind? They did not seem to be jealous of the newest girl who had no idea that her time was limited and that she would soon be joining them on the wrong side of the bench. To listen to him, love was bullshit, marriage an ignominy and children just a dirty trick. In China, a spectacular revolution was taking place that would shatter the way mankind behaved by abolishing the dictatorial laws of the market and destructive male-female relationships. The elimination of feeling, the sweeping away of love had begun. We were going to be free of the secular tyranny of the couple. But even though he proclaimed the contrary, I believe he preferred women to revolution – and by a long way.

He maintained that, given what a mess the species had made of things, virtually all of mankind should be forbidden to reproduce. He hoped that scientific and biological progress would put an end to the reproductive anarchy of the foolish masses. On this point, his theory was in the process of elaboration. He had found a name for it. It would be called 'Saint-Justisme' in homage to the revolutionary and to his celebrated 'No freedom for the enemies of freedom'. According to his fevered explanations, our ills stemmed from democracy, from the idiotic multitude being given the right to vote. He wanted to replace the republic of the masses by that of the wise. Individual liberty must be suppressed and replaced with a collective order in which only the most competent and the best educated could decide society's future. He was counting on the free time he would have in Algeria to write an important and seminal book on the subject. He would use the opportunity given him by national service to try to find an alternative solution to the physical elimination of opponents, though he felt it might be difficult to achieve his aims without becoming another Stalin.

'There may be other solutions to how to deal with the majority. But we won't be able to avoid killing a whole load of them. To set an example.'

Pierre's collection of rock'n'roll albums was unique. He owned records of all the American singers, without a single exception. Priceless imports. He was generous and would lend them without any hesitation. He had an advantage over us. He understood the words of the songs. In our case, we loved the music and the beat. We picked up one or two words here and there, but the meanings were lost on us and we couldn't care less. While we listened to the songs he translated the words for us. At times, we found it hard to believe him: 'Are you sure he's talking about blue suede shoes?'

We were disappointed by the lyrics, and preferred for him not to translate them any longer. One day he talked to me about a new disc by Jerry Lee Lewis, his favourite singer. I went to his home to collect it and record it. I was expecting an attic room on the seventh floor without a lift, but he lived in a huge apartment on quai des Grands-Augustins, with a view over Notre-Dame. His drawing room alone was the size of our flat, and there were labyrinthine corridors which he strode along with perfect ease. When I went into raptures about the furniture, he told me: 'It's not mine, little bugger, it's my parents'.'

He had a Schimmel grand piano, which he played wonderfully well. He put on the record, hurried over to the piano and had fun reproducing Jerry Lee's trills at the same speed and with the same flair, but he didn't sing as well as Lewis did.

Pierre had all the attributes bar one. He didn't know how to play baby-foot and he was determined to learn. On the evening he bought me a shandy after my altercation with Franck, he insisted we should play a game. I teamed up with my brother. It was the first time we had played together. Pierre copied what his opponent did, which is a mistake. If you want to block your opponent, you move as little as possible. Franck played to the rules whereas Pierre played any old how and also used the rods to perform windmills, which is forbidden. He burst out laughing. The more I asked him to stop, the more he went on, and the more irritated I got, the more excited he became. He was beyond redemption as a player.

On the evening prior to his call-up, Pierre organized a surprise party with his pals. When he invited me, Franck responded for me: 'The parents wouldn't hear of it.'

I protested as a matter of form. That evening, I gave it a try. My mother looked at me in alarm.

'Michel, you're twelve years old!'

I tried the classic arguments: I would go and come back with Franck, I would return home early, before midnight, before eleven o'clock, before ten, I'd just go and come back. But there was nothing doing. My father, who usually supported me, made things worse. He had not been allowed out until he was eighteen. And what's more in Baptiste's day they were working. Seeing my disappointment, he comforted me: 'Soon you'll be able to, when you're older.'

I did not press the point. After dinner, we sat down in front of the television. I pretended to be enjoying a ghastly variety programme.

Franck left us at nine o'clock. My mother told him not to come home too late. I went to bed as though nothing were the matter. My mother came in to see me. Néron was asleep, rolled up in a ball against my leg. She glanced at my book, Zola's *La Faute de l'abbé Mouret*. I began to talk to her about it enthusiastically. She was tired. She did not remember having read it. She advised me to go to sleep. I obeyed and switched off the light. She kissed me affectionately and left the room. I waited in the darkness. I got dressed again. I got back into bed. I waited, alert to the slightest noise. Silence reigned. Néron looked at me with his enigmatic expression. I got up, my ears pricked. The parents were asleep. From their bedroom, at the end of the corridor, I could hear my father snoring. I tiptoed past the kitchen. With the utmost care, I unlocked the door to the service stairs. I locked it again with the key. I put on my shoes on the landing. I walked down the staircase in the dark, crossed the deserted courtyard, then, like a cat, I slipped through the entrance hall, without the caretakers noticing me. I opened the entrance door. I waited for a few seconds. I left without looking back.

Paris at night. *La belle vie!* I felt ten years older, and light as a swallow. I was surprised by the mass of people in the street and in the bars. The boulevard Saint-Michel was packed. People seemed happy to be alive. I was frightened of being spotted. But nobody had noticed me. I looked older than my age. I could pass for a student like anyone else. I shoved my hands in my pockets and drew up the collar of my jacket. On quai des Grands-Augustins, the music could be heard from the pavement. Carl Perkins was waking up the early-to-beds. I rang the bell. A young woman I did not know opened the door. She was slim, with regular features, very short black hair, brown eyes opened wide in surprise, and a mocking smile. She stood aside to invite me in. I had scarcely set foot inside than Pierre walked over and made the introductions: 'D'you know my sister, little bugger?'

I stammered.

'Cécile, this is Michel, the best baby-foot player on the Left Bank. He's like you. He never stops reading. Cécile is doing a literature degree. She adores Aragon, can you imagine? Aragon!'

Her smile grew wider. She turned and vanished into the crowd who were rocking away to 'Hound Dog'.

'I didn't know you had a sister.'

Pierre put his hand on my shoulder and dragged me in, followed by two of his previous girlfriends as well as the current one, and introduced me as if I were his best friend. He reeked of alcohol and was smoking a Cuban cigar he had bought in Geneva. He spluttered smoke into my face. He offered me a fat cigar and a glass of whisky. I declined. One of his exes held the bottle in order to serve him as soon as he requested. He gazed at me solemnly.

'I'm glad you came, Michel. May I ask you a favour?'

I swore that he could ask me anything. He was leaving for Algeria for a long time and did not know when he was coming back. Not for a year at least, perhaps longer. You could no longer go on leave in the city. He wanted to entrust a small treasure to me. According to him, I was the only person worthy of guarding it until his return. I protested: it was a heavy responsibility. He cut short my prevarications by laying his hand on two boxes of rock albums. Fifty-nine exactly. His American imports, acquired for a fortune. I stood there speechless and open-mouthed.

'It would be a pity for no one to make use of them. I've no intention of playing the hero for the French army. It'll give me time to write my book. I'll get myself discharged at the first opportunity. In six months' time, I'll be home again. That's my little plan.'

I wanted us to make a list of the albums he was lending me. It was pointless. He knew them by heart.

'May I lend them to Franck?'

Pierre drew on his cigar, shrugged his shoulders and turned away. I pressed him.

'Couldn't care less!'

I caught up with him. I swore to him that he could trust me completely.

'By the way, do you like science-fiction, little bugger?'

I was rather taken off guard. I wondered what he was driving at. I shook my head.

'Do you know Bradbury?'

I had to confess my ignorance. He picked up a book, which he shoved in my pocket.

'It's the finest novel I've read. Straightforward, unfussy stuff.'

I froze, rooted to the spot by what I saw. In the midst of the intertwined couples, Cécile was dancing to a soppy Platters tune, pressed against Franck. They were kissing one another passionately. My gaze turned from the couple to Pierre, convinced that he was about to pounce on them and smash Franck's face in. On the contrary, he appeared to be amused. I panicked: 'Pierre, you mustn't be angry with him.'

He had not heard and was yelling at the deejay: 'We're fed up with the slow stuff!'

He shook his finger vindictively at me: 'In the new world, those who don't dance to rock'n'roll will be executed!'

A lively rock'n'roll number broke the cocoon-like spell. Suddenly, Franck noticed me. He rushed over towards us, grabbed me by the arm and began shaking me roughly.

'What the fucking hell are you doing here?'

Pierre stepped brusquely between us: 'Leave him alone! Tonight, it's party-time.'

Franck let go of me in a fury. Looking slightly anxious, Cécile joined us. Pierre completed the introductions. She turned towards Franck: 'I didn't know you had a brother.'

He took her hand and dragged her off to dance. Pierre knocked back his glass and, with a far-away look in his eyes, murmured: 'Nowadays, people speak to one another and they don't say anything.'

I attended my first party rather as an entomologist might examine a colony of unknown ants. I sat on a stool, drinking a glass of vodka and orange that made me dizzy. In order to feel more confident, I accepted a yellow Boyard cigarette from the person beside me. The first drag exploded in my lungs. Franck took no notice of me. Cécile shot me occasional half-smiles. At around midnight, I decided to go home. Pierre was slumped on a sofa, dead drunk. Ought I to take his albums? He had made me this offer while he was semi-intoxicated. When he came down to earth, he might have changed his mind. I slipped away without anyone noticing.

I returned home by another route. With the same careful attention to detail as when I left, I opened the service door and stood on the landing, peering around. The flat was silent. The parents were asleep. Carrying my shoes, I walked into the kitchen, which was lit by the moon shining through the fanlight, I locked the door and, without making a sound, was on the point of returning to my bedroom when the light was switched on. My mother stood in front of me. Before I could make a move, a monumental smack caused me to whirl full circle, then my mother grabbed hold of me and laid into me. I was given the biggest hiding of my life. She hit me all the harder because she had been so frightened. She yelled and beat me and kicked me. I curled myself into a ball. It went on and on. She thumped me on the head so many times that I thought I was going to die. She also hit my father, who was trying to separate us. He had to use all his strength to prevent her from crippling me. He managed to control her and drag her away. She was hysterical.

'Think of the neighbours!' he yelled.

She calmed down. He hurled me into my bedroom. The door slammed shut. My mother was wailing about the ingratitude of men in general and of her sons in particular. My father kept on telling her that it didn't matter. Eventually silence was restored. My heart was pounding away, my cheeks were on fire and my bottom ached. I lay there in the dark recovering my breath. I waited for sleep that never came. In spite of the thrashing and the punishments that would follow, I did not regret a single moment of the escapade. I felt in my pocket for the novel that Pierre had given me. I turned on my bedside light: *Fahrenheit 451*. It was not a long book. It had not been damaged by my mother's fury. Various passages had been underlined by Pierre. I started to read at random:

> … I plunk the children in school nine days out of ten. I put up
> with them when they come home three days a month; it's not bad
> at all. You heave them into the 'parlour' and turn the switch. It's
> like washing clothes; stuff laundry in and slam the lid… Better to
> keep it in the old heads, where no one can see it or suspect it…
> Why, there's one town in Maryland, only twenty-seven people,

no bomb'll ever touch that town, is the complete essays of a man named Bertrand Russell…

Certain paragraphs had been annotated, but Pierre's spidery scrawl was illegible.

6

The weeks that followed were tedious. I became a sort of pariah. The family and the neighbours gave me sideways looks, as though I were a delinquent. Maria, normally so friendly, glared at me as if I had spat on the Cross. Old Mother Bardon, the caretaker of the building, regarded me with a pained expression. Her husband, an usher at the Paris City Council, took the liberty of making comments in my mother's presence such as: 'You'll have to take care to wipe your feet on the doormat, young man, you've got to respect other people's work.'

My mother backed him up: 'Monsieur Bardon's right, Michel, you don't respect anything.'

I was more irritated by the jibes from this Poujadist than I was by the many restrictions I had to endure. (I took my revenge. Every time I noticed any dog shit, I deliberately stepped on it and then wiped my feet on his doormat.) On Thursdays, I was not allowed to watch television and had to spend the whole evening doing homework in my bedroom. If I displayed the slightest urge to disobey orders, Maria had been told to phone my mother immediately, which resulted in my being bawled at and given official warnings. I made my situation worse by refusing to admit I was to blame or to look downcast. The small amount of freedom I had obtained had disappeared. Once again I became a child whose mother took him to school and came to collect him. In a panic, I asked my father to intercede. He hesitated and changed his mind several times before remarking in a half-convinced way: 'That's the way it is and that's the way it's going to be.'

My mother would not allow anyone else the job of tightening the screw on me. She had decided to take charge of my education. But if you are going to educate someone, it takes two of you, and I was determined not to play my part. My father had suggested he pick me up in the evenings as he often came home before her. He was given a categorical refusal and did not press the matter any further. Franck pleaded my cause. Because of the bad company he kept, she considered him as being partly responsible, and she put him in his place. Behind her artificial smile, she ran the household as she did the Delaunay business: as an energetic woman who was used to being obeyed. For a while, I had hopes that her schedule would prevent her coming along when classes were over, but she arranged with the principal that I should stay behind studying until seven o'clock. The baby-foot and the pals were over. I did not work any harder. I took the opportunity to read. Because I had no other choice, I made use of the school library, which was pathetic, consisting solely of books given as end-of-year prizes.

Pierre's book enthralled me. Reading Bradbury prompted me to embark on a trial of strength. You've got to know how to resist, not to compromise or give in or accept the dominance of force as inevitable. The decision was obvious and simple: I would stop speaking. To anybody. This would be my way of punishing them. I took refuge in a protective silence and I answered in mumbles. When I left school at the end of the day, my mother would be waiting for me in the car, and I would get in without replying to her questions about what I had done during the day. The short journey took place in a wonderfully weighty silence. I went to the table and sat down there with my eyes glued to my plate, experiencing pleasure at the awkwardness I was creating. I left the table without any warning and rushed off to my bedroom without appearing again.

To begin with, I was playing with them and they did not realize. In the little game of 'How long can you live without talking to your parents?' I was capable of holding out for a long time. They would give in before me. But then I was rather pleased to discover an unsuspected power within me. I would never have believed how unsettling silence could be. Néron paid the price and, starved of communication, he deserted me and found refuge in Juliette's bedroom; she was delighted to have him back. After a fortnight had passed, I began to sense signs of weariness. My mother and father had rows about me, though never in my presence. I loved hearing the sound of them arguing. My mother was not ready for this insidious warfare. I ignored her covert overtures and her peace initiatives. I watched them getting worked up, giving me sideways glances, talking about me as if I were crazy – 'Perhaps there's a problem that's not obvious?' – and wondering whether they should consult a psychologist. Franck was the only one not to be taken in. He urged me to stop 'arsing around'.

Grandfather Delaunay asked one of his friends to intervene, a professor of medicine, whom they invited to lunch one Sunday. He observed me from a distance for two hours. I heard via Juliette that he had considered me tired and depressed. He advised some sporting activity and a course of vitamins. After that I was entitled to a glass of squeezed orange juice every morning. But I refused to join the football team. And still, to every question that was put to me, I waited, shrugged my shoulders, unable to make up my mind, and returned to my bedroom to read.

Juliette sometimes came and joined me. She sat at the side of the bed and Néron placed himself between us. She told me about her life in detail. I continued with my reading. I didn't listen to her. Only Néron looked as though he were following her. After an hour or two, I stopped her: 'Juliette, I'm going to sleep.'

She stopped, gazed at me sympathetically and gave me a kiss: 'It's nice when we talk to one another from time to time.'

One evening, over dinner, my mother raised the possibility of going to the cinema on Sunday afternoon to see John Wayne's *The Alamo*, the film everyone was talking about. I was longing to go. Several months before the film was released, I had declared my admiration for Davy Crockett and my father had given me the cap with the fox tail made of artificial fur. My mother knew I would find it hard to resist. My father pretended that he had not been expecting this suggestion and declared that it was a wonderful idea. Before the showing, we would go and have lunch at the Grand Comptoir. He wanted to go to a cinema on one of the central boulevards. The film would look splendid on its giant screen. They looked at me and waited for a response that never came. I stood up without saying a word. I left the table. As I was going out of the door, I had an inspiration. I turned round. I opened my mouth as if about to say something. I held back so as to make the pleasure last. I only had to say yes for hostilities to cease and for life to go on as it had before, with an exciting film into the bargain, but I had developed a taste for masochism and provocation. I rammed the point home: 'Next year, I'd like to go to boarding school.'

My father appeared bewildered. My mother sat open-mouthed, unable to understand. Franck looked surprised. I said nothing more. I couldn't give a damn about their response, positive or negative. Had they agreed on the spot, it would have been all the same to me. They looked at each other without knowing what to say. My mother asked me: 'Why?'

I paused in order to produce the maximum impact: 'So that I won't have to see you any more.'

I left the dining room. And that is why I missed seeing *The Alamo* on a panoramic screen. It immediately made me feel sick. My only consolation was that they did not see it either. I stayed in my room, hesitating. I came within a hair's breadth of admitting my errors. I was on the point of giving in. With my ear glued to the wall, I could hear a more than usually fierce quarrel going on between my parents. It was the first time my father had gone out, slamming the front door violently behind him. My mother came into the bedroom. I pretended to be immersed in reading *La Condition humaine*. My cheeks were ablaze. My heart was thumping. I was doing all I could not to show how upset I was. She sat down at the side of the bed. She gazed at me in silence. I went on reading without taking in a word.

'Michel, we have to talk.'

I put the book down.

'Haven't you gone to the cinema?'

She gazed at me intently, trying to understand me. But how could she when I reacted without thinking? Her confusion was palpable. I pretended to go on reading.

'You frighten me. If you go on like this, you'll find yourself on a slippery slope. You'll ruin your life. I won't be able to do anything for you.'

I looked up from my book as if surprised to see her there.

'About boarding school, you weren't being serious?'

I replied that that was what I wanted. She shook her head several times: 'What's the matter with you, Michel?'

I almost burst out laughing and told her that it was a bad joke and that I didn't mean it. But something stronger urged me on: 'I'd prefer it. It would be better, wouldn't it?'

I turned away from her. I began reading again. I sensed her get to her feet. I did not hear her leave the room. She must be waiting. I turned around. She looked at me. We remained there, face to face. I knew instinctively that the first one to speak would have lost. I held her gaze without arrogance or insolence. The telephone began to ring in the dining room. No one picked it up. They had gone out. There were just the two of us. The ringing went on endlessly. We looked at one another without a word. The ringing stopped. The silence between us was restored. I saw her raise her arm. It remained in suspension with a slight quivering. I did not move. She hurled it with force. It was Malraux who bore the brunt. My book hurtled against the wall. She rubbed her hand and left the room. The front door slammed. I heard her steps growing fainter as she went downstairs. I was alone in the empty flat. The telephone rang again. I let it ring. That evening, Néron decided that our separation had lasted long enough. He returned to my bedroom and reclaimed his position at the end of my bed.

The following morning, Maria announced that I would be going to school on my own. My mother would not be coming to collect me any longer. During the afternoon, Sherlock, the head supervisor summoned me. He was a cold, sharp-featured man, with a natural authority. At the mere sight of him, you stopped talking. You stopped running and you bowed your head when you passed him. He had a way of scrutinizing you that made you feel guilty. And yet he had never been heard to raise his voice or mistreat a pupil. Pierre Vermont liked him very much and swore that he was one of the most cultured of men, a philosophy graduate who had given up teaching to go into administration. Sherlock asked me for my pupil's pass. He looked at it suspiciously. He had my school record open in front of him. He glanced back and forth between his figures and me, while I shifted from foot to foot.

'Marini, your results are not up to the mark. Especially in maths. If this continues, you're going to have to repeat a year. You've got the final term to pull yourself together. You're a year ahead, it would be a pity to waste it.'

He tore up the yellow card and replaced it with a pale green one, signed it, removed my photograph, which he stapled on, and rubber-stamped it. The green card indicated that I was free to leave after the last class. He handed me the pass. Just as I was taking it, he kept hold of it.

'I don't want to see you hanging around in bars any more. Is that clear?'

At five o'clock, I waited. Nobody came to collect me. For a moment, I felt like going to see my mother at the shop to tell her that I was sorry. I hesitated. I decided to go home. Nicolas was the first to be surprised at my change of attitude when I refused to go with him to the Balto or the Narval. I did not mention Sherlock, just said I had to get down to work or else… Nicolas was a realistic boy who spoke without any ulterior motives: 'You and maths, it's a hopeless case. But don't worry, there are masses of jobs that don't require maths.'

If God exists, he's my witness that I tried. Truly. I applied myself. I spent ages at it. So did Franck. He did everything he could to knock the wretched syllabus into my head. In my mind, it was worse than a blockage, it was emptiness. I would feel that I'd understood and was making progress, but as soon as he left me on my own, I plummeted. He persisted: 'It's not complicated. Don't get worked up. Any idiot is capable of solving these problems! You must get there and you will.'

We spent entire evenings, Saturdays, Sundays and holidays at it. We didn't succeed. When he explained a theorem to me, it all seemed obvious, but I was incapable of working it out on my own. A couple of his pals did their best but then gave up.

'Don't worry. It's a matter of time and work.'

One day, even he gave up. He had his own exams to prepare for. I didn't blame him for stopping. He had done all that a brother could do. Maths and me, we just didn't get along together. There was nothing anyone could do. It wouldn't be the first time inexplicable things occurred on this earth, nor the last time. I preferred not to think about what would happen if I had to repeat a year. I put the maths book back on the shelf and set off to meet Nicolas. Blow the consequences. We began to play baby-foot once more. We were given some drubbings and we handed out even more. That's life, after all.

One evening, Nicolas wanted to change venues. Because he was so insistent, we went to the Narval. I had not been back there since Pierre left, three months ago. I did not want to come across Franck, who was convinced that I was racking my brains over Euclid, harmonic beams and quadratic equations. When he saw me at the baby-foot with Nicolas, he muttered 'I see' in a way that spoke volumes. I behaved as if nothing were the matter. My bad mood affected my opponents, who were given a thrashing. A group of spectators congregated around the baby-foot table. When we swapped teams, I glanced over hurriedly at Franck's table. He had left the bistro without a word. I felt a hand on my shoulder. I turned round. Cécile was smiling at me.

'Did you go missing?'

I realized that Franck had not told her anything about my family tribulations. I did not reckon it was worth expanding on the matter and adopted an evasive air: 'I've had... a lot of work to do.'

Her eyes sparkled. I felt like I was melting into a warm puddle. I was dripping with sweat. For the first time in my life, I skipped my turn at baby-foot. The incredulous expression on the face of Nicolas, who had acquired a new attacker, increased my discomfort.

'What'll you have?'

We found ourselves at the bar. I had a café au lait, like her.

'You know Pierre has left his records for you. I'm not going to cart them over to your place.'

Even though I protested and came up with a string of excuses, it was to no avail. I promised to come round one Saturday to collect them. As she left, she gave me a kiss on the cheek. I caught the smell of her lemony perfume. That night, I slept badly. Maria told me one should not drink café au lait late in the evening.

7

For some time, I kept a low profile. I could sense my mother holding back. The business was going through its tax audit and the inspector was asking awkward questions that she could not answer. Her smile had disappeared. She spent a huge amount of time plugging the holes and she feared a harsh penalty. My father, who worked as a sales director, knew nothing about management. She never missed an opportunity to remind him that she could not rely on him and had to cope with the unrewarding task of managing the business on her own. She spent hours on the telephone to Maurice, who gave her useful advice. For Mother's Day, my father arranged for an enormous bunch of thirty-nine red roses to be delivered, and he booked a table at La Coupole. When my mother returned home in a hurry, shortly before midday, I wished her a happy Mother's Day and showed her the wonderful bouquet. She scarcely glanced at it, she was so preoccupied about getting back to the shop to resolve some details with the chartered accountant before a meeting she was due to have with the inspector the following day. She left us without a word and rushed off without saying thank you for the flowers, which remained on the table. My father behaved as if nothing were the matter and cursed the sadistic officials, who had no consideration for wives and mothers whom they obliged to work on Sundays. He put the flowers in a crystal vase without removing the wrapping. We set off for lunch without her. Her absence ruined our appetites. When she came home in the evening, she never touched the bouquet, which remained in its cellophane paper. After two days the roses withered and Maria threw them away.

For her birthday, I had wanted to tell her about my moving up to the third year, without letting it be known that this had been achieved thanks to Nicolas. I told myself that only the result mattered. But I did not mention it; either then, or on any other day. She never asked me the question. For her, it was a given. My father, on the other hand, who had given up his studies after taking the school certificate, was proud and happy. He announced the good news to every neighbour he came across with as much delight as if I had been accepted at the Ecole Polytechnique. He invited us to the cinema. Juliette and I wanted to see *Le Voyage en ballon*. He was not keen. He preferred *Ben Hur*. It was sold out. He resigned himself to *Le Voyage*. Outside the cinema, people were queuing round the block. My father tried to jump the queue, but despite his skill at easing himself into the crowd discreetly and without a fuss, he was spotted by some moaners. We strolled along the boulevards. We came to a cinema where *A bout de souffle* was showing. Franck had talked enthusiastically to us about it. No one was waiting. The woman at the box office advised us against it. It was not a film for children. My father thrust us into the auditorium nonetheless. He and Juliette loathed the film. We left before the end.

'How could Franck have liked such a load of rubbish?' he moaned.

I acted dumb. Deep down, I knew why Franck had liked the film so much. And I loved it for the same reasons.

Once the baccalauréat exams had started, school became less important. Nicolas and I spent our days in the Luxembourg gardens, reading, dawdling or rescuing boats that were stuck in the pond. When evening came, we went to the Balto for our daily game of baby-foot. I still now and then noticed the door with the green velvet curtain at the back of the restaurant, behind the benches where the lovers sat. It was a place one did not enter. Odd-looking men, never women, came to the Balto and simply vanished behind the curtain. I often wondered where the door led. None of my baby-foot friends knew. Old father Marcusot fobbed me off with a 'You're not old enough', which disheartened me. Jacky used to disappear in there with drinks. When I questioned him, he shrugged his shoulders. Nicolas had brushed me off, saying: 'What the hell does it matter to you what's behind that door?'

'Come on now, you donkeys, are you playing or dreaming?' Samy called out, cocksure as ever, and off we went for another game.

8

At the end of June, what I had been dreading finally happened. Cécile was walking towards me up the Boulevard Saint-Michel. I could not avoid her. She rushed over to me. She was excited and spoke without finishing her sentences. She talked at the same frenetic speed as her brother. She asked me to come with her to the Sorbonne in a voice that brooked no opposition. Without waiting for an answer, she took me by the arm and dragged me into the university building. I was surprised by the continuous flow of students who walked up and down the stairs, amidst a pandemonium that required you to shout to make yourself heard. She hesitated, looking panic-stricken and ready to run away, then she gripped my hand very tightly. We went up to the first floor. She walked straight ahead, tense, head held high, pale, forcing her way through the dense mass of bodies with difficulty.

'Michel, go and look over there, please,' she said plaintively.

I turned around and saw a group of students congregated around some noticeboards on which the exam results were displayed. Some of them were cock-a-hoop and were waving their hands in triumph, others had collapsed or were in tears. I shoved my way through and searched for her name among the endless lists. Sudden surges of the crowd moved me several feet away. I used my shoulders and elbows to steady myself with as much determination as if I were the one involved. Her name appeared: 'Cécile Vermont: pass, with merit'. I struggled to extricate myself. Her eyes were closed. I yelled: 'Cécile, you've passed!'

I rushed over to her. We fell into each other's arms. She hugged me until I almost suffocated. I could feel her body, her panting breath on my neck, her smell, her shudders of joy. The embrace seemed to last for an eternity. My head was spinning. We remained pressed to one another for a few seconds longer than the mere explosion of delight at the results warranted. She took my face in her hands and murmured: 'Thanks, little brother, thanks.'

It was the first time she had called me that. This new intimacy agreed with me wonderfully. When she kissed me on the cheek, my heart thumped. We walked back through the university in a jubilant mood. Up on her cloud, Cécile laughed, hopped from one foot to another, hugged everybody and cheered up those who had not got through. As if to emphasize her joy, she introduced me just by my first name. Several students gave me a puzzled look. I could sense them staring behind my back. I felt as light as a sparrow. We found ourselves on the Place de la Sorbonne once more among groups of students discussing their results. Cécile gradually recovered her natural calm. She spotted Franck before he saw her. As soon as he saw her looking so happy, he realized and took her in his arms. He whirled her round. They spent a long time kissing. Franck offered us a drink in a jam-packed café. Cécile began to talk about her exams and the traps she had known how to avoid. It was impossible to interrupt her. We didn't want to. With her short hair and her tomboyish figure, she looked the spitting image of Jean Seberg. Just as beautiful, just as radiant, with the same grace and the same fragile intensity, except that Cécile had dark hair and large brown eyes.

She wanted us to go and pick up the records that Franck had left for me. My protests were useless, as were Franck's. We found ourselves in the huge apartment on the quai des Grands-Augustins, which might have seemed gloomy had it not been for the cheerful amount of clutter everywhere. Cécile had not touched a thing since Pierre's farewell party: the empty bottles of alcohol, the books piled up, the overflowing ashtrays, the dirty plates and the paintings lying all over the floor produced a strange atmosphere in this empty place, which was far too big for her. She cleared away the clothes that were heaped on the sofa and shoved them onto the floor to make room for us to sit down. She went to look for the records. We could hear her rummaging in the cupboards as she moaned about the mess everywhere. She reappeared and then vanished immediately. Franck put his arm around my shoulder.

'Apparently you didn't care for *A bout de souffle*?'

'I liked it personally. It was Papa and Juliette who didn't. They couldn't understand why you had liked the film.'

Franck looked thoughtful: 'I love a girl who's got a very pretty neck, very pretty breasts, a very pretty voice, very pretty wrists, a very pretty head, very pretty knees…'

His eyes were moist and there was a furtive smile on his lips. Cécile entered the room carrying a box of records in her arms. There were far too many. I was embarrassed to take them. Cécile spelled out her brother's intentions: 'Pierre's not giving them to you. He's lending them to you.'

Since I looked doubtful, she grabbed a bundle of envelopes held together by a rubber band and read us his most recent letter:

Dearest Cécile,

The holidays drag on. The weather's perfect. At night, we freeze. We're still at our base camp at Souk-Ahras. Since the Morice line has turned out to be completely useless, they're reinforcing it with the Challe line. This is serious stuff. The fence is electrified all the way along with five thousand volts and at certain points it's over thirty thousand. Best not to touch it. I'm working with a guy from Electricité de France who knows all about high voltage and, what with my military skills, if I don't find a job in management, I could retrain in electricity. As incredible as it may seem, the French army has learnt lessons from past mistakes. The heavy and supposedly impassable Maginot line-style fortifications are no more, the Challe line is a simple cordon used to detect break-ins and, as such, it's pretty diabolical. We have a system that enables us to identify where the line has been cut and we can send out units straight away to step in and prevent people infiltrating from Tunisia. As soon as there's an alert, we fire off star shells. What with surveillance radar and the mined barbed-wire system, the place has become too quiet. For weeks, nothing has happened. You'd think you were a character in The Desert of the Tartars. I think of myself as Lieutenant Drogo. Except I've got nobody here with whom I can discuss anything. Buzzati's book is unrealistic. His fortress has an unbelievable number of intellectuals per square metre. Here, it's real life: nothing but thickos. We look ahead of us. The enemy's over there. We wonder where. There's nothing but shrubs and scree. Perhaps they're somewhere else. We spend our days waiting for the guys from the ALN and we get bored to death. I spend hours monitoring the echoes on the radar. The only time we got the alert, it was a wild boar that had managed to get itself trapped. This at least improves the rations. Finally, what bugs me most is that I'm starting to alter my views. I was convinced that we were all bastards, that the local inhabitants were against us and wanted independence. Now I realise you shouldn't listen to the pet theories of people miles away/nowhere near the conflict. You have to see what's going on in these places. The army is doing a real job here and you mustn't believe the crap you hear. There are nothing but bad solutions to choose from. Few people can have spoken such crap as I have. Apart from Franck, perhaps. That was in Paris. Here, it's different. We're not in a café chatting, we've got our hands in the shit. I feel as if I'm a windsock. I keep on changing my mind. At times, I ask myself what the hell we're doing here and afterwards I realize that, if we leave, there's going to be a ghastly mess. They're not joking, the guys confronting us. But they're not just coming to pick a quarrel with us, they know that we're well equipped. They never attack from the front.

The Saint-Justisme is taking shape. After some tedious starts, I've filled two exercise books that I found at a nearby school whose pupils were evacuated over a year ago. I am more and more convinced that democracy is nothing but a hoax invented by the bourgeoisie so they can run the system permanently. We're going to have to smash everything, without regard or discussion. Individual freedoms are snares and fantasies. What's the use of being free to say what you think if you have a bloody awful salary and you live like a dog? You express yourself, you enjoy the so-called freedoms of the pseudo-democracy, but your life is rotten. We've had revolutions and wars. We've overthrown governments. Nothing changes. The rich remain rich and the poor just as poor. It's always the same people who are exploited. The only freedom that should be given to citizens is economic freedom. We've got to get back to basics: 'To each according to his means, to each according to his needs.' More than ever, the only real power is economic and that's what we have to take back. It won't be by fair means, but by foul. Too bad if, once again, we have to eliminate the supporters of the old order. If we have failed to create a new revolution and not sent to the guillotine those who have usurped economic power, we shall have done nothing but gossip. Elections are merely a sham.

I'm longing to know the results of your exams. I'm not in the least worried – you'll pass with flying colours as usual. You have to learn to have self-confidence. As soon as you've got your results, let me know. Did that little bugger Michel come by to take the records? I don't understand what he's waiting for. If he doesn't make the most of the opportunity, too bad for him. I'm not going to lend them to anyone else, except Franck. It's up to you. I'm not giving them, I'm lending them…

Cécile wanted to reassure me: 'You know, when Pierre says "little bugger", he doesn't mean it unkindly.'

I did not want to take the lot. I made my selection. I counted out thirty-nine of them. Cécile refused to make a list.

'Don't worry, you can return them when he comes home. He's not giving them to you.'

I left twenty behind. They could be swapped if I wanted. True to form, Franck stuck his oar in. Pierre's letter must have made him feel uncomfortable. He put on his bad-tempered expression.

'You'd be better off swotting up your maths instead of listening to rock. What's happened to your good resolutions? Vanished. Have you given up already? You'll get failed next year and you'll regret it all your life. Pierre's right, you're just a little bugger.'

On the spur of the moment, I thought I was going to grab hold of him. Cécile came to my defence. We had something in common, she said. She was allergic to maths as well. She suffered from a basic incomprehension. Pierre had struggled with it for years. He had tried everything possible to help her improve. He had shouted. He had shaken her like a plum tree. In vain. She had been lucky to get herself out of it by doing a literature degree. Franck didn't miss a trick: 'Right! Is that what you want to do? A literature degree?'

Cécile gave him a strange look. She was not amused. Because of me, the maths and the literature degree, they started to quarrel. The sound of their voices grew louder and increasingly sharp. Eventually they sounded like two watchdogs barking at one another. He went out, slamming the door. Cécile was annoyed. So was I. We sat on the sofa in silence. We thought Franck would come back. He did not come back.

'Why do we have this problem?' she murmured.

'You mustn't be cross with him; he's not very smart at times. He doesn't think about what he's saying.'

'I'm talking to you about maths, little bro'. We don't understand a thing. It's not normal!'

'It's in our nature. It's nothing to be ashamed of. In general, maths brains are useless in literary matters and they're proud of it.'

But she was so resistant to my explanations that I gave up. She insisted that we had to resolve this problem. Since it was one we shared, we would join forces. If a guy who was gifted was incapable of teaching maths to an idiot, then perhaps two idiots could manage if they were taught together. She did not want to remain a failure. I was not convinced by her reasoning. If a lame man runs with two crutches, it doesn't make him a sprinter. But I was in no position to refuse. I agreed to her suggestion of our taking maths lessons together in a spirit of hypocrisy.

'It's a very good idea.'

When I brought the records home, there was a fuss. My mother wanted to know where they came from, who had given them to me and why, on the pretext that she herself had never been given anything, neither records, nor anything else. Franck managed to reassure her. Because of the neighbours, she forced me to play them quietly, which, for rock'n'roll, is an aberration. On several occasions, I lugged the record player and the discs over to Nicolas's place, since he lived in a modern building. We took the opportunity to listen to Elvis and Jerry Lee Lewis until our ears were buzzing. Despite his insistent requests, I refused to lend the records to him. Then, our neighbours, who lived above us, moved home and their flat remained empty for several months. I waited until my mother went out and then I turned up the sound; just before she came home, I lowered it to the approved volume. It was a breath of oxygen in a monastic world. I spent hours on my bed listening to records, and, even though I didn't understand a thing, I knew the words by heart. Maria couldn't have cared less. Juliette felt obliged to make comments. To begin with, being very keen on variety shows, she used to enjoy Gilbert Bécaud. She changed her mind, and eventually came to adore rock. It produced a miraculous effect on her: she kept quiet. We turned up the sound. Up to the normal volume at which you need to listen to rock: as loud as the speaker would allow. There was a ring at the door. I switched off the sound. The woman who lived on the fourth floor wanted to know whether, by any chance, it was from our flat that…

Juliette showed herself in an unexpected new light. She lied better than me, and I was an expert. With her natural ingenuity, she opened her eyes wide, and put on a bemused, open-mouthed expression to protest about this infernal din. Seeing her looking so innocent, no one on this earth would have imagined that anything but the absolute truth could come from the lips of this angelic face. I couldn't resist the pleasure of making fun of a girl who went to mass every Sunday, went to confession on Thursdays and was in the priest's good books: 'What does Father Strano say? Do you confess your fibs?'

She merely smiled, with an ambiguous expression. Bardon and certain neighbours still had their doubts about me, so Juliette had a splendid idea. She switched the record player on while I was out and turned it up to the maximum. I would arrive down below, all unsuspecting, and complain to Bardon about this racket that was preventing me from working.

'Do we no longer have the right to be quiet in our own home? It's unbelievable!'

On several occasions, she also warned me about our mother arriving home unexpectedly. Our little game lasted for a long time. But this trifling episode, which ought to have brought us closer, paradoxically set us a little further apart. Whether I lied was of no consequence. These were the tools a man resorted to in order to survive; but that a young girl, not yet an adolescent, who was the image of purity, could deceive people and do so with such nerve, opened up frightening new perspectives for me on the human soul. If she was capable of lying with this alarming sincerity, capable of making me doubt myself, how could I know when she was telling the truth? Who could I believe? I could no longer trust anyone. It was a horrible revelation.

9

The Balto was packed. Ten people were clustered around the baby-foot table. I was in dazzling form. Opponents followed one after another, powerless. True to our custom, we played with our heads down. We saw his leather wristbands before we heard his husky voice: 'Hi there, nitwits. You've improved, haven't you?'

Samy tossed his coin on the table. He was wearing his smug expression. Nicolas and I gave each other a quick glance. We were determined to deal with him unceremoniously. We were the ones on fire, not him, and we intended to make the most of our advantage. Samy got round my midfielders, but Nicolas played the game of his life. He stopped almost everything. He held his centre-back at a slightly straighter angle so as to block shots from Samy, who was getting irritated. Nicolas scored four goals with his backs, three of them off the side. I was the one who was useless. As soon as I got the ball back to the forwards, Samy blocked my shots almost as if he had guessed what I was going to do beforehand. I scored one miserable goal by shooting when he had barely laid hands on his rods. It was a bit iffy. Samy, in lordly fashion, did not protest. On match point, he played around with us and lined up a rebound shot that was so quick we didn't see the white ball disappear into the goal. We heard a metallic *clack* followed by 'Take that, morons!' Nicolas was furious with me. There were seven coins in the ashtrays. He inserted one. Three quarters of an hour waiting for our turn, just to be trounced by Samy. Nicolas had a go at pinball on the Liberty Belle. He challenged me to a game. But while he started to play, I sat on the terrace reading. I was dripping with sweat.

At the far end of the restaurant, facing me, and behind the benches, was the door with the green curtain. Jacky was coming through it with cups and empty glasses. I shrank back into the corner. He passed by without seeing me. An unshaven man in a stained, threadbare raincoat disappeared behind the curtain. What was he doing dressed like that at this time of year? It hadn't rained for weeks. Stirred by curiosity, I drew back the curtain. In sprawling handwriting, someone had written on the door: 'Incorrigible Optimists Club'. Heart racing, I moved forward cautiously. I got the greatest surprise of my life. I had walked into a chess club. There were some ten men absorbed in games. Half a dozen more were following the matches, either standing or sitting. Others were chatting in hushed voices. Neon lights lit up the room, the two windows of which gave onto boulevard Raspail. It also served as a storage room for old father Marcusot, who kept spare tables, folding chairs, parasols, worn-out benches and crates of glasses there. Two men were making use of the armchairs to read foreign newspapers. No one had noticed me coming in.

It was not the chess club that was the surprise. It was seeing Jean-Paul Sartre and Joseph Kessel playing together in the smoky backroom of this working-class bistro. I recognized them from television. These were famous people. I was fascinated. They were joking away like schoolboys. I've often wondered what could have made Sartre and Kessel laugh so much. I never found out. Imré, one of the pillars of the Club, maintained that Sartre used to play like a dimwit. They did it for fun. I don't know how long I remained there, in the doorway, watching them. Neither of them took any notice of me. Nicolas came to look for me: 'It's our turn.'

He didn't know there was a chess club there and he wasn't in the least interested. As for Kessel or Sartre, their names meant nothing to him. Nicolas didn't have a television and reading was not his strong point.

'I don't want to play any more.'

He stared at me in disbelief: 'Are you crazy?'

'I'm going home.'

I rushed off to tell Franck and Cécile my story. I would have done better not to say a word. Because of me, they started arguing again. To begin with, I kept them guessing. They went through a list of a whole string of celebrities. Franck had deduced that the men playing chess were intellectuals. Eventually he hit on Sartre. He couldn't get over the fact that I had seen him. They didn't get Kessel. They couldn't imagine that these two could be playing and joking with one another. The problem was that Franck swore by Sartre, and Cécile didn't in the least. She adored Camus. Franck loathed him. I hadn't yet realized that it was like being for Reims or the Racing Club de Paris, Renault or Peugeot, Bordeaux wine or Beaujolais, the Russians or the Americans, you had to choose which side you were on and stick to it. There must have been one hell of a disagreement between the two men for their voices to rise so sharply. Certain nuances of the exchange eluded me. The words: narrow-minded, history, complicit, blind, lucidity, bad faith, cowardice, morality, commitment and conscience reoccurred on both sides. Cécile gained the upper hand. Her machine-gun delivery and her vivaciousness may have prevented Franck from responding at first. Unable to contain himself, he countered with: 'You're a petit-bourgeois moralist and you always will be. Like Camus.'

Cécile seethed. Quite calmly, she retorted: 'As for you, you're a pretentious little bugger and you always will be. Like Sartre.'

Franck left, slamming the door. Cécile and I sat waiting for him. He did not come back. Cécile was not annoyed with me. I tried to console her and to plead Franck's case. She was turning this discussion into a matter of principle; something fundamental and of prime importance. I did not see why it was so crucial. She said to me: 'Don't go on about it. He's wrong.'

From one of the piles of books stacked up in the drawing room, she picked up a thick book and handed it to me.

'*L'Homme révolté* by Albert Camus.'

'I may not understand it.'

She opened the book. I read the first line: 'What is a rebel? A man who says no.' It didn't seem very complicated. I felt involved. Did this mean that I was a rebel?

'Read it. You'll see. What bugs them is that Camus is readable. And brilliant. Sartre isn't. They loathe Camus because he's right, even though I don't agree with him on everything. He's a bit too humanist for my taste. Sometimes, one has to be more radical. Do you follow?'

At the dinner table that evening I could not resist announcing: 'Guess who I saw playing chess?'

Franck gave me a dirty look. I pretended I had not seen him. My father was amazed and felt obliged to explain to my mother that Sartre was a famous communist philosopher.

'He's not a communist. He's an existentialist.'

'It's the same thing.'

'Not at all.'

She looked to Franck for support, who confirmed: 'He's close to the communists. He's not a card carrier. He's primarily an intellectual.'

My father sensed that he should not step into this minefield. Persuaded to be a good chess player in spite of the thrashings Enzo gave him, he took it upon himself to explain the subtleties of the game to her and was shot down with: 'I'd remind you that in our last game I had you checkmate.'

'That was after the war. Perhaps I'll go and take a look at this club one of these days.'

He could see from the look on my mother's face that she did not want him wasting his time in a chess club. I could feel the storm brewing.

'And you, what were you doing in this bar? I've told you a hundred times that I don't want you hanging around out of doors! Have you seen your maths marks? I forbid you to go there! Is that understood?'

She turned and walked away. Franck wore a smile from ear to ear. My father tried to comfort me: 'That's the way it is and that's the way it's going to be.'

That is how, on the same day, I discovered Kessel, Sartre and Camus.

10

Of course, I went back. Very gradually, I got to know the members of the Club. They were virtually all from Eastern Europe. Hungarians, Poles, Romanians, East Germans, Yugoslavs, Czechs, Russians, sorry, Soviets, to take just a few. There were also a Chinese and a Greek. The large majority shared a passion for chess. Two or three of them hated it and yet came every day. They had nowhere else to go. The Hungarians played a card game for which they alone knew the rules, which were incomprehensible to anyone who was not Hungarian even after they had explained them to you. In one corner there was a small table with a draughts board. No one played the game apart from Werner and old father Marcusot. Whenever one of the members wanted to wind up his partner, he would point to the table and say: 'Chess is too complicated for you. You ought to play draughts instead.'

They had several things in common. They had fled their countries in dramatic or quite incredible circumstances, often crossing over to the West during a business trip or a diplomatic visit. Some of them had never been communists and had kept their opinions to themselves for years. Others had been communists from the start, convinced deep down that they were acting for the good of the world before becoming aware of the horrors of the system and discovering that they had been hoist on their own petard. Some of them still were, even though they had been disowned and thrown out by their party and by the French Communist Party, which regarded them as traitors. Worse still, Franck told me: as renegades! They embarked upon endless discussions or tried to justify themselves and asked themselves questions that were impossible to resolve: why did it fail? Where did we go wrong? Had Trotsky been right? Was it purely Stalin's fault or are we all complicit? Which meant: are we monsters? Are we to blame? And worst of all: might not social democracy be the solution? It led to animated, drawn-out, hate-filled and impassioned discussions. Frequently, they would peter out for lack of vocabulary. Igor, one of the two founders of the Club, ruled that French should be the common language. He was a stickler about this and was constantly reprimanding them: 'We're in France, so we speak French. If you want to speak Polish, go back to Poland. Me, I'm Russian. I want to understand what you're saying.'

In opting for freedom, they had abandoned wives, children, family and friends. It was for this reason that there were no women in this club. They had left them behind in their own countries. They were shadows, pariahs, without any means of support, and with degrees that were not recognized. Their wives, their children and their homelands belonged in a corner of their hearts and their minds and they remained loyal to them. But they spoke little of the past, more preoccupied with earning their living and finding a justification for their lives. By going over to the West, they had given up comfortable homes and good jobs. They had not imagined that the future was going to be so tough. Some of them had fallen, within a few hours, from the status of top-ranking civil servant in a protected job or manager of a public company with everything one could wish for, to that of someone of no fixed abode. This downfall was as unbearable as the loneliness or nostalgia that gnawed at them. Often after endless journeying, they had found themselves in France, where they had been given political asylum. It was better to be here than in the countries that had rejected them. This was the land of the rights of man, as long as you kept your mouth shut and were not too demanding. They had nothing, they were nothing, but they were alive. Among them, this refrain was like a leitmotif: 'We're alive and we're free'. As Sacha said to me the other day: 'the difference between us and other people is that they are alive and we survive. When you've survived, you're not allowed to complain about your lot, for you would be insulting those who stayed behind.'

At the Club, they had no need to explain themselves or to justify themselves. They were among exiles and they were not obliged to talk in order to be understood. They were in the same boat. Pavel declared that they could be proud of finally realizing the communist ideal: they were equals.

'What'll you have, son?'

The first person to speak to me was Virgil, a Romanian with a rolling, sing-song accent that made me smile. This was something they had in common: odd accents that caused them to swallow half their words, conjugate verbs in the infinitive, place them at the beginning of sentences, gobble up their pronouns, mix up homonyms, and ignore the masculine and the feminine or else use them in risky combinations. Occasionally, one of them would make a correction and take it upon himself to give a lesson in French grammar that was riddled with mistakes. Endless and pointless discussions would ensue and, even after years, pronunciation and grammar did not improve. Nevertheless, they understood one another and they managed to have rows in French whenever they discussed politics or commented on the news, which was their principal activity.

'May I stay?'

'If shut up, no possible kibitz.'

He could see that I had no idea what that meant.

'Follow game without speak. No interrupt.'

Silence was inherent to the Club. In actual fact, it was not so much the silence as tranquillity. You could hear the pieces being moved on the chessboard, the breathing and the deep sighs, the stifled whispers, the cracking of fingers, the sneering laughter of the victors, the rustling of newspapers and, from time to time, the regular snoring of a player who had fallen asleep. They sat so close that they could touch one another. Only the movements of their lips and their cocked ears made one realize they were conversing. Some of them still had the habit of putting their hands to their mouths as if to conceal what they were saying. You had to get used to this hissing noise that made it sound as though they were plotting. Igor used to say it was a habit acquired over there, on the other side of the world, where the slightest word could send you to prison or the cemetery, where you had to be wary of your best friend, your brother, your own shadow. Whenever one of them began to raise his voice, there was surprise and it took the rest a second to remind themselves that they were in Paris; then, as in a lively allegro, they began to have tremendous fun. Voices suddenly grew louder and then died down equally quickly. Without thinking, I developed the habit of slipping in between the tables, sitting in my corner without anyone noticing me, talking in such a low voice as to be inaudible, and expressing myself with a glance, or a movement of my eyebrows.

There were afternoons when the periods of silence were brief and the laughter devastating. Igor, Pavel, Vladimir, Imré and Leonid were joyful companions who took nothing seriously and made fun of everything, especially themselves. They were the first to scoff at a grumpy player who requested quiet. They knew an endless number of communist jokes that made them choke with laughter. It took me some time to realize that their absurd jibes were not far from the reality. But in spite of their humdrum lives, they were neither sad nor melancholy. On the contrary, they displayed constant good humour and appeared carefree and unburdened by any memories. Woe to him who was depressed and manifested his anxiety; he would be called to order and told: 'You're boring us stiff with your problems. You're alive, make the most of it and live.'

With them, it was either heaven or hell. There was no in-between. All of a sudden, there would be a flare-up between those who hated the system and those who believed in the future of the human race. Two or three of them would begin raising their voices. Then they forgot their French and started to speak in their native tongues, disobeying the rule laid down by Igor. They took sides, even those who had no idea what had caused the altercation. For ten minutes, there was a shambles of Babel-like proportions. They insulted one another, gave the impression they were about to smash each other's faces in, called each other by every name imaginable and spat out the most appalling insults. When I asked Igor to translate for me, he replied with a smile: 'Best not to. They're not nice. There's nothing to be done: we're either severed or unsevered.'

One day, Igor explained to me this fine distinction that divided members of the Club into two eternally irreconcilable categories: those who were nostalgic and had cut ties with socialism, and those who still believed in it and remained bogged down in insoluble dilemmas. The wounds were raw and painful. These rows were as violent as a hurricane that destroys a town as it passes through, except that they were over as quickly as they had begun and caused no damage. Age-old quarrels and ancient resentment rose to the surface. The Poles hated the Russians, who in turn loathed them; the Bulgarians detested the Hungarians, who ignored them; the Germans abhorred the Czechs, who despised the Romanians, who could not care a damn. Here, they were all stateless and equals in adversity. Once they had unburdened themselves, those who had been scrapping calmed down miraculously and got on with their game of chess. Five minutes later, they were joking with one another without any thought of revenge. They drank without moderation. Both good and bad news was justification enough to clink glasses and down a few bottles. Since the price of vodka was prohibitive in those days, they had discovered local beverages and enjoyed calvados, armagnac and brandy. They bought each other 102s, double pastis 51s at the drop of a hat and happily returned the favour. They had retained an expression used by Leonid Krivoshein who, when he arrived in Paris, did not speak French. He did not know how to say: 'I'd like to buy you a drink' and would say instead: 'Shall we knock back a bottle?' Ever since, they knocked back bottles. By common consent, Leonid had no rival as a drinker. No one had ever seen him the worse for wear. Even when he sank back one or two 204s.

Having been used to reading only one newspaper, they rightly enjoyed being able to choose the paper that corresponded to their own views. They read whatever came to hand, and were astonished that a journalist could criticize a minister without being arrested or shot, or that a newspaper could challenge government decrees without being banned. Wednesday was the day for the *Canard*. Vladimir, Imré or Pavel read aloud the article by Morvan Lebesque, whom they praised to the skies for his forthright views, his inexhaustible capacity for rebelliousness and 'his brawling poetry'. They were all in agreement with the polemicist's column and his combative writing.

'This guy ought to be given a public health award,' Werner maintained.

I should also add that they survived thanks to the money given them by Kessel and Sartre, who were rich, famous, generous and discreet. They recommended their pals to Gaston Gallimard and to other publishers for translation work, although there wasn't much available. I lived among them for years without being aware of any of them getting a great deal of work. I learnt the truth, by chance, fifteen years after the Club had closed down, when I came across Pavel at Sartre's funeral.

I abandoned my baby-foot mates and became the youngest member of the Club. I struck up a friendship with Igor Markish, a Russian doctor who taught me to play chess. He had a son of my age in Leningrad. He introduced me to his pal Kessel with whom he spoke Russian. That was how I came to know Sartre. My testimony contradicts all the biographies. Sartre joked, he was humorous, he cheated at chess by stealing pawns, and he burst out laughing when Kessel surprised him by asking what had happened to his knight on f5. He did not come often. He could sense the animosity of several members of the Club, who criticized him for his communist sympathies, but accepted his money. He would spend the afternoon writing on his notepad, never looking up, absorbed in his work, dragging on his cigarette down to the filter, and nobody dared disturb him. We gazed at him from a distance, slightly intimidated, feeling we were privileged witnesses of creativity in action, and even those who disliked him watched in silence: 'Let's not make any noise. Sartre's working.'

11

The end of the year was gloomy and Paris imprisoned beneath grey skies and freezing weather. For the first time, we did not celebrate Christmas with the family. Something that held us together had become loosened. Franck, who was training to join the school of reserve officers, had been called up for a month. He was traipsing around in the snow in deepest Germany. Wild and contradictory rumours were circulating about Algeria. Grandfather Philippe had decided to go there himself to make up his mind. People said that the newspapers were all corrupt and that you could not trust any of them, apart from *L'Aurore*, and even that was unreliable. Despite being busy at the shop, my mother went with him, glad to be with her beloved brother again and to make the most of a bit of blue sky. Juliette joined them. I did not want to go. I made the excuse that I was behind with school work.

'As you wish,' my mother said, without dwelling on the matter.

My father and I stayed at home like two bachelors. I looked after him, did the shopping and went to pick him up every evening from avenue des Gobelins where he kept an eye on the enormous building site that was going to affect the family business drastically. I would go with him to a little café in rue des Fossés-Saint-Jacques that he used to patronize. He would meet his mates for a game of tarot in the back room. To begin with, I found it hard to understand the rules. Suddenly, it all became clear. I was sitting behind him, and when he hesitated about what he ought to do, he looked at me questioningly to find out whether he should attempt a 'take' or a 'guard' and whether he should push the 'small' to the end. The unpleasant comments of his partners didn't bother him: 'At the Marinis, we play as a family.'

Together, we won frequently. Afterwards, we would go out. He loved Chinese food. Every evening, we used to go to a little restaurant in rue Monsieur-le-Prince.

For the first time, we skipped Christmas Mass at Saint-Etienne-du-Mont because it was so cold that the square outside the Panthéon had turned into a skating-rink. We spent the evening in front of the television, stuffing ourselves with Grand Marnier-flavoured Yule log, chocolates from Murat's and marrons glacés, and bursting out laughing whenever we imagined the people we knew in the neighbourhood who were going to get frozen stiff as they emerged from Midnight Mass. It's not very Christian to speak badly about good Christians, but it's fun.

'We'll have to tell your mother that we did go. We stayed at the back of the church, the congregation was so big.'

'Why not the truth?'

'It'll avoid arguments.'

'We can say that I was ill and that you were looking after me. There's a flu epidemic.'

Before Christmas, my father had given himself the very finest of presents: a Citroën DS19 Prestige. He had been talking about it for a year. My mother did not want one and preferred a sturdy 403, but he disregarded the maternal veto. One evening, he announced quite casually that he had bought it.

'That's the way it is and that's the way it's going to be.'

He had pulled out all the stops in order to have the delivery speeded up and he had managed to get it three months early. We went to collect the car from the dealers on boulevard Arago. At the ceremony of the handing-over of the keys, one might wonder whether the word 'car' was appropriate. Priests celebrating the holy sacraments could not have behaved more ostentatiously. The car was a gleaming black, as shiny as a mirror, feline and alive. We walked around it, trying to absorb the fact that it was ours, not daring to touch it. The manager of the show-room explained to my father how everything worked. Papa made him go through everything several times and he repeated all the instructions so as to get them into his head. There were buttons everywhere, a stereo radio and cushions that were as comfortable as armchairs. To start with it was rather heavy going. My father had difficulties with the gear lever on the dashboard behind the steering wheel. The car moved forward in jerks like a horse that rears up and won't allow itself to be mounted. My father kept stalling it and grew irritable. And then, he got the hang of it and the DS was off. The car drove itself, accelerated, braked, overtook. All you had to do was let it go. We set off along the outer boulevards. People turned round to watch it go by. We took the motorway at porte d'Italie and the DS flew along, free as a bird in the sky. No other car put up any resistance. She gobbled them up like mosquitoes. My father was the happiest man in the world. He began making fun of Grandfather Phillipe, adopting the cheeky, mocking accent of Jean Gabin, whom he imitated wonderfully. I burst out laughing, and the more I laughed, the more he carried on. I was given the full repertory of Pierre Fresnay, Michel Simon and Tino Rossi. I had tears in my eyes. He switched on the radio. We were treated to a Brassens song. We took up the chorus:

> *Les amoureux qui s'bécotent sur les bancs publics, bancs publics,*
> *bancs publics ont des p'tites gueules bien sympathiques.*

On Christmas evening, my father had arranged a surprise for me. He took me to the Opéra de Paris. Since he had only had the idea at the last moment, he had paid a fortune for tickets at an agency. He dressed up for the occasion, and when I arrived in my creased suit, he looked at me in bewilderment.

'Haven't you got anything else to put on? We're going to the Opéra.'

'It's all I've got.'

'I'm going to tell your mother to buy you some things. Come on, we're going to be late.'

We found ourselves in the upper circle, at the side. Despite his protests, I let him sit in the proper seat. I took the folding one. You had to dislocate your neck to get a view of the stage. The Opéra was packed, the women in evening gowns and the men in dinner jackets. He was excited. Even the programme was exorbitant.

'Your grandfather would have given anything to see *Rigoletto*.'

When the lights were dimmed, there was some coughing. The orchestra started to play. The music was beautiful. Nothing happened. We waited in the dark before the curtain rose on the ducal palace at Mantua. Had I not read the programme I wouldn't have known what was going on. They sang in Italian. The audience appeared to understand what they were saying. My father was ecstatic and drank in the words. I watched him humming along with the Duke. In the darkness, I couldn't read the programme. I was bored to death. It was interminable.

'Tell me, Papa, is it much longer?'

'Make the most of it, my boy, make the most of it. Look, it's going to be marvellous.'

The problem was that I didn't know what I should be making the most of. I was confused by the characters who stood there like turnips, listening to the singing, and who then carried on themselves, with great fervour, for hours. I wriggled about in my seat, as if I had ants in my pants. 'Sssh,' hissed the woman next to me in an aggressive voice. My father leaned over to me and whispered in my ear: 'Close your eyes, Michel. Listen. Let yourself go with the music.'

He was right. It was better with your eyes closed. The next thing I knew, I woke up in the DS, being driven along, without knowing how I had ended up there.

'Did you enjoy it?'

'Oh, yes, very much. A bit long perhaps. Especially the end.'

'For me, it could have gone on all night.'

For New Year's Day, we had planned to go to Lens, to Grandfather Enzo's house, but two days beforehand, he cancelled. Grandmother Jeanne was tired and had to rest. My father felt thwarted. It wasn't just that his mother was unwell. He was longing to show off the DS to his father and he had marked out the route we would take. He had planned to have drinks with his old friends in the area. He felt piqued to be left in the lurch. When my father's elder brother Baptiste telephoned, I was the one who answered, convinced it was my mother. I was surprised. He never rang up. My father and he did not get on. Caught unawares, my father accepted his invitation without thinking. One of them must have felt obliged to make a gesture, and the other to accept it. There was a year's difference in age, but Baptiste gave the impression of being older. When you saw them side by side, you would never imagine they could be brothers, so different were they. My father had bought toys for his nephews and a fine briar pipe for his brother. My uncle had not bought anything and reproached my father for showing him up. He had not wanted any presents and he refused to allow his children to open them.

'Should have warned me earlier. I would have bought some presents. You didn't say anything to me.'

My father kept a low profile. My cousins were dying to open the parcels and were awaiting paternal authorization.

'Baptiste, we're not going to get all worked up on a day like this.'

'Paul, you know I'm not well off. You wanted to upset me.'

'It was for the children. You can't refuse my presents.'

'You're making our lives a misery with your presents. We don't need them. What are you trying to prove, that you're rich? OK, you win. I reckon you've got a big problem with money.'

'You're talking rubbish!'

'You've forgotten where you come from, Paul, that's your problem.'

'I move with the times. I make the most out of life and I try to help my family to do so. I want people to be happy. What's wrong with that?'

'You've gone over to the other side! You're a bourgeois!'

My father reddened. He clenched his fists. I thought he was going to hit him.

'To be the right sort of guy, you've got to earn a shitty salary, get bored to death in a lousy job and—'

He didn't finish his sentence. There was a strange smell. While they were quibbling, the turkey had continued to cook. Black smoke brought us back to reality. My father rushed over to the window to air the room. Baptiste burned himself getting the dish out of the oven. The bird was completely charred. The scorched chestnuts looked like jacks from a game of pétanque. By digging away at the ribs, Baptiste pulled out slivers that were grey and inedible.

'If you had accepted these gifts without making a fuss about everything, we would have eaten in peace. I'm sick and tired of your petty preaching. You're suffocating us!'

'If you had remained like us, nothing would have happened.'

My father was chewing a recalcitrant chestnut. He spat it out onto the plate.

'I haven't changed! It's the world that is changing. Are you incapable of understanding that with your tiny commie brain? That's it, I've had enough, we're leaving!'

He stood up, threw his napkin on the table, picked up his coat from the chair and went out without turning round. Baptiste rushed over and caught him by the arm.

'Wait, Paulo, I'm going to make some spaghetti.'

'Don't ever call me Paulo again! Do you hear? My name is Paul! Paulo is finished! You've spoiled my appetite! If you don't want the presents for the kids, throw them in the dustbin! This is the last time I set foot in your place.'

He left the flat in a fury. I followed close behind him. Baptiste pursued us down the stairs, the cousins behind him.

'Come on, Paul, don't be like this.'

My father was not listening. We caught up with one another in the street. He was walking ahead very quickly. I pulled on his sleeve to restrain him. Behind us, Baptiste was trying to make amends, but to no avail. My father was searching for his car keys and couldn't open the door.

'What is this banger?'

'It would have given me pleasure to show it to you, and now I'm ashamed to.'

'Do you know how long I would have needed to work in order to buy myself a car like that? Five years, at least.'

'For me, it took three months. That's the difference between us. And if you saw the shop that I'm in the process of doing up, you'd die of jealousy.'

We climbed in. He slammed the door shut. He drove off, drew level with Baptiste, wound down the window and yelled at him: 'This is no banger, it's a DS. If you're not capable of understanding that, you'll stay a bloody prole for ever!'

He set off at full tilt. My father was driving very fast. He did not seem very happy. We went to have lunch at the Chinese in rue Monsieur-le-Prince. Throughout the meal, he never spoke. When we were finished, he asked me: 'Michel, was I wrong?'

'The cousins loved the presents.'

'Poor kids, Baptiste has always been a killjoy. I'm beginning to understand a lot of things.'

'What about?'

'Old stories. Best not to talk about them.'

'Tell me.'

'When you're grown up. By the way, what do you want to do later on? The future lies in television and household appliances. Think about it.'

One evening, Baptiste telephoned to wish him a happy birthday. When Juliette tried to hand the phone over to him, my father said in a loud voice so that he could be heard: 'Tell him I'm not here. There's no point in him calling back.'

He did not invite him to the opening of the shop. They did not see one another again until the day of my grandmother's funeral and even then, they avoided one another.

12

I didn't want to leave Paris. I just wanted to be with Cécile whom Franck had deserted to become an officer. Since she was on her own, I suggested she come to have dinner with us. She didn't want to meet my father. I insisted, but she refused to make her relationship with Franck official. She preferred to work on her thesis, which she wanted to submit the following year. She didn't mind solitude, quite the contrary. She liked to spend entire days without setting foot outside. I went shopping for her, bought her milk, instant coffee, gruyère, gingerbread, apples and chocolate. I don't know how she managed to eat so much without feeling ill. I tried to make her go out and suggested going to the cinema. But it was cold outside and she didn't want to budge from her home. She gave me a bunch of keys, but I didn't like to use them. I avoided coming round too early. Often, I would ring the bell for ages. She would appear at the door half asleep, dressed in one of Pierre's white woollen, cable-stitch sweaters that came down to the middle of her thighs, wrapped in a rug.

'What time is it, little bro'?'

'Eleven o'clock.'

'It's not possible!'

She took a shower while I prepared her breakfast. She gulped down endless cups of café au lait throughout the day. Every evening, she wrote me a little list of the things she needed; she gave me money for them and refused to accept any change. She felt the cold, so we would make up a log fire and spend our afternoons in the vast drawing-cum-dining room that overlooked the Palais de Justice. From time to time, she would give me a book and urgently demand to know what I thought of it. When I talked to her about it two or three days later, she no longer remembered or hadn't the time. I spent a lot of time slumped in the armchair, reading. As soon as there was a glimmer of sunshine, Cécile had to get out. We would go for a walk. She searched the bookstalls for the rare bargain, for a book no one had heard of. We talked as we paced up and down the banks of the Seine or did the full circuit of the Luxembourg. The park drew her like a magnet. We sat beneath the plane trees by the Médicis fountain. That was her spot, the place where she liked to hide away and work. We looked for somewhere out of the way, by the pool, and preferably on the right so as to catch the sun. For her, it was by far the most beautiful monument in Paris. She could spend a long time there, peering at it as if it held a hidden secret. For me, it was a pretty fountain. She murmured in a dreamy voice: 'This fountain is an impossible dream made up of water, stone and light. It serves no purpose except to please the eyes. You can walk past it without noticing it. As soon as you spot it, you are captivated. It's a Florentine goddess who casts her spells and enthrals you. Her proportions are ideal, her perspective perfect. She makes you romantic, even if you are not. Observe Acis and Galatea, the separated lovers, never to be reunited. It's a landmark for lovers and poets, the guardian of secrets and the witness of eternal vows. One day you will bring the person you love here and you will recite a poem to her.'

'I'd be surprised.'

'It would be a pity if you didn't come.'

'You're not going to tell me that Franck recited a poem to you?'

In response she gave me an enigmatic look.

'He wrote one for you? No, I don't believe you. Not Franck.'

'Don't forget. This fountain has a power. It makes us better people.'

I took photographs of the fountain. From close up, from afar; details; columns; carvings. I took a considerable number. It cost me a fortune. All for nothing. I wasn't able to capture the view of the pond, which was blurred without my realizing why.

She read piles of books for her thesis and she took notes. Sometimes we spent a whole day, each of us in our corner, without speaking to one another. I spent a great deal of time observing her work, scrutinizing her every movement. As soon as she stirred, I dived into my book. I tried to imagine what she was reading, what she was thinking, what she was going to write. She was capable of spending an afternoon with her nose stuck in her photocopied notes. Occasionally, she would glance up, deep in thought, appear to notice me then smile at me.

'Supposing we made ourselves a café au lait?'

Each day she waited impatiently for the postman. I had a key to her mailbox and checking it was the first thing I did every morning. Was there a letter? Pierre wrote once a week. In one month, Franck had sent a black-and-white postcard from Mayence on the Rhine, with 'Love, Franck' on the back.

'You wouldn't say he's over-exerting himself.'

'Franck hates writing.'

She concealed her anxiety behind a smile.

'What if we did a bit of maths today?'

'Do you think we should?'

We immersed ourselves in *The Principles of Algebra and Geometry*. We tried to do the exercises. This pair of torturers had boundless imagination and Cécile had particular requirements. Among the pile of possible exercises, she chose one involving a cyclist.

'We'll feel as though we're in the countryside.'

'I didn't think you liked the countryside.'

'It would be more fun, wouldn't it? The leaking bathtubs, that's depressing, and the trains that pass one another, there's no point unless you work for the rail company. You'll see, it's easy: "A cyclist sets out on a journey consisting of 36 km over flat ground, 24 of them uphill and 48 downhill. When he is climbing, his hourly speed decreases by 12 km an hour; on the descents, it increases by 15 km an hour. Knowing that the length of the journey over flat ground is one third of the total duration of the trip and that the circumference of the wheel is 83 cm: 1) find out the hourly speed of the cyclist over flat ground; 2) what is the total duration of the trip, the average speed achieved and the number of times the wheels revolve."'

We were in a slight panic. We weren't told the age of the cyclist, nor the time of his departure, nor whether he had a three-speed or pedalled on the downhill bits.

'Perhaps if we took a Michelin map, it would be easier.'

We both worked away, lined up the numbers, thought hard, and weighed up the pros and the cons. We agreed about the method. We were pleased. This cyclist was not going to give us any difficulty. We were going to win our bet and become wizards at maths. Cécile left the multiplication and division to me. I'm good at calculations. I worked out the numbers easily.

'He's travelling at… 4645 km per hour!'

'You must have forgotten to divide by a hundred. There must be a rule of three method somewhere.'

We searched. We didn't find it. We started again. We arrived at the same result. She wanted to do the calculations once more. She came up with 4316 km per hour. I suggested to Cécile that we should bring the decimal point forward. She refused. I didn't see the point in persisting with the same mistake. It seemed that this wretched cyclist was pedalling at 46.45 km per hour even when he was climbing, which demonstrated his exceptional athletic abilities and a certain mathematical perversity.

'No one will know.'

'I'll know!'

'The important thing is the result.'

'The important thing is to work it out properly!'

'They're the same thing.'

'They're the very opposite!'

I couldn't see the difference. As far as she was concerned, there was just one way and it had to measure up. Cécile seemed worried.

'That's where there's this barrier between men and women, do you see, little bro'. We don't reason in the same way.'

Traditional processes having shown up their limitations, Cécile decided to experiment on me with a new teaching method which would revolutionize education and transform idiots like me into mathematical geniuses. She developed a personal theory of learning mathematics based not on reflection and progression, but on analytical memory and subconscious work. We had to allow our intelligence to work in its own way. If mathematics were logical, there must be a different approach to it that would pass through the subconscious. We needed to find the right path. Cécile based her ideas on an American study on learning languages while you sleep, in which a tape recorder repeated sentences that fixed themselves in the recesses of the memory. One ought to be able to do the same with mathematics. I made her read aloud from the book, which she learnt by heart as if she were reciting it. After several readings, it was my turn. And so we went on. We ended up learning the theorems mechanically like a calculus table. I have to admit that, in part, it worked. My maths teacher, the ghastly Lachaume, would have been amazed to hear me casually describing: 'The product of the symmetry in relation to a figure P and the symmetry in relation to a point O of this figure is the symmetry in relation to the straight line D perpendicular in O to figure P.'

But basically, this method produced no results. Cécile maintained that our subconscious was blocked, which frequently happens, and that education could be reduced to the basics of plumbing, which consists of unblocking obstructed canals. But after a few weeks of repeating the same things, we had to face up to the facts: the method was useless. This did not mean to say that it was wrong, it might eventually have succeeded with other people, but rather that mathematics, and any method derived from psychoanalysis for learning maths, was a closed book to me. She was insistent, convinced that we needed time for our subconscious to appropriate the theorems and that they would re-emerge sooner or later like a resurgence or a bright flash. But nothing was ever triggered nor was any connection made. After two weeks, even though I deluded myself by being able to recite my maths book by heart, I was downright incapable of doing an exercise. Worse, and incomprehensibly, the speed of the cyclist had risen from 4645 to 4817 km per hour! We started again. But now he was going along at 4817 km per hour. We spent a long time searching for the doorway to psychological mathematics. We did not find it. Cécile, who was so convinced by this method, felt piqued. I comforted her as best I could, though I never was much good at comforting. Psychology has nothing to do with mathematics, any more than faith can move mountains.

'You must have a problem with your father, no?'

'We get along fine.'

'Mathematics represents authority. When people have a blockage in maths, it's because they have a problem with their father and with authority.'

I tried to fix this reasoning firmly in my mind, but the more I thought about it, the less clear it became.

'At home, it tends to be my mother who represents authority.'

'You mean she's the one who wears the trousers?'

'My father isn't someone who's authoritarian. She's the one in charge. He couldn't care less. Quite the opposite: for him the important thing in life is to make the most of it. He tells jokes, he smiles and he can sell anything. If what you say is true, I shouldn't have any problems with maths.'

'Have you got problems with your mother?'

'Things haven't been great for some time.'

'She represents authority instead of your father. She has substituted herself in his image. That's why you are blocked. You'd do better to choose a creative path. What would suit you?'

'Maybe a photographer. When did you know what you wanted to do?'

She did not answer. She remained silent. She screwed up her eyes as though she were searching her memory.

'I don't know.'

'It's not bad being a teacher.'

'All of a sudden, it bothers me. Can you imagine, little bro', an entire life confronted with idiots like us? You bust your guts for them and they loathe you.'

'It's strange, on Sunday my father asked me the same question. He wants me to go to business school. He says the future is in household goods.'

'How awful! No one can enjoy selling baths and washing machines.'

'He earns a lot of money.'

'Is that what you want?... I can't believe it, Michel! Not you!'

The following day, Cécile told me that she was stopping her studies. She couldn't see herself being a literature teacher all her life.

'Psychology studies, perhaps.'

I wasn't sure whether that would be a good idea. I said nothing.

'It's thanks to you, little bro'.'

'What have I done?'

'It's because we talked to one another. You're the only person I really speak to.'

'And to Franck?'

She looked at me with that sad smile that did something to me and she shrugged her shoulders as though nothing were of any importance. Then her expression altered. In a flash, that bitterness had disappeared and she was radiant.

'Cécile, may I take your photo?'

'If you like. You don't know how relieved I am not to be dragging around that thesis any longer.'

'You seemed to believe in it.'

'My supervisor is a communist and wants to please Aragon, whom he bumps into from time to time. Had he supported Maréchal Pétain, he would have suggested I did Claudel. It's literature I love, not teaching. One has to have a vocation and I don't have one.'

Then she received a card from Franck, still on the Rhine at Mayence, who in his telegraphic style announced that he would be returning home shortly. There was also a long letter from Pierre. She unsealed the flap of the envelope without tearing it and carefully removed the two sheets of paper. I could hear Pierre's voice as I watched her lips:

My dear Cécile,

We've not heard or seen a fellagha for two weeks now. Our detection and interception system is so efficient that we stop virtually a hundred per cent of the attempts at break-in. They go along the coast or via Tébassa, further north, but with us and in the Souk-Ahras region, it's quiet. We've had one wounded, a stupid fellow who fell from a roof trying to connect a radio mast. Our main job consists of removing the mines in the area around the Challe line. We find two or three mines occasionally. However much we suffocate ourselves, that is to say keep ourselves hidden for two days at a stretch, we never manage to catch the fellaghas. Obviously, they avoid us like the plague. When they fire at us, it's from so far away that we're not aware of it. We don't complain. We prefer to be here than trying to maintain order in Algiers or in Oran. If the government gave us permission to cross the frontier, we would already have made mincemeat of them. They're on the other side, facing us, and they know we're not allowed to go after them. We feel as if we're tucked away behind our barbed wire fences and our watchtowers when in actual fact we're hemmed in by a frontier, by a simple line in the desert, which separates us from Tunisia where they calmly go and take refuge. These guys are cowards, capable of torturing and murdering defenceless farmers or peasants. As soon as they see us, they scuttle away like rabbits. We used to say that with the arrival of De Gaulle, it would change, that we would set about them and crush them like flies once and for all, but nothing happens. Nobody understands anything.

You will have some idea of the degree of decrepitude into which I have fallen when I tell you that I spend my days and part of my nights playing cards with three guys who I reckoned were mentally retarded six months ago and who are now my best friends. I've decided to test the basic principles of Saint-Justisme on them. After all, if one has to fight for the oppressed, one might as well ask them their opinions and what they want. That would avoid us making the same unfortunate mistakes again. I'm lucky to have with me an ideal sample of the broad mass of the French working class: a farmer's son from the Ardèche, a toolmaker who works in an engineering factory in Saint-Etienne and a truck driver from Le Havre. Educational level: bac minus six. Their conversation is mainly about girls, soccer and old bangers. Their main preoccupation is food. They couldn't care less about politics. All the more reason to try and discover what's in their heads.

My book progresses. I've just finished the third exercise book. Two more and my theory will be coherent and irrefutable. The pace is slowing. I have to resolve some problems that have serious consequences. I had not weighed up the extent of Saint-Just's phrase: 'Many opponents will have to be killed for this cause to triumph.' I hoped that we would be able to confine ourselves to a few hard core facts, to the symbols of the old order. We must have no illusions as to the enemy's capacity to resist, for he will use all means available to hang on to power. It will be a real revolution or none at all. Many will die, and I don't know whether people are prepared to spill so much blood nowadays. Will it be worth our while? Certainly. Will the people be with us? I am less sure. Oppressed as they are, they won't dare rebel for fear of losing the miserable advantages the bourgeoisie has granted them. Why fight for slaves who lick the hands of their masters? To tell the truth, I'm in quite a state about this question. How far should we go to make men happy in spite of themselves? What's happening in China is instructive and promising and will serve as a guideline. A profound revolution is taking place and we cannot measure its consequences. As soon as I am demobbed, I shall go there in order to see what they're doing. Perhaps it's my Western over-sensitivity that prevents me from keeping up with the pace of the revolution. An intermediary stage may be necessary.

Remind that little bugger Michel of what Albert Einstein said: 'Don't worry about your difficulties with maths, I can assure you that mine are far greater.' They have reopened the school which had been closed for over a year and the commanding officer has asked me to give a lesson on the binomial system to the local children with a lieutenant from Poitiers who is teaching them French and has decided to stage Racine's Bérénice. These kids are eager to learn and they grasp things very quickly. We're doing one term's syllabus in a month. We find ourselves educating the children of our enemies. Is that logical?

It makes me laugh to think of Franck freezing his balls off in Germany. The war will be over before he gets here. I've written to him. He hasn't replied. I don't know whether he got my letter…

Cécile stopped reading. She remained pensive. I took the letter. I reread it with difficulty. Pierre's handwriting was like a doctor's.

'You mustn't worry. He's in a quiet spot.'

'There's something that's not quite right. There must be another approach. One has to find the right key. Meanwhile, ask your father to pay for private lessons.'

Cécile went off to make some café au lait. The coffee pot was heating up. She had made a shopping list.

'You could go yourself.'

'Don't you want to do it for me any more?'

'You don't get out of your house any more. It's at least a week since you set foot outside.'

'Are you going to do the shopping for me or not?'

She handed me the list with two ten-franc notes.

'Don't bother with the list. I know it. Coffee, milk, honey bread and apples. You're going to get ill eventually if you don't eat anything else.'

'Don't you start too.'

She took me by the shoulders and shook me. She was unexpectedly strong for her size.

'Listen to me, little bro'. I don't need to be looked after, or to be protected. Not by you, not by anyone. I'm old enough to look after myself. If you want us to remain friends, never ever tell me what I must do! Is that clear?'

'As you wish. But you're too thin.'

She pushed me onto the sofa, threw herself on me and started to tickle me. Cécile loved tickling me because I'm very ticklish. She laughed as much as I did. The more I tried to protect myself, the more she went on. I couldn't do the same to her. She's not ticklish. In between hiccups and howls, I managed to free myself by hoisting her up at arm's length. I held her there, suspended. I was perspiring and out of breath. So was she. My arms were trembling. I held on for ten seconds. I let go. She fell on top of me. We were still laughing, helplessly glued to one another, exhausted and happy. We drank our umpteenth café au lait of the day with her Breton biscuits and her honey bread.

'You haven't told me what you thought of Pierre's theory, about Saint-Justisme.'

'He's absolutely right.'

'It will be a dictatorship!'

'What is it these days? A democracy?' '

'It's not possible. You can't have a programme to slaughter people.'

'You have to know what you want in life!'

It was a dangerous subject. It was best to change the conversation. I didn't want to argue with her.

'I must go. My mother's coming back this evening.'

*

On Saturday, we did a photographic session in the Luxembourg. I only had one roll of film. She posed in front of the Médicis fountain, the sculptures in the park, and beneath the bandstand. It was a fine day. I took my time focusing, finding the correct angle and getting the light right. She was on edge. She told me to hurry up, that she would look horrible and she would tear up the photos. She sat down by the side of the pond. I shot her from close up, thirty centimetres away from her face. Her hair was tousled. There was a ray of sunshine that lit her from the side. At that moment, she smiled. Her eyes smiled. She stood out against the sky and the trees. She was calm and radiant. I caught her sideways glance. They're the best photographs I've taken of her. I showed them to her. She didn't tear them up.

13

My mother and Juliette returned from Algeria looking tanned. While we froze under leaden skies, they had sunshine all the time. We questioned them about the incidents there. They had not seen very much. Except for Juliette. But my father forbade her to open her mouth.

'Am I not allowed to speak?'

'I don't want to hear you.'

'You'll never know what I've seen!'

Only my mother was allowed to express herself. There were parachutists at every crossroads. From time to time, they were woken in the middle of the night by explosions from bomb attacks and they tried to figure out in which part of the town the explosion had occurred. Once, on the Avenue Bugeaud, they were doing the rounds of the shops with Louise when someone wearing a white cap fired twice at a man who was sitting on a bench reading a newspaper. The gunman dashed off in a Peugeot 203 that shot away at top speed. The man on the bench slumped down. No one came to his aid. The passers-by walked around him as though he did not exist. A stream of blood flowed along the pavement as far as the gutter. But everyone went on their way. Apart from that, it was peaceful. Philippe had returned from Algeria feeling reassured. The French army had the situation in hand. You could put your trust both in it and in De Gaulle. Very soon, there would be no further incidents.

'We'll never hand over a French department. The uprising has bled itself dry. Their leaders are in prison.'

Maurice and he even reckoned it was a good time to invest in Algeria. There was a lot of money to be made. Most people were prepared to sell their furniture for a crust of bread, but everything had to be carried out discreetly, in collusion with the OAS, the paramilitary organisation which did not want the French to leave or give up their properties. My father did not agree. But he was not allowed to have his say. If it were a question of investing, he would have preferred to open a branch there.

'My dear Paul, you've got ideas above your station,' Philippe maintained. 'You've embarked on Pharaonic building works, and I'm not the pharaoh. I won't pay one franc more than the estimate. Anything in excess, you'll have to pay from your own pocket. Mind you, it's my own fault; because of your education, you know nothing about business. I should not have left you in charge of this project on your own.'

My father turned towards my mother, who said nothing.

'Paul, you should have thought about it,' she acknowledged. 'How could you have commissioned these building works without asking us our opinion? Where's it all going to end? You've put us in an impossible situation.'

I cleared the table after dinner, and, in the kitchen, my mother stared at me: 'You don't look well, Michel, what have you been doing during the holidays?'

'Maths.'

She looked at me in surprise. She didn't believe me.

'Every day. I learned my book by heart. I can recite it for you, if you like.'

'Have you made progress?'

'It's a complicated thing, maths. It's not through learning that you understand, and when you don't understand, you don't know why. I've been told I have a psychological blockage.'

'Is that all?'

'Apparently, I'm not responsible for it.'

'Whose fault is it then?'

My father had joined us in the kitchen with a pile of plates. I almost replied that it was a problem of authority, but it was best to keep my mouth shut so as not to get into endless explanations. The two causes of my mathematical blockage gazed at me and awaited my answer. I shrugged my shoulders. That's the disadvantage of psychoanalysis — knowing the cause of the problem doesn't resolve it.

14

When I arrived at the Balto, I sensed an unusual atmosphere. The baby-foot tables were unoccupied and so were the pinball machines. Everyone was leaning against the bar and talking in hushed voices. At the Club, nobody was playing chess. They were there, sitting side by side, in silence, being careful not to make any noise. Silence was the norm there, but this was strained. Sartre was sitting alone at a table, looking pensive. A cigarette at the corner of his lips had gone out without him taking a puff. A length of ash drooped from it. In front of him were two empty glasses and a third which he drained down to the last drop. Jacky came in, his tray laden with drinks, which he distributed to each table with unaccustomed delicacy. When he passed close to the table at which Sartre sat, he held out his empty glass. Jacky stood stock still, stared at him in an apologetic manner, and left the Club. He returned a few moments later with a bottle of Black and White, which he placed on the table. Sartre looked up. Jacky filled his glass with whisky. Sartre nodded in gratitude, began to drink in small sips, then stopped and didn't move, his eyes staring into space; his shoulders slumped, and he looked tired. His right hand, which lay on his lap, held the empty glass. Those who came in to the Club melted into the all-pervading silence. They stared at Sartre sympathetically. He picked up a pen and scribbled something in a shaky hand. I went over to Igor Markish, whom I had got along with during the holidays. He gave me a knowing smile and laid his hand on my shoulder as if to console me. I whispered in his ear: 'Has there been a death in his family?'

Igor looked surprised by my question and replied in a barely audible voice: 'Camus is dead.'

'Albert Camus?'

'In a car. He died instantly. Terrible loss.'

'He looks shattered. They must have been very close.'

'After the war, they were friends. When *L'Homme révolté* came out, Sartre demolished Camus. He was contemptuous and hurtful. They fell out.'

'A girlfriend gave me the book. I've not read it yet.'

Sartre was scribbling away nervously. You could hear the furious scratching of his pen on the paper. He kept crossing out and starting again. He stood up wearing a gloomy expression and knocked back his glass in one. He seemed restless and he departed, leaving the sheet of paper on the small table.

Together with Igor and the others, we walked over to the table to see what he had written. The page was almost illegible, with crossings-out everywhere. A few lines stood out. Igor began to read:

… We had quarrels, he and I. A quarrel doesn't matter – even if you never see one another again – it is just another way of living together without losing sight of one another in the narrow world that is given to us. This did not prevent me from thinking of him, from sensing his gaze on the book, or the newspaper that he read, and wondering: What does he think of it? What does he think of it at this moment? … His stubborn humanism, narrow and pure, austere and sensual, waged an uncertain war against the massive and shapeless events of the times. But conversely, through his dogged rejections, he reasserted, at the height of our age, against the Machiavellians, against the golden calf of realism, the existence of the moral act…

As though he did not believe what he had just heard, Pavel took the sheet of paper from Igor and deciphered it for him. Vladimir read it next and handed it to Werner. The sheet went round the group. Everyone had a different view. Imré did not understand: 'I thought they were enemies? What does "another way of living together without losing touch" mean? Either you're angry or you're not!'

'It's a bit late to have regrets,' said Vladimir.

They started to discuss as they usually did, talking without taking the trouble to listen to one another, but lowering their voices. Virgil was inveighing against Sartre. Gregorios supported him. When they argued among themselves, they didn't bother with the French that they coped with more or less proficiently and reverted to their native tongues, thus enabling them to insult each other more easily. Sartre returned, accompanied by Jacky. The noise died down immediately. He saw us huddled together, reading what he had just written. He did not look pleased, and he hurried over towards us, grabbed the page from Leonid's hands, put it in his briefcase, took out a handful of banknotes with which to pay the bill and left the Club without a word. They all stood there, transfixed. I asked Igor why they looked so shocked.

'Because herein lie all our problems.'

15

For several weeks, the apartment rustled with the launching of the new shop. The eighth wonder of the world. My father had had to do battle with Philippe, who did not see the point of spending so much money on improvements.

'It's all for show. The house of Delaunay has a reputation. A lick of paint to make it clean, that's normal. To demolish everything just for the sake of it; out of the question!'

My father would not have prevailed in the fight over the shop had my mother not tipped the balance in his favour: 'Listen, Papa, you left the shop to me. Now, I'm in charge. As you've seen, it's going well. Paul's right, we need to modernize.'

'Spending millions on a window giving onto the street, marble and neon lighting everywhere, sliding doors, moving the offices to the first floor, the shop to the courtyard, and replacing my shop sign which was as good as new, now there, my girl, I do not agree. Playing music! What is this nonsense? We're not near the Opéra. You may be in charge of the shop, but I'm the shareholder. It's too big, it's too smart. Our clientele is working-class. We mustn't forget that. Luxury doesn't suit the neighbourhood. In business, just as in life, one mustn't have ideas above one's station.'

When people thwart her, my mother is not the sort of woman to answer back. She keeps mum and patiently endures the smouldering flames. But you can't depend on her silence. She had supported my father for years. This Sunday afternoon, as Philippe was venting his spleen, my mother's face hardened.

'Papa, I'm sorry, I'm the boss now. I've decided. This is the way it's going to be and that's that!'

My father, Juliette and I glanced at one another, flabbergasted that she should be using one of father's expressions. Philippe had looked taken aback and, despite their disagreement, my father tried to console him:

'It flatters people to shop in a place that looks flashy. We're going to blow them away. Small businesses today, they're finished. We're going to sell with smaller margins. We'll have two or three times the number of orders. We're going to make more profit than we do now. We're going to advertise.'

'Neighbourhood advertisements, you mean.'

'Advertising. On the radio and in the evening paper!'

Philippe stood up, stared at us as if we were a load of halfwits and, followed like a shadow by Grandma Alice, he left looking very offended. It was six months before we saw them again. They refused to come to the opening.

I walked along avenue des Gobelins. The old shop sign that had seemed huge to me had been replaced by one twice as tall and glittery, which kept flashing at rapid intervals, and gave the time and the temperature. You could see it from place d'Italie. On the day before the opening, the construction work was completed in an atmosphere of complete chaos. The grubby and austere old store, which had not altered in half a century, had made way for a bright and ultra-modern shop with a white marble façade which served as an exhibition space for baths, bathrooms and kitchen equipment. The place was buzzing and bustling as though it belonged in a Charlie Chaplin movie. My mother was pursuing my father because we were heading for disaster and because she should have listened to her father, my father was pursuing the architect because nothing was ready. He was threatening him with a ruinous lawsuit once he had smashed his face in. The architect was complaining to the workers because things were not moving quickly enough, the workers were swearing that the delay was due to the electricians perched upon ladders and inside the false ceilings, which they never stopped touching up, and whom nobody said anything to because their foreman, an Italian who was well over six foot tall, was yelling in his giant's voice to drown the musical drizzle of the chorus from *Bridge over the River Kwai* that emanated from the ceiling. He did not look very easy to get on with. He was a former lighting engineer who took his job seriously and rushed around the spotlights, illuminating every cooker with love and inspiration as if it were a starlet. The future sales staff were whistling the tune '*Hello, le soleil brille, brille, brille*' in unison and were bustling about, unpacking and installing the equipment, and cleaning and polishing it. My father was directing affairs as though he were on the parade ground, issuing his instructions on the move. A shrill, piercing sound made us jump. The man who was mending the loudspeakers panicked and disconnected the sound system. After several fruitless attempts, he managed to get the orchestra started again and struggled to reduce the deafening whistling noise. The architect was running after my father, brandishing twenty or so sheets of paper which my father refused to look at. He despatched him to my mother who scrutinized the pile with a mistrustful eye. The architect handed her his ballpoint pen for her to sign the sheets.

'What is this?'

'The additional charges for the work.'

'Turn the sound down!' yelled my father.

She leafed through the invoices, distraught.

'It's not true. It's not possible! I won't sign. It's daylight robbery! Do you hear?'

'Your husband told me that—'

'Ask him to pay you! I'm not paying for a penny more than the original estimate!'

They started shouting, and each of them tried to drown out the other's voice. My mother was not the kind of woman to allow herself to be impressed by an architect, even if he was employed by the government, even though he weighed twice as much as her. My father, who did not concern himself with management problems, remembered that he had an urgent meeting elsewhere and vanished through the back door. My mother and the architect searched for him. No one had seen him leave. His disappearance inflamed them. The architect was convinced he was being taken for an imbecile. My mother could not bear the slightest trace of suspicion. They swore they would summon their lawyers, who were formidable, and they threatened one another with the foulest legal actions. Furthermore, they were sure of winning: the architect was influential, and my mother had relatives in high places. Listening to them, you could tell one of the two was going to regret this for the rest of his or her life. My mother picked up the phone and dialled a number. Her lawyer was not there. She refused to let the architect ring his lawyer from the office. The architect ordered the workers to leave the building. My mother threatened not to pay them unless they completed the work and, caught in two minds, they were not sure what to do. My father chose this moment to resurface. Far from restoring calm, his presence increased the fury of the architect, my mother and the Italian foreman, who wanted to be paid immediately. In the face of this panic, I abandoned ship. I returned home and started *L'Homme révolté*.

My father returned home in the early morning, exhausted. The shop was ready, apart from the sound system. He looked pleased. The problem – the furious architect and the additional charges – must have been settled. They did not discuss the matter. He went to bed for two hours to rest before the final assault. My mother never stopped deliberating about her appearance after she had asked for my opinion. I did not have any precise view, not knowing whether it was preferable to wear a smart, unbusinesslike outfit, or whether to maintain a discreet appearance that did not suggest this was a decisive new beginning for the future of the family. While I was deliberating on this dilemma, she glared at me as though she had never seen me before.

'And you, what are you going to wear?'

'Well, this.'

'Jeans. The boy's crazy.'

She rummaged through my cupboard. I had three pairs of grey trousers that reached the bottom of my calves and a worn Terylene suit that was patched at the knees and too small for me.

'What do you wear to go to school?'

'One of those. You're not allowed to wear jeans.'

'That's all I need. It's my fault. I don't take enough care of you.'

We dashed off to a shop in boulevard Saint-Michel. The proprietor attended to us. She took the opportunity to invite him to the opening, he and his wife.

'He needs clothes. The problem is that he never stops growing.'

'You've got to get the stretchy new material, it's the latest thing in trousers.'

I found myself kitted out with three pairs of trousers that were supposed to grow with me. We waited until the alterations were ready.

'Did you reach an agreement with the architect?'

'How do you know about that?'

'I came along to the shop yesterday evening.'

'We reached a compromise with him. I'm satisfied.'

'Didn't you settle all this beforehand?'

'What with the additional work, he was trying to take advantage of your father's gullibility. We let him try it on and we caught him.'

'I wouldn't have thought that—'

'It's business, Michel. One day you'll understand.'

I nodded knowingly.

'By the way, where's your brother? We don't see him any more. He's disappeared.'

'Franck doesn't tell me what he's doing.'

'Perhaps he's with… that girl.'

'He doesn't tell her anything either.'

'Is he at her home?'

'I don't think so.'

'Then it can't be serious between them. Perhaps he's changed girlfriends.'

I was slightly on my guard. My mother never spoke in the spontaneous way that my father or most other people did. Enzo once told her that she expressed herself with her head, as though she had ulterior motives. She had not been pleased. This impression was accentuated by the permanent smile on her face. She continued to interrogate me. Whether I knew her, what she was like and what did she do. I didn't want to discuss any of this with her. Even if I had found the words, she wouldn't have been able to understand Cécile. They were light years apart from one another. They could only ever disagree where Franck was concerned. I acted dumb. She persisted. She knew a great deal, or pretended she did. She was aware that

Cécile's brother was a lieutenant in Algeria, that I had been to the farewell party at their place on the famous evening when I had crept out of the flat, that they had lived on their own since the death of their parents in a motoring accident. Franck had given her a few explanations. I opened my eyes wide, adopted an innocent expression and shrugged my shoulders. Silence fell. She looked impatiently at her watch several times. She was worried about missing her appointment at the hairdresser.

16

As if to keep misfortune at bay, my father had chosen 22 November, the date of their wedding anniversary, for the opening. My mother categorically refused, because it was the day of her brother Daniel's death. Confronted with my father's insistence, she had pretended to give in, but my father should not have deluded himself into believing that he had imposed his views. In actual fact, she had already foreseen that, given the additional costs, she would kill two birds with one stone: the opening was to be delayed by several weeks at least, and this would free her from Philippe's intrusive supervision.

The opening was scheduled to start at four o'clock in the afternoon and would run on into the evening. I came home to get ready. Juliette, jealous of the bags that I had brought home, struck up the old tune of 'I've got nothing to wear' and was told to pack it in by my father who was making phone calls to make sure that journalists would be present. To listen to him – and he knew how to be convincing – it was the most important commercial event in Paris since the opening of the Drugstore. He hung up in excitement.

'*L'Aurore* is sending someone from the newspaper!'

He immersed himself in his list again and rang up *Elle*.

Juliette came into my bedroom and pretended she couldn't make up her mind. She had a huge range of clothes to choose from in her model wardrobe. I threw her out and unpacked my things under the expectant eye of Néron. My new suit made me look like a man. With the tie, if I combed my hair flat and pulled back my shoulders, put my hands in my pockets and didn't smile, I could pass for sixteen or seventeen. My mother came back with a blonde perm, crimped and lacquered, which she was very proud of. I was turning to and fro so that she could admire the results of her purchases when her face suddenly fell. From the bathroom, we could hear my father singing at the top of his voice:

'*La donna è mobile, qual piuma al vento, muta d'accento, e di pensiero…*'

She leapt to her feet. I could hear their loud voices arguing: 'Are you crazy singing so loudly? The whole building will hear you.'

'Am I no longer allowed to sing?'

'Not in Italian. I don't want to have the neighbours making remarks.'

'It's *Rigoletto*. It's Verdi!'

The bathroom door slammed. My mother's footsteps echoed in the corridor. He began singing '*La donna e mobile*' again in his tenor voice.

My mother had the rare ability to shout without raising her voice.

'Paul, stop immediately!'

Ever since his return from Germany, Franck had been evasive. We hardly saw one another. He would drop in, rush over to the fridge to eat whatever he found there, lock himself in his bedroom, spend hours on the telephone looking as though he were plotting something, and then disappear without warning. Cécile pursued him. She rang up frequently and blamed me for not passing on her messages to him. She didn't hear from him. He didn't sleep at home. He wasn't with her. She seemed anxious. Nobody knew what he was up to.

He had reappeared on the day of the opening. He was in one of his foul moods, with rings under his eyes and a week's growth of beard. My mother shouted at him. He didn't hesitate to come to my father's defence.

'For years now you've been boring us stiff with your neighbours. We couldn't give a damn what they think. We're suffocating here. We have to walk around in slippers. We have to turn down the radio. I've had enough!'

My mother was outraged.

'We should respect our neighbours. They're decent people and I'm not going to allow you to—'

Franck paid no further attention and sat down at the kitchen table to consume what remained of the roast chicken. She made an effort to control her anger.

'I'm glad you've come home. You must get ready for the opening.'

'Oh, it's not a good day. I won't be coming.'

'May I know why?'

'We've got a cell meeting. I have to prepare for it.'

'Obviously, you're not going to spare any time for me.'

'Whether I come or not won't change anything. You don't need me. The party, on the other hand, does need me.'

'So because of your bloody party meeting you're going to let your family down?'

'This bloody party was the party that was being fired upon while others were lining their pockets on the black market, if you see what I mean.'

'No, I don't see,' said my mother in an icy tone. 'What are you trying to say?'

'Ah, it's true, I forgot that the Delaunays behaved like heroes during the war. Brave Uncle Daniel. That fellow didn't die in vain.'

'I'm not going to allow this! You're a disgrace.'

'Didn't the Delaunays get wealthy during the war?'

'That's incorrect! We were exonerated.'

My father felt that the discussion was taking a dangerous turn and tried to calm things down.

'Franck, it's in the past. Me, I had to put up with four years of prison camp and yet today, we're friends with the Germans. We've turned the page and so much the better. I think of the future and of the family. You should do the same.'

'Listen, Papa, I've got to go to this meeting. It's important.'

'What can be more important than the opening, may I ask?'

'You'll see!'

It might have remained there. A family row like millions of others. Everyone sulks in his own corner and, three days later, it's all forgotten. Nothing unpleasant would have come of it. Everything would have continued as before. But my mother rose to her full height and, weighing every word, said to him:

'You will apologize, Franck. You will withdraw what you have said.'

There was a long silence. Her eyes were gleaming, her face impassive. I knew what Franck's reply would be and, deep down it was what I hoped for, which proves just how stupid one can be at that age.

'I will not apologize. It's the absolute truth.'

'You will take back what you have just said or you will leave!'

Franck stood up, his chicken thigh in his hand. My father made a final attempt: 'All right, let's calm down Listen, Hélène, there's no point in getting angry. If he doesn't wish to go to this opening, it's his bad luck, he won't have any champagne.'

'I've no intention of feeding a viper. You will apologize immediately!'

Franck hurled the chicken thigh across the kitchen.

'You won't be seeing me again in a hurry!'

He rushed off to his bedroom and filled a bag with clothing. He left, slamming the door behind him. We tried to come to terms with what had just happened. At moments of tension, one has to learn to keep one's mouth shut. The first person to speak has lost. My father grumbled: 'You shouldn't have said that to him!'

She exploded. It was my father who took the brunt of it. The neighbours heard everything. That he had gone badly wrong, that we were now paying the price for his poor education and the Marinis' political views. Say what you will, but you would never hear a child speak to his mother in that tone at the Delaunays, and his father just sit there like a vegetable, without reacting. Then an unusual thing happened. Instead of grinning and bearing it, and waiting for the storm to pass, my father beat his fist on the table. So hard that the Baccarat crystal vase fell over. The water spilled on to the wooden floor. No one dreamed of intervening.

'Shut up!' he yelled. 'You've driven your son out! Are you satisfied?'

'Don't worry, he'll be back.'

'Idiot!'

My mother remained speechless and so did we. My father returned to the bathroom. He did not sing.

One hour later, we were all together again in the entrance hall. My father had put on his best suit, made of black alpaca, and had sprayed himself with cologne. Juliette was waiting, sitting beside him on the sofa in the corridor, swinging her feet. She was holding my father's hand. I joined them. They pushed up to make space for me. I took his other hand. My mother arrived in her Chanel suit. She walked past us without a glance. We stood up.

'We're late,' my father remarked in a neutral voice.

We didn't look as though we were going to the opening of our new shop, but to our own funeral. We were out on the landing when the telephone rang. My father rushed to take the call. We thought it was Franck. He held out the receiver to me.

'It's for you.'

It was Cécile. Her voice was hoarse.

'Michel, I beg you. Come!'

'What is it?' I shouted.

'Come, I'm going to die!'

She didn't need to tell me twice. I shot off down the stairs. I could hear my mother cry out: 'Where's he going?'

I ran like a lunatic. I jostled those who didn't get of the way quickly enough. I hurtled down boulevard Saint-Michel without stopping. I reached quai des Grands-Augustins. I bounded up the stairs three at a time. On the landing, my lungs were ready to burst. I rang and hammered at the door as I recovered my breath. No one answered. I opened the door with my key. The lights were on in all the rooms. I began to call out her name as I made my way around the vast apartment. I found Cécile on the bathroom floor, unconscious. I yelled, I shouted her name. There was no reaction. She looked pale. I shook her vigorously. She was as limp as a rag doll. I put my ear to her heart. It was scarcely beating. I was bewildered. I was expecting her to stir, to stand up. She lay there unconscious. My legs were trembling. A voice inside me said: You little bugger, this is no time to panic. I rang the emergency services. A man asked me for the address and told me that they were on their way. They were the longest twenty minutes of my life. I placed a flannel rinsed in cold water on Cécile's forehead. I kissed her hand. I stroked her face. I murmured a prayer in her ear: Don't go, Cécile, stay with me, I beg you. I pressed myself to her. I took her in my arms, hugging her as tightly as I could, to keep her, to stop her from going under. I cradled her like a child. It was then that I saw the small bottle that had rolled under the washbasin. The ambulancemen arrived and put an oxygen mask on her. I gave them the bottle. They rummaged through the medicine cupboard, which was crammed with boxes of pills. The older of the ambulancemen asked me whether she was ill. I wanted to say no to him, but I couldn't speak. They gave her an injection. He took out a plastic bag and emptied the contents of the cupboard into it. They carried her downstairs on a stretcher. We crossed Paris at a crazy speed. The siren was making a deafening noise. I sat up front, and through the window I could see Cécile, who was swaying about, held in place by two ambulancemen. At the Cochin Hospital, she was taken to casualty. A young doctor in a white coat, accompanied by a nurse, came to ask me questions. I was not able to tell them anything useful apart from the fact that I was a friend and that she had telephoned me. If I understood correctly, she possessed loads of medicines at home that she shouldn't have had. I stayed sitting at the entrance to the casualty department. The ambulancemen and the police deposited their sad cargo of dying or wounded people covered in blood, before setting off again in a constant shuttling to and fro. A nurse gave me a hospital admission form to fill in. There was a mass of information required that I couldn't supply. A man brought in a woman who was screaming, her stomach streaming with blood. From what I heard, she had tried to perform her own abortion. I closed my eyes.

Down an endless dark corridor, I set off in search of Cécile. I pushed open the doors. The hospital rooms were empty. In some of them there were smears of blood on the walls. Loud cries of pain guided me along this deserted labyrinth of corridors and staircases and ceased the moment I stopped to work out where they were coming from. A vile smell overwhelmed me. I was horrified to discover that my hands were covered in shit. All of a sudden, a dazed-looking man passed close to me, without seeing me, his arm torn from his shoulder. Cécile was yelling and calling for me. I could not find her. At the far end, I noticed the green light of an emergency exit. I rushed down it so as to get away. But the more I ran, the more the light withdrew. I could hear Cécile's cries and I turned my back on them. I arrived at the emergency exit. I pushed open the door to get away. An enormous hand grabbed me by the shoulder and shook me. I jumped and came to my senses, numb with sleep. The young doctor peered at me, with one eyebrow raised.

'Monsieur, Monsieur... Your friend has pulled through. For the time being.'

'Is there a problem?'

'She had taken enough pills to put an elephant to sleep. We've given her an enema. We'll see when she wakes up.'

'Are there any complications?'

'She's as well as she can be.'

'May I see her?'

'No. She's sleeping. Come back tomorrow.'

'I won't leave without seeing her.'

The doctor let out a long sigh to let me know that I belonged to the category of bloody nuisances. He turned and walked away without a word. He held open the swing-door for me. Cécile was in a ward with five other patients. An old woman was tossing about deliriously on the next bed. Cécile was asleep, her breathing regular, her expression calm. Her right arm was connected to a drip.

'What time will she wake up?'

'In the late morning.'

I got home at four in the morning. I rang the bell and the door opened immediately. My father took me in his arms.

'Are you all right, son?'

My mother pestered me with questions. Where had I come from? What had I been doing? Did I realize how worried she had been? What had she done to the Good Lord to deserve such sons? My father told her to be quiet and leave me alone. She went on like a machine. Why had I left? Was I with Franck? With Cécile? Why had she phoned me? What had happened? I told her in a calm voice: 'Nothing has happened.'

I went to my bedroom. I closed the door. They were behind it, listening out for every move and sound that I made. I heard them walk away. I wasn't sleepy. I remained sitting on my bed with Néron pressed against me.

It had been one of those bleak and bitter days when your life topples over into absurdity, when it runs away from you like sand through a fist. A bit like my parents' disastrous wedding day when they heard that Uncle Daniel had died. This day had been just as gloomy, not merely on account of the ruined opening and Cécile's suicide attempt, but because of the quarrel between my mother and Franck. Nobody had really taken much notice of it to begin with, my disappearance having distracted them from their row. Even though it had been the worst altercation ever, they thought that it would all calm down. It had been a ridiculous argument of the kind that occurs in every family: a bit of tension, irritation, tiredness, raised voices, an unpleasant remark, unpardonable words which one doesn't really mean and then the great reconciliation scene in Act III. But my mother and Franck are very intense characters, neither of them prepared to make concessions. They did not see or speak to one another for twenty-five years. During that lost life, they must have thought about that day and asked themselves how and why things had reached such a point and whether it was worth bearing such a huge grudge on account of trivialities, things you've said that you eventually can't even remember. Our memory is made in such a way that it wipes out unhappy recollections and only preserves the best of them. Twenty years later, while chatting to my father, he asked me what the cause of the argument had been because he had forgotten. I had to make an effort to remember. Had they known, they would have patched things up, but no one is capable of predicting the future. We live from day to day. Our expectations, our best-laid plans turn out to be pathetic and vague. My mother's little schemes proved to be disastrous. This opening, which should have been a day of celebration and hope for our family, turned out to be one when the fine building began to show cracks.

17

Igor Markish had lived in France for the past seven years. He had left Leningrad in circumstances that he refused to describe. Like the others, it appears to have been for political reasons. When I raised the subject, he put on a distant smile. Along with Werner Toller, he was one of the founders of the Club. The two of them provided an information service on administrative matters. The members of the Club had just one purpose in mind: to have their papers, not to be arrested during a straightforward identification check, not to be deported, to be able to lay down their bags at last, leave the past behind them, begin a new life again, and to work. To be in order, that was their obsession. Only those who have been in an illegal situation can understand the permanent anxiety of the refugee who, after having saved his own skin, has to do battle with this mysterious adversary: the clerk of the Préfecture. The members often discussed their respective authorities in order to find out which was the most fussy, unpredictable and nightmarish. Each of them passionately promoted his own country as deserving the unenviable title of the most foolish administration in the world. They told quite incredible stories about what they had witnessed or suffered: having to prove that you were not dead or that you were not related to someone of the same name who was a traitor to his country, or that you were not guilty of innumerable charges was endless. A Czech would recount an unbelievable case that earned him first prize until a Pole or a Hungarian stole it from him. In the end they decided that the Russian administration was the worst of all.

Leonid Krivoshein, in the most solemn voice imaginable, told of an incident that happened to him: 'I found myself in a cell with two other Russians who did not understand the reason for their arrest. "I arrived five minutes late," said a fellow from Kiev, "I was accused of sabotage." "I was five minutes early," explained a man who came from Novgorod,

"I was accused of spying." "I arrived on time," Leonid asserted, "and I was accused of buying my watch in the West."'

We burst out laughing. Leonid swore that it was not a joke, but a true story. As proof, he showed us his watch, a Lip Président with a magnifying glass case, which he had been given during a stopover in Paris when he was flying the Moscow–London route. De Gaulle and Eisenhower wore the same one. He looked upset that we didn't believe him. That was part of the game. Leonid never stopped joking. You could never tell with him when he was telling the truth.

'You're making fun of us,' Tibor asserted. 'You've never been arrested in your life. I don't know whether you're an utter liar or an utter dimwit.'

Leonid stopped laughing, drained his glass and stared at Tibor, his eyes gleaming.

'If you ever say that word again, I'll kill you. I promise you. I'll strangle you with these hands. Believe me, I won't be playing games.'

The Palme d'or for exceptional absurdity had been attributed by this jury of connoisseurs to Tomasz Zagielovski, who had been a reporter on a mass circulation national paper and who held the enviable title of victim (first class) of the Polish authorities. He had been summoned to his local town hall, in the Warsaw suburbs. A woman civil servant had asked him suspiciously who he was. When he had refused to identify himself, she had treated him as an impostor. It turned out the real Tomasz Zagielovski had been held for three months in the Bialoleka, the State prison. Tomasz realized the police had mistakenly arrested instead of him an unfortunate fellow who had protested his innocence in vain, and who had claimed his name was Piotr Levinsky. There had, in actual fact, been a terrible misunderstanding: this Levinsky was a good communist. Tomasz thought he was finished and was expecting to be arrested when the civil servant, who was not immune to his charms (he had been told to behave as though he were irresistible to women), had revealed to him that Zagielovski had eventually confessed his errors and had been sentenced to ten years in prison for treason! Tomasz got away with it by telling her that he was the real Piotr Levinsky. Occasionally, he went by the name of Tomasz Zagielovski. He lived at the latter's home, being his wife's lover. The civil servant had slight doubts, but Tomasz's case was black and white: 'If I were Tomasz Zagielovski, do you think I would have risked coming here, knowing that I was guilty of treason? Look at me, do I look like the sort of idiot who would throw himself into the lion's jaws?'

She could say nothing in the face of such irrefutable logic. He would even prove it to her by going home to search for his papers. The civil servant had allowed him to leave. He took the opportunity to flee immediately, with just the clothes on his back. As soon as he arrived in France, Tomasz had written to the Polish authorities to point out the mistake. He did not know what repercussions his letter had had, and the members of the Club were certain that his initiative had been pointless.

The authorities hate to admit their errors and to lose face. And as Jan Paczkowski, a former Warsaw lawyer, had observed, when a sentence had been pronounced there was no second chance, it was irreversible, especially in a communist country. This story sent a chill up my spine. I imagined the wretched Piotr Levinsky, who had not merely been convicted for his errors, but had had his name taken away from him. I could not understand why he had confessed to another's offences. Igor had explained to me: 'For us, a suspicion is a certainty. It's the underlying basis of the system. You're guilty because they suspect you. This Piotr had something to feel guilty about.'

'He was innocent!'

'That's not enough. We would have needed a bit of luck as well. It's what we'd been lacking. Piotr didn't have any luck either.'

After his epic flight from Poland, Tomasz had found work as a salesman in a clothes shop on the Champs-Elysées where he made a good living. A fine-looking man, who dressed elegantly, and an inveterate charmer, he spent his Sundays in the dance clubs in rue de Lappe and he never failed to tell us of his conquests, even though we never saw him with anyone.

By common consent, the French authorities were a model of clarity and simplicity compared to the Eastern-bloc countries. But woe betide anyone who encountered a wily enemy lurking in the shadow of the administrative woods: the communist clerk who loathed the traitor denigrating the USSR and its brother countries, the land of happy workers.

The supreme objective, the key, was to obtain political refugee status. Logically, it should have been the simplest document to obtain, given that you came, as they did, from the other side of the iron curtain. But there was an unforeseen obstacle and one that it was impossible to overlook: the appalling Patrick Rousseau, the unctuous head of the bureau that worked on behalf of the political refugee. His warm smile and apparent compassion were deceptive; weapons deployed in order to destroy you more effectively. Vladimir had come across him reading *L'Humanité* at the bar of a local café and, taken aback, Rousseau had told him that the only political refugees worthy of that name came from Spain or Portugal, where fascist dictators were in power. This pervert took it upon himself to block or reject the files from Eastern Europe 'whose delinquents and outcasts were dumped on us', as he described it. There was always a paper or a rubber stamp or a certificate missing and when, after twenty attempts, you thought the file was completed, a document was lost or no longer valid, and you had to begin over again. Rousseau had even succeeded in causing the calm and phlegmatic Pavel Cibulka, who would have strangled him had Igor not been with him, to lose his temper. Rousseau demanded a certificate of civilian status from him (something which was impossible for an exiled person to obtain), simply because he had been born in Bohemia and the status of political refugee was not granted to gypsies. For a former ambassador to Bulgaria, this was a deadly insult that earned Rousseau a monumental slap and meant that Pavel had to wait three more years to obtain the status. Igor knew every department of the Préfecture, the town hall and certain ministries, the papers that needed to be acquired and how many copies, the names of the clerks to avoid and those who could be bought. To judge by the difficulties encountered in obtaining their papers, they concluded that the clerks in the resident permit department of the Paris Préfecture were virulent trade union members.

Igor spoke French with a slight accent. He was often taken for an Alsatian. He came from a background where people learned French before Russian. His father rented a villa every year in Nice and he remembered his summer holidays there when he was a child. This was before the war, the first one. Igor didn't like recalling his memories. He had made a great effort to begin a new life and he did not wish to be reminded of his past. His family was wealthy. His father was a well-known surgeon who had a private clinic in St Petersburg. Their life had been swept away by the revolution from one day to the next. But he had had no regrets. A new world was beginning. Everyone joined in to build socialism. After his degree, Igor had worked as a doctor in a hospital, but had not succeeded in becoming a heart specialist. He no longer had time to continue his studies and he had to provide for his family. They were happy. And then, the Earth had stopped turning and had then exploded. Late one Sunday afternoon, he had lifted the veil slightly: 'During the siege and at the front, I acted as surgeon. I even performed a caesarean during the bombing of Gostiny Dvor. For anaesthetic, all we had was vodka. The mother and the child came through. You've no idea of the operations. If anyone had told me beforehand, I would have sworn it was impossible. And yet I coped. I saw nurses amputating limbs with white-hot instruments. You don't need degrees to operate in wartime. The important thing is to survive, isn't it?'

The war had destroyed his city. He had fought as a doctor in the Red Army, miraculously surviving the siege, after which he had taken part in the German campaign. He had worked for six months as a labourer rebuilding the hospital. That was what stayed with him for ever. The destruction of Leningrad. Rubble everywhere, as far as the eye could see. Hordes of half-starved skeletons in rags fighting with one another to eat a stray dog or the bark from trees. The streets, the avenues and the canals had disappeared. They were going to rebuild them. As before. Even better, larger and more beautiful. A vast building site worthy of Russia. Igor didn't want to talk about this period any more. You had to force him.

'Why did you go over to the West?'

'If I hadn't fled, I wouldn't be alive today.'

'Why did you leave? Tell me.'

'If I explained, you wouldn't understand. It's complicated. Come on now, it's your turn. You're like an old woman with all your chatter.'

I started to play again. A little later, I asked him another question. He pretended to be engrossed by the game. Occasionally, he would come out with snatches, bracing himself against his memories. It was up to me to put together the pieces of a puzzle in which the main bits were missing. He had left a mother over there, a wife, a son of my age and a daughter who was younger. He had had no news of them for eight years.

'I've lived several lives that I've forgotten.'

'You don't just decide to forget with a click of your fingers.'

'You do. You forget or you die.'

He had decided not to think about it any more. His life, the only one which he was prepared to recall, began with his arrival in France. Igor was warm-hearted, relaxed and bore no ulterior motive. He had a spontaneous manner, which put people at their ease. I never heard anyone speak ill of him. On the contrary, everyone liked and respected him. He was a good-looking man who, with his impressive build, his wavy hair, his blue eyes and friendly smile, did not go unnoticed. He looked a little bit like Burt Lancaster. People never stopped teasing him about that.

'You should become a film star.'

'Impossible, I don't know how to lie.'

Igor taught me how to play chess. He was the first person to approach me and suggest a game: 'Do you know how to play?'

'A bit.'

'Sit down there.'

I found myself looking at a chessboard with the white pieces in place. I had never played before in my life. At random, I moved a pawn forward two squares as I had seen others do. He placed his pawn in front of mine. I made two foolish moves, then I moved my knight as if it were a pawn.

'You don't know how to play!'

'Not really.'

'I'm going to teach you.'

He was a good teacher. After a few days, I mastered the rules and began to get the hang of it. I didn't understand when he said to me: 'There, you know how to play chess. Now, you need to become a player. That will take longer.'

'How long?'

'That depends on you. Five years, ten years, more? Look at Imré. He's fifty years old and he's been knocking the pieces around the board for thirty-five of them. With a little practice you could beat him. Remember: lots of concentration and a bit of imagination.'

We would meet in the early evening for one or two quick games. Most of the time we played in silence.

'If you want to talk, go to the café next door.'

We spent hours barely speaking to one another. He always won. However much I thought until my head ached, made plans, tried to position my pieces, devised a strategy and concealed my moves, he read my game like an open book. He could see my little plan a mile off. My attempts at tactical play amused him.

'It's right to want to open up your rook, but be careful not to leave the diagonal free for my queen, otherwise you'll be checkmate in three moves.'

'How did you know that I wanted to move my rook?'

'There's nothing else you can do. Don't move so quickly. You attack in a disorderly way. Protect your position. It's easier to defend.'

'If I don't attack, I won't win.'

Igor looked aggrieved and shook his head.

'You're nothing but an ass. And that's not fair on asses, they're intelligent animals. Not like you. You don't listen. You ought to take notes.'

To improve, he told me, I needed to follow games, copy out each player's moves and replay them on a pocket chess-set. From time to time, Igor dived into his little notebook. He managed to reconstruct games just from his notes, and a string of moves such as: 1.e4 c5 2.Knf3 e6 3.g3; 3...d5 4.exd5 exd5 5.Bg2 Qe7 6.Kf1; 6... Knc6 7.d4 Knf6 8.Knc3 Be6 caused him to say things like: 'He hasn't improved at all, Vladimir. Still just as over-elaborate.'

'He won.'

'It's Pavel who lost. If you want to get better, watch Leonid. He's the best. Simple and effective.'

For two years, he was my one and only partner. Those who knew how to play or thought they did had no wish to waste their time with a beginner. When I suggested a game, they replied: 'We'll play with you when you know how to play.'

They accepted me because Igor had accepted me. Anyone who wanted to could come in and play at the Club, but it was he or Werner who decided who should be a member. There was no other criterion apart from their good will. When an unsuitable person sought to join, they knew how to dissuade him or get rid of him tactfully: 'It's a private club. We're not taking any more members. You'll have to go on the waiting list.'

After two years, we played a game which reached a stalemate. It was a draw. There was neither a winner nor a loser. For me, it was a victory. Igor sensed this.

'Another two or three years, my lad, and you'll manage to win a game.'

It took me a year to beat him. He had an excuse. It was a day when he was doubled up with sciatica. He found it hard to sit in his chair. When he arrived in France, Igor had tried to establish himself as a doctor. He had been turned down because his degree was not recognized in France and there was no way of obtaining an equivalent one. He had left Leningrad in a hurry, without any official papers or documents, with nothing that could prove his assertions. His service during the war as a military doctor and his medals were of no use. The only solution, as a member of the medical association had amiably suggested, was to start at the beginning. But it's not easy to start studying for seven years when you are aged fifty. As well as being penniless, Igor had to endure a dreadful problem: he had been an insomniac ever since his flight from the USSR in March 1952. When he arrived in Helsinki, he went eleven days without sleeping, hoping that he would eventually collapse from exhaustion and be able to break this curse. His body had resisted beyond what is possible. He continued to be wide awake, with a wild look in his eyes, and his head in a fog. He began having attacks of delirium in the middle of the traffic, walking around bare-chested in temperatures of minus ten, and singing at the top of his voice. He had been injected with a sedative. When he woke up, he had refused to take the sleeping tablets he had been prescribed, until a doctor who had himself suffered from interminable insomnia gave him the solution: 'If you're not able to sleep at night, it's because your biological clock has been reversed. The reason? We don't know, but we have our suspicions. How can you start sleeping again? No idea. Go back to Leningrad perhaps? The cure is likely to be worse than the disease. Do as I do. Sleep during the day. Work at night.'

Igor had followed his advice and rediscovered a regular pattern of life. When he arrived in Paris the following month, he had worked as a packer at Les Halles for a fruit and vegetable firm, while awaiting a reply from the medical association. Then, because his back hurt him, he had found a job as a nightwatchman at a hotel near the Madeleine. He was bored to death. For two years after that he had been a night porter at La Pitié Hospital. He was wondering what terrible sin he could have committed to deserve this fate when, that very night, he met the two men who were to change his life.

Count Victor Anatolievitch Volodine was driving his gleaming Simca Vedette Régence like an aristocrat and exercising the noble profession of chauffeur, second-class — which is to say he was a qualified taxi driver. On rue de Tolbiac, he had picked up a blood-stained vagrant who had been beaten up and left for dead. He had almost run over his body, but had braked in the nick of time. During the civil war, Victor had had occasion to see many wounded people and corpses. He had cut off the nose and ears of several Reds. He knew about such things. This dying man looked pretty bad. People could say what they wanted about Victor Volodine, that he was a prig, a rascal and a liar, that he had never been a count, nor had he served the Tsar of Holy Russia, and nor was he the cousin and close friend of Felix Yussupov, Rasputin's murderer, as he related with such conviction and force to his astonished customers. His yarns explain the errors in certain books by historians of repute who had taken his flagrant lies at face value. Victor had merely had the opportunity to be the prince's driver when he was in Paris. Yussupov refused to give his views about Russia, but he agreed to speak Russian with a compatriot, convinced that the conversation would be about the inevitable and speedy collapse of the communist regime and of their own triumphant return to their homeland. Victor Volodine had just been a simple soldier in the Tsar's army and Staff Sergeant in the White army under that idiot Denikin and then under Wrangel, who was no softy. Then, in the middle of the night, he had dropped off the two passengers whom he had collected from the Folies-Bergère in Pigalle and picked up the future corpse in order to deposit it at the nearest hospital.

At twenty-five past one, Igor, the porter, was helping him carry the wounded man out of his taxi when he heard Victor let out an expletive on discovering that the white seat of his car was spattered with blood. Even if you have lived in France for thirty-three years and speak the language like a Parisian, when you hit the roof and let out a stream of abuse, you do so in your native tongue. And when two fellow countrymen who have been thrown out of their native land meet in a foreign country, they are happy to get together and the past is no longer of any importance. Igor and Victor were programmed to loathe and destroy one another, but they fell into each other's arms. It was good to hear one's patronymic. In France, people just used the first name. Suddenly, it was as if a little of the smell, the music and the light of their homeland had returned, even though one was a White Russian, a practising Orthodox, an anti-Semite and a misogynist, who hated the Bolshies, and the other the former enemy, a keen, committed and enthusiastic Red, who had been involved in establishing communism. These sorts of differences that made you tear out one another's throats at home vanished here. Especially where two Russian insomniacs were concerned.

18

For the first time in my life, I skipped school. The idea would never have occurred to me before. Even when lessons were deadly boring, I endured them resignedly. But there was no question of leaving Cécile on her own. I left the flat as though nothing were the matter and set off to the Cochin Hospital. Anyone can just walk in. There were only three patients in her ward. I asked the nurse which department she had been transferred to. She looked at me as if she did not understand and hurried off into the ward. She looked dumbfounded as she stood there in front of the deserted bed and the empty cupboard.

'She's gone!'

She grabbed the telephone and, in a panic, notified security of Cécile's disappearance. She gave a brief description. Nobody had seen her. A professor arrived with a group of students who followed him like his shadow. With a crestfallen expression, she told him the bad news. A quarter of an hour earlier, she had been passing through the ward, she was still asleep and then... She did not finish her sentence. The professor called her every name under the sun and was unbelievably aggressive, insulting her without her reacting. He turned towards the students and yelled at them: 'What the fuck are you doing here, you bunch of idiots, eh? When are you going to get a move on?'

The professor went into a room, slamming the door behind him, without even glancing at me. The students and the nurse dispersed like a flock of sparrows. They questioned visitors and patients, but Cécile had vanished into thin air. I left the hospital. I searched for her in the cafés opposite. I asked the waiters, nobody had seen her. I walked down rue Saint-Jacques as far as the Seine, peering inside the bistros. No sign of Cécile. I had the insane hope that I might bump into her. I went to her home, on quai des Grands-Augustins. The apartment was in the same state as the previous night, after the emergency services had arrived. I felt ill at ease, rather like a novice burglar. I waited a long time for her, walking round in circles. Surely she would not be long. In an alcove, there was a Franche-Comté type of clock. I told myself 'She'll be here at ten o'clock.'

When the chimes struck, I turned towards the entrance hall, convinced she was about to appear, as though by a wave of a magic wand. Nothing happened. Through the window, I searched for her among the crowd. At half past ten, the grandfather clock caught me off guard, with my nose glued to the window-pane. 'She'll be here at eleven o'clock. She can't not come.'

On the eleventh stroke, my hope vanished. She wouldn't come. I had been foolish to believe she would. I left the flat, placing my bunch of keys under the doormat. I had the unpleasant, gnawing feeling that she would not be coming back here. If she did anything foolish again, I wouldn't know. On a piece of paper that I slipped beneath the door, I'd scribbled: 'If anything happens, inform me: Michel Marini', and I gave my telephone number. I scoured the neighbourhood, the cafés and shops she used to go to, rue Saint-André-des-Arts and the area around Saint-Sulpice. Nobody had seen her. Head down, I skirted the railings of the Luxembourg. Back to square one. I turned in the direction of Henri-IV. There was nothing to feel cheerful about. I searched for an excuse to give Sherlock. Something indisputable, cast-iron, which would be the spitting image of a genuine one, and which no head supervisor, even a crafty one like him, would think of questioning or checking up on. In this eternal game of cat and mouse, I was a small, panic-stricken creature with a pitiful imagination. For every cause of absence I dreamed up, it would only take a second for the old tomcat to catch me out on. I was getting ready to be crucified when I arrived at the park gates near the Odéon theatre. I was a few yards away from the Médicis fountain. I risked missing the two o'clock bell. I continued on my route. I stopped. 'If she is not there, I shall never see her again.'

I turned around. Another five minutes won't make much difference. I ran towards the fountain. All I saw were readers and the usual pairs of peaceful lovers. No Cécile. Suddenly, I noticed two patches, green and white, like a casket, in the midst of the fountain. Without being able to say how or why, I found myself entranced too. I couldn't take my eyes off Polyphemus, so fine and so monstrous, so pitiful when he surprises Galatea and Acis and is about to kill the shepherd. An obligatory yet pointless crime. As I arrived at the edge of the pond, I was full of compassion for this poor, desperate and despised one-eyed man. Then I spotted Cécile, in a secluded corner. She was asleep in a chair, her head tilted back and her arms dangling. She looked extremely pale, her cheeks were hollow, and her skin was waxy. No breath stirred in her chest. I placed the palm of my hand on her forehead. I felt her warmth. I covered her with my jacket and sat down beside her. Cécile opened her eyes. She wasn't surprised to see me, she gave me a shy smile and held out her hand to me. I took it and clasped it in mine.

'You took your time,' she murmured.

'I looked for you everywhere.'

'I was frightened you wouldn't come.'

'I'm here.'

'Please don't leave me.'

'Don't worry. Do you want to go home?'

She shook her head. We stayed sitting beside the fountain. I did not know whether she was sleeping or resting. I stared at Galatea, draped over Acis, alone in the world and blissfully happy. Cécile watched me carefully.

'They're beautiful, aren't they?'

'They're unaware of the danger that threatens them.'

'They're happy to be alive. They love one another. Nothing else is important. Danger doesn't exist for them. They will remain in love for eternity. Have you any money?'

'A little.'

'Will you buy me a coffee?'

She got to her feet with difficulty. She moved forward in small steps and leant on me. After twenty yards, she no longer needed my support. We went and had a café au lait at the Petit-Suisse, the bistro opposite. We sat at an outside table.

'I'm hungry.'

'That's a good sign.'

She devoured two croissants in no time at all and asked for another café au lait. She wanted to say something, and then hesitated.

'… Can I trust you, Michel?'

'Of course.'

'Nothing happened to me. Do you understand? Nothing at all. We'll never speak about it again. We'll behave as if it never happened.'

'… If you want.'

'Promise?'

'Promise.'

She noticed my awkward silence and pursed lips.

'Nothing has happened! To anybody. Franck mustn't know.'

'I can't not tell him. If he found out one day, he would kill me.'

'If you don't tell him, if I don't tell him, he'll never know. In any case, it doesn't matter any more. We're no longer together.'

'What!'

'It's over between us.'

'Since when?'

'I don't know. We don't see each other any more. He's… vanished.'

'At home too, he's disappeared.'

'When you are with someone, you don't leave them without any news for weeks unless there's a good reason. I've called him hundreds of times. I've spoken to your father, your mother, you and your sister. I don't know how many times I've left the same message, but he's never called me back. The only time I managed to catch him on the phone, it lasted thirty seconds. He was on the doorstep, in a hurry. He was going to ring me in the evening. Three weeks went by. Generally, when a man behaves like that with a woman, when he is… elusive, it means he's met another woman and he doesn't dare tell her about it.'

'That's impossible. Not Franck.'

'Do you swear you don't know anything?'

'I swear.'

'Can you think of an explanation for his disappearance?'

'There must be one. I know he loves you.'

'Did he tell you?'

'He's given me to understand he does.'

'When was that?'

'We were at your place.'

'I'm sure there's another woman in his life.'

I was no great expert in love affairs. My only experience came from my reading. I could see no reason for his constant absence. Ever since he returned from Germany, he had slept no more than three or four nights at the flat. I was careful not to talk to him about it.

'If he did that, he's a real bastard.'

She shrugged her shoulders and tried to smile. Her cheeks were flushed and her eyes were red. She bit her lip, sniffed and caught her breath, and choked back her sorrow.

'You've got to be bloody stupid to try to kill yourself for a guy! Now, it's over. I've got to be stronger.'

'I just can't believe it. It's not possible.'

'That's the way life is. Yet I could have sworn that… I'm going home.'

The waiter brought us the bill. Cécile hadn't a penny on her and I was two francs sixty short. I didn't know where to put myself. The waiter was a decent fellow.

'It's not a small amount. Bring it to me. I'll trust you. It's just that I have to pay the boss cash.'

'I'll bring it tomorrow, without fail,' I promised.

'Excuse me,' she asked him, 'you wouldn't have a cigarette?'

He gave her a Gitane. He struck a match. She puffed at it with infinite pleasure.

'I don't know whether that's a very good idea.'

'Listen, Michel, get out of this habit of telling me what I ought to do.'

I accompanied her back home. We didn't feel like talking. She stopped twice, tired by the walk.

'Perhaps it would be best for you to go back to the hospital?'

'Michel, I'm telling you again, I don't need a nursemaid.'

I managed to go up the stairs ahead of her. I removed the little note I'd slipped under the door without her seeing me. I retrieved my bunch of keys from under the doormat. She went inside. I stayed on the landing.

'Don't worry. It'll be all right.'

'Do you want me to give you back your keys?'

'No, keep them. Unless you don't want to come any more.'

'That's not what I meant.'

She kissed me on the cheek.

'Thank you, little bro'. Thank you for everything.'

'I'll come by tomorrow maybe.'

'Whenever you like.'

Once again, I did the round of the bars, in search of Franck this time. Nobody had seen him. Two people made fun of me: 'Maybe your brother's with Cécile?'

'If I do find Cécile, I'm not going to tell your brother.'

I took no notice. Everywhere, I left the same message: 'If you see him, tell him to get in touch with his brother. It's urgent.'

I called on Richard, his best friend, who lived behind the mosque. They were members of the same cell and sold the Sunday edition of *L'Humanité* together in the market on rue Mouffetard. He seemed confused to see me. He had had a crew cut.

'Did you have a problem?'

'What with?'

'Your hair?'

'Michel, I'm busy, what is it you want?'

'I was hoping that Franck was at your place.'

'I haven't seen him for some time. Did he tell you he was sleeping here?'

'He has done occasionally. I thought—'

'He must be at Cécile's.'

'If you see him, tell him to get in touch with me. It's important.'

'Definitely.'

We stood there confronting one another for two seconds too long. Richard, normally so warm and spontaneous, was on his guard. He was doing his best to keep his composure. There was an unpleasant stiffness in his manner. Good liars keep their heads held high. They fear nothing. Bad ones look away, as if to protect themselves. It's something I must remember.

'That hairstyle doesn't suit you. You looked better before.'

To put my mind at rest, I called on two other friends of Franck's. They didn't know where he was and promised to give him the message when they next saw him.

During dinner, my mother asked me: 'How was it at school today?'

'Same as usual.'

'What did you do?'

'In our English lesson, we continued with Shakespeare, and in French, we started Racine's *Les Plaideurs*.'

'Are you ready for your maths test?'

'I've worked with Nicolas a lot.'

'It's a pity we don't see him any more,' my father continued. 'You should invite him one Sunday.'

I spent part of the night devising a list of reasonable excuses to give Sherlock without him over-reacting, being doubtful in any way or needing to check up, but feared I wouldn't be able to slip through his net. I slept badly. In the morning, I was resigned to a trip to the doghouse when, in my jacket pocket, I found the hospital admittance form that the nurse had asked me to fill in when Cécile was being admitted to casualty. I saw it as a sign of fate. A sort of delay of execution. It could succeed because it was far-fetched. I hesitated about tampering with this document, but I had no alternative solution. I took a black ballpoint pen and I filled it in with my name. I used a minimum of detail. In the space for 'wounds', I put 'minor bruising'. For 'cause of accident', I put 'knocked down by a cyclist'. I made sure I wrote in small, illegible letters like a doctor. I signed with a scrawl. My heart was thumping as I handed him this note of apology. He examined it without casting doubts on its authenticity and enquired about my health.

'Nowadays, you have to be careful of everything: cars, buses and cyclists. It's a good lesson.'

I felt I had to add: 'And he didn't even stop!'

'It's disgraceful. What century are we living in?'

'It's not serious, you know. As the doctor said, I was more shaken than hurt.'

Thanks to Nicolas, the maths test went well. He was not obliged to help me, but he allowed me to copy, as he always had done. What with all this business, I had rather neglected him. He bore no grudges. In order to say sorry, I suggested we play baby-foot. We went to Maubert. I had not been near the game for three months, but baby-foot's rather like riding a bike, it's not something you forget.

19

After having left the dying man with the duty houseman, who was snowed under and didn't know which part of the wretched man he should examine, Igor and Victor set off to the Canon d'Austerlitz to get to know one another. Very soon, the stocks of vodka were exhausted.

'Have you drunk whisky before, Igor Emilievitch?'

'Never.'

'It's got a strange taste, but you quickly get used to it.'

'I'm not very keen on anything American.'

'Be careful, real whisky is Scottish.'

Igor drank his first glass of whisky in the Russian way. Not as pleasant as vodka, but not bad even so. The two men swore eternal brotherhood, vowed never to part and recounted the stories of their lives to one another. Victor was cunning. He knew that a fellow-countryman would soon uncover his fibs. He told the truth. Quite simply. He knew that after the euphoria of their reunion would come the moment of suspicion about the historical enemy. Like all liars, Victor could not believe that people told the truth, and he did not believe Igor: 'No, you're not a doctor. I don't believe you.'

'I swear to you. I graduated from the Leningrad Medical Institute. The degree isn't recognized in France. I specialised in cardiology. I practised for fifteen years. I held a consultancy at the Tarnovsky Hospital in Leningrad. During the war, I was a military doctor in Zhukov's army with the rank of lieutenant. I was a good doctor. My patients adored me.'

'You're talking nonsense. You're a porter! You know a bit about medicine through seeing sick people and listening to doctors. No one fools father Victor. We're alike, you and I. Clever guys can diddle both the ignorant and the stupid. Stop taking the piss, comrade.'

Igor found himself confronted by an insoluble problem. How could he prove that he had been a doctor? His attempts at explanations and corroboration, and his sketches, were all met by a wall of incredulity. Victor wanted real proof. On embossed paper, with official rubber stamps in colour, on headed paper and with ministerial signatures. The degree certificate was still in Leningrad. Victor smiled.

'You're no more a doctor than I'm Prince Yusupov's cousin!'

'You... Prince Yusupov's cousin!'

'I tell the tourists that for fun. I have to admit you've got the knack. The important thing is to look the part. I know grand dukes and counts who look like housekeepers or cobblers. When they let it be known that they're from the nobility, they're treated as liars. In my case, everyone believes me.'

Igor no longer had a combative nature. His flight from the USSR and his wanderings had led him to see notions such as truth or lying from a different viewpoint. At present, he was unsure about anything apart from the fact that he was alive. For him, it was the one and only truth on this earth: you were either alive or you were dead. The rest was nothing but belief or hypothesis.

'Believe whatever you like, it's all the same to me. You're right, here I'm not a doctor, I'm a porter.'

Victor took this rapid renunciation as proof that Igor was a downright liar and that he would therefore make a good taxi driver.

'How much do you earn on this job?'

'Not much.'

'Would you like to earn a decent living, pay yourself whatever you want and be free?'

'Who would say no to such an offer? If it's honest, I accept.'

'Are you insulting me or joking? I'm a former officer in the army of the Tsar, and don't forget it. I hope you're not Jewish?'

'I'm alive, isn't that enough for you? I agree to work for you on one condition: that I work at night. I only sleep during the daytime.'

'It's not that simple. Driving at night requires special skills.'

'Take it or leave it, Victor Anatolievitch.'

'My wife will be grateful. The guy who works for me during the day-time rips me off. With you, I won't have to worry. The one good thing

132

about Commies is that they're honest. What should I take to get to sleep at night?'

'I'm not familiar with French medicaments. I refuse to take sleeping pills. How long have you had insomnia?'

'I haven't slept since I first arrived in Paris. In my youth, I was scrawny and slept like a log. You're one hell of a liar, if you were a doctor you'd know how to cure insomnia.'

Igor became a taxi driver and worked for Victor, who had a flexible notion of honesty and paid scant attention to his customers, especially the foreigners.

'You're wrong to bother about these minor details, Igor Emilievitch. You know me, I'm a believer and I respect the commandments. If God created mugs, it's in order that they should be ripped off.'

Igor took some time to become a real Parisian taxi driver. Paris was a vast city, Parisian men were stark raving mad, Parisian women were hotheads, the suburbs were snarled up and those who lived there were skinflints. But thanks to his doctor's memory, he eventually came to know the street map by heart. The traffic jams were inescapable, though.

'In the old days, the traffic moved. At the time of the Liberation, it was perfect. After that, the 2CVs came and wrecked our lives and ever since Renault invented the Dauphine for these ladies it's been a shambles.'

Victor taught him the various ways of making a little extra on the side that had enabled him to afford the white house he was so proud of on the heights of L'Haÿ-les-Roses from where he had a view over Paris, the Eiffel Tower and the Sacré Coeur. Up until Victor's death twelve years later, during the événements of May 1968 — caused by a heart attack in a gigantic traffic jam on the Nationale 7 near Orly, when he was driving a Texan who was yelling because he had been caught up for two hours in the southern suburbs — he was convinced that Igor was an inveterate liar and had never been a doctor in his life. After making him swear on the Novodievichny icon not to tell anyone, not even his confessor, he revealed to him the art of distracting the customer's attention and turning full circle while appearing to drive straight ahead; how to lengthen the journey by catching the red traffic lights; which streets were used by the dustbin lorries so that you could get delayed behind them; the route followed three times a week by the horses of the Republican guards; the advantages of taking the avenues in which there were roadworks rather than those which were free of traffic; how to get yourself stuck behind a delivery or removal lorry without the customer suspecting, and the thousand and one ruses that allowed you to buy yourself a fine detached house in the course of twenty years of honest labour. He also taught him how to avoid like the plague those sadistic taxi policemen whom the Préfecture despatched in pursuit of cab drivers so as to harass them under any pretext – taught him how to recognize them and how to come to an agreement with them when you could not do otherwise.

'There's a flawless way of spotting them: they only drive around in black 403s. As soon as you have one on your tail, turn your sign back on. You're lucky, they don't often work at night.'

Igor and Victor hadn't any need to sign a contract. They had done a deal and they'd embraced. Igor grumbled that he was being exploited by Victor, but he continued to work for him. He never followed any of his advice, and he took his passengers on the most direct and economical route. He could have worked for himself, but in effect he was his own boss and he made his living without any worries. That was what mattered to him. Unlike Victor, who used it to blow his own trumpet, he never told any of his customers that he was Russian. Sometimes he drove Soviet Communist Party dignitaries, who loved the Russian cabarets in Paris. He overheard secret conversations murmured in the back of his taxi. Thus was how he was able to inform us four days beforehand that Nikita Khrushchev was about to be dismissed and replaced by Leonid Brezhnev and that, during his visits to Paris, the unremovable and Buster Keaton-like Andrey Gromyko took the opportunity to call on a very dear ladyfriend whose name was Martine.

20

Franck was leaning against a wall at the church of Saint-Etienne-du-Mont and smoking a cigarette. He was waiting for the classes at Henri-IV to come out. He had been at school there himself, and seven years later I encountered the same teachers, who examined me doubtfully.

'Are you related to Franck Marini?'

'Yes, Madame, he's my brother.'

'He was more talented than you are.'

Ten days previously, he had left the flat, slamming the door behind him. I crossed over the road to join him and instead of shaking hands he kissed me on the cheek. I put that down to emotion.

'I got your message. Supposing we go for a drink? Have you got time?'

We crossed back over rue Clovis. We bumped into Sherlock who, as a good supervisor should, was presiding over the pupils leaving school. He came over to us and shook hands with Franck in a friendly way.

'How are you, Marini?'

'Very well, Monsieur Masson. And how's Michel getting on?'

'His accident has had no repercussions, thank God.'

'You had an accident?' exclaimed Franck.

My legs began to wobble. I came out in goose pimples. I managed to stammer out: 'It... it's nothing. I'll explain to you.'

'You've got to be vigilant, Michel,' said Sherlock. 'I was observing you when you crossed the road with your brother. You didn't look.'

'I swear to you that I'll be careful, Monsieur.'

'It's incredible, he's taller than you, Franck, but he's not in the least like you. He does the basic minimum. The average is good enough for him.'

'It's not for lack of trying, believe me, Monsieur.'

'I get the impression he's more gifted at baby-foot.'

'Ah, baby-foot's over, it's chess now.'

'Chess? How very interesting, my dear Michel, you must show me one of these days.'

We left to go and have a drink at La Chope, in place de la Contrescarpe.

'What's all this about an accident?'

'Just a story I told him to justify my being away one day.'

'You're out of your mind!'

'Oh, I'm careful.'

'You could be expelled from Henri-IV for a prank like that! Can you imagine our parents?'

'Are you worried on their account?'

'It's for your sake I'm saying this. You've got to stop playing the fool and think about your future a little. You've got to swot if you want to make it.'

The waiter put a half of beer on the table for Franck and a really weak lemonade shandy for me.

'What about you, do you never fool around?'

'I've got my degree. I do as I want. What's all the hurry about? If it's for the parents, there's no point.'

'Cécile… Have you forgotten her already?'

'What's the matter with Cécile?'

'The matter is she's unhappy. You told her you'd ring her back. You didn't ring her back. For weeks, she's not heard a word from you. She doesn't understand what's going on.'

'What's it got to do with you?'

'I thought you loved her.'

'Mind your own business.'

'She's an extraordinary, wonderful girl… "I love a girl who's got a very pretty neck, very pretty breasts, a very pretty voice, very pretty wrists, a very pretty head, very pretty knees…" Do you remember?'

'Stop it! What's your game? Did she ask you to come and find me? To preach at me?'

'She's convinced that you're with someone else and that you haven't the guts to tell her to her face!'

'These are old wives' ravings. I'm not with anyone.'

'Are you ditching her?'

Franck didn't answer me. His head dropped. He shot me occasional dark glances. He took out a Gitane and lit it before realizing that there was already one alight in the ashtray. He stubbed it out.

'Are you able to keep a secret?'

'You're not going to join up too.'

'I've brought forward my call-up. I've enlisted. I'm leaving for Algeria.'

'You're a student.'

'I've withdrawn my reprieve.'

'You're crazy!'

'Try to explain to a woman that you're leaving her to join the army. You could spend years trying. I haven't said anything to her. There was no point. Beyond my capabilities.'

'She thinks you're deserting her for another woman!'

'I did that deliberately. So that she could free herself from me.'

'Why didn't you explain that to her face to face?'

'Because I love her, you stupid bastard! I wouldn't have been able to. I don't want her to wait for me. I don't want to be tied down. I'd decided to leave without talking about it.'

'And so why are you telling me?'

'You've alerted the whole of Paris! I thought something serious had happened.'

'Something did happen!'

'What?'

'Fuck off! You don't deserve her!'

I stood up and left the bistro. Franck caught up with me at the square. He grabbed me by the lapels of my jacket and yelled as he shook me: 'What has happened, for God's sake?'

I had never seen him looking so tense. We sat down on a bench. A tramp was sprawled at the side of the road, asleep. I told him everything. He allowed me to speak without asking a single question. He looked distraught. By the end, he was deep in thought, his shoulders drooping. He was crushed. His head nodded gently.

'Thank you,' he said feebly. 'Has... has she come through it all?'

'It would have been better had she spent a day or two under observation at the hospital. She doesn't listen to anyone.'

We heard a sepulchral voice coming from the ground: 'You're a real bastard!'

The tramp was sitting up, he had listened to what was being said and, sitting on the edge of the pavement, he was gazing at Franck with a look of disdain and pointing his finger.

'Got to be a complete moron to join the French army and ditch your girlfriend. The guy's a nutcase! Ah, you can be proud of yourself!'

Franck was furious. I thought he was going to hit him.

'Mind your own business! Go on, get lost or I'll give you a hiding!'

The tramp picked up his bags and his bottle of wine. He wandered off, grumbling to himself and taking his sour smell with him.

'Morons! They're all morons!'

He disappeared down rue Mouffetard, shouting and insulting the passers-by.

'Are you going to see her?'

He shook his head.

'Franck, it's Cécile!'

'It was a difficult decision. Face to face with her, I wouldn't have had the courage.'

'She could have died because of you!'

'I'm sorry and I feel bad about it. It's too late. I'm leaving in four days time. When I get there, I'll write to her to explain myself. When I get back, we'll see.'

'Do you think she'll wait for you? She loathes you!'

'It's my life, Michel! I have to do it.'

'Bloody hell, Franck, you're a real arsehole!'

'I beg you not to say anything to her. Not before I leave. Let me deal with it.'

'You're out of your mind. You'll regret it all your life.'

'Give it a rest! Come on, let's go and get a bite to eat.'

'I don't want to. I'm going home.'

I hesitated about leaving him standing there. He seemed confused.

I still hoped to be able to persuade him.

'I'll phone and say that I'm staying at Nicolas's place for dinner.'

He took me to the Volcan, a small Greek restaurant where the owner cooked as they do in Salonika. We went into the kitchen where we lifted up the lids and chose according to the aroma. The dishes smelled of aubergines, courgettes and peppers stewed with caramelized onions, cumin and bay leaves. That evening, Franck told me the history of our family, our parents' meeting, the war, his birth, their five years of separation, their reunion and their forced marriage. He needed to get things off his chest. I didn't utter a word. Children don't know about their parents' lives. When they are young, they don't think about such things because the world only began with them. Their parents have no history and have the bad habit of only talking to their children about the future, never the past. It's a serious mistake. When they fail to do so, they always leave a gaping hole.

'She hates me. It's taken me a while to admit it. Because of me, she was obliged to marry our father and she's made a mess of her life. Had I not been born, she would have made a good marriage, to a man from her own background.'

He was right. I could raise no objection.

'And me, does she hate me?'

'With you, it's not your fault. Later on, she wanted a family. For her, you're a Marini, not a Delaunay. Don't forget that. I don't say it to turn you against her. I'm not angry with her. You needed to know.'

Now there was an even greater difference between us. But I didn't feel concerned. There was nothing I could do to change anything. I was only interested in Cécile.

'Why did you join up?'

'If you don't do anything, you leave the path wide open to the fascists. It may be too late. At least I shall have tried.'

'Do you think you're going to be able to change society on your own?'

'I'm not alone.'

'And Papa? . . . He doesn't hate you. You can't leave without telling him. It's not fair.'

'Papa, I agree. But not a word to Cécile!'

I was shocked and powerless. To conceal his enlisting from her struck me as disgraceful. But if I let her know about it, I lost my brother. He had made his choice and it wasn't Cécile. I felt besmirched, trapped and full of anger. Had I been stronger, I would have smashed his face in. I have a problem with logic. I've never understood how people can say one thing and do the opposite. Swear they love someone and then hurt them, have a friend and then forget him, claim to belong to the same family and then treat one another like strangers, hold lofty principles and then not practise them, profess that they believe in God and act as though he did not exist, think of themselves as heroes when they behave like bastards.

21

I gor did not like to drink. He couldn't cope with alcohol. When he did happen to drink, he made up for the bottles he had missed and he started to philosophize, even though he loathed philosophy and philosophers.

'You've got to keep your feet on the ground,' he would say. 'Every time you raise yourself up a bit, you fall from a height.'

The night he met Victor, he returned reeling to the La Pitié Hospital and was told off by the matron, who was greatly admired by her colleagues for the impressive height of her back-combed chignon. She didn't give a damn about his having met a fellow-countryman and she was going to have him reported for leaving his post and drunkenness while on duty. Igor laughed out loud in her face. He went to collect his belongings from his locker and was about to leave the foul-smelling world of the hospital when, in the corridor, he noticed the man whom Victor had brought in. He had been lying on the stretcher ever since he arrived. No one was bothering to look after him. No duty doctor was available. The department head would not be there until eight o'clock and the man was going to die. He was unconscious. Igor examined his pupils, took his pulse and checked his blood pressure. His nose had been crushed and it was preventing him breathing, his lower jaw was fractured, several teeth were broken and his face was covered in blood. Igor tried to open his jaws. The man groaned. Igor thrust his hand into his mouth, removed the broken teeth and unblocked the windpipe. He grabbed a pair of scissors and cut through the man's clothing. He palpated the thorax. One particular spot was hurting him, at the level of the plexus. A protuberance indicated a thoracic fracture. The nurse arrived.

'What are you doing? Stop this! You're mad! You're not allowed to do this!'

'I'm a doctor! This man has a haemothorax. He's going to die unless he is given a pleural drainage. Find me a drain, and quickly. I need some iodised spirit and some xylocaine.'

'I've no anaesthetic.'

'We'll manage without.'

Igor had difficulty undressing the injured man. The nurse returned with a semi-rigid drain on a mandrel and a flask of iodised spirit.

'It's all I could find.'

'Help me to lift him up. Hold him under his armpits and lean against him.'

They lifted up the man, who was unconscious. Igor made him sit down, cleaned his shoulder blade with spirit, located the second intercostal gap and swiftly thrust in the needle. The patient recoiled. The nurse held him down. Igor removed the mandrel, fitted the needle, thrust it in and tapped the blood with the syringe. The drainage lasted several minutes. Igor withdrew the needle smartly and cleaned up the man's numerous wounds. The nurse rushed into the waiting room and started shouting down the telephone, threatening the person she was talking to that she would call the police and sue him for failure to assist a person in danger if he did not arrive within five minutes. What's more, she swore that she would scratch his eyes out. Igor went over to her.

'He's continuing to bleed. We have to operate, perform a thoracotomy. Either they operate immediately or else I'll do it, with or without anaesthetic.'

Two housemen arrived five minutes later to take over and had the man wheeled to the surgical block. The nurse turned to Igor, who looked pale and exhausted. His clothes were stained with blood.

'Why didn't you tell me you were a doctor?'

'I'm a porter.'

'Don't worry, I won't report you.'

Igor hesitated for a second, then shrugged his shoulders.

'I'm through now. Good luck.'

He left the hospital, tossed his white coat into a dustbin and went to have a last café-calvados at the Canon d'Austerlitz. When he paid, he came across the telephone number that Victor Volodine had scribbled on a packet of Gitanes. It was a dark night. He asked the cashier for a token and, from the payphone, rang Victor, who had just arrived home.

'It's to tell you that I'll take the position. When do I start?'

'To begin with, I'll show you the ropes. You'll come with me for a few nights, if that's OK.'

'No problem.'

'Let's meet tomorrow, or rather this evening, at seven o'clock. Do you know Le Royal, on place de la Nation?'

'I'll find it. Good night, Victor Anatolievitch.'

'You too, Igor Emilevitch, sleep well.'

Igor gave up his career as a porter without any regrets. As he removed his white coat, he swore to himself that he would never set foot in a hospital and never attend to anyone again. He began his new life as a taxi driver that same evening, and he felt quite happy about it.

Victor was a chatterbox. With him, you never had to wonder what you were going to talk about. He kept the conversation flowing himself. Sitting in the front, Igor listened to him recounting to an astonished English passenger how he had narrowly missed taking part in the murder of Rasputin with his cousin Felix Yusupov. How he had caught violent bronchitis because of the icy cold and the secret meetings in the draughty, badly heated corridors, and how his wife, Countess Tatiana, who was the daughter of Archduke Orlov, and was related to Rostopchin, had forbidden him to leave their palace on the banks of the Neva to join the conspirators. They were parked in place Vendôme, outside the Ritz, with the engine turned off and the meter ticking over for one hour and twenty minutes. It was not his record. Merely enough time for a magical story. Victor Volodine was not an inveterate liar. He was a raconteur. He added unexpected and little known details, morbid and obscene information, which conferred an aura of truth to what he said. When his customers merited it — they had to be English or American — he took out from the glove compartment a piece of mauve velvet embroidered with gold thread, which he unfolded religiously and, as though he were revealing a secret, displayed to the fortunate tourists the Cossack dagger, encrusted with diamonds, that had slain Rasputin and which Yusupov had given him as a token of friendship. The Englishmen had paid the largest taxi fare in their lives without batting an eyelid and had given this impoverished aristocrat, a victim of the Bolsheviks, a princely tip. Nothing could fluster Victor. He had a cheek that no one British could resist.

'What age were you at the time of Rasputin's murder? You can't have been very old?' asked the man, without meaning any harm.

Victor put on his best smile. Meanwhile, he worked out the dates.

'How old would you say I was, sir?'

'About fifty-five, which would mean that you were about sixteen at the time of Rasputin's death, in 1916, I believe.'

'I thank you for your kindness, my lord. Life has not spared me. I'm going to be seventy-one in two month's time and am still obliged to work to feed my family.'

'Good heavens, you don't look it.'

The weather was like summer in this month of April '56. Victor Volodine wound down the window of the Régence and breathed in with pleasure. He was just fifty-six. No Englishman, be he a lord and peer of the Realm, was going to catch him out.

'Look how fine it is,' he said to Igor.

The place Vendôme belonged to them.

'You would think we were in St Petersburg.'

'For me, it's called Leningrad.'

'If you want us to be friends, never utter that word in my presence.'

Igor was not going to quarrel with his boss on his first day of work over a matter of vocabulary. Whatever its name was, they had the same town in mind.

'Tell me, Igor Emilievitch, is it true that the city is destroyed?'

'There was a siege that lasted nine hundred days, and there were almost as many bombing and shelling attacks. A million dead, at least. Look at Hiroshima. It's the same thing. They're rebuilding it. It will be more beautiful than before.'

Victor offered him a Gitane. They smoked, dreaming of the Winter Palace before the war. Igor was spellbound and disappointed to learn that the Cossack dagger in the glove compartment had not killed Rasputin. It was a Berber knife and Victor had bought it for the modest sum of three hundred and fifty francs during the 1931 Colonial Exhibition. Ever since, he had acquired his supply from a Moroccan shop in Montreuil where he bought them by the dozen and gave them to his friends for their birthdays. Victor had sworn to a quiet couple of dumbfounded Bordeaux winegrowers, on the heads of the children he did not have, that he had set eyes on the Archduchess Anastasia. There was no doubt or mystery about her. She was, beyond all dispute, the last descendant of the Romanovs. May God protect her. They had played as children in the gardens of the Petrodvorets Palace where his family was often invited.

'It's not complicated, you see. The more far-fetched it is, the bigger the tip.'

'It's the way I've been brought up. I don't know how to lie.'

'I don't lie. I tell them a story.'

'I'm not sure I could manage it.'

'Well then, say goodbye to large tips, and too bad for you. I'm not surprised with that fucking commie education.'

That first night, Victor was so pleased with his takings that he decided to stop work earlier than usual. Igor found himself dumped, at about four in the morning, not far from his little hotel near the Bastille. He was not sleepy. He thought again about the man he had treated the previous night, wondered whether he had survived and, even though he had sworn never to set foot there again, he returned to La Pitié. When she saw him, the matron thought he was coming to ask for his job back. Igor wanted news of the wounded man.

'He's alive for the time being. He was operated on for five hours by Mazerin himself. He hasn't regained consciousness. Prognosis pending. The professor said you saved his life. Since he has no identity papers on him, they don't know his name. Do you really not want to come back?'

'May I see him?'

'Charcot wing, room 112.'

The man with the swollen face was in a ground-floor room on his own. He had a drip attached to his right arm, and was intubated and under cardiac and respiratory supervision. With his head swathed in bandages, he looked like a mummy. Igor checked his health record and the post-operative report. Not brilliant. He sat down near him. It was quiet and unbearably hot in this department. He held the man's left hand. It was grey, cold and wrinkled. Igor warmed it by blowing on it and rubbing it. It took on a little colour. What sort of struggle was taking place inside this faltering body? What more could he do? Was there anything new, some unknown remedy that could save him? Was his helpless condition unpreventable? Had his time come? Would he manage to swim back to the surface or would he let himself sink? Igor rediscovered that forgotten feeling a doctor has when confronted with death, remembered the unspoken urge to fight against it, to challenge its prerogative, that supreme pleasure of snatching away its prey. Once more he saw the fingers clenching the mattresses, the crazed eyes, the countless fears, the inevitable asphyxiations, the faces of those he had been unable to save, who had slipped through his hands during the interminable siege of Leningrad and on the front line, the vast crowd of abandoned, sacrificial victims, who counted for nothing, who were of no importance. He rediscovered that visceral repulsion, that bitterness that always welled up again within him and with which he always struggled. This inert man, suspended between life and death, was closer to him than anyone else. A human brother. This was someone he would look after. He squeezed his hand and said to him in Russian: 'I swear to you that you're going to live.'

He was aware just how much he missed his profession. A little over four years. Would he have to leave France to practise again? Set off for Africa? South America, perhaps? In which countries would his degree be recognized? He ought to find out, not content himself with merely surviving, not allow himself to become resigned. At five o'clock, the night nurse came by on her rounds. He introduced himself to her. At six o'clock, she found Igor asleep, slumped in the armchair. He was holding the man's hand. At seven o'clock, the day nurse woke him inadvertently. He apologized and slipped away. He came back in the evening. He spent a moment beside the man, who was in a coma. He returned again after his night's work and stayed with him for an hour, holding his hand, speaking to him in a low voice. He got into the habit of visiting twice a day. He asked the nursing staff for news of the patient and the response was: 'Stable.'

A nurse informed him that, during the day, a police inspector from the Gobelins station had called in to question the patient about the assault. Seeing the man's condition, he went away again.

Igor made the acquaintance of the senior consultant, Professor Mazerin, a fairly young man, who was portly and wore superb bow ties. Mazerin had realized that Igor was a doctor and he plied him with questions: how had he managed to carry out such a perfect pleural tapping? Where did he come from? Who was he? Igor did not reply to any of the questions. Instead he asked questions of his own. No one could say when the man would emerge from the coma or what state he would be in. He had suffered a cranial trauma, but his spine had not been broken. The one piece of good news was that his blood pressure, which had been low, was normal again. Mazerin was hesitant about whether to try out a new Canadian product that enabled the intracranial pressure to be reduced. Igor studied the specifications and ventured the opinion that there would be no point, the problem was not a cerebral hypoventilation. One had to wait. Perhaps he would be lucky?

Igor came every day. He examined the medical sheet, sat himself down in the armchair and took the man's hand. He recounted Victor's fairy tales, told him about the passengers' reactions, the amount of tips, the new areas he was discovering during the course of his journeys. With his exam in mind, he took the guide to the Paris streets and the suburbs with him and learned it by heart. Victor had suggested that he start with the maps of the métro lines and the bus routes and use them as landmarks. The night nurse made him revise and acted as his examiner. She was a hard taskmistress. She knew Paris like the back of her hand, and she explained the layout of the arrondissements and their significance, which were middle-class districts and which were not. When she heard the bell on the ward, she rushed off to the patient's bedside. Suzanne was a true Parisienne, a brunette with a high-pitched voice who had always lived in Buttes-Chaumont. She never stopped talking, and she was delighted to meet someone she could chat to at last.

'I don't know whether you'll pass your taxi exam. If you fail, you can join the RATP.'

She was not impervious to his charm; she started to ask him about his life and suggested they visit the city together on Sunday. But he soon put an end to her attempts to ingratiate herself. He told her he was married and had numerous children. Suzanne was upset and stormed off. On the nights that followed, she ignored him, scarcely addressing a word to him. He continued to spend his mornings and evenings there. He liked the hospital atmosphere — the way it smelt of bleach and ether, the way it buzzed with activity. Luxury, profusion and modernity abounded here. And yet the staff and patients both whinged and grumbled. They should have done a course at the Tarnovsky, which was not the worst of Russian hospitals, and they would have discovered what poverty and despair really meant and stopped complaining. People did not realize how lucky they were, least of all the patients.

'You shouldn't be allowed to moan when you're fortunate; it's an insult to those who have nothing.'

'Don't forget, Igor,' Mazerin retorted, 'that the French are congenital moaners.'

Igor passed his exam at the first attempt and began his life as a Parisian taxi driver. Victor lent him the Simca Régence at nights. They would meet in the evenings at Nation, and Igor would return the car to him in the morning, along with a cut of the takings.

The weeks went by. Hope that the man would regain consciousness had become infinitesimal. Suzanne had resigned herself and was now talking to him again. To her mind, he was wasting his time. The man would not wake up. He would get worse, complications would accumulate and he would suffer a cardiac arrest. But Igor refused to give in to fatalism. He had witnessed inexplicable miracles on the front line. He had seen operations that were doomed beforehand turn out well, hearts that started to beat again, and dead men crawling out of the burial pit. He no longer came across Mazerin, nor any of the doctors. He didn't give up; he sat down beside the wounded man, took his left hand and told him about his night's work in detail. Sometimes, he had the impression that the man was reacting. Sometimes, Igor nodded off without realizing and spoke in Russian before pulling himself together. Eventually, he would fall asleep. Irène, the day nurse, woke him when she came on duty.

On the fifty-ninth day, the stranger emerged from his coma. Igor had just arrived and he was telling him about a road accident involving three cars that he had witnessed at the Étoile roundabout when he felt pressure on his hand. The man was stirring. He called Irène. The man had opened his eyes and was gazing vacantly at them. Igor did not return to his hotel that day. They asked the man questions. He remained prostrate. For Mazerin, this aphasia was disturbing. If he did not recover his speech within twenty-four hours, it would mean that there were irreversible injuries to the brain.

After a week, the injured man had still not said a word. Management was considering admitting him to a care home. But Igor observed some improvements. The man was raising both hands and was moving his legs. He could drink from a glass of water on his own. He had smiled at Igor on several occasions. Igor massaged him vigorously. His muscles had disappeared. Each of them holding one of his arms, he and Irène had succeeded in making him take three or four steps. Every day, they walked a yard further.

One evening, Igor was reading *Le Monde* when the man sneezed.

'Bless you,' Igor said automatically.

'Thank you,' the other man answered.

Igor jumped.

'You... you've just spoken.'

'Where am I?'

'You're in the Charcot wing, at La Pitié Hospital.'

Igor dashed on to the ward.

'He's talking!'

Irène came back to the room with him and questioned the man: 'Who are you, Monsieur? What is your name?'

'I don't know,' he replied.

The nurse looked at him suspiciously.

'Don't you think he's got a funny accent?' she asked Igor.

'I didn't notice anything.'

'What's your name, Monsieur? Do you remember your first name?'

'My name? My first name? I don't remember. I don't remember any-thing,' said the man, with a strong German accent.

'Shit, he's a Boche!' Irène exclaimed.

22

Cécile had decided to change. We often wish that our lives could be different. We dream of something else, but nothing materializes. We make promises to ourselves. We progress through life with ifs and buts. We wait, we put off the moment when our existence will improve, and the days and the years go by with our pledges replaced or faded away. Cécile no longer made any plans. On the landing, I heard the sound of a truck. With my ear glued to the door, I tried to discover where this din came from. I put the keys back in my pocket. I rang the bell and drummed on the door. The engine noise stopped. Cécile appeared, black as a chimney sweep, her hair awry, dressed in one of Pierre's shirts that came half way down her thighs, and clutching a duster.

'What are you doing?'

She gazed at me, frowning, and with a solemn expression.

'I've had a major spring-clean in my life and I'm having a major spring-clean in my flat.'

She stood aside to let me pass and I found myself in an unfamiliar room. It was tidy and neatly arranged, as if a good genie had come out of an oil lamp and, with a stroke of a magic wand, had transformed this place where hitherto only disorder reigned, where no duster had touched any furniture for years, where piles of dirty plates from past parties had still been stacked up amid overflowing ashtrays, empty beer and spirits bottles; where newspapers were piled up on top of lecture notes, beside unpacked boxes, half-opened letters, crumpled leaflets, 33 and 45 rpm records whose sleeves were scattered everywhere, and vases filled with dead flowers. The sofa had been well and truly flayed. The cushions had been stripped. The stained and torn covers lay on the floor waiting for the upholsterer. There was a smell of fresh wax. The room sparkled and shone like those advertisements at an Ideal Home exhibition extolling the happiness of the modern woman.

'What do you reckon?'

'Incredible.'

'It's spotless, you mean. I spent a day and night doing it. I threw out ten sacks of rubbish from the sitting room alone. The things you cling onto become oppressive. I can breathe. Can't you? I'm worn out.'

I walked round the sitting room, where every object was back in its original place. The bookshelves, which covered two walls from floor to ceiling, used to be invisible beneath the books, papers and magazines that were stacked up on them. Now everything was neatly arranged. A dozen piles of books were waiting in the hall to be taken to the dustbin.

'You're not going to throw away books!'

'If I keep the ones I love and Pierre's, I don't know where to put them. I'm not touching his records, they're sacred. As for the rest, he agrees, be ruthless.'

'Did you get a letter? How is he?'

'He asks whether the little bugger has made any progress in maths.'

'Did… did you tell him about Franck?'

'I told him everything.'

'What did he say?'

She took the letter from her pocket, unfolded it, and searched through it: '"… we must discard things that clutter us up. Spring-clean. Get rid of what is useless…"'

She crumpled up the letter and tossed it in the waste-paper basket.

'If there are any books that interest you, take them. Otherwise, we'll chuck them out.'

'That's crazy. We can take them to Gibert's. They take second-hand books.'

'I'll give them to you, if you want. Sell them. And, in future, don't talk to me any more about Franck! Is that clear?'

I came to a sudden halt in front of a machine a metre high, with a headlight on its front and a bulky red bag hanging from an enormous chrome frame.

'What on earth is that?'

'It's a vacuum cleaner. A Hoover. My father bought it in the United

States before the war. I came across it by chance in the bottom of a cupboard. I plugged it in. It started straight away. He hadn't used it for over ten years. It's noisy, but efficient.'

'You can't keep it. It sounds like a pneumatic drill.'

'It was a present from my father to my mother.'

I bent down to examine the machine. It was a collector's piece that belonged in a museum.

'Anyway, the neighbours can get stuffed. Fancy a café au lait?'

She had not touched the kitchen, which was hard to get in to. She removed two bowls from the pile of crockery overflowing from the sink and washed them. We waited for the coffee to percolate and, as usual, I made a bit of room for myself by pushing away the plates and bottles. Cécile grabbed a dustbin bag and threw endless packages and boxes into it. That made space on the table.

'I can't go on like this.'

'I have to admit it's a bit cluttered.'

'We'll get rid of the packaging.'

'I'll take it down.'

'Can you do me a favour?'

'With pleasure.'

'Would you give me a hand cleaning the flat?'

I hesitated for half a second. Time to reflect on the mountain of work in store.

'Do you want to clean the whole flat from top to bottom? It's going to take... months. There are parts of it that are dreadful. You should treat yourself to a cleaning lady.'

'I want to do it myself. I want it to be as it once was. Afterwards, when everything's clean, I'll ask the housekeeper to look after it.'

'The job's going to kill us.'

'Look, Michel, I've been thinking. I've taken a wrong turning. I'm starting again from scratch. I've let things get on top of me. It's over. I'm starting a new life. I'm tidying the flat. I'm finishing my thesis... or else I'll do psychology. And... I'm taking up sport.'

'You?'

'I've begun. One hour's gymnastics each morning, windows open.'

'I don't believe you.'

'We'll do it together.'

'Me? I loathe it.'

'If you go on like that, in twenty years' time you'll have a pot belly. We're too concerned with our heads.'

'I'm excused from gym.'

She gave me a sharp little punch in the tummy, which made me double-up.

'You've got no stomach muscles. You're a softy. Bloody hell, Michel, you've got to do something!'

'So what sport should we do?'

'Skating. In the open air, at Molitor. In winter, we'll go to swim at the Lutetia pool, and in summer, at Deligny.'

'Cécile, skating's dangerous.'

'Stop talking nonsense. We're going to come alive again.'

23

S ince Igor was the only one to show him a little kindness and care, the man awaited his arrival impatiently. His memories only went back to the moment he awoke. What preceded this had vanished, the blackboard of his memory erased by an unknown hand. Nothing remained, or very little – just tiny fragments of a vast jigsaw puzzle, like those ghostly frescoes on the walls of churches where only shadowy figures and vague outlines remain. Igor did not ask any direct questions. He tried to stir up images and associations of ideas. He had bought a card game for children aged three to five, and showed him pictures of animals and objects to name, in the hope of triggering a cerebral reaction. The stranger paused, screwed up his eyes, searched the back of his mind, braced his neck and probed until he began to shake. Igor had the feeling that he was close to succeeding, that it required very little for him to pierce through the darkness into light, that a connection was being made, like a spring ready to burst forth. But then his face and his shoulders slumped and he fell back into his vacuum. In spite of his efforts, he was not making any progress. Vague, scattered snatches of speech, illogical and incoherent, were emitted. There was nothing to do but wait and hope, find the key that would open the mysterious door. He was a German or an Austrian and he remembered nothing. The little he did manage to convey was spoken in the coarse, abrasive accent which aroused bleak memories. They had considered other nationalities, but each time they arrived at the same conclusion. In those years, it did not do to be a German in France. Too much bitterness, too much resentment. Every week there was a film shown that stigmatized Nazi barbarities and informed the French of the heroism of the Resistance, and those who had had so little courage soon convinced themselves that they had all been heroes. All the more reason to settle scores with anyone you could lay hands on. This man, who was about forty-five and must have been born between 1910 and 1920, was bound to have served in the German army.

'We had them for four years, we managed to get rid of them, and we don't want to see them over here any more.'

The nurses who were so adorable, the theatre attendants who were so devoted, the doctors who were so kindly, harped on, without exception, in the same way: out with him, and the sooner the better. It was unanimous. Sitting in an armchair all day and left on his own, the man was unaware of the uneasy atmosphere he created. When Igor arrived in the evening, he had to wash him and feed him like a child. No nurse wanted to tend to him. Igor was unable to curb the wave of hatred. He did his best to prevail upon them but came up against a brick wall.

'It may well be that he's a Swiss German.'

'He's a Boche!' Mazerin fulminated. 'You know that as well as I do.'

'You haven't the right to throw out a sick man!'

'Physically, this fellow's as fit as a fiddle. We don't know how to treat amnesia. It can last ten years or for ever. This is a hospital, not a hospice. I'll give you twenty-four hours. After that, I'm kicking him out. I don't want to find myself with a strike on my hands because of this guy.'

He went out, slamming the door. The stranger smiled. Hard to make him understand that they hated him because of what happened more than ten years ago, when all he could remember were the last five days.

'Where to begin? How can I explain the war to you?'

Someone knocked at the door. A black man with an athletic build came in and showed his police card.

'Inspector Daniel Mahaut. Gobelins Police Station.'

The policeman had come to question the injured man about the attack on him. He had asked to be informed before the man left the hospital. Igor told him about the general anger and the thoughtless deportation. The inspector leant over towards the seated man.

'I'm from the police. We're making investigations. Do you wish to bring proceedings?... Do you remember the assault on you, Monsieur?... Do you know who did this to you?'

The man stared at him before replying, a faint smile on his face.

'An assault, you say? I don't remember.'

'These people will never change!' moaned the inspector. 'If his memory

156

does come back, he can drop by at the station. We're behind the town hall of the thirteenth arrondissement.'

A little later, Mazerin came by to tell him that he needed the bed and that he would have the patient thrown out the following morning. He would not countenance any delay and he turned round and walked away. The man said nothing. He stared at Igor with a trusting expression.

'I earn barely enough to pay for my small hotel room. I won't be able to look after you. Maybe you're an absolute bastard, but that doesn't matter any more. Don't worry, I'm not going to desert you. You can move in with me. We'll manage, and if the boss doesn't like it, we'll go somewhere else.'

24

'Not a word to our mother either. I don't want to hear about her again. Do you understand? Work it out for yourself, otherwise…'

Franck had left me no alternative. With Cécile, all I had to do was keep my mouth shut and behave as though I knew nothing. At home, it was different. Ever since he had left, slamming the door behind him, Franck was a taboo subject. It was as if he had never existed. And yet he was all around us. In the way we said hello and in the way we looked at one another, whenever we said: 'How are you?' or: 'What did you do today?' In a family you are attached to one another by invisible strings that bind you even when you sever them. Nobody explained the rules of the game to Juliette or me. We followed them instinctively. My father was fully taken up with the new shop. We did not see him any more. He spent his life there. We had dinner without him, not saying a word. He came home late and tired. I would find him in the kitchen reheating the remains of the meal. He ate in silence, a vacant expression on his face, pretending to listen to me, but with his mind elsewhere. I wanted to talk to him about Franck without the risk of my mother coming in, but it was impossible to do so in the flat and at the shop. I had to wait for the right moment. Time went by. I never managed to be alone with him. There were only two days left before Franck's departure when, one morning at breakfast, my mother came in, all spruced up in one of the Chanel suits she brought out for important occasions. She was going on a three-day 'Develop your leadership' course. One of those American seminars recommended by Maurice.

My parents at least had one cause for satisfaction. The opening of the new shop had earned us a photo on page eight of *France-Soir*, which my father had had enlarged, made into a prospectus and distributed to letter-boxes in the fifth, sixth and eighth arrondissements. It did not take long to have an effect. The success far exceeded his most optimistic expectations.

They had the greatest difficulty in supplying the orders and delivering to customers. My father managed his team effortlessly, keeping an eye on everything, smiling, relaxed, joking, settling disputes between the salesmen in their garnet-coloured jackets, suggesting to customers who did not have the means to pay cash that they spread out their payments by laying out a modest sum each month. He had had to insist in order to foist this idea on my mother who, in spite of her seminars, remained attached to the old-fashioned principles of commercial trade.

'Since the poor are more numerous than the rich, if you want to sell a lot, you have to sell to those who have no money and who long to buy what they can't afford to give themselves. You have to provide them with credit accounts.'

Philippe Delaunay had rejoined the firm and was giving a helping hand because of the demand. Among his acquaintances, he shamelessly claimed credit for the success of the venture. But you could sense his bitterness about certain aspects. He was conscious of the total immorality and deep injustice of commerce: that an idiot such as Paul Marini, a self-made man without any education could make a fortune with a good idea. Business was not what it once was. People no longer needed to have read the classics in order to succeed. Tomorrow's world would belong to the parvenus and the wily. My father never missed an opportunity to remind him of his dire predictions and took pleasure in turning the knife in the wound by pointing out that he had increased the turnover tenfold and the profit by fifteen. My mother did the accounts. The electronic calculator crackled away and never stopped producing lists of figures that left her flushed with happiness. There was talk of opening another shop. My father had found premises in avenue du Général-Leclerc. When he mentioned the selling price, my mother had backtracked, terrified by the magnitude of the investment, and they began arguing. He had not given up and he had an eye on a place in rue de Passy too, in the fashionable district, while he waited to be able to realize his life's dream: opening a shop in Versailles.

'Being poor and not having money is not too bad, being rich and having a bit is better.'

*

When I entered the shop, my father spotted me and left his customers with a salesman.

'It's lovely to see you here.'

'I must speak to you. It's important. Come.'

I dragged him outside. We walked down avenue des Gobelins. I found it hard to explain things to him. He never stopped interrupting me and asking me questions. I lost the thread of what I wanted to say. We sat down on a bench, close to Saint-Médard church.

'Why should we wait till tomorrow?'

'That's what he asked.'

'Where is he?'

'I don't know.'

'What's he playing at? Eh? He had a deferment. It's because of his girl-friend, is that it?'

'She doesn't know. She's desperate. She tried to commit suicide!'

'What? I'm your father. Do you know what that means? I'm the only person you can trust and you treat me like a stranger!'

'I've only known for two days. Before that, I thought he had another girlfriend.'

'I don't believe it! You don't enlist like that! Me, I was obliged to. It was a general call-up. We had no choice. If I could, I wouldn't have gone. No one's so bloody stupid to enlist out of idealism. He doesn't know what war is. It's not a game.'

'If you knew Cécile, you'd say he's completely crazy.'

'I'm going to call Philippe, he knows people at the Ministry of Defence.'

'There wouldn't be any point. He'll refuse.'

'So we can't help him?'

'He'll be waiting for us tomorrow at four o'clock at the Terminus, it's by the exit from the Château-de-Vincennes métro... Oh, by the way, he doesn't want you to talk to Mother about it.'

'Because of that row about the opening?'

'Because of... I'm not too sure. You must ask him.'

'I've got a massive amount of work tomorrow, but I'll come to give him a kiss.'

25

After his night's work, Igor went back to the hospital to take the man home with him. He stopped by to see Suzanne to ask which medicines he should take to treat him or whether he could have a prescription, but she shrugged her shoulders.

'There are no medicines!'

She left the nurses' area, grabbing him by the arm.

Igor was in the process of putting the things he had bought for the man into a plastic bag when there was a knock at the door of the room. Inspector Mahaut appeared, with a sheet of paper in his hand.

'I was bothered by this business. I put in a search request at the missing persons department at police headquarters. I've a West Indian friend who works there. He's from Martinique, but when we can, we do favours for one another. He spent the night there. In the file containing descriptions of people who had disappeared but who were of no cause for concern, he came across a landlady who had reported that her lodger, a stateless person of German origin, was missing. That's all we have.'

'You think that…'

'I thought we might go and call on her. It's not far. It would be quicker than summoning her to the station. At least we'd be certain.'

'Let's go. What's his name supposed to be?'

Inspector Mahaut put on his spectacles and read the scribbled name on the paper.

'Wener Teul… Werner Toller.'

Igor took the man's hand and smiled at him.

'Are you Werner Toller? … Is that your name?'

The man considered the matter.

'Werner Toller?… It means nothing to me. I don't know any Werner Toller.'

'Perhaps it's not him,' the inspector opined.

The month of May was dreadfully dreary, with leaden skies and drizzle. They got on the métro at Saint-Marcel. The inspector did not have his police car. During the short journey, he questioned Igor, appearing sceptical: 'If I've understood correctly, you were a porter when a Russian taxi driver brought in this injured man to the hospital, and you took a liking to this fellow countryman of yours. Now, you work for him as a night driver.'

'He has French nationality. I don't. Yes, that's what happened.'

'It's a bit odd, don't you think?'

'That's life. I've been obliged to adapt.'

'Why are you taking care of him?'

The inspector jutted his chin at the supposed Werner Toller who, with his nose pressed to the window, was making the most of the elevated railway line to store up images of the strange city that was flashing past.

'He was alone. I was alone.'

'You're...'

'Homosexual? Oh no, not in the least. In Russia, I had a family, and I still would if I had not had to escape in order to save my life.'

'Really, you didn't know him beforehand?'

'I swear to you.'

'If it's true, he was lucky to come across you.'

They got off at Denfert-Rochereau. The man seemed unfamiliar with the area. The woman who had reported the missing person was supposed to live at 110 avenue Denfert-Rochereau, but the name Toller did not figure on the list of residents of the building and the concierge was out.

'You've no idea how much time is wasted searching for information,' Mahaut observed. 'It's only in films that it happens quickly. Come on, we'll ask in the bistro and I'll buy you a *café crème*. We've deserved it.'

He pushed open the door of the large café that stood at the corner of the two boulevards. It smelled of *boeuf bourguignon* and fried onions. At this hour of the morning, a few regulars were chatting at the counter. Four students were battling away around the two baby-foot tables. A man of about fifty with a paunch rushed over towards them.

'Werner! Where were you?'

He took him in his arms, glad to have found him, and gave him a warm hug. Werner remained impervious to this outburst. He clearly did not recognize him. The man eventually relaxed his grip, turned round and announced in a loud voice: 'Madeleine… It's Werner! He's come back!'

Igor and Mahaut watched as a large woman in a white apron appeared. She stood stock still at the kitchen door, behind the counter, her face lit up.

'Werner! It's you!'

Thrilled and moved to tears, she clasped him in her plump arms and raised him off the ground as she hugged him.

'Well, what's the matter with him?' she said.

Inspector Mahaut introduced himself. The owners of the Balto recognized the man known as Werner Toller without a moment's hesitation and explained they had been renting a studio flat in rue du Val-de-Grâce to him for over ten years. They all sat down in the backroom of the Balto. Werner sat on the bench, a little further away, uninvolved with the conversation. Igor told the Marcusots about his amnesia and his disturbing condition.

'It's not like him to leave without warning,' Madeleine pointed out. 'We suspected something odd. At the Edgar-Quinet police station, they didn't believe us. They said he'd gone back to Germany. We knew that was impossible. By the way, is he going to regain his memory?'

'No one can answer that question,' replied Igor. 'He suffered a cranial trauma during his attack. As to how deep the injury is, or whether it is serious or irreversible? Nobody knows. His memory may return tomorrow morning when he wakes up, or in six months, ten years, or never.'

Igor described how Werner had been thrown out of the hospital because he was German. Albert Marcusot turned red, and he declared loudly: 'I don't believe it! It's crazy! Tell me I'm dreaming! Werner Toller is a German who's anti-Nazi! In the Monnaie network, he specialised in infiltrating German intelligence. He's been decorated by the Resistance and his Forces Françaises de l'Intérieur card was signed by Kriegel-Valrimont himself. What country are we living in?'

'I didn't know there had been any Germans in the Resistance,' said Mahaut.

'At the beginning of the war, there were Austrians and Germans here, at least three or four thousand of them, who had fled their countries in the thirties. Many of them did an enormous amount of work providing information, they served as liaison officers, as translators, they recruited deserters from the Wehrmacht, they provided a mass of information to the resistance movements, and they were turned in by the French police. Most of them were Jews or Communists. But there were also Christians and Social Democrats, or ordinary people who disagreed with the Nazis. Before the war started, Werner had already had experience in resisting. He knew what was going to happen to us. We didn't. You could write a book about what he did and how he slipped through the net. He disowned his country. After the war, he didn't want to go back there. It's not easy to have next door neighbours or office colleagues who denounced you or arrested you and cheered on the oppressors. He refuses to speak German. He still has that wretched accent. He hasn't managed to get rid of it. It sticks to his tongue. When he tries, he can get by. We were once stopped by a patrol. I heard him speaking to his fellow countrymen in a Parisian accent. He's no longer German, he's not French; he's what's called a stateless person.'

'What does he do for a living?' Mahaut asked.

'He's a projectionist at a cinema in rue Champollion,' replied Albert Marcusot. 'The owner knew him in the Resistance and, with a job like that, he doesn't speak to anyone. After his work, he comes and has supper with us. He's almost one of the family. Every evening we play draughts together.'

'Did Werner have any enemies?'

'Not to my knowledge.'

'Before he went missing, did he have a quarrel or a disagreement with anyone?'

'He said nothing to me. What about you?'

'He's a quiet, very ordinary man,' Madeleine confirmed.

'And yet he was beaten up and left for dead.'

'That really frightens me. You see motiveless acts nowadays that didn't happen before. It may have nothing to do with the war or Werner's past.'

'I'd like to believe you, Madame. But in our job, there are never coincidences, or very seldom.'

During this time, Werner sat there, beside them, on the bench, as though not involved. It was hard to believe that he was the man the Marcusots were talking about. Igor went and sat down opposite him.

'How are you, Werner?'

'Fine.'

'Are you glad to be back in this bistro? You're at home here.'

'I don't know.'

'Don't you recognize them?'

He shook his head. His gaze fell on the nearby table where several games – a chessboard with pieces in a box, a game of draughts with black and white counters, a game of tarot and a Yams/421 board – were all piled up in a jumble.

'Do you want to play?' Igor asked.

His eyes glued on the table where the games were, Werner did not answer.

'A round of belote?'

Igor waited for a reply which was slow in coming.

'Or 421? Do you know the rules? Could you show me? We can play for the apéritif, if you like?'

Werner remained silent.

'Or a game of chess, perhaps? I haven't played for four years, but I used to get by reasonably well.'

Werner continued to gaze at the table, in silence. Igor turned round, unsure what to do. Madeleine nodded in agreement. Igor took the chessboard and placed it between them. He laid out the pieces in the box.

'We could have a quick game? That would be fun, wouldn't it? Here, I'll let you play white. It's an advantage. Your go.'

Werner stared at the chessboard, not moving, not speaking. Igor waited. The others, at the neighbouring table, followed this game that took ages to begin, in religious silence. The shouting and yelling of the baby-foot players, and the ball slamming against the metal goals, could be heard in the background. It didn't disturb them. Madeleine and Albert had pins and needles in their legs. Igor had a bad back. Nobody moved. They were waiting for Werner to move, but Werner didn't move. He sat there with his eyes fixed on the chessboard, his eyebrows arched, face taut, rigid as a marble statue. Opposite him, Igor sat patiently, not fidgeting or showing any sign of irritation, a slightly knowing smile on his lips, as befits a player worthy of the name who allows his opponent to determine his strategy and to reflect a little before making his first move. Except that there wasn't one. After two hours and countless glances between them, Igor could feel weariness gaining the upper hand, there was somewhat heavy sighing, much clearing of the throat and coughing, and the bench creaked beneath painful posteriors. He was convinced that nothing would happen. They might remain face to face for years without Werner reacting. This game was not a good idea, thought Igor, nodding gently, his lips clenched, his eyelids flickering. Then he made an unpremeditated move. He advanced his black pawn two squares on the board. It was an incongruity, an absurdity. No player since the game of chess was invented several centuries ago has begun a game playing black. It was a sacrilege. An impossibility. Something that couldn't be done or imagined. Playing white first was an organic, integral aspect of chess. Werner sat up straight, astounded and perplexed. His mouth was agape, his eyes wide open, and he was staring at Igor. He shook his head and grunted, as if to point out that what he had done was unbelievable. Then, without further ado, he took his white pawn and moved it two squares so that it was opposite Igor's black pawn. The game had begun. Igor followed with another black pawn. Werner responded similarly. When Igor continued with his third black pawn, Werner moved his knight. Any player will tell you, including beginners, that when you bring out your knight on the third move, it indicates hostile intentions. And everyone knows that when you are aggressive you can't be feeling too bad. Werner took two pawns with this knight. They played another twenty or so moves and then, to everybody's surprise, Werner castled and put Igor in a dangerous position.

'I've got the feeling it's not going too well,' Igor admitted.

'You'll be mate in four moves.'

'You've won and I'm delighted,' said Igor as he toppled over his king.

'May I be permitted an observation?'

'Please.'

'You're not allowed to open with black. It's not allowed.'

They were astounded by this memory that had come back like a flash of lightning. They surrounded him. They congratulated him. They embraced him. They plied him with questions. Werner now remembered almost everything. He remembered his life both before and after his recovery. But nothing about the assault of which he had been the victim, or about its perpetrators. Inspector Mahaut looked piqued. Igor tried to cheer him up: 'The important thing is that it should end well.'

'Werner's not telling the truth. He knows his assailants.'

'What makes you think that?'

'The way he hesitates when he talks about it. He has thought carefully and invented this memory lapse.'

'I'd be very surprised. He's constantly searching for his words. A man doesn't think of lying when he's got his memory back.'

Albert offered everyone some Clairette de Die that could easily be mistaken for the best champagne. Jacky, the waiter, opened half a dozen bottles and twenty or more customers made the most of them. Some thought that Albert must have won the lottery to behave so generously. He didn't have a reputation for splashing out lavishly. Igor advised Werner against drinking sparkling wine. He followed his advice and ordered a glass of beer without any froth. Madeleine never stopped repeating that it was a sign from Heaven, where she was seriously in debt. As she grew older, she had returned to religion, though she never set foot in a church, Sunday mornings being taken up with her work at the Balto. She felt bad about her negligence and was convinced that sooner or later she would pay for her thoughtlessness and her casual behaviour. She promised herself she would light a large candle to thank St Anthony for his intervention. As far as Werner was concerned, the Good Lord had nothing to do with his cure, which was as speedy as it was miraculous. Werner was a poor prospect. Not the kind whom the Lord would reward.

'It's not good to blaspheme, Werner. God sees everything.'

'If it's true, Madeleine, he's got no excuse. If I need to thank anyone, it's Igor and him alone. He looked after me and he found the key. Thank you, Igor.'

They hugged one another. Whether it was the effect of the Clairette or the emotion, Igor's head was spinning slightly.

'I've done nothing extraordinary. The credit is due to Inspector Mahaut.'

This citation in despatches at the Balto brought him a round of applause and the eternal gratitude of those present. He was deeply moved. It was not every day that he was cheered. Usually, it was the opposite. In those days, the police and police officers were not liked. Igor proposed a toast. This suggestion pleased everybody. Jacky filled the glasses to the brim.

'To Werner's good health!' Igor cried, before downing the contents of his glass in one and then hurling it to the ground where it shattered on the floor.

Everyone imitated him; they all drank their glasses dry and threw them down in an infectious outburst, where they broke into a thousand slivers — with the exception of Albert, Madeleine and Jacky, who gazed in horror at the damage done to their glassware. Ever since that day, they continue to celebrate important events at the Balto, but Russian toasts are forbidden by the owners.

Heated discussions took place in small groups. There were two opposing camps: the mystics who saw this as divine intervention and the unbelievers who regarded it merely as yet another mystery concerning the human body. Was this inexplicable cure to do with the supernatural? Or was it conclusive proof of our ignorance? Did physical, even bodily materialism exist in the way that historical materialism did? Voices were raised. People interrupted. They grew excited. None of them was short of edifying arguments and examples. It was sad to observe that not one of these magnificent outbursts had any effect. Our inability to convince others is absolute proof of the value, according to our means, of the scornful insult, the punch, the sharpened knife, the automatic pistol, the stick of dynamite tied to a detonator, or the nuclear aircraft-carrier. Our misfortunes have only one cause: our opinions are sacred. Those who change their points of view are idiots and so too are those who allow themselves to be persuaded.

Seated on the bench, Igor and Werner were talking about their past lives and they remained uninvolved in this uproar.

'It can't have been easy for you,' Igor said to him.

'It can't have been easy for you either.'

'The important thing is to be alive, isn't it?'

'Yes, we have to think of the future.'

'If we ourselves are not optimists, who will be?'

The official launch of the Club dates from 30 May 1956. Apart from occasional headaches, Werner did not suffer any after-effects from the attack on him and he did not speak about it again. The following day, he resumed his job as a projectionist. Igor and he became friends; they got into the habit of meeting one another at the Balto for their games of chess and the only thing that ever kept them apart was the fact that Werner was an early riser and Igor a nightbird. Very soon, Igor became part of the family and acquired the habit of dining with Werner, the Marcusots and Jacky. He would get in touch with Victor Volodine, who allowed him to have the taxi for the night. He had arranged with Victor that from now on the handover should take place at Denfert and no longer at Nation.

The first time he went to the Balto, Victor set eyes again on the man whom he had picked up, half-dead, on the Rue de Tolbiac and taken to the hospital. He demanded repayment for the cleaning of his blood-stained white car seat. Igor thought he was joking. Victor was in earnest. Werner reckoned the bill was somewhat steep, but he made it a point of honour to repay Victor down to the last centime and refused to let Igor contribute. Each of us must pay our debts. This explains why Victor was not admitted as a member of the Club.

When, four years later, Igor recounted this episode to me, I made a pathetically trite observation: 'It's unimaginable.'

'There is no adjective that describes this story, no words that can portray what doesn't exist and what can't be imagined. Werner's recovery was inconceivable a few seconds beforehand,' Igor explained to me. 'On the contrary, the story causes us to put our imaginative capacity, which we think is infinite, into context and to question ourselves about the frailty of our imagination, which we often confuse with understanding. There is nothing unimaginable about the gulag, genocides, death camps or atomic bombs. They are human creations, rooted within us, and it is only their enormity that overwhelms us. They go beyond our understanding, destroy our willingness to believe in man, and reflect our own images of monsters back at us. They are, in reality, the most accomplished forms of our inability to convince. The apex of our creative ability. We can imagine such unimaginable things as travelling in space-time, or discovering what the lottery numbers are in advance, or meeting the ideal or perfect man or woman, for after all, people have invented abstract painting and concrete music; we can imagine everything, but not that. Not a miraculous cure. That is purely a matter of chance or luck.'

As I was walking along rue Champollion, I spotted Werner. The projection room looked out onto the sloping street, and he was opening the door to air the room. His boss had acquired the cinema next door and he was looking after both theatres. He had twice the amount of work, but since the screenings were staggered, this did not bother him. When he had a moment of quiet in between changing reels, he would smoke a cigarette on the doorstep. We exchanged pleasantries. He offered to let me see the films free of charge. Usually I declined his invitation. At the Club, he occasionally informed us about a masterpiece that shouldn't be missed under any circumstances. But it wasn't very comfortable in his narrow room and the projectors made a noise. When the cinema wasn't full, he arranged for his friend the usherette to give us a folding seat. The foreign, subtitled films that were shown at his cinema were long-winded and deadly dull. He went into raptures as he talked about them. I didn't dare tell him that they bored me stiff and I avoided rue Champollion. He must have been aware of this and kept his distance. There are books that we ought to be forbidden to read too early. We should avoid them or pass them by. And films too. They ought to carry a label: Not to be seen or read before one has lived.

26

As I arrived at Cardinal-Lemoine métro station, I bumped into Sherlock, who was standing there reading *Le Figaro*. Hard to find a plausible excuse. He looked me up and down with his eagle eye.

'Haven't you a maths class, Marini?

'I've a very bad back, Monsieur. I'm going to the Cochin Hospital.'

'I'll come with you, my lad.'

'I may be there all afternoon.'

'I hope it's nothing serious. Bring me a note from your parents. In fact, for Cochin, it's not the right métro line, you'd do better to catch the bus. The 27. You'll get there quicker.'

He was obliging enough to wait for the bus with me. When I reached the Terminus, Franck wasn't there. Two conscripts were fooling around by one of the baby-foot tables. I inserted my coin and found them standing opposite me.

'Are you playing on your own?' the elder of the two asked.

'Does that bother you?'

I pulled out all the stops. Like Samy. I hadn't practised for three weeks, but I felt more energetic than I'd ever felt before. I passed them at will. A real pro. There was a respectful silence as the balls slammed in. I thrashed them without even giving them a glance. Others followed the same path. I strung together seven successive games. My powers were fading. A hand was laid on my shoulder. Franck was standing in front of me, his head shaved.

'Looks like you've improved.'

We sat down on the terrace. It was a quarter to four. He put his large bag down on the ground and ordered drinks: 'A beer and a really weak lemonade shandy.'

'Well, they certainly did a good job on you.'

'It'll grow again.'

'Papa will be here soon. Do you know where you'll be posted?'

'That's the army for you. We don't know a thing. We may find ourselves in Algiers, in Djibouti or in Berlin. We assume it'll be Algeria. That's where they need non-commissioned officers.'

'Will you let me know where you are?'

Franck considered the matter.

'No.'

'Why?'

'I don't want Mama to know where I am. I've cut all ties with her.'

'You promised to write to Cécile.'

'How is she?'

'If you want to know about her, you only have to ask her!'

'Please, Michel, talk to me about her. What's she up to? Has she gone back to uni? Has she made any progress on her thesis?'

'She wants to quit.'

'What's this all about?'

'Didn't you know? She doesn't know where she is. She's not sure whether to go on. She likes the idea of psychology. She's good at that.'

'What is all this nonsense? With her thesis, she'll be able to teach literature. It's a fine job, it's what she loves and it means security. Psychology's a leap in the dark. There are no jobs. You've got to stop her doing such a crazy thing.'

'If you're so keen, go and tell her yourself. She won't listen to me.'

Franck was furious. Head bowed, he considered the matter. His right hand drummed on the table feverishly.

'The only person who can do anything is Pierre. I'm going to write to him.'

'Do you know where he is?'

'He's based in Souk-Ahras. Psychology's not his thing.'

'When he writes to her, he mustn't mention you, or me. She's become oversensitive. As soon as you give her any advice, she jumps on you.'

'You've become her friend. Has she… has she confided in you?'

'She doesn't want to hear about you any longer. Don't ask me about her any more.'

'You'll have to look after her.'

'Don't worry. She doesn't need anybody.'

'We share the same views. She's even more outspoken than I am, on a mass of things. Rather like Pierre. This war's not going to last long. De Gaulle's going to deal with Algeria. I'll be back home soon and we'll sort it out. She'll be proud of what I've done. It's far from being over between us.'

'She won't forgive you for having deserted her. If you'd had the courage to tell her to her face, she would have understood and she would have waited for you. You stabbed her in the back. She wasn't expecting it. She's erased you from her life. Don't delude yourself, you won't find her again when you return.'

'I'm sorry Michel, but you know nothing about women. They say one thing in the morning, another in the evening, and the following day they've changed their mind. Right now, she's feeling livid. When I get back, we'll discuss it all again.'

Franck glanced at the clock. Twenty-five past four.

'Did you really tell Papa?'

'He won't be long.'

'I have to be there at five.'

We had two more drinks. He offered me a Gitane.

'I don't smoke. May I ask you a question?'

He didn't answer, but allowed me to continue: 'Why are you going there? What with self-rule, we know how it'll all end. What's the point? The game's over.'

'You're wrong. The game is over if you play by their rules. I don't want to talk about it.'

'How can you treat us this way?'

Franck paused. He was searching for words. It seemed too complicated to explain or impossible to get to grips with.

'If I say to you… revolution, what does that mean to you?'

'You want there to be a revolution?'

'I haven't time to explain. We can never fill the gulf between the profiteers and those who get screwed. It's the one and only question:

173

what side are we on? There'll be no peace on earth and no settlement, no progress, no dialogue and no social breakthrough. The time has come to act.'

'We can improve things, bit by bit. Try to understand one another, even when we don't agree.'

'Respect is what the bourgeoisie has invented to achieve its ends. No one respects the proletariat.'

'You're going to fight for people who couldn't give a damn.'

'The world's moving on. People are fed up. And not just in France, everywhere. The Third World War has begun. This time they're not going to steal our victory from us.'

'You're either dreaming or indulging in wishful thinking: the vast majority of people wouldn't go along with you.'

'We don't think in the same way. That's why there's no point in discussing it.'

It was as though there were a brick wall between us. We sat there not knowing what to say to each other. I heard the door open. Franck's face lit up. I looked round. Richard was coming in, carrying a large bag. My brother stood up.

'I can't wait.'

He paid for the drinks. The three of us left. We set off towards Fort de Vincennes. Some young conscripts were there, showing their call-up papers to one of the soldiers on duty who was allowing them in. I was watching out for my father, but there was only a crowd of anonymous people. We arrived at the small drawbridge.

'There must have been a problem.'

'It's too late, Michel.'

He grabbed me by the shoulders and clasped me to him. We couldn't stop patting one another on the back.

'Take care of yourself.'

He picked up his bag and crossed the drawbridge. Richard followed close behind. The soldier checked their papers and let them pass through the metal gate. He went in without looking back. By my watch, it was exactly five o'clock. I turned round. My eyes were stinging.

A taxi screeched to a halt in front of the entrance. My father got out, yelling at the driver and threw him a hundred-franc note through the open window.

'If you don't know how to drive, take lessons! I've never seen such a numbskull!'

He saw me and hurried over.

'Where is he? Hasn't he arrived yet?'

'Papa, he's gone in.'

My father looked up and gazed at the dark and hostile fortress.

'It's not true!'

'Why are you late?'

'That bitch of a DS broke down! The clutch has gone. On the way out of Versailles. Bloody old banger! Try finding a taxi in the middle of the forest! I tried hitching, but no one gave me a lift. I walked ten kilometres. And I did find a taxi! A real slowcoach, I'm not joking. He was driving along at forty! He stopped at every traffic light! I could have strangled him!'

Before I could utter another word, he had stepped over the draw-bridge. I followed him. He went to see the soldier on duty, who told him that he was there to check the conscripts' papers. He set off in search of the duty officer. Five minutes later, he came back with a man built like a house who looked like Chéri Bibi.* My father tried to explain to him, but he went about it in the wrong way. He began with the shop he had visited in Versailles, a good deal, a bit pricey; the DS, which was under guarantee and blew up right in the middle of the Marly forest; and the novice taxi driver. Chéri Bibi interrupted him. Three conscripts who were late were waiting to get past.

'You're interfering with procedures.'

'It's for my son.'

'Where is he?'

'Inside. I should have liked to give him a kiss before he goes away.'

'Kiss him?... That's over, Monsieur. You must get off the gangway.'

'I'll be five minutes.'

* The hero of Gaston Leroux's serial adventures.

'You're in a military zone. You're forbidden to stay here.'

'Five minutes. That's not going to alter the course of the war.'

'There is no war. If you don't leave, I'll call the military police and they'll arrest you.'

'And for what reason, may I ask?'

'For obstructing the conscription of recruits. Get out of the way!'

I pulled at my father's sleeve. We moved back and found ourselves on the pavement once more.

'What an arsehole!' he yelled. 'Good luck to the lad. If they're all like that, he's going to have a tough time.'

The sergeant glared down at us. My father held his gaze. We were in front of the entrance to the fortress. My father was smiling at him arrogantly, hands on hips. The sergeant, arms folded, stood still as a statue. A sort of arm wrestling. It began to rain heavily. The sergeant stepped back inside the sentry box. A mocking smile lit up his square-jawed face. All of a sudden, the crowd dispersed. We were the only two left, getting soaked, like two lonely, forgotten leeks.

'Papa, he's not going to let us see him.'

'Why did he do that?'

'I don't know. Come on, let's go home.'

Cars, trucks and buses, making a deafening din, were snarled up as far as the eye could see. There was a stench of petrol and exhaust fumes. Drivers were getting irritated, pushing their way through, blocking each other, sounding their horns and yelling insults. An everyday traffic-jam in the heavy, dismal Paris rain. We searched for a taxi. They were all occupied and there was no point in waiting. We walked up avenue de Paris for two kilometres as far as porte de Vincennes. We were moving faster than the stationary cars. We were soaked. In spite of my insistence, my father refused to take the métro and was searching for a taxi.

'I haven't taken the métro for over fifteen years and I'm not going to start now.'

Eventually, we did grab a taxi. Paris was at a standstill.

'I'll go along tomorrow to see about the DS. They're going to hear about this at Citroën.'

'Papa, you must write me a note for school.'

'Why?'

'Because of Sherlock.... of Monsieur Masson, the supervisor. I told him I was going to the hospital to get treatment. I couldn't tell him the truth: that my brother's a communist — that would have gone down very badly. He supports French Algeria.'

He wasn't listening to me. He was gazing out through the streaming window. His lips were moving. He was mumbling some inaudible words. He stared at me distractedly.

'What did he say to you?'

'Nothing of interest.'

'He might have waited for me.'

'Whatever you do, not a word to mother.'

He began nodding his head up and down as if to convince himself.

'You have to believe that that's the way it is and that's the way they're going to be,' he murmured.

Delighted by her seminar, my mother was unstoppable over dinner and she tried to make us share her enthusiasm. My father didn't eat. On two or three occasions, he tried to talk to her. I shuddered and had a fit of sneezing. A filthy cold that dragged on.

I spent a week at home, reading. My father wrote the note. Everything returned to normal. I didn't say anything to Cécile. She didn't ask any questions. When we cleaned the balconies or polished the wooden floors, she became dreamy and would stop rubbing. I didn't need to ask what she was thinking about. I was waiting for Franck to send her the promised letter. I didn't want to circumvent him. He had to reflect, weigh up each word, mull over his sentences to explain the why and the wherefore, ask to be forgiven, and persuade her that their relationship wasn't over and that there was a future for them. The months went by. Love and revolution must be incompatible. He never wrote to her.

JANUARY–DECEMBER 1961

1

Martha Balazs was a flighty girl who was bored to death in Debrecen, a godforsaken hole in the depths of Hungary, to where Edgar, her husband, chief engineer of the Magyar railways, had been transferred in 1927 as regional manager. She missed her carefree life as a singer of operetta, when she lost herself in Offenbach and Lehar. The breathtaking stage-fright before the curtain rose, the thrill that ran through the audience when well-known pieces were sung, the jolly dinners with the cast after the show, the endless tours by train or the bus journeys to Bratislava and Bucharest, to Austria and to Germany, the applause of the spectators that caused her to come out in goose pimples, and the curtain calls, as many as seventeen of them, that made her head reel in Zagreb. She kept the newspaper articles in two large Venetian blue exercise books and, even though she didn't understand the language, she could find her name. These yellowing cuttings mentioned her, her spiralling soprano voice that reached such high notes that it should have opened the doors of the Opera to her, the real one where Verdi and Bizet are sung, if … if … she was no longer really sure, she had had a bit more luck, or courage, or had spoken out a bit. She could have gone on for a few more years if she had not had that panic about the future and about becoming one of those bloated old singers who make up the herd of backstage choruses and who tend to be dismissed unceremoniously. Martha had been able to pull out in time, make a good marriage, and she had maintained her position in society while scorning the uncultured petit-bourgeois women of Debrecen with their hoarse Hajdu accent, that remote province where there was nothing but yokels, bears and forests.

In her exile, Martha had two passions, her little Tibor, who was admired by everyone for his beauty, his angelic smile and his sweet nature, and France. Martha had gone to Paris after the war. She had been marked for the rest of her life by the Roaring Twenties, which, in her case, had only lasted for six months. She still spoke about them with emotion as being the great period of her life. Each month she received French fashion magazines as though they were gifts from heaven. It was the light of the banks of the Seine that illuminated her life and those of the three friends she had converted to her religion: being a Parisienne. Living, talking, walking, eating, dressing like a Parisienne. Martha cultivated refinement in all its forms. In this country where the culinary peak was over-boiled stew, she did her best to carry the flag for French gastronomy and, in time, she had become an exceptional cook. She despised the mocking smiles of the local flibbertigibbets who got their clothes from the seamstress on Arpad Square, and who thought that the centre of the world was Vienna. Martha had her clothes sent from Madeleine Vionnet, whom she worshipped for her corolla skirts, her slanting cuts and the friendly little messages she sent along with her New Year wishes. Martha had been the first Hungarian woman to have an Eton crop. She was mad about cloche hats and she maintained the tradition of wearing ribbons as codes, but Hungarians were graceless folk for whom a hat had no other purpose than to cover the head. They did not know that a ribbon with flounces meant that the lady was engaged to be married, or that a rose wrapped in a ribbon signified that she was unattached. Martha read French novels that were sent to her by a bookseller in rue du Bac. Her gods were Radiguet, Cocteau and Léon-Paul Fargue, an ardent and elusive poet she had met at a party in Montparnasse, and with whom she had had an affair. He had shown her Paris. He was funny, inexhaustible, and he knew everybody. Thanks to him, she had met Modigliani, Picasso and Erik Satie. She preserved as though it were a holy relic a small collection of love poems he had written for her, just for her, and which she knew by heart. They had corresponded for two years, after which he no longer replied to her letters. That's often the way with late-night poets.

Tibor Balazs knew how to speak French before he knew Hungarian. But Martha never succeeded in ridding him of that accent which exasperated her. She tried relentlessly to correct his pronunciation. Little Tibor never managed to do so. She wrote a begging letter to Cocteau, who had such a beautiful voice, to ask his advice. She never received a reply. She told herself that it would disappear once he grew up and went to live in Paris. She could not imagine that he would live anywhere else. She spoke to him for hours in French. The father could not stand all the whispering, of which he understood nothing, but he was not capable of standing up to Martha and he left her to her Parisian whims, even though he found the monthly bill a little steep. She did her best to develop the artistic qualities of her son, who entered the Budapest drama school and was about to embark on a brilliant career, when Europe was set ablaze.

It was just a matter of time and, once peace had been restored, despite the advent of the Communist regime, Tibor became the juvenile lead whom Hungarian directors fought over. For ten years his agent, Imré Faludy, staged the French and German classics for him. Tibor triumphed in *Dom Juan*, *Bérénice*, *Lorenzaccio* and *The Prince of Homburg*. The few producers who managed to make films took him on. Tibor had his actor's card.

In 1952, one of his films, *The Return of the Travelling Players*, directed by István Tamás, was selected for the Cannes film festival. The film was well received by the critics, but less warmly by the public. Festival goers had avid discussions as to whether this was a subtle propaganda film or an ode to lost freedom. For a week Tibor was tipped for the prize for best male performance for his role as a pathetic bastard. What with climbing the steps to the sound of applause and the flashes from the photographers' bulbs, it was the apotheosis of his career. Everything was possible. The world belonged to him. But they were up against *Viva Zapata* and the fact that all the actors seemed old-fashioned. Marlon Brando walked off with the prize and Tibor was forgotten. On the night of the awards, Imré tried to use Tibor's new celebrity to procure political asylum in France. He had had proposals for him from Italian producers for a cloak and dagger film starting in September and for a gangster film early the following year. The screenplay was adapted from a novel by Chester Himes. Tibor agreed enthusiastically. The fee was not huge, with just a share of the takings, but for a small-budget film, one could not be choosy. The main thing was to get work.

'And Mama?'

'You must realize that...'

Tibor was aware that if he went over to the West, he would never see her again. There is a threshold of vile behaviour beyond which no man can go. He imagined her, alone, in Debrecen, endlessly wondering why her beloved son had deserted her. With heavy hearts, they returned to the land of happy workers, where Tibor was regarded as a national hero, the finest of actors and a victim of imperialist injustice, and he succeeded at last in staging his *Galileo*.

In Hungary, the number of those who knew the truth could be counted on the fingers of one hand. Dashing Tibor, the most popular actor in the country, for whom Hungarian women would have sold their souls, was madly in love with his agent Imré. Their love was as secretive as it was passionate. In those years, the party did not treat social outcasts and their anti-proletarian love affairs lightly. Imré went so far as to arrange for the man of his life to marry his female assistant, thus confirming rumours that were circulating about him, much to the despair of millions of Hungarian women.

There were cracks in the leaden sky. Small, unexpected openings, unknown spaces where a whiff of liberty blew in. You take a step. You wait for the policeman to blow his whistle. There is no policeman. You take a second step, a third and still another. There comes a moment when you have moved so far forward that you can't go back. You have to continue, come what may. It's called a revolution. Tibor had put on *Galileo Galilei* at the Vigszinhaz theatre. It was not the first play of Brecht's in which he had acted. Imré had obtained the official approvals. There was no reason to be anxious. He was a Marxist writer and a much admired one. On its third performance, the play was suspended without explanation, the authorities foolishly mirroring the intolerance and dogmatism in the play. Previously, this ban would have gone unnoticed. It would not have occurred to anyone to mention it. But it took place on 16 October 1956, during a wave of agitation and popular protest, and the students demonstrated against the censorship. Within three days, Tibor became the symbol of violated freedom. He gave several interviews, expressed his solidarity with the protesters, burned his actor's card in public and encouraged his fellow countrymen to rise up and resist. Like others, he was convinced that it was the end of the hated regime and they were about to regain their liberty. Elated, the actors in the company unanimously decided to perform the play. Every evening, in the great amphitheatre of the university, they defied the ban in front of an enthusiastic crowd who constantly interrupted, booed the Inquisition court and applauded *Galileo*. Tibor was not a hero. Nothing in his previous life had prepared him to carry the flag. He allowed himself to be borne along by the wave of rebellion that was overrunning the country. When the Russians laid siege to Budapest on 4 November, he realized there was no point in resisting. You don't fight an army of seventy-five thousand men with two thousand six hundred T54 tanks, and armed with coaxial machine-guns, with your bare hands.

For a week, the resistance was heroic, desperate and useless. Tibor set off for Debrecen to search for Martha. What with strikes, people taking flight and panic, it turned out to be a futile quest. During 6 November, men were consumed by folly. British and French parachutists were dropped over the Suez Canal in order to recapture it. As soon as the Russians and Americans glared at them, they gave up the idea and retired, tails between their legs, and while the Russians were threatening them with strikes from their atomic rockets, no one bothered about what was going on in Hungary.

On the ninth, after three days watching and lying in wait in the snow and the cold, Tibor and Imré succeeded in fleeing to Austria. They left their belongings behind them and found themselves in Vienna without a penny. By selling the car, they managed to subsist for a month. What work could they hope for in this bleak city that resembled a set for an operetta and where thousands of their compatriots were wandering around looking crazed and lost? 'In Paris, they know me,' declared Tibor who remembered his reception in Cannes.

2

I loathed sport. I loathed those who engaged in sport. They were idiots and they stank. Nevertheless, I ran like lightning behind Cécile, who romped along in spite of her two packs of fags a day. I was about to faint. My heart was thumping, my head was on fire, my legs felt like cotton wool, and I didn't smoke. From time to time, she glanced back and slowed down and allowed me to catch up. As soon as I drew level with her, without pausing for breath, she asked me: 'All right?'

I was crimson and dripping with sweat. Steam was rising from my head. My nose was dripping like a fountain. I had given up answering her because she never waited and would set off again at a trot. I was holding up Pierre's shorts, which were threatening to fall down, with both hands.

'Are we never going to stop?'

However much I shouted, she pressed on. And just supposing, behind this silly need to exercise, there was something else? Supposing, behind that angelic aspect, there was a hypocritical smile lurking? Might she want to avenge herself on me for what Franck had done to her? One only had to read Racine's *Iphigénie*. It could not be ruled out. I slumped onto a bench. She was disappearing from view. Once she could no longer see me, she would be obliged to come back. I was fed up with running circuits of the Luxembourg in the dust. These were gardens that were meant to be walked in. Not a race track. A park in which to dream and read beside the Médicis fountain. Not in which to clown around in a pair of shorts that was too big for me.

That morning, I had rung the bell for ten minutes in order to drag her from her bed. I had made her a very strong café au lait. She appeared in lemon-yellow woollen leggings.

'What do you reckon?'

'They're original.'

'They're American. I paid a fortune for them. Where are your things?'

'I thought we were going to go for a walk in the Luxembourg.'

'You'll need some clothes.'

She dragged me off into Pierre's bedroom. Ever since his departure, fourteen months ago, I had not set foot in there. It was in the same state he had left it in. The bed unmade, the blankets rolled in a ball, two squashed pillows, ten or more piles of books, a record player on the floor with 45s lying everywhere, clothing strewn about and, on the table, a bottle of brandy with its cork removed and two empty glasses. This clutter and the dust that covered every object gave the impression of a room that was dead, as if Pierre had not lived in it. Cécile opened the cupboard and pulled out masses of pullovers and shirts, which she piled on the floor. She grabbed hold of a pair of white shorts with violet trim and handed them to me like a trophy.

'You're not expecting me to wear those?'

'They're Pierre's shorts. Stop sniffling, it gets on my nerves.'

'I'm trying to get better. Two of me could fit into those.'

'They'll be fine, with a belt.'

I found myself kitted out with these white shorts and an enormous white, mud-stained Paris University Club rugby shirt with a violet collar, with the number 14 on the back. When I saw myself in the mirror I looked like a clown.

'You look like a real rugby player,' she announced.

'Wouldn't you prefer us to do housework? I could tackle his bedroom. He'll be glad to find it neat and tidy on his return.'

'We'll do it later. I must sort out his books.'

The doorbell rang. It was the concierge bringing the post. There was a letter from Pierre. Cécile tore open the envelope eagerly and started to read it. Her smile vanished. Her eyebrows knitted and before I could say a word, her face had turned crimson, she had torn up the letter and had thrown it in the dustbin.

'What's it got to do with him? Do I involve myself in his affairs? He's another one who pisses me off!'

She left the room in a fury. I picked up the torn pieces and, with some difficulty pieced the letter together again on the coffee table, like a jigsaw puzzle.

My dear Cécile,

Nothing to report since my last letter. It's damned cold, just as it is in Paris. We spend our time glued to the radio, trying to follow events in Algiers. You probably know as much as I do. I've resolved none of the questions I posed myself. Time doesn't matter here. I don't know whether it's the landscape that is affecting me, but I'm becoming fatalistic. I explained my theory to my three friends with whom I play belote. They consider me a lunatic. In between games, I have long discussions with them. I've read several passages of my book to them. I thought they would praise and encourage me. They don't understand a thing I'm saying, nor why I'm busting my gut working on a theory of revolution. They just don't want to know. It's all the more interesting because they're workers, peasants, or guys who have no jobs. Before immersing myself in writing the final part, I'm going to conduct an enquiry in depth. I think I'll manage to do this because my men regard me as an exceptional NCO, and because I don't insult them and don't yell at them from morn till night. I'm expecting a great deal from this full-scale survey to clarify what I do next.

How's your thesis going? I'd like you to tell me a bit about it. I'm waiting impatiently to see how you tackle the question of Aragon, surrealism and his break with Breton. You may have to ask yourself what the historical basis for surrealism was and who betrayed what or whom. Send me a few pages. You'll have to buckle down to it. I know you. You're going to want to make a change. That would be a great mistake. Your thesis is the priority. You must pass with distinction. You could do psychology afterwards. Doing so now would be the height of stupidity. You haven't the right to sacrifice years of effort on a whim. With psychology, you're not sure of finding work, whereas with your doctorate, you would get a position as a teacher and even though you may grumble, it's a real job. You're made for it...

There was almost a page in the same vein. Pierre wasn't exactly subtle. I was in the process of deciphering the rest of it when Cécile came back in like a fury.

'Was it you who told him?'

'No!'

'You're the only one I've talked to about it!'

'I haven't said a thing. I haven't written to him.'

'How does he know that I want to give up my thesis?'

'I really don't know.'

'I don't believe you, Michel. You're lying!'

'He's talking about it in the conditional tense, as if it were a hypothesis. The proof of it is that you haven't made up your mind. You're thinking of stopping. It's normal for your brother to give you advice.'

'He and his lousy advice can get stuffed!'

'Pick up your pen and write and tell him that. It would please him.'

'What's it got to do with you? Did I ask you for your opinion? I'm sure it was you. You're a sly little rascal who does things sneakily.'

'How could I have mentioned it to him, I haven't got his address?'

'Swear to me that you didn't write to him.'

'I swear to you!'

'Word of honour? Look me in the eyes.'

'You have my word, Cécile. Whether you do literature or psychology, it's all the same to me.'

'He's pretty sharp, the kid brother.'

'He knows you.'

'He hasn't got a hope of reading my thesis. Come on, let's go for a run.'

On the bench, I got my breath back. Cécile was retracing her steps.

'You're not going to keep stopping every five minutes.'

'I'm exhausted. And these shorts keep slipping down.'

'I'm fed up. You've spent the entire time moaning!'

'And you're nice to be with, are you? You're a pain in the neck! A real bitch! If you want to go running, go on... have fun. Without me!'

'Pierre's right, you're just an arsehole!'

In a fury, I made my way out of the park. We had occasionally clashed before, but never to this extent. I reached the gates without hearing the sound of her voice. I turned round. Cécile had disappeared. I couldn't go back home dressed like this. I'd left my things at her place. I was obliged to go there. I waited for her for a good hour, sitting on a stair. She was surprised to see me.

'What are you doing here?'

'My clothes are inside.'

'Come on, let's go and have a coffee.'

'I don't want any.'

'Shall I make you a chocolate, then?'

'Listen, Cécile, I'm going to change and I'll leave straight away.'

'Aren't you my little bro' any more?'

I didn't feel like fighting. She knew it.

'You've become a real bore.'

'I've stopped smoking.'

'It's not true! Since when?'

'I haven't touched a pack for a week. You're the only one I can take it out on.'

She swept up the scraps of Pierre's letter that were on the table, put her foot on the dustbin pedal, and threw them in. We found ourselves sitting down facing one another with our café au lait. She had run out of chocolate.

'Couldn't you have told me?'

'Why do you think I started doing sport? I've put on over a kilo.'

'You're looking flabby.'

'I'm going to put on seven kilos. Definitely. I've got a friend who's put on ten. I'm going to have a spare tyre. Do you find that attractive?'

'Maybe it won't show much.'

'There's no way!'

She disappeared. She returned with a photograph album. She took out a photo.

'That's my mother, before her marriage. She weighed forty-eight kilos.'

She flipped through the pages at speed, stopped towards the end of the album, and pointed to a black and white photo in which her mother was posing in a fur coat somewhere near the Acropolis.

'Fifteen years later, weighing thirty kilos more. I don't want to become like her.'

'It's not automatic.'

'Yes it is, girls end up looking like their mothers and boys like their fathers. That's why we have problems.'

'I don't have any problems with my father.'

'You will have. Pierre tried to escape from them. Few boys have put so much effort into driving their families to despair. He was drawn to misfortune like a magnet. They couldn't agree about anything, and yet they thought alike. The same mechanism, but in the opposite direction. He's become as boring as Papa.'

'You never speak about your parents.'

'They're dead and buried. There's nothing to say about them.'

'Will you show me the album?'

'Out of the question. Personally, I'd have thrown it away. Pierre insisted on keeping it. You see what I'm saying. We always get hoodwinked by our feelings.'

There was someone else who got hoodwinked. Twice a week, I found myself running like an imbecile around the Luxembourg. Cécile gave me a tracksuit that was my size. To begin with, it was hell. After a month, I managed to complete a circuit without stopping. I couldn't believe it. We ran on Thursdays and Saturdays for one hour, and on Sundays I did the housework. With practice, it became easy. I ran for Cécile's sake, to help her keep her promise never to touch a cigarette again. But she would fall back into bad habits at the slightest provocation and she always had a good reason. When I arrived at her home, I could smell the stale tobacco even though she had opened the windows wide to air the flat. It was her thesis, which was not progressing, that was to blame, or Pierre, who wrote to her saying he wanted to read it, or a girlfriend who had been ditched by some bastard, or the enjoyment of smoking… It was impossible to reason with her.

But then an unforeseen transformation took place. It was a Thursday afternoon, towards the end of March. It was cold and drizzling. The

Luxembourg was deserted, swept by a north wind that bit into our cheeks. As usual, she was running ahead of me, and I was trotting along at her heels. I drew up alongside her. She accelerated. I didn't slacken. I could hear her panting. I'd never felt so light. We remained elbow to elbow. I upped the pace. She was unable to follow me. I overtook her. I could hear her straining behind me. I took a ten metre lead, then twenty. I waited for her to come back at me. She was out of breath. I accelerated.

'Stop, Michel, I can't go on.'

She was doubled up, her hands pressed to her knees, trying to catch her breath. It took her two minutes to do so. I waited, smiling to myself.

'You look great.'

'Do you think so?' she murmured, breathing rapidly.

'Pity I haven't got my camera. You could see how you look.'

'I feel as if I weigh a ton.'

'Are you sure that running makes you lose weight? Perhaps, in your case, it has the opposite effect.'

She turned scarlet. I set off without waiting for her reply.

'You little bastard!'

3

Tibor soon became disenchanted. The world of Paris theatre was split into two groups of equal importance who loathed one another passionately: the scoundrels, who put on interesting plays, and the turncoats, who operated on the boulevards; certain moonlighters laid claim to both labels. The majority of directors belonged to the communist party, which enthusiastically supported the Soviet invasion. During an audition, a well-known director referred to Tibor as a fascist and had him removed from the room by his assistants. Another one told him of the disdain he felt for petits-bourgeois like him who took advantage of the working class. Everywhere, all he encountered was hatred, snubs and rebuffs. Those who were not communists hadn't heard of him and had nothing to offer an unknown actor with a strange and unpleasant accent. With others his past reputation stood him in bad stead. The only two directors who were willing to help him and offer him parts failed to understand why he turned them down and classified him in the boring and pretentious category. It's true that modesty was not Tibor's prime virtue.

Imré and he submitted an application asking for political refugee status. The hypocritical Rousseau, who ran the department, went out of his way to throw a spanner in the works for the Hungarians who flooded in. How could you prove you were a refugee and that your life was threatened when you left your country in a panic?

'I need evidence, do you understand? It's easy to say that you were hounded out by the political police. If the Soviets intervened, it was at the request of the Hungarian government, as far as I know, and to save the country from the counter-revolution led by small landowners. The vast majority of your fellow-countrymen approve. It may be that you have fled Hungary because you've broken the law or haven't paid your taxes. It's up to you to provide me with evidence, not me. For the time

193

being, your file is empty. When it goes before the committee, you would be well advised to have something important inside it. Otherwise, you'll be refused. France is not a haven for foreign crooks! We've got enough of our own.'

When they arrived, at the beginning of 1957, they were alarmed by the price of hotels in Paris and they moved into a brothel in rue Saint-Denis. The manager threw them out the following day.

'I don't want any queers!'

'But whores are allowed?' Imré protested.

'It's not the same. I don't want any trouble with the police.'

Tibor couldn't find any work. They sold their watches and their cufflinks, they ate dry bread, and they moved out of the shady hotels they could no longer afford without paying their bills. Imré found a job as a packer with a butter, eggs and cheese agent in Les Halles who was a decent man, even if he paid him on the black market at half the going rate. It wasn't as though there was any lack of Hungarians for the wretched job. At least he allowed him to take home the produce that had travelled badly. Tibor could also have found work at Les Halles, but he had to preserve his energy for auditions and he did nothing while he waited for Imré to finish his backbreaking night shift. Because they constantly left without paying the bill, they were banned from the district around Les Halles and had ended up in a small hotel in rue de la Huchette.

One Monday evening, they were sharing a coffee on the terrace of a brasserie on rue des Écoles. They were in low spirits. Imré had a painful shoulder and his hands were cracked. Tibor was in despair. He had spent the entire day waiting to audition for a Feydeau play. After four hours hanging around in a draught, an assistant came along to inform them that they had filled all the parts.

'I'll never find a part in this land of arseholes. Supposing we went to England? They don't make a fuss about letting foreigners in.'

'I don't speak English,' Imré protested.

'You think only of yourself!' moaned Tibor, despite the fact that gratitude was not his strong point. 'I'm about to die here.'

'I'm killing myself for you. All you do is blame me. Do you think it amuses me to squelch around in cheese. I smell of cheese, don't I?'

'You stink of cheese! You should have worked at a florist's. Let's leave right away, Imré. They'll give me some interesting parts in London.'

'The only thing the English will offer you is their bloody contempt.'

'I've played *Macbeth* and *Othello*.'

'The fact that you play Shakespeare in Hungarian is one thing, for you to play it in their country would be considered a crime of *lèse-majesté* or a joke in poor taste. As soon as you opened your mouth, they'd burst out laughing. That fucking accent would cling to you there too.'

'That's not true, I speak English.'

'Not as they do in Oxford! For them, you're a Hungarian, that's to say a savage.'

'There's not just the theatre. I can make films. You're always putting me down.'

'Why not try America while you're about it?'

'And Bela Lugosi? Didn't he succeed in Hollywood? His Hungarian accent didn't prevent him acting in dozens of films.'

'For playing Dracula in vampire films, it's indispensable. Is that your aim? You? In lousy films?'

'I want to act. I'm an artist! Not some flunkey!'

Their voices rose. Customers began staring at these two foreigners who were squabbling in an incomprehensible language. A man came up to them and peered at Tibor.

'Excuse me, Monsieur, are you not Tibor Balazs?'

'What do you want?' he asked guardedly.

'I'm one of your admirers. I adored *The Return of the Travelling Players*. I've seen it dozens of times. It's a wonderful film.'

In the four months since he had arrived in France, it was the first time anyone had recognized him. For an actor, recognition is what distinguishes you from other mortals. Tibor had been fortunate enough to come across the only Parisian film buff capable of remembering an obscure Hungarian film that had gone unnoticed when it was released four years previously. In his eyes he could see the same glimmer of joy he had been accustomed to observing among his Hungarian admirers.

'You've seen *The Return of the Travelling Players* dozens of times? Are you making fun of me?'

'I'm a projectionist at a cinema in the Quartier Latin. We had the film on for six weeks, with five showings a day...'

'Do you watch the films you show?'

'When it's a good film, it's the great thing about the job.'

Werner Toller was delighted to meet Tibor, especially since he loved actors, never met any of them, and, despite his introvert character, was starry-eyed by nature.

'You're not French. You have a slight accent.'

'I'm German, but I'm not going back to Germany.'

'We're Hungarian, but we're not going back to Hungary.'

'Gentlemen, may I be allowed to invite you to dinner? We shall talk cinema.'

Who could refuse such an invitation? When Tibor and Imré walked into the Balto, they sniffed the air. It was a long time since they had smelled anything so delicious. Igor was sitting on the bench, reading *L'Express*. Werner made the introductions. Igor took him at his word when he introduced Tibor to him as the greatest living Hungarian actor. He had not seen *The Return of the Travelling Players*, nor any Hungarian film, but Werner was never wrong. Hearing Tibor and Imré, Igor was reminded of himself four years ago, when he arrived in Paris. The same doubts, the same fears, the same story to tell. Within a few minutes, it was as though they had always known one another. The Marcusots joined them for dinner. Madeleine, who loved the cinema, seldom went, because of Albert. Just once a year, on 1 May, the one day the restaurant was closed. She had stood firm for the day in honour of working women, even when there was a lot of work on. Since she could not bring herself to waste such an occasion, she usually carefully made her selection from the romantic category, and watched films such as *Gone with the Wind*. She had loved this film so much that she had gone back to see it the following year. But she remembered that Werner had insisted she should come and see *The Return of the Travelling Players*. The fact that a movie star, even a

Hungarian one, and such a handsome man too, should come to dine at her table filled her with joy.

'It's a sign from God that you're here.'

'Madeleine, please,' Igor reprimanded her, 'leave God out of it. If Tibor and Imré are here, it's not thanks to God, but because of Monsieur Khrushchev, and I don't think he's acting on the advice of the Lord or thinking of him.'

Jacky laid the table. The plates were steaming and full. They ate in silence.

'It's delicious. I love this. What is it?' asked Imré.

Good cooks are like movie stars. They love compliments. Generally speaking, when customers enjoyed her cooking, they were rather sparing with their praise. Imré won Madeleine Marcusot over.

'It's a *daube à la provençale*, cooked in my way.'

'What do you put in it to give it that taste?'

Madeleine lowered her voice, looked to left and to right. Nobody must discover her secret: 'Some cloves and… some cumin.'

'But that taste? Behind the cloves and the cumin.'

'You won't repeat it to anyone?'

'I promise you.'

'Everyone adds Gamay or Côtes-du-Rhône. In my case, I use a fruited wine. I marinate the beef in some Saumur-Champigny and, at the end, I add a little bit of kirsch.'

'It's divine. Do you know how to make goulash? The real one, in the Hungarian way?'

'Have you got a good recipe?'

'There's one…'

He stared at Tibor, who took a moment to understand.

'It's my mother, Martha's recipe. She, who loved Paris so much, would be glad for you to give it to her.'

'Real goulash is made with beef, never pork. It's the poor or the Austrians who use pork. Shin or chuck. Five hundred grams of fresh onions, some sweet paprika, a large soup-spoonful of each, finely chopped fresh chervil, oregano, Cayenne pepper, two sweet peppers, five hundred grams of tomatoes. You need some *galuska*, a small Hungarian pasta. You make it with flour, water and salt. You fry the onions, you peel the tomatoes, you cut up the meat into small chunks—'

'Imré,' Madeleine interrupted, 'come and make your goulash for us. For me, where cooking's concerned, I have to see it. You've made my mouth water.'

'You'd like me to come and cook goulash for you?'

'Whenever you like.'

Imré's culinary gifts were limited to what it took for an ordinary bachelor to survive. Omelette, ham and spaghetti. He had gone a little too far with Madeleine and he found himself in the kitchen at the Balto feeling somewhat anxious. She had prepared everything according to his instructions. He had whispered the secret of Martha's goulash in her ear: 'You have to put in the paprika ten minutes before the end of the cooking. It mustn't boil and mustn't stick. It's best when it's reheated. Nobody knows why.'

Werner, Igor, Albert, Jacky and Madeleine tasted it. Tibor and Imré awaited the verdict.

'I think it's delicious. What about you?' asked Madeleine.

'It's wonderful,' Werner remarked.

'Nothing need be said,' added Albert, the expert.

From his lips, this single observation amounted to a compliment. He looked questioningly at his wife. She turned to Imré.

'Would you mind if I included this on the menu? The customers are fed up with *blanquette*.'

'On behalf of my country, I should be honoured,' Imré replied.

'For you,' said Albert, 'Thursday lunches will henceforth be free. I'd like you to put in a little less paprika. It's too spicy for the neighbourhood. And I'd thicken the sauce with a bit of flour.'

The goulash made its appearance the following Thursday as the dish of the day and, by twenty past one, there was no more left. Imré and Tibor became regulars at the Balto. The Club doubled its membership. Over the weeks, a new clientele appeared. Exiled Hungarians had passed on the good news. There was a bistro at Denfert where they served a goulash like that in Budapest, plentiful and not expensive, even if it was not spicy enough, but you couldn't have everything. After lunch, they got into the habit of staying behind in the restaurant. They had the time and they loved playing chess. This was how the little business got under way. By word of mouth.

4

Life and survival are dependent on unforeseeable details. On a bout of flu, for instance. I had recovered from my cold but, in that dismal winter when the rivers overflowed their banks and floods paralysed the country, the ghastly virus struck. Not me personally. I would have preferred that it had, but I was spared. Nicolas, who was as strong as an ox and who hadn't been ill since his first year at primary school, caught it. Like millions of others. With Nicolas absent, the door to disaster was opened. Without him, I was lost. Lachaume, our maths teacher, whom we called 'Shrivel-face', and who, with his eternal black scarf wrapped around his neck, elicited more pity than envy, avoided the epidemic.

I went to call on Nicolas, who was touched by my thoughtfulness and my concern for his health. I didn't dare speak to him about the fateful moment that was approaching, inexorably and menacingly: the maths exam. Philosophers, psychiatrists and ministers of education have never been concerned about the primitive fears, the traumatic nightmares and the irreversible damage caused by exams in general and by maths exams in particular. I was perched over the chasm and the world cared not a damn. I had spent a fortune at Mère Bonbon's in the Luxembourg. I took Nicolas an assortment of the sweets that he loved. An enormous packet of liquorice whirls, caramel bars, Coco Boers, boiled sweets, Mistrals, gingerbread bears and chocolate cigarettes. And Malabars, which he adored because of the transfers that went with them. I hoped this would buck him up and help towards a speedy recovery. Instead he felt queasy. I didn't want to bother Cécile, who was doing her housework and spent her time changing her mind about whether to go on with her thesis or to study psychology.

I worked like a lunatic, but the more I crammed, the less I understood and the more depressed I became. I had to confront the mother of all ordeals on my own and without a safety net. For we French, Berezina and Waterloo are synonymous with bitter and painful defeats. But at least there had been battles. We had been crushed. But we had fought with bravery or desperation and our enemies, even the English, recognized our courage. Here, I felt total shame. I stared uncomprehendingly at the wording of the exam question as though it were in Chinese. Shrivel must have chosen the wrong subject. I watched my classmates slogging away, heads down, without any qualms. I spent an hour staring into the infinite space of my incompetence. The lamb arriving at the abattoir must be in this state of mind. It awaits the knife as deliverance from its torment. I handed in a blank paper, unsullied by any mathematical reasoning. Shrivel could criticize me for many things, except having given him work to do.

We can try to escape from reality, put on a front, hide behind the mask of virtue, bury our heads in the sand, make up excuses and pretexts, prevaricate and postpone, yet our future depends on the way we cope with life's greatest dilemmas and our good fortune in controlling our own lack of courage. The truth comes back with the speed of a boomerang. If you decide not to run away, you're on the edge of the abyss. If you don't jump, you'll have to pay the price.

At dinner that evening, I waited apprehensively for the dreaded question. My mother seemed to have forgotten. My father had had bad news about grandmother Jeanne, who had just had to go into hospital for the second time because of her heart condition. He was planning to drive up to Lens the following Sunday and wanted someone to go with him. Juliette had to go to friend's birthday party and I gave the excuse of having to revise for the history-geography exam.

'By the way, Michel, how did that maths test go?' asked my mother as she served the vegetable soup.

She was expecting the usual answer: 'Didn't seem too bad, we'll have to wait and see.' Don't claim victory and be modest: two virtues that are rooted in the Delaunay family.

'It was… a disaster.'

'Why?'

I had prepared an explanation that had to do with resounding defeats, with Trafalgar and the Maginot Line, with famous thrashings and with great men, well-known dimwits whom their parents had despaired of, who had been awarded the Nobel Prize and had been buried in the Panthéon. I got into a muddle. I drew a blank. No excuses. The truth. Judgement Day.

'Einstein… in his youth… during the battle… with Pasteur… Churchill too… like Nicolas… It's not serious, a bad dose of flu… I've been copying from him for years.'

My mother dropped the ladle into the soup bowl. The tablecloth was spattered with soup. She stared at me open-mouthed, transfixed, not knowing whether I was being serious or playing my usual silly jokes.

'I handed in a blank sheet. I didn't even understand the question.'

'About Nicolas, you're joking?'

'I've been cheating for years. I'm fed up with lying.'

If I had told her that I was a prostitute or that I was planting bombs for the FLN, it would have had less of an effect on her. She walked round the table and came up to me, blazing with anger. I saw her right hand rise up. I didn't move, didn't try to avoid it or to protect myself. I knew she hit hard. The slap was part of the payment. Her arm remained in the air, quivering.

'Hélène! That's enough!' my father yelled as he rushed over.

She should have hit me. That would have wiped the slate clean. This was a matter between the two of us and it had now become a family affair. He intervened. Her raised arm was a threat to my father. He stared at her impassively. Eventually, she lowered it.

'It's not a reason to hit him,' said my father in a tone that was intended to be persuasive.

She was shaking feverishly and was having difficulty controlling her mounting exasperation.

'Your son admits he's a cheat and a liar and you think that's normal!'

They usually argued in private, in their bedroom. They were keen to keep up appearances and we would pretend we hadn't heard anything.

'You say nothing! You do nothing! You don't react. You let them get away with everything. My father wouldn't have tolerated this disgrace for a moment. He knew how to run his house. People were afraid of him. And woe betide you when he brought out his belt. At the Delaunays' house there were standards. Children obeyed their parents. We've seen the results. My brother Daniel behaved like a hero, Maurice succeeded in—'

'Come off it! He married the heiress to one of the largest fortunes in Algeria.'

'And you, what have you done? Didn't you marry the boss's daughter?'

'What you're saying is disgraceful.'

'Maurice looks after his children. Yours behave badly. They have no respect for anything. They're not afraid of you.'

'In my house, we don't beat children. When they do something stupid, we discuss it, we talk to one another. My father always said—'

'Education is a wonderful thing at the Marinis!' she interrupted. 'We've seen what it did for Franck. Michel's going the same way.'

'You muddle up everything.'

'I know what you're like. One must understand, forgive. Perhaps he's entitled to congratulations?'

'I've never hit my children and I'm not going to start today.'

'I don't agree.'

'That's the way it is and that's the way it's going to be.'

She went out, slamming the dining room door. Juliette was frightened and got up and followed her. My father sat down beside me and put his hand on my shoulder.

'Don't worry, son, she's upset. She'll calm down.'

'I'm sorry, I didn't mean to—'

'Never mind, I'm here. What's going on at school?'

'It's the maths. I'm absolutely hopeless.'

'You used to get good results before.'

'My good marks were thanks to Nicolas.'

'It's a strange thing. I would have thought that... It doesn't matter. In life, once you know how to read, write and count, it's enough. Maths, physics, philosophy, they're a load of rubbish. I got my school certificate. At school, I was bottom of the class. Always last, except at gym. Have I needed the baccalaureate or diplomas to succeed?'

*

We walked around the neighbourhood for an hour. He had his hand on my shoulder. I'd been roaming around the area for years and no one had ever noticed me, whereas he knew everybody, shopkeepers, concierges, passers-by. He greeted them, said good evening to them, smiled, joked, chatted, introduced me as his second son who had grown up too quickly and was already taller than him, but isn't it typical of that generation. Anyone would have thought he was a member of parliament in the market square.

'Have you had any news of Franck?'

'None.'

'And his girlfriend, has she heard?'

'She's no longer his girlfriend, Papa. They separated before he left.'

'Doesn't mean you don't let people have news now and then.'

'Franck doesn't like to write. When he went away on holiday, he never used to send postcards.'

'This isn't the same, there's a war on.'

A couple asked him what was happening with the installation of their bathroom, which was two weeks overdue. He explained to them that these days, things weren't like they used to be. It was due to the flu and to workers being ill. He promised to look into it personally. They thanked him as they set off again.

'We've got so much work on that I'm not going to be able to send anyone to them before goodness knows when. Later on, you could go to a business school.'

'You always say that business is not something that can be learnt.'

'Business is easy, what's complicated is the accountancy, the law, the taxes and the paperwork.'

'You didn't study and yet you've succeeded. You could teach me what you know.'

'It's true, business can't be taught. It's a game, nothing but a game.'

'I don't understand.'

'You're the cat, and the customer is the mouse. A mouse is cunning. A cat is patient. And above all, since he wants to eat the mouse, the cat puts himself in the mouse's place. In order to think like a mouse. The cat must have a great deal of imagination to catch the mouse. It's up to you to know whether you want to be a cat or a mouse. And imagination is not something that can be taught in business schools. What's your view?'

'If there's no maths involved, then I'm all for it.'

'Wonderful! You'll have a great life, believe me. I've got some major projects in mind. Together, we'll make a killing.'

When I spoke about this to Igor, he told me that I was a little arsehole and that I'd continue to be one.

'My father's got a point, you can earn a lot of money in business.'

'And you're going to spend your life slaving for money? Is that your dream?'

''What do you expect me to do? I'm hopeless at maths!'

'I'll tell you, Michel, being a taxi driver is the best job in the world.'

Igor was persuasive. But there were three of them at the Club who were taxi drivers and they did not share his view. It was a fine occupation as long as your back didn't hurt. They had sciatica and slipped discs, they breathed in exhaust fumes from dawn till dusk, got irritated in traffic jams, were terrified they might have their throats cut by some crook who wanted to steal their takings, and were harassed by policemen who were lying in wait so that they could give them fines.

'You've got to work at night. There aren't many of us. You don't have your boss on your back. You feel free. No traffic. No cops. And crooks have more lucrative jobs than assaulting taxi drivers. It's different at night.'

Igor had built up a clientele of regular customers; night owls, restaurant and club owners, or performers whom he drove home in the early hours.

'People who stay out late at night know how to live. They're not stingy. The tips are often larger than the price of the journey. At night, you make friends. Real ones. In the daytime, people don't have time to talk or listen to one another.'

A few months after he had started, shortly before midnight, Igor had picked up a passenger in rue Falguière and had taken him to Franklin-Roosevelt. During the journey, the man hadn't uttered a word. Some passengers are not very talkative. When the time came to pay, the man asked him: 'Are you Russian?'

Igor stared at him. He had never seen him before. The man was impressively tall, had thick hair, and the chiselled features of a convict on the run. He nodded suspiciously. The man continued in Russian: 'Where are you from?'

'From Leningrad.'

'I was born in Argentina. When I was young, I lived in Orenburg, do you know it?'

'Is it in the Urals?'

'My father was a doctor there. We came to France before the revolution.'

'I was a doctor in Leningrad. My name's Igor.'

'Mine's Jef.'

In the car, Igor and Joseph Kessel talked about their homeland for two hours. Kessel invited him to have a drink at his place and they continued their discussion until dawn. In Russian. About the war, about Paris, about music, Dostoevsky, chess and a thousand other things. It was as if they had always known each other. Igor became more than his regular driver. They would often have dinner together. He introduced him as one of his old friends. Jef invited him in, but he paid the exact fare. You don't give a tip to a pal. On more than one occasion, Igor whispered in his ear that it was time for him to go home and he accompanied him to his door. He didn't treat him like a customer. Kessel was the only person allowed to sit in the front seat. He inscribed his books to him in Russian and often turned up at the Balto. Madeleine was very proud, and she cooked dishes just for him. He struck up friendships with most of the members of the Club and some of them came to recognize themselves as characters in his books. The first time Victor Volodine noticed him, Igor and Kessel were playing chess. It was hard to believe that Igor should be on first-name terms with such a famous person. He clicked his heels together as he introduced himself to Kessel.

'Count Victor Anatolievich Volodine of the Tsar's guards cadets.'

Victor had probably made a mess of his career and should have been an actor. Kessel was totally taken in by him and, had Igor not been there, he would have bought Rasputin's dagger. When, a little later, Igor told him the truth of the matter, he had the greatest difficulty persuading him, so convincing was Victor in his role of the aristocrat fallen on hard times.

5

W hat could an unknown Hungarian actor, whom no director wanted to employ because of an accent that made people laugh as soon as he opened his mouth, do in Paris? Nothing. Ridding himself of his accent became Tibor's obsession. It was an indelible mark that clung to his vocal cords like one of those bad viruses that consume you from inside. Imré declared that it was a hopeless cause, that Hungarians never lost their nasal twang, and that only years of relentless daily work could remove it. Tibor had neither the time nor the patience, but there is nothing worse than an actor condemned to silence. Igor and Werner set about the task. Together, then each in turn. They could not agree either on the method or the exercises. It was mission impossible. Pity versus charity. How can you make progress when the teacher has not understood the lesson? Werner, who carried his German phraseology around with him as though it were a punishment, was in the worst position to assist him. By speaking extremely slowly, Igor managed to conceal his origins. As soon as he relaxed, it was as though the Volga had overflowed its banks.

'Igor, I'm sorry, you remind me of the swimming teacher I had at school in Cologne. He taught us by reading the instruction manual, he couldn't swim himself.'

'With you, he's going to pick up your Teutonic accent.'

'We're like two eunuchs talking about love.'

'A French person would be the ideal.'

'And one who's a teacher.'

There was only one person among their acquaintances who fitted the bill. They both thought of him at the same time.

'He wouldn't want to.'

Gregorios Petroulas was a special case at the Club. He had fled his country because the communists were being expelled and wiped out there. He had left Greece in 1949, at the end of the civil war. A price had been put on his head by extremists from a royalist movement that had murdered his two brothers. Gregorios was a communist both committed and frustrated, which made him unpredictable, even among his close friends. He was reputed to be temperamental, a man who went from elation to dejection and from garrulousness to submission in a flash without anyone knowing why. He was warm-hearted and he would give you a hug, then, a moment later, he would call you an idiot, scum, and a fascist, which, he swore, was a pleonasm, or redundant expression, from the Greek *pleonasmos*, which means excess. Gregorios could not utter a sentence without recalling the etymology of any Greek word, an obvious sign that our civilization was Greek and that we owed our identity to him, without our being in the least grateful or cognizant of the fact, from the Latin *cognoscere*, but this was an exception.

'I'm ashamed of what I've done,' he sometimes said, absorbed in his memories.

'What did you do?'

He looked up and shrugged his shoulders.

'It's over. Nobody gives a damn. So, are you playing?'

Gregorios taught Latin and Ancient Greek on ten or more private tuition courses. This activity had him running from one end of Paris to the other to dispense his precious knowledge. The only schools that offered him work were run by priests or nuns, who made it a point of principle to keep alive the teaching of dead languages, but Gregorios loathed churches in general and priests in particular. When, as the former French teacher at the Patissia School in Athens, he arrived in Paris, Gregorios had expected to be welcomed with open arms. But the Ministry of Education informed him that he did not have the necessary degrees to teach in France. The only job he could find was at Sainte-Thérèse, an institution for well-to-do young ladies in the sixteenth arrondissement. His recruitment had been miraculously swift. The rector had bid him sit down in front of him, had looked him up and down and, without further ado, had begun to talk to him in Latin. Gregorios had responded in a trice and they had chatted together for an hour. The rector had engaged him immediately, trusting him with Greek, a language he himself did not speak. Every time they encountered one another, they conversed in the tongue of Virgil.

'As long as we speak it together,' he said to him in Latin, 'it won't be a dead language.'

Gregorios must have had a very personal and lively way of teaching. In the baccalaureate, his pupils obtained marks that exceeded, and by a long way, their normal pitiful results. This was the starting-point for his new career. The rector, who had grown fond of him, obtained residence and work permits in no time. He was so happy with what Gregorios had done that he recommended him to his colleagues in Catholic education. Among religious institutions in the archbishopric of Paris, Gregorios became the essential point of contact for the humanities. The more in demand he was, the more it put him in a fury bordering on apoplexy. He concealed his repulsion for men of the cloth and their sermonizing, and for those *bien pensant* families for whom the catechism was basic knowledge, by telling himself, in order to sustain his daily ordeal, that these members of religious orders were not Greeks and had nothing to do with the terrible deeds that had been committed and sanctioned in his own country by the Orthodox Church. He was poorly paid and he supplemented his income by giving private lessons to his less able pupils. This was how he got to know the desperate father of one of these ignoramuses who was amazed at his knowledge and asked him to become his speechwriter. Gregorios hesitated. The man was an ignorant, foolish and uncultivated Poujadist member of parliament whose sole conviction was that he loathed the Reds. But he agreed under pressure from his wife and because it was the Greeks who had invented discourse. It was his way of continuing the work of Demosthenes and Pericles. He peppered the politician's speeches with Greek and Latin quotations that were unanimously admired by his fellow members of parliament, who warmly applauded this highly cultured colleague. He called on us as witnesses to his problems of conscience and moral dilemmas. Pavel, who was his best friend and chosen chess partner, listened to him politely. All too soon, Gregorios's soliloquies ended as follows: 'If I were to say what I think about priests, they would kick me out. I'm trapped.'

'It doesn't matter,' Pavel replied. 'You're not the first or the last person to sell yourself for a mess of potage.'

'I'm not corrupt. What would you do in my position?'

'I'd play the game. The clock is ticking down. You're going to find yourself out of time and lose as a result.'

'It's not cowardice, Pavel. You know me. The worst thing is that they think of me as one of them when I actually hate them. The only thing I don't regret is having killed a few of them.'

Gregorios could have returned to Greece after the amnesty. But he had fallen in love with Pilar, an unassuming young woman with delicate features, who was the daughter of Republican refugees, and who taught Spanish on one of these private courses. It was the sort of family he liked to associate with. They could tell each other about the betrayals, the horrors and the ignominies of their respective civil wars. Gregorios was not surprised to discover that the Spanish Catholic Church rivalled the Greek Orthodox Church as far as appalling deeds and vile behaviour were concerned. For the sake of Pilar, who did not wish to leave her family, and because of her beautiful eyes, he gave up the idea of returning home and became a Parisian. They married and, to please her and despite his convictions, he agreed to a religious wedding. His friends made fun of him. They moved into a small flat at Porte de Vanves and had three children. Pilar changed into an unexpected and uncompromising religious zealot, who dragged him off to mass and to vespers without asking his opinion, never missed a single feast day, and pledged a mystical veneration to John XXIII. What with Pilar, his member of parliament who had become a left-wing Gaullist, and his nurturing priests, Gregorios was frightened of retracting his views and ending up like some holy Joe, and so he endured this triple calamity as he would a curse, a burden that he bore like Sisyphus, for the Greeks, in addition to sculpture, literature, philosophy, architecture, politics, strategy, sport and sporting competitions, had also invented mythology. Like any true teacher, he could not prevent himself from reluctantly desiring the happiness of the pupils.

'Do you do Latin, Michel?'

'No.'

'It's vital to learn Latin, even if it's a less interesting language than Greek and has borrowed a great deal from it.'

'My problem is maths.'

'It was the Greeks who invented mathematics: Euclid, Pythagoras, Archimedes, Thales. Such geniuses. I'll teach you Greek, if you like.'

'Listen, Gregorios, I don't understand a thing, even in French.'

'Tough on you. You'll remain a barbarian. From the Greek *barbaros*, which means stupid.'

When Igor and Werner asked him to help Tibor, Gregorios refused. He worked to the tightest of schedules and hadn't a moment to give to a new pupil.

'That's just as well, he's got no money and he can't pay you,' Werner remarked. 'Make an effort, Gregorios. You know his situation. You're the only one with perfect diction. People take you for a Parisian.'

'You're an excellent teacher. Your pupils get exceptional marks,' Igor continued.

'For pity's sake, my friends, don't take away this breath of oxygen. The only respite I get in my crazy life is the time I spend here, among normal people, who are not religious freaks. You've no idea what I have to put up with.'

They insisted, but all their pleas met with a firm and polite refusal from Gregorios. His daily game of chess was vital to him. He refused to sacrifice this brief moment of freedom. Werner had given up and was looking for an alternative solution when he noticed that Igor's head was nodding, his lips were pursed and his eyelids were blinking.

'There's one vital reason,' Igor murmured.

'I'm sorry, friends. Nothing and nobody are going to make me change my mind.'

'Tibor has been approached to play Oedipus, and what with his pronunciation, he hasn't got a hope.'

'Oedipus in *Oedipus Rex*?'

'Can you imagine Oedipus with a Hungarian accent?'

'That's true, it's not possible. If you could have heard Sophocles in Greek, you would have understood what theatre is. The *Oresteia* of Aeschylus is a tragic poem in which the words are music. In French, it's grotesque.'

Igor dashed over to the payphone and warned Imré, who told Tibor that Gregorios was going to give him lessons free of charge so that he could be rid of that hissing accent. Imré repeated to him what Igor had told him: 'A director is thinking of you for the part of Oedipus.'

'Oedipus? That's wonderful. My mother used to tell me it was an exceptional play. She saw it when it was first put on in Budapest. Which director? Which theatre?' asked Tibor excitedly.

'There's no rush. Rehearse your lines, so that the audition will be perfect.'

Perhaps Imré should have reflected a little more, been more precise or taken precautions. So delighted was he to have found a solution, he left Tibor and Gregorios on their own.

'I'm grateful for your kindness, Gregorios. You haven't got much time. I appreciate what you are doing for me. I hope to be able to speak French like you one day.'

'The Greeks have no accent. We invented diction. Don't worry, Tibor, I won't make you speak with a potato in your mouth.'

'I shall be your best pupil. For me, it's a matter of life or death.'

'If you want to lose your nasal twang, Tibor, you must speak slowly. As though you were considering what you are about to say. Separate each syllable, keep the same tone of voice and lay the stress on the ending or when your breath gives out. For example, when you say "*j'ai commandé*", put the stress on the *dé*; when you say "*un thé au lait*", accentuate the *lait*.'

'*J'ai commandé un thé au lait.*'

'Put your fingers in your mouth, pull your lips towards your ears and let the sound come from your belly.'

'*J'ai com-man-dé un thé au lait.*'

'That's perfect! We'll work on the text. It'll be more useful.'

Gregorios took out two pamphlets from his briefcase and gave one to Tibor, who looked at it in surprise.

'It would be best to use the proper text.'

'It's the right one. The translation's excellent.'

'There's no need. We're working on *La Machine infernale*.'

'What are you talking about?'

'About Cocteau's play.'

'You're acting in *Oedipus Rex*, the play by Sophocles.'

'I'm not acting in that old-fashioned stuff, but in Cocteau's play about Oedipus!'

'How dare you compare the miserable buffoonery of that old queen with *Oedipus Rex*, one of the greatest plays known to man?'

'It's tedious, outdated, pompous, stilted.'

'We invented theatre and psychology twenty-four centuries before Freud.'

'The problem is that you haven't invented anything since. The world has changed, and you haven't realized.'

'How could a Hungarian possibly understand Sophocles?'

Gregorios rose to his feet with dignity, gathered up his pamphlets and left without paying the bill.

'You know what the old queens say about you? You're just a priest's lackey!' yelled Tibor as he hurled his *thé au lait* at him.

These misunderstandings explain why Tibor retained his accent. Gregorios and he never spoke again and ostentatiously ignored one another. Imré managed to find minor roles for him. Tibor accepted them. He needed to get himself known and noticed. He played the part of a police inspector in the series *Les Cinq Dernières Minutes*, in which he was Superintendent Bourrel's assistant. His only piece of dialogue consisted of saying 'OK, boss' four or five times, which he managed to pronounce like a Frenchman, thanks to lengthy rehearsals with Igor. Despite the minimal text, it was well paid, despite the fact that Tibor made the mistake of arguing with the director and requesting that his part be expanded.

He had high hopes when he was taken on at the Comédie-Française. He played the halberdier in *Athalie*, a Roman soldier and a senator in *Bérénice*, a Spanish grandee and a valet in *Ruy Blas*, and a Moorish prince, a merchant and a gondolier in *La Bonne Mère*. They were non-speaking, purely walk-on parts. Even though he took a few paces towards the front of the stage, he remained unknown and it was killing him.

Then Imré had the idea of changing his name. It wasn't easy to make him agree to it, but everyone encouraged him to do so. After a good deal of trial and error, it was reckoned that François Limousin sounded one hundred per cent French and that Tibor shouldn't mention his nationality again. In spite of his new name, the director of the play in question noticed that a particular little phrase grated on the ear and he discussed with his assistant as to whether it was Alsatian or Belgian, or perhaps from the Limousin. François Limousin found no more work than Tibor Balazs did. The pseudonym was dropped after two years of pointless struggles, and Tibor reverted to his own name. Thanks to a fellow-countryman who worked in a dubbing studio in Boulogne-Billancourt, Imré found two parts for him: that of King Hubert in Walt Disney's *Sleeping Beauty* and that of Brutus in twenty or more instalments of *Popeye*, in which the characters' pronunciation was unimportant.

Imré had found a job as a warehouseman at a clothes wholesaler in rue d'Aboukir. He humped piles of cuttings and rolls of cloth on a trolley from one end of the Sentier neighbourhood to the other. He couldn't take working on Tibor's behalf any longer, and it was wearing him out. He wanted him to relieve matters by taking a small job. Tibor was furious at being cornered like this. Imré had given an ultimatum: 'I'll give you six months to find a real part.'

At the end of the year, the part Tibor had hoped for had been given to someone else. He wasn't going to accept a real job with a boss who shouted at you and colleagues who were disagreeable. Thanks to Igor, he found employment as a night porter at L'Acapulco, a striptease and 'international attractions' joint in Pigalle. From the early evening, he paced up and down boulevard de Clichy, dressed in the uniform and turquoise-blue cap of an officer of the imperial guard – it wasn't known which one – and he hailed passers-by, preferably foreigners, offering them reduced price tickets for drinks and 50 per cent off bottles of champagne. It wasn't an unpleasant job, except in March, when it was so cold, or when it rained. His boss was pleased with him. He preserved a little of his strength during the day so that he could attend auditions. He wasn't offered a single part, even on distant provincial tours, but between the dubbing of cartoons and L'Acapulco, he didn't manage too badly. But he didn't know how to count or to economize – he found figures irritating. He smoked Dunhills, at least two packs a day. He only took three puffs and then stubbed them out without finishing them. As soon as he had a few pennies, he would buy himself ruinously expensive clothing. Imré, on the other hand, who worked for a pittance, never bought himself anything. And yet he must have needed to. He would pick up clothes during his wanderings around the Sentier neighbourhood. At the Balto, Tibor ordered from the menu without bothering about the price. Jacky, who knew of their difficulties and the amounts they owed, peered at Imré, who would eventually give a nod. Jacky served him the *steak au poivre* with his favourite potato dish.

'Aren't you eating anything?' asked Tibor with his mouth full.

'I'm not hungry,' Imré replied casually.

At the Balto, Tibor enjoyed special treatment because of his status as a star, even if he no longer was one. As far as Madeleine was concerned, a screen actor could not be tied down to the material circumstances of just anyone. He was allowed to run up the largest bill by far. When it exceeded the limit, Jacky warned Albert, who alerted Madeleine who, because it was Tibor, never refused excessive spending. He was the only one to enjoy such benefits. When the bill reached breaking point, she had a word with Imré who reduced it to an acceptable level and suffered in silence. From time to time, he wavered: 'You should watch what you eat, Tibor. You're putting on weight.'

'Do you think so?'

'In France, charmers are slim. If you want to play young male leads, you'll have to lose four or five kilos.'

Tibor went on a diet. But he had no will power. He no longer ate anything at the Balto but was invited out by the dancers and technicians from L'Acapulco with whom he had got on well and who adored him. In time, Tibor's little ruse was discovered.

'It's being out of work that makes me get fat! In Hungary, I ate whatever I wanted without putting on an ounce. All this wasted time. What's happening about this offer of a tour in Brittany?'

Imré had received a negative response a week previously.

'They're having trouble making ends meet.'

'In this country, nothing ever comes of anything. Let's go to the United States. Over there, they make hundreds of films each year. Bela Lugosi will lend me a hand. Hungarians help one another out.'

'Tibor, if you want to try your luck, do so. I'm not going. I don't speak English. In France, I've a chance of pulling through.'

6

It was a sad and gloomy Sunday. The rain was bucketing down. Everyone was lost in his own thoughts. Imré was reading Morvan Lebesque's article in *Le Canard enchaîné* to Jan and Gregorios. They wouldn't have missed his columns under any circumstances. Igor and Leonid considered him too moralistic and preferred the cartoons in *Hérisson*. Tibor was watching the rain falling. Tomasz was daydreaming. Pavel was continuing to translate and modify his book on the treaty of Brest-Litovsk. Kessel had arranged a meeting for him with a publisher who had asked for cuts. In a corner, Vladimir was doing a shopkeeper's accounts. Werner and Piotr were conversing in low voices like plotters. Leonid and Virgil were playing chess. Igor and I were sitting together and following the game in silence. Monsieur Lognon, standing as was his wont, was nodding his head in appreciation. Leonid was the best player in the Club. Nobody had succeeded in beating him. To obtain a draw against him was considered an achievement. Only Igor and Werner had achieved this. At one point, not so long ago, he had been ranked among the forty best players in the USSR. In thirty-third place. This put him above any champion of France. He had won the Aeroflot pilots tournament on four consecutive years and had had the signal honour of playing two games against Stalin. He had been forewarned. He had allowed Stalin to win after having initially put him in a difficult position, which had earned him a friendly tap on the shoulder and helped him be promoted to captain on board a Tupolev aircraft. I jotted down their respective moves in my notebook. Virgil Cancicov was a good player, but he could not compete with Leonid. He launched into frenzied attacks that left Leonid impervious. Virgil wore himself out against an impenetrable defence and lost his pieces one by one. Leonid had the patience of a cat and waited to deal the deathblow. Virgil could feel the inevitable moment of execution approaching, and he retreated. Unexpectedly, he sacrificed a bishop. Leonid frowned and thought carefully, stroking his chin. He advanced his rook and Igor smiled. I made a note of the position. Monsieur Lognon's features puckered in admiration.

He had been coming to the Club for some months without being a member. He had not been seen coming in and no one had noticed him. He stood there, hands crossed behind his back, stomach protruding, with an unlit pipe in his mouth. He did not disturb anyone and he possessed a quality that everyone appreciated: he knew how to listen. He spent hours on end watching Pavel, Tomasz, Imré, Vladimir, or whoever it might be, with a thoughtful and affable expression, without interrupting or asking any questions. He listened with interest. He nodded with the good-natured air of a sympathetic pensioner. From time to time, he filled or relit his pipe. All one ever heard him say were things like 'Well, my dear fellow' or 'It's unbelievable, what's happened to you', or commonplace remarks of this kind. Monsieur Lognon was not chatty. Three or four facts that he had let slip were known about him: he had retired from Electricité de France, his wife was a caretaker, the days were long, and coming to watch the games took his mind off things. He ordered a half of beer with as little froth as possible and spent the afternoon sipping it. Without ever asking to be one, he had become a de facto member, even though he didn't play. The perfect kibitzer, he never bothered anyone. When someone suggested he join in, he replied that he didn't play well enough and that his passion was *belote bridgée*, a card game that wasn't played at the Club. When he was asked how he was, he always replied: 'Fine, thank you, and you?'

The only occasion when there was any awkwardness was when Werner asked him what his first name was. It was the custom at the Club.

'If you don't mind, Monsieur Werner, I prefer to be called by my surname. I don't like my first name. At Electricité de France my colleagues called me Lognon. My friends too.'

We had a good laugh, when he wasn't present, imagining what ridiculous first name his parents might have chosen for him. Tomasz searched in a post office calendar. We found some that nobody knew: Paterne, Guénolé, Fulbert or Fiacre. It became a game between Pavel, Tomasz and Tibor. They would throw out a name at random and wait to see whether he reacted: 'Er, Léonce... Ignace... Landry.' 'Oh, Enguerran, um … Parfait… Aymard.' 'Hey, Romaric, no Barnabé.' They never found out. Lognon remained imperturbable. They tried Adolphe, Benito and Rodrigue. According to Leonid who reasoned like an engineer, he could be called Anicet or Casimir and behave as though he hadn't heard, or else it was a name that was missing from the calendar. In due course, we came to forget Lognon's mysterious first name and grew accustomed to his presence, except that we never heard him approach and would discover him standing slightly set back from the table, following the game, and he would disappear as if by magic.

'There are some people whose first names we do know and who get on our nerves,' said Werner, who appreciated his discretion. 'Each of us has his little secrets. He's not a bad guy.'

Inspector Daniel Mahaut rarely appeared at the Club, busy as he was with his investigations that required him to work irregular hours, and, since he lived in the suburbs, the moment he had a bit of spare time, he went home to spend it with his family. He remained close to Igor and to Werner, whom he invited on Sundays to the house in Corbeil that he had done up. He was waiting for the transfer that would send him back to his native Guadeloupe, though his daughters did not want to return home. From time to time, he would appear and have a drink. There was always some-one who had a problem with the administration or a fine they wanted to be rid of. Daniel did favours without making any fuss and when he shook his head, we knew it was impossible. We were surprised to see him on this wet Sunday. He had spent the night watching a house and had just been relieved. Igor asked him what he wanted to drink. Daniel froze when he noticed the massive form of Lognon, who had his back turned to him and was following a game between Pavel and Virgil.

'Oh, Désiré!'

Lognon's head shot up and he looked round, amazed that anyone should be calling him by his first name.

'Mahaut!'

'What are you doing there?'

'Well, what about you?'

'Do you play chess?'

'You know each other?' asked Igor.

Daniel didn't reply. There was a long silence. He stared at Lognon and hesitated. He didn't know what he had said, or what he was doing there.

'You know each other?' Werner repeated.

Lognon walked over to Daniel and whispered a few words in his ear.

'It's not true!' Daniel exclaimed. 'I'm dreaming. You're crazy!'

'Do you know him?' Igor persevered.

'Gentlemen,' Daniel continued after a moment's consideration, 'I'd like you to meet Inspector Désiré Lognon of the Secret Intelligence branch.'

'Don't be an ass!' said Lognon.

'His job is to keep an eye on you. I hadn't realized, but you're a gang of terrorists who threaten the security of the Eastern bloc and Franco-Russian relations.'

Of the various feelings that swept through the group, incredulity was predominant. Only Leonid asked Lognon to step out of the Balto so that he could smash his face in without further ado. It was the general opinion that this solution offered more drawbacks than advantages. Striking an official, an officer on duty what is more, could cost them dearly. Their respective situations did not afford them this type of pleasure. What should be done about Lognon? Should he be expelled from the Club? The word 'expulsion' resonated in their ears uncomfortably and brought back unfortunate memories. Surely they were not going to start behaving like them? Furthermore, could a police inspector be expelled? In their own countries, that would have been impossible, for the police were everywhere. In France, people were unaware of them. Police logic required that it should stay that way.

'Who's got a criminal record?' exclaimed Tomasz aggressively.

'Pavel maybe?' remarked Vladimir with a half-smile. 'The State Department has refused him a visa for America. Perhaps he's an ex-convict.'

'That's wrong, I'm the victim of a witch-hunt!' roared Pavel, before realizing that he was making fun of him.

Lognon was called upon to explain himself to this group that was well accustomed to collective confessions. No, he hadn't noticed anything of importance, apart from secrets about the art of castling at the right moment or the best way of obtaining a stalemate. No, he did not discuss the results of the games. The higher echelons were not interested. Yes, he wrote bimonthly reports for his superiors. They contained no useful information. He was blamed for this. He couldn't invent things. Yes, it was normal to keep a watch on foreigners, communists and political refugees. No, they weren't dangerous. No, he hadn't told them that in his opinion it wasn't worth keeping a watch on them: he had no wish to be sent elsewhere, to infiltrate workers, students or *fellaghas*. It was cushy here. Lognon was asked whether he was ashamed of what he did. He thought about this and shook his head. No, he was obeying a legitimate order given by a legitimate authority. He had not manipulated, nor deceived, nor struck anyone. He was happy just to be there and keep his ears open. He had been chosen because, with his air of a next door neighbour who knew how to integrate himself into groups like a chameleon without being noticed, he inspired trust. People weren't suspicious when you didn't ask them a single question. It's questioning that marks out a cop. He himself never asked any. That was his technique. Put people at their ease and keep your mouth shut. It took longer, but it was effective. Generally, people need and want to talk. As soon as they find an attentive ear, there's no need to ask questions. You need patience. You just have to wait. He could influence them without their realizing merely with facial expressions: astonishment, surprise, bewilderment, interest, compassion. Above all, compassion. Yes, he would continue doing this as long as he was asked to do so. Better that it should be him than anyone else. He feared reprisals if he were to reveal that he had been unmasked, and he didn't like having to implicate a colleague. They asked him to leave the room. The group pondered the matter with Daniel Mahaut.

'Have we the right to prevent him setting foot in the Balto?' asked Werner.

'It's incredible that we didn't spot anything,' Vladimir observed. 'That we weren't aware of anything. We're getting soft. It comes from living in France. Over there, we mistrusted everyone and we were on our guard. Here, we don't mistrust anyone. That's how we get conned.'

'And when you were on your guard, what difference did it make?' said Pavel.

'If they're keeping watch on us,' Leonid observed, 'it's because they're frightened of us. We represent a threat, otherwise why would they keep watch on us?'

Cock-a-hoop, Imré stared at Tibor: 'Do you remember what I told you?'

'You're not going to have us believe that you'd guessed he was a cop!' Pavel exclaimed.

'It's true, Imré said to me: "This guy's odd, he's got big lugs,"' Tibor replied.

We thought about Lognon's ears. They suddenly struck us as immense, protruding and, now, threatening, what with their lobes that looked as if they had been artificially enlarged. We had never seen such large ones. We exchanged dubious glances as though we were annoyed with one another for not having noticed or been suspicious of anything.

'This cop must not set foot in the Club again!' announced Gregorios.

Before anyone else could have a say in the matter, Daniel Mahaut intervened: 'That would be the worst mistake you could make!'

'He's spying on us,' Imré objected.

'The most important thing is to be aware of that. If you're aware of your opponent's tactics in advance, you're sure of being able to beat him, aren't you?'

This reasoning, aimed at the established chess players, left them unmoved.

'What do you suggest?' asked Igor.

'I know the chap. He's as slippery as an eel. You can come to an understanding with him. Ask him to submit his report to Igor or Werner.'

Lognon hesitated a few moments before refusing.

'Out of the question. If I submit a report to you, it proves nothing. I could write one behind your back. If there were a problem, I'd undertake to warn you beforehand. Either take it or leave it.'

They accepted. Lognon walked over to Daniel: 'It's you who put this stupid notion into their heads.'

'I advised them to be reasonable. You should be grateful to me.'

'I've infiltrated a number of groups and networks. It's the first time my identity has been disclosed. Because of you.'

'You should think of retiring, Désiré, you're getting old.'

Lognon turned to Leonid and to Virgil: 'How about finishing your game? Go on. I won't disturb you. Behave as though I weren't here.'

'Watch out, Big Ears,' Gregorios said slowly, 'if any single one of us ever has problems because of you, I'll track you down. Wherever you are. First, I'll cut off your ears, and afterwards, I prefer not to say what I'd do with you.'

'You're not allowed to, I'm a civil servant.'

'My dear fellow, if you knew what I'd done to civil servants during the civil war, you'd run a mile. Don't forget that for the Greeks the punishment for treason is to have your eyes put out.'

'I won't cause you any harm, I promise you.'

Now, whenever he came in, people were aware of him, voices dropped and conversations ceased. It brought back memories of their homelands and of their chess clubs. Somewhat the same atmosphere, but less oppressive. Lognon had not wanted to be called by his first name, which he loathed. That was understandable. We called him Big Ears instead. Scarcely anything changed. After a few months, we noticed that he turned up less frequently. He would come by at the weekend and ask rather gloomily for news of each of us. Nobody answered him. He was worried about what he would say in his report.

'Say we're quiet and peaceful and behaving like good citizens, and that we're not involved in any politics,' said Gregorios. 'And remember that it was the Greeks who invented revenge!'

After that, we spotted him only four or five times a year. He was unpredictable and discreet; we never saw him enter or leave. He would be there, following a game, without any of us knowing whether he came out of duty or for pleasure. When one of the players lost his temper, said something stupid, or moaned about the government or the authorities, they would look around to see whether he was there and would be relieved not to see him. Leonid or Pavel threatened whoever was grumbling: 'Watch it, if you go on causing trouble, I'll denounce you to Big Ears!'

7

I opened the door with my bunch of keys and put the shopping on the kitchen table. I heard her voice, coming from the far end of the flat: 'Is that you, Michel?'

'Who do you think it is?'

Cécile was in the bath and was speaking to me through the door.

'You can come in, if you like.'

'I'll wait for you in the sitting room.'

After changing her mind several times, Cécile had decided to finish her thesis on Aragon and to follow this with a degree in psychology. Pierre's request to read her dissertation had stuck in her throat and she had returned to the subject on various occasions.

The spring-cleaning of the flat was progressing slowly and was hampered by technical difficulties that had nothing to do with good old-fashioned housework. What appeared simple became complicated. Each room revealed a problem we did not know how to resolve. Could one rescue antiquated wooden shutters? Carpets stained by goodness knows what? Water marks on the wall? Why did the gas burner above the sink no longer light up? It rattled when touched. Were we going to be suddenly asphyxiated or would you smell it beforehand? How could one remove painted wallpaper with a knife without loosening the rendering? Why did this vacuum cleaner no longer vacuum? Cécile refused to call in professionals on principle.

'They're Poujadistes! I wouldn't pay them a penny.'

We asked the advice of Monsieur Bisson, from the ironmonger's shop in rue de Buci, who had sold us half of his shop. Either the goods were defective, or else we didn't know how to use them, or we didn't have the right equipment. She lost heart.

'I'll let you finish it, Michel. I've got to work on my dissertation.'

Aragon always got the blame. She spent her time dissecting his books, his articles and his speeches, taking notes, sorting them, filling in index cards, and filing them in wooden boxes with coloured dividers, and she spent hours on the telephone to her friend Sylvie, curled up on the sofa, swapping the latest bits of gossip from the Sorbonne. When I asked whether I could read her work, she told me to get lost: 'Why are you pestering me like this? You'll read it when I've finished.'

'You need to come and look under the sink.'

'What is it now?'

'Mice.'

Were those tiny black balls mice droppings? According to Monsieur Bisson, they certainly were. He suggested either a one-kilo box of rat poison – very effective, although once they got used to it they wouldn't eat any more of it – or the traditional mousetrap with a blade on a spring like a guillotine, sold without the cheese that lured them. The best solution would be to take both. Cécile refused: 'If a mouse gets decapitated, will you pick it up?'

'If you like, I'll lend you Néron. There are no more mice at home and he's getting bored.'

'I don't like cats.'

We hid the food in two top cupboards that could be locked. I had no talent for DIY. I abandoned it so that I could go and read in an armchair in the sitting-room while she worked nearby. Sometimes I observed her when she wasn't looking. She wasn't working. She looked thoughtful, a vacant expression in her eyes.

'And you haven't talked to Franck at all?' she asked me out of the blue, one day when I was scrubbing the parquet floorboards with wire wool to get rid of some stains.

'I haven't written since he's been away. He hasn't either.'

'Hasn't he phoned you? Haven't you had a single letter?'

'Not one. He'll write to you eventually, that's for sure.'

She didn't reply. She immersed herself in her book again. I could see she wasn't reading.

'Aren't you fed up with working? How about going for a run?' I suggested.

'I don't feel like it.'

'How about going to play chess?'

'I can't see the fun in sitting on your bum for hours on a chair just moving pawns about and hanging around. Personally, I find board games a drag.'

'I'll introduce you to my friends. You'll get on well with them. They're former communists. Well, not all of them. Some of them aren't communists. Others are. You'll understand. Some of them know a great deal about literature. You might see Kessel or Sartre.'

'Do they come often?'

'In the evening, generally. Sometimes during the day.'

'Let's go.'

We caught the number twenty-one bus. In ten minutes, we were at Denfert. I had not picked a good day. The room was buzzing with noisy excitement.

'Is it a chess club?' Cécile asked me in a low voice.

'Normally, it's silent.'

We had arrived in the middle of a slanging match. You could spend several weeks in complete quiet and then suddenly an outburst and confrontation would flare up. In this case, there was no way you could remain uninvolved. Those looking for peace and calm had to cross the square and move to another café. When, on 12 April 1961, Yuri Gagarin made the first human flight into space, aboard the rocket *Vostok*, the entire world realized that this was one of those major events that change the history of mankind. But what gave rise to admiration and unanimity elsewhere produced, at the Club, cries and the gnashing of teeth among the 'severed' and the 'unsevered', as Igor used to say. That is to say among those who loathed the leftward-leaning ideology and looked towards America, and those who had escaped from the Eastern-bloc countries, but had continued to be socialists. For the latter, it was merely the system that had gone wrong. The principle remained eternal and the ideal exciting. They were caught in a net of their own contradictions, going into great raptures about the breakthroughs and victories of a country where they were pariahs, and where they would have been done away with had they not gone over to the West. The planetary struggle of the USA versus the USSR would interrupt their games of chess and their reading, and the best of friends would trade insults and hurl invective at one another. Between these two factions of equal importance and eternal irreconcilability, there were countless opportunities for such rows. From Gagarin, who had just screwed the Americans, to Botvinnik, who had crushed his rivals for the umpteenth consecutive time with depressing ease and who was going to remain chess champion of the world for decades, by way of the influence of Lenin's philosophy on the invincibility of the Russian hockey team and the Soviet hammer throwers who threw higher and further thanks to the quality of Russian steel and the coaching of the masses.

'It really is absolute proof, isn't it?'

'I thought you were against the system.'

'I try to be impartial, to admit the rightful value of the results.'

'It's the system that produces them.'

'I respect those who are admired by decent folk.'

'You said you agreed with this system.'

'I didn't say that.'

'Yes, you did!'

'No! This system is an aberration. It crushes man and does not respect him. I'm a Marxist, not a Communist.'

'Communists and Marxists are shits and bastards!'

'And as for you, you're nothing but a dirty fascist!'

They were at it again. People were divided into two camps, with nothing in between. Everybody got involved and contributed his own testimony and his own experiences. No one knew who had said what. No one was listening any longer. Voices soared like a geyser. They ended up shouting at one another in Russian, in German, in Hungarian and in Polish.

Cécile made the foolish mistake of intervening. I would never have imagined that she would do such a thing and there was nothing I could do to stop her.

'If I may be allowed,' she ventured, interrupting Tomasz. 'I think one has to place this event in its historical perspective and consider the

revolutionary nature of this technological feat from the point of view
of where the USSR has come from. They have created a space industry
within fifteen years. It's the result of a planned approach and research—'

Cécile did not complete her sentence.

'Who's she?' yelled Tomasz.

'I agree with you, Mademoiselle,' Pavel chimed in. 'But it should be
made clear that most of this research was provided by friendly countries
and particularly by—'

'Who are you?' yelled Tomasz, beside himself.

'She's a friend, I brought her,' I explained.

'Women are not allowed in the club! It's bad enough to have to deal
with these old commies without having to put up with a woman as well!'

'The woman says fuck off! You're just an old reactionary!'

Cécile shouldn't have hit Tomasz. The slap resounded like a clash of
cymbals. There were two or perhaps three seconds of complete silence,
astonishment and alarm. We tried to come to terms with what had just
happened. We watched his stunned face slowly turning red with the mark
of her fingers imprinted on it. Later on, Leonid explained that this very
brief interval was necessary for the impact of the pain to rise from Tomasz's
cheek to his brain. Leonid didn't care for the Poles. Tomasz hurled himself
at Cécile and tried to strangle her. She was quick and avoided him. The
din reached fever pitch. Tables were knocked over, games of chess were
interrupted for good, pieces were stepped on, and glasses were smashed.
With difficulty, I managed to haul Cécile away by the arm before Tomasz,
who was being restrained by Pavel and Leonid, could tear her to pieces.

'What's got into you? Are you crazy?' I exclaimed.

'That beats everything! Are you going to defend that prick? You're a
real friend!'

Before I was able to respond, she was making her way across boulevard Raspail, where cars were slamming on their brakes and hooting their
horns. I saw her disappear into the métro. I went back to the Balto. A new
subject for dispute had been added to the recurring rift. Were women
allowed to come to the Club? The problem was no longer one of left—
right confrontation. Those who had agreed a few moments beforehand

229

were now confronting one another and joining forces with their former enemies.

'There's no rule in this club that forbids a woman coming along,' Igor confirmed, speaking with the authority of the founding member.

'The rules are those of democracy and the majority,' said Gregorios. 'I would remind you that it was the Greeks who invented democracy. Let's vote! And I'm voting against. It's peaceful just among men.'

It was the first time Imré and Tibor had expressed their disagreement in public.

'We're not in an English club,' Imré explained. 'Here, the only rule is liberty.'

'We can't allow the communists to take over and spoil everything.'

'You're talking nonsense, Tibor.'

'The real problem is women and Gagarin!'

One sensed that a harmful topic had just been raised, like an unknown virus that contaminates without one being aware of it. The few who played conciliatory roles and wanted to avoid the point of no return were reviled by both sides. Were they going to come to blows? Allow ideology to decide what we wanted instead of us? Forget who our friends were? Were politics and women going to be the cause of our misfortunes once more? Could there be such an important discussion without there being a winner?

'We have no reason to quarrel. Our wives have forgotten us and nobody wants us.'

'Are you playing games or fomenting revolution?'

Silence returned, until the next victory or the following defeat. I slipped out. I had let the wolf into the fold and I was expecting to bear the consequences. But as paradoxical as it may be, nobody held it against me.

Next day, I rang Cécile's bell. She opened the door with an enormous smile on her face and greeted me as though nothing had happened. When I set foot in the Club again, nobody made any comment, apart from telling me I was useless at chess. Which just goes to show that notions of fault and blame are relative. Grandfather Delaunay proclaims loud and clear that there is nothing worse than wanting the best for people against their will. But for me the worst thing is not wanting to make others happy or giving up trying to do so. No one could say that I hadn't tried. Perhaps if Gagarin had waited for a day or two before looping the loop in the firmament, Cécile would have been welcomed with open arms.

8

I was in a nasty situation. Not desperate, no, but damned difficult. When I moved my bishop from g2 to c6 to put Tomasz's queen in check, I thought I had struck a superb blow, but I play too quickly without considering all the possibilities. Igor shook his head in sorrow. He had seen my mistake before I did. Tomasz sensed the danger. On my right, Pavel was following the game impassively, his head resting on his fists. Tomasz had the reputation of being a good player. He played very little. He preferred to watch and make comments even though kibitzers were not allowed to speak. In reality, he avoided pitting himself against the best players and he did not play against Leonid or Igor. Tomasz hesitated. All he had to do was to move his rook to f4 to checkmate me the following move. It was glaringly obvious. He reached over to his queen, as though it was in danger, and kept his hand poised in the air.

'You're playing like an ass,' Pavel moaned.

'Right, and I suppose you're Botvinnik?' Tomasz replied.

'Michel's a beginner. How can you play so badly?'

Tomasz glared at the chessboard. His face lit up.

'Now that I can't allow,' I protested. 'If there are two of you against me, it's no longer a game.'

Tomasz's hand was reaching over towards his rook and he was about to pick it up when the door slammed. We jumped. Vladimir came in, excited and animated, and so out of breath that he broke one of the rules of the Club. He spoke to Igor in Russian – a few bellowed words that caused Igor and Pavel, who spoke Russian fluently, to leap to their feet.

'It's Nureyev. He's gone over to the West!' Igor translated for us.

'When the plane landed at Le Bourget airport,' continued Vladimir frenetically, 'he shoved aside the two KGB agents who were accompanying him. He jumped over the barrier and he ran like a madman, pursued by other KGB agents. He managed to take refuge in one of the French customs offices. Nureyev is free!'

'Who is he?' asked Tomasz.

'You don't know Nureyev?' said Igor in surprise.

'How could he know the greatest dancer in the world?' Leonid exclaimed. 'What do the Poles know about dance?'

'Leonid, Vladimir and I went to see him dance last week in *La Bayadère* at l'Opéra de Paris,' said Igor. 'We had tears in our eyes. In the third act a frisson went through the audience. He began to carry out a series of leaps, twirls in the air and running steps with incredible grace and at an amazing speed. No one had ever seen anything like it. Nureyev is not a dancer, he's a bird. A seagull. He doesn't touch the ground. Weight doesn't affect him. He flies. He filled the vast stage of the Kirov on his own. There's just him, the light and the music. He pirouettes in the air. You follow him with your eyes and he transports you with his spins. Today we're going to crack a few bottles. Jacky, bring some champagne.'

'Wouldn't you prefer the sparkling wine? It's the same thing.'

'The best, the Cristal!'

'Some Roederer? It's expensive.'

'Give us two bottles!'

Old Marcusot brought over the champagne with plastic cups.

'You're not expecting to make us drink from these?' said Leonid in a fury.

'Your little parties cost me a fortune.'

'Don't worry about that. Today's an important day.'

'I'll have a beer,' said Tomasz.

That afternoon, Albert Marcusot had his best takings of the year; he finished his stock of champagne and sparkling wine, and renewed half of his glassware. The little party cost Igor, Leonid and Vladimir a fortune. But Nureyev's freedom had no price. Igor requested silence for a toast to the Kirov, the best ballet company in the world. He raised his glass in the air and was interrupted by Vladimir: 'I agree that we should drink a toast to Nureyev, who is an exceptional dancer, but the best ballet company is the Bolshoi!'

'You're joking, I trust. The Kirov is the absolute benchmark.'

Vladimir called on the gathering to be his witness; scarcely any of them knew the work of either company.

'In the past, perhaps; nowadays the Bolshoi is everyone's choice.'

'You Muscovites are simply jealous. The Marinsky is so vast that you could fit the Opéra de Paris inside it twice over.'

'I'm not talking about the size of the theatre, but the reputation of the ballet.'

'Diaghilev, Nijinsky and Vaganova, have you heard of them in Moscow?'

'They retired thirty years ago.'

'The Ballets Russes, who created them?'

'That was before the war. Ask whoever you like, ask the connoisseurs, and they'll tell you the Bolshoi is the best by far.'

'Oh, really? And Nureyev? Where's he from? From Moscow? No, my dear fellow, he's from Leningrad! When he was about fifteen or sixteen, when he wanted to join the Bolshoi, you didn't want him. Are you aware of that? The Bolshoi passed Nureyev over! They didn't spot his talent. The poor guy slept in the street like a pauper. It was the Kirov that welcomed him and made him famous. When his genius erupted in *Le Corsaire*, the Bolshoi tried to lure him away, but it was the Kirov he signed up with! Name me one dancer from the Bolshoi to compare with Nureyev? Even in the last twenty or thirty years.'

Vladimir reflected and could not come up with any. Leonid went further: 'I've seen the Bolshoi twice and the Kirov ten times. Igor's right. I don't say that just because I'm from Leningrad. Nothing can surpass the Kirov in beauty.'

Vladimir shrugged his shoulders.

'One can't discuss the matter with you lot. You're in cahoots.'

'You disappoint me, Volodia. The Kirov is beyond compare. It's quite obvious. To be forgiven, you must buy a bottle,' Leonid concluded.

Tomasz came to find me so that we could finish our game of chess. I pretended I didn't have the time.

'We're discussing important matters.'

'I was on the point of winning.'

'Didn't you see you were about to be checkmate?'

He stared at me incredulously. It was time to deal the final thrust, as I'd often seen Pavel or Leonid do: 'There's no hope for you. You'll always be a small-time player from the suburbs.'

Tomasz sat down at the chessboard and spent the rest of the afternoon looking at the game from every angle without being able to understand, and rightly so, where the danger was coming from.

9

Imré was weeping and there was nothing to be done. In actual fact, he was not weeping, but tears flowed whenever he spoke about Budapest.

'There's no point in getting yourself into such a state,' said Tibor, putting his arm round his shoulder to comfort him.

I also tried to make him feel better. Imré had that look of blank astonishment of those who are having nightmares with their eyes open. In his mind's eye, he could see the besieged Corvin cinema, where students were making Molotov cocktails on an assembly line, machine-guns were firing at civilians taking refuge beneath the arcades and amongst the heaps of tangled corpses. He could hear the growl of the tanks' tracks make a whooshing sound on the asphalt and the uncomprehending yells from the desperate crowd.

'I had a friend at the Corvin cinema whose name was Odon,' said Imré, 'and he climbed up onto the tanks like an acrobat, hurled his lighted cocktail at the turret and jumped down before the tank caught fire. He knocked out two dozen of them on his own. I don't know what became of him. We fled from the cinema when they began firing at it.'

Every man commits a certain number of errors in his life. He searches and finds good or bad reasons for them, often excuses or pretexts. The worst of all reasons is the discovery of his profound foolishness. After the tragic events that had brought bloodshed to Hungary, Tibor, Imré, and the majority of their one hundred and sixty thousand compatriots who had fled the country, asked themselves the same question: were the Hungarians imbeciles? Had they mistaken their desires for realities? Were they like credulous children? Could they have avoided this catastrophe that had killed twenty-five thousand of them? How could they have underestimated their enemy to this extent? On each occasion, after endless discussions, and having gone over the various phases of the rout, they concluded that it was unavoidable. For Imré, there was no room for doubt. The blaze had not been lit spontaneously. But nobody had understood how it had ignited. Someone had certainly blown on the embers. During the preceding months, Radio Free Europe, which broadcast in Hungarian from Austria and was picked up in virtually the whole country, had not ceased encouraging the Hungarians to rebel, promising that help would come from the West. The people must show its determination and rise up. They could count on the support of the European nations and of the Americans, whose bases in Germany were less than an hour by plane from Budapest. Millions of Hungarians had listened to this broadcast and had become convinced that the Western armies would help them free themselves from the Soviet yoke and that they should revolt. The young and the students took advantage of the indecision of the leadership of the communist party, and later the temporary retreat of the Soviet troops, which was interpreted as confirmation of Radio Free Europe's theories. To begin with, they were dead scared at having dared to revolt. After 23 October, the fear had vanished. They felt as though they were reliving the revolution of 1848. The country wasn't being led and nor was the revolution. For a brief week, Hungary was in the hands of the rioters and liberty had been achieved. There was no organization and great confusion reigned. They could pull down the statue of Stalin without being fired upon. The French and the British, bogged down in the Suez crisis, had no more intention of intervening than did Eisenhower, who was thinking only about his re-election. Radio Free Europe, which was financed by the CIA, could not give a damn about the Hungarians.

'The majority of peoples on this earth have been hoodwinked either by the Russians, or by the Americans,' said Imré, sniffing as he explained to me. 'We're the only ones to have been conned by both of them. Never listen to the rubbish they tell you on the radio.'

Imré was weeping because the world had changed. At the Club, consensus was rare. They liked to quibble and squabble. Nowadays, there was no recurrence of the events that had taken place in Budapest. On this, they were all agreed. The Hungarians had died in vain. Those who said nothing were annoyed they could produce no counter argument. All the signs, both positive and objective, were leading inexorably towards democratization.

'It's irreversible,' Vladimir explained.

The grim kind of communism, that of the rigged trials, the camps, the KGB and Stalin, was in the process of disappearing, just as ice melts in the sunshine and day follows night; these two allegories being those used by Vladimir and Pavel respectively. Tomasz mentioned the chrysalis that becomes a butterfly and Gregorios the pain that goes with child-birth. Whatever images were used, they all led to one conclusion. In that glorious summer of 1961, communism was changing. At last! Thanks to Little Father Khrushchev, writers and poets who had been shot or had vanished in the camps were rehabilitated. With him, there was hope. In the countries of the East, free newspapers with independent journalists were flourishing. People weren't arrested or imprisoned when they suggested getting rid of absurd and authoritarian projects or restoring a degree of liberalism to the economy, or when they spoke of democracy, free elections, creating political parties and trade unions to defend the rights of workers, and doing away with the secret police. Everywhere, these newspapers were arguing heatedly. Books that had been circulating in secret were now published officially. Khrushchev had even allowed Solzhenitsyn, a former prisoner, to publish a remarkable novel that was set in a gulag.

'It's the way History is moving,' Pavel had asserted.

But on the morning of 13 August 1961, the sky collapsed over their heads and they woke with a hangover that would set them back several years. During the night, the authorities in the German Democratic Republic had closed sixty-nine of the eighty-eight checkpoints between the Soviet and the Western zones, building an initial wall of barbed wire and bricks that extended for 155 kilometres around Berlin, followed by 112 others between the two Germanies; they bricked up the windows and doors of houses situated on the line of a wall that was 3.60 metres high and was sunk 2.10 metres into the ground, crammed with 96 watchtowers, 302 control towers, 20 bunkers, and 259 units with guard dogs. What puzzled the Club members most was not the brutality and the ignominy of the methods used, nor their ideological justifications, the dictatorial behaviour, the disdain for human beings, the shattered lives; no, all of this they were familiar with. What upset them was their mistaken analysis, their collective blindness, their failure to understand, the desire to uphold their conviction that the system could get better. There is nothing worse for a Marxist than not understanding historical materialism. There was no possible hope of return now. This wall was like a new prison into which they were shut. They were rather like the inmate who is expecting to be released at any moment and who is then told that his sentence is to be extended to life.

'For our families, it's all over,' said Vladimir, devastated by grief.

'This time, we're cut off for ever. We'll never see our homeland again,' muttered Igor.

'We're idiots. We'll never change,' Imré chimed in.

As usual, whether it was good news or bad, they greeted the event with bottles of Clairette-de-Die.

'As long as we can drink, let's make the most of it while we're alive,' added Leonid.

'I raise my glass,' said Werner, who did not usually wax lyrical, 'to all those bastards who make us seem so friendly.'

Imré was relieved to note that it was not just the Hungarians who had been screwed.

During the weeks that followed, a number of confused Germans turned up at the Club. Those who spoke French settled in Paris. Those who spoke English suffered further hardship by emigrating to London. Nikita Khrushchev was appointed a life member of the Club for his enduring contribution to its development.

10

Tibor had not been seen for two days. Imré had given the alert and Igor had informed Daniel Mahaut, who had launched some enquiries at the Préfecture, but with no results. Imré was beside himself. According to Jacky, Tibor was depressed; he was eating nothing and was drinking more than usual. Imré confirmed that he had not been sleeping and had been having morbid thoughts. The idea that he had done away with himself gathered momentum, though his body had not been found. The worrying thing was that Tibor had taken nothing with him. None of the clothes he was so fond of. Neither his crocodile skin shoes, nor his suede jacket, nor his suit from Christian Dior in Prince of Wales check that had cost him an arm and a leg. His personal money, the fruits of his tips, was still in the biscuit tin, which meant he had not left of his own free will.

From these observations, Daniel Mahaut had concluded that his disappearance gave cause for concern. He made enquiries in the hospitals and nursing homes in the Paris region, but to no avail. Tibor had left his job at L'Acapulco at about four o'clock in the morning. Nobody had noticed anything abnormal or unusual about his behaviour. He had not returned home. There may have been an encounter with the wrong kind of people in Pigalle, where crooks proliferated, especially at night. God knows what sordid racket he may have got involved in. Lognon got down to work. Along with Special Branch, they had their sources. He had promised us he would search for him, but eventually he was forced to admit that Tibor really had disappeared. When people vanished without leaving any trace, it was not a good omen. Mahaut and two of his colleagues embarked on the titanic job of checking registration forms at hotels and furnished apartments. Imré informed us that Hungarians used to commit suicide by throwing themselves in the turbulent torrents of the Danube, which was not blue, but muddy. He feared Tibor might have drowned himself in the Seine. By now his body may be drifting in the North Sea.

Days and weeks passed and we began to speak of him in the past tense. None of us was aware of the fact, except Imré, who left the Club, slamming the door behind him. We didn't see him again for three days. Igor went to call on him to apologize and bring him back to the Balto, to be with his friends.

Old father Marcusot had a real cause for concern: Tibor had bequeathed him the largest bill any Auvergnat bistro owner had ever consented to.

'That may well be why he's disappeared,' he reflected one evening.

'Albert, it's shameful to think of anything so horrible,' replied Madeleine. 'Poor Tibor. He, who was so gullible and so kind. He must have had an accident.'

'He's met the man of his life and hasn't dared tell Imré!' suggested Jacky. 'I know Tibor, what he lacks is not acting parts, but cash. He's found someone that's filthy rich and he's now billing and cooing beside a swimming pool on the Côte d'Azur. I've seen the way guys look at him and even though he has put on twenty kilos, he's still a handsome fellow. He's a star, someone who attracts people. It's true though, when all's said and done, they're just like us.'

If Madeleine protested out of principle, no one found Jacky's idea ridiculous. We had all thought of it. Apart from Imré. He sat there alone on a chair, with his newspaper on the table, lost in thought, and no one dared disturb him. I went and sat down beside him and asked him to talk to me about Tibor. I hadn't known him very well. I didn't know who he was. But when I'd greeted Imré, he'd looked at me as though I were an Iroquois. He did nothing during the day except eat croissants that were intended for customers, read the newspaper, smoke his pipe, daydream as he drank milky tea, and begin translations that no one had asked him for. He always dressed with care and elegance. He no longer played chess. Madeleine overlooked his tantrums and fed him generously, good meals being the best cure for melancholia. He recited poems to her in Hungarian. She didn't understand a single word. He had translated Rilke from German into Hungarian and he retranslated it for her into French. She found it very beautiful, and swore to him that he didn't have the slightest accent. This strengthened him in his conviction that he was the victim of a conspiracy.

The news broke unexpectedly and should have made them happy. When you're convinced that someone is dead and you discover he's alive, you ought to jump for joy and display your relief, but when the members of the Club heard that Tibor was alive, they were filled with consternation. Even Imré would have preferred him to be living it up in Saint-Tropez without him. The reason for their concern was splashed over the front page of *France-Soir*, which reported his triumphant arrival in Budapest. Tibor Balazs had returned home! It was the first time that a man who had fled from a communist regime had made the journey in the reverse direction. And, far from harassing him or instituting legal proceedings against him, Hungary welcomed him like the prodigal son who testified to the superiority of popular democracy over imperialism. It was a spontaneous and voluntary act that surprised everyone, including the Hungarian authorities, who did their utmost to prevent their own people from escaping and were not accustomed to a move in the other direction. Tibor had arrived at the Austrian border and a few minutes later, the response came from Budapest: 'Allow him in!' He was interviewed by the State radio and declared: 'I've come back to Hungary. Life in the West is unbearable and loathsome. I couldn't stand being far away from my country and my mother any longer. I ask the Hungarian people for forgiveness.'

His return was resounding proof that the West was squalid, nothing but a mirage created through propaganda, and that the emigrants were going to return to their homeland. Not only was Tibor not put in prison or bothered by the authorities, he was feted and celebrated as a national hero. He returned to Debrecen and found Martha again. She had never given up hope. She knew that he would come back and would not abandon her. He was appointed professor of drama at the Budapest conservatory and, later, appeared in several Hungarian films.

Tibor left a considerable bill unpaid. Some said it was one thousand five hundred francs, others said far more. The fact remains that, shortly after Tibor's reappearance, Albert put up a framed notice: 'Credit is dead, the bad debtors have killed it.' Imré decided he would pay this debt down to the last centime, but Albert refused. Imré wasn't the one who had ordered the food and drink and Albert knew his financial position was difficult. Imré was adamant. If Albert refused, he would not set foot in the Balto again. Albert relented. Imré made used of the eight hundred and seventy-one francs that Tibor had left in the biscuit tin and he took over a year to pay off the rest.

Try as he might, Imré could not bring himself to forget Tibor and he arranged for him to come back, much later, in the most unexpected guise. The Club made it a point of honour not to talk about him any more, even though everyone envied him for having the courage to do what they dreamed of doing: to return home.

11

My mother wanted to spend the Christmas holidays in Algiers, at her brother Maurice's house. It had become a tradition and there was no question of breaking with it. My father disagreed. He reckoned there was no point in courting danger. There had been assassination attempts in Paris, but no one felt threatened. Down there, there were explosions every day, though no one knew whether it was the FLN or the OAS that was planting the bombs. On the one hand, the government proclaimed loud and clear that it had the situation under control, and on the other, no one believed them. During a Sunday lunch, he had been adamant: 'If you want to go, I can't prevent you. But Juliette will not go, I forbid it.'

Grandfather Delaunay also thought it was unwise and, faced with this unusual alliance, my mother gave up the idea.

Cécile received a letter from Pierre who, out in the sticks somewhere near Constantine, seemed to be living on another planet, far removed from what was going on. He had heard about events through the radio and the newspapers, and he was waiting to go on leave. He didn't tell us where. Cécile was hoping that he would come back to Paris, until we received a postcard depicting two camels in the palm grove at Tébessa that left us confused.

Dear Cécile,
      We thought we'd go for a swim. We were allowed to spend seven
      days a hundred kilometres away from our base. It's a paradise on
      earth here. We spend our days stuffing ourselves with Barbary figs
      and dates and playing jokari. We had an inter-army tournament and
      I lost in the semi-finals against an arsehole of a legionnaire who has
      three lungs and never stops farting as he runs. I got on well with
      him. In doubles, I play with my pal Jacquot. We qualified for the final

which takes place tomorrow. We're going to smash them. I'm still waiting to read your thesis. Don't forget that Aragon's a man in love.

'I can't imagine Pierre playing jokari,' I remarked.

'Nor can I imagine him getting on well with a legionnaire.'

We looked at one another. We both thought of the same thing. I waited for her to talk to me about it.

'And supposing we scrubbed the shutters? The ones that give onto the little courtyard,' she suggested.

'Did you see the state they're in? They're beyond repair. They haven't been cleaned since the First World War.'

'You're always complaining. You'll never change.'

She threw herself on top of me and started tickling me. From time to time, the mood came over her. It amused her. I'd have preferred to stay calm just so as to annoy her, but I didn't resist for long before I collapsed laughing. She laughed just as much as me. I took a series of photographs of her that day while she was getting on with odds and ends and scraping off the wallpaper in the corridor. She was in a joyful mood and was fooling around with the broom and the vacuum cleaner. She didn't like posing. I waited for the right moment to snap her unawares. I was correct about the shutters. When we opened the right-hand one, it was rotten and came off its hinges.

No news of Franck. Fifteen months of silence. We didn't know whether he was in Algeria, in France or in Germany. When my father made enquiries at the Ministry of Defence, he received a reply saying it was up to Lieutenant Franck Marini to provide his family with news. Maurice resolved the problem by deciding that this year they would come and spend the holidays in Paris. The moment he set eyes on me, he addressed me in English: 'Hi Callaghan, how do you do?'

'Very good, Uncle.'

I earned the right to a friendly chuck on the chin.

'How are things at school?'

'Fine.'

'Apparently they don't want you at Polytéchnique because you're too clever?'

He burst out laughing. I didn't like his making fun of me in front of the cousins. I wished I could have answered him back and shut him up. I replied curtly. My mother showed him around the shop, which he hadn't seen before. They had needed to expand and had taken over the next door shop, which was used as a workshop and after-sales service office. Maurice came on a busy day and was flabbergasted by the number of people who were queuing and taking a ticket from the dispenser. My father didn't make much of an effort.

'Forgive me, Maurice, I must look after these ladies and gentlemen.'

A couple were signing a purchase order. The man handed a cheque to my father. He stapled it casually and showed the file to Maurice whose eyes opened wide in amazement when he saw the amount.

'Ten grand! I don't believe it!'

My mother proudly explained to him how the different services functioned and how difficult it was recruiting competent technicians to do the various jobs.

'I'm amazed. You're terrific!'

When she told him the turnover they had achieved that year, he couldn't believe her.

'And even then, we're missing out on sales. If we could find the staff, we could make thirty or forty per cent more. And I'm not going to tell you what our profit margin is.'

'Well, Hélène, all I can say is bravo, bravo, bravo! I'm glad to see that those management seminars have borne fruit.'

'They've helped me a lot,' my mother admitted.

'You should attend the seminar on "Soldering success in plumbing jobs" said my father, making a dig at her, 'you could open a shop in the Casbah.'

Over the two following days, we spent our time shopping for the Christmas Eve dinner, which promised to be sumptuous.

Cécile decided to go away for two weeks to stay with her uncle who lived near Strasbourg, the only family she still had. She wrote a letter to

Pierre, enclosing a copy on onion-skin paper of the first chapter of her thesis. She didn't want me to read it.

'When he sends it back to me, I'll give it to you. Do you want to send a note?'

I had so much to tell him. It was the first time I had written since he had gone away. I thanked him for the records, which I listened to every day, thinking of him. Many of my friends were extremely envious. I would give them back on his return. I gave him a bit of news about Henri-IV, about Sherlock and Shrivel-face, and told him about my mathematics mishaps. I told him about the people I had met at the Club. I laid it on a bit by saying that they were a group of revolutionaries whom Special Branch was keeping an eye on. I was sure that would interest him. I took the opportunity to ask him whether, in his position, he could obtain news of Franck and, if there was any, to let me know. I'd have liked to tell him that it seemed as though he had been away for ever and that I missed our discussions, but I remembered that he hated people flaunting their feelings. I scratched out two lines and avoided saying anything personal. Cécile was curious: 'You're writing a book. What are you saying to him?'

She tried to read over my shoulder, but I slipped the letter into the envelope without her having read it.

In spite of the cold weather, we went for a run in the Luxembourg. We managed five complete circuits, then I accompanied her to the Gare de l'Est. As I was leaving, I noticed a baby-foot table in a café on the other side of the street. I couldn't resist.

My mother was keen that her brother should come and stay with us.

'Why pay for a hotel? We've got room.'

I had to move into Juliette's bedroom and vacate mine for the cousins. Maurice and Louise moved into Franck's room. It was a bit like camping. It felt like being on holiday. There was a queue for the bathroom and the lavatories. 'Well, we'll just have to make the best of things,' my father would say, being the only one not to enjoy this merry shambles. He set off at dawn and came home late, having telephoned to tell us not to wait for him at dinner. He had work to do at the shop. He then used the

247

excuse that grandmother Jeanne was ill in order to go to Lens for three days. During the fortnight we were obliged to cohabit, Juliette prevented me from sleeping. She snored. No one had ever realized before. However much I shook her, she rolled over and started again five minutes later. When I told her about this, she was offended and made out that I was lying. One night I went to fetch my cousins, Thomas and François. They discovered I was telling the truth. Juliette was obliged to admit she snored and she was very annoyed with me.

Whenever he came to Paris, Maurice had only one thing on his agenda: to see as many films as possible; and this time we were allowed to go with him. He set out his conditions: he would choose the film and the cinema. And no cartoon movies. In Algiers, he hadn't the time and it was danger-ous. Bombs were exploding in the cinemas. The films were dubbed and, for him, that was a crime. John Wayne in French was a joke, and as for Clark Gable, it was enough to make one weep. Every day, while Louise and my mother wandered around the department stores and shops of the Faubourg-Saint-Honoré, we would go and see an American film in its original version. Each time Louise dragged him off to see a French film, he would fall asleep. There, that proves it, doesn't it? He strolled down the Champs-Elysées, with his nose in the air, fully trusting the poster, the stars and the title, and he scanned the photographs to determine whether we would be bored or not.

'This will be great. It's a French film, with a plot like an American one.'

I realized where my nickname came from when we went to see *Callaghan remet ça*, the sequel, as he explained to me later, to *A toi de jouer Callaghan* and *Plus de whisky pour Callaghan*, humorous and action-packed thrillers that featured at the top of his pantheon of movies alongside *Lemmy Caution* with Eddie Constantine, both featuring heroes adapted from books by Peter Cheyney. As we came out, I earned a little punch on the chin: 'At least we weren't bored.'

After the film, we went and had an ice cream at the Drugstore. He loved its wild-west, saloon-style decor. He bumped into a pied-noir friend, a shoeshop owner, whom he had not seen for two years. He had managed to sell his shop in a suburb of Algiers and to buy one on boulevard Voltaire. He advised him to follow his example. Maurice went red in the face.

'Bloody hell! Do you think I've been waiting for your lousy advice? You're wrong, you great moron! Mine's not a twenty-square-metres shop at Saint-Eugène. I own thirty-two buildings! If I sell anything at all, it will be the cemetery. I've been warned! There's nothing I can do. I'm trapped. We'll find a way out of it, believe me. We're going to smash them! We're going to stay in our own country!'

A customer got involved. Voices rose. The guy called him a fascist and a dirty colonialist. Maurice had not attended seminars on diplomacy. He spat in his face and called him a filthy commie motherfucker. The man did not appreciate this. They grabbed each other by the neck and shook each other, then attempted to hit one another. Some waiters intervened. We were accompanied unceremoniously to the door of the Drugstore, without having finished our ice creams. There was one consolation: he had not paid for them.

12

The Christmas Eve feast *was* sumptuous. As far back as the Delaunays could remember, no one had ever seen such a fine table, with gleaming silverware, Limoges china, lace place mats and Baccarat crystal glasses. No one mentioned the Drugstore incident. We were not going to ruin the party for the sake of a few idiots. Some of Louise's relatives joined us. We were fifteen, but we could have fed twice the number. My mother and Louise had planned everything down to the smallest detail. The meal was scheduled to last two hours. We had to be at Saint-Etienne-du-Mont for midnight mass at eleven o'clock.

'If you can find a way of getting out of it,' my father whispered to me over the apéritif, 'I'll pay for your Circuit 24.'

It was an incredible offer. My mother refused to buy the car racing game for me. She thought it was ridiculous and that I didn't deserve it. We spoke to one another like conspirators, in a low voice and out of the corners of our mouths.

'I'm going to say that I'm not feeling well and that you're going to have to look after me.'

'She won't believe you.'

'Oysters, they made me ill when we went to La Baule. And I'll drink white wine. I can't bear white wine.'

'She'll realize.'

'What are you two plotting?' asked grandfather Philippe as he sat himself down between us.

'I was telling him about the film we saw this afternoon. It was great.'

'Michel, there are other words in the French language besides "great". Can't you alter your vocabulary?'

'You're right. I won't say "great" any more.'

'I was told that your mother was tired,' he said to my father. 'I hope it's nothing serious.'

'It's her heart. The doctor wants her to go on a diet.'

'It's an obsession!' he exclaimed. 'They're going to kill us with their diets.'

'It's not much fun being in hospital over Christmas. Papa is with her this evening.'

'Don't worry, she'll be back on her feet again.'

'Let's sit down,' my mother announced as she brought in an enormous smoked salmon.

There was an infectious good atmosphere. Perhaps the Gewürztraminer contributed. I held out my glass. Maurice filled it. Not bad. I was allowed a second round before anyone realized, apart from my father, who tried to dissuade me with a glance. In the news, the only item of topical interest that captured people's attention was the acquittal of the serial poisoner, Marie Besnard.

'She bumped them off. She's awesome,' my grandfather stated.

'She's innocent,' suggested Louise.

'Landru also protested his innocence. If she's innocent, I'm the pope,' protested Maurice.

'The experts have said that—'

'I tell you what I would have done to her,' announced Philippe peremptorily, 'I would have made her drink her own arsenic, which they found in her garage, and as she was dying, before she snuffed it, off to the guillotine with her!'

'What you're saying is appalling,' exclaimed Louise.

'And those whom she poisoned so that she could pinch their inheritance, I suppose that's not so horrible?'

'She was acquitted! And—'

'Holy mackerel! A lot you know about criminals, my dear girl!'

Nobody gave her time to explain. You could never discuss anything. If you didn't agree with grandpa, you were simply stupid. He shook his head and raised his eyes to heaven. She gave in. She should have known that you weren't allowed to go it alone. At the Delaunays, you hunted in a pack and you shared the same opinions.

'I hope you haven't put any arsenic in the salmon,' my father asked my mother.

'A little in the oysters,' she answered.

They laughed for a couple of minutes. The centre of the table was cleared. Between them, my mother and Maria carried in a pyramid of silvery oysters. Fifteen hands reached out simultaneously, seized hold of the oysters and poured a little shallot dressing over them, and they were swallowed down in a jiffy. You would have thought it was a competition to see who could eat the most oysters in the fastest time. There were so many of them that the heap appeared to remain intact for a long while. My mind was made up. I was going to stuff myself with oysters. How many could one eat before collapsing? Two, three dozen? More? I decided that at about ten o'clock I would pretend I had a stomach ache and writhe about in pain. My father would stay with me and the others would set off to mass. I needed to drink some white wine. A little more. It was worth taking a few risks for a Circuit 24.

'I reckon this one has a strange taste,' said Philippe, examining his oyster suspiciously.

'What's the matter with it?' exclaimed my mother anxiously.

'It smells slightly of arsenic. A little bitter and not unpleasant,' he said, feeling rather pleased with himself.

'You fool,' she said, relieved.

'Watch out, Paul, you've just eaten an oyster stuffed with arsenic,' announced Maurice.

'I'm not bothered on that score. What I leave behind me is of no consequence. But don't trust your husband, Louise. He's not going to miss out.'

I was the first to hear the doorbell, for the ring was muffled by the laughter and the din.

'Papa, I think someone rang the bell.'

'I didn't hear anything.'

There was silence. The bell rang. Several long rings.

'Michel, go and answer the door. I wonder who it could be at this hour.'

'It must be the caretaker,' said my mother as I left the table.

I opened the door. I stood rooted to the spot. On the landing, four policemen in uniform were looking me up and down. My father came over and put his hand on my shoulder.

'Gentlemen, what is it you want?'

'Monsieur Paul Marini?' asked the oldest of them.

'That's me.'

'We're looking for Franck Marini.'

'Franck? He's not here. He's in Algeria. He's doing his military service.'

'No, Monsieur. Your son has deserted.'

'What?'

My mother had joined us.

'What's going on?'

'I don't know. They're saying that Franck has deserted.'

'I don't believe it!'

The policeman drew a bundle of papers out of his briefcase, and read from the top page, weighing each word: 'We act in accordance with letters rogatory issued by Monsieur Hontaa, the examining military magistrate at the permanent military tribunal of the armed forces at the ZNA in Algiers…'

He stumbled over ZNA* and did not appear to know what it stood for. I could feel my father's fingers digging into my shoulder. The policeman glanced inquiringly at his colleague, who grimaced uncertainly, and he began to read again: '… who has issued an arrest warrant in respect of Franck Philippe Marini, born in Paris XIV on 25 May 1940, and has ordered a search of his home address.'

He walked in, followed by his three colleagues. My mother hurriedly closed the door behind them. The others wanted explanations. The conversations grew confused. No one knew who was replying to whom. We shuffled around the hallway and the corridor. Grandfather Delaunay mentioned his connections at the Ministry. The comment did not please the chief policeman. He would later make a note of it in his report . They made us go back into the sitting room. One of the policemen, stationed by the door, kept watch over us. His colleagues carried out a search in my father's presence. We remained standing, not speaking, and glancing

---

* The ZNA (Zone Nord-Algérois) was one of the many sectors of the country in which French troops were billeted during the Algerian War (1954–62). Tr.

at one another. My mother muttered something in Maurice's ear. We began to talk to each other in whispers. After ten minutes, a policeman appeared at the half-open door. He wanted his colleague to note down the identities of those present and he asked Maurice to follow him.

'Why me? I've got nothing to do with him.'

'If you please!'

They went out. Muddled noises reached us from the other side of the wall. Maurice returned. Since he and Louise were occupying Franck's bedroom, the police wanted to know what belonged to them. My father walked in with the policemen, who had finished their search. They had confiscated files, books and notebooks, magazines and a diary, and had placed them in plastic bags that were sealed with red wax and an official stamp. They made my father sign the official sequestration paper, and the chief policeman handed him a summons to report to the police station at Reuilly barracks on 27 December at three o'clock to make a statement.

'A statement, what for?' my mother asked.

'About your son, Madame.'

'That's easy: I've had no news of him since he left for Algeria and I don't want any.'

The chief policeman felt awkward. He spoke in a hushed voice to one of his colleagues, who nodded.

'If you prefer, I can take your statement straight away.'

They sat down in the kitchen. They made some room on the cluttered table. My father offered them a drink. They accepted a coffee, but they didn't want anything to eat. Apparently one of the policemen, the fair-haired one, took down their statements by hand. My parents were given no information. The policemen explained they were not privy to the details of the case.

'A judge in Algiers has initiated proceedings. You should get in touch with him. There's a problem with these papers. Normally, they issue a summons. When it's an arrest warrant, it's more serious. If you're in touch with him, tell him it's in his own interest to give himself up to the authorities. We catch them all, in any case. Sooner or later.'

They left so quickly that grandfather, who looked dazed and had collapsed into an armchair, wondered whether he had had a bad dream. Louise sat down and patted his hand. Maurice kept repeating: 'I can't get over it!' Maria ought not to have interrupted in order to ask cheerfully whether she could serve the vol-au-vents. My mother told her off in no uncertain terms. Even we, the children, who had no idea what a permanent armed forces military tribunal, or arrest warrants, or searches might mean, were appalled. Our anxiety was heightened by our parents' concern and confusion. We realized instinctively that it was a disaster for the family, and a major threat, that it was linked to current events, to the war and to whatever it was that was being concealed from us. There's nothing like the arrival of a quartet of policemen to ruin a Christmas Eve party. In my mind's eye I could see Franck at our moment of farewell at the bistro in Vincennes. His desertion was impossible to understand. I wondered how I was going to break the news to Cécile. Maurice sat down at the table.

'Boys and girls, if we don't want to miss mass, we'll have to get a move on.'

My mother walked over to my father and said to him: 'You see, I told you so. I was right.'

'What are you talking about?'

'It's your fault.'

'It's not my fault! It's not yours! And it's not his! It's this fucking war.'

'It's because of his shitty party and those lousy ideas they've filled his head with. If you'd done something, this wouldn't have happened.'

'This is sheer madness! I forbid you to say that!'

'You can't forbid me anything! You're the one who's responsible!'

We waited for him to react, for the voices to rise, for an explosion. He stood there, with an uncomprehending look on his face, and then his expression grew hazy. Absorbed in his thoughts, he sighed, and, head bowed, he turned around, opened the cupboard, took out his overcoat, and left, closing the door without a sound.

'You're going too far, Hélène,' grandfather snapped. 'It's not his fault. You should go and talk to him.'

'Never!'

'Be careful what you say. You seem to me to be rather fraught. You should take a holiday.'

'Papa, it's—'

'That's enough! Get a grip on yourself. Come on, let's get ready. We've had enough to eat as it is.'

There was no question of a jolly meal. They put on their coats in silence.

'Michel, what are you waiting for?'

'Mama, I'm going to be sick.'

'It's the oysters,' she observed, 'he can't eat them.'

'He drank too much white wine, said Louise.

'White wine at his age! Now we've seen it all.'

'Maurice, did you give him white wine?'

'He's a grown-up now. He drank one glass.'

'Two,' I specified.

'It's unbelievable,' Louise went on. 'You don't serve wine to a child. You don't think at all.'

'Go to bed,' said my mother. 'I'm going to give you a little bicarbonate of soda.'

I lay down on the sofa. Juliette came to see me. I thought it was to cheer me up. With a broad smile, she whispered in my ear:

'You're going to die of poisoning.'

They set off for church. From their expressions, one would have thought they were going to celebrate a burial, not a birth. I waited for ten minutes. I had a good hour and a half ahead of me. I got dressed and opened the door carefully. The building was silent. I went down the stairs in the dark so as not to arouse the attention of the concierges. It was freezing cold outside. The wind was stirring up gusts of snow and the rare passers-by hurried on, their coat collars turned up.

I searched for him everywhere. The streets were deserted. I walked up rue Gay-Lussac as far as the Luxembourg. The restaurants and cafés were closed. Rue Soufflot was empty and the place du Panthéon was swept by icy squalls. I found him in his workers' dive in rue des Fossés-Saint-Jacques, the only place open on this Christmas night. It was a bistro for infidels who played tarot and joked as they knocked back the booze. He was watching the game attentively. I sat down next to him. He was a bit surprised to discover me there and put his arm round my shoulder.

'Would you like a beer?'

'No, thanks.'

'Have a Coke.'

He spoke to the owner: 'Jeannot, bring us two Cokes, please.'

'I'd prefer a really weak lemonade shandy.'

The others suggested he play tarot with them. He declined the invitation.

'Thanks, fellows. We prefer to watch.'

He drained his glass, then leaned over and asked: 'Have they left?'

I nodded. He got up and paid the bill.

'Come on, let's go home.'

We found ourselves out in the cold once more. He shielded me in his overcoat.

'Papa, maybe now's the time, if ever there was one, to go to mass and light a candle for Franck.'

'You know, Michel, if God's as great as that and sees everything, he doesn't need us to ask him something in order to make up his mind, but if you want to, we'll go.'

For a long time, I felt annoyed with myself for not having gone to church. When you think about what happened afterwards, one candle isn't much to ask. If there are that many people in the world who light candles or night-lights, you have to believe they serve a purpose and that, from time to time, in the midst of the masses of flickering flames, there must be one that catches his notice, otherwise we are only lighting them to reassure ourselves in our human darkness. But when you think of the millions and millions of candles that have been lit since mankind began, and of all the prayers and bowing and scraping, you could also say that God, if he exists, doesn't expect anything of us.

JANUARY–DECEMBER 1962

1

There are some tasks, such as confronting reality, telling the truth, or acknowledging our mistakes, that are insuperable. We delay, we avoid them, we move on to something else and we adopt the Jesuits' maxim that a lie of omission is not a lie. When Cécile returned from holiday, I said nothing to her.

'How did it go?'

'Like any family party.'

We wished each other a happy New Year and much happiness.

'What's your dearest wish, Michel?' she asked me as she cut some *kugelhopf* she had brought back from Strasbourg.

'Apart from a Circuit 24, it would be taking a photograph of you.'

'You've taken masses and they're not great.'

'I could take some photos of you in your bath.'

'Are you joking?'

'They would be artistic.'

'Can't you think of anything more original?'

'If we can't even joke any more... What would your wish be?'

'I don't want anything. A wish is something sad and impossible. I don't feel like dreaming.'

'You could think of Pierre, wish for the war to end and for him to come home.'

'I do think of Pierre, the war will end and he will come home.'

'What about your thesis?'

'It'll be finished on time and I'll pass. You haven't answered me.'

I hesitated to tell her about the visit from the police. We would have concocted hypotheses and come up with explanations that did not stand up. We would have wished for the same thing. I knew what she was like. She would have put on her most casual air and replied that she couldn't care less, that it was no longer her problem.

'What I really want is a little more *kugelhopf*.'

She had invited me for a hot chocolate and had forgotten to buy any. She made a café au lait. We finished the *kugelhopf*.

'My uncle runs a restaurant. I can't tell you what I've eaten in the past two weeks. Do you reckon I've put on weight?'

'Since we're leaving things unsaid, I'd prefer not to answer that. We'll start going on runs again.'

What would have been the point of talking about Franck? For over a year she had avoided raising the question. And besides, what would I say? We knew nothing. Maurice had some connections, but they were useless. An invisible and insurmountable wall descended the moment he mentioned the words 'deserter' and 'examining magistrate'. His contacts promised to call him back. He spent hours by the telephone waiting for a call that never came. Those we did receive were not the ones he was expecting. He spent his time hanging up on people. He had arranged for someone to be constantly by the phone. We were told not to use it, in case someone might be contacting him. When he returned the calls that had come in, there was nobody there and he left pointless messages. Grandfather Delaunay had decided to take over the reins before we ended up in the ditch, but the people in high places whom he once knew had all retired. No one remembered him. De Gaulle had had a clear-out in the ministries and placed his own men everywhere.

The holidays came to an end without our having any news. Maurice, Louise and the cousins had left to go back to Algiers. Maurice appeared optimistic. He had his networks down there and he would soon obtain information. But his friends in Algeria were like his friends here, they shrugged their shoulders fatalistically and advised him not to dwell on the matter. At the court in Algiers, he was sent from one office to another. Even his friend Fernand, whom he regarded as a brother, and who was a head of department at the Préfecture, seemed to be evasive and elusive. 'Drop it, Maurice,' he said finally, unable to help, 'Don't get involved.'

Two words summed up the tragedy: military justice. It was secret. Like a hidden danger or a shameful illness, it was spoken of in hushed voices. We couldn't let anyone else know, otherwise we would be courting endless trouble. Whenever Maurice rang, my father rushed over to the phone, my mother listened in, and they conducted a three-way discussion. The examining magistrate at the permanent military tribunal of the armed forces had refused to see him. He had not been allowed to enter the El-Biar barracks and he had been obliged to wait in the blazing sun. A parachutist had told him that he was wasting his time and that he should not come back. For a month, our lives revolved around these nightly calls. Whatever my father might say about Maurice, my uncle spared no effort to obtain information. Then he came up with a solution. My mother was firmly opposed to it. Maurice knew 'a very nice person' who ran a hotel at Bab-el-Oued that was frequented by Massu, Bigeard and half the general staff. In spite of my father's exhortations, she refused to allow her brother to ask this woman for help. It required Philippe to become involved for her to give way: 'You're boring us stiff, Hélène, with your qualms! Let Maurice deal with it. This is for men to sort out!'

'It's our last chance,' Maurice explained, trying to persuade her. 'She knows everyone in Algiers.'

Igor, Werner, Pavel or Gregorios had faced up to impossible situations and endured the cruellest ordeals without panicking. When I walked into the Club, Big Ears was chatting to Tomasz. I was convinced they were going to guess what my problems were from my expression or my demeanour, but apparently one can endure the worst torments without anyone suspecting. I sat down and made comments about the game being played. I waited for one of them to ask me: 'What's the matter, Michel?'

Nobody noticed a thing. I kept my secret to myself. Yet what was the point of having so many friends if you couldn't talk to them? I made up my mind to ask Igor. He was someone who would understand and he would know what to do. I was sure that Big Ears would not be there on a Sunday. When I arrived at the Balto, there was a group of people congregated around Madeleine and Imré, listening to the radio. Albert was switching impatiently from one station to another.

'What's going on?'

'Haven't you heard?' Imré replied.

'About what?'

'There's been an attempt on Sartre's life. He may have been killed!' Jacky exclaimed.

On that 7 January 1962 a bomb attack by the OAS had destroyed the small flat on the fourth floor of 42 Rue Bonaparte where Jean-Paul Sartre had lived with his mother since 1946. Another bomb, the previous year, had caused some damage. This time, the flat had been wrecked, his piano demolished, and his manuscripts scattered.

Thanks to old Marcusot's Auvergne grapevine, the following day Sartre found a studio flat to rent that was very close to the Balto, on the tenth floor of a modern building at 222 Boulevard Raspail. He moved in as unobtrusively as possible for fear of another attack. The tenants were scared stiff about having him as a neighbour and ten of them signed a petition, which the estate agent threw in the bin. Sartre started coming to the Balto and the local bistros more frequently. He had his table in the dining room, close to the door to the Club. He spent his mornings writing and no one dared to disturb him apart from Jacky, who served him a *café crème* as soon as he arrived, and brought him another whenever he waved his hand. Occasionally, he would sit down next to Sartre and they would chat. We wondered what they could possibly be saying to one another. Jacky had only one topic of conversation: the Stade de Reims football team. We deduced that Jean-Paul Sartre liked football too. One day, we asked Jacky: 'What can you have to say to one another?'

'What are you talking about?'

'You and Sartre have been chatting for an hour. What did he say to you? Is he interested in soccer?'

'Oh, he's a complicated guy. He never stops asking me questions about my job.'

'About your job?'

'Yeah. He thinks that compared to other café waiters, I'm not playing at being a waiter. I interest him a great deal. He says that I'm genuine, that I'm not pretending, that I'm not acting a part in relation to what I do, but that I am living in reality as far as who I am. Apparently I'm the only waiter he knows who doesn't use his social background to achieve his position, yet I am, essentially, a café waiter, and that astonishes him. The guy's really got a lot of time on his hands, hasn't he? What'll you have?'

Sartre would sometimes spend the afternoon working in the dining room without coming into the Club. Although Igor, Leonid and Gregorios had huge admiration for him, Imré, Vladimir, Tomasz, Piotr or Pavel detested him on account of his defence of Stalin's communism, his double standards over events in Budapest, and because he had asserted at the time of the Kravchenko trial that all anti-communists were dogs. They walked past him without looking at him or saying hello. Sartre did not glance at them. As for me, every time I saw him, I gave a nod. He replied with a little bob of his head. On one occasion, he ran out of matches. I offered to go and get him some.

'Yes, please.'

I brought him a book of matches.

'Thank you very much.'

He smiled at me. I didn't dare address myself to the former pupil of the Lycée Henri-IV and tell him that we had that in common. I wanted to say something more original, I was not sure what. How could you be intelligent in front of Jean-Paul Sartre?

'Did you hear what happened yesterday? Racing thrashed Stade de Reims yet again. Things aren't what they used to be.'

He stared at me in astonishment. He said nothing, lit his cigarette, went back to his work and started writing. I concluded from this that I had blundered and that he was a Stade de Reims supporter. On another occasion, I picked up one of his sheets of paper that had fallen on the floor. In his metallic voice, he said to me: 'Thank you, young man.'

'I'm at the Lycée Henri-IV, you know.'

'We had a lot of fun there. I have good memories of it.'

I was very proud of this exchange. I repeated it to Cécile. I told her she would be welcome to come and see him, but her contact with the Club had been so unfortunate that she did not want to set foot there again.

The great writers have pointed out that women are superior to men and have attributed to them instinctive psychological skills. At the Club, nobody had detected anything different in my attitude, but eventually,

Cécile noticed something unusual about my behaviour. We had completed our run round the Luxembourg and were resting by the Médicis fountain.

'What's the matter with you, Michel?'

'I'm a bit out of breath.'

'You look as if something's wrong.'

'Oh, really?'

'Have you got problems?'

'No.'

'Something at school?'

She was insistent. The great writers have subtly observed that women are insistent. Until they obtain satisfaction and the hero confesses. Which can give rise to an outburst. Having read a great deal, I decided not to admit to anything. After closely analysing Isabel Archer, Jane Eyre and Marguerite Gautier, I was forewarned that they could have recourse to weapons that men were unable to resist.

'You're not allowed to fib to me, little bro'.'

'I'm not fibbing.'

'If it was important, would you tell me?'

'Stop it, Cécile. Come on, let's do another circuit.'

We set off at a trot. I could see from her expression that she did not believe me. The great writers have often solved their hero's problems with a convenient escape, but I'd never read anything in which the two protagonists set off running together.

'Whatever you say. You've got a strange look on your face.'

I said nothing to Cécile. I said nothing to Igor. Every evening, I hoped for an answer. When the telephone rang, we rushed over. But Maurice's efforts were proving to be unsuccessful. The acquaintances of his woman friend at the hotel were taking a lot of persuading. She would continue to make enquiries. Still nobody was able to tell us why Franck had deserted and what had become of him.

2

'Those who have never flown in a Sturmovik 2 will never experience the delightful sensation of piloting a steam iron,' Leonid explained to me. 'Especially when there's a Messerschmitt 109, which is almost two tons lighter, flying at 200 km per hour faster and clinging to your tail like a magnet. Then, you really do start to sweat and your balls shrink to nothing. You can hear the bullets whistling around you, making holes in the cockpit; your machine-gunner lies bleeding, your joy-stick no longer works. You don't know what to do. No one can teach you how to extricate yourself from this hornet's nest because no one has come out of it alive. Your only god is called Parachute. Believe it or not, I never ever thought to myself that I was finished. Twice, I was able to land, one of them a crash landing. I was wounded seven times. I always trusted in my lucky star. Two or three times, I had close shaves. To begin with, we had no rear-gunner. Afterwards, when Ilyushin put one in for us, beneath an extended canopy, it was worse. The plane was as unsteady as a legless man on a scooter. The recoil from our 37mm guns gave us no accuracy. Little Father Stalin had a tantrum. He knew what this meant. They slaved away day and night. We switched to a two-seater, with new engines and armour-plated structures. By the end of forty-two, we began getting decent Ilyushas, with 20mm guns, and then we were able to do them some damage. Our bombs mopped up everything over an area of a thousand square metres. We knocked out their tanks and their Stukas as though we were showing off. It was in the Urals that the war tipped the other way.'

'Did you really know Stalin?'

'I was introduced to him during the battle of Prokhorovka. I'd been wounded in the shoulder when my plane was shot down. He congratulated me on my bravery, decorated me with the order of Koutouzov, which he had just instigated, and decreed that I was a hero. Others were frightened of him. I didn't fear him myself. He could sense this and it pleased him. I spoke to him as if to a friend, as I would to anyone else. He said to me: "Leonid Mikhaïlovitch, apparently nobody knows as many jokes as you do." I'm not sure how he knew this. He asked me to tell him a few. I started off as I did every evening with my pals. He roared with laughter – not something that happened very often. His staff officers laughed too. We drank quite a lot, celebrating our victory. We were happy. We knew that we were going to win the war. He asked me whether I knew any jokes about him. They stopped laughing. What could I reply? My general was quaking. If I told him I did, I risked being shot on the spot or sent goodness knows where. If I said I didn't, he wouldn't have believed me. I didn't get flustered. I told him that I only knew one. He asked me to tell it to him. That's how we became friends.'

'What story was it?... No, Leonid, don't tell me it was the joke about the sun that rises in the daytime and goes over to the West.'

'Yes, he loved it and asked me to tell it on several occasions. Each time, it produced the same effect. The staff officers were terrified. As for him, he had tears in his eyes. He said it along with me, he repeated it back to me, and he added details. He choked himself laughing. One day, a general informed him that he was shocked by this insolence and that it didn't make him laugh. Stalin replied that heroes were entitled to small privileges and that one could make exceptions for them. It was said that he had infinite patience and that he was as wily as a fox. One day, he asked me who had told me the joke. I told him that it was a friend, a lieutenant who had died in battle. I could see he didn't believe me, but he wasn't angry with me. Thanks to him, I was made a colonel and I received the gold star of Hero of the Soviet Union. The decoration wasn't given as a favour, but for an air battle in which I brought down three Messerschmitt 109s and a Junkers 87, one of their fucking Stukas, by causing a deliberate mid-air collision. That was fairly common in the Soviet air force. There were hundreds of them. We were fighting for our homeland and we weren't afraid of dying. The Japanese kamikaze invented nothing new. My parachute opened. It was the highest distinction that a Russian serviceman can be given. I had the huge honour of being awarded it twice. The second time was after the battle for Berlin. That's one I'm not so proud of.'

My father never talked about the war. He spent forty months in a prisoner of war camp, bored to death. When Leonid Krivoshein told me about his war, it was like an all-action film. We jumped back twenty years into the past. Pilot's licence at the Perm Air Academy, posted as a sub-lieutenant to the Garde air squadron, he achieved 278 missions, 91 accredited victories, of which 65 were individual and 26 in combination, as well as knocking out 96 tanks, 151 anti-aircraft guns and 17 locomotives on the ground, and 25 decorations and military awards. His rapid advancement was due to his courage and to the slaughter of the Soviet troops that had left him, at the end of the conflict, as the sole survivor of his year.

To begin with, I found it hard to believe him. In spite of his dark, tired eyes, he seemed scarcely older than Franck. With his white skin, his tousled blond hair and his smooth cheeks, he looked more like a youthful English aristocrat than a Russian airman. I would have reckoned him to be about thirty when he was actually nearly fifty. Igor held him in high regard and confirmed that he was speaking the truth. As soon as he started describing the battle of Koursk, when he had destroyed two enemy planes before being shot down by a Henschel 129, or the terrible Polish campaign, though, the others jumped on him. Vladimir Gorenko was the harshest: 'You can't go on being such a pain in the arse, Leonid. You've won. You got a pack of medals. Stalin embraced you and decorated you. Ilyushin said you were the best pilot in the world and Tupolev thought of you as his son. Streets and school have been named after you. You were a hero of the Soviet Union. Bravo, comrade, but today you're just an arsehole of a Parisian taxi driver. Stop boring us stiff with this fucking war. We don't want to hear about it any more!'

Leonid stood up to the rebuffs without getting annoyed and countered immediately: 'If I don't speak about it, Vladimir, if I don't talk about what we went through, who will know?'

From time to time, he suffered from bouts of sniffing, as if an unpleasant smell were bothering him, and he peered at his colleagues to see whether they were aware of it. He took a small opaque glass phial from his pocket and poured five drops onto a handkerchief then used it to dab at his nostrils. I didn't dare ask him questions and so I asked Igor.

'It's nothing. He's got a slight medical problem with his nose. He's sniffing some medicine.'

Summer and winter, he wore the same black cashmere pullover with a loose-fitting polo neck, and a worn Burberry bought in London when he was at his peak. On his right wrist he wore his Lip Président watch, which, in over ten years, had kept perfect time with the talking clock. It was his most precious possession. Every day, Leonid took away two sandwiches, one made with ham and one with Gruyere cheese, lovingly prepared for him by Madeleine, who gave him double portions. She wrapped them in a cloth bag which he slipped into the inside pocket of his raincoat. More than once, Madeleine discovered an entire sandwich and told him off for not eating it. Leonid smiled as if to apologize. He wasn't hungry. The alcohol was enough for him. He was renowned for his exceptional ability to hold his drink, and more than one idiot who had wanted to test his stamina had slumped beneath the counter while Leonid had walked nonchalantly away, shrugging his shoulders, then climbed into his taxi and driven off without swerving an inch. Even when he was in an awkward position or had drunk a lot, he managed to extricate himself by playing for a stalemate. His fame had spread, and more than one player would push open the door of the Club to take him on. Students from the neighbouring *grandes écoles*, Centrale or Polytechnique would turn up hoping to beat him. Leonid wouldn't agree to any game without a bet on either a bottle of Côtes-du-Rhône, drinks all round, or an apéritif. Those who took him on would frequently stagger away again, having made fools of themselves. Apart from his best friends, Igor and Werner, and Virgil, who longed to defeat him, the others in the Club had given up challenging him. The losers had to endure his sarcastic comments: 'You've made progress, Tibor, but backwards', or 'You're just a small-time player from the suburbs, Imré', or, to Gregorios, who had no sense of humour: 'On the scale of 1 to 10, you're minus zero.'

The worst chess insults were reserved for those who dared contest his supremacy, whom he treated as pathetic idiots. I had tried on several occasions to get him to take me on. He evaded the matter with a smile:

'In ten years' time, when you know how to play, we'll discuss it again. Practise with Imré or Vladimir. When you beat them every time, come and see me.'

I spent hours observing him, noting down his moves and asking him questions. Leonid was a fanatic and had no need of a board or of pieces. He played in his head. He claimed to know two hundred and eighty-seven games by heart, the most useful ones, as well as several hundred of the best openings and endings. He had not counted them, which was amazing for he was always absolutely precise. He would memorize each move and describe a series of identical exchanges, comparing them with a particular sequence in a well-known tournament, and then wonder what Alekhine, the complete master, who knew more than a thousand games, and against whom he had had the honour of playing on three occasions without beating him, or Botvinnik, the champion of champions, who had always thrashed him, would have done in this situation. I followed him as best I could. I only understood about half of what he said. One day, seeing me looking downcast, he set out some pieces: 'This one's easy. You've got to checkmate in four moves.'

He left me feeling useless. The pieces shifted around in a pointless ballet. Pavel and Virgil joined me. We thought long and hard before coming to the obvious conclusion that this time he had got it wrong.

'Did he say in four moves?' asked Virgil.

'There aren't thirty-six solutions. We're not idiots,' Pavel declared. 'He's taking the piss out of you.'

'Go and ask the champion how he does it in four moves,' Virgil suggested. 'I maintain it's not possible. In five perhaps, but not four.'

'He's playing at the moment.'

'We don't care a damn,' Pavel replied. 'Who does he think he is, after all?'

I dared go and disturb him while he was playing a game with a student. Leonid had just made his move and pressed the button on the time clock.

'Hey, Leonid, are you sure you didn't get it wrong? Mate in four moves is impossible. We all agree.'

'Can't you wait? I've told you that you should never disturb a player except if there's a fire in the Club. In the past, we would add: or if the Germans are attacking. There's no danger? Then get the hell out of here!'

I followed the game. To judge by his tense expression, his young opponent could not see a way of extricating himself from the position he was in. From time to time, he glanced at the minute hand of the clock which was approaching the fateful XII. Then he let out a long sigh, shook his head as though it were weighing him down, and toppled over his king.

'Bravo,' he murmured sharply.

He reached out his hand to Leonid, who shook it with his fingertips.

'Jacky,' Leonid called, 'bring a bottle of Côtes. The gentleman is inviting us. Won't you have a drink, young man?' he added.

'No thanks.'

'Whenever you want,' said Leonid as he poured himself a large glass of Côtes-du-Rhône.

He knocked it back in one gulp and filled the glass again.

Then, rubbing his back, he dragged himself to his feet and deigned to move over to our table.

'They're weird, these kids from Polytechnique. Good at maths and not great at chess. That guy could make it, but he plays with a tight ass. He's too frightened of losing.'

'Are you offering us a drink?' asked Pavel.

'I'll buy you one when you've improved. And it's not going to happen in a hurry.'

'This time, you've got it wrong!' announced Virgil, coming over to the table.

'You're just a load of wet blankets,' said Leonid as he made four moves with the black and white pieces. 'Mate. Not even my cat would want to play with you lot.'

Virgil and Pavel slipped away without saying anything.

'As for you,' Leonid told me, 'you're going to finish the game and try to understand why this dumb ass gave in. He at least saw what was coming.'

I leant over his chessboard and stood the king up.

'He was in a reasonable position, wasn't he?'

'It's not complicated. Not obvious, but fairly straightforward. I'll give you a clue. We had an identical set of moves last week, but there was one knight fewer.'

I stood staring at the chessboard for twenty minutes as though I was trying to discover the secret of some hieroglyphics.

'You're a great guy, Leonid. But I'll never understand it. Chess is like maths, I just don't get it.'

'The day you start using the brain you've got in your head, you'll get better.'

'That's all I ask for. How do I do it?'

'If I knew the answer, I'd give up the taxi. And my pockets would be full of dough.'

'Have you ever been really drunk?'

He thought about it, recalling distant memories.

'Dead drunk, you mean? Two or three times, when I was young, I felt a bit dizzy. During the war, I had quite a few. I stayed on my feet.'

Madeleine and Igor were scheming to make him eat the dish of the day, but he hardly ate any of it. He was polishing off the bottle of Côtes, and woe betide anyone who refused to serve him when he asked for another one.

'I'm paying. I'm not drunk. I'm not making a scene. Do your job and give us something to drink.'

'Leonid,' Igor would say, 'You're not eating anything. You're getting thin and people no longer recognize you. I wonder how you manage to go on. One day, you won't have the strength to drive.'

'I've never had an accident in my life.'

'It's none of my business,' Madeleine went on doggedly. 'But you're all skin and bone. You're a good-looking man, Leonid. If you go on like this, no woman will want you.'

'That's one thing less to bother about.'

'I think you have a problem with alcohol.'

'Madeleine, it's when I have no alcohol that I have problems. As my father used to say: as long as your hands don't shake, life is fine. It's when you start to fall over that things get serious. Vodka warms the heart. It's the only alcohol that doesn't freeze... Did I tell you the joke about Lenin and Gorky?'

They tried to remember and shook their heads one after the other.

'One day, Gorky is visiting his old friend Lenin and invites him to drink a rouble's worth of vodka. Lenin reminds him of the restrictions imposed by the revolution and refuses to drink more than half a rouble's worth. Gorky knows him well. He had invited him to Capri before the war. They had had one hell of a time. He insists and points out that two people with their level of eminence can give themselves a little extra. No one would dream of saying anything to them. Lenin is determined to resist and Gorky asks him the real reason why he is so obstinate. Lenin puts his head in his hands: "You see, Alexis Maximovitch, the last time I shared a rouble of vodka with a friend, it had such an effect on me that as I left I felt obliged to make a speech to the workers who were waiting there for me and, at this moment, I'm still trying to understand what I could have said for them to have behaved so bloody stupidly."'

3

Often I didn't have time to go to the Club after school, and I didn't feel like going home. I would call by at the city library, especially after Christiane started working there. Her husband had been transferred by his firm from Toulouse to Paris, where she knew nobody. The transition had been sudden. She hadn't managed to adapt to the city and its grim weather, nor to Marie-Pierre, the chief librarian, who didn't like her, she wasn't sure why, and made her do the least pleasant jobs such as sorting out the books or fining readers one centime for every day they were late with their returns. Christiane complied without making a fuss. As soon as she spoke, you noticed her accent. The first time, I thought she was being funny. And she didn't simply stamp the cards as Marie-Pierre did; every loan came with a comment: 'A very good choice', or 'You'll love it, it's one of his best novels.' And when she did not like a book or an author, she would merely remark: 'It's a book about which there's a great deal to say.'

I got to know her at the beginning of my Dostoevsky period. After *The Gambler*, I had felt so moved that I decided to embark on his entire oeuvre. It was the least I could do to show my gratitude. There were twenty-nine of the forty novels by the great Fyodor on the shelf, as well as some other writing. I took five of them and put them down on her table.

'Ah, *Poor Folk*, not bad for a first novel,' Christiane remarked. 'But I've never liked epistolary novels. You should read *Notes from Underground*. It's the sequel, twenty years later. It's a dreadful tragedy, about cynicism and self-hatred. One of Nietzsche's favourite novels.'

She carefully stamped the cards and then stamped the yellow sheets that were glued to the flyleaf with the date four weeks later, which was the last day for the books to be brought back.

'*The Double*? I haven't read it.'

'Why doesn't the public library have the entire works of Dostoevsky? Something must have happened. Why are eleven missing?'

'I don't really know. I agree something must have happened. I'll find out.'

About ten days later, I brought back the five books and took out five others.

'You're not going to tell me that you've read five novels in eleven days?' she asked in her sing-song accent.

'I read all the time, even in class.'

'In class?' she repeated incredulously.

'I put the book on my lap. I pretend to be listening and I manage to read in peace. The lessons are so boring.'

Almost every evening, we discussed books. She tried to persuade me to give up this habit of reading an author's entire works in one burst.

'It's silly. You've got to stick to the best, go for the classic ones. At least half of what Balzac, Dostoevsky, Dickens or Zola wrote is of no interest. You're wasting your time reading their bad books.'

'How will I know if I don't read them? You might praise a novel to the skies, and I wouldn't. I loved *White Nights* and you're telling me it's Dostoevsky's worst book. Who's right?'

But then I followed her advice and gave up reading writers systematically. She urged me towards contemporary novels, but we didn't share the same tastes.

'You should read *Portrait of a Lady*,' she suggested to me one evening when I had mentioned the mysteries of Anna Karenina's suicide. Before I could reply, she had got down from her platform, disappeared between two sets of shelves and returned with a book in a beige cover.

'Tell me what you think of it.'

I knew neither the title nor the author of this novel. I leafed through it and stopped at a random paragraph. I read three lots of ten lines, fifty pages apart. There is something irrational about reading. Before you read a book, you can know immediately whether or not you are going to like it, just as with people, you can tell just from looking at them whether or not you'll be their friend. You smell it, you sniff it, you wonder whether it's worth spending time in its company. The pages of a book have an invisible alchemy that imprints itself on our brain. A book is a living creature.

Christiane could tell that I was hooked. She couldn't stop herself adding, 'I don't want to anticipate. But compared to Isabel Archer, Karenina isn't worth the candle.'

Portrait of a Lady, and afterwards *The Wings of the Dove*, each earned me three days of detention. I still had the old habit of reading as I walked to school. But this time, I stood glued to the pavement, beside a zebra crossing, transported to Gardencourt:

> It stood upon a low hill, above the river – the river being the
> Thames at some forty miles from London. A long gabled front of
> red brick, with the complexion of which time and the weather
> had played all sorts of pictorial tricks, only, however, to improve
> and refine it, presented to the lawn its patches of ivy, its clustered
> chimneys, its windows smothered in creepers...

My repeated lateness incurred the wrath of Sherlock, who was convinced that I was a dilettante or someone who couldn't care less – the type he loathed. How could I explain to him that I couldn't help it? I was late. Whatever he said – that's all there is to it, there's no excuse, you'll do me three hours detention – it didn't matter to me. And I managed to keep all this from my parents. I would intercept the letter informing them of the detention and on Thursday afternoon, I'd be able to read in peace.

Cécile was the only one who knew about my habit. We were due to meet by the Médicis fountain before going for a run in the Luxembourg. I was standing facing the gardens, waiting for Isabel Archer to sort out her problem with Gilbert Osmond before I crossed the road. Eventually, I started walking. I heard Cécile yelling: 'You're crazy!'

'What's the matter?'

'Did you see how you crossed over?'

'How?'

'Reading! When you cross the road, you look: to left and to right. You crossed on the green light, with your nose stuck in your book. You nearly got run over by three cars. One of them had to swerve, didn't you notice?'

'Well, no.'

'Are you all right, Michel?'

'Not specially.'

'Are you taking the piss?'

'I've been doing it for years. Nothing has happened to me. Apart from being late and getting a detention.'

'You're stark raving mad!'

'I'm not the only one. There are lots of people who read while they walk.'

'How can you see them if you're reading? I've never seen anybody reading in the street. Sometimes people read the headlines of the newspaper. But they're standing still. When they start walking, they don't read. I can't believe it. It's madness. Pure and simple.'

'I have a radar.'

'You've got to swear to me that you won't read any more when you walk!'

The great novelists have frequently observed that women have a compelling need for certainty. Long passages of their narratives are to do with obtaining a promise. Their female characters mount fresh attacks, they insist over and over again, they make it a matter of life and death, and the men eventually yield.

'As you wish.'

'Swear to me.'

'Maybe we don't need to go quite so far.'

'Swear! Or else there's no point saying we're friends.'

'I swear to you.'

Cécile favoured me with one of those smiles of hers that made me melt. She kissed me as though I had just saved her life. She didn't bother to ask me what I was reading. We did four circuits of the Luxembourg then she bought us each a waffle with chestnut puree. The great novelists have observed that if women obtain clear-cut pledges from men, the men usually go on to break them For some writers betrayal is a matter of great importance, while for others it is less so. Those who cope with it successfully have material for a second book. Perhaps the originality of the modern novel, the mirror of its age, lies in the fact that it has allowed women, too, to break their promises, to be as disloyal as men are, and to become lonely.

4

'I t's a very important matter! What does that mean?' my father yelled at the telephone.

'Paul, there's no point shouting like that. The entire building can hear you,' complained my mother, who was holding the earpiece.

'I don't care! I couldn't give a damn. What is it that's so important?' he continued berating Maurice, who had just phoned us. 'Did your madame from the brothel tell you that?'

'Paul, the children,' said my mother.

'What about the children? What's wrong with the children? Don't they know what a whore is? Michel, do you know what a whore is?'

'I think so, yes. It's—'

'That's enough! Go to bed, children,' cried my mother, taking the receiver and handing him the earpiece.

'Maurice, it's me... What do you mean by: "it's not a simple matter of desertion"?'

My father snatched the phone from my mother.

'What's this bloody story all about? Where are we? On the moon? We're in France! There are laws, fucking hell. I've a right to know what's happened to him. Do you understand? I've a right!... Are there still lawyers in Algiers? You haven't killed them all? What are you waiting for before you get off your arse and go and call on the best lawyer in the fucking city?... They can get stuffed, the court, the judge and the whole of the French army! It's not the Gestapo! I'm going to show them that this is a lad who's got some balls!'

He put the phone down unceremoniously.

'I'm leaving for Algiers tomorrow morning!'

'Let's let Maurice deal with it.'

'He does nothing. Apart from going for a shag in the brothel.'

'Paul, please.'

'My son's in difficulty. I'm not just going to sit here twiddling my thumbs. He needs help.'

'We have to know where he is in order to help him. How are you going to find him? Do you think it will just happen? He had a deferral, the idiot. No one obliged him to join up. He was lucky to be able to study. He's only got himself to blame. He's no longer a child, he's a man.'

'I have to go there. That's the way it is and that's the way it's going to be!'

My father left the next day. For five days, we heard no news of him. Maurice had gone to meet him at Maison-Blanche, the airport for Algiers, but my father had told him that he intended to manage without him. Maurice had watched him get into a taxi and he didn't know where he was. My mother continued to work as though nothing had happened. We listened to the news on the radio and, between the bombs and the assassination attempts, what we heard was not reassuring.

Cécile telephoned when I failed to turn up for our meeting in the Luxembourg. I told her that I was ill. I could tell from the sound of her voice that she didn't believe me.

'What's wrong, Michel?'

'Nothing.'

'You've got a strange voice.'

'It's this chronic bronchitis.'

'I'll be at the Luxembourg tomorrow, if you can make it.'

I called in at the Balto. I wanted to tell Igor everything. He was playing a game with Werner, which Imré was watching attentively. I sat down opposite him, waiting for an opportune moment.

'What a face you're making,' Imré said.

'What's the matter?' asked Werner.

'I don't want to bore you with my problems.'

'You look as if you're going to a funeral,' said Igor.

'Did someone die at home?' Imré continued.

'It's not that.'

'If no one's dead, don't make that face,' Igor concluded.

'You're overdoing it,' replied Werner. 'Let him speak.'

I was about to begin when I noticed Lognon. There he was, in between Werner and Igor, and, as usual, no one had seen or heard him arrive. We had just noticed his presence, without knowing how long he had been there.

'So, Big Ears, still nosing around?' asked Imré.

'Forget it,' said Igor. 'It's best not to talk here.'

'That's true,' Lognon responded in a low voice, looking at me. 'Particularly on the telephone. But if we don't talk to one another, life's going to become rather sad, don't you think?'

He turned and slipped away stealthily to the nearby table where Vladimir and Tomasz were playing and were not aware that he was kibitzing.

'What did he mean?' Werner asked.

'I think I know,' I said, staring at Big Ears' massive silhouette.

That evening, we waited in vain for a call from my father. Juliette was clearly anxious.

'There's no point worrying about your father, my girl. He'll phone us when he can.'

To reassure her, my mother rang Maurice, who had no news.

'You see what I was saying to you. How can he think he'll do better than Uncle Maurice with all his connections? He always thinks he knows best.'

I decided to tell Cécile what was going on and I met her at the Médicis fountain. No sooner had I arrived than she took out of her pocket a letter from Pierre.

'So, he's replied to you at last.'

My Cécile,

Sorry for the delay, I'm failing in my epistolary duties. I was feeling a bit low. The first chapter of your thesis reassures me about your involvement but I'm not sure you're on the right track when you mention that old bore. You do him a favour by suggesting he was subject to all those influences you credit him with. Be careful not to over-interpret: communism is neither a variant of nor a development of surrealism as you imply. I would take advantage of the fact that the old croc is still alive to go and ask him a few questions that will make him appear less attractive. I'll wait impatiently to hear what happens next.

The poll carried out among my belote and jokari friends has proved a disaster. They couldn't care less about politics. The fabulous invention of democracy is capitalism's ultimate way of preserving the existing order. The exploited are neither numbed nor worn out, they are bought. They are given crumbs and they hurl themselves at them like starving rats. They trust in de Gaulle to guide them, especially since there's talk of sending our regiment home to metropolitan France. What they want is to make the most of it. They're not interested in hearing about the revolution. Today's working class dreams of pressure-cookers, cars with caravans, and televisions. How can you create a revolution with guys like that? I've lost any desire I had to write anything. My great book on the happiness of the world vanished on the high plateaux south of Constantine. Saint-Justisme was simply crap. Even Saint-Just didn't dare make a theory out of it. What's the point of trying to prove you're right when reality just comes down to surviving or dying? Here, you realize that humanism is a load of rubbish. There's no point in respecting others. They have to be crushed. It's a matter of life or death. It's the law of evolution. I had filled three notebooks of one hundred and twenty pages each to demonstrate that the imbeciles and the enemies of freedom have to be bumped off remorselessly and prevented from doing harm, and I had written a mass of drivel about the revolution, the crassness of democracy and how disgraceful it is for the load of morons that surround us to have the right to vote. Yesterday evening, on our return from patrol, I destroyed the lot. Saint-Justisme was a fine dream, it has vanished for ever in the flames of a camp fire.

Yesterday, I became a shit, just like the other guys. I killed a man I didn't know. I lined him up in my sights and I had a choice. To shoot or not to shoot. He didn't suspect a thing. I wondered what he was thinking, what his opinions were, whether he was rich or poor, whether he had parents, a wife, children. I had no answer to these questions. His mistake was to be a fellagha and so I fired. From about a kilometre away, his head exploded. We got eight of them but it won't change a thing.

As for you, Michel, I'm interested in meeting your revolutionary pals. I didn't know any still existed. Do me a favour. Ask them before they forget: what's the best way of making a Molotov cocktail? It might well come in handy. I'd be glad to play a few games of chess with them. Better take some lessons, you little bugger, because I was a champion even though it's been donkey's years since I've played. What I have improved at is baby-foot. There's a table at the mess and I am the goalkeeper selected by a lieutenant in the Legion who's a baby-foot champion. We won the match against the paras from Constantine. No comment. Have you had any news of your ass of a brother? He's vanished into thin air…

I handed the letter back to Cécile. She paused. I was expecting her to ask me for an explanation, but she didn't want to pose the question. She got to her feet and set off at a trot. I followed close behind. As usual. Sport is a common escape from communication.

That evening my father called. My mother picked up the phone. There was a moment's hesitation. I rushed over and grabbed the earpiece.

'He mustn't speak, he mustn't say anything!' I yelled. 'They're listening to us!'

'What?'

'He mustn't say anything on the phone. The police are listening to us!'

'Paul, Michel's here and he's saying that you shouldn't speak.'

'Why?'

'You mustn't tell him, Mama.'

'If I don't tell him, he won't know. And—'

'Hello? Hello? Can you hear me?'

'Paul, have you any news?'

'It's a disaster. They're prosecuting Franck for the murder of an officer. That's why he deserted.'

'What is this all about?'

283

'He killed a captain in the parachute regiment. I've engaged the best lawyer in Algiers. Franck vanished two months ago.'

My mother slumped back into her chair.

'It's unbelievable! Are you... are you sure of what you're saying?'

'According to the lawyer, he may have gone over to the FLN. That's why they can't find him.'

'I don't believe it!'

'We haven't actually been able to get hold of his case file. We managed to get some information from—'

I took the receiver out of my mother's hand.

'Papa, it's Michel. How are you?'

'Don't worry, my boy.'

'When are you coming home?'

'I don't know. We must find him before the military police do. Apparently, deserters—'

'Is it dangerous? Are there bomb attacks?'

'Sometimes you can hear explosions. You don't know where they're coming from. I'm at the Aletti Hotel in the centre of town, and it's just like Paris. People go out in the evening, they go to the restaurant, they stroll about with their families and eat ice cream. I speak to a lot of people. They're convinced they're going to stay put. They haven't understood a thing. You wouldn't think you were in a country that's at war.'

'Look after yourself, Papa.'

I gave the phone back to my mother.

'Listen, I don't know what he's on about, but you can't stay away for long. There's nothing we can do for him. There are masses of orders to deal with. This is where you are needed.'

'Have you understood nothing, Hélène? I've come to look for my son. I won't leave until I've found him.'

She put down the receiver, shrugged her shoulders and stared at me suspiciously.

'What's all this business about phone tapping?'

'With modern devices, the police can record calls. You have to be discreet on the phone.'

'How do you know this?'

'I've read about it. In a novel.'

'You read too much, Michel. You'd do better to get on with your work.'

I was reading in my bedroom when Juliette came in.

'Am I disturbing you?'

'Juliette, I've told you a hundred times to knock before you come in.'

She sat down on the side of my bed. Néron joined us and began washing himself.

'What are you reading?'

'*Le Lion* by Kessel. A friend lent it to me. Kessel inscribed it to him: "To Igor Emilievitch Markish. For our wonderful past evenings and the even better ones still to come. With my best wishes. Jef." I can't let you have it, but you'll find it in the library.'

'I don't like library books. They're not clean.'

'You're more at risk when catching the bus or going to the cinema.'

'Is the book good?'

'There's not much plot and the story is magical. It takes place in a game reserve in Kenya with Masai warriors everywhere. It's about a girl of your age who makes friends with a lion. He's not tame. He's a monster. She knows how to live with wild animals but not with humans.'

I handed her the book. She had a faraway look in her eyes.

'Does this mean that Franck has killed someone? Is that it?'

'For the time being, he's disappeared. He's in hiding. Papa's taking care of it.'

'What are they going to do to him if they catch him?'

'I think he'll go to prison.'

She continued to look thoughtful. Néron rolled himself into a ball at the foot of the bed and went to sleep.

'For how long?'

'That depends on what he's done.'

'Will it be awkward for us?'

'I don't know.'

'If he doesn't find him, will Papa not come back?'

'He has to look after the shop.'

'May I sleep with you this evening?'

When I woke up, Juliette was no longer in my bedroom. Néron and *Le Lion* had disappeared. I had two hours of maths with Shrivel-face and I couldn't make up my mind whether to go in. I almost rang Cécile to find out whether I should ask about how to make a Molotov cocktail and whether she wanted to go for a run. But I told myself that it wasn't the right day to see her. I could never have kept anything from her. I grabbed *L'Arrache-coeur* by Boris Vian, which I kept hidden, and set off for school.

I'd just reached place du Panthéon when, immediately behind me, I heard a voice I knew: 'Keep walking. Don't turn around. Take rue Valette, to the right. Look ahead of you. You shouldn't read when you're walking!'

I began walking down rue Valette. Lots of pupils were waiting outside the Collège Sainte-Barbe.

'Stop! Go into this building!'

I pushed open the door of number 13. I walked down a poorly lit corridor and turned round at the corner. In front of me stood Franck.

5

One day, the fighting had stopped. No more bombardments, no more shelling from dive-bombers, no more explosions, or the blasts of tanks and guns; no more acrid smells of oil or burning wood, no more yelling. Peace, at last. No cries of victory, nothing. A disturbing silence. Cities destroyed as far as the eye could see, transformed into vast piles of rubble. Crazed-looking civilians who found that nothing remained. Streets that had disappeared. Corpses nobody had the strength to bury. Endless lines of bearded, filthy and unkempt prisoners. Why? Who? Was it all going to begin again? During the Polish campaign, a few months earlier, the camps had been liberated, revealing things impossible to name and understand: the discovery of mass graves, the death industry, the hordes of living skeletons, the typhus, the victors who were more bitter than those they had conquered. The shame, the hatred, the madness. And, up until April, in Germany, hideous camps on the outskirts of the cities. Then acts of vengeance against the captured German soldiers and the civilian populations.

On 8 May, Leonid's squadron had been the last to return to base. For him, it was not an evening of celebration. He had had to wait weeks before he took part in the victory parade on Red Square on Sunday 24 June. In spite of the gloomy skies, it had been the biggest military parade of all time. A glorious occasion, the like of which had not been since ancient Rome. The drums in their hundreds and a host of brass fanfares of *A Slave's Farewell* had given the millions of delirious survivors goose pimples, as had the vast army marching past the marshals who were standing side by side – Zhukov on his white horse and Rokossovsky on his black horse – and the way the standards of the defeated armies of the Reich had been thrown pell-mell at the feet of the victor, perched on top of Lenin's mausoleum. Leading his Yak 9 squadron, Leonid had flown three times over Moscow. That evening, he had received from the hands of the Little Father of the Russian people his second gold star as a Hero of the Soviet Union.

After forty-seven months of uninterrupted fighting, Colonel Leonid Mikhaïlovitch Krivoshein had returned to find his homeland devastated, his city, Leningrad, razed to the ground, his parents dead from hunger, cold and disease, and an endless list of friends killed in the fighting or from the bombing. He had not been able to find his girlfriend, Olga Anatolievna Pirojkova. He had had no news of her and he hadn't written to her for over three years.

Two years after Leonid returned home, a nightmare left him sweating and his heart thumping. His plane was on fire, spiralling downwards like a spinning top, and he was a prisoner in the cockpit and could see the ground coming closer by the second. During the nights that followed, the demons of the war came back to torment him, and in his mind's eye he saw once more the slaughter of civilians and soldiers. Images of the gunfire, the raping, the brutality and the spectres of concentration camp prisoners haunted him and woke him with a start at exactly half past two every morning, and he remained awake, unable to get back to sleep. He refused the sleeping pills prescribed by the doctor, Major Rovine. Taking medicine meant that you were ill and, in spite of this weariness, he felt in good health. He waited in the surgery, sitting opposite the young doctor, who consulted numerous specialist books in the hope of finding a treatment then asked him two or three questions before immersing himself in his books once more. In the medical corps, Dimitri Vladimirovitch Rovine had lived through the same battles as Leonid. They wondered how they had managed to survive and not come across one another. He was a doctor who did not believe in the power of medicine and who was convinced that we ourselves are the sole cause of our illnesses. 'We're living in the Stone Age,' he used to say, as if to apologize.

He prescribed his remedies with a sceptical and perplexed air and seemed surprised when they succeeded. Very soon, the two men became inseparable. Rovine had three attributes that made him a good friend: he talked constantly about the war, he knocked back his drink and he was a remarkable chess player.

Eventually Rovine admitted: 'I know of no cure for you.'

Leonid decided to exhaust himself physically in order to be able to sleep. To fight against himself. He walked until daybreak without meeting a living soul. At the first call of the clarion, he joined the marines in their training sessions, said to be the toughest in the army. He found hidden strength to keep up with the ferocious pace demanded of the privates by the Staff Sergeants. During the day, he went to the air base to establish exactly how many spare parts the air force had, an interminable and pointless task that no one had asked him to do. He dared to do battle with the military bureaucracy in order to stop them ordering just anything and, since it was rumoured that he might be appointed divisional squadron leader, they promised him they would do what was necessary. Sergei Ilyushin personally invited him to join his research consultancy to work on the project for a long-range aircraft that would be capable of raids deep into the rear of the enemy. Leonid couldn't imagine himself being a sedentary engineer, especially in Moscow, and he dreamed of only one thing: piloting his plane. Ilyushin insisted. Leonid agreed on condition that he would be the number one test pilot but received no reply.

In the evening he drank and played chess with Rovine. The drink had no effect on him. He increased the dose. He consumed several bottles of vodka with his chess partner, who succumbed before he had been beaten, and he eventually collapsed, numb with tiredness, only to spring out of his slumber an hour later. His eyelids were swollen, his temples heavy, and there was an anvil at the back of his skull and a blacksmith who kept hammering at his forehead. Only the bags of crushed ice that he pressed to his brow from dusk till dawn afforded him slight comfort.

One evening as he was strolling along the River Neva, the smell came, insidious and hard to identify. He returned to his bedroom. The smell followed him.

'Can you smell something horrible?' he asked his colleagues at the barracks, who sniffed but could not detect anything apart from the cabbage that was cooking. 'No, not that one. There are some rotting corpses somewhere.'

They searched, but in vain. The stench remained, clinging and acrid. No one suspected him. He was a hero of the Soviet Union, one of the most decorated men in the land, a close friend of Stalin's. The generals and the political commissars spoke of him with respect and esteem. They looked again, they searched the cellars and the most hidden recesses of the fortress; they checked the riverbanks and the destroyed mansions nearby. They thought that a concealed mass grave might be uncovered, but they found no trace of one. The smell persisted and it was unbearable, even when the north wind blew and swept away everything in its path, or when he pressed a pile of handkerchiefs to his nose, or when he wore a gas mask. The smell permeated everything; it prevented him sleeping, it suffocated him. The treatments prescribed by the most eminent university professors proved ineffectual. The only means of relief he found was to soak a handkerchief with vodka, so that the alcohol obliterated the stench. But breathing it in made him drunk, and the odour seeped in beneath the alcohol. He wondered whether he might be rotting internally. When yet another well-known professor confessed his own helplessness and admitted that the only possible treatment was a course of therapy that could take years without guaranteed success, Leonid decided he'd had enough. He hadn't survived four years of war in order to die a lingering death. He took this decision in a flash. It was obvious. It was the only solution. He put his affairs in order, wrote a letter to his sister who lived in Moscow, to whom he bequeathed the little he owned, and asked to be buried at the Tikhvine cemetery at the Nevsky monastery. He prepared himself. He had thought it would be agonizing, that he would feel deeply distressed and be racked with regrets, but he felt calm and serene. He downed a flask of vodka and tidied his office. Before leaving, he asked himself what were the ten most beautiful things that he had seen during his life and he decided that he would pull the trigger after the tenth. He thought of his mother Marina, of her smile that forgave him everything, and of his sister's infectious laughter. And memories came back to him of Leningrad before the war, before the most beautiful city in the world was destroyed. He saw once more the images of his youth, the northern lights over frozen Lake Ladoga, the Hermitage and its vanished treasures,

Petrodvorets and its hanging gardens, Saint Nicholas the Sailor with its thousands of twinkling icons, and Smolny, the white and the blue, with its delicate golden domes in the pristine sky. He was disconcerted to notice that all the wonders of his city dated from the time of the Tsars and the clergy, and that his own generation had brought nothing but destruction. He didn't deserve to live after allowing such a disaster to occur. He counted on his fingers.

He had reached eight when, in spite of the late hour, there was knocking at his door. He opened the door to Rovine, who had seen the light on in his window. He was holding a large, white porcelain teapot and he wanted Leonid to drink the potion he had prepared for him. He insisted, pushed him away with his arm, sat down on a chair without asking, requested that he close the windows, and poured some dark green liquid into a bowl.

'What is it?'

'Tea.'

'Your tea has a smell of ether.'

'It's been difficult to get hold of. I've been searching for some for a month. Drink.'

Leonid drank the burning liquid in small sips.

'Supposing we played a game?'

'Thank you, Dimitri Vladimirovitch, but it's not the right moment.'

'Are you tired, perhaps?'

'I've got work to do.'

'You know what they say in the kolkhozes? One should always put off till tomorrow what can be done today. Perhaps you're frightened I'll beat you?'

Leonid told himself that chess had been his one real pleasure in life and that a final game would be a good way to go. What's more, he had to win it. Rovine was a tough player who didn't attack much, hid behind an impenetrable defence and, being an excellent finisher, waited for his opponent to make a mistake without taking any risks himself. Rovine set out the pieces on the chessboard. Leonid grabbed a bottle of vodka and two glasses.

'Are you joking? No alcohol! You're drinking tea. I, on the other hand, will have some with pleasure.'

Rovine picked up the handkerchief soaked in vodka that Leonid was using and threw it in the dustbin. He poured some tea into Leonid's bowl and some vodka into his own glass.

'Why are you doing that? This tea's disgusting. What is it?'

'Don't ask pointless questions and just play. I'll let you have white. You'll need them. I'm intending to teach you a lesson.'

Leonid hesitated between two pieces, changed his mind, then advanced a pawn two squares and started the clock. Rovine took his own pawn and placed it opposite Leonid's.

'I don't mean to be rude to you,' Rovine remarked. 'But this game is only interesting if one observes two or three rules. In chess, a piece that is touched is a piece that has been played. I'd like you to remember that.'

'You're right, Dimitri Vladimirovitch, I won't do it again. While we're on the subject of rules, I'd remind you that you should press the button of the clock with the hand that has just made the move.'

They played without talking, absorbed in the game. With an instinctive gesture, Leonid picked up the bottle of vodka. Rovine was quicker than him and poured him what was left in the teapot. The game lasted close to two hours. The pointer of the clock was close to XII. Taken aback by Rovine's cast-iron defence, Leonid was showing signs of irritation.

'You've taken advantage of the condition I'm in to gain the upper hand. That's unfair.'

'Three minutes more and you'll be out of time'

'You're playing for time. It's really boring.'

'The important thing is to win. If I'd attacked, you'd have beaten me.'

'Are you ignoring the rule that forbids a subaltern from beating his senior officer? At least I allowed Stalin to win the game.'

'That's the difference between us. If it were me, I'd have beaten him. And you're not my senior officer.'

Leonid put his hands to his head and stared at the board intently, searching for a miraculous solution that would get him out of this hornets' nest. His position was desperate and there was no sign of any dramatic change. He was on the point of knocking over his king when he sniffed several times.

'I no longer smell anything!'

'I'm pleased for you.'

'Is it what you gave me to drink? What did you put in the teapot?'

'Some simple things.'

Leonid stood up, opened the window wide and breathed the freezing night air into his lungs.

'It's extraordinary, I no longer smell anything! Tell me, Dimitri Vladimirovitch, am I cured?'

'I'm sorry, Leonid Mikhaïlovitch, but this smell will come back. We don't know how to cure what is wrong with you. A psychoanalyst might perhaps, but it's not the kind of thing we deal with. When the smell returns, sniff this.'

From his pocket he took a small brown phial and gave it to him.

'It's pure essence of eucalyptus. When the smell comes back, you must drink eucalyptus tea twice a day. It's not nice, but there's no other treatment. Morning and evening, you must have eucalyptus fumigations. The hardest thing will be to find some.'

'Why didn't you give me any before?'

'At the university they look down on this type of remedy. An old woman who sells herbal teas recommended it. I had to move heaven and earth to find any.'

Rovine gave him a tablet to soothe his headache without telling him it was a sleeping pill.

'Thank you, Dimitri Vladimirovitch. It's the first time that I'm happy to lose a game.'

That night, Leonid slept like a child.

6

W e stood there face to face for a few seconds, then we hugged one
another. He clasped me tightly to him and didn't let me go. I
could smell his strange aroma of damp earth and tobacco.

'I'm glad to see you.'

'So am I. We wondered where you were. How are you?'

Over the sixteen months, his hair had grown and was now curly.
Several days' growth of beard made him look stern. He was thinner. His
crumpled, dust-covered jacket was too big for him.

'How long have you been back?'

He was on the qui vive, straining to listen. He put his finger to his
lips and drew me into the recess beneath the staircase. Somebody was
coming down. He shoved me against the cellar door. The sound of footsteps had ceased. The metallic sound of a key in the lock could be heard.
An old woman, with a stick, was taking her post from the letterbox.
She walked away down the corridor and left the building. The light had
gone out. I wanted to switch it on again, but he grabbed my hand and
stopped me.

'Don't make any noise,' he whispered. 'We'll go that way. There's an
exit from the building onto rue Laplace.'

We moved forward in the darkness, guided by the beam of light from
the other entrance.

'Walk along as though nothing's the matter and keep an eye out for a
cop or a guy in civilian clothes who's hanging around or who looks odd.
Go and stand in front of the window of the baker's shop and look to right
and left. Do you have a bit of cash on you?'

I rooted around in my pocket and brought out some small change.

'Two francs fifty. It's not much. Take rue Laplace. Stop a little further
along. We'll go to the Bois-Charbon.'

The street was deserted. I noticed nothing unusual and set off down towards the École Polytechnique, putting on a casual air. Franck followed close behind.

'It's on the left.'

We walked into a small café where the owner was playing a game of 421 with a customer. We went and sat down at the back of the restaurant. Some regulars were chatting at the bar and took no notice of us.

'Two *crèmes*,' Franck asked the owner.

We sat there without speaking. He brought us the coffees.

'The police came to the apartment. They did a search.'

'When was that?'

'Christmas Eve.'

'They didn't hang around.'

'It caused quite a fuss, I can tell you.'

'I imagine. And Papa, where is he? I've been watching out for him for several days.'

'Papa? He's in Algeria.'

'What the hell is he doing there?'

'He's looking for you.'

'When did he leave?'

'About a month ago. We expected Maurice to find things out, but he wasn't able to, so Papa went there to find you. Mama didn't want him to go, but once he's made up his mind there's no way of stopping him.'

'He doesn't realize. It's not France down there, it's the Far West. You must let him know I'm here.'

'It's not going to be easy. Our phone's being tapped. They must be doing it at his hotel, too.'

'How do you know that?'

'I've been warned that we should be discreet on the phone. I'm going to try and find a way.'

He drank his *café crème*, blowing on it to cool it down. His fingers were stained yellow from nicotine.

'I need money, Michel.'

'I haven't got any. I've got my savings bank book, but if I touch it, Mama will see and ask me why.'

'I'm hungry. I've not had a bite to eat since yesterday morning.'

'I can't believe it!'

'So how do you think I'm going to be able to buy anything to eat?'

'I thought you had friends.'

'My friends want to hand me over to the cops. I'm on my own. There's only you and Papa.'

He drew aside the flaps of his overcoat and I could see the butt of a revolver tucked into his belt.

'I've got nothing more to lose.'

'You're crazy, Franck! I've got a bit of money I'd kept for... I've not spent my pocket money. I'm going to give you—'

'That won't be enough!' he shouted irritably.

He pulled himself together immediately. The owner glared at us and frowned.

'I need cash,' he continued in a low voice. 'I've got to get away, and quickly. Otherwise, they'll catch me.'

'OK, I know where to get some. It's not a problem. There are some people who'll help me. Until Papa returns. You'll have a bit tomorrow. Where can I find you?'

'I've got no address. I sleep in cellars, mate. I swap around every night. I've really got no choice. If you borrow any money, no one must know it's for me. If you need to talk to me, put your book under your left arm. If it's urgent, under the right arm. And stop reading while you're walking! Do you want to get run over or something?'

'It's funny, that's exactly what Cécile said to me. Word for word.'

'Do you still see her? Is she all right?'

'Do you really want to know?'

He paused and let out a sigh.

'No, not really. Got any fags?'

'I don't smoke.'

'The money, can you bring me some this evening?'

'I'm going to try.'

'We'll meet here after your classes are over. If you don't see me, it means there's a problem. I'll get in touch again when I can. And above

296

all, say nothing to Cécile, or to Mama. Or anyone. Leave me your money.'

'Did you really kill someone?'

He nodded his head in a continuous motion.

'He was a bastard! I don't regret a thing.'

'What happened?'

'I'd prefer not to talk about it.'

I got to my feet, put my two francs fifty on the table and I left the bar. I had missed two hours of maths and I wouldn't hear the end of it. How was I supposed to make progress under these conditions? There are some obligations you simply can't escape from. It was like a sort of curse. I made a detour through Maubert and boulevard Saint-Michel so as not to risk bumping into Sherlock and I avoided the Luxembourg in case I met Cécile. I was going to have to come up with a cast-iron explanation to justify a day's absence. The future of the boys in our family didn't look very bright. I set off for Igor's place. I had only been there twice before, the previous year, when he had decided to go and live in a small fourth-floor apartment not far from Werner's home, overlooking the courtyard of a brick building on rue Henri-Barbusse. He had appealed for volunteers to help him move and to paint everything from the floor to the ceiling in white. I rang the bell for five minutes. I was on the point of going downstairs again when I heard the door open and Igor appeared, wearing pyjamas, with dishevelled hair and a crazed expression on his face.

'What time is it?'

'Eleven o'clock.'

'In the morning! Oh shit! You're crazy waking me up. Don't you know I work nights? I went to bed at eight. And with the racket that bastard upstairs makes, I couldn't get to sleep.'

'I've got a problem, Igor.'

He peered at me, his eyes asquint, rubbing his forehead.

'I couldn't give a damn, Michel. I need to sleep, do you understand?'

'It's a serious problem.'

He turned around and made as if to go back into his apartment.

'What are you waiting for? Come on in!'

He slammed the door behind me. I went and sat down in the kitchen.

I could hear the noise of the shower. Igor came back, dripping wet, wrapped in a bath towel like a Roman emperor. He was in a bad mood and made himself some coffee.

'I hope for your sake that you've got a really serious problem,' he grumbled.

7

To hell with principles if a pill was all it took to lead a normal life. Once he had slept, Leonid regained his lost vitality and felt ten years younger. He went out with his friends once more and began to have fun again. He was the old pre-war Leonid, handsome and charming, who could enthral a gathering until the small hours with his funny stories. In the aftermath of wars, especially ones as brutal as this one, women are more numerous than men and this unmarried colonel, adorned with his prestigious decorations, was a good catch. Leonid had no intention of allowing himself to be led to the altar and made the most of his good fortune. His company was sought after. He was invited to the numerous parties that enlivened the Leningrad nights. The survivors needed to make up for lost time and get the most out of life.

People devoted all their energy to the reconstruction of the city and its destroyed monuments. During a reception to mark the start of works at the Kirov, he met Sonia Viktorovna Petrovna, who was working on the restoration of the plasterwork at the Winter Palace. It was hard to imagine a more different couple, and no one understood how they had come to be attracted to one another. They shared no common tastes or ideas and disagreed about everything, but two things brought them close: Leonid admired Sonia because she drank as much as he did without getting drunk, and they had a perfect physical understanding. They got married two months later. The registrar and the guests were impressed by the warm message of congratulations sent to them by Stalin. It was a simple wedding in the Soviet style, washed down with vodka, with the traditional photograph in front of the equestrian statue of Peter the Great that had just been restored.

Leonid was a pragmatic military man, a son of the revolution, a steadfast communist for whom the question of whether the party was right was as absurd as asking whether one and one made three. Sonia was an idealist who had seen her family and friends decimated by the war and the arrests, and who loathed the communists. For her Leonid was not like the others. There was a fragility and vulnerability about this colonel with his string of decorations that moved her deeply. He snuggled up to her and forgot his anxieties. She was always cold, even in mid-summer. He took her in his arms and he warmed her. He often fell asleep at daybreak. She didn't dare wake him.

Leonid knew that a technological revolution was under way and he wanted to be part of it. Since the end of the war, thanks to the German equipment reclaimed by the Red Army and the German research workers who were now part of the NKVD's* department of scientific operations, Soviet manufacturers had been hell-bent on being the first to fly a jet plane. After lengthy prevarications, the Defence Board had selected two research consultancies to develop a fighter plane capable of attaining an altitude of 12,500 metres, achieving a flight range of at least 700 kilometres and flying at more than 850 kilometres per hour, a speed and specifications that were insane, but which would give the country a decisive advantage in the likely event of a war against its former allies. Leonid had to make a strategic choice. Which constructor should he apply to work for? To the well-established Yakovlev, or to the young engineers, Mikoyan and Gourevitch, who appeared to possess limitless means and connections? Wonderful things were said about their new Mig, but he had had no contact with them, whereas Leonid knew Alexander Yakovlev. He had flown all his planes, from the Yak 1 at the beginning of the war to the latest version of the Yak 3, and Leonid had given him valuable advice as to how they might evolve. Yakovlev was not surprised by Leonid's request. He knew his good qualities and agreed to include him in his team of test pilots. He showed him the prototype of the jet plane of the future, the Yak 15. Leonid gave no explanation to Sonia other than that his new duties called him to Moscow. She would not be allowed to accompany him. He expected reproaches, but she resigned herself to a

---

* The NKVD, the Soviet Security Service and Secret police, would be broken up into the MGB and MVD in 1946 and renamed the KGB in 1953. Tr.

long separation. He was preparing the administrative formalities for his departure when he received a phone call from Yakovlev: 'There's a problem, Leonid Mikhaïlovitch. I am obliged to cancel our project.'

'Why?'

'It's an order from Timoshenko. I'm sorry.'

The People's Commissar of Defence had a dreadful reputation. Rovine advised Leonid against seeking clarification, but Leonid was furious, and was determined to disregard the decision and join Yakovlev's team. He got an appointment and made the journey to Moscow, where Semyon Timoshenko received him politely.

'It's not possible to allow you to join the Mig or the Yakovlev teams. The death rate among test pilots is so high that there's no question of a Hero of the Soviet Union risking his life in such a dangerous activity.'

'I've taken greater risks every day of the war.'

'Of the eighty pilots of your year, you're the only one who survived. You're among the 5 per cent of Russian military survivors to have begun the war. Imagine what would be said if there was an accident. We have to make way for the young. And test pilots are bachelors.'

'I'll get divorced tomorrow morning.'

'No point.'

'I can still serve my country.'

'You shall have the opportunity to do so.'

'I want to fly. I'm going to be forced to speak to you know who.'

'He told me that he would hold me responsible if anything happened to you.'

Leonid was offered command of an air squadron. It was an honour for a man of his age, but he was not overjoyed at the thought of this promotion. Obedience among military men is often merely resignation. He should have understood that the time had come for him to settle down. But in spite of his fame and his medals, he wanted to be at the controls of a plane and to fly, to find himself in solitary communion once more with the immensity of the sky. His friends told him he should move on to something else, give Sonia some children, start a family. He replied that he felt like a caged bird and would die of boredom if he were shut up in an office.

In the autumn of '46, Leonid heard that the civil aviation company Aeroflot was looking for pilots to operate the new routes that were about to be opened. He applied, convinced that he would be welcomed with open arms. He was turned down. He had no civil licence. He asked for leave and enrolled at the Civil Aeronautical Institute in Leningrad. The hardest thing was learning to speak English. He obtained his licence at the first attempt. The company rejected his application again on the pretext that it was draconian as far as the soberness of its pilots was concerned, a decision which made them all laugh heartily on the tarmac of Cheremetievo airport. This time, he applied to the proper quarters. Leonid Krivoshein then became one of the few pilots, the only one of this rank, to resign from the Red Army and join Aeroflot, where he was taken on as second in command on the new Ilyushin 12, which had just been put into service on the Moscow–London route.

The following year, he was promoted to chief pilot. At the controls of his plane, he was the happiest man in the world. To his proud achievements, he added a justified reputation as a real charmer. Aeroflot used him as a symbol in its new campaign and a photograph of him, dressed in his fine navy blue uniform, adorned the company's advertising posters. Leonid was a hero. All Russians knew his name and his brave deeds. Children imitated him when they played. His photo was in the schoolbooks. He was spoken of with the respect men pay to demi-gods and he would still be a hero of the people had he not, during a stopover at Orly, met Milène Reynolds.

8

It was midday. Igor had listened to me carefully, asked three questions and had finished the coffee in the pot.

'You could have talked to me about it before.'

'I tried to. It's not easy to come in and pour out your problems like some sales rep. Is it serious, do you reckon?'

'How can one tell? With the army, it's the same in every country. Secrecy. Even when it serves no purpose. The main thing is to warn your father. If you ring him at his hotel, the police will know your brother's in Paris. You've got to speak to him somewhere else.'

'At my Uncle Maurice's.'

'Too risky. You have to be quicker than the police. Give me a bit of time. I'm going to ask an expert for some tips.'

'I think I know who it is.'

'If you know, forget about it.'

He left the kitchen and came back with a wad of banknotes, which he laid on the table.

'There's seventy thousand francs.'

'Seven hundred francs, you mean.'

'I can't get the hang of *nouveaux francs*.'

'It's a lot. I'll take three hundred francs. That should be enough for him until my father returns.'

'Take it all. You never know what may happen. If he needs it, it will be of some help.'

'It's a lot of money. I don't know whether I'll be able to pay you back and I can't promise my father will.'

'It doesn't matter. It's only money.'

'I'm really grateful to you, Igor, for what you're doing. I won't forget it.'

'You're lucky, Michel, but it's not for you that I'm doing this.'

'It's not for my brother, you don't know him.'

Igor poured the last dregs of coffee into his cup, stood up and started making some more.

'You see, when I left the USSR, ten years ago, I hadn't planned my departure. I had to get out very quickly. I abandoned my wife, my children, my job. It took me a minute to decide. Either I left immediately, or else it was the firing squad. I had nothing. I left with a loaf of bread. I was lucky. On the way, I met someone who helped me. A peasant from a forestry collective in Karelia. He knew I was on the run. He could have shot me or handed me over, but he showed me the way to Finland, avoiding the frontier guards. He gave me some biscuits and some dried herrings. When I asked him his name in order to thank him, he told me that I didn't need to know it, that had he been able to do so he would have come with me, and he asked me to remember him back there.'

'You never talk about your family.'

'I don't, and neither do the others. We think about them every day, every hour. We haven't any hope of seeing them again. It's impossible, unrealistic and dangerous. We say nothing. We keep them deep in our minds. There's not a moment when I don't wonder what my wife and children are doing. I know they're also thinking of me. And it's unbearable.'

He remained silent, his eyes lowered.

'Take this cash and stop boring me stiff with your moods. We'll leave a message for one another at the Balto.'

There was no point in turning up at school without a letter of explanation. I couldn't imagine what I could possibly say to Sherlock to account for this unjustifiable absence. Without a note from my father, I would need a convincing excuse or a medical certificate. Two things that were impossible to produce. I would have to keep an eye on the post over the coming days in order to intercept the letter from school. I went to the Balto. I waited in my corner. I was unable to concentrate on *L'Arrache-coeur*, the book I was reading. At about three o'clock, Igor arrived.

'Don't worry. I know how we'll go about it.'

'How?'

He took from his coat pocket a sheet of paper that was filled on both sides with small handwriting.

'I took some notes. Come on, let's give it a try.'

We went to the post office on the Avenue du Général-Leclerc. Igor asked the telephone operator for a number in Algiers. We got through after a quarter of an hour.

'Hotel Aletti, good afternoon.'

'I'd like to speak to Monsieur Marini, please.'

'He's gone out. His key's hanging up.'

'Do you know when he's due back?'

'He hasn't told us anything. He often goes to the Amirauté restaurant for lunch.'

'Is that far from you?'

'One kilometre.'

'Thank you. I'll call back.'

Igor put the phone down.

'You could have asked for the number of the restaurant.'

'It's not possible. I've got the number of a bar five minutes from his hotel. He'll have to go there. The police won't have time to tap the phone.'

We tried every twenty minutes. The operator knew the number by heart and the hotel receptionist shortened his response to 'Sorry, sir, still not back'. We waited anxiously as the time went by. Igor had to pick up his taxi. I had to meet Franck at six o'clock and be back before my mother. At a quarter past five, we tried again.

'He's here. Hold the line, I'll put you through.'

We waited for a few moments. I could hear my father's voice: 'Paul Marini here.'

'Monsieur Marini, I'm a friend. I have some news for you.'

'Who are you?'

'I'm with someone who was with you at the time your son Franck was conscripted. You arrived late because your DS broke down. You came back on foot and the rain was bucketing down. Do you know who I'm talking about?'

'Yes. What do you want?'

'You must go immediately to the Grand Café. Let's allow ten minutes. We'll meet there. At the bar. OK?'

'I'll be there.'

Igor hung up and asked the operator to put him through to the Grand Café in Algiers, but for some unknown reason it was impossible to connect him. The lines were jammed. Or else there may have been a bomb attack. No need to get worked up, the operator reassured him, it happens twenty times a day. Time passed and we became increasingly anxious. It was twenty to six. I could see that I was going to have to leave Igor without being able to speak to my father.

'Never mind,' Igor said to me. 'If we haven't got through to him ten minutes from now, go and meet your brother and give him the money. That's the most urgent thing. I'll speak to your father. Let's hope he'll wait.'

A pensioner complained. We were monopolizing the telephone counter. He was getting impatient about not being able to gain access to the operator.

'The lines are jammed.'

'I just want to call Amiens.'

'You'll wait your turn, Monsieur,' Igor replied, without getting flustered. 'A little patience.'

'Igor, may I ask you one other thing?'

'If it's legal, you may.'

'It's about school. I've missed the whole day and I've got no excuse. If I fool around, I risk being kicked out.'

'Don't count on me to forge your father's signature.'

'What if I gambled on speaking frankly to Sherlock? I'll go to see him in his office. I'll tell him the truth: "Well, Franck is on the run, a deserter. He's asked me to help him. I couldn't just leave him." He knows him and likes him. A supervisor ought to be able to understand that. No?'

'You might as well go and denounce him to the police. There's one basic rule for survival on this earth. If you had lived on the other side, it would be etched firmly in your head: never trust people! Anyone! Do you hear me? It's a lethal word, trust. It's killed thousands of nutcases like you.'

'Not even someone you know?'

'Not even your father, your mother, your brother or your wife.'

'I'm trusting you.'

'I'd have nothing to gain by informing on you. Do you think I'd hesitate for a second about ratting on you, you and your family, if the police were threatening to take away my political refugee card?'

I stared at him. His expression was impassive.

'Are you joking, Igor?'

'Cabin 5 for Algiers,' called out the operator.

We hurried over to the cabin. Igor picked up the phone and I took the earpiece.

'Grand Café here,' said a woman's voice.

'Hello, Madame, I'd like to speak to one of your customers, Monsieur Marini. He's at the bar.'

We could hear the woman asking: 'Is there a Monsieur Marini here?'

'Yes, that's me.' The phone was passed over.

'What are you doing?' my father yelled. 'I was about to leave.'

'There was no connection,' Igor explained, passing the receiver to me.

'Papa, it's me. I'm with a friend. The hotel phone is being tapped, and so is the one at the flat. We have to watch what we say. Here, they can't listen to us. Franck is in Paris. I saw him this morning.'

'How is he?'

'He seems tired and strained. He needs money. He'd eaten nothing since yesterday.'

'Give him whatever you have.'

'May I ask Mama for some?'

'Best not. Give him whatever cash you have, I'm going to come back.'

'The gentleman who spoke to you can give me some money for Franck. Will you repay him?'

'Of course. I'm returning to Paris as soon as I can get a seat on the plane.'

Igor took the phone from me and glanced at his sheet of paper as he spoke: 'Monsieur, I'm Michel's friend. You mustn't go by plane. The police will know. Furthermore, the flights are full. Go back to your hotel. Say that you have had some news of your son, that he's managed to cross over into Morocco and that you are off to find him. If the receptionist asks you questions, tell her that he's in Tangiers. Don't give any details. Don't take a taxi. Make sure you're not being followed. Go to the port of Algiers. There's a ship, the *Lyautey*, that's leaving for Marseilles this evening at nine o'clock. They don't ask for identity papers when you embark. Buy a second-class ticket and pay in cash. Don't speak to anyone. At Marseilles, take the train to Paris. Do you want me to repeat this?'

'Do you belong to the secret service, or something?'

I rushed to rue Laplace. I arrived at the Bois-Charbon shortly after six o'clock. Franck was not there. I sat down at the back of the café at the table we had sat at in the morning and ordered a really weak lemonade shandy. The owner was playing 421 with the same customer and I recognized the same sinister-looking faces at the bar. Perhaps they were cops and they were about to pounce on me. I waited. Franck didn't come. Had he had a problem? How would I know if he had been arrested? It would be difficult to ask the owner whether he had seen him. I waited until the last possible moment. I had to be back by a quarter to seven. I only had the money that Igor had given me. The owner looked at the twenty-franc banknote suspiciously. He handed me back the change without saying anything. On the way home, I turned around several times. I didn't see him. I arrived five minutes before my mother. I went to see her in the kitchen where she was preparing dinner.

'What did you do today, Michel?'

'We had Maths and French. The English teacher's ill.'

'Still!'

'And you, everything all right at the shop?'

'We just don't know how to cope. With your father away, we're losing orders every day.'

'I think he'll be back soon.'

'Let's hope so. What's more, I've got a seminar next week and I don't want to miss it.'

'Tell me something, Mama, are you really angry with Franck?'

'Angry? ... No.'

'You don't talk about him. You don't seem to be bothered.'

'There's nothing more I can do for him. But he's my son, and he always will be, whatever he may have done.'

'If he got in touch with you, what would you do?'

'I'd tell him he has to be responsible for himself.'

'What if he asked you for help?'

'I'd advise him to give himself up to the police and to trust in the law of his country. There's no other solution for him. Why these questions?'

'We've never talked about it. I didn't know what you thought.'

My mother rang the Hôtel Aletti. She was told that my father had left the hotel. She was surprised to discover that he had left for Morocco.

9

Ever since Moscow, the Ilyushin 12 had been flying above a dense mass of clouds. To the east, a white sun shone in a limpid sky. Gazing at this magical spectacle, Leonid and Sergei, his co-pilot, forgot about the mind-numbing din of the engines.

'Have you any plans for this evening?' Leonid asked.

'I'd like to go to the cinema. At least one can see American films in London.'

He turned towards the radio operator, at the rear of the flight deck, who was absorbed in his work and, for once, was not listening to their conversation. Alexandra, the new air hostess who, quite rightly, was said to have the finest bottom in the company, brought them scalding tea and some biscuits. At the very moment she was handing the cup to Leonid, he pricked up his ears anxiously.

'Do you hear anything, Alexandra Viktorovna?'

'Nothing in particular, captain.'

'I've already told you, girl, call me Leonid.'

'Captain, there's a strange noise coming from engine number 2, as though there was a guy banging with a small hammer!' Sergei announced in a panic.

Leonid listened intently and concern twisted his lips.

'Comrade co-pilot, you'll have to confiscate the hammer from the guy at engine number 2!'

Sergei fiddled with some buttons. Some warning lights came on and went out.

'Small hammer confiscated from guy at engine number 2, captain.'

'There you are, Alexandra. No more noise. You're very lucky to have me aboard this plane.'

'Captain, I can hear groans coming from engine number 2.'

'Sergei Ivanovitch, the time has come to give back the little hammer to the guy at engine number 2.'

Sergei fiddled with the same buttons.

'Hammer returned, captain. The guy's asking for a sickle.'

They burst out laughing. The radio operator stood up and handed Leonid a telegram.

'Bad news from London, captain,' said the radio operator.

If the smog of the winter of 1952 was the most deadly ever, with four thousand deaths caused by the sulphurous gas from exhaust fumes and industrial waste and hundreds of thousands of coal-fired furnaces, that of the winter of 1951 would remain in the record books as one of the worst the British capital had ever experienced. From a distance of twenty metres, nothing was visible and there was a stench of rotten eggs. Londoners, who had seen many such winters, told each other jokes about unexpected baths in the Thames – a little chilly at this time of year, don't you find? – and cheered each other up by reminding themselves that, thanks to this ghostly fog, Claude Monet had invented Impressionism. On several occasions, London was cut off from the rest of the world when no planes could land at Heathrow. On this Tuesday 9 January, when Leonid was given the order to reroute to Paris, he thought he would land at Le Bourget, but the Paris airport was paralysed by these unscheduled arrivals and he was diverted to Orly. It was late in the day and nobody could give him any idea of how long they would be held up. Leonid was worried about his passengers becoming bad-tempered, but the announcement of the delay did not provoke any negative response in the cabin. Among the two dozen Russians Leonid had on board there were a deputy minister and a delegation of seven members of the Supreme Soviet who decided to make the most of the unexpected bad weather by fostering Franco-Soviet relationships. Taxis and a hotel had to be found for the delegation. Would there be any rooms at the Meurice?

Inside the air terminal, the delegation from the Supreme Soviet stormed the only counter that was open, where no plans had been made to welcome them. A haughty young woman, dressed in the petrol-blue woollen serge Air France jacket and its felt beret, smiled imperturbably. Two of the people's representatives had a basic knowledge of French, which she deliberately chose not to understand.

'You're at Air France here. Not at the tourist office,' she replied, still maintaining her exasperating smile.

'Where tourist office?'

'It's closed at this hour. Try on the Champs-Elysées.'

'You telephone Champs-Elysées.'

'You may use the public booths, a little further along in the hall.'

They went there. The Post Office and Telecommunications kept the same opening hours as the rest of the country. The operator had closed her metal shutter. The Air France official refused to allow her telephone to be used.

'It's an internal line for company use only.'

'Me complain company,' roared the deputy minister.

'You should speak to the complaints department.'

'Where department?'

'On the first floor. It's closed. It will be open tomorrow,'

Leonid arrived at the Air France counter with the four members of his crew at the very moment the deputy minister was insulting the official in Russian. Leonid spent a moment scrutinizing this woman's statuesque beauty. She had a wide forehead, long auburn hair that fell in ringlets over her shoulders, turquoise blue eyes and widely arched eyebrows. He had the vague notion that he had seen her before. If I had ever met this woman, I would know when and where it was. I would not have forgotten this face, he thought. She looked like an American actress. At the cinema, Leonid never remembered the names of the stars, apart from Chaplin, and Laurel and Hardy. The only actress he recognized was Greta Garbo. This woman was quite unlike her. With the deputy minister yelling at him, he promised him that he would sort things out with her.

'Me no speak French,' he told her, putting on his most persuasive smile.

He carried on in his aeronautical English. His laborious explanations came up against a wall. She spoke English without an accent.

'You, French or English?'

'My nationality is no concern of yours.'

'Can you speak less quickly?'

'I'll tell you again one more time. You are at Orly, not at Le Bourget.'

312

'It's because of fog over London.'

'I've received no instructions. My shift is over.'

'You must help us.'

'You are at Air France, not Aeroflot.'

'We are lost, we don't know where to go.'

'I am not a travel agency.'

'I am going to be obliged to inform the embassy.'

'You can telephone the Pope and the President of the United States. And stop smiling at me in that idiotic way, do you think you're Cary Grant?'

The woman pulled down the shutter at her counter and disappeared into an office. The deputy minister and the delegation put this incident down to the spicy temperament of French women, which led them to expect a more enjoyable stay than in London. The air terminal was emptying. They rushed outside and piled into taxis. The five members of the crew were left with the last cab, and the driver refused to take them all: there were only four available seats. They insisted and promised him a large tip. He refused and made it a point of honour to justify the reputation of Paris taxi drivers.

'Three in the back and one in front. Hurry up or I'm leaving!'

A captain must ensure the safety of his crew. He saw them off and waited for a taxi that had little chance of coming. He was resigned to whiling away his time when he saw a white Peugeot 203 go past him, stop and reverse. The window of the passenger door was wound down and the Air France official appeared. Leonid felt a wave of optimism run through him. He stepped forward.

'Are you going to Paris?' she asked him with an enigmatic smile.

'You've saved my life.'

'Sorry, I'm not a taxi. Since I'm in a good mood, I'm going to tell you the way. You go straight on and you'll come to the motorway. Turn right and you may find a taxi or a bus. Otherwise, it's not far to Paris. You can't go wrong. You're lucky, it's not raining. You see, it doesn't take much for a man to stop being cocky. I wonder why that is!'

She drove off. He watched her disappear. He came to the main road where the cars were hurtling by. He stuck out his thumb. Nothing stopped. He continued on his way. As he walked, he hitch-hiked. After half an hour, at a crossroad, there was a sign that read: 'Paris: 11 km'. He drew up the collar of his jacket. On the right side of the road, he noticed a patch of white, which, on closer inspection, took the shape of a car. The 203 was sitting on the verge of the road, its left front tyre burst. The woman was waving at the cars, which were whistling past her. Her coattails were flying. When she saw Leonid, she stood stock-still and rearranged her clothes.

'Good evening,' she said. 'I didn't expect to see you so soon.'

'You're lucky, it's not raining.'

'I didn't see the pot-hole.'

'I thought that holes in the road only happened in Russia. I'll be careful in future, thanks to you. Aren't you going to change the wheel? There must be an instruction manual in the glove-box.'

She showed him the crank, which lay near the burst tyre.

'It's impossible. I can't do it. Can you help me?'

'Sorry, I'm a captain, not a breakdown mechanic.'

'You're not much of a gentleman.'

'Me! On the contrary! I'm going to do you a favour. You need to find a mechanic. If you continue along this road, you'll find a garage. They're closed now. They'll fix it for you tomorrow morning.'

'Make the most of it. Take it out on me.'

'A small puncture, and all of a sudden, oops: a smile.'

This woman had an expression that flustered him. Leonid felt very small. Often, during the years that followed, and throughout his life, he would think back to this precise moment when his life was turned upside down. He remembered the endless silence that followed this remark; he remembered hesitating, and his guardian angel saying to him: 'Do something, Leonid Mikhaïlovitch. She's going to make a fool of you. You're no match for her. She'll eat you alive. Continue towards Paris. Save yourself. Let her cope with her burst tyre.' Why hadn't he listened? As time went by, his responses to this question changed. For a long time, he told himself that we should ignore our conscience, otherwise, remorse would not exist, and a life without regrets is of no interest. Later on, he had come to the view that no man could resist such a smile, or if he did, he wasn't a man. Nowadays, he told himself that he had been bloody stupid, just as all men become bloody stupid when a woman smiles at them. Leonid bent down, picked up the crank to change the wheel, and his troubles began.

It was impossible to remove the hubcap, to unscrew the nuts, to find the right slot in which to stick the jack, to raise the car up with the crank. You would have thought some sadistic engineer had vowed to murder anyone who might try to help a woman in trouble. During the war, Leonid had dismantled engines that weighed half a ton, changed aircraft wheels that were heavier than him, fixed undercarriages that were in pieces, adjusted and reconnected incompatible parts, and no Peugeot was going to make him look ridiculous. He braced himself, cricked his back, shouted, tore the skin from his fingers, but he could not make the nuts budge — it was as if they were soldered on. He yelled, he could hear his vertebrae cracking. His muscles were tearing. His blood froze in his brain. Air drained from his lungs. A second before his heart was about to explode, he managed to move one nut. The three others required just as much effort.

An hour later, he was dripping with sweat, his knees were bruised, his face and hands black with filth and oil, his shirt and trousers spattered with mud, grease and sweat. He got to his feet, shaking and out of breath.

'You wouldn't have managed,' he remarked, exhausted.

She came over to him and wiped his sweating forehead. Her hand stroked his face. She thrust herself against him. He caught a whiff of a perfume he had never smelled before, a distant scent of the Orient and of a horizon ablaze. She put her hands around his shoulders, drew him to her and pressed her lips to his. With the strength that remained in him, he took her in his arms. It was a time when kisses went on for ages. Theirs lasted an eternity. Passing cars hooted their horns. They didn't hear a thing.

After the longest kiss of his life, came the longest night. Leonid, who had known many such nights, in Leningrad and in Moscow, which he had described as sublime, phenomenal, staggering, memorable or amazing, could find no adjective to describe this night. It had left him speechless. It was as if, in the darkness, he had approached the forbidden tabernacle and been marked for ever by a red-hot iron.

10

My father arrived at the wrong moment. Superintendent Bourrel was about to reveal the name of the murderer. We were waiting impatiently for the last five minutes of the detective mystery and, at the crucial point, the front door slammed and he swept into the flat. He looked like a man who hadn't slept for two nights, who had travelled standing up in a packed corridor, unshaven and dishevelled. Without replying to my mother's questions, he rushed into the shower and we waited for half an hour by the bathroom door.

'Well, Paul?' my mother asked.

'I haven't found him.'

'I told you so. It was pointless going there. What a waste of time.'

They went off to bed. We felt irritated, for we would never know who had killed the cheesemonger.

In the middle of the night, my father came into my bedroom. I felt his hand on my shoulder. He didn't want to switch the light on. In a low voice, I told him what had happened after Igor's telephone call. How I had missed Franck and how he had suddenly turned up the following morning on the way to Henri-IV.

'I skipped lessons on Thursday, Friday and Saturday morning. It wasn't my fault. I managed to intercept the letter from school. You've got to do something.'

'I'll deal with it. Where is he?'

'He lives in cellars and he changes his whereabouts each day.'

'And his friends?'

'He told me that they would hand him over to the police. We're the only ones he can rely on. He's frightened. He's suspicious and on his guard. He's got a gun.'

'What for?'

'He said he wasn't going to let himself get caught.'

317

My father was silent. I could hear his deep breathing. 'I can't believe it,' he murmured. 'How did you manage to meet?'

I didn't see Franck on my way to school, but when I had reached Place du Panthéon, I heard him; he was three or four yards behind me. That was the way he did things. He guided me. We walked down rue Mouffetard, in single file. We went into a small bar in rue Censier. I asked him whether he'd had a problem the previous day.

'Got some cash?' he asked me, still on the alert.

I handed Igor's seven hundred francs to him under the table. Franck wasn't expecting so much money.

'Where's this cash come from?'

'A friend lent it to me.'

'Did you say it was for me?'

'What else could I do? He managed to get in touch with Papa, who'll be here tomorrow or the next day.'

'If his phone's being tapped at the hotel, the cops will know I'm in Paris.'

'Can you see any cops? Aren't you taking enough care?'

He didn't look happy. He walked over to the owner and gave him some money. Perhaps he was running up a bill. He was restless.

'We've got to get out of here.'

Instead of parting, we waited by the entrance to the métro. We pretended to be talking to one another, while Franck watched the bar. He relaxed a bit. We separated, then met again in the botanical gardens. He was chain-smoking Celtiques. He offered me one.

'I don't smoke. What happened?'

He didn't answer. It started to rain. We sheltered in the Natural History Museum. There was nobody there apart from us and two wardens who were putting out some bowls to collect water spilling from the glass roof. We sat down in the large hall opposite a stuffed giraffe.

'We were in the hinterland south of Oran, on the high plateaux. We controlled the region. There were small bands of very mobile *fellaghas*. We weren't able to corner them. We turned up in villages. We picked up a few of them. The intelligence officers questioned them and we could hear them screaming from a hundred yards away. They were butchering them. Sometimes they were dragged into helicopters that returned empty. After the interrogation, they were taken for a ride in the country. They were told to get lost. They set off running, or in whatever way they could, and they were shot.'

'Do you mean you fired at them?'

'Here, that seems unbelievable, there it was run-of-the-mill. It's the way this war is. On their side, they don't give a damn about committing atrocities either. You're caught in a trap: if you don't force them to speak, you're accepting the attacks and the French people who have had their throats slit. You end up convincing yourself that you've got to do a dirty job so as to avoid anything worse.'

He couldn't speak any more. I waited for him to continue, but he was no longer with me.

'What happened, Franck?'

'The company captain asked for volunteers to gather wood.* No one offered. He couldn't go on his own. There were seven *fellaghas*. Three had been beaten up and two of them could hardly walk. Since I was a lieutenant, he chose me to accompany him. One of the Arabs had a kid aged ten or twelve who was supporting him. It was late November and in the full sunlight the heat was stifling. My combat uniform was sticking to my skin. We went about a kilometre. He told them to get lost. He shot two of them. I asked him to spare the kid. He took aim. The others were hiding behind a tree. He was waiting for them to appear before lining them up. I yelled at him to stop. He didn't listen to me. He got the father. I shot him in the head. That's what happened. Then I hotfooted it. They did everything they could to find me, but I slipped through the net.'

'In France, there are judges. It's not the same thing.'

'In the military court, they have you standing to attention. They don't make judgements, they issue orders, and then you're supposed to get back

---

* 'Gathering wood' or 'wood duty' was an expression used by French soldiers to denote the summary execution of prisoners during the war in Algeria. Tr.

into your kennel. With a conventional examining magistrate and a civil court, I might have had a chance. There, I hadn't a hope. Look what happened in October, when they chucked hundreds of Arabs into the Seine: who protested? No one. Everybody keeps quiet. The press as well as the trade unions. They do whatever they like. They're not going to get me. I've got to get out of France. Go to a country where they won't be able to find me. Papa will have to help me. I need cash.'

'He's really uptight. I'd never seen him like that. He's gone away. He'll get in touch with you.'

'You must sleep, lad. You did well. We'll help him. We can be proud of him.'

He kissed me in the darkness. I didn't hear him leave my bedroom. I didn't know whether he was still there. I switched on my bedside light. He was no longer there.

11

Leonid sighed, his gaze lost in the wispy cirrocumulus clouds. Sergei watched him furtively. His captain was not talking to him, not responding to any of his jokes, and he had stopped admiring young Alexandra's sumptuous bottom. The radio operator confirmed the landing in London. Good weather awaited them.

'Fucking Met Office,' Leonid moaned.

At the airport, he let his crew leave without him.

'I'll join you in the hotel as soon as I can.'

He managed to get in touch with Milène at Orly, courtesy of the Air France manager at Heathrow. She was not expecting his call.

'Milène, it's me.'

'Where are you?'

'I've just arrived in London. I'm so glad to hear your voice. I've not stopped thinking of you.'

'Neither have I.'

'I've got thirty hours before the return flight.'

'It's not long.'

'Perhaps we can see each other?'

'I'm waiting for you.'

'What can we do? I can't come to Paris. I haven't got a visa. If I fly over, they'll find out.'

'I'd thought of that. I was convinced it was over between us.'

'Milène, we can't not see each other any more. Don't you want us to meet again?'

'Don't say that.'

'I can't go anywhere. You're the one who'll have to come.'

'I finish my shift at eight o'clock this evening. I could catch the plane for London. Wait, I'm checking... It's not possible, the last flight's just left.'

'If you can't come to London and I can't go to Paris, we won't see each other again.'

'If you did Moscow–Paris, it would be easy.'

'Aeroflot has no flight to Paris. Milène, I need you. Do you understand?'

'Leonid, I don't enjoy saying this to you. Our affair is an impossible one. We've experienced something very beautiful. To continue would be madness. Do you realize that we're trapped? We can't take on the entire world.'

'I couldn't give a damn. Nothing and nobody will prevent us seeing each other again.'

'There's nothing we can do, Leonid. It's impossible.'

'Give us just one chance, at least.'

'We live in different and incompatible worlds.'

'Tell me that you don't feel anything and I'll stop.'

'It's complicated with us. It won't work.'

'I've met you only once. I don't know you, and you don't know me, but what happened between us is stronger than everything. It's the first time this has happened to me. What about you?'

There was a long silence. What was going on inside Milène's head? Was she frightened of missing out on a remarkable experience? Or was it pride? Was she saying to herself: I'll succeed where others have failed? Or had she suddenly stopped thinking things through? Didn't she wonder why obstacles that seemed insurmountable a moment ago had now vanished, as though removed by a magic wand?

'What hotel are you staying at?'

'The Hyde Park Hotel. It's in the centre.'

'Go there.'

Milène arrived at two in the morning. Leonid had fallen asleep, fully dressed, with the lights on. He heard gentle tapping at his door, got to his feet with difficulty and, half asleep, opened the door. It took a few seconds for him to realize that she was there, in front of him, wearing that smile that overwhelmed him. She rushed into his arms.

Late that morning, worried that he had not seen Leonid, who was always the first to be up, Sergei went to find out what had happened. Leonid came to the door, his hair tousled, wrapped in the bedside rug, unaware of the time, the day, or where he was. Through the half-open door, Sergei could make out a shapely leg protruding from the sheets, and he heard a female voice asking: 'What's happening, darling?' and concluded that it was not the right moment to suggest visiting the Tower of London.

The return flight was cheerful and relaxed. Alexandra was granted the complete set of jokes about air hostesses who were frozen at high altitude.

From now on, the Tuesday flight to London was a jolly affair. Nobody was in any doubt as to the reasons for Leonid's good mood. He disappeared as soon as they arrived and only returned for the boarding formalities. Nobody was concerned by this. Informed of the situation by the radio operator, the MGB* found nothing to object to. A hero of the Soviet Union was entitled to have fun. The routine enquiry, initiated by the military attaché at the Soviet embassy, was pushed through by an overworked official. There was nothing to fear from Milène Reynolds, a Frenchwoman, *née* Girard, the wife of the manager of an insurance company in the City. Nothing in his report about her separation from her husband. Nothing either about Milène's rejoining Air France. It was a recent development. Since neither Milene nor Leonid had access to strategic information, this concise dossier was filed away, especially since one of them had connections in high places.

Once a week, Leonid and Milène got together. He waited in the pilots' room at the Heathrow air terminal for the late-night arrival of the DC3 mail plane which delivered and collected the post. Milène had succeeded in persuading the crew to allow her to board the cargo plane even though carrying passengers was forbidden by the company. But what would any flight captain not have done for the sake of Milène's lovely eyes? She knew how to ask, and no man could refuse her. She made the journey sitting on a folding metal seat and she made good use of the postal bags for padding. On the tarmac at Heathrow, Leonid could make out the sound of the Dakota before it became visible and began its descent. Over time, it became a habit. Except, of course, when there was smog.

* Created in 1946, the MGB, the Soviet Ministry for State Security, would merge with the Ministry of Internal Affairs, the MVD, and would be renamed KGB in March 1953. Tr.

Sometimes, their time was limited, because of the weather, in which case, instead of going into London they would remain in a corner of the air terminal, talking and holding hands. Whenever they parted, it was both a wrench and a worry. A week to wait. Leonid's thoughts were filled with Milène. No woman had ever obsessed him so. She was with him night and day. Her presence was sweet. He spoke to her, he smiled at her, he caressed her from three thousand kilometres away. She replied that she thought of him continually. She had rented a small house in Hounslow. They could spend two days and nights at a stretch in bed, inseparable, scarcely bothering to eat. They walked around London's parks like a couple of students. Milène preferred Greenwich because of its huge cedars and the intrepid squirrels that would come and eat from the palm of her hand. She took him to the British Museum, but Leonid got bored in museums.

She introduced him to American movies. They went to the Odeon in Richmond, which showed two films at each session. He didn't understand everything. The actors spoke quickly. She explained by whispering in his ear. Once, they went to Covent Garden. Leonid adored the ballet. To begin with, she was astonished by the amount of whisky he absorbed without being affected by it. The first two bottles had no effect on him. By the third, his eyes lit up and he laughed at the slightest thing, but he could walk straight and keep his head. Leonid didn't like drinking on his own and Milène didn't drink. Her lips barely skimmed the glass. When he was with her, he refrained from drinking so much. They often spent part of the evening at the Black Fox, the local pub. One couldn't tell them apart from the regulars. They would leave at the last minute, amazed to discover how late it was, and rush off to Heathrow, she to return to Paris and he to Moscow: see you next week.

Periods of leave spent in Leningrad, once something he looked forward to, became dreary. The games of chess with Dimitri Rovine, who supplied him with pure eucalyptus oil, seemed interminable and Leonid was not bothered if he lost them.

'You're making beginners' mistakes. What's the matter? You seem preoccupied.'

'Dimitri Vladimirovitch, can I tell you a secret?'

'If it's a secret, Leonid Mikhaïlovitch, it's best not to tell me anything. In our country, everyone should keep their secrets to themselves.'

'I've met someone.'

'In the five years I've known you, you must have had a hundred affairs, perhaps more, no? I'm going to confess a real secret to you, I envy you.'

'This one's not the same.'

'That's the main concern of women. Imagine if they were all alike. There would be no need to change. What's different about her?'

'Everything.'

'You're lucky to have met a different kind of woman.'

'We can't live together.'

'Is she married?'

'They're separated.'

'If there's no husband, what's the problem?'

'She's French. She lives in Paris.'

'Leonid Mikhaïlovitch, you're crazy! Didn't you have enough women here?'

'I had no choice. Neither did she.'

'How long has it been going on?'

'Six months. I do the Moscow–London run and she works in Paris. She slips over on the sly and we see each other during my stopovers.'

'What are you going to do?'

'What do you expect me to do?'

'My poor Leonid Mikhaïlovitch, when all's said and done, I wouldn't like to be in your shoes.'

12

'Cécile, I've got something to tell you.'
She stopped running, bent down and, with her arms dangling, she got her breath back. She had phoned me in the morning, surprised that I was no longer coming to the Luxembourg.

'What's the matter, Michel? Have you forgotten me? Have you got a girlfriend or something?'

I couldn't talk properly: 'I don't have one. I'm weighed down with work.'

'Wait a moment, I'm going to sit down and I want you to say that again.'

The previous Monday, my father had come with me to school. He had seen Sherlock and had explained that my absence was due to a death in the family and a burial in the country. He lied with such conviction that for a moment I wondered whether someone had died without anyone telling me. That night, my father had come to my bedroom. Franck had got in touch with him as he was leaving a client's office. They had had a long discussion. He had tried to persuade him to give himself up, but this idea was met with categorical refusal. Franck wanted money in order to escape abroad. My father had promised to help him.

It had become a routine: when the house was asleep, my father would come and wake me up and keep me informed. The only difference was that Néron would join us for these nocturnal confabs and, to prevent himself stepping on the cat's tail, my father used to switch on the bedside light. When he didn't come, I waited for us to be alone at breakfast; I would give him a questioning look and he would shake his head, which signified that nothing had happened.

One night, he came in with a damn stupid idea. The sort of idea you think is brilliant on the spur of the moment and that turns out to be such a disaster that you wonder how it could have taken shape in a sane mind in the first place.

'What if you talked to his girlfriend?'

'To Cécile?'

'She might manage to persuade him.'

'They broke up two years ago. He dropped her in a really unpleasant way. He didn't dare tell her to her face that he was joining up and that it was over between them. He told me he would write to her to explain, but he never has. You just don't behave like that. She doesn't want to talk about it any more. Every time I've raised the subject, she's switched off.'

'You know nothing about women. It's when they say no that they are thinking yes.'

'Oh, really?'

'Believe me. I know. We've got nothing to lose. If she refuses, at least we'll have tried. She may manage to persuade him not to leave and to stand up for himself. She could do that in memory of their relationship. There's no need to love a person in order to help him. There are lots of people who were once together, who separate and who remain friends.'

'Let's suppose she agrees. How would she manage to meet him? He's in hiding. He won't want to see her.'

'Do you remember Sanchez?'

'Your engineer who took retirement?'

'Franck is at his place. Sanchez lives alone at a house in Cachan. He's always worked for the Delaunays. I trust him. He hasn't asked any questions.'

'I think she'll refuse.'

Cécile sat down beside me on a bench facing the tennis courts.

'So, Michel, what is it?'

I told her about the police arriving on Christmas Eve, my father's departure for Algeria, Franck coming back and his life as a fugitive. She glared at me in a way that made me feel rather uncomfortable. She expressed no criticism. She heard me through.

'You were right to talk to me about it.'

'It's only natural. If I hadn't said anything to you, I would have blamed myself for it all my life.'

Her hand brushed my cheek.

'Thanks, little bro'.'

I ought to have felt like a shit. It's shameful to lie to someone who trusts you. I didn't feel I was to blame though, quite the reverse. Later on, I realized that it hadn't mattered at all whether I told Cécile or not, and that whether this idea came from me or my father, I was merely a messenger. It was she who took the decision. Had she wanted to, she could have shrugged her shoulders and carried on with her life. She decided to go to Cachan. I did my best to dissuade her with arguments worthy of *L'Armée des ombres.**

'Why all this crazy fuss? We've got to stop being paranoid.'

She caught the Sceaux line train and didn't want me to go with her. I don't know what went on there. The following day, she asked to see my father. We met again near her flat, at the Alsatian brasserie on Place Saint-André-des-Arts.

'I've seen Franck. He told me you were preparing for his departure.'

'It's what he's asked me to do. I can't go into details. It's harder than we thought.'

'He agrees to the notion of giving himself up. He wants to see a lawyer.'

'We could consult Maître Floriot. He's the best.'

'Franck wants a lawyer from the Human Rights League. It will be a political trial.'

Both lawyers had been to see them, but it didn't mean they were any further forward. The lawyers could not give a view without knowing what was in the file and they were both of the same opinion: the allegations were serious. Murder and desertion in the course of fighting the enemy were punishable by death. Were Franck to be granted extenuating circumstances, he risked life imprisonment or a twenty year sentence with possible release after ten years. Sanchez was used as an intermediary. Franck didn't leave the house. My father gave me no details; he no longer came to my bedroom in the evening.

* Jean-Pierre Melville's 1969 film based on Joseph Kessel's book of the same title about his experiences in the Resistance. Tr.

328

On several occasions, I called on Cécile, but to no avail. I had my bunch of keys, but I felt embarrassed to use them. I phoned her. She wasn't at home. One evening, I rang the bell without much hope of finding her in.

'Michel! I'm glad to see you.'

'You disappeared. I wondered what had become of you.'

'Didn't your father tell you?'

'He doesn't tell me anything. What's going on?'

'I'm going away with Franck.'

'What?'

'We're leaving France.'

'I thought you…'

'So did I…'

'It's crazy.'

'I saw another lawyer. What with the new court martial where they try you without a preliminary enquiry, he's not very optimistic. Franck's taking a huge risk. He's not going to ruin his life and serve fifteen years for having killed some bastard.'

'You're putting yourself in an impossible situation.'

'I'll go with him, but I'll come back whenever I want. They can't prevent me. We'll go to a country where there's no extradition. We'll live freely in a free country. We're back together again. Do you understand, Michel? Why poison your life when you can be happy? We're not disappearing. We're going to live somewhere else. You can come and see us. Your father and his friends are trying to find us a cargo boat that will take us to South America. We'll probably leave from Rotterdam.'

'When's that?'

'Any moment. I feel sorry on Pierre's account. I won't be able to write to him any more. When we're in Holland, I'll drop him a line so that he doesn't worry. I'll tell him I'm going away for a few months. I won't give him any details. The post might be opened. We can never be too careful. When he gets back, you can explain to him. Can I count on you?'

13

At about ten o'clock at night, Leonid left the pilots' lounge. He never tired of watching the planes land. Two hours to wait before she arrived. He wandered around the air terminal where there were fewer and fewer people. An electrician was laying cables and two joiners were busy working at the Pan Am stand. The main indicator board was still showing yesterday's flights. The mail planes were not listed. He passed the deserted customs desk and walked out onto the tarmac. Silvery reflections came from the aircraft lined up in a row. He strolled around, inspecting them, unbothered by the rain. He walked over to the new Super Constellation and admired it with an expert eye. He pricked his ears. To the east, he caught a familiar sound. Just above the second runway, two yellow dots appeared in the darkness, and the Dakota mail plane hovered, landed and rolled towards its hangar. A lorry drew up and the unloading of the post began. Leonid walked over to the DC3 and recognized the co-pilot, Jean-Philippe, with whom he got on well. He waited for Milène to appear at the front door.

'How are you, Jean-Philippe?'

'We were blown about over the North Sea. We were overloaded.'

'As usual.'

'There's nothing we can do. However much we moan, they couldn't give a damn. It felt like being inside a drum.'

'I can imagine. You've got to climb high. Isn't Milène with you?'

'We haven't seen her.'

Leonid walked back to the air terminal. They were filling up with fuel and loading the hold with post for the continent. Why wasn't she there? Was she ill? Had she missed the flight? Why hadn't she warned him? There would be news at the hotel.

He hurried, and caught the last shuttle. There was no message. He asked the receptionist to contact Milène in Paris. They called him in his bedroom to say she wasn't at home. He felt a strange throbbing at the base of his neck. He had nothing left to drink. The receptionist refused to open the bar. Not even a beer. He offered money. The man remained adamant.

Leonid went out, walked around the neighbourhood and remembered that, in this country, the pubs closed very early. Back in the hotel, he woke Sergei and grabbed his bottle of vodka from him. Leonid asked them to try Milène's number again. Twice, he let the telephone ring for ten minutes without her answering. He felt hot and sweaty. He opened the window wide and the freezing air soothed him. He sat down in the armchair. He felt anxious, without knowing what it was he should be frightened of. He fell asleep. He had a restless dream about planes droning around amid flashes of lightning, and drunken receptionists. And the unbearable noise of the bell ringing. Like the siren of a ship in distress. The telephone cord was wrapped around his neck, it was suffocating him and burning his skin. The interminable ringing was earsplitting. He opened his eyes. The telephone was ringing and ringing. He rushed over and picked up the receiver.

'Ah, I was afraid you might be asleep, sir,' said the receptionist. 'I'm putting you through to Paris.'

'Hello, Leonid, this is Milène.'

'At last. I'm so glad to hear you. What happened?'

'I tried to reach you at Heathrow. They couldn't find you.'

'I went for a walk while waiting for you. Why haven't you come?'

'I won't be coming any more, Leonid.'

'What?'

'It's over between us.'

'What are you saying?'

'It's finished.'

'That's not possible!'

'I've had enough of this lopsided life. I've had enough.'

'You know the situation I'm in. I've got no choice.'

'It's too complicated, Leonid. I was hoping for something else for us.'

'We can't part like this. You should have talked to me about it.'

'For months, every time I've raised the subject, you've replied that we love each other and that the important thing is the present moment.'

'Isn't that true?'

'We've no future, Leonid. When you love someone, you live together. We're in an impasse. The longer we wait, the harder it will be. How long can we go on like this? Two years? Five years? Longer? I want a man for every day of my life, to make plans with, to create something that lasts. Time goes by so quickly, we can't waste it. We could have had a wonderful life. We're not enjoying anything. It's best to stop now.'

'Why didn't you tell me this to my face?'

'I wouldn't have had the courage.'

'I love you, Milène.'

'I love you too, Leonid, and I'm leaving you.'

'We can talk about it. Try to find a solution.'

'There is no solution. We know that.'

'We can't part like this, not on the telephone!'

'I won't be coming to London any more. It's over, Leonid, over. Forget me, I beg you.'

Milène hung up. For a long time, he stood there with the receiver beeping in his hand. He left the hotel and walked around a deserted London. Early glimmers of daylight appeared. The milk floats began their rounds. Later on a delivery man noticed that an off-licence had had its window smashed with a stone and several bottles of spirits were missing.

In the afternoon, Leonid embarked for the return flight. He looked as though he were in a filthy mood. Sergei discussed purely technical matters with him.

'This is my last London flight, Sergei Ivanovitch, I'm going to ask to be transferred to domestic flights. The essential thing is to be above the clouds, and they are the same everywhere.'

Sergei knew him well and knew that he shouldn't reply. Alexandra brought tea and biscuits. Leonid was in a foul mood. He looked tense and he kept sniffing.

'This plane stinks! There's a body rotting inside it! Can't you smell it?'

'No, captain.'

'You could clean it up instead of putting on airs!'

14

Cécile was not at home over the next few days. I didn't know where she was. I was waiting for my father to say something to me, but he was employing his usual tactic: he left at dawn, came home late and went to bed immediately.

One morning at about five o'clock, I managed to pull myself out of bed. I joined him in the kitchen where he was having his breakfast standing up.

'What are you doing here? Go back to bed.'

'What's going on?'

'I've told you; the less you know about it, Michel, the better.'

'Why?'

'You're not old enough.'

'It's not fair.'

'What are you on about? Do you think I enjoy playing at spies? We're going to be in the shit, and I don't want you to be mixed up in it. You're going to promise me that, whatever happens, if anyone asks you whether you have seen or heard word of Franck, the answer is no. I insist, Michel. Whoever it is. Do you hear? You know nothing. I want a promise, man to man.'

When my father extracted a man to man promise, it was a solemn matter. Anyone who failed to observe it would bring down everlasting wrath on himself and be reduced to the status of a worm without honour, despised by the whole of mankind. He looked me straight in the eye. I had no choice but to swear and go back to bed.

The following evening, my father came home earlier and we had a family dinner.

'How long are you going to stay there?' my mother asked him.

'It should be settled in two or three days' time. It's a one-off opportunity.'

'We're already finding it hard to supply our customers, if we have to fit two hundred bathrooms, we won't be able to cope.'

'We'll manage. If we want the company to expand, we have to acquire large building sites.'

My mother didn't appear convinced. She got up to clear the table and went back into the kitchen. Juliette was keen to know more.

'What is this building site, Papa?'

'A development for two hundred houses. They grow like mushrooms up there.'

'And where is that?'

'In the north of France.'

I no longer understood a thing.

'Weren't you going to Rot—'

I was given a kick under the table.

'It's in the suburbs of Lille, my darling.'

My mother summoned Juliette to come and bring in the salad. My father winked at me and put his finger to his lips.

At breakfast, my mother mentioned that she had not realized my father had left. I was sorry not to have been able to see Franck and Cécile, to say goodbye to them. I imagined them in the port of Rotterdam, surrounded by sailors, ships and cranes. I called in at the Club. Virgil was playing chess with Vladimir and didn't know where the others were.

In the middle of the night, the telephone rang. I struggled out of bed. When I got to the sitting room, the ringing had stopped. I picked up the receiver. There was no one there. My mother was in a bad mood at being dragged from her slumber.

'That must be your father. He's out of his mind calling us at three in the morning. I'm not going to be able to get back to sleep. Leave it off the hook, I don't want it to ring again.'

The following evening, I got the shock of my life. Outside Henri-IV, on the opposite pavement, Cécile was waiting for me. It couldn't possibly be her. She was meant to be in Rotterdam with Franck and my father, or somewhere else, not here. Although it was late April, the weather was cold, and people were dressed as if for winter. She was wearing the flimsiest of pullovers and was standing there frozen, on the corner of rue Clovis.

I saw her before she saw me. I waved to her. From her strained expression, I could tell that nothing had gone as planned. I was shivering. I couldn't get across the road because of the traffic. She was yelling at me, but I couldn't hear a thing. I almost got myself run over trying to reach her.

'Where's Franck? He's no longer in Cachan!'

I realized that my father hadn't been thinking of my mother when he made me swear not to say anything. He had tricked me with his bloody stupid promise.

'I don't know.'

'Don't lie to me, Michel! Where is he?'

A small group had gathered around us. I took off my duffel coat and put it round her shoulders.

'Come.'

Watched by my classmates, we set off towards place de la Contrescarpe. We sat down at one of the tables outside La Chope, and I ordered two *grands crèmes*. She was shivering.

'Franck's disappeared. Your father must know where he is.'

'My father didn't tell me anything. When I asked him, he didn't answer me.'

'Is your father at home?'

The waiter brought our coffees. She put her hands on the cup to warm herself. I wondered whether I should tell the truth, but which truth? Should I break my promise and compromise my father and Franck? Or lie to Cécile and lose her trust?

'He must be at the shop.'

'Are you sure?'

'He may be with customers.'

'Did you see him this morning?'

'He leaves before we get up. He's got a lot of work on. Why these questions?'

'Yesterday, we were due to meet. Ready to leave. At midday, in a bistro at porte de Pantin. I waited. They didn't come.'

'Who?'

'Your father and Franck. We were due to go to Holland then take a boat for Argentina. I waited until four o'clock. I couldn't ring, there's no telephone. I went to Cachan. The house was shut up.'

'Was it you who rang last night?'

'I wanted to talk to your father. This morning, I went back. Still nobody. Where are they?'

'They must have changed hiding place.'

'They didn't warn me. There's something wrong.'

'There may have been a hitch.'

'I must speak to your father.'

'As soon as I see him, I'll tell him to call you.'

'If there was anything, you'd tell me?'

'Cécile, go home.'

She took my hand and squeezed it tightly.

'Don't be like that, Michel.'

'Come on, I'll take you home.'

My father came back late. We were watching TV. The look on his face made my mother exclaim: 'Looks like it went wrong!'

'They wanted to make us slave away for nothing. I told them they shouldn't mess around with us.'

'You're right, Paul. We've got enough of that sort of work.'

I caught up with my father in the bathroom. He sent me packing.

'Now's not the time. Go to bed!'

During the night, I felt a hand shaking me in the darkness. I switched on the bedside light. My father was sitting on the side of the bed. Néron had joined us and had begun washing himself methodically.

'Franck has gone.'

'Where to?'

'Far away.'

'To Argentina?'

'That's not for you to know.'

'He's left without Cécile!'

'It was his decision. She wanted to go with him. I personally saw nothing wrong with that. He changed his mind.'

'Why didn't he say anything to her?'

'It was fairly complicated as it was. I don't think he wanted to foist that kind of life on her.'

'How can he behave like that?'

'I wanted to talk to him over those two days, but it was impossible. He wouldn't open up.'

'We can't leave her in the lurch. You must phone her. Explain things to her. Tell her that I knew nothing.'

My father took out a white envelope from the pocket of his dressing gown and handed it to me.

'Give her this.'

Written on the envelope were the words: 'For Cécile'. I recognized Franck's handwriting.

'He spent an age writing it. He finished it sitting on the gangway. He threw the rough drafts in the water. A sailor shouted at him to come up. He slipped the sheet of paper into an envelope and walked over to me. He told me that you would deliver it to her.'

'Don't rely on me, Papa.'

'I'll send it to her in the post.'

I took the envelope. My father stood up.

'He's a strange fellow, your brother. When he boarded the ship, he didn't turn round. He disappeared inside. I waited on the quayside like an idiot. The ship set sail. He didn't wave to me. I couldn't believe my eyes. I told myself: "He'll show up. It's not possible for him to set off without saying goodbye to me." I wasn't asking him to thank me. Just a glance, a little smile and a farewell wave.'

Cécile was unpredictable. She might throw herself out of the window or swallow half her medicine chest. I was awake all night. I turned the envelope over and over in every direction. What had he said to her? If I steamed it open and resealed it, she wouldn't notice. I could soften the blow. Or else not give it to her. Tell her some tall story. That he had to escape with the police on his tail. That he had had no other option and that he would be in touch with her soon. Gain time. Give her hope.

15

Leonid made his way across Leningrad. In these late March days, a mild spell had turned the snow into blackish mud. The city was one gigantic construction site. Everything had been destroyed and had then been rebuilt in identical fashion. He had reached the huge Moskovskaïa Square and was walking in the direction of the House of the Soviets when he stopped. His legs were shaking and he could feel the throbbing at the base of his neck. He hesitated and turned round. He had pinned his twenty-seven decorations to his flight captain's uniform. They covered the left side of his chest and, on the right side he had attached the two gold stars he had been awarded as Hero of the Soviet Union. Passers-by stared at him warily. He sat down on the wall of the Griboedova Canal, which was frozen over.

On his return from London, he asked for leave and spent four days drinking as he had never drunk before. He drank vodka to try to drown the foul stench that was suffocating him. He had run out of eucalyptus oil and was unable to obtain any. Dimitri Rovine had vanished and no one knew his whereabouts. He knocked back half of a small bottle and began breathing again. For a few minutes, the smell of the vodka blotted out the stench of decay that gradually returned, gnawing and insidious. He took freezing cold showers, rubbed himself with a brush and coal tar soap until his skin turned red, before resorting to the one remedy that soothed him. He soaked a piece of material in vodka, shoved it under his nose and inhaled in short breaths until he felt giddy. He slumped, naked, onto his alcohol-drenched bed, with the windows open, and sank into a troubled sleep from which he was soon awoken by that foul smell.

On the morning of the fifth day, a knocking at the door dragged him from his nightmare. He got up with difficulty, put on a dressing gown and opened the door to a woman of about sixty. Her white hair protruded from a black scarf decorated with a multi-coloured floral pattern. Irina

Ivanovna Rovine introduced herself. He asked Dimitri's mother into his room. She sniffed and appeared not to notice anything.

'I need your support, Leonid Mikhaïlovitch.'

He was flabbergasted when she told him of Dimitri's arrest. Three militiamen had come to look for him at the military hospital. For nineteen days, she had had no news. By chance, she had discovered that he was being held in the gloomy Kresty prison. She had spent a day sitting on a bench, waiting. A clerk from the Ministry for Internal Affairs had informed her that her son was liable under Article 58 without giving her any further details, except that it concerned a matter of State Security. Her attempts to find out more had hit a wall. Merely asking the question aroused suspicion. Dimitri's colleagues refused to become involved. The director of the hospital had unshakeable trust in officialdom and, since in this country people were not arrested without some reason, there must be one. If Rovine was suspected of treason and counter-revolutionary activity, it meant he was guilty. She had climbed dozens of staircases, knocked at hundreds of doors, told his story a hundred times over, but as soon as she mentioned the words 'Article 58' the interview was brought to an end and she was sent to another department.

'Dimitri described you to me as his best friend and told me that you were a hero decorated by comrade Stalin. I'm asking you to help us. I don't require any special favour. I want to know what he is accused of. If he has done something wrong, he must pay for it. But I'm convinced he is innocent. My son is not a traitor.'

'I'm astonished by this accusation. During the war, Dimitri conducted himself in exemplary fashion. He was decorated with the Order of the Red Flag. I'm in a good position to know that this award is not given to just anybody. I can't imagine what treason he could be accused of. He spends his life in hospital looking after the sick conscientiously and with exceptional devotion. He's an unusually effective doctor. Without him, I don't know what would have become of me. Had he been a bad Soviet, I would have been aware of it. Tomorrow, I'm going to make some enquiries. If I get no answer, I'll go to Moscow to see the People's Commissar and, if necessary, I'll approach comrade Stalin in person. You can trust me. I won't let him down. Dimitri is a great friend. I'm sure there's been a mistake.'

Irina rushed over to him, knelt down, clasped his hand and kissed it three times. He helped her to her feet. She was in tears. He took her in his arms and clasped her to him.

'I promise you, Irina Ivanovna, Dimitri will soon be free.'

Men don't cry. Especially not heroes. Sitting on the canal wall, Leonid wept. He didn't wipe away his tears, and he was unconcerned by the passers-by who stared at this serviceman clad in a strange uniform covered in decorations. He thought of Milène. What was she doing? Was she at work or at home? Was she thinking of him? Could you love somebody yet part from him? He sniffed. The foul smell had disappeared. He stood up, determined to confront the security services of the House of Soviets. What was the purpose of arresting a man who had done nothing but care devotedly for others? He thought of their last meeting when he had told him of his love for Milène, and he shuddered. Supposing Rovine were to denounce him? Supposing he told them about his affair with this Frenchwoman and their secret meetings in London? What would they think? Would they not reckon that he was a traitor too? His military past and his medals would be worth nothing. People more highly decorated and ranked higher than he had been arrested and shot. Rovine would not betray him. Cowards don't wait, they denounce the whole world as soon as they are arrested and he would have been asked to account for himself as soon as he returned to Moscow. Leonid was a good bargaining weapon, a small fish for a big one. Could it perhaps have been Rovine's idea? Supposing it had occurred to him, deep in his loathsome Kresty prison cell, as a way of extricating himself? Who could say whether he would hold out? Whether he might not hand over his best friend or his brother if his life were at risk? Rovine knew of Leonid's connections. If he were to continue to remain in prison, would he not resent him for not standing up for him? What was the point of a friend if he didn't offer a helping hand when you needed it? Might Rovine not come to the conclusion that Leonid was a coward and that he could ditch him without any compunction? What would he do in his position?

If he had a hope of evading the MGB or the fearsome MVD? If it were me, I wouldn't give it a second thought, Leonid said to himself as he walked away. Who knew what he had done? People aren't arrested without a valid reason. No one can do anything for him where he is now. By intervening, I'll compromise myself. Each of us has a duty to save his own skin. He hasn't betrayed me yet, but sooner or later he will.

Leonid set off for the Aeroflot building and declared that he was ready to go back to work. He returned home and waited. Each time someone knocked at his door, he feared it might be militiamen. Rovine couldn't have resented him sufficiently to denounce him, or else he knew that this wasn't going to save him.

One morning, when he was getting ready to go out, he noticed Irina Rovine coming up the stairs. He went back inside his flat and let her ring the bell without opening the door. He had nothing to say to her. Five days later, he was given his orders. He was back on the London route. In his travelling bag, he packed his few belongings, that is to say virtually nothing. Three pieces of jewellery that had been left to him by his mother, three shirts, his decorations, his pilot's licence, his Leica, a stack of photographs, and the medals his father had been awarded during the Great War. Knowing he would never see the city again, he went for a last walk and strolled up and down the Nevsky Prospekt, which was cluttered with building sites, as far as the Anitchkov bridge whose four bronze horses had just been returned, then he arrived in Smolny. All that was left were the crumbling walls and the gutted onion domes. He could still picture it in its pre-war splendour.

At Moscow Airport, he met his crew again as though nothing had been amiss. From London, Leonid phoned Orly.

'Milène, it's me.'

'Leonid, I'm glad to hear you. How are you?'

'I've not stopped thinking of you.'

'Please, don't go on at me.'

'I'm in London. I'm defecting to the West.'

'What?'

'I've made up my mind.'

'It's crazy.'

'I'm coming back to you. I want us to live together.'

'Don't. I know you, you'll regret it.'

'If you want me, I'll be the happiest man alive.'

'You don't realize what'll happen.'

'We'll make plans. We'll have a future. You'll have me with you every day and every night and not just on Tuesdays. Except when you don't want to.'

'I don't know what to say.'

'You're not going to let me go again? It's an opportunity for us. We deserve some happiness. Do you love me? Tell me what you think?'

Milène stared at the receiver.

'Do you want me?… Answer me, Milène, I beg you.'

'I'm waiting for you, Leonid.'

'I love you.'

'So do I.'

On Tuesday 2 April, Colonel Leonid Mikhaïlovitch reported to the airport police at Heathrow and asked for political asylum in Britain. He was taken to London. For three days, he replied to questions from members of the British secret service, who verified his statements and granted his request. No senior Soviet military officer had ever defected to the West before. Normally, the British and French press would have run this story of a defector on the front page. Instead, the story was given five lines in the news-in-brief column on the inside pages. The few editors who considered devoting an article to the matter decided against it and wondered whether, by any chance, it might be a ruse by the Soviet secret services. Leonid had not chosen the best moment. On 5 April 1951, a civil court in New York State sentenced Ethel and Julius Rosenberg to death for spying on behalf of the USSR. This conviction provoked horror and indignation all over the world. There were thousands of demonstrations to protest against this legal farce, a grim mirror of the Moscow trials, but the international protests were powerless to prevent two innocent people being electrocuted.

In the DC4 that was taking off for Paris, Leonid was not thinking of the Rosenbergs because he had never heard of them, but rather of Dimitri Rovine, who was rotting in a Siberian prison camp. He was annoyed with himself for not having tried to help his friend. He tried to persuade himself that it would have been pointless. Dimitri's face disappeared, blotted out by Milène's. They say it is not necessary to be certain of success in order to begin something, and it's a profound truth. Things that are a matter of conviction and hope are beyond all logic. When a man achieves his dream, there is neither reason, nor failure, nor victory. What is most important in the Promised Land is not the land, but the promise.

16

Cécile had read the letter by the window. A torn page from a spiral notebook, written with a blue ballpoint pen in a sloping hand. For five interminable minutes, she had stood gazing into space. The letter had slipped from her hands. She had picked it up and handed it to me without appearing to be upset. She was unexpectedly calm.

'I'm going to make us some coffee.'

I'd arrived at about half past seven in the morning. I hadn't rung the bell. I'd used my bunch of keys. She was asleep, curled up on the sofa in the sitting room. I'd sat down on the floor, facing her. I stared at her, not daring to wake her. Eventually, she had opened one eye and hadn't been surprised to see me there. I'd left the envelope on the sofa without saying a word.

Cécile,

You know I don't like writing so I won't be long. You mustn't expect anything of me. I'm off. I'm leaving without you. Without telling you to your face. As usual. A few days ago, you'd persuaded me to stay. It was nice to think of our future and that we were going to leave this war behind. I wanted to talk to you at that moment, but there's not going to be any amnesty for what I've done. I don't want to inflict the life I shall have on you. I lied to you. I'm not a hero. Would that I were.

I met a young Algerian, a Kabylian girl. She was employed at the barracks canteen. I feel wretched writing to you about this. I know the pain I'm going to cause you. Djamila's family didn't want us to see one another. She became pregnant. We decided to run away together. But in this country, that's not possible. It's forbidden. Her father forced her to go to their village in the djebel. When I went to see the French authorities, they told me that he was entitled to do this. I had to keep quiet about it. They had better things to do than bother about my little problems. I didn't agree. I decided to go and search for her. I deserted. I lived like a dog. I managed to find her. We were captured near Tlemcen. We were hiding in an abandoned village. We were waiting for the right moment to cross into Morocco. The simoom started to blow and when we saw them, it was too late. They caught us on the road to Oujda. We had no papers. They wanted to take us to the checkpoint. I had no choice. When a young conscript wasn't paying attention, I seized the opportunity to grab his machine-gun. Why the fuck was this little captain bothering about us? He should have let us go. He could see we weren't terrorists. He ordered his harkis to arrest us but they didn't move. He walked over to disarm me. I yelled at him to stop. He was about to pick up his FM. I fired. The guys from the patrol fired back. I got another one. Djamila was wounded. They took her away. I escaped. I should have told you before. I couldn't bring myself to do so.

I'm being called, I must go.

Franck

I found Cécile in the kitchen sitting in front of a bowl of steaming coffee. I sat down opposite her. I put the letter on the table. I poured myself some coffee and some milk. I waited for it to cool. We stayed there, in the half-light, with Franck in between us. We didn't know what to say about Franck because his escape had deadened us and crushed us. I looked at her. Was she thinking of him? Perhaps not. What does one do at such moments? One ought to express what one feels and what one thinks. I felt nothing and I thought of nothing. I don't believe Cécile did either. I don't know how long we remained like that. I didn't look at my watch. We said nothing. I stood up. Cécile didn't move. I left.

17

Leonid was reunited with Milène and it was the happiest day of his life. Ten years later, he still spoke about it with tears in his eyes. She had to wait a long time before the inspectors from the Sûreté nationale granted him a pass. When he left the customs office, she rushed over and threw herself in his arms and they remained huddled together in an endless embrace. They drove away in the white 203 and were held up in a traffic jam on quai de la Tournelle by a demonstration in support of the Rosenbergs. Milène told him their story. Outraged at their conviction, she wanted to park the car and join the demonstrators. The notion that one could march with placards and banners, yelling insane nonsense against the government, the police and a country that was an ally struck Leonid as incongruous, for he had only ever known official demonstrations in which one walked in neat and orderly rows.

'What difference does it make to you French people that these two Americans have been convicted?'

'They're innocent! It's a disgrace! A scandal!'

'They're spies. They've betrayed their country. They deserve to be shot.'

'How can you say such awful things? It's appalling!'

'They've been convicted. That's proof. Especially in the United States.'

This was their first argument and a frequent subject of disagreement between them.

'You don't know the Americans. You don't know what they're capable of!' she shouted.

'Compared to us, they're choirboys.'

Leonid ought to have been more circumspect. His fate, through the most mysterious of coincidences, would be compounded with that of the Rosenbergs, whom he couldn't care less about.

*

Milène lived in a flat on the top floor of a fine building in avenue Bosquet. They rediscovered their London devotion to one another and marvelled that every day could be a Tuesday. She wanted him to feel at home, so she emptied a cupboard and fitted out an office for him. She showed him around Paris, taught him French, basic cooking, how to shop and how to watch out for the tradesmen in rue Clerc who forgot to give change. She took him along to the large stores, dressed him from head to toe, and bought him so many clothes that she had to give up another cupboard to him. These were months of carefree happiness. Milène worked long hours and Leonid waited impatiently for the evening. She told him in detail about how she spent her days and he asked her hundreds of questions to do with planes and airlines that she was unable to answer.

For several months, when Air France left Le Bourget airport to go to Orly, she left home early and returned at about midnight, and she would retire to bed, exhausted, without touching the meal he had prepared for her. He stood leaning over the balcony, smoking Gauloises, admiring the glass partitions of the Grand Palais and, with his nose in the air, the Eiffel Tower. He walked around Paris from morn till night, methodically visiting each neighbourhood, without ever managing to get used to the traffic or to cars that paid no attention to pedestrians. When he arrived, Leonid had a handful of roubles that were worthless, and fifteen dollars. Milène put some money in a purse. He took from it what he needed. When it was empty, she added more without his having to ask. He did the shopping and looked after the flat. She never criticized him. One day, she asked him to buy some mimosa. She loved this flower and its scent. He got into the habit of filling the flat with mimosa and he made it a matter of honour to find some even when it was out of season.

For the holidays, in August, they spent two weeks in Corsica, and Leonid fell in love with Bonifacio. On the evening before they returned home, they were dining at the port. He took her hand and squeezed it.

'I can't go on, Milène. I'm bored to death. I'm useless. I need to work.'

'If it's because of money, don't worry.'

'A man must work, do you understand? Not wait for his wife to bring in the money and live off her.'

'It doesn't bother me.'

'It does me!'

They sought a solution but what job could a former Soviet pilot do? Through a friend who was one of the company's directors, she obtained an interview with the personnel manager who, impressed by his record of service, made him take the physical aptitude and accreditation tests. For six months, Leonid waited. When he phoned to find out what was happening about his application, he was unable to obtain an answer. He went along to the head office of Air France and asked to see the personnel manager. He was told he was unavailable. Losing his patience, Leonid kicked up a fuss. Without giving him any explanation, they informed him that his application was unsuccessful.

Milène kept to herself what her friend who was a director had told her: that the company could not risk being on bad terms with the Soviet authorities. She encouraged him to apply to other large airlines, but most of them only recruited their own nationals. Leonid got in touch with Sabena, BOAC and KLM, filled in a pile of applications, subjected himself to a string of exams, identity checks and interviews, and he waited.

To celebrate the first anniversary of their getting together again, she invited him to La Tour d'Argent and gave him a Lip watch that cost a fortune. It was an exact replica of the one created for General de Gaulle and given by him to President Dwight Eisenhower. She thought he would be pleased with this present, but quite the reverse.

'I've got nothing to give you. I'm not going to buy you a present with your own money.'

'I don't need one. You are my present.'

She took his hand but, because she was sitting opposite him, she took the wrong arm and put the watch on his right wrist. Leonid thought that this was the custom in France and he always wore it in this way. He gave her his pilot's watch with its eagle rampant, the insignia of the Chasseurs of the Guard regiment, the only one in the Red Army to have the imperial coat of arms engraved on the dial beneath the hammer and the sickle. She removed her watch. He attached his to her right wrist. She swore that she would always wear it.

She smiled at him and nothing else mattered. She asked him hundreds of questions about his war. He gave her secret information that he had never told anybody. He went on talking until daybreak. She listened to him in fascination, eager for precise details. She wanted to know everything about his life. When he questioned her about her own past, she refused to answer. In solemn tones, she said she had lived through hard times and did not wish to be reminded of them.

'Let's think of ourselves and our own happiness.'

She took him in her arms, kissed him and made love to him as though every embrace were the first. When he woke up, she had left to go to work. He found himself wandering around this affluent area with nothing to do. He started to drink again. Nobody took any notice of him. How could you get away from booze in a city where there was a bar on every street corner and countless sympathetic ears that would listen to him, especially as he was the one paying for drinks? He had known hardship this Russian, even though few believed him when he described the hellish years of his patriotic war. His colleagues at the bar wondered which film he'd got the aerial battle scenes from.

After fifteen months of waiting, Leonid received a positive reply from KLM.

'I'd stopped believing,' she confessed.

'I've never stopped believing. Luck changes. You've got to learn how to be patient.'

They gave a memorable party with their friends and Leonid astonished a gathering of connoisseurs by downing a bottle of Dom-Pérignon as though it were a glass of water. Milène bought him a suit made of Prince of Wales check and decided they must leave nothing to chance. For two days, she worked on him, playing the role of the person doing the recruiting, asking him questions that were delicate, embarrassing or ambiguous, and making him learn the correct answers by heart.

On Saturday 22 November, she went with him to Amsterdam. She allowed him to drive the 203 and, during the journey, she made him revise. At the company's head office, Leonid froze and was unable to answer a question. He was recruited for Garuda Indonesian Airways and told he would have to take up his post in Djakarta before the end of the month. The terms were favourable, and they were surprised by his refusal. The return journey was gloomy. Leonid didn't utter a word. Milène tried to lift his spirits: 'It doesn't matter. We'll go on searching.'

'We've tried all the European companies. I've had it.'

'Perhaps you should have accepted.'

'Would you have followed me there?'

Milène took her attention off the road for a second. The car swerved. They didn't say another word to one another until they reached the outskirts of Compiègne. Leonid started sniffing.

'It stinks in this car.'

'It's the tobacco. Open the window and let some air in.'

Leonid was the most precise man I've ever met. Diabolically precise. It was as though he kept a minutely detailed private diary. Every event in his life was engraved deep in his memory. He remembered each moment of every hour and day spent with Milène. What they had done together and where they had gone. What they had said to one another. And the following day. And every day of the two years and two months they spent living together.

'It was after Thursday 27 November 1952, on our return from Amsterdam, that I went off the rails. I didn't realize what I was doing. I moaned from morning till night. I no longer looked for jobs that I was certain I wouldn't get. I spent my time in bars, boozing. In Leningrad, there were no repercussions, and I had no one to vent my anger on. In Paris, I became odious. I ruined her life with my foul temper. She said nothing. Not one word, not one complaint. She should have put me in my place. She let me belch and curse, and I never realized just how impossible I was to live with. The more I drank, the worse I became. I blamed her for having dragged me into this disastrous state, I heaped my bitterness on her and she took it without saying a word. Perhaps if she had yelled at me and put me in my place, that might have saved us, but she endured it in silence. I could no longer sleep. I had nightmares. I woke her up at night. I opened the windows wide to get rid of the smell that pursued me. I refused to look after myself. On Saturday 18 April, over a dinner with eight of her friends and her cousin from Nantes, I started to insult her because the roast was overcooked, telling her she was incompetent and useless. One of her friends, an air steward, intervened. I gave him a clout. His nose started bleeding. Not only did I not apologize but I threatened to smash in the face of all the arseholes like him who bored me stiff. She didn't comment. On Tuesday 12 May, I took her car without telling her. She didn't want me to drive it. Later I never understood what had happened. Somehow I braked too hard and got stuck under a lorry. But I escaped without a scratch. I wrecked the lovely white 203. In those days, they didn't prosecute drink-drivers. I expected Milène to blow her top, but she didn't hold anything against me. The only thing she said was: "It doesn't matter in the least, the main thing is that you're not injured…" Look, Michel, you have before you the biggest fool of all time. I had the best and most beautiful woman in the world. I messed up my chances with my arrogance and my stupidity. Not to mention the shitty life I made her lead. I'm not proud of it. And then, on Friday 19 June 1953, she came home. She looked distraught. I was slumped on the sofa, in the process of tackling another bottle of Muscadet. She sat down on the edge of the cushion and poured herself a glass of wine, which she drank in one gulp. Her eyes were gleaming. I hadn't noticed she was crying. "They've killed the Rosenbergs," she announced.

"'They did the right thing."

"'What you're saying is horrible!"

"'They're traitors. They got what they deserved."

"'Get out!"

"'What?"

"'Out! I don't want to see you ever again!'"

18

For a week, I hadn't dared ring Cécile. I hoped I might bump into her at the Luxembourg, but I didn't spot her there. I regretted having given her that letter. If I had had the courage to open it, I would have burned it. She would have been left in a state of uncertainty, which would have been preferable to this wreckage. He, who never ever wrote, had written just one fucking letter in his life and it would have been better if he had died that day, because then he would still have been the person she loved. He destroyed our illusions with his lies, his mistrust and his hypocrisy. If he had told the truth: I'm in love with someone else and we're going to have a child, it would not have altered anything and we would have helped him, even Cécile. It was the deception that was unforgivable.

Almost two weeks went by. I rang her home morning and evening. She didn't answer. At lunchtime, I waited for her by the Médicis fountain. I tried to read Kessel's *Fortune carrée*. I couldn't concentrate. For a change, I took some photographs of the sculptures that were illuminated by the sun filtering through the foliage. Suddenly, as I was staring at the statue of Acis and Galatea, I understood. She hated me. She was angry with me. I had brought her the bad news and I was the brother of a complete shit. I needed to tell her that I had nothing in common with him, that we were different, and that he was a nonentity who didn't deserve any respect. That she had to forget him, dump him, think of him not as a treasured memory, but as a rotten bastard; that he was no longer my brother, and that I was disowning him and eliminating him from my life and my mind. I wanted to persuade her that we should live as though he had never existed and promise each other never to utter his name, that she deserved a thousand times better, that she should turn over a new leaf and think of her future. I ran over to her apartment. I rang the bell for ten minutes, then opened the door with my bunch of keys. It was dark inside the flat, and impossible to tell whether Cécile had gone away for a long time or not.

Lessons continued, as boring as ever. I finished *Le Lion* and *Fortune carrée* and returned them to Igor, who lent me some other novels by Kessel, all of them inscribed. These books were precious to him. He thought that I read too quickly and didn't get the most out of them. We had to negotiate. For the time being, he lent them to me two at a time. We discussed them passionately. We disagreed about their strengths: he liked Kessel's lyricism and the books' mysterious atmosphere whereas I admired his very pure documentary style and his psychological analysis. I read during lessons, with the book propped up on my lap. I was quite sure I was not wasting my time. Nicolas warned me with a thump on the elbow or knee if the teacher had just moved or if my posture looked odd.

A bell rang out, chiming at regular intervals. Not the school bell. The bell on the Clovis tower. The school porter came in and whispered something in the ear of the Spanish teacher.

'Gentlemen, put away your things,' said the latter, getting to his feet. 'We are going down to the courtyard. And in silence!'

The pupils surged down the corridors and staircases. The monitors split us into two groups: the *lycéens* in the main courtyard and the *collégiens* in the cloister. When the bell rang for a general assembly, it was a bad sign. It had happened only once in the past four years. That time, Beynette, the headmaster, surrounded by the teachers, had announced with great reverence the name of someone who had died for his country. The choir had sung the *Marseillaise*. There was a minute's silence and we went back to our classrooms.

The bell stopped chiming. The microphone crackled and the voice of the headmaster echoed through the loudspeakers: 'My children, it is with great sadness that I have gathered you together on the day before the start of the holidays. I had hoped I would never have to summon this sad assembly again. I have just learned that Lieutenant Pierre Vermont was killed the day before yesterday in a skirmish with enemy forces. This death is a great sadness for us. He spent his schooldays in this establishment. He was a brilliant young man and a remarkable student who, shortly before he joined up, had told me of his desire to become a member of the teaching staff. Pierre Vermont had only friends here…'

He continued, but I no longer heard him. It took me a moment to understand, to realize that he was talking about my Pierre. I left my row and went up to a monitor.

'He's not talking about Pierre Vermont, is he?'

'Go back to your place, there's about to be the minute's silence.'

I stood stock still. I could visualize Pierre jiving. I could hear him laughing and raging against the holy trinity of the couple, the flag and money, or proving with conviction and passion that every priest, religious leader and rabbi on earth ought to be killed, and that the only concession he would make was that their deaths should be quick and gentle. But I couldn't imagine him lifeless and bleeding. I felt no emotion, no sadness. His death was a mere statistic. It was the absurdity that shocked me. Not so much that he was dead, but that he should have been killed four days before the end of the war. As though the last death should be any more idiotic than the first. His dying should have shattered me. I was alarmed at my own indifference. I thought of Cécile. Who would inform her of her brother's death? How would she react? The *Marseillaise* rang out. I had goosebumps all over my body. I set off at a run and the school porter, who wanted to prevent me leaving, was pushed back unceremoniously. I shot down rue Saint-Jacques like an arrow, down to quai des Grands-Augustins. I tore up the stairs four at a time and hammered at the door. No one answered. I sat on the bottom step and I waited in the dark for a long time. She didn't come. As I left, I knocked at the concierge's lodge.

'Excuse me, Madame, do you know where Cécile Vermont is?'

'She left a fortnight ago. I'm collecting her post.'

'Is she at her uncle's, in Strasbourg?'

'She didn't say anything to me. Are you not feeling well, young man? Do you want to sit down? You're white as a sheet.'

I went to Denfert. I didn't go into the Balto. Through the window, I could see Samy playing baby-foot and, at the bar, Imré was chatting with

Werner. I didn't feel like talking to anyone. It was late when I got home. They were having dinner, watching the television news.

'Do you know what time it is?' my mother called out. 'Go and wash your hands before sitting down at the table.'

'I'm not hungry.'

My father came up to me in the corridor.

'What's the matter, Michel?'

'Do you remember Pierre Vermont? Cécile's brother.'

'The one who gave you those records?'

'No, he lent them to me. He's dead. In Algeria. In a skirmish.'

'Shit! How old was he?'

'I don't know.'

'How did the poor girl react?'

'She doesn't know.'

'That's terrible. At the end of the war, it's so crazy.'

'And now she's on her own.'

'She's unlucky.'

'You know, they say it's the shits who come out alive and the brave guys who die there. It's true. It's Pierre I would have liked to have as a brother. A guy who behaves like a hero and who everyone talks about with respect.'

'You've no right to judge Franck. You don't know what he's been through.'

'I haven't got a brother any more. For me, he's dead!'

I went to my bedroom and slammed the door. I wanted to be left alone. Nobody came to look for me. I got into bed and switched off the light. I wasn't able to sleep. I could hear Pierre's laughter in the Maubert bar. He had given me so much and I, for my part, had given him nothing. I felt frustrated by this debt. And then I saw him, in a halo of sunshine, on the ramparts of his fortress, on the edge of the desert, peering into space. In his shabby uniform, his collar turned up, the flaps of his tunic open and blowing in the wind. His hair was white and his face was lined. He was smiling.

19

Through the window, in the distance, Cécile caught sight of a mountain covered in forests. She turned round and looked intently at the man in the white coat sitting opposite her, behind a metal table. He was checking through a pile of papers. He was taking his time and examining the figures carefully. She searched for the slightest sign on his impassive face. He wore a satisfied expression.

'Your tests have been excellent and I give my consent. But we must respect our laws. We're going to make an appointment in the afternoon with a colleague who will give you a second opinion. My secretary will give you his contact details. Afterwards, we'll do the operation. You'll come in the morning, having fasted, and you'll leave again in the afternoon.'

'And what if there's a problem?'

'We've never had any problem.'

'The sooner the better.'

The doctor consulted his diary.

'Friday morning, if you like.'

'That's fine.'

'The day before, you must take this sachet in a glass of water and these two pills.'

'Afterwards, what should I do?'

'Spend some time in the fresh air so that you can rest. You have slightly high blood pressure. A week at least, two would be ideal.'

Cécile walked along a path lined with chestnut trees in blossom. The setting sun lit up the lake and the mountains. She sat down on a bench and gazed at the huge jet of water that rose up, turned to spray in the breeze and vanished into the sky. Five wild swans were flying in single file. It was dark when she entered an imposing hotel surrounded by parkland. She went up to the reception desk and, when he spotted her, the receptionist passed over her key. She walked over to the lift, hesitated, turned around and came back towards him.

'I'd like to phone Paris. Will it take long?'

'The connection is quick today,' the employee replied in a heavy accent.

'Odéon 27 53.'

'I'll put you through in a few minutes.'

Cécile entered the phone booth and lay down her things on the chair. The telephone rang. She picked up the receiver.

'Hello, good evening, I'd like to speak to Michel.'

'Hang on, I'll go and get him,' a girl's voice replied.

Juliette went into her brother's bedroom.

'There's someone on the phone for you.'

'Who is it?'

'I don't know. A lady.'

Michel picked up the receiver.

'Hello?'

'Michel? It's me. How are you?'

'Well... it's...'

'I'm OK.'

'Are you at home?'

'I'm... I'm on holiday. I needed to get away for a bit, do you understand?'

'Your concierge told me that you'd gone to stay with your uncle.'

'Er... yes... And I went to see a girlfriend. You must do something for me, Michel. You're the only one I can ask.'

'Go ahead.'

'Can you go to my place? You've got my keys?'

'Yes.'

'Take my thesis and send it to me. It's in my bedroom, in the right-hand drawer of the desk. The key's in the little Greek vase on the radiator. I'm going to get down to it again. I must get on. I've got some time to work on it. Is that possible?'

'No problem.'

'Can you send me some books? I don't want to have to buy them again.'

'Wait, I'll get a pen.'

'I need *Les Voyageurs de l'impériale*, *Les Beaux Quartiers*, *Aurélien*, *Le Crève-coeur*, the *Cantique* and *Les Yeux d'Elsa*. They're on the shelves. They're annotated. Put them in a cardboard box and send them to me by post. There's a box with my card notes. I need that too. I'll give you the address. I'll pay you back.'

'Are you joking?'

'Wait. Don't bother with *Les Voyageurs* and *Les Beaux Quartiers*. The others are enough. You should read them yourself.'

'Really? May I?'

'Take any books you want. I'll give you my address. Are you ready?'

'I'm listening. Go on.'

'Send the parcel to me at... poste restante, Evian.'

'Don't you want me to send it to your friend's address?'

'The post office is more convenient.'

'As you wish. Which region is it?'

'Mmm... Savoie, I think. What about you, is school OK?'

'Cécile, I've got to talk to you.'

'Yes?'

'Something has happened.'

'What?'

'It's Pierre.'

'Pierre? What's wrong with him?'

'He's been... he's...'

'He's been what?'

'He's been... He's been killed.'

'What are you talking about?'

'In an ambush.'

'What?'

'Cécile, he's dead.'

'Stop it, Michel!'

'I swear to you.'

'It's not possible!'

'It happened five days ago.'

'It's not true! The war's over!'

She could feel her head spinning. A hot flush rose to her face and prevented her from breathing. She tried to get her breath back and collapsed in a heap.

'Hello… Hello?… Cécile!… Answer me! What's going on? Cécile?' Michel yelled down the receiver which swung in mid-air.

20

At the Club, Leonid was a special case. He was the only one, along with Gregorios, to have remained a hard-line communist, a committed Soviet. He defended Khrushchev and later Brezhnev through thick and thin, and he read *Pravda*, which he bought every day from a kiosk in rue La Fayette. He hadn't fled for political reasons or because he was threatened, but for love. He had retained his opinions and he was proud to proclaim them. And those who had narrowly escaped with their lives and had been ground down by the system held his orthodoxy against him.

Imré and Vladimir were reading *Le Canard enchaîné*, as they did every Wednesday, each holding one side of the newspaper, and commenting on the headlines. They started to snigger.

'Did you hear Jeanson's latest?' asked Vladimir merrily. 'Why are the generals so bloody stupid?'

We came up with hypotheses that were logical, absurd, cranky and daft. We wondered whether it was directed at de Gaulle, Massu or Franco. Eventually we conceded defeat.

'Because they're selected from among the colonels!' Vladimir continued.

Everybody burst out laughing, except Leonid.

I was the only person Leonid talked to about his life. No one else listened to him. Igor reckoned that bringing up the past made one melancholy and that it was the chief cause of his alcoholism. It was hard not to unpack one's baggage, hard to suppress the old, worn-out memories that were only too eager to stream forth at the first beat of the blues and some Côtes-du-Rhône. But Leonid had no excuse. The alcohol had no effect on him.

'You're boring us stiff with your damned memories! Find yourself a woman, a real one, and give her a child while you can still get a hard-on,' Vladimir complained.

'You'd have done better to think of your own children before you got out. A fat lot of good it does them now having a father like you!'

'We agreed that we'd only talk about the present and the future,' Werner reminded them.

'The kid wanted to know.'

'The kid's a pain in the arse, he ought to be playing baby-foot!' moaned Gregorios.

'He's my guest. And I talk about what I want with my friends.'

To be raised to the rank of a friend of Leonid's was a passport to respect and I felt rather pleased.

'They're jealous. They ran away with their tails between their legs. I'm the only one to have chosen liberty for the love of a woman. No one forced me to do it.'

'Don't you regret it?'

'If you'd known Milène, you wouldn't have asked the question. And since I'm always thinking of her even now, every moment of my life is a happy one.'

'When she threw you out of her flat, didn't you try to go back?'

'I found myself on the landing, feeling like an absolute idiot. I reacted in the worst possible way. I went on down. I was convinced that she'd run after me. You can imagine just how stupid and arrogant I was. I waited for half an hour outside the building. She didn't come to look for me. When I went back up, my things were on the stairs. I've always fought to save my bacon. When my plane caught fire, when I was hit by a hail of machine-gun bullets, and when I crashed behind enemy lines, I never gave up. In that instant, I realized it was over, that there was no point in discussing, protesting, begging, or asking her forgiveness. It's all or nothing with that kind of woman. The problem is that by the time you realize it, it's too late. If a thing's broken, you can't glue it together again. And I still had a little pride left. Do you understand what I mean, Michel?'

'I would have tried my luck.'

Leonid polished off the jug of Côtes and asked Jacky for another. He poured out two large glasses one after the other. He offered one of them to me.

'I don't drink alcohol.'

'What would you like?'

'A half of really weak lemonade shandy.'

Jacky grumbled. Orders were being passed to him without being grouped together, and he was weary.

'I'm telling you fibs. I did, in fact, try to win her back. I fought, but she was stronger than me. But when you're in love, you have no pride. I still hoped to make a fresh start. That evening, I don't know if I've told you, it was a Friday, and I found myself in the street with my belongings. I left them at the Gare d'Orsay, which was nearby. I spent my first night out of doors, opposite her flat. She switched off the light at twenty-five past one. For the past few days, she had been reading *Léon Morin, prêtre* by Béatrix Beck. She loved that book. In the morning, when she left, I rushed across the road. I was almost run over by a lorry. She got into her car. She had just been to collect it. I knocked twice on the window. She was surprised to see me. She lowered the window. 'Milène, we must talk.'

She wound up the window, started the engine and drove off. I stood there on the pavement like a dummy. I waited for five endless days. She didn't come back. I didn't want to go away, for fear of missing her. I had no money on me. Not a penny. On the first day, the concierge at the building took pity on me and left something on his window sill for me to eat. After that, he refused to open his door to me and waved me away as though I were a dog. I didn't shave, I didn't wash. I had to beg. Because of the way I looked, people were frightened of me and avoided me. I was so hungry that I ate food from dustbins. I was filthy. I couldn't change my clothes. I had no money to pay the left luggage at the station. I was picked up by the police for vagrancy. On the second day, a guy came to see me at the police station. He was dressed in a very elegant suit. I didn't know him. The sergeant opened the door of the cell for him. He sat down beside me on the straw mattress. He had a brandy flask in the inside pocket of his overcoat. He took a sip and offered me some. He had a very slight accent. I grabbed the flask from him. No drink has ever given me so much pleasure. It did wonders for me. I could feel the alcohol trickling down my throat. I drained his flask. He offered me a

Winston. We sat there side by side smoking our fags like two old buddies. He knew everything about me. Who I was and what I had done. From his other inside pocket, he took out an enormous bundle of banknotes. He proposed a deal. He would give me this money if I promised not to see Milène again. To begin with, I didn't understand what it was he wanted. He explained the conditions to me. One hundred thousand francs, and in those days that was one hell of a lot, for me not to speak to her again. I told him that I could take this money and fail to keep my word. He replied that he trusted me to be honest. The choice was either to have a bit of money to sort myself out or not to have a bean. In either case, I had lost her. He gave me another cigarette and allowed me to think matters through while I smoked it. I made up my mind to agree to the promise, to take the cash and to come back later to plead my cause. When I told him that I agreed, he extracted the piece of paper wrapped round the notes and held in place by an elastic band. It was a brief note written in French and in English so as to be sure that I understood it. He asked me whether I believed in God. I replied that I didn't. He said to me: "It doesn't matter. You're Orthodox, you will read out this document and swear to it by raising your left hand." I raised it. I hesitated. I found it hard to speak the words. He said nothing. He waited for me to decide. I'd never seen a man so calm and self-assured. I had my left hand in the air. I gave in. I promised. In that instant, I knew I had lost her. He told me that I had made the right decision, that he trusted me, and he gave me the money. I left the police station. And since that time, I've never seen Milène again. I sold her for a bit of cash. I didn't deserve her.'

'What was this promise?

Leonid took out his black leather wallet and, from a flap, removed a piece of faded paper, worn at the folds, creased, stained and torn, and stuck together with adhesive tape, and handed it to me. It was difficult to decipher. The four lines, printed in red on a typewriter, were blurred:

I, Leonid Mikhaïlovitch Krivoshein, give my word never to see
Milène Reynolds again, never to contact her and to respect her
wishes until the end of my days. I make this solemn promise on my

honour as a serviceman who bears the two gold stars of Hero of the Soviet Union. Signed in Paris, Thursday 25th of June 1953.

He showed me the watch on his right wrist and stroked the glass.

'I look at it a hundred times a day. It hasn't lost a second against the speaking clock. Isn't life strange? And all because of those bloody Rosenbergs. If their death sentence had been commuted to life imprisonment, we'd still be together.'

'Leonid, they were innocent!'

'They were criminals! They knew what they were risking. We don't have the right to betray our country. They don't convict innocent people in the United States. It was inevitable. What happened, however, was not their fault, it was mine. There are some people here who think that I regret having lost my job and wasted my life for a short-lived affair. As I've told you, I don't regret a thing. What I experienced with her over 794 days was so unusual and so intense that I've had my lifetime's satisfaction. If I had to go through it again, I'd do so without hesitation. I'm not one to complain about my misfortune. I was lucky enough to meet Igor – without him I'd be a tramp – and to make a few friends, and friends are for life. If ever you come across a woman by the side of the road, and she waves at you to ask for help, whatever you do, don't stop. Changing a wheel is a mechanic's job. Those fellows are tough. They don't mix work with feelings. If I had respected the good old Marxist principles about the division of labour, I wouldn't be where I am now. They stuff our minds with useless principles such as politeness and gallantry and they don't teach us the basic rule: beware of women who smile, for they are concealing ulterior motives. It's when a woman doesn't smile that she's at her most natural. If she falls in the water and cries for help, throw her a lifebelt and go on your way. These are the basic rules that a father should pass to his son in order to protect him from the perils of life. Mine never warned me.'

'There's one thing I don't understand, Leonid. How can you love a woman and not fight to be with her?'

'I gave my word. It's my fate, my own way of being faithful to her. You don't need to be loved in order to love. For the past nine years, on 5 April each year, she has received a bunch of mimosa. An anonymous bunch. She knows it's from me. It would be entirely up to her if she wanted to see me again. All she would have to do is go to the florist, who would give her my address. She doesn't want to. I respect my promise. Maybe she'll change her mind one day.'

'You've been apart for ten years. You can't possibly go on believing that she might.'

'I would have preferred to put it behind me. But you don't decide whether to love or forget. The thought never leaves you. I live with her during the day, and at night, when I wake up, I think of her. I'm as much in love as I was on the first day. You can grow tired of a woman and want someone else. That's not love, it's desire. Because love, real love, is intellectual. It's in the mind that it takes place, and there are days when I tell myself that it would have been better if I'd forgotten her. Jacky, give me a 102.'

Whether it was for the hundreds of games of chess of which he had memorized every move and which made him a much-feared player, or for his affair with Milène every detail of which remained vivid to him, Leonid was admired and envied for his exceptional memory, and yet this was the very cause of his unhappiness. It would have been better for him to have been like the rest of us and to have remembered just two or three games, if that, and to have retained only the sunnier moments of his love life. We always fear losing our memory, yet it's the source of our troubles. Happy people forget. This regrettable story explains why Leonid was the only Paris taxi driver who refused to take passengers to Orly airport, even though it was a lucrative fare. Ten years later, he still doggedly refused. As though he feared an unpleasant encounter there.

21

In the game of 'Happy Families', I'm collecting the repatriates. It's hard to imagine how any single family could accumulate so much misfortune. The Delaunays disembarked from Algeria. Maurice, Louise and the cousins Thomas and François, with their suitcases, their spaniel Toby, their pied noir accent and their bitterness. They had left behind their thirty-two buildings, their businesses, their cars, their furniture and their sunshine.

'Right up to the end, we believed them. We hoped for a miracle. France abandoned us. It was a stampede. Panic everywhere. We fought to climb aboard the boats. We left without anything. Without a bean. They took everything from us,' explained Maurice dejectedly.

'Over there, you were rich. Here, you're poor. If it were me, I would have stayed,' my father asserted.

A few years beforehand, grandfather Philippe had divided his will between his two children. My mother had inherited our flat and the family business. Uncle Maurice had invested his share in buildings in the centre of Algiers and Oran. He had borrowed money and given his personal guarantee. He was going to have to go on paying it back over ten years and he no longer received any rent.

'All we're left with are our debts and our eyes to cry with,' moaned Louise.

'We're in it together! It's when there are problems that the family is important,' asserted my mother, trying to raise their spirits. 'You're at home here.'

They moved in. When they had come during the holidays, the mood used to be joyful. We laughed and concentrated on having fun and making the most of everything. But now the atmosphere was no longer fun. The flat was transformed into a disorganized camping site. If we had been able to voice our opinion, we would have preferred them to live somewhere else. It was a bad moment to arrive, for reasons we didn't wish to talk about. I made an effort. Thomas and François only read comics. I recommended books to them, but they looked at me as though I were retarded.

Maria was an energetic woman with an exalted notion of her role. She was part of the family. My mother left the day to day running of the house to her, and, from morning till evening, she did so without having anyone nagging her. From one day to the next, she found herself landed with the Delaunay tribe, who never lifted a finger, thought they were in a hotel and gave her orders that she refused to carry out. She loathed them and considered them intruders. The old resentment between pieds noirs and Spaniards rose to the surface. Louise grumbled about her bad temper. As far as my mother was concerned, Maria was a gem. It all exploded after the washing machine gave up the ghost. Maria declared she had too much work and gave a week's notice. My mother kept her by giving her a pay rise, but she continued to moan.

Juliette had pinned great hopes on the arrival of the cousins: someone to talk to at last. But the *chiacchierona* was disappointed. Louise never stopped crying and exhausted her with her constant complaining. The cousins cold-shouldered her. They spent their time in front of the telly and she irritated them. So Juliette continued talking to herself and she took her revenge on the cousins, who took baths every morning, by emptying the hot-water-tank and leaving them with ice-cold water.

No one could have foreseen the battle that would break out between Toby and Néron. Our cat was furious about the presence of this slobbering creature that left hairs everywhere and barked for no reason. The moment they were introduced, they hated one another. They had to be shut in separate rooms. Toby never left Franck's former bedroom, and Néron remained in Juliette's room. But we kept forgetting to close the doors and every time we did so they laid into each other. Toby set about Néron intending to kill him, had his snout ripped open by an angry claw, and howled the entire night. Subsequently, even this dog we had reckoned was stupid realized that he had to give our cat a wide berth.

★

Worries shouldn't be kept to yourself – they should be shared with friends. I spoke about mine to Leonid, who was playing chess with Igor. I was in luck. On matters to do with distress, misfortune and adversity, they were experts. They explained to me what in mathematics is known as the 'law of series'. An American by the name of Murphy had given an example that bore it out with incontrovertible logic. If I have understood correctly it goes like this: a slice of bread always falls jam side up or it remains stuck to the ceiling and, when it falls down again, it lands on the carpet, your face or your tie.

'If, by the most unlikely chance, it falls on the non-buttered side,' Igor continued, 'it's because you've buttered it on the wrong side.'

'I've tried it with blinis and taramasalata, and the same thing happens,' Leonid continued.

One way or another, they succeeded in persuading me that the Delaunays' moving into our home was a godsend and that I should be pleased about it.

'We don't want to depress you, Michel, but at your age, you should learn to appreciate the present moment. The worst is ahead of you. Compared to what awaits you, the present, whatever it may be like, is easy.'

'But be careful, you shouldn't lack interest in everyday matters, you must just keep away from them. That way, nothing can affect you.'

This conversation made me feel happy. I was delighted to have understood a scientific concept. I changed my attitude towards my cousins. They were not aware of anything different and still kept themselves glued to the television.

After two weeks, a sort of organized disorder set in. My father went back to his old habit of leaving at dawn and returning home as late as possible. My mother did much the same. The family had grown larger and we had to resign ourselves. Louise was the only one not to have understood that certain questions ought not to be asked, for fear of upsetting this delicate balance.

'What's become of Franck?' she asked. 'Where is he?'

She tried this on my father, who left without responding; on my mother, who gave her a dirty look; on Juliette, who didn't know; on me, who pretended I hadn't heard her; and on Maria, who never spoke to her. She tried again at lunchtime one Sunday, while my father was carving the chicken, and Grandfather Philippe cut her short: 'You're boring us stiff, Louise, with your bloody questions. Franck's travelling!'

Every time the phone rang, I rushed to pick up the call. It was never usually for me. But one evening, Cécile got in touch. She had come back. It was late, and she sounded tired, a bit absent-minded. She didn't want us to meet. She had to arrange Pierre's funeral, which would take place in the country, at the family tomb.

'I can come, if you like.'

'It's not worth it.'

'I'd like to be with you.'

'There's going to be family there. People I haven't seen for years.'

'But we'll be together. I've had a lot of problems too.'

'Don't go on, Michel, I want to be alone with Pierre. The others are strangers to me. I'm tired; I need to rest. I'll be there for a brief while and we'll see each other when I get back. Will you be around?'

'Guess what: the Delaunays from Algeria have landed. The house is a pigsty. We won't be going on holiday this year, so we can have some time together in August. Cécile, I'm your brother now.'

'Yes, you're my kid brother. I'll call you.'

It was early July. My mother had not come home. We were slightly concerned. She never went away without warning us. She had left the shop in the late afternoon without saying where she was going. We phoned my grandfather, but she wasn't with him. We began supper without her. Then the front door slammed and my mother entered the room in a fury. We were gathered round the table. Maria was serving us.

'Paul, five million in Treasury bonds are missing at the bank! Where are they?'

My father got to his feet. His napkin fell into his soup plate. He stood there, open-mouthed, caught off-guard.

'What have you done with them?'

When my mother reverted to old francs, it meant there was a problem.

'Er... Ah yes, the five million. I wanted to talk to you about that.'

'Are you making fun of me?'

'Listen, we can talk about this later. Privately.'

'Immediately!'

The Delaunays from Algeria witnessed the row. Juliette and I didn't know where to put ourselves.

'Listen, Hélène, it would be better if we discussed this on our own.'

'I want an explanation!'

'I can't tell you anything.'

'What? You take five million francs from the bank without my knowledge. You forge my signature and yet you can't tell me anything?'

'I needed it.'

'Five million? What for?... Are you taking me for a ride? It's family money. I wanted to give it to my brother. He needs it. It's all gone!'

'It's money I've earned! I was entitled to take it. And stop using that tone in front of the children.'

'I'll talk in whatever tone I want. I'm not blaming you for taking the money! I'm blaming you for concealing it from me. And for forging my signature!'

'I'll pay you back.'

'Oh really? What with? With my money, perhaps?'

'Don't you believe me?'

'Who's to say that you didn't just pocket this money? That you haven't got a mistress? That you didn't lose it at the races or at cards?'

'As if you didn't know what I do all day long.'

'Tell me the truth!'

'I can't, Hélène.'

'I hope it's not for Franck? It's not for him, is it?'

'No.'

'Was that why you made the trip to the Nord? Do you take me for an idiot? I suspected as much. You've seen Franck. You've helped him.'

'Never!'

My mother turned towards me. She looked me straight in the eye.

'Michel, have you seen your brother?'

A shiver ran through me. I felt as though my hair were standing on end and I blushed. But I held her gaze and tried to remain calm. My father's head was down. I immediately remembered the promise that he had insisted I make, man to man. I was trapped. I could still hear his words: 'Whatever happens and whoever it may be.'

'No, I haven't seen him,' I said in an offhand way.

'You haven't spoken to him?'

'I would have told you, Mama.'

'And you, Juliette?'

'Mama, I promise you. We haven't seen Franck.'

She glared at my father.

'If it's not for him, you're going to have to explain to me. You know me, when I've got a bee in my bonnet, I don't give up. I won't stand for it, believe me!'

My father put on his coat and went out. In the morning, when we got up, he wasn't there. After that, the Treasury bonds were never mentioned again. I didn't know whether my father had used them to pay for the cost of the journey or whether he had given them to Franck for future use. But the subject was closed.

My mother declared that the *fellaghas* would never lay down the law in our house. We would not alter our plans or habits in any way. We would spend our holidays in Perros-Guirrec as we did every August. I phoned Cécile on several occasions, but she didn't reply. I went round to her place, and the concierge confirmed that she hadn't come back and that she didn't know where she was.

Just as we were taking our baggage downstairs, a policeman arrived, and my father was summoned to the police station. Two inspectors asked him the same questions over and over again. Why had he returned to France? He had mentioned Tangier. Was his son in Morocco? Diplomacy not being his forte, he told them that they could go to hell, they and the entire French army. They detained him for two days. We had to delay our departure.

The day after we arrived in Brittany, my father deserted us, with the excuse that he had work to do, and returned to Paris. We had to endure a month of rain interspersed with winds and icy squalls. It was impossible to swim, to stay on the beach or to walk along the coastal path, which had turned into a bog, without risking breaking our necks. We watched the rain pour down. We played Monopoly. The Delaunays from Algeria didn't know how to play chess, but they loved buying houses and hotels. I made several calls to Cécile, without getting through.

My father came back to collect us and we returned earlier than planned. Because their school records had been burnt in a fire at the Lycée Bugeaud, the cousins had to take an exam to get into Henri-IV. They failed. Their accent must have counted against them. They were so pleased with themselves that I didn't feel sorry for them. Grandfather tried to use his connections, but to no avail. Louise wanted to register them at Stanislas, which had an excellent reputation, but they no longer had the means. The cousins were also turned down at Montaigne and at Buffon, and eventually ended up at Charlemagne, which took settlers without an exam.

On 15 September, I got a call from Cécile. I hadn't heard a word from her for two months.

'I'm glad to hear from you. I went to your place. Your concierge told you, didn't she?'

'We have to see one another, Michel.'

'We can meet in the Luxembourg tomorrow.'

'We've got to meet straight away.'

'I'm in the middle of making my cousins from Algeria do some work. They were turned down by Henri-IV. They're absolutely useless.'

'It's urgent.'

'Can't you wait a bit?'

'No!'

Half an hour later, I rang her doorbell. She opened the door. She had changed. She was wearing Pierre's white Scottish pullover, which came down to the middle of her thighs. It was the first time I'd seen her in a skirt. She had a new hairstyle, with an uneven fringe. Her dark hair fell over her shoulders. She had that gloomy expression she wore when she was in a bad mood. She didn't reply when I said, 'Hello, how are you?' She turned around and leant against the drawing room table. A cardboard box lay on top of it.

'These are Pierre's personal belongings. I've just received them.'

She put her hand in the box and brought out a batch of letters. With a nervous gesture, she threw them down.

'Do you want to read them?'

I stared in bewilderment at the letters scattered over the table.

'What's wrong?'

'When I asked you whether you had warned Pierre that I was giving up my thesis, you swore to me that you hadn't written to him.'

'It's true.'

'It was your fucking brother who wrote to him! You talked to him about it before he joined up!'

She took out an envelope from inside a notebook. I recognized Franck's handwriting.

'Would you like me to read it to you? It's touchingly thoughtful.'

'Wait, I'll explain.'

'So you've got an explanation as well!'

She stood up and grabbed a large bundle of envelopes, which she threw at my face. I caught it.

'You were the only person I trusted and you've betrayed me. You! You lied to me. You Marinis, you're all the same!'

'It's not true.'

'You had no right!'

'It's just that—'

'Get the hell out!'

'I didn't want to—'

'Get out! I never want to see you again!'

I left. I waited on the landing for her to call me back. I shut the door behind me. It was finished. I couldn't get over it.

Over the next few days, I hoped I would bump into her so that we could talk. I hung around the Luxembourg and the quai des Grands-Augustins, but I didn't see her. Judging by results, lying is totally pointless. All you get is a hell of a lot of trouble. If I had broken that bloody man to man promise, my father would not have held it against me. My mother might have understood that my father had no choice other than to help his son and she would have forgiven him. If I had told her the truth, Cécile would have kept her trust in me. I felt like a tightrope walker looking for something to hang on to before he falls and discovers the void beneath his feet.

After several months in hospital, Grandmother Jeanne died in her sleep. Grandfather Enzo was asleep in the armchair beside her and was not aware of anything. When my father received the phone call telling him the news, he was getting ready to go to work. He collapsed in a heap on the chair and began to weep. He had not been to see his parents since the end of August. He asked me whether I wanted to go to the funeral with him. My mother answered for me, saying that it was the week of the exams and that I couldn't miss them. She advised him to go with Baptiste. My father refused to call his brother.

'He's a railwayman. He'll go by train.'

He set off for Lens immediately. I phoned my grandfather. There was no reply. I wrote to say I was sorry I couldn't be with him and that I was thinking a lot about him and Grandmother Jeanne. Juliette signed the letter.

My father returned ten days later. I asked him how Grandfather Enzo was.

'I don't know. I hope he's not losing his marbles.'

'Why do you say that?'

'He's got some funny ideas.'

He didn't want to tell me what they were.

It was only at the Club that I found some respite. Thursday 22 November was a very special day: Kessel was elected to the Académie Française. It's not every day that a friend becomes an academician. We knew he was a candidate, but there had been such opposition to this son of multi-ethnic Jewish émigrés that we were sure Brion would be elected instead.

We were gathered around the radio, and when the news came on and the reporter announced his election, we exploded with joy. Before he arrived, the champagne corks were popping. Even Jacky and old father Marcusot stood their rounds. When he arrived, there was hysteria. Everyone congratulated him and wanted to embrace him. Sartre joined us and stood a bottle. Kessel clinked glasses with each one of us.

'We were afraid that the hatred of certain academicians would prevent you from being elected,' Igor said to him.

'You can always achieve more than you think,' Kessel replied with his huge grin.

It was late. Reluctantly, I had to go home. I was told that the party had continued until dawn and that Marcusot had ordered a new set of glassware. By common consent, it was the greatest party ever in the history of the Balto.

Every passing day made Cécile's absence harder to bear. Leonid tried to persuade me that you had to hope, force the hand of destiny, and wait for the right moment.

'You've got to be tenacious,' he began. 'She won't be the first woman to change her mind.'

'I'm sorry to contradict you,' Igor interrupted. 'But there's no point in deluding yourself. When it's important, they don't change their minds.'

'That's not true,' yelled Leonid.

They embarked on an endless and heated discussion. Without realizing it, they were speaking in Russian. Igor was the first to become aware of it and he reverted to French.

'We're never going to agree. We don't know whether it's better to wait and hope, or to resign oneself and give up.'

'Tomorrow will be better. I'm sorry to have to point this out, Igor Emilievitch, but you are negative. Me, I'm an optimist.'

'I'm an optimist too,' Igor replied. 'The worst is ahead of us. Let's rejoice in what we have.'

JANUARY–SEPTEMBER 1963

1

At the Club, there was one man who kept to himself, separate from everyone else. He never spoke to anyone. He stood watching the others playing chess without saying anything. Everyone avoided him. On several occasions, I asked who he was, but I just got the reply 'I don't know' or 'Don't concern yourself.'

He would turn up occasionally, rather like Lognon. He appeared without anyone realizing, and disappeared for several weeks without anyone noticing. He was slim, almost thin, his face was emaciated and bore a three-day growth of beard, he had dark wavy hair, a bulging forehead, protruding cheekbones, dark brown eyes sunk deep in their sockets, a slender nose and a dimpled chin. He chain-smoked. Summer and winter, he wore a shabby grey overcoat that was too big for him. You could glimpse the cuffs of his stained, threadbare nylon shirt. With his baggy trousers and his worn shoes, you could have mistaken him for a tramp. Jacky, so attentive to orders and refills, didn't ask whether he wanted a drink. Leonid never missed the opportunity to jostle his shoulder whenever he walked past him. The man didn't respond, neither did he avoid him. At the party celebrating Kessel's election, I was witness to an incident that went otherwise unnoticed.

The man was standing apart from the group. Kessel saw him, picked up a glass, filled it with champagne and went over to him. Leonid noticed this and, with a nod of the chin, pointed it out to Igor who approached Kessel at the very moment he was handing the glass to the man. Igor put his hand on Kessel's arm and kept it there. For a few seconds, neither of them moved. Neither of them said a word to each other. Kessel stopped what he was doing, placed the glass on the table and turned around. With a clumsy movement, Igor brushed against the glass. It fell to the floor and shattered. The man stepped back, cast his gaze over the jolly gathering that was rejecting him, and disappeared.

I missed Cécile. In early January, I told myself it was time for us to get back together again, time for me to be forgiven. I phoned her. A voice replied that the number I was calling had changed and that I should consult the directory or the information centre. I went round to her place, but there was nobody there. Her concierge had not seen her for two months. No post arrived for her any more. Last January, we had wished each other a happy new year and it had been the worst one in our lives. Even if you know there's no point, that's what wishes are for — to wipe away the past. But perhaps compared to what awaited us, the year that had just passed would come to seem happy to us.

Every day, I would go and sit by the Médicis fountain. There is nothing more idiotic than these rituals we impose on ourselves, as though they could keep misfortune at bay. I was convinced that sooner or later this would be the place where I would find Cécile again. It was merely a question of being patient. If she had left Paris, sooner or later she would return and would come past this spot. I brought a book and would read beside the pond. I took a photo from time to time. I used to pick out a detail and wait for the light to lend the statues an unusual aspect. Nicolas had suggested that I change my subject matter, but for me there was no shortage of material in the Luxembourg. Over five years, I had taken hundreds of photographs of this fountain and its surroundings. Dreamers, strollers, readers sitting on benches, students, retired people, gardeners and policemen. And Acis and Galatea lying beneath the rock. There was an aura of inexplicable and fascinating mystery about it, and until I understood its meaning, I had no wish to do anything different.

I recognized him from his round shoulders and his weary gait. He stopped by a rubbish bin, picked out a newspaper, sat down on a chair and began to read *France-Soir*, beginning with the back page, the one with the comic strips. Then he stuffed it into his pocket and sat down facing the pale January sunshine. With his legs outstretched, he appeared to be asleep. An attendant came up, holding her book of tickets, and tapped him on the shoulder. He woke with a start, got to his feet and set off grumbling in the direction of the fountain, without paying her. When he drew level with me, he stopped. I didn't know whether he was pretending not to recognize me or whether he was trying to recollect where he had seen me before.

'I noticed you at the Club,' I ventured.

'Your face is familiar. Are you a regular at that old folks' home?'

'I'm learning to play chess.'

'You should be having fun with people of your own age. Anyway, they don't know how to play.'

'Leonid's a champion. People come from all over Paris to take him on. He never loses. Even against students from the Polytechnique.'

'Do you know Leonid?'

'I know them all.'

'My congratulations. The place was beginning to smell of stale herrings. A bit of new blood would do them no harm. May I?'

He didn't wait for me to reply before sitting down on a nearby chair, stretching out his legs on another one, and continuing his siesta. A ray of sunshine lit up his bearded face. He spoke impeccable French. This distinguished him from the other members of the Club, who offered a full array of Central and Eastern European accents. I was struck by the elegance and whiteness of his hands. He folded them over his threadbare overcoat. The attendant came up. He didn't stir. I paid for the three chairs.

'You shouldn't have,' he said without opening his eyes.

'You can't get out of it. Or else you have to sit on a bench.'

'And what's more, he's law-abiding. The sort of people you mix with have rubbed off on you. It's outrageous to have to pay for the right to sit down in a park, don't you think?'

'Yes.'

'With people like you around, they don't have to worry. Me, I refuse. One day, they'll make you pay for the air that you breathe.'

He hadn't opened an eyelid. His breathing was calm and regular. I started to read again and paid him no further attention.

'What are you reading?' he asked, his eyes still closed.

I held up the cover so as to make him sit up.

'*Témoin parmi les hommes*. Happy reading.'

'And inscribed by Kessel. Not to me. To one of my friends.'

'He gave me a copy too.'

'I was there when they celebrated his election.'

'I'm glad for him. He deserved it. It's a great honour.'

'Igor prevented him from giving you a glass of champagne.'

'I don't remember.'

He sat up and shrugged his shoulders. He took out a pack of Gauloises from his coat pocket, offered me a cigarette that I refused, and lit one for himself.

'They don't seem to like you.'

'I wasn't aware of it.'

'Why don't they like you?… They don't talk to you. They ignore you. Leonid jostles you. Igor stops you clinking glasses and Kessel doesn't say a word.'

'To be a member of a club, you have to pay a subscription. I didn't want to subscribe. I'm a bit stingy.'

'There's no subscription in this club.'

'I find it hard to make friends.'

'Nobody forces you to go there.'

'The days are long. I call in when it's raining. I'm still slightly hopeful. But I must have a face that puts them off. Do I frighten you?'

'No.'

'You believe me, at least?'

'I know Igor. He wouldn't do anything without a reason. Neither would Leonid.'

'At your age, you ought to know the reasons why men quarrel. For money: we're all broke. I don't owe them anything. For a woman: I've given up on that score. Or for an idea, and there we're all in the same boat.'

'You're the only one they treat like that.'

'The truth is simple. When I enter a room, people stop talking. When I walk in, they disperse.'

'Are you from the police?'

'Look at me. Do I look like a cop? Be honest, do I make you feel uneasy?'

'No.'

'What's your name?'

'Marini. Michel Marini.'

'I'm glad to have made your acquaintance, young man.'

He stood up and walked away. I had forgotten to ask him his name.

2

'*La donna è mobile*' was back again. My father no longer went to work. He spent his time on the sitting room sofa listening to his favourite tune. He switched the gramophone arm to 'repeat' and played it continuously. He knew the words by heart and sang softly to himself, barely audible. He didn't disturb anyone, but we weren't used to seeing him at home during the week. Sometimes he left without anyone noticing, leaving the turntable spinning. He spent his afternoons in the little café on rue des Fossés-Saint-Jacques playing tarot with his pals. I would go and find him there and sit down beside him. Occasionally, he would ask my opinion: 'What shall I play: a *petite*, a *pousse* or a *garde*?'

He was a good player, cunning and teasing. When he asked me the question, it was just to fool his opponents. They played for drinks. Some of them weren't able to afford it and he paid for the round.

'Pity we're not playing one franc per point, I'd have made some dosh today.'

I returned home as usual before seven o'clock. He came back after dinner, rummaged around in the fridge and put on his record without paying any attention to us. This little game went on for four months. The disappearance of the Treasury bonds had had unexpected consequences, but he refused to justify himself. My mother wouldn't accept this. On two occasions, she went back on the offensive and cross-questioned me. Trapped by the promise I had made to my father, I stood my ground. She was not convinced by my reply. The presence of the Delaunays from Algeria did not make communication any easier. Perhaps if my parents had been on their own, they might have been able to overcome this ordeal and stand up for themselves. He would have had the courage to reveal the truth and she would have been able to accept it. Louise gave bad advice, urging my mother to stand firm and pretend to be shocked and upset. She put her own interests first, and advised my mother not to forgive and to discover the truth at all costs. My father had made the mistake of giving ground to them and returning to Paris over the summer holidays. I overheard their conversations during damp walks along the coastal path: 'After all you have done for him it's outrageous that he behaves like that behind your back. It's theft. He's treating you like an imbecile. I wouldn't have allowed my husband to do something like that to me. Your brother's a man of stronger calibre. He's been educated. Who's to know whether he's not keeping someone. Five million, it's a huge sum. And what if he did it again?'

At the beginning of October, my mother had announced that her brother would work with her in the business. Maurice had been appointed manager of the shop. My father had no say in the matter. To begin with, the division of duties was clear-cut. Maurice would look after the running of the business and the administration with my mother, who wanted to step back a little. My father would continue to manage the commercial department. His reaction was immediate: he switched off completely. Instead of struggling to find new customers, he waited for them to get in touch with him. Three months went by before they realized that the order book was looking empty. My father calmed them down: 'It's because of the slump.'

We lived in a state of chaos. Maria had left the family in the lurch. In the rush of her departure, it was hard to understand who had died: her father or her brother. She had announced one morning that she was going to Spain for the funeral and had jumped on the bus for Valencia. We thought she would come back after a week, but she didn't turn up. We made calculations about the length of mourning in Spain, which was longer than in France, where you started work the day after the funeral. My mother didn't have her contact details. She made enquiries among other Spanish cleaning ladies in the neighbourhood. In actual fact, Maria had had enough of the Delaunays from Algeria and had invented an excuse to get away. The apartment was in a pitiful condition. The dishes accumulated, and neither broom nor cleaning cloth, nor feather duster, was used. The dirty clothes piled up. My father blamed Louise, who never lifted a finger.

'My health is delicate. After all the hardships we've had to endure, I don't intend becoming your skivvy!'

The climax came when my mother tried to do the laundry using the washing machine bought at the Ideal Home Exhibition. Maria was the only one who knew how to use it, and the kitchen and the neighbour's flat below were flooded. Maurice, realizing that the atmosphere was becoming highly charged, cleared the table and did the washing-up. He suggested that my father might help him. My father sent him packing. 'The last time I washed up other people's plates was in the German prison camp. Unless the war's started again without anyone telling me, you won't see me with a washing-up brush in a hurry.'

One particular incident triggered hostilities. Néron had disappeared. We looked for him everywhere: under the beds, in the cupboards where he sometimes hid, among the furniture, in drawers, inside the washing machine and the fridge. We turned the place upside down, to no avail. We worked out that he must have managed to slip out through the front door. We asked the neighbours, but no one had seen him. It was a real mystery. Juliette and I searched the cellars, the courtyard and the service stairs. No tomcat. We asked old Bardon, the concierge, who revealed the truth of what had happened. In the morning, he had seen the cousins leave the building, carrying Néron. They swore that he was mistaken, that he was lying, and that they loved all animals, especially cats. But the harm had been done. We scribbled out fifty or so little notices which we pinned up all over the neighbourhood. Juliette became hysterical and she began to hate the Delaunays and to make their lives impossible.

In early December, they found a flat in Daumesnil in the remotest part of the twelfth arrondissement, an unfamiliar district, which we had been through only once, when we went to the zoo at Vincennes. They moved in without any help from us. Juliette and I refused to go to the house-warming party. My mother went on her own.

After their departure, we hoped that family life would return to normal, but nothing was the same any more. At dinner times there was a deathly silence. Our parents didn't open their mouths. They no longer asked us what we had done at school, so we switched on the television.

Maria didn't come back. My mother started to do the housework, from dawn till dusk, and from floor to ceiling. Louise came to have tea with her and watched her polishing, scrubbing, sweeping and ironing. My mother wore her apron all day long. She didn't want to go out any more and she no longer wished to go with Louise to the shops. At the beginning of the year, Maurice went on the offensive. He rejected signed orders on the grounds that they were not cost-effective. My father did not appreciate his work being called into question. My mother sided with her brother: we did not have enough customers to waste time on those who brought in no money. Maurice asked my father to organize a daily 'debriefing' on his market expectations and to put in a 'report' on his activities.

'A what?'

My father told him to get lost. He stopped working.

'In a firm, it's the person who brings in the cheques who's the boss.'

He listened to *Rigoletto*. He bought himself *La Traviata*, with la Callas, and played it over and over again. He played tarot, believing it was just a matter of time before they would come to beg him on bended knee to return. But Maurice came up with a riposte. He hired three sales reps, who were paid on commission. He didn't ask my father for his opinion. Business took off without him. When I think about it, I can see he didn't have much luck with his sons. At a time when he could have done with a helping hand, I was no support to him. Feeling obsessively gloomy about Cécile's absence, I didn't notice what was happening and I did nothing to help him. We never spoke about it.

Amid this wreckage, there was one piece of good news. A woman phoned. She had seen one of our notices. Néron had been found. He had taken shelter with a hairdresser in Jussieu. He had lost two or three kilos. He showed no joy at seeing us again, nor any gratitude. He spent his time by the front door, hoping to escape each time it was opened. Shortly afterwards, Maria came back from Spain and started work again.

3

Getting my photographs developed was costing me a small fortune. I couldn't get away from the standard, skimpy format. For anything over 9 x 11 cm, the prices were prohibitive, but it wasn't a good time to ask for a rise in pocket money. I confined myself to one roll of film per month. Nicolas's father recommended a shop where the current prices were attractive, especially for large formats. Wedged between two shops selling religious knick-knacks in rue Saint-Sulpice, Fotorama did not just sell equipment. The two windows displayed a couple of dozen large prints that were of remarkable quality. Many passers-by stopped to admire them. The window on the right was set aside for traditional commissions: weddings, first communions, individual or group portraits. They avoided looking clichéd thanks to the use of flattering lighting, which disguised facial blemishes but still allowed character to show. In the left-hand window were black and white photographs of country landscapes in the snow, trees covered in white, and ice-covered telegraph posts and wires. I was examining another set of photographs, taken in the desert, showing Touaregs with furrowed faces, when the window panel opened. A technician in a white coat was placing a print of an encampment at dusk on a small easel. With his rounded shoulders and his weary manner, I recognized the man from the Club whom I had talked to in the Luxembourg a fortnight ago. I stood aside; he didn't see me. He laid out the photographs in a different order, alternating the brighter and the darker prints. I set off with my film in my pocket. When I was opposite the Sénat, I realized that I had been wrong to walk away. It was a good opportunity to get to know him. I retraced my steps. I went into the shop. A man in a suit was serving a customer and explaining to him how to charge his camera. I admired the pictures displayed on the walls while I waited for him to finish.

'May I help you?'

I lay my film down on the counter.

'What format would you like them? And glossy or matt?'

'May I see your technician, please?'

'Who are you talking about?'

'I want to see the person who was putting the photographs in the window.'

'I don't know who you mean.'

'He was here a quarter of an hour ago. He was wearing a white coat.'

'I'm the only person who serves in this shop.'

'I saw him, I can assure you.'

'You must be mistaken, young man.'

He gave me back the film. Puzzled, I left the shop and waited a little further away, but I didn't see anyone come out. Adamant though he may have been, I knew I was not mistaken.

It had been three or four months since we had seen him. One Sunday afternoon, Leonid and Tomasz Zagielovski were involved in a ferocious game. There were half a dozen of us kibitzing round the table. Leonid was playing black and he was in danger. He had lost a bishop and a knight. Tomasz was making his moves and Leonid was not responding. Igor and Imré exchanged questioning glances. We noticed Lognon at the same moment. He was standing behind us, his hands behind his back.

'What's Big Ears doing here?' moaned Gregorios.

'How are you, Monsieur Petroulas? I congratulate you on your last speech. It gave much pleasure in high places. You raise the general tone.'

'Why do you come here? You're wasting your time with us. Haven't you a wife and children to spend Sunday with?'

'If you didn't see me, you'd forget about me and you'd get bored. Nice play, Monsieur Zagielovski. You're going to win.'

'He's check-mate in three moves,' Leonid muttered.

'It's not possible!' said Tomasz.

'Three moves. Whatever you do.'

We stared at the chessboard. Each of us tried to work out how it was possible. There were about twenty pieces on the board. After a few minutes' consideration, it was agreed all round that it was impossible.

'You'll never get anywhere,' Leonid said. 'You're just a gang of small-time players from the suburbs.'

'You're bragging,' Lognon replied.

'Are you betting?'

'You know we don't play for money here,' said Igor.

'That's a rule for Club members. He's not one of them, as far as I know? If you're so sure of yourself, Monsieur Lognon, how much are you willing to stake?'

'I'm going to teach you a lesson. You're a conceited fellow, Monsieur Krivoshein.'

He took out his wallet and drew out three hundred and thirty francs in notes, which he counted and placed under a glass.

'I'm prepared to pay one hundred francs more if you want. On condition that you win in three moves.'

'Bet taken.'

Leonid picked up the beer-mat beneath his glass and scribbled three lines on the back of it.

'I suggest that Michel takes my place. He will play the three moves that I've just jotted down. Is that agreeable, Monsieur Lognon?'

'It's fair.'

He stood up and handed me the mat. I sat down in his seat, opposite Tomasz.

'Go on,' said Tomasz.

I followed Leonid's written instructions. Tomasz responded. I carried out my moves, took his rook and saw his face become anxious. He placed his chin on his fists and reflected for so long that he drew a comment from Gregorios: 'Are you determined to send us to sleep, or something?'

He was trapped. He couldn't take my knight. His bishop was blocking it. He moved a pawn. I advanced my queen as Leonid had foreseen.

'Check and mate!'

A murmur ran through the group. They congratulated Leonid, who feigned indifference.

'Thank you, my friends. It wasn't so difficult. You should have spotted it.'

He took the money and fingered each banknote with conspicuous pleasure.

'I'm glad you came, Monsieur Lognon. It's always pleasant to have good players watching one. You should come more often.'

'I admit it was well played,' said the policeman, his jaws clenched.

'You owe me a hundred francs. Don't forget to bring the money. If I'm not here, you can leave it with Jacky. We'll drink to your health. Don't go. And a bottle of champagne, courtesy of the Préfecture.'

'We've got Cristal-Roederer, if you'd like. Special vintage,' said Jacky.

'If it's special, bring us two. It'll save you the journey. And no paper cups!'

Jacky disappeared. I followed him with my eyes and noticed the man standing a little way away, by the door. He smiled at me and gave a little wave. He stood aside when Jacky brought the bottles of champagne. Leonid poured some for everyone, including Lognon, but not for him. They drank toasts to one another, wished each other good health, drained their glasses and paid no attention to him. It was as though no one saw him. I clinked glasses with Igor and Imré. I turned round. In a flash, he had vanished. Leonid tapped me on the back.

'I'd like to give you a present, Michel. What would give you pleasure? Thanks to our friend Lognon, I've got some money, make the most of it. Hurry up.'

'Can we have a game one evening?'

'You're asking a lot.'

'It won't cost you anything.'

'Playing against a bad player is a drag. Come on, sit yourself down and, for once, play well.'

'Not this evening. My head's in a whirl. I must go home. We can do it another time.'

I left the Balto, leaving them to drink Lognon's health. Outside, I searched for the man, but couldn't see him. When I reached the Port-Royal crossroads, there he was, sitting on a bench. I went up to him.

'Was it you who created panic at the shop?' he asked me.

'Why did he say you weren't there?'

'Because I'm not supposed to be there. I work there occasionally. I help out. It's off the record. Yesterday, you brought the boss out in a cold sweat. Don't do it again. I need that job.'

'You're not registered, is that it?'

'One can't hide anything from you.'

He shrugged his shoulders in a resigned way. With his creased, cat-like eyes, he looked as though he was smiling.

I sat down on the bench with him. He took out a pack of Gauloises and offered me one.

'I don't smoke, thanks. Are you… are you a foreigner?'

He nodded.

'One wouldn't think so. You haven't any accent.'

'I learnt when I was young. With a Frenchman. When there are cops around, I put on a Vosges accent.'

'Haven't you any papers?'

'I'm drowning in papers, but they're not the right ones.'

'Don't you have political asylum?'

'I filled in a form a long time ago. They lost it. I've let the matter drop.'

'What's your name?'

He smoked his cigarette down to the filter, in no rush, threw it to the ground and trampled on it.

'My name's Sacha,' he said absent-mindedly, staring at his dusty shoes.

'Why do the others cold-shoulder you?'

'I've told you, I don't know. I've committed no offence. Nothing objectionable. You'd better ask them that question.'

'I did ask Igor again. He didn't reply.'

'They haven't understood that here we're free men in a free country. Everyone has the right to do as he pleases and go where he wants. Give me your film. I'll get it developed for you – for free. I'll bring the photos back to you. I know where to find you. You're often at the Médicis fountain, I believe?'

I handed him the film. He screwed up his face as he took it.

'What do you use?'

'A Kodak Brownie.'

'It's not ideal.'

'It's for family photos.'

'I won't promise anything.'

He pointed with his chin. I followed his gaze. On the other side of the avenue, Lognon was gesticulating, followed by Tomasz Zagielovski, who seemed rather frantic.

'He must be furious to have lost so much money,' I said to Sacha. 'Tomasz must feel annoyed to have been the cause.'

'That's too bad for them. When you don't know how to play chess, you learn it.'

'It wasn't obvious. No one would have thought Leonid was going to turn it around. He's a champion.'

'Tartacover against Bernstein, Paris competition, 1937. Leonid knows his classic matches.'

'So do you.'

'He has the selective memory that survivors have. What we find inconvenient or doesn't interest us, we forget. We retain what's useful to us, otherwise we have no hope of surviving.'

They crossed the road, Lognon grumbling and Tomasz apologizing. They disappeared down boulevard Saint-Michel.

'It's strange that that guy's got big ears,' Sacha observed. 'It's a tell-tale sign, isn't it?'

He lit a Gauloise and amused himself by blowing smoke rings.

4

When I came back from school, Grandfather Enzo was sitting in the drawing room in an armchair, with a suitcase on either side of him and a bag wrapped in string. Maria had made him a café au lait and given him some home-made shortbread. He was smoking his pipe while he waited for us. He hadn't warned us of his arrival and we were surprised to see him. He had come to Paris for three or four days to settle a few things. My father insisted that he sleep at our house. My mother didn't want this. We could hear them discussing the matter in the kitchen without understanding what they were saying. Eventually, she agreed. They offered him Franck's bedroom.

Over dinner, he revealed the reason why he had come to Paris. We were stunned. He had decided to leave France and return to Italy. Because of grandmother's illness, he had delayed this project that had been on his mind for a long time. His father came originally from Fontanellato, a village near Parma. He hadn't had any difficulty tracing the members of the family who had stayed behind when his father and two younger brothers had emigrated to France in search of work. His cousin, the son of the eldest of the Marinis, had taken over the family farm. He had been in touch with him and Ricardo Marini had invited him to come back home, where his bedroom and his family awaited him.

'Are you mad? You're out of your mind!' my father exclaimed.

'Paul, there's nothing extraordinary about it.'

'You've always told us that France was our country.'

'I miss Italy.'

'If you'd ever gone there at least, even if it was just once, during the holidays, I would understand. You've never set foot there. All of a sudden, you feel the lure of the homeland, is that it?'

'Your mother and I talked about it. She wanted us to go to Venice or Rome but we weren't able to. I started to learn Italian. I can cope quite well, I just need practice.'

'How will I manage when you're down there? Will you tell me that?'

'Manage what?'

'Looking after you!'

'Your mother and I didn't see you very often in Lens.'

'You're getting to an age when you may need help.'

'I'm not relying on you. Nor on your brother. You have your own lives. If you want to see me, it's not as if I'm going to Australia.'

'What does the cousin do?'

'He's retired. His children look after the farm. They grow tomatoes. And they keep pigs.'

'Do they make Parma ham?' Juliette asked.

Grandfather Enzo moved into Franck's bedroom. He didn't ask any questions.

The following day, when he woke up, I was having my breakfast. My father was about to leave. Grandfather joined us in the kitchen.

'You leave early for work.'

'You have to get on with life.'

'I'm going to see your brother today.'

'Good.'

'You're wrong to be like that with him. He's had bad luck. You have to understand him.'

'I have problems too, Papa.'

'Can I help you, Paul?'

'If there was a solution, I'd know what it was.'

'We need to see each other before I go. On our own.'

'If you leave, we won't see one another again.'

'In the seven years since I've retired, I've been coming to Paris once a month. I came with your mother and she used to go and see your brother. The only member of the family I saw was Michel. We would go to the Louvre together. You never had the time.'

'I work, Papa. I've got a business to run. And museums bore me.'

'I don't blame you for anything. I want to make the most of the time left to me. I want to visit Italy.'

'Why?'

'What do you expect me to do? Go to the park, watch telly, play pétan-que? Life's dull here. I need light. Now I want to see in reality what I've admired in books. In my retirement, I have the opportunity to live as I please. To take my time. I'm fortunate to be in good health. Cousin Ricardo is a decent man. The farm at Fontanellato is large. You can come to see me whenever you want. During the holidays, anyway.'

'Who knows, I may come earlier.'

My father left.

'He's got a huge amount of work,' I said in order to excuse him. 'I'm going to get your breakfast ready.'

'Are you sure you have time?'

'I don't have any lessons this afternoon and, if you like, we can go to the Louvre.'

'Before I leave, there's something I'd like to see again.'

On the front of the building at 4 rue Marie-Rose, not far from the Porte d'Orléans, there was a marble plaque: 'Here, Vladimir Ilyich Ulyanov, known as Lenin, lived from July 1909 to June 1912.' We made our way into a middle-class property that smelled strongly of polish. He went ahead of me. We climbed up two floors. He rang a bell. We heard a bolt and a chain being removed. An elderly man with a huge paunch appeared.

'Good morning, comrade,' he said as he shook grandfather's hand. 'Don't make a noise. The neighbours don't care for visitors.'

He closed the door carefully, went and sat down on a chair by the window, and began to read his book again as though we were not there. The apartment was gloomy and old-fashioned. I was expecting my grand-father to show me round, but he was standing silent and motionless in front of a gilt mirror on which some old photographs and yellowing papers had been stuck, and he seemed to be trying to decipher them. In the corridor, there was a dusty red flag and two glass cases filled with objects, lit by a bulb whose glow was so feeble that we could scarcely see a thing. At the end of the corridor, Lenin's bedroom was decorated with peeling, crinkled floral-patterned wallpaper. A game of chess lay on the bed. Above it hung a framed photograph of Karl Marx. On the wooden desk was a pencil box, some sheets of paper, some envelopes addressed to him and an oil lamp. The bookcase was stacked with ancient volumes. I drew closer to see what he read. The books were dummies and contained only blank paper. The bedroom in which Lenin's wife, Krupskaya, slept, with its single bed, was austere and smelt of mildew. The walls were covered in photographs and facsimiles of letters. In a dark corner were two children's beds. In the kitchen overlooking the courtyard was a stove with a cast-iron pot on top of it. My grandfather came over to me.

'Michel, we're going.'

We were on the point of leaving when the old man asked us: 'Would you like to sign the visitor's book? We had Monsieur Chou En-lai here last month.'

My grandfather shook his head.

'Don't make a noise on the stairs,' the caretaker said as he closed the door.

Once outside, after being in this stale-smelling building, trapped in time, we felt we were breathing pure air. Grandfather walked along avenue du Général-Leclerc at quite a pace. I had a hard time keeping up with him. His eyes were red.

'All right? What's the matter?'

He stopped.

'I shouldn't have gone back there.'

At the junction with rue d'Alésia, he hurried into a smoky café where they were betting on the races. He ordered a coffee and a *calva*, and I had a half of beer. The barman placed our orders on the counter. Grandfather put three lumps of sugar in his coffee and stirred it slowly.

'What happened with Franck?'

I couldn't not talk to him about it. In the hubbub, I outlined the basic details. He listened without looking at me and knocked back his glass of *calva*.

'Is he well at least?'

'I don't know. I tell myself that if there'd been a problem, we would have known about it.'

397

'Where is he?'

'Papa didn't want to tell me anything.'

'How did it go down at home?'

'Mama hasn't forgiven him for the Treasury bonds business. Papa is trapped. He knows that Mama will never forgive Franck for what he did, or forgive Papa for having helped him. And it's not much fun with Maurice.'

'Keep me informed with news of the family, write to me, my boy. The address is Enzo Marini, care of Ricardo Marini at Fontanellato, Emilia-Romagna. Will you remember?'

'We're not far from the chess club. Do you remember? I told you about it. Would you like to go there?'

'I don't feel like it.'

'Another day.'

'I'm going away, Michel. The day after tomorrow.'

'You could stay. You don't have to go. We could play chess together.'

'Look at this foul weather. Down there, it's sunny. You come and see me in Italy and we'll play chess all day long. You'd better keep on improving. I'll take you to Florence and to Siena. You'll see, it's the most beautiful country in the world.'

My father, Juliette and I accompanied him to the Gare de Lyon. We arrived there one hour early. He wasn't a railwayman for nothing! He examined the locomotive with a critical eye. He knew the journey, the timetable and the changes of train. He had planned to stop off for a week in Milan to see the city.

'It costs an arm and a leg!' he remarked to the clerk behind the counter.

'You get a reduction on the French rail network. In Italy, you pay the full whack.'

'I'm a former railwayman.'

'The Italians couldn't care less.'

'You see, children,' he said in a fit of pique, 'there's no international solidarity. It's every man for himself. How are we expected to manage?'

My father put his suitcases on the rack and settled him into his compartment. We waited on the platform for him to appear at the window, blow us kisses and wave us goodbye, but the train moved off and disappeared without our seeing him. My father was furious.

'What the hell is he going to do down there? Eh? Can you tell me that? For years, he's bored us to death telling us over and over again that we were French. One hundred per cent pure butter, as he put it. He had a fight with a neighbour who called him Macaroni. And the very first thing he does when he's able to do so is go back to the land of his birth. What sort of nonsense is that? It's where you live that you put down roots. They're in the earth beneath your feet. Not in Italy. He's a foreigner down there. I'll give him six months before he's back again. Now that he's sold his home, where will he go? I can't look after him. He'll just have to go to Baptiste's. He can read *Railway Magazine*. They can tell each other jokes about the Trades Union and swap the latest party gossip.'

'Talking about the party, we went to the Lenin museum.'

'Oh really!'

'He seemed upset. Why?'

'You'll have to ask him.'

'He's gone to Italy.'

'That's the way it is and that's the way it's always been.'

Two days after Grandfather Enzo's departure, my father arrived late for dinner. He was carrying a parcel wrapped in white paper. He laid it on the table, as though it were a present for my mother.

'It's for you.'

'What is it?'

'Open it and see.'

My mother untied the string, pulled open the wrapping, and discovered a shoebox. Inside it were around ten bundles of one hundred franc notes. Bonapartes.

'There's five million there. I'm giving you back the Treasury bonds money, with the children as witnesses. You won't be able to say that I took anything from you. You can count it.'

'Where has it come from?'

'Let's just say that I borrowed it and now I'm returning it to you.'

'Do you think I'm just some sort of weathercock? You take the money without telling me! You refuse to tell me what you've used it for! You bring it back as though nothing had happened. Am I some little goose you can play around with as though I were sixteen years old? Do you think I'm going to put up with this?'

She took the box and disappeared into her bedroom, slamming the door. Juliette went and joined her.

'It's unbelievable!' my father exclaimed. 'She's never happy. I take the money, she grumbles. I bring it back, she grumbles. I don't know what else I can do.'

'You could have told her the truth.'

'She mustn't know for your brother's sake. You promised, Michel.'

'I've said nothing. And where did you get this money? It wasn't Franck who gave it back to you.'

He hesitated.

'It's your grandfather.'

'Grandfather Enzo?'

'He sold his house in Lens and the furniture. He divided the sum into three parts, one for Baptiste, one for me and one for himself.'

'There's no reason to hide it from Mama.'

'You don't understand. Taking the Treasury bonds put me in an appalling position. This way, I've patched things up without appearing to do so.'

'You should have talked to her about it.'

'I'm not going to take lessons from a kid!'

'I'm trying to help you.'

'You're not helping me. You're pissing me off!'

The repayment of the money did not help his situation. Quite the reverse, matters only got worse. He would have done better to keep it. When I spoke about it to Igor, he told me that my father had been wrong. When you do something stupid, you never patch it up. You have to follow things through to the end and hope you get a chance to extricate yourself. Otherwise, you pay twice over. Both for the stupid deed and for having tried to extricate yourself.

*

Grandfather Enzo did not come back. He toured Italy by bus in a methodical manner and he found a clever way of doing so. He slept in monasteries, of which there are countless numbers there. They were clean, you could eat your fill, and it cost almost nothing. It made him laugh, he who loathed priests, to be taking advantage of this. He sent us postcards of the *duomo* in each little town to make us feel envious. It was more beautiful than he had imagined. He also wrote to us on our birthdays. He was happy and had been made very welcome. He gave a helping hand to Ricardo's children picking the tomatoes or the corn. They got on well and it was as if they had always known one another. He sent us a photograph of Fontanellato in which we could see them all in an arcaded square. In the background were a brick castle and a park. It's true that they did look like a family. The notion of returning was not mentioned. On the contrary, he asked us to come and see him and to discover our country. Apparently he spoke Italian with a Romagna accent, and no one noticed that he was French.

5

Nicolas put pressure on me to lend him Pierre's records. He insisted. I stood firm. But you can't go on saying no to your best friend, otherwise, as he kept repeating to me, it means you're not friends.

'You're a rotten swine, Michel, I lend you mine!'

'These ones aren't mine. I'm the trustee.'

'You're making fun of me! They're yours. Pierre's dead and his sister has cleared off!'

It wasn't an easy situation to cope with. Especially when the friend was gifted at maths and sat beside you. I went round to his place and took along two or three of the records. We listened to them eagerly, with our eyes closed, and I took them back with me when I left. He had a passion for Fats Domino and knew the words by heart.

He eventually came up with an ingenious solution. For his birthday, his parents had given him a Philips tape-recorder with a reversible magnetic tape. I couldn't refuse to allow him to record them. But in spite of repeated efforts, the results varied from mediocre to bad. Try as we might to avoid making noises, there were still crackling, hissing, squeaking sounds and a grainy background sound. We asked his brothers for total silence. The windows were shut tightly and we held our breath. We took refuge in the bathroom that overlooked the courtyard. I held the pick-up arm. He pressed the 'record' button. We remained stock-still until the end of the song. But we couldn't get rid of the interference. We had to make do.

'It's better than nothing. Between now and the end of the year, we'll have recorded the lot.'

Above a certain volume, you could no longer hear the static. That's the advantage of rock'n'roll. Nothing can drown it out. We tried to play the record and the recording at the same time, but we never managed to synchronize the two. We also got an echoing effect.

As I left Nicolas's house, I spotted Sacha, sitting on a bench in place Maubert. He was smoking and blowing rings. He watched me with his ambiguous smile as I approached.

'Paris is a small world,' I said to him.

'We live in the same neighbourhood. I'm five minutes away.'

'I didn't know that.'

'I've got your photos. If you wait for me, I'll go and get them.'

'There's no hurry.'

'They're wonderful.'

'Do you think so?'

'I know a bit about it. I was surprised. Three or four of them are really good. Come on, let's go and get them.'

I followed him. Sacha lived in an attractive building on rue Monge, but his room was on the seventh floor and there was no lift. The back staircase was filthy and had not been cleaned for years. The wooden steps were bare and the damp had caused plaster to peel off the walls. The paintwork was blistering. Electric wires were dangling. There were no lamp-bulbs on the first and second floors. It was a long, slow climb. Sacha was panting. When we arrived at the top, he was red in the face. He fanned himself with his hand and caught his breath.

'No more cigarettes.'

A dark, narrow corridor led to a dozen attic rooms. Sacha opened the third door. We entered an austerely furnished room of about twelve square metres, lit by a skylight high above. There were a neatly made single bed, a shelf full of books, a rectangular table with odd bits of crockery, a fruit bowl with two apples, an overflowing ashtray, a chair, a wardrobe lacking a door with a few clothes inside, no decoration, and all arranged with fastidious neatness. The only apparent luxury was an ancient crystal set placed on a stool, and an old gramophone with a pile of 78 records.

'It's not big and it's not expensive.'

'Have you lived here for a long time?'

'A year after I arrived in France, Kessel found me this place.'

'Do you know him?'

'A bit. He gives us all a helping hand from time to time.'

He took off his overcoat and threw it on the bed.

'Are you thirsty? I can't offer a choice. All I've got is water.'

He picked up a bottle and left the room to fill it from the tap at the end of the corridor. I cast an eye over his bookshelf. Authors I'd never heard of. He returned, poured out two glasses and handed me one of them.

'What nationality are you?'

'What would you say?'

'There's nothing to go by. There are only books in French.'

'When I left Russia, I hadn't time to take anything with me. To find Russian books in Paris, you've got to have money. If I want interesting novels, I go to the public library.'

'I've never seen you there.'

'For you, it's somewhere you pass through. You return your books, you take away others. You chat to Christiane for five minutes and you rush off. Me, I'm not in a hurry. I sit down. I do my reading there, in the warmth. I stay there and make the most of it until closing time. There's no central heating here.'

'It must get cold. Especially at night.'

'When you've lived in Leningrad, you're accustomed to polar temperatures. Our hides are tough. Do you want to see the photos?'

'I'd love to.'

He went out of the room and looked up and down the deserted corridor. There wasn't a sound. He waited for the light to go out. He put his hand to his mouth.

'Follow me,' he whispered.

He moved forward on tiptoes. We went down a few steps in the darkness. On the half landing, he opened a door with care. He walked into a room full of hole-in-the-ground lavatories. He motioned me to follow him. I hesitated for a moment. He noticed my reluctance.

'Don't be frightened of anything,' he muttered.

I followed him inside. He bolted the door. He put his hand inside his shirt and drew out a thin cord from around his neck. On it was a pointed key with sharp edges. He stood on the concrete ledge and raised himself up with great agility. Balancing, he unlocked a panel in the wall with the key and pushed aside the metal cover. He put his hand inside, felt around and brought out a cardboard folder. He handed it to me. I took it. He replaced the metal cover, locked the panel and climbed down again. He wiped the palms of his hands and put the cord back inside his shirt. We left the toilets. He was still on the alert. Reassured by the silence, he moved forward, without switching on the light. We walked down the stairs and emerged onto the street. He dived into the adjoining entrance. We came out in the Arènes de Lutèce. We sat down on a bench in the sunshine. He pointed out the building to me. He lit a cigarette.

'That's where I live. If you put the chair on the table, climb up on it and hoist yourself onto the roof, you get a marvellous view over Paris.'

'May I ask you why you put that in the toilets?'

'Did you see the door of my room? It's paper-thin. One shove of the shoulder and you're in there. People who live on this floor go out to work. During the daytime, the place is deserted. The rooms are often burgled. The woman next door to me, who works at the baker's shop on place Monge, they even stole her lipstick and her iron. Do you know what they took from me? My electric radiator! And what's more they're vandals. So that's where I hide my treasures and I do what Alyona Ivanovna, the old pawnbroker in *Crime and Punishment* did, I keep the key of my casket round my neck. No one would think of searching in the bog, would they?'

'Why are you telling me this?'

'I trust you.'

'Really?'

'Don't talk to anyone about it.'

'OK.'

'You mustn't tell your friends at the Club that we know each other.'

'As you wish.'

'It will be a secret between us.'

He took the cardboard folder and opened it. He took out my prints. The photographs of the Médicis fountain had been laid on stiff card and on top he had pasted on a mount that brought out the black and white details. I was gobsmacked.

405

'They're 18 x 24. It's a good format. Several of them have come out really well.'

'Do you think so?'

'You've got talent, Michel. I know about these things. Believe me. Any fool can press a button and take photos. But there aren't many photographers. You know how to frame a shot, pick out the main focus, find the most effective angle, look for the right sort of light and decide on the best moment to take it.'

'You don't know how pleased I am. It's the first time anyone's told me that.'

'And I'm not someone who pays compliments.'

'The card helps bring out the best in them.'

'Don't get me wrong. It's not like a frame for a painting. I don't use it to make it look pretty. It's to help focus the view and make the photo stand out. Nothing should interfere with it. If the photo's no good, it won't make it any better.'

'You don't think I'm too close?'

'On the contrary, that's what's interesting: you don't make the beginner's mistake of trying to control the perspective. You avoid the high and low-angle shots that distort or dwarf the subject matter. The camera should interact with the eye and remain at the same level. It shouldn't be performing gymnastics.'

'When they look like this, they're wonderful. The problem is that I can't pay you for them.'

'I'm not asking you for money. I don't let my friends pay.'

'Why do you say we're friends?'

'Aren't we friends?'

'Yes… but…'

'What's the matter, Michel? Don't you feel at ease with me?'

'What bothers me is that we address each other as "*vous*". I use "*tu*" with my friends. I'd feel more comfortable if we said "*tu*" when we speak to one another.'

'I hate using "*tu*". I'd prefer to go on as we are. We can be friends without being over-familiar.'

'As you wish.'

'In time, maybe. If you don't mind, I'll take a couple of them.'

'You want my photos?'

'I like grouping photographs together on a particular theme. I'm going to organize a small exhibition of photos of open-air sculptures. I'll put them in the window, with your agreement.'

'I'd be delighted.'

'I can't decide between these two.'

He was looking at two close-up, right-side profile prints of Polyphemus. A patch of sunlight dappled the bronze face, expressing its never-ending sorrow.

'One has the feeling he's alive. I'm choosing this one. I'll give it back to you after the exhibition.'

Sacha was different. He didn't have the Slav temperament. He didn't get irritated, he spoke in a soft, calm, slightly weary voice, and he looked at you with a mocking smile. I wondered whether he tried to cultivate this enigmatic aspect. I don't think so. He hung around the neighbourhood. I used to see him sitting on a bench in the Luxembourg, reading, surrounded by sparrows that came to peck from his hand the crumbs from his baguette. We would bump into one another all over the place. We'd spend hours chatting on the pavement. He worked at Fotorama when he felt like it. Had he wanted to, he could have had his papers put in order, but he took no steps to get a regular job. On several occasions, I tried once more to discover why the members of the Club disliked him. He shrugged his shoulders in a resigned sort of way.

'I've done them no harm. I'm like the others: if I hadn't escaped, I'd be in the wastes of Siberia down some icy hole. I make the most of each day as though it were a gift. For years, I worked like a lunatic, without counting the hours spent, without taking a rest. For nothing. That time was given to me and I lost it. Nowadays, I read, I sleep, I listen to concerts on the radio, I roam around Paris, I chat to people, I go to the cinema, I take siestas, I feed the cats in the neighbourhood and when I've not got a penny left, I either get by or get myself a job. I have the bare necessities and I've never been so happy in my life. What's shocking is not the exploitation, it's our bloody stupidity. These constraints we impose on ourselves to have things that are superfluous and useless. The worst thing is the silly fools who work for peanuts. It's not the bosses who are the problem, it's money that makes us all slaves. On the great day of judgement, the one who will come out on top is not the silly bugger who's come down from the trees to become *sapiens*, it's the ape who's continued to pick fruit while he scratches his belly. Man has understood nothing about Evolution. A person who works is a complete moron.'

6

We never saw it coming. Juliette and I had believed what we'd been told. One evening, my father did not come back for dinner. That happened, occasionally. We spent the evening without him, watching television. He came back late from the shop and had a bite to eat in the kitchen. We caught a glimpse of him the following morning, hurrying to get ready. That was normal. On the second evening, we thought he was overdoing it. On the third, my mother said he was away on a business trip. She spoke in that odd, slightly dry tone of voice that meant: 'Don't push me, I'm not in the mood.'

On Friday, they came home together. We were glad to see them. They both had gloomy expressions. We sat down in the drawing room. Just as we did when guests were there.

'Go on,' my mother said.

'Children, we have to talk to you. You must have noticed that, for some time, there have been problems at home.'

'Oh really?' said Juliette.

My father glared at my mother, shaking his head in a helpless sort of way.

'My darling,' my mother continued, 'your father and I have decided that it would be better if we separated.'

'What?' Juliette exclaimed, getting up from the chair. 'What does that mean?'

'We thought it best.'

'You're going to divorce?'

'Nothing is decided. For the time being, we're thinking. We're taking stock. You're grown-up. There's nothing unusual, these days, about parents that separate. You're not involved. We'll always be there for you. You'll continue to see your father, but we won't live together any more.'

'You can't do that!' cried Juliette.

She ran out of the room. We heard her bedroom door slam. My father rushed along to her. She had locked the door.

'Juliette, open up. I'm going to explain to you.'

'There's nothing to explain!' yelled Juliette through the door.

'Be reasonable, darling. You're really upsetting me.'

'And what about me? Do you suppose I'm not upset?'

'Please, my Juliette.'

'I'm not your Juliette!'

For an hour, they tried to persuade her to open the door. She didn't reply. They took turns, using the same arguments alternately, from begging her to threatening her and being angry.

'I don't know what to do any more,' said my father in a drained voice. 'I told you that we should have gone about it gently.'

'There's no perfect solution!' my mother exclaimed. 'When you have an abscess, you have to burst it! It hurts and afterwards, it's over. We've prevaricated, and this is the result. She'll get over it.'

They considered whether my father ought to barge open the door with his shoulder. Eventually, they concluded that this was not advisable. They needed to give her time for it to sink in. They spoke in my presence as though I were not concerned. My father packed two suitcases. He came to see me in my bedroom.

'I'm off now, Michel.'

'Where are you going?'

'I'm at the Hôtel des Mimosas, by the Gare de Lyon.'

'Are you leaving Paris?'

'The owner is a friend. He's helping me out until I find myself a flat. We'll see each other, don't worry, but I'm going to be fairly busy.'

'Why do you say that?'

'I've not got any work, my boy. It's over.'

'What about the shop?'

'It's your mother's. I've got nothing.'

'That's not possible.'

'That's the way it is, and that's the way it's going to be.'

'It's not right. You're the one who's done everything.'

'The shop doesn't matter. I'll always manage. What bothers me is you and your sister.'

'Are you… are you going to get divorced?'

'We're deliberating, because of you. We're going to see if we can come up with a solution. I believe she's right. There comes a time when you have to know when to say stop.'

'What'll you do?'

'I'll get back on my feet. I've got a few ideas. As for the other guy who's incapable of signing up a customer, I wouldn't give them six months before they file for bankruptcy.'

He put his hand on my shoulder. He squeezed it.

'We'll get ourselves organized. Listen, Michel, you mustn't judge your mother. Do you understand? What's happened to us, it's just life. I'm counting on you.'

He took me in his arms and we gave each other a hug. He left the room and switched off the light. I strained to listen. There wasn't a sound. In the middle of the night, I felt a hand shaking me. I turned on the bedside light. It was Juliette, her eyes red and her hair awry, her pillow under her arm.

'May I sleep with you?'

I lifted up my blanket. She lay down and snuggled up to me. I put my arms around her.

'Are we going away too?'

'No, we're staying in our home. It's Papa who's going. You mustn't worry.'

'Mama told me it wasn't serious.'

'You know, Juliette, you mustn't always believe what your parents say. Brothers and sisters are for life. I won't ever let you down.'

'I won't either.'

Two days later, my mother and grandfather Philippe arrived, accompanied by a man in a dark suit whom they addressed with the greatest deference. They showed him around the flat. He was a bailiff. He noted that my father had departed the marital home, that he had taken his clothes and his personal effects. Maria certified that Monsieur had left with two large suitcases. The concierges confirmed this. My father ought to have been more wary of my mother, who told him that they would both be able to think more clearly if they were on their own. When you become a couple, you shouldn't think clearly.

7

On Sunday in the early afternoon, Vladimir, assisted by Pavel, arrived at the Balto with two or three crates overflowing with food. The shopkeepers in rue Daguerre had waited for the market to be over to pay him in kind. He spread out the provisions over the tables. The souk was open. 'It makes us feel young again,' said Igor. 'It's as though we were back in the days of the New Economic Policy.'

They shared out the fruits of Vladimir's accounting labours according to the neo-Marxist principle: To each according to his desires and his pleasure, which was a matter for subtle negotiations.

'Take the *pâté en croute*. Next week, you can let me have the knuckle of ham.'

'Who wants some quiche Lorraine? I've got too much. I'll swap half of it with you for some gruyère.'

The shopkeepers made up generously for the low fees they paid him for keeping their accounts. Vladimir Gorenko had been wrong to treat the objectives set by the Commissioner for Planning as unrealistic and utopian and he had clashed with a vice-commissioner whom he had criticized for never having set foot in a factory in his life and for being a narrow-minded apparatchik. The moment he uttered those words, he had regretted them and knew that his fate was sealed. On his return to Odessa, he had been summoned to the headquarters of the Ministry for Internal Affairs. He had escaped in the hold of a cargo boat and found himself in Istanbul. Once he reached Paris, he had searched in vain for work and had gone back to being an accountant again. His experience as a weary administrator in manipulating accounts to disguise colossal losses and transform them into proletarian success stories gave him a long head start on French clerks. He had no equal in detecting inconsistencies in administrative schedules or fiscal regulations and he had built up a clientele of small shopkeepers for whom paying taxes and national insurance was extortion.

To those who didn't have any cash, Vladimir gave what he brought back. He made others pay a third or a quarter of the price. They obtained camembert from Normandy for one franc, sausage from the Ardèche for five francs a kilo, roast chickens from Bresse at ten francs apiece, and as much loose sauerkraut and sardines as they wanted for nothing at all.

That Sunday, a few protests could be heard.

'I haven't had any rabbit pâté for months,' Gregorio grumbled.

'Who's pinched the sausages from the sauerkraut?' asked Pavel.

'It's not right that Werner should have the rillons,' Tomasz moaned.

'Do you know why you should gather ceps when they're small?' asked Leonid, who had taken a Bayonne ham bone on which there was masses left over.

We spent five minutes trying to come up with an answer.

'They're more tasty?'

'They cook better?'

'There are very few of them?'

'You can't have been to the forest very often,' Leonid concluded. 'If you wait, there's someone who'll pick them before you do. In life, it's the early bird that catches the worm.'

'And what about democracy?' Tomasz protested.

'You're getting confused with equality. Democracy is an unfair system. They ask idiots like you for their opinion. Be happy with what you've got. There might be nothing else. And say thank you to Vladimir.'

Imré was the last to arrive. There were six eggs left. Vladimir gave them to him.

'I'll make an omelette with white beans. That should be good, shouldn't it?'

'In Hungary, maybe,' said Vladimir.

Imré was a melancholy bachelor. When he got home, he didn't feel like cooking. It's not much fun eating on one's own. He found it hard to endure the silence. He turned up the volume on the radio and paid no heed to the neighbours. He opened the windows of his modest two rooms in Montrouge that overlooked the busy highway, and enjoyed the hellish noise of the traffic. It didn't prevent him from sleeping with the windows open. No one had taken the place of Tibor, who haunted him like a ghost. He had resigned himself. He preserved this emptiness deep within himself. It wasn't unpleasant. For Imré, eating was a dreary functional activity, to be carried out quickly, mainly involving tinned food: lentils or white haricot beans, with vinaigrette in summer, or heated in the bain-marie in winter. At home or in the street, Imré would speak to himself. He held proper discussions with Tibor. They told each other about their lives and their worries, they asked one another's advice, they joked and they quarrelled. Passers-by were not surprised to hear him. They no longer took any notice of him. There are countless lonely people. Whom should they talk to, if not to themselves?

'I know you don't like flageolet beans. They make you fat. You put on kilos the older you get. It's normal. I don't feel like salad. Tomatoes are outrageously expensive at the moment. You'll never change.'

For the sake of doing something different, Imré decided to fry the eggs that Vladimir had given him. He took out his frying pan, put in a little butter, broke open one egg, and then a second. When he broke the third, he heard a shrill, repeated 'tweet-tweet' sound. He thought that a pigeon was sending him a message. He leant out of the window. There was nothing but traffic as far as the eye could see. Pigeons don't say 'tweet-tweet' he told himself. He was about to empty the contents of the third egg into the pan when he noticed an unusual yellow patch in the shell. He saw the chick. Alive! Taken aback, his arm wobbled and the creature fell in. Without thinking, he caught hold of the little thing before it burnt its feet. At that very moment, something happened, such as happens only once or twice in a lifetime: love at first sight. There is no other term to describe what occurred between them. They gazed at each other for ages. Imré was spellbound. The eggs were burnt. It was Saturday evening. He opened a tin of beans in tomato sauce for himself.

How and why did it get there? Raymond Martineau, the cheesemonger in rue Daguerre to whom Vladimir put the question, refused to believe it. It wasn't possible. In twenty-nine years in the business, he had never heard of such a ridiculous thing.

'If you're telling me that so you can get an extra egg, you're making a mistake, my lad. You don't fool old Martineau with stories like that.'

Perhaps it was a particularly hardy bird with a knack for staying alive. For Imré, it was a miracle. A real one. He could see no other explanation. He mentioned it to the priest at Saint-Pierre-du-Petit-Montrouge, the church he walked past each day. The priest asked him whether he was making fun of him and asked him to stop blaspheming in God's house. This did not reconcile Imré to the Catholic Church. For him, it was proof that it knew nothing about miracles and that it was blind to reality and to signs from the Lord. When he told us the story the following day, we were convinced that he would get rid of the chick, but he decided to keep it.

'A chicken is less of a nuisance than a dog. You don't catch cold going out two or three times a day and it's less tiring than a cat. There's no lit-ter-tray to change and it doesn't go on at you all day long asking for food.'

'If it gives you pleasure, you're right. What will you call it?' asked Igor, who was very broadminded.

'I haven't thought about that.'

We wondered what you could call a chicken. We were used to the sort of names given to cats and dogs. Médor, Toby, Rex, Kiki, Mimine, Minette, Bibi, Pilou and others of that kind didn't seem right.

'An animal that's a companion needs a name,' Werner asserted.

'You'll just have to call it "my Chick",' declared Gregorios, who had little imagination.

'What about "Cocotte"? That's perfect,' Virgil Cancicov suggested.

'Call it "my sweetheart", that'll make a change for you,' said Tomasz, who had a nasty sense of humour.

'I don't like that. I'm going to call it... Tibor.'

'I don't believe it!'

'You can't do that!'

'He shall be called Tibor!'

We looked for a resemblance. There wasn't one. The creature was tiny and fragile, with its downy feathers and it's very faint tweeting call. Imré took it to the Club on several occasions. Igor and Werner made an exception for it, since animals were not permitted. It was a baby that suffered from loneliness and needed affection. Imré put it inside his overcoat pocket. It proved to be a lively and mischievous pet. We took it in our hands and stroked it. It tweeted at us. After four months, it had reached a respectable size and could be left at Imré's home on its own.

'It keeps me company, but I'm looking ahead. A cat or a dog produces nothing. A hen is useful and productive. It gives eggs. One just has to wait. Hens are unjustly despised creatures. They have a different sort of intelligence to ours. There's a complex hierarchical organization in the farmyard that prevents conflicts. When the hen finds food, she alerts her chicks with a chirping sound. If there's a danger, she gives out a different call according to whether the threat comes from the ground or the air. When I say "Bi, bi, bi, bi", it rushes over to eat. And if I say "Bou, bou, bou, bou", it knows we're going out.'

He fed it with the leftovers from his meals: bits of bread and white beans that the creature pecked at delicately.

'Say what you will. There's nothing like a chick. They're affectionate, discreet, humorous and clean. When I'm sad and don't feel like talking, it stays on its cushion and respects my silence.'

The creature prospered on this diet and grew into a magnificent white hen that never laid an egg. Imré didn't mind. On the contrary. She followed and obeyed him like a lapdog. They communed and had a relationship that few people experience. When Imré went away on holiday he took his hen with him to the Noirmoutier camping site. We felt awkward. Nobody dared ask how he was. It embarrassed us to ask him questions, for fear of having to say 'And how is Tibor?'

We hesitated to mention his strange companion, though we spoke about it when he wasn't there.

'He could have chosen another name,' Virgil maintained.

'It's embarrassing, it's true.' Igor agreed.

'It's you who have a problem. Not Imré,' Gregorios explained. 'Because he's homosexual and loves a hen. It bothers you that he's happy with Tibor.'

'In my opinion, he ought to consult a specialist!' said Tomasz.

'Don't forget, you moronic Pole, that it was we Greeks who invented psychology. From the Greek *psukhê* which means "soul", and *logos* which means "science". When you give affection, you receive it in return. You ought to be able to understand that?'

8

The mornings had changed. Previously, when I got out of bed, he was in the kitchen finishing his breakfast. He was listening quietly to the news on the radio and smoking his first cigarette. I would sit down beside him. Adopting Gabin's, Jouvet's or Bourvil's voice, he would ask me whether I had slept well. We didn't say much to one another. He was always in fine fettle. There we were, together. If he wasn't in a rush, he would make me my café au lait. He waited for the weather report and he left. In a hurry, as he did every day. Because of this bloody ring-road, which was never going to be finished and created a shambles everywhere. He had depots all over Paris, customers to see in the suburbs, he had his sights on a big deal, there were Italian goods that had not been delivered, and he didn't know how he was going to cope with getting everything done. That's life. See you this evening, my boy, and work hard.

Now, the flat was quiet. It no longer smelt of tobacco. I couldn't care less about the weather. I drank my coffee in deathly silence. I gulped down my bowl and I rushed off. So I didn't have to see anyone. So I'd left before they got up. I didn't take a shower. I was out of the house one hour earlier. I read my book, in peace. It was the Kazantzakis period. Christiane had recommended him to me. She had ordered all the titles of his that were published in France. I wasn't keen on reading *Christ Recrucified*. I assumed he was one of those conservative Christian writers who preached the catechism. She forced it on me.

'If you don't read it, you'd better not set foot in this library again!'

I fell under the spell of this story of hopeless redemption. But I felt confused. At times, my mind wandered off like a breeze. It took me two months to finish the book. I had a sort of aversion to it. I stopped reading frequently. I wasn't in the mood. I felt tired and listless. I sat down all day. It was a real slump. I had *Freedom and Death* on my lap, but my mind was elsewhere. I didn't manage to finish the first chapter. I started again.

I switched off. I had had no news of my father for two weeks. A few days earlier, I had asked my mother about him.

'It's not my job to keep an eye on him. What he does is no concern of mine.'

I called at the Hôtel des Mimosas by the Gare de Lyon. I was taken aback. It was a gloomy, old-fashioned building with a spiral staircase. The receptionist didn't know him. He consulted his register and found his name; he had stayed there for two nights three weeks ago.

'He told me the owner was a friend.'

'I'm the owner. I don't remember him. Because of the railway station, a lot of people come here. If I see him, I'll tell him you were looking for him.'

I was convinced that he'd left, that he'd caught a train. Where to? And what if he'd gone to be with Franck? Would I ever see him again? Perhaps he was dead, had had an accident, or he had committed suicide and they didn't want to tell us. Otherwise, he would have phoned. What other explanation was there for his silence? If he wasn't dead and he had simply deserted us, then he was no longer my father. It reminded me of the novels of Dickens. Literature is not just stories. It's based on truth.

I was in my bedroom, lying on my bed. I was peering at the paintwork on the ceiling and listening to Jerry Lee Lewis. My mother came in, wearing a grim expression.

'Michel, have you seen the state you're in? I've told you a hundred times not to put your shoes on the bed. What's this you're wearing? How long is it since you've changed? I won't have you wearing dirty clothes. What *do* you look like? You must go to the barber. And turn off this barbaric music when I'm talking to you!'

I rolled my eyes and sighed as loudly as I could.

'You're going to have to change your attitude! If you think I'm going to put up with your tantrums, you're mistaken. I want you to show some respect to your grandfather.'

I turned and faced the wall. I let her continue: 'Are you ill?... We're not going to have all that again!... You could at least answer me! I don't know what to do with you any more!'

The record wailed like an endless sob. The music stopped. She had pulled out the electric plug. I leapt off the bed.

'Are you satisfied now? It's scratched! It's not my record!'

'You'll tidy this room. And take a shower. It smells like a pig-sty in here!'

'I couldn't give a damn. I'm not going to his birthday party!'

'We'll see about that!'

She slammed the door. I examined the record under the light. Fortunately, it wasn't scratched. I put it back on the turntable and turned up the volume so that the neighbours could enjoy it. Juliette joined me. She sat down on the bed. We listened until the record finished.

'I'd love to play the piano like him.'

'Is it true you don't want to go to grandpa's birthday party?'

'Did Mama send you?'

I didn't have the heart to conceal the truth from her: 'I'm not going because... Papa's dead and I'm in mourning for him.'

'It can't be true?'

I nodded my head in confirmation.

'There's no other explanation, my dear Juliette.'

She burst into tears, jumped up and ran out of the room. Girls have no guts. I lay down on my bed. I was reading the flyleaf of *Zorba the Greek* when my mother came in like a fury.

'What's all this about?' she yelled.

She grabbed my arm and dragged me into the sitting room before I could stop her. She picked up the phone and dialled a number.

'Is that you?' she said.

She passed the receiver to me.

I heard my father's voice saying: 'Hello? ... Hello, Hélène? What's going on?'

He was alive. I put the receiver down. In a flash, I felt something snap. It was worse than if he was dead. My mother said something. I didn't hear her. She took my hand. I pushed hers away. My face was burning. I slammed the door as I left the flat. I found myself outside. I walked without knowing where I was going. I was furious. With him, with her, with myself and with the whole world. The bastard! He had no right to forget me. He had abandoned me. If he had said to me: 'I'm going far away, I've got some problems, we're not going to see each other for a few months', I would have understood. I realized that I meant nothing to him. I played no part in his decisions. What seemed unbelievable to me a few minutes earlier now struck me as overwhelmingly obvious. He had struck me out of his life, without any warning. I was surrounded by desert. One by one those I loved had died, gone away or abandoned me. Perhaps it was my fault? Maybe there was nothing about me that merited their affection. Maybe I was worthless. But you can't cut yourself off from those you love. I was falling down a deep well and there was no one to cling on to.

I took the métro to Gobelins on the Porte de la Villette line. If I were to disappear, nobody would realize. There weren't many people on the train. There wasn't any point in going on under these circumstances. There was no hope, no light at the end of the tunnel. Who would miss me? I opened the carriage door. The dark wall of the tunnel rushed by. The electric wires swayed. One second of courage and I wouldn't have to think about it any more. I felt complete indifference. I was going to crush myself between the carriage and the wall. There would be shreds of me left. I smiled to think of their horror when they saw the bits of my body. They would cry from grief and shame. They would blame one another and tear themselves apart over my coffin. People would point the finger at them for having driven their son to despair. They would be haunted by guilt until the end of their days, which would be soon. No, it would be better if it gnawed at them for as long as possible, better if they died slowly from grief and bitterness. I pulled the door a little further. A cold, damp draught blew into my face. My hand trembled. It suddenly occurred to me that I didn't have my papers. They would find an unrecognizable body, without a name. And I would end up as an anonymous corpse in a communal ditch. They would think that I had run away from home. If you're going to do away with yourself, you need to have your identity card on you. Otherwise, there's no point. I got off at Châtelet.

*

422

I was quite close to the quai des Grands-Augustins. If she had returned, that would alter everything. I hadn't been back there for two months. I had the keys to the flat, but I didn't want to use them. Each time I did, I went away feeling depressed. And there was no point speaking to the concierge. As soon as she saw me, she gave a negative wave. I stayed on the embankment, unconcerned by the passers-by staring at me or the cries from the tourists on the riverboats. I found myself in the Luxembourg. I looked away as I passed the Médicis fountain. I sat down by the pond. I started to blub. 'Only sissies cry,' my father used to joke. I didn't want to cry. Not for him. I couldn't give a damn about his piddling morality, his shitty promises and his bloody stupid remarks. He could make fun and act the tough guy. It was all his fault. I would never see him again. Too bad. I was holding my head between my hands, trying to create some order in the clutter in my brain when I heard: 'You're going to catch a filthy cold going out in a sweater in such chilly weather.'

I sat up. Sacha was standing in front of me, his hands in his overcoat pockets.

'I left home in a bit of a hurry.'

He sat down on a nearby chair. We remained there, side by side, without saying anything, watching the kids playing with their boats on the pond and pushing them with their poles. One of the boats had become stuck beneath the water spouting from the fountain. Sacha took out a Gauloise, held out the crumpled pack to me and gave a flick with his thumb to make one of the cigarettes emerge. I took it. He struck a match. I leaned over to light it while he cupped the flame in the hollow of his hands. That was how I came to smoke my first fag. Because of my father, my mother, and in order to keep myself warm. And besides, you had to begin sometime, take the plunge, cut the ties, push off without your stabilizers, fall off, get up and start again. The cigarette had a bitter taste that clung to my palate and burned my throat, and an unpleasant smell of charred leather. We smoked them in silence and stubbed them out on the ground.

'You're looking out of sorts, Michel. You seem preoccupied.'

'What's there to laugh about?'

'At your age I never stopped. And yet it was a grim time. There was nothing to eat. We had nothing to keep ourselves warm. But what fun we had with our pals. The grown-ups wore gloomy expressions, whereas we made the most of things. We were right. Have you got problems?'

I hesitated to tell him where to get off. What business was it of his? There was nothing he could do to change the situation. He looked on kindly and waited.

'My parents are separating. My father has forgotten me. My mother takes no notice of me. My brother has run away. My best friend has disappeared. Her brother died in Algeria. My grandfather has returned to Italy. And I'm hoping I haven't lost my identity card.'

'I'm not someone who gives advice, Michel. But where troubles are concerned, I'm an expert. To get rid of something that's upsetting you, there are three cures. You've got to eat. A good meal, cakes, chocolate. Then listen to music. You should always have some with you. It makes you forget. There are few sorrows that some time with Shostakovich has not removed, even a few minutes. Though you should avoid music when you are eating.'

'And the third cure is to get thoroughly plastered?'

'A big mistake. Alcohol doesn't make you forget. Quite the reverse. My own favourite method is the cinema. A whole day. Three or four films one after the other. That way, you forget everything.'

'It's expensive.'

'You're quite right. I can't afford it. Come on, I'll take you.'

We walked up rue Soufflot as far as the Panthéon. We turned right into rue d'Ulm. A little further and I would have given up and gone home.

'Do you know the Cinémathèque?'

I'd walked past a hundred times without noticing it. I'd seen groups of people chatting on the pavement, laughing or arguing. Nothing unusual about that in this area. But I didn't know that it existed, or what its purpose was. Tickets weren't expensive. Forty-seven centimes. I could have paid that myself. Sacha insisted on taking me.

'What are we going to see?'

'If you're interested, there's a poster in the window showing the programme. Personally, I don't want to know. It's of no importance. It'll be a surprise.'

As we walked in, he shook the hand of a huge man with an enormous forehead and tousled hair who was talking to two students.

'Hello, Henri, how are you?'

'I'm furious. We've got two copies of Fritz Lang's *Fury*. There's one in English, without subtitles, and in poor condition. It keeps breaking. The other is dubbed in Italian, with subtitles in Spanish, and it's seven minutes shorter than the original version.'

I had just walked into a madhouse. The people at the Cinémathèque couldn't care less about the language. We were given the Italian version. I have to admit, to my great surprise, that after the first few minutes it didn't bother me. The subtleties of the dialogue passed me by, but I was so enthralled that these incomprehensible films have remained rooted in my memory far more than those I saw last year and which I have forgotten. It was a small room with wooden seats that banged when you stood up. It was packed during the week, with retired folk or people who didn't have enough money to go to the local cinema, with those aspiring to make movies, who took notes in the dark about what was the correct thing to do or not to do, with students who were skipping courses, fighting with one another to be in the front row and take it all in, or to sit on the floor. We got to see *Los Olvidados* dubbed in Portuguese with subtitles in German. It was luminously clear. We finished with Raoul Walsh's *The Tall Men*, a magnificent western and in French: bliss.

Sacha was right. The cinema makes you forget. It's the best cure for depression. Preferably a film that ends happily, that makes you feel better, that gives hope, featuring a hero who's on his knees, abandoned by his friends, who's human and humorous and who has a beguiling smile, whose best mate dies in his arms, who withstands the blows with unbelievable resilience, triumphs over the bad guys and their schemes, ensures justice for the widow and the oppressed, finds his beloved, a splendid blue-eyed blonde, once more, and who rescues the town or the country to the sound of rousing music. On the way out, members of the audience lingered on the pavement or in the smoke-filled cafés on place de la Contrescarpe trying to work out whether it was a great film or a very great film, with byzantine subtleties in its hidden meanings, its setting and what was left unspoken, and the minute details that they alone had noticed. There were passionate discussions that broke up old friendships, gave rise to life-long bonds with a perfect stranger, or that created immense dislikes and stubborn grudges. They fought with one another trying to decide who was the best, the most innovative or the most creative director of his kind. The same American, Japanese or Italian names came up again like leitmotivs. Sacha taught me to rank films in two categories: those you could talk about for hours after you'd seen them and those about which there was nothing to be said.

9

In return for the match won against Tomasz and paid for by Lognon, Leonid owed me a game of chess. It was stupid of me to want to take him on. Nothing would be resolved and there would be no surprises. The only question that arose was: how long would it last? I had pestered him about it again: 'I've no desire to waste my time with a pisser like you!'

'You promised, Leonid!'

'Improve a bit, then, in a few years' time, come and find me and we'll have a game.'

I should have seized the opportunity the day he suggested it, but I resigned myself to his turning me down. To show my displeasure, I no longer spoke to him and ignored his greetings. At the beginning of March, he sought me out: 'Michel, we'll play our game, the one I promised you. And you're going to beat me.'

'I don't believe you!'

His eyes were twinkling. Despite his resistance to alcohol, I wondered whether his immoderate consumption of Côtes-du-Rhône had not got the better of him.

'I've got an idea. We'll have some fun.'

'You'll thrash me.'

'Do you remember the story of David and Goliath? Who was it who won?'

'Why do you ask me that?'

'Apart from him, do you know many Davids who win? It's a biblical fraud. They want to make us believe that David was clever, but they weren't fighting on equal terms. The puny fellow had a lethal weapon. Put them in a ring with gloves on. Who's the winner? In real life, it's Goliath who wins. But for once, in a real match, on equal terms, David is going to beat Goliath.'

He described, in the smallest detail, something unimaginable. Something that would remain in the Club's annals for ever. A game that was rigged. No one would know. They would ask themselves how an arsehole of a schoolboy had been able to beat the thirty-third ranked Russian player. It would be like a whippersnapper fighting with his bare hands against a first-rate soldier with a Kalashnikov.

'Sorry, Leonid, but I don't see the point. I wanted to play a game with you. A proper one. With the aim of holding out for as long as I could. For fun. They know me at the Club. They know I'm not capable of beating Imré or Tomasz. Not to mention you. They wouldn't believe it.'

'Michel, are you able to keep a secret?'

'Do I look as if I'm two-faced or something?'

'Would you like to earn a bit of money?'

I hesitated.

'You could buy yourself whatever you want.'

'We'll have to see.'

Much has been written about the lure of money. I'd like to add my own contribution. It begins early on. In my defence, I'd like to make it clear that I was taken in by a professional. I was not up to confronting Victor Volodine. I was actually the willing victim of the well-known 'coincidence' that fills prisons and ensures a constant number of customers for the guillotines and the electric chairs. I'm not greedy. I longed to have my own Circuit 24. I went to the Bazar de l'Hôtel de Ville where the game was being demonstrated on a model display of the Le Mans Grand Prix and there, for two brief minutes, having waited patiently amid the pushing and shoving in an endless queue, I was allowed access to the controls of a Ferrari TR60 and the chance to pit myself against three competitors. For several months, I had been asking my parents for this very special game. The family upheavals had reduced birthday and Christmas presents to a minimum. My mother reckoned it cost a ridiculous amount and that, considering my results, I didn't deserve anything.

I had only seen Victor Volodine once, two years previously. It was a rainy Sunday. Igor and Vladimir were involved in a closely fought return match. Several of us were gathered round the board, following the game.

Sacha was standing in the background. At that time, I hadn't yet met him. Suddenly, the door opened, and Victor Volodine appeared, soaking wet and in an excited state. He spoke in Russian.

'Victor Anatolievitch, we speak in French here. For politeness' sake,' said Igor.

'I've got to talk to you. It's urgent. Let's get into my car.'

'Have you seen the weather?'

Victor was red in the face and continued speaking in Russian. Vladimir addressed Igor in French: 'Tell your boss that he's just spilled water over the chessboard and that if he continues to drench me, I'll take great pleasure in removing the old fart with a kick in the arse.'

'Did you hear what my friend Vladimir Tikhonovitch Gorenko said? We'll see each other tomorrow.'

'Fuck you, fuck him, and all the communists on earth! I'm warning you, Igor Emilievitch, if you don't come, I'll sack you!'

'I couldn't give a damn. You can find yourself another driver to exploit. I'm leaving France. In Portugal, my medical degree is recognized!'

We looked at one another in surprise.

'You're not leaving?' Vladimir asked.

'I've started the process of obtaining an equivalent rating. It's not ready yet. Where paperwork's concerned, there's no one to beat them.'

'You don't speak Portuguese,' Leonid remarked.

'I'll learn. It can't be very complicated. I'm a doctor, not a taxi driver. I'll be able to practise my profession there. It's important to me.'

'Tell me, Monsieur Volodine,' asked Imré, 'you appear to have shrunk. You're ten centimetres shorter.'

'It's the taxi drivers' disease. Because we spend our time in cars, we put on weight and we shrink. I've got a major problem, Igor. You've got to help me. Come outside so that I can explain. I've always been good to you. You can't refuse to help me.'

'I'm involved in a fierce contest, Victor. If you've something to tell me, you can speak openly, they're friends.'

Victor pulled up a chair. He mopped his brow and no one knew whether it was rain or sweat. Leonid picked up his bottle of Côtes-du-Rhône, filled his glass to the brim and handed it to Victor who knocked it back in one gulp.

'Thanks, Leonid Mikhailovitch. I'm finished,' he said in a hollow and desperate voice.

'Are you unwell, Victor Anatolievitch?'

'I would prefer to... I was summoned to report to the police station. I went along. I thought it was a problem to do with taxis. It's a disaster.'

'What happened?' asked Igor.

'You know me. I've done nothing but good in my life. Except during the civil war. But that was for God and the Tsar.'

'If you've nothing on your conscience, you've got nothing to worry about,' Leonid concluded.

'It's because of Rasputin's dagger.'

'You're still selling them!' Igor exclaimed.

'Very few. And they're not expensive.'

'I thought that was over.'

'I'd never sold one to a Canadian. I said to myself ... if that makes him happy.'

'Where's the problem?'

'Given the price that he paid, he must have thought it was real.'

'How much did you sell it to him for?'

'... Two thousand, five hundred dollars.'

'You're crazy!'

'They were Canadian dollars. They had Queen Elizabeth on them. He was a lawyer from Toronto. A decent fellow. To begin with, I played the part of the guy who refused to sell and who regarded his moving and historical trophy as the apple of his eye. For an hour and twenty minutes, with the meter running, he persisted. I gave in. He'll put it in his display cabinet, I thought. He'll show it to his friends. The usual thing. This damn fool wanted to show off. He donated it to the Toronto Museum. They realized that the Metropolitan in New York had the same one. The Canadian was not amused. He filed a complaint. So did both museums.'

'Did the police question you?'

'I denied it. I told them that it couldn't be me, given that the original was in the Russian Museum in St Petersburg.'

'The name of the city is Leningrad!' objected Igor.

'Never! It shall always be called St Petersburg! It was the Tsars who built it, not the commies!'

'We're not going to argue about that again!' Leonid interrupted.

'Your pal the police inspector, he's been promoted. Couldn't he look into the matter and sort it out?'

'Daniel Mahaut?' said Igor. 'Don't depend on it.'

'Be careful, if I get into trouble and they take away my licence, it will affect you.'

'Igor, I can't afford to lose my job!' said Leonid.

'Victor Anatolievitch, if I intervene, it's not because of you. I warn you, this is the last time. You're lying through your teeth. You're abusing your customers' trust. I don't want to be your accomplice.'

'My dear Igor, you've understood nothing about life. Coming from a materialist, that doesn't surprise me. It's like St Anthony's relics, Corot's paintings or Napoleon's hats. What the hell does the truth matter? The important thing is to dream. There's more to life than money!'

I don't know what Igor did, but the matter went no further and we never heard about it again. The museums withdrew their complaints. According to Pavel, they realized it would have a negative effect on donations. In the United States and Canada apparently ridicule is fatal. Victor stopped selling people the daggers that assassinated Rasputin. Apart from to a Congolese minister, a fellow from Zurich, a Brazilian Miss Universe and a Greek arms dealer.

Two months later, Igor received a positive response. His degree was recognized and valid. He stood a round of drinks to celebrate the news. Our smiles and encouragement were strained. He set off for Portugal to go through the formalities. We were sad to think we wouldn't see him again, but we didn't show it. The thought that he would be practising his profession in Lisbon made him happy. He invited us to come and see him whenever we wanted. Three day later, he was back again. He had the gloomy look of a man of whom it is best not to ask questions. In actual fact, the Portuguese authorities were taking him on as a military doctor to look after the colonial troops in the war in Angola. He had refused. Werner told us that he had lost his temper and insulted an army colonel who was a doctor. He took up his job as a taxi driver once more and continued his search to find a country that would accept his degree.

During the past two years, Victor Volodine had put on weight and developed a double chin. He ate a great deal, did no exercise, and made it a matter of principle to spend his money on lavish meals with plenty to drink, made-to-measure houndstooth suits with waistcoats, American braces and crocodile skin boots. Since the episode of the Rasputin daggers, we had not seen him at the Club. His company owned several taxi licences. He could have stopped work and taken life as it comes, but he refused to retire and continued to clock up eleven hours a day. Igor and Leonid worked for him and did not complain. Victor had a poor opinion of Igor, who followed none of his recommendations. Leonid had taken advantage of his advice and had realized that being a taxi driver was not synonymous with public service. Their preferred target was foreign tourists, ideally those who spoke no French, whom they picked up near the big hotels around the Opéra and the Champs-Elysées and drove around Paris, on the most congested routes. Victor explained the scheme he had worked out with Leonid to me. He was going to arrange for bets on our game of chess. Nobody would risk a centime on me, but he would place a bet on me at ten to one. They were going to earn a lot of money and I would have my share.

'It's a rip-off!'

'You mustn't exaggerate. We're going to extract a bit of cash from people who don't need it and who must not suspect that they're going to be hoodwinked. As I always say: if God, in his infinite mercy has created mugs, it's in order that they should be taken for a ride. Had he, for whom all is possible, not wished for this, he would have made them less stupid. What would you like, my boy?'

He had put me on the spot.

'An hour with some brazen little hussy? How would you like that? At

432

your age, they couldn't stop me. I know two or three who aren't shy. You could choose: a blonde, a black girl? How do you like them? How about both, young fellow?'

Overcome by panic and confusion, I blushed and stammered. This podgy fellow revolted me with his impudence and self-importance. I searched for something I might say that would be like a slap in the face; that would express my anger, my contempt, my revulsion, my indignation, my loathing. Something that would be cutting and scornful, that would make him feel ashamed throughout his life; that would remind him of his despicable behaviour, his mediocrity and his vile remarks. I wanted to yell at him that I was different; that I would not betray my friends; that I had nothing in common with a grasping reactionary like him; that his whole being disgusted me; that only pity and his one hundred and twenty kilos prevented me from spitting in his face.

'I want a Circuit 24.'

10

Many bad things are said about the excessive number of postal workers and clerks in the City of Paris. These comments are unfair. In my neighbourhood, there was one area in which they were beyond reproach: punctuality. For many years, the postman deposited the mail for the building on the concierges' doormat between 7.38 and 7.40 in the morning. Old Bardon left at 7.45 for his job as usher at the Paris city hall where he started work at 8.15. He would open the door of his porters' lodge, scoop up the pile of letters and newspapers, put them inside and, having taken leave of old mother Bardon with a 'See you this evening, my sweet', he would set off. This endearment must have had its origins in some distant past when she was not shaped like a beer barrel and did not have arms like those of a removal man. She would reply: 'Have a lovely day, little goat', though no one who had encountered this embittered and vindictive nutcase would venture to compare him to a kid goat. I had a five-minute window. I left the flat at 7.30 in order to arrive at school by 7.59. I sat on the staircase, with the lights out, huddled up on the first-floor landing and pressed against the inner courtyard window so that I could read in peace, waiting for the postman to throw the mail on the doormat and leave. I hurried down on tiptoes. In a flash, I spotted the letter marked Lycée Henri-IV on the envelope, snapped it up and slipped it into my pocket. The end-of-term reports with their 'Could do better if he wished but he doesn't want to', 'Constant in his inconstancy', and other cynical and unpleasant comments, as well as the endless regulations, warnings and boring letters, never reached my parents. From the start of the school year, I had been forging my father's signature. I had no trouble imitating his scrawl. I allowed letters to go through when there wasn't any risk. It was the only way I had found of achieving total peace. My parents never suspected a thing. That's where my fondness for postmen comes from.

Lessons were deadly boring. The weather was fine. Stuck in the back of the class, by the window, I could see the grey dome of the Panthéon. Why is there never an earthquake in Paris? I wanted to be outside. I looked at my watch. Every minute of this afternoon seemed to go on for ever. Sitting beside me, Nicolas was swotting. He was faithfully writing everything down, and underlining it with his ruler and four-colour ballpoint pen. He was a sight to behold, totally enthralled, rather like some unknown species of insect discovered by a scientist. He was keen to learn and eagerly absorbed these tiresome litanies. I couldn't care less about my notes, about being promoted to the higher class or about the future that beckoned. I continued reading, with my book on my lap and my satchel open beneath it so that I could let the book drop into it in the rare event of the teacher coming to stretch his legs in the aisle. I was having difficulties with Kazantzakis. It was impossible to concentrate on *Freedom or Death*. My mind wandered. I thought of Cécile. Where was she? What was she doing? Was she still angry with me? When would I see her again? I wondered how you could find someone who has disappeared when you're not a family member. Perhaps Sacha would have some idea? There were two knocks on the door. The English master paused. The school porter came in.

'Marini,' he announced. 'You are summoned to M. Masson's office.'

I got to my feet. Kazantzakis fell into the satchel. Nicolas stood up to let me pass. He gave me a pat on the back to spur me on. I followed the porter.

'What does he want me for?' I asked.

'When he summons someone in the middle of a lesson, it's not a good sign,' he replied.

Walking along the endless corridor, I realized what had happened. It was the postman, the post office or my mother. Or the neighbour from the fifth floor, whom I hadn't heard coming and who had caught me unaware, sitting on the stairs, last week and had not understood my muddled explanation. They had discovered my secret. I was going to have a difficult time. It was going to be hard to deny it or pretend that the post had got lost. This was known as: misappropriation of correspondence by a halfwit hoist on his own petard. It was bound to mean the disciplinary committee and expulsion. Shame and degradation, the path to the guil-lotine. I searched for attenuating circumstances. Perhaps if I cried, and pleaded utter idiocy and family trauma, the sentence would be restricted to a three-day expulsion. I had an irresistible longing to have a pee. And to escape. If I ran, no one would catch me. Where would I go? The draw-back about running away is that it doesn't take you far from where you started. It's like a boomerang. You have to face up to things. Going down the main staircase, I thought of Isabel Archer and of Alexis Zorba. Could the difference between men and women possibly be that women tackle their problems courageously, whereas men always find a bad reason for putting up with them? We had reached the supervisor's office. The porter knocked twice. 'Come in,' we heard. He opened the door. I closed my eyes. Like the man about to be shot who hears the word: 'Fire!'

'What's the matter, Michel?'

Sherlock was standing in front of me in the doorway, smiling. Was he a sadist? Did he want to seem all matey and lay a trap for me so that I would confess?

'I think you know why you're here?' he said in a solemn tone.

I searched through an endless list. If I opened my mouth, I risked con-fessing to something that had not been discovered. It was like chess. When you don't know your opponent, you play a tentative move to allow him to reveal himself. Adopting a contrite expression, I nodded.

'I think so, Monsieur.'

'I don't imagine it's easy for you. If you would like to talk about it, I'm always available, and you won't ever be disturbing me.'

He clutched my shoulders in both his arms and then went out. There was my father sitting on the other side of his desk.

'I'll leave you,' Sherlock had said.

He had closed the door behind him.

'What on earth are you doing there?'

He came towards me.

'I didn't know what time you came out. Nor whether you had classes. So I made enquiries.'

'You gave me the fright of my life!'

'Michel, I'm sorry, I ought to have warned you.'

It took me a few seconds to realize that we were talking at cross purposes. Where is anger hidden? In what recess of our brain does it lie festering? Why do we enjoy wounding those we love? Was it the strain accumulated over weeks or the terrible fright I had just had? Or was there another reason, deeper and more personal, that I did not wish to own up to?

'I'm talking about the fact that you've forgotten us! You couldn't give a damn about us! I would never have imagined that you'd be capable of doing something like that to us. You've deserted us!'

'Don't say that. Please. I found myself in an impossible situation.'

'It's your fault. Mama's right.'

'I didn't want it to happen like this.'

'How could you let six weeks go by without letting us know whether you were alive? Do you think that's normal?'

'It's more complicated than I thought.'

'A phone call, that's all we wanted. Just to say you were well and that you'd see us next week.'

'You're right, I should have called. Did your mother not say anything to you?'

'We say hello in the morning, good evening when she gets back from the shop, and good night.'

'It's not easy for her either. I need to talk to you. The thing is… I'm living in Bar-le-Duc.'

'Where's that?'

'In the East. It's the principal town of the Meuse.'

'What are you doing in Bar-le-Duc?'

'I'm in the process of starting a business. I've found a partner. I wanted to move to Versailles. That's where he's from. He reckons that if it takes off in Bar-le-Duc, it'll succeed everywhere.'

'Haven't they got a telephone in that dump?'

'I've got a crazy amount of work. You can't imagine.'

'I couldn't care less! That's no reason. The family's finished!'

I slammed the door as I left the room. Sherlock was in the corridor and was talking to the school porter. My father caught up with me, and they

437

watched us with troubled expressions as we passed them. They had had no need to listen carefully in order to follow our conversation. We found ourselves outside. We started walking.

'Michel, I came so that we could talk.'

'There's nothing more to be said. The harm's done.'

'You're grown-up. You can understand.'

'You've forsaken us. That's all there is to it!'

'I took the day off. We're up to our eyes with problems and jobs to be done. I'm catching the 17.54 train. Can I buy you a half of lemonade shandy?'

'I don't feel like one!'

'What *do* you feel like?'

'I want a Circuit 24.'

'You want me to buy you a Circuit 24? What does it cost?'

It was too expensive. Not at this moment. In a few months' time, perhaps, if things went as he hoped. For the time being, he was living on a tight budget and could not allow himself any unnecessary expenditure.

'It's now that I need it. Not in ten years' time!'

'You could ask your mother.'

'She told me that she didn't have any money, that business was going badly and that I should ask my father!'

'Things are going badly! I suspected as much. Maurice is useless.'

'She also says that you're not paying the maintenance that had been agreed.'

'What with? She knows my position. In fifteen years I haven't asked for a penny for my work. I paid back what I borrowed with my share of the legacy. I left with just my clothing. I need time to re-establish myself. I'll make up for what I owe, both the capital and the interest. Don't worry on her account, nor on yours. You'll want for nothing. I don't want her involving you in our troubles.'

He was on edge. He took out his pack of Gitanes and put a cigarette to his lips. I held out my hand. He let me take one. He lit them both.

'Do you smoke?'

'I have for a while.'

438

'Really. Listen, I'll phone you once a week.'

'Don't feel you're obliged to.'

'That way we'll be able to talk. On Sunday evenings, would that suit you?'

'I don't know whether I'll be there. When are you coming back to Paris?'

'As soon as possible. Trust me.'

'I must go. I've got work to do.'

'We've still got an hour to spare.'

He looked at me with his big round eyes and his bathroom salesman's smile. In five seconds, he was going to adopt Gabin's or Jouvet's voice. I turned round and went out. Without shaking his hand. Without kissing him. I didn't look back. It was my turn.

11

So as to be quite sure that no member of the Club knew, Leonid chose the game played in the final of the little-known Sverdlovsk tournament won in 1943 by Botvinnik, the one and only representative of God on earth, who had handed out a thrashing to the formidable Alexander Konstantinopolsky, an advocate of trench warfare and cast-iron defence. The opponent used all his might to attack an unassailable citadel. Once he had lost several pawns and major pieces, Botvinnik brought his own men into play using the steamroller tactic. No risk. An apparatchik's game. Deadly boring. I spent two weeks learning this game by heart. I played it over dozens of times. There was no way I could make a mistake. I learned the fifty-two moves made by Botvinnik with white and memorized the fifty-one made by Konstantinopolsky, to be played by Leonid. I was practising the moves on my pocket chessboard by the Médicis fountain when Sacha appeared. He guessed I would be there and he suggested I go with him to the Cinémathèque. I slipped the piece of paper with the game on it into my pocket.

'Not today. I'm in training. I'm playing Leonid on Sunday.'

'You won't win.'

'I'm telling you I will! There are some people who want to take bets on it.'

'It's not possible. If I had any money, I'd bet against you and I'd win.'

'Please, don't bet on Leonid. I'm the one you should bet on. I've analysed his game. He has weaknesses. I'm using the Caro-Kann defence.'

'No one's played that for twenty years.'

'All the more reason to. He won't suspect it.'

'I didn't know you played so well. I'll come and watch that.'

Leonid and Victor had chosen their day carefully. It fell on 31 March, the eve of 1 April. They were already laughing about it. Leonid refused to allow me to discuss the matter with Igor.

'They're your friends, Leonid. Aren't you embarrassed to play a trick like that on them?'

'They're not rich. They won't lose a lot of money.'

'In Igor's case, it bothers me. Especially him.'

'Don't worry. He never bets.'

We arranged to meet the day before, opposite the Bon Marché. I got into his taxi for a dress rehearsal. He wanted to be sure about my memory. We played the game in his car in record time, as though it were blitz chess. On the fortieth move, he stopped, looking pensive. He frowned and seemed frustrated. His naturally lean features accentuated his concern.

'Leonid, is there a problem?'

He shook his head and went on with the game. On the fifty-second move, I placed my knight on e6. Check mate! Botvinnik had turned around a game that was lost and had won in style.

'We should play it less quickly,' he said in a distracted voice.

'Is there anything wrong?'

'No.'

'We can swap, if you'd rather. I'll have black. It doesn't matter if I lose. It would be logical.'

'We won't change a thing!'

'No one will believe that I can beat you.'

'They still think that the communist party defends the workers. They're soft in the head. They're prepared to swallow anything.'

'Even if you were dead drunk, I'd never manage it. The deception is too great. They'll realize.'

'Victor's cunning. He's thought of everything. See you tomorrow.'

The great day had arrived. During the week, Leonid had prepared the ground by announcing that Volodine was out of his mind: he had decided to bet on little Michel and to accept bets at ten to one. Igor didn't like this.

'We don't play for money in this club.'

'If this idiot Victor wants to throw away his money, why not make the most of it?' pleaded Vladimir.

'It's the principle. And principles are made to be respected.'

441

'It's a rule that's valid among ourselves,' Pavel retorted. 'Victor Volodine doesn't belong to the Club.'

'It strikes me as unlikely that he'd bet on Michel. He hasn't a hope. Not one in a million.'

'At the races, Victor plays for high stakes,' Leonid explained. 'He likes to go for big money.'

'I find that hard to believe.'

'Michel has improved,' Leonid pointed out.

'I hadn't noticed,' said Igor.

'You say that Leonid's a man who's got no standards. We're going to teach him a good lesson,' said Virgil.

'It's the exception that will prove the rule,' Gregorios concluded. 'All against Victor Volodine!'

Apart from Werner who was working at his cinema in rue Champollion, all the members of the Club were there. Even Lognon, who had not been seen for two months. Victor arrived at about three in the afternoon, squeezed into a rather tight made-to-measure suit. You could smell his eau de Cologne two metres away.

'How are you, Victor?' asked Pavel. 'We don't often see you.'

'On Sundays, I don't hang around in a place that stinks of tobacco and beer. I get fresh air into my lungs. I go to Longchamp or Auteuil. Horses, there's nothing like them. I've just bought one with a friend, a baron from the old nobility. A crack horse of the future. We're going to run him at the country racecourses.'

'Have you robbed a perfume shop?' asked Pavel.

'I take my precautions when I come here.'

'Apparently you're betting on Michel against Leonid?' asked Virgil.

'Do you take me for a mug? He hasn't got a chance in a million. It would be like putting a young girl in the ring against a heavyweight.'

They looked at one another in confusion. Their hope of winning any money was disappearing.

'I'll bet on little Michel on two conditions.'

'What are they?'

'That he plays white.'

This is called baiting the hook. Putting forward as an obstacle what everyone else accepts unreservedly. Nobody raised any objection.

'And Leonid will play with these.'

From the inside pocket of his suit, he pulled out a pair of spectacles of the type that welders wear to protect their eyes from being spattered and which let no light in between the skin and the outside of the frames. The lenses were covered in black paint.

'He won't see anything. He'll play blind. From memory. It'll be a slight handicap. It'll restore the balance. Under these conditions, gentlemen, I will take bets. For Michel and against Leonid.'

'That changes everything.'

'It's not the same thing.'

They started arguing. Could Leonid memorize the positions in a game, or not? He had never done so before. You could be a great player and still not remember the position of your own pieces and those of your opponent, even if he was a beginner. There was much humming and hawing, prevarication and quibbling, and it would have gone on until the bar closed had not Leonid taken control of proceedings:

'Victor Anatolievitch, it's Sunday today, you're not my boss and I'm going to speak my mind. You're nothing but a bloody lily-livered fascist. If you think that your pathetic trick is going to make me lose, you've got your finger up your arsehole. I've played and won hundreds of games blindfold. And against champions.'

He took out of his coat a bundle of fifty and one hundred franc notes.

'There's eight hundred and fifty francs. You can count it! How much are we playing for?'

'Two to one.'

'You're just someone who sucks the blood of the poor. It doesn't surprise me in a White Russian!'

He was about to put his money back in his pocket when Victor stopped him: 'Four to one. I'll go no further.'

'If I'm blindfold, I'm playing seven to one.'

'Are you crazy?'

'Are you scared? Go back to your horses.'

'If you're quite sure of yourself, it's five to one. Final offer.'

'You're on!'

This released the others. Wallets were taken out. Banknotes appeared. Everyone placed his bet. Victor and Vladimir jotted down the amounts in a notebook. Lognon laid three wads of banknotes on the table and kept his hand on them.

'Tell me, Monsieur Volodine, do you think I've got large ears?'

We looked at one another. Nobody had ever mentioned this in front of him. How could he know? We looked for an escape route.

'I've seen bigger,' Victor replied opportunely. 'Cossacks have huge ones.'

'If God gave me large ears, it's so that I can hear from a distance. Did you say five to one?'

'I did indeed.'

'I'll stake three thousand. I've also got one hell of a nose. You who are a specialist in dagger thrusts, you've got it coming to you.'

'Are you quite sure of yourself?' Imré asked Leonid.

'I've got hundreds of games in my head.'

'I don't want to lose.'

'It's now or never if you want to make a pile of money. At five to one!'

'The little fellow hasn't got a chance!' yelled Tomasz. 'I thrashed him twice this week. I'll thrash him again afterwards, if you like.'

Imré produced two hundred and forty francs. The Club had filled up with customers from the Balto who were laying bets on Leonid. Old father Marcusot, drawn by the crowd, made an appearance and used the opportunity to take orders.

'Albert, are you going to have a bet?' Vladimir called out to him. 'Michel can't win.'

'I never gamble.'

'You've got the money, father Marcusot, you could allow yourself a bet,' said Victor.

'The dosh is all here,' he said, tapping his paunch with both hands. No one's going to take it away from me. Gentlemen, we eat and drink here, and I'm ready for your orders.'

Igor was overwhelmed and was scratching his chin.

'Aren't you betting?' he asked me.

'Er… I haven't any money… He's going to win.'

'May I help Michel?' Igor asked.

'Come off it!' Leonid groaned.

Sacha came over. He had a hundred franc note in his hand and was about to put it on the table when Leonid grabbed his arm.

'You're not placing a bet!' he said.

'Get out!' Igor continued. 'How many times do you have to be told? We don't want you in this club!'

'We live in a republic here. We're free, so fuck off!'

He went and sat down, picked up a newspaper that was lying around and began to read it. Gregorios tapped me on the shoulder with a fatherly smile.

'Don't worry, Michel. It's not serious.'

They were gazing at me with kindly faces. They were wondering how long I was going to hold out against the ogre, even if he was blindfold. They knew that I didn't have a chance against Leonid. They weren't worried about their outlay. The notion that I might win was totally inconceivable. As improbable as a martyr devouring the lion, or a man flying away waving his arms, or a Liechtenstein victory over the Red Army. I shuddered and had an almost irresistible desire to pee. If I were going to escape, it was now or never. You can't play when you're not feeling well and your bladder's about to explode. Then in a sort of flash I saw them there, with their gleaming eyes and their mocking smiles revealing teeth that were ready to bite. They couldn't give a damn about me. They were wondering how they would spend their stake multiplied by five thanks to this ass Victor. The fat slob must be stupid. They were no better than him. Life is a casino. On the one side, there are those who think that luck exists and who are going to lose, and on the other those who don't believe in it and who win every time. Today, the croupier was Victor, who wore a compassionate, funereal air, knowing that he was going to fleece them but ought not to show his overwhelming delight.

'Relax,' Vladimir advised me.

I sat down at the chessboard. Leonid drained Tomasz's 102 and ordered a bottle of Côtes from Jacky.

'I hope I'm going to be proud of you,' Igor said to me.

'Leonid, don't forget we've bet on you,' announced Imré. 'We need some cash.'

'Michel, play as normal,' Tomasz said.

'It would be best if we played in silence. I've got to concentrate.'

Gregorios picked up the spectacles and tried them on.

'You can't see a thing.'

'They're specially chosen,' Victor explained in a warm voice.

One should be wary of small fat men and chubby-faced jovial people with their angelic air of first communicants. They are the most dangerous. Leonid joined me. He laid his glass down on the table. He put on the jet-black spectacles. He looked up as though he was searching for the light, reached out his hand aimlessly, groped around and almost knocked over his queen.

'I'll move your pieces for you, if you like,' said Pavel. 'You tell me where to put them.'

'Pavel's going to win a game for once,' Tomasz joked.

'I need silence too,' said Leonid. 'Whenever you're ready, Michel.'

They all fell silent and waited for the opening move. I gave it some thought. Like a player who begins and then wonders what his second move will be. Except that I was Botvinnik, the best player in the world. I moved my pawn on e2 to e4. That bloody fool Konstantinopolsky replied with his pawn on c7 to c6. The contest was starting in an original manner. I responded with d2 to d4 and he blocked me with d7 to d5. Don't play too quickly, whatever you do. 'It must look natural,' Leonid had said to me the previous day. Leonid gave his instructions for each move and Pavel placed the piece for him. On the ninth move, I castled on the king's side. I could hear a murmur among the spectators.

'The little fellow's playing well.'

'He's not doing badly.'

If ever I find myself without a job, I could join the Comédie-Française. I didn't play a part, but I acted out a role in which I knew every line beforehand, with an opponent who had the words at his fingertips. We gave our cues like two old hams. We took great care. We weren't pretending any more. We really were our characters, in all their sincerity, their spontaneity, their level of intensity, their slight hesitations, pauses, frowns, outbursts of glee and sighs of regret, moments of astonishment and deep reflection. All the others saw was the passion. Leonid was a convincing blind man placed in difficulty on the twenty-eighth move by my knight's e2 to e4. By yielding control of the king's file, his rook allowed my white king to reach the centre of the board. Leonid slowed down his game. You could sense there was a problem. He reached out his hand into space.

'What move are you making?' Pavel asked.

'I want my glass damn it!'

Pavel handed him his glass of Côtes, which he knocked back. The tension was mounting. There was much sighing, clearing of throats and handkerchiefs wiping glistening foreheads.

'It's amazing that he can remember all the pieces. What a memory!' Tomasz said.

'Shut up!' muttered Vladimir.

'I'm thirsty,' said Leonid. 'Pour me some more!'

Pavel filled his glass. Leonid drank half the wine and kept the glass in his hand.

'What was the kid's last move?' he asked in a strange voice.

'He moved his knight from c3 and took the pawn on b5.'

From this moment on, nothing went as planned. On the forty-first move, I was supposed to take his black rook and force an exchange of rooks in order to capture his remaining bishop. He waited. Drips of sweat were running down his temples. He was clutching his face in both hands. He remained hunched over for minutes on end, wrought up, fingers kneading his hair.

'It's not possible!' he exclaimed.

'Yes it is, I assure you,' said Pavel.

I had nothing to do with what happened next. I had done what had been agreed. It was Leonid who changed his mind. Instead of moving his rook on g1 to f1 as Konstantinopolsky had done, he moved his queen to c6. I didn't know how to respond. This was not expected! No one around us had noticed the change. I gave him a kick under the table. He smiled. I suddenly realized. He had found a better move than Botvinnik's. He couldn't help it. He wasn't able to prevent himself. He knew it was going to cost him a small fortune. He played against himself. None of the thousands of players who had studied and dissected this game had seen that Konstantinopolsky could win. Leonid was more talented than his master. I knew for sure that I wasn't going to be able to extricate myself. Botvinnik was going to lose. Among the onlookers, some had begun to sense that things were beginning to go badly for me. Igor gazed at me with a regretful expression. I did what I could so as not to lose face. This game would be consistent with morality. Goliath would win and David would take a hammering.

Victor Volodine racked his brain for memories of this wretched game. His last match had taken place during the civil war, at the siege of Perekop in October 1920 before he was evacuated with Wrangel's army. He had been twenty and now had not played for forty-three years. He realized from the joyful bubble of excitement running through the spectators and their rude comments that things were going wrong.

'Are you losing your touch, Victor?'

'You're usually much craftier.'

'What a crazy idea, betting on the kid'

'I was worried for a while. The boy played well. He put him in difficulties. Leonid turned things round.'

'Get the cash ready, Victor.'

'We're going to drink your health!'

'What's going on?' asked Victor. 'The boy's going to win.'

'He's checkmate in three moves. He can't get out of it,' Vladimir confirmed.

'I don't believe it!'

On the fiftieth move, just as I was about to be beaten by Leonid, Victor, in a rage, swept the board over with his hand and sent the pieces scattering around the room. Before we could recover from our astonishment,

448

Leonid took off his spectacles, observed the damage done, grabbed Victor and punched him several times in the face. He was hitting him furiously. We realized he was going to kill him. It took several people to separate them. He was kicking him in the stomach. With unexpected spirit for a man of his size, Victor got to his feet. He had a black eye. He was bleeding profusely from above the eye. He left without further ado. They let Leonid go. His shirt was red with his boss's blood.

'I was about to beat him!' Leonid yelled.

'That's obvious. You don't get any credit for beating Michel,' said Pavel.

'Idiot! It was Botvinnik I was about to beat!'

Nobody understood. Apart from me. Since the game had not been completed, after long discussion they reckoned there was no reason to pay out or claim the bets. Everyone remained where they were, not unhappy to have escaped lightly.

'You don't play too badly, after all,' commented Vladimir.

'You've improved,' said Igor. 'I'm glad.'

'He's become like us,' Leonid concluded.

And he was consumed by a continuous bout of nervous laughter that was contagious. A full-throated roar that he was unable to stop. He had tears in his eyes and was hiccupping. We no longer knew whether he was laughing or contorted in pain.

'My cousin, she had epileptic fits. They're rather similar,' Virgil remarked.

'It's not epilepsy,' Igor stated. 'It's a strange kind of mad laughter.'

They reckoned that he had lost the plot as certain great players do. They achieve such a high degree of intellectual purity and cerebral concentration that they tip over the edge. The most intelligent among us use only 5 or 6 per cent of their grey matter's potential. These others, who attained this extra percentage, moved into a world where the average mortal could not follow. This enabled them to play against Jesus Christ, Napoleon, Einstein or themselves. The story was told of a Spanish grandmaster who, having thrashed Freud and Marx a few times, had spent the last seventeen years playing a game that was full of new developments against the Devil himself. The latter was soon in a tight spot. Leonid joined us again fairly quickly. He was pale, exhausted and trembling. His lower lip was quivering. He was crying like a small boy.

'I beat Botvinnik!'

I took the opportunity to slip away. It was drizzling outside. I felt I needed a cigarette. I was wondering whether to buy myself a pack. Sacha was waiting at the zebra crossing. I stayed at the doorway. I didn't want to speak to him. The lights turned to red. He didn't cross the road. He turned round, spotted me and smiled. He walked over towards me.

'You're much improved, my dear Michel, I congratulate you. Or else that poor Leonid is getting soft in the head.'

For a second, I was frightened that he might have recognized the game.

'I don't know whether it was Leonid who had drunk too much or you who were inspired. I found it hard to believe. Luck plays no part in chess. How did you manage to stand up to him? I thought you were going to beat him. It was inevitable. You've got to be talented to put him in difficulties. For forty moves you played like a grandmaster, and then, everything collapsed. He pirouetted out of it and you played like a numbskull. As if you no longer knew what to do? And that swine Volodine who was betting on you and against Leonid, even though he was playing blind, it was surreal. You're lucky the others are so hopelessly gullible.'

With a smile on his lips and his eyes narrowed, he was waiting for an answer from me. He offered me a Gauloise and lit it for me. To confess that it was a rigged game would be to admit that I was rubbish. If I told the truth, he would feel appalled to have a cheat as a friend. I inhaled deeply and held his gaze. I was about to tell him the truth when I was rescued by the arrival of Igor.

'What the hell are you doing with this guy?'

'We're not doing any harm. We're discussing.'

'That's not possible, Michel. You're either with him or with us.'

I looked from one to the other. Sacha remained imperturbable. Igor was red in the face. I was frightened he might attack him.

'If you told me why, I'd be able to understand.'

'They're old stories that don't concern you. I'll only say one thing: beware of him.'

Sacha made up my mind for me: 'Don't go to the trouble, Michel.'

'I warn you,' Igor threatened. 'We don't want to see you here again. The next time you show up, I'll smash your face in. This is the last warning!'

Sacha smiled and shrugged his shoulders.

'I'm terrified. I'm not going to be able to sleep at night,' he replied calmly.

He turned around and set off at a steady pace down avenue Denfert-Rochereau.

'You're free to go with him,' Igor told me. 'But you wouldn't be able to come back to this club.'

'I'm with you, Igor.'

He put his hand on my shoulder and clasped me to him.

'I'm pleased to hear it, Michel. You've improved one hell of a lot. Have I ever told you about my son?'

'Not much.'

'He's your age. You would get on well together. Do you smoke now? Is that recent?'

'The occasional one.'

Igor told us about how the boss and his employee had got back on friendly terms. Victor had his arm in a sling, one eye that was closed, a split lip, a face that had swollen to a fine shade of violet, two missing teeth and a crooked mouth that caused him to lisp. He was about to inform Leonid that he had been dismissed for the very serious offence of inflicting bodily harm that might have led to the death of his immediate superior. Leonid did not allow him to finish.

'If you sack me, I'll bleed you like the pig you are. I'll use the Rasputin dagger you gave me. I dare not say what I'll do to you with it. You know me, Victor Anatolievitch, I'm not joking. Do you remember what we did to the Whites when we caught one? You'll suffer before you die.'

After thinking about it, Victor decided not to sack him. He behaved as though nothing had happened and told people that he had slipped on the stairs of his house at L'Haÿ-les-Roses.

12

In June, a memorable event occurred. I'm trying to find other adjectives to describe this episode: staggering, outrageous, amazing. Except that I was the only one to notice it. When I first heard about it, I thought I would get an admiring response. I expected people to come and seek me out, shake me by the hand and pat me on the shoulder. I waited for a week. Nothing happened. It was impossible for it to go unnoticed. It was incredible, illogical and unjust. I had to harden myself. After all, Van Gogh didn't sell a single picture during his lifetime, Kafka died unknown and Rimbaud vanished into general indifference.

'Would you like to see something extraordinary?' I asked Juliette once she had finished her chattering.

'What is it?'

When she has something on her mind, Juliette is capable of repeating the same request twenty times and then asking it again in different ways. She instinctively and successfully employs the technique of near annihilation by means of exhaustion. For the sake of peace, you eventually give in. I resisted.

The sky was limpid. The air was sweet. We crossed the Luxembourg and walked down rue Bonaparte as far as Saint-Sulpice. We reached Fotorama. I stopped in front of the window. She looked in it without understanding why.

'What is it?'

'Take a look at the photographs.'

She stared carefully at the prints on display. She stood rooted to the spot.

'I don't believe it!'

'Yes, it's true!'

Set upon small stands were two black and white photographs of Acis and Galatea. There was a white label on the card and on it, written in large letters: 'Michel Marini'.

'Did you take those photos?' Juliette exclaimed.

'And there are others inside.'

'It's wonderful!'

'What do you think of them?'

'They're marvellous. Where did you take them?'

'It's the Médicis fountain. At the Luxembourg.'

The door of the shop opened. Sacha appeared, dressed in a white overall.

'How are you, Michel?'

I introduced them. Sacha impressed Juliette with his serious voice, his calm manner and the sensitive way he moved his hands.

'You have a very talented brother. I couldn't take such beautiful photographs at his age.'

The gleam of admiration that I saw in Juliette's eyes made me love Sacha for the rest of my days. With my cheeks on fire and a tingling up my spine, I was in a state close to weightlessness.

'I'm not the only one to admire them,' Sacha continued. 'We've sold your work.'

I stood open-mouthed. So did Juliette.

'A connoisseur bought the series of the five photos of the fountain. It was the boss who sold them. He was delighted. I've put these two prints in the window, but I don't think they show up the contrasts very well. It's the beginning of fame. Come in, I'll pay you.'

My face was burning. We followed him into the shop. He took out a white envelope from the drawer.

'The boss asked for the display price. For five pictures, he would have offered a reduction, but the customer didn't bargain and paid cash. Connoisseurs don't quibble. He sold them for thirty francs each, less the cost of printing and the exhibition fee. You get eighteen francs per picture, which comes to ninety francs in total.'

He laid five notes down on the counter. One Henri-IV and four Richelieus. I didn't dare pick them up. I stared at Sacha.

'And what about you? I'd like to pay you.'

'You're joking, Michel. I'm paid for my work. Keep your money. You'll need it to buy yourself a good camera.'

'Which would you advise?'

'Best of all is the Rolleicord. But you need experience and they're expensive. The single-lens reflex or compact cameras are a bit less expensive and easier to use. Second-hand ones can be found at attractive prices.'

'How many photographs would I have to sell in order to buy myself one?'

He thought for a moment.

'Between forty and fifty.'

'I've got other expenses to think about. I wouldn't be able to afford it.'

'You're in no hurry. Make the most of your money.'

We shook hands over the counter. I gathered up my banknotes. I arranged them in my wallet. He accompanied us to the door and stood aside to let us pass.

'Take some lovely photos for us, Michel, and we'll sell them for you.'

'He's nice, that man,' said Juliette in the street outside.

I tried to work it out in my head. How many photographs in order to buy a Circuit 24, a proper camera and the two dozen LPs that were indispensable for basic survival? A terrifying number. Two hundred? More? Given that my catalogue consisted of no more than five photographs and that a passing American might buy two or three of them on a good day, how many would I have to take in order to achieve this vast objective? Perhaps I ought to take an interest in the Sacré-Coeur and the Arc de Triomphe so as to increase sales? But I didn't want to get involved with postcards. Perhaps if I searched through my stock, I might find some photos that I had passed over which Sacha might agree to exhibit. Or some of Cécile perhaps? Did I have the right to use them? What had become of her? I turned round as though I was about to glimpse her behind me.

'Michel, you're getting on my nerves, do you never listen to what I'm saying?'

Juliette brought me back to reality.

'I have ears only for you.'

She had found herself a role. She was going to make my fortune and hers. She was going to talk about the photos to the fathers of her best

454

friends. She knew about twenty or more of them who didn't know what to do with their money. She went through them one by one.

'Nathalie's father, with his hairdressing saloon, he's rolling in it. Sylvie's has bought a property in the Midi. Her mother's rushing round the shops in order to decorate it. I'm going to explain to her that you're a photographic genius and that she should hurry up and buy them before they become prohibitively expensive. I'll take care of your publicity. But we'll have to look for another gallery. That one's not great. Your friend's nice, but you can't let feelings get in the way of business. We must be able to find a cheaper commission fee, don't you think?'

I didn't have time to reply to her.

'May I show you something?'

She led me to the window of a clothes shop in rue du Four.

'There it is.'

I searched for what I was supposed to look at. She pointed out a pink and white hairband.

'Please, Michel. I want it so much. Isabelle's got the same one.'

Her face was tearful and anxious. I reckoned that if it made her happy, I could buy her a hairband. I'd never given her a present. An artist who earns money can give his sister a hairband.

The shop assistant carefully removed it from the window, without upsetting anything.

'It's the last one we have left.'

Juliette tried it on and looked at herself in the mirror. She turned from side to side. She was beaming with joy.

'What do you think?'

'It looks lovely on you. I'll buy it for you.'

She threw her arms around my neck and kissed me. When I went to the till to pay and the shop assistant told me the price, I couldn't believe my ears.

'You must have made a mistake. I don't believe it. A headband can't cost thirty francs.'

'It's a designer label!' Juliette exclaimed. 'It's not expensive for a top designer.'

455

'It's exorbitant.'

'You don't know anything about it. And what's more, you're stingy!'

I dithered for a few seconds. I was caught in a trap. I felt as if she was robbing me. For a sum like that, I could buy myself ten rolls of film or a couple of rock albums. Juliette was glaring at me. She was white in the face. Did I really need to get angry with her and make her loathe me for saying no to her? I took out my wallet. I smiled as I paid, but each note weighed a ton.

'Thank you,' Juliette said. 'Did you see the scarf that goes with it?'

'Are you making fun of me?'

'It's not expensive.'

'If I may be permitted,' ventured the shop assistant, 'for a scarf of this quality…'

I left the shop with my head down and Juliette right behind me.

'Keep your money! I warn you: I won't speak to anybody about your lousy exhibition. I won't do any publicity for you. No one will know who you are! Tough on you!'

This tiresome incident was proof that sisters have no gratitude. No feminine equivalent exists in the French language for the word 'fraternal'. Nobody needed one. The truth is that it's because of squalid stories involving belts, earrings and trinkets that several geniuses have remained unacknowledged. Especially in photography.

I made the most of my unexpected wealth to invest in *With the Beatles*, their second album, which had just come out. I could lose myself for hours in this divine music. I listened non-stop to *All my Loving*. I was on my way to heaven when Juliette tried to intrude: ''What is this record?'

'Get out!'

I dreamed up grandiose plans. Taking into account my various expenses, I still had thirty-five francs, which represented a little less than a tenth of a Circuit 24. My hopes rested on Sacha. Reckoning on a modest and reasonable rate, I would need a good year to put together the necessary funds. I would have to increase my production. I picked out the photographs that seemed worth showing. I withheld seven of them. I called by at Fotorama to get his opinion, but his boss said he would not be seeing him until the weekend. I popped in at his place. He wasn't there. I slid the photographs under the door with a brief note: 'Thanks for telling me what you think of them. Michel.'

At the Balto, there was a party to celebrate Kessel's award. Igor offered me a glass of champagne. I toasted his election to the Académie française, planned for the following year. He filled it again. Everyone had something to say in tribute and, to great applause and much encouragement, each of them commented on what a great writer and what a kind-hearted man he was and how lucky we were to have him as a friend. We awaited his arrival. We raised our glasses and drank his health. They were looking at me. They were waiting for me to speak next. I found myself standing there like an idiot, with all of them staring at me. I was caught off my guard. I had the choice of repeating what had just been said or trotting out a set of platitudes. I reacted in the worst possible way. I threw caution to the wind. Had I come out with the same commonplaces as Vladimir or Tomasz, no one would have minded. I showed off: 'In order to speak about Kessel, I would need time, and I prefer to celebrate him in a fitting manner: I'll pay for my round of drinks in his honour!'

I had scarcely finished before applause rang out.

'Michel's paying for a round!'

'We've seen it all.'

Igor leant over and whispered in my ear.

'Are you sure?'

'Don't worry, I've got some money.'

'Champagne or sparkling wine?' Jacky asked.

'I prefer the sparkling, it's better.'

It was a fine party. Vladimir, Leonid and Igor sang *Le Chant des partisans* in Russian. They sang it in rather a slow way, full of anger and bitterness. On the second verse, the others took it up in French. The two versions coincided exactly. I had goose pimples.

When my bottle arrived, they touched it to ascertain whether it was a mirage or a miracle. They all wanted to drink some to see what it tasted like. Apparently, it was the best sparkling wine they had ever drunk.

In thirty seconds, it had disappeared. Leonid ordered three more bottles immediately and recounted his stories. He was unstoppable.

'When Khrushchev went to New York for the United Nations Assembly, he challenged Kennedy to a bicycle race. In spite of his bad back, Kennedy came in a good first. The front page headline in *Pravda* ran: "Soviet triumph in New York: Khrushchev second, Kennedy next to last".'

We almost died laughing. Pavel choked and Gregorios was thumping him on the back.

'And do you know what a Soviet string quartet is?'

We all searched for the answer. It was a pointless contest.

'A symphony orchestra back from a tour in the West!'

Pavel fell to his knees with tears in his eyes. He was groaning and unable to get his breath back.

'Stop, Leonid, you're going to kill him.'

Werner threw a jug of water in Pavel's face. Jacky handed me the bill. I paid twenty-two francs for my first round. If I compare it to those I have paid for since, this was the jolliest. Igor passed a hat round for contributions to the Académie sword. Everyone put his hand inside so that nobody could see what was being given. Out of my previous fortune, ten francs remained. I hesitated for a moment. I kept half of it. A Victor Hugo note struck me as an appropriate amount.

I was convinced that I had lost my father, that he had gone away for ever to some inaccessible land. We no longer spoke except on the telephone. Marooned as he was in the back of beyond, he hadn't seen my photos exhibited. He didn't know about them. Neither did my mother. She didn't have time. One evening, I covered the walls of my bedroom with my photographs. The good ones, the bad ones and the others. I didn't count them. There was a packet full of them. I used up two boxes of two hundred gold-coloured drawing pins. It was an exhibition of the Médicis fountain from every angle, like some imperfect, haphazard mosaic. There was also a board with forty-two pictures of Cécile. At her home, in the kitchen, on the balcony, doing the housework, running, reading beside the fountain. I preferred her in these stolen portraits. There was one in particular that I loved. In it her tousled hair and her eyes scarcely protruded above her knees, which she held clenched close to her face. She looked like a film star posing. As though she didn't want to be seen. I hadn't given Sacha any photographs of her. He would have liked this one. I didn't want to show it, or exhibit it or, above all, sell it to anyone. No one would ever see it. I was glad to have found it. We could spend hours side by side once more. I could read sitting beside her. She was with me.

At twelve o'clock on Saturday morning, I told my mother that I wanted to show her something. She had hardly come through the door when she froze and then exploded. She was furious with me for 'wrecking' my bedroom, and ordered me to remove the photos immediately. I refused. Voices became raised. I yelled that I didn't want to stay in this house any longer, that she was stifling me, that I wanted to go and live with my father. She burst out laughing.

'There's only one problem. Your father isn't even able to buy a train ticket to Paris. If you think he can afford to look after you, you're mistaken. As long as you're here, you'll do as I tell you. You're going to learn to obey! I'm in charge here, whether you like it or not. You'll take those ghastly things down at once!'

Since I didn't react, she began to rip them down one by one. Because she hadn't removed the drawing pins, she was tearing them. I didn't want her to touch the ones of Cécile.

'I'll do it,' I shouted.

On our return from holiday in Brittany, I went through a miserable patch. Feeling disorientated, I went to call on Sacha to invite him to the Cinémathèque, but he was weighed down with work so I went on my own. They were showing an Indian film dubbed in English, the story of an elderly, impoverished aristocrat who spends his last penny hiring musicians to put on a private concert for himself. As I left, I had an accident. It was sudden and unexpected. It was unbelievable; my guardian angel must have been protecting me. I had taken a few steps along the pavement of rue d'Ulm. I was searching for the paragraph that I had previously been reading when someone suddenly crashed into me. I found myself on the ground, confused and in pain. I had banged my head. Against what, I didn't know. I pulled myself together. Then I saw her. Right in front of me. She was rubbing her forehead, which was hidden behind her curly hair. She seemed surprised, almost distraught. We were like two lost travellers who find themselves on a desert island and discover one another. She was wearing jeans and gym shoes. She had been reading *Le Matin des magiciens* and I, *Bonjour tristesse*. I didn't stand a chance.

SEPTEMBER 1963–JUNE 1964

1

Stories have to start somewhere. Ours began like a silent movie. We sat staring at one another for a moment, trying to understand what had just happened to us. Amid the hubbub of a world reduced to ground level, with the audience leaving the Cinémathèque stepping over us. We were still in shock, our hearts still racing. We were in pain and we wanted to laugh. We could have yelled out 'You idiot!', or been annoyed, we could have grumbled, been unpleasant, or moaned 'Can't you watch where you're going!' as people do in the métro a million times a day. A group of people stopped. We could see each other between their legs. We could hear snatches of conversation about the use of music as a constructive element in the dramatic art of the Indian cinema. They were in vehement discussion over whether it should be used in the background or implied. We burst out laughing at the same time. It served as our calling card.

'What are you reading?'

I showed her the cover.

'Any good?'

'Not bad.'

'My father said it's corny.'

'Have you seen Carné's *Quai des brumes*?'

'On telly.'

'At one moment, Gabin is in some cheap restaurant in the middle of nowhere. He meets a crazy painter played by Le Vigan. He says to him: "I can't help painting the things that are behind things. For me, a swimmer is already a drowned man." Do you remember?'

'Not really.'

'Sagan is like that. She describes trivial social things. If you go by appearances, it's a rather syrupy novel. Except that she's describing the real things that are hidden behind these things. They're genuine love stories. It was the librarian who recommended her to me. Normally, it's not my kind of book. When I discover an author, I begin with the first novel and then I read all of them one after another.'

'That's funny, so do I. And who have you read?'

'I'm emerging from my Greek period. Kazantzakis, do you know him? He's extraordinary. That's why I needed something a bit lighter. What about you, what are you reading?'

'Only American authors, or almost only.'

She smiled. I'd never seen anyone smile in the way she did. American literature was a corner of the library in which I had not set foot, a mine to be prospected once I had completed the Sagan shelf.

Overhead, the group was becoming lively. Someone was asserting that in a proper film there was no point in music because there was no music in real life. They moved away, arguing heatedly about the influence of the soundtrack.

'It's odd what they're saying,' she observed.

'At the Cinémathèque, they spend more time discussing films than watching them. It's when there's nothing to say about a film that there's a problem.'

I was the first to get to my feet. I held out my hand. She took it. I pulled her up. She wasn't heavy. She was massaging the bone above her eyelid and I was rubbing my nose. I picked up her book as well as mine.

'And what's *Le Matin des magiciens* like?'

'Brilliant! It's revolutionary. You have to read it.'

'I've heard of it. They must have it at the library. Did I hurt you?'

'It was my fault. I was reading while walking.'

'So was I. That's why I didn't see you. It's a strange coincidence, isn't it?'

'It's not a coincidence. It was predictable that we'd meet today.'

'I reckon it's more of an accident. Neither of us was looking where we were going.'

'There are encounters that are bound to happen and others that never will. What sign are you?'

'I'm Libra.'

'With what in the ascendant?'

'I don't know. What do you mean?'

'There's a close relationship between the position of the planets at the time you were born and your place of birth, what you'll do and what will happen to you.'

'Is that the newspaper horoscope? It's a joke.'

'I'm talking to you about matters that are serious and have been proved.'

'Do you believe in that?'

'Totally. The stars have a genuine influence on our behaviour.'

'I can't believe it! There are thousands of influences and circumstances that alter your destiny. Ten minutes ago, I was sitting quietly in the Cinémathèque. I was about to watch a second film, a western with French subtitles. And at the last minute, I changed my mind and said to myself: You've been indoors long enough, go and take a walk. I left. And smack! It's not all written down.'

'The most recent research proves the opposite. Studies carried out on thousands of cases have shown that the position of Mars has an effect on athletes, that Jupiter affects actors, and Saturn, scientists. It's an inexplicable statistical anomaly. At this quantitative stage, it's not possible that chance alone should have established this connection. We're only at the beginning, but if we were able to analyse in depth, we could read our lives beforehand and we would see that it was predicted that you would change your mind and that we would meet at this precise moment and at this particular place on rue d'Ulm.'

'That's incredible! So someone like me, who's useless at maths, it could all be due to the stars?'

'You should have your birth chart drawn up. It wouldn't surprise me.'

'It's impossible to understand. I've slogged away like a maniac. With my brother, with my former best friend, with a girlfriend and even on my own. Result: a disaster. According to this girl, it was psychological. Due to a problem with my father and my mother. I wondered whether it wasn't just that I was stupid. Now, if there's an outside influence, it explains everything. It's even logical. I should have thought about it earlier.'

We talked for an hour on the pavement, but I can't remember what about. Everything is muddled up. She spoke with her hands, and I listened to her with conviction. I nodded. She looked at her watch.

'Oh, it's late, I must go.'

'Bye.'

She turned round and left. Like the idiot I am, I watched her walk away. I had an excuse. I was suffering from shock at the staggering revelation that my incompetence at maths was due to fate. She disappeared round the corner of the place du Panthéon. I realized I knew nothing about this girl. I hadn't even thought to ask what her name was. How could I have failed to do that? Not to have asked her where she lived, which school she went to, what she did, whether we could see each other again. Really pathetic.

I ran. She had gone. I looked in every direction. She had vanished into thin air. How could I find her again when I hadn't a clue who she was? Had chance brought us together? Or the planets? Fortune only knocks once. If you don't grasp it, tough. I had wasted a unique opportunity and I could only blame myself. I felt more annoyed with myself than ever before. But if everything was pre-ordained, it may have been decreed that we were bound to bump into one another, that I would let her leave without knowing her first name or her surname and that I would wander around searching for her until the end of time. Perhaps I would meet her again in seventy years' time. I would be bald, toothless and pot-bellied. She wrinkled and crippled. I would walk with a stick. She would be glad to see me. We would realize that we had spent years combing the neighbourhood looking for one another without success, missing each other by a few seconds. She would have thought about me frequently before marrying out of unrequited love and having six children. We would know each other's names at last. I would take her frail hand. We would smile tenderly at one another.

2

During the summer holidays, I thought I had hit rock bottom. On 3 July, my father had eventually opened his electrical goods business and discovered to his consternation that in the part of the country in which he was living, paid holidays were all the rage. The few curious-minded people who ventured into his empty shop considered it attractive but expensive. Business was tough.

He wanted to introduce us to Bar-le-Duc. Up until the last moment, I had hoped to escape the cousins. Ever since they had been repatriated to France two years previously, we saw one another frequently. For reasons that were incomprehensible, they never stopped demonstrating their affection and their friendship. I couldn't bear them. Not just because of their crass ignorance and their loyalty to French Algeria, but also because of their relentless pied noir accent which never left them. I suspected that they made it a point of honour to retain it and cultivate it. To begin with, I made fun of them by adopting it myself. That had them in stitches.

My father had given up his plan to spend the holidays locally. I had therefore been allowed to spend the period from 15 July until the end of August with the delighted Delaunays at Perros-Guirec, with its freezing waters, its rubbery crêpes, the constant spray from the sea, its cliff path that had been turned into a skating-rink, its endless games of Monopoly and, worst chore of all, holiday homework. The cousins made between ten and twenty mistakes per page. To everyone's total lack of interest, I had just passed my mock examinations with a slightly above average mark. Every morning, for the sake of family solidarity, I had to put up with dictation for halfwits. When I pointed out that spelling mistakes could be overcome by daily reading, they looked at me as though I were speaking Chinese. On 30 July, I couldn't take it any longer. On the menu was 'a marvellous passage' by Paul Bourget, or so said Grandfather Philippe, who regarded him as the greatest French writer of the twentieth century and whose *Le Disciple* was the book he read and re-read. I sent them packing and went out slamming the door. It was the feast of Saint Juliette and she was furious with me for ruining her feast day. She was convinced that I had picked on that day just to annoy her. In spite of my mother ordering me to do so, I refused to admit I had been rude or to apologize and, to make matters worse, I no longer joined in the daily dictations or in purchasing hotels on rue de la Paix.

One day, my mother asked me why I never took photographs of the family or of Brittany. I didn't answer.

'I'm sorry I tore your photos. Things had got on my nerves. I was tired.'

'I've thrown away my camera!'

'Why? It was given to you for your birthday.'

'It took lousy photos.'

'I'll buy you another one, if you'd like.'

'You'd be better off buying postcards.'

She bought a Polaroid. It produced foul-smelling photographs with drab colours that made them hop about with excitement. They spent their time snapping away and roaring with laughter at the images of themselves.

'Hey, Callaghan, why do you sneak off every time we take a family photograph?' asked Maurice.

'Because I don't want to be in a photograph next to you.'

We spent a month mumbling nonsensical words at one another. I wandered about on the heath alone, unable to read because of the gale, and I understood why there were so many roadside crucifixes in Brittany. Every afternoon, there was tea in a crêperie. They consumed tons of pancakes.

'Goodness gracious me, I can't believe how good this crêpe is!'

'Have you tried this one, my boy?'

'You're pied noir, you are' observed the woman who ran the crêperie, who wore her Bigouden headgear in the shape of a sugarloaf.

'Yes, Madame, and we're proud of it!'

They gave her a snapshot of herself. She reckoned there was no stopping progress. At Paimpol, on one occasion, I don't know what came over them, but it may have been due to the dry cider, they started singing: 'We are Africans and we've come from afar...'

The prospect of returning to school had made me feel unusually excited and enthusiastic. But on the first day of term, the sky had fallen in. Nicolas had vanished. My oldest friend. My chosen pal, with whom I shared everything or almost everything. Who was invited home for birthday parties. Whose father had told me, one Thursday evening, to cheer me up, that I was part of the family and that I should consider myself at home in his house. With whom I worked in harmony and mutual respect. Disappeared. Taken flight. Melted away. I had been promoted from the C stream to the A stream. He should have been in a different form to me, but no one had had any news of him. I went to their flat in the Maubert district. They had moved out at the end of July. The concierge didn't know where they had gone. They had left without warning. I didn't believe her. I rushed into the nearest bar. I bought a token for the payphone. I dialled his number. A female voice replied: 'The number you have dialled has not been recognized. Please check in the directory or with the information service.'

It made me shake with anger. A week before I went away on holiday, we had recorded a Little Richard album and another by Jerry Lee Lewis. I had saved him a fortune and he thanked me by ditching me, without telling me he was leaving. Especially since I had lent him a Fats Domino record from Pierre's collection. An imported disc you couldn't find anywhere. He used to spend his holidays with his grandparents in a godforsaken hole in the Deux-Sèvres, renowned for being deadly boring and for days that never ended. He was hoping to benefit from the complete silence to achieve a perfect recording. He had made a subtle threat, full of innuendo:

'Next year, if we're still together, I won't be able to let you go on cribbing during maths tests. With Shrivel-face, it was easy. With Peretti, it'll be another matter. He's a swine. He never stops walking up and down the aisles. He knows all the tricks.'

It was the sort of argument that makes you think. I gave in. I lent him *Blueberry Hill*. There was a strange little smile on his face when I gave it to him.

'You can trust me.'

I lost my Fats Domino. He knew he would be leaving Paris. No goodbye. No regrets. Not the least sadness. As though I were a stranger. I would never have believed it possible. Not with Nicolas. I felt as though my years of friendship had been stolen from me. He had no right to do that. One day we would see each other again and he had another thing coming. I'd smash him in the face. Worst of all was that I now found myself sitting next to Bertrand Cléry, who was frightened of his own shadow, would raise his left hand to conceal his precious work from me and, when that wasn't enough, he would create a barrier with his shoulder. Each time I sat down, I would take the opportunity to nudge him with my elbow or else tread on his foot. I don't know whether it was Peretti's influence, whether the standard had dropped, or whether it was a stroke of luck, but I found myself slightly above the average and, for once, was no longer the butt of everyone's jokes.

At Henri-IV, I derived a certain satisfaction from steering clear of my colleagues. Each morning, I gave myself an objective. Not to say good morning to anyone. Not to open my mouth all day. Not to reply to a single question. Not to shake anyone's hand. To try to be an invisible man. The result surpassed my expectations. Nobody spoke to me at school apart from Sherlock, whom I was duty bound to acknowledge. I was alone at last. I could read without being disturbed. Cléry had the good sense to move to the front row. Nicolas's place was empty. My mood swung between anger and resentment. After a week, I reckoned the time had come to meet my real friends. I went back to the Balto.

Igor and Leonid were playing baby-foot, whirling the rods around like a couple of chumps. They roared with laughter whenever the ball went into the goal.

'What are you doing?'

'Hello, stranger, we thought you'd moved,' said Igor, keeping his eye on the game.

'We're taking a bit of exercise,' Leonid continued.

'Teach us to play,' Igor asked.

'You're too old. You've got to start young.'

'You little devil, I can run faster than you!' said Leonid.

'We gave you lessons in chess and that wasn't much fun for us.'

That was how I came to give them their first lesson in baby-foot. They loved it. It became their favourite pastime. Every evening, before playing chess, they would have two or three games. You can play baby-foot at any age. Within a few weeks, they had formed a partnership known as the 'Bolchos', and became famous for their dishonesty and their endless challenges. Igor, playing at the back, became a decent goalkeeper, and Leonid was the attacker, even though they found it hard to abide by certain rules such as being forbidden from talking in Russian in order to distract the opponent, or knocking the ball about endlessly before shooting. Occasionally, Leonid made loud protests. When he was told he was not allowed to do this, he started to sneeze violently and would then shoot while he was doing so. It was unsporting behaviour, but you couldn't stop them: they pretended they didn't understand French.

'You're looking a bit out of sorts,' Igor remarked.

'I've got an issue with my best friend. He's cleared off without saying anything.'

'And is that why you've got such a gloomy expression?' said Leonid. 'Come on, let's have a drink.'

I told them about Nicolas's betrayal. They knew him by sight.

'What your Nicolas has done, that's nothing. I've done far worse,' Leonid explained, filling his glass. 'I deserted my best friend, Dimitri Rovine. An outstanding doctor, who saved my life. He was arrested. His mother begged me to intervene, to use my connections to lessen his sentence. I could have tried to save him, but I told myself that it wasn't worth it, that I risked compromising myself. I left him to his fate.'

'Who knows, it may have been pointless and you would have taken an unnecessary risk,' Igor said.

'What would you have done, Igor Emilievitch?'

'It was a time when people were disappearing without anyone knowing why. It was like a kind of epidemic, but one you felt ashamed to talk about. I did what the others did, Leonid, I looked the other way. You mustn't worry. At worst, he spent a few years in jail and was freed in 1953, after Stalin's death. Today, he's practising as a doctor in a hospital in

Leningrad or somewhere else and he's no longer thinking of you.'

Leonid poured himself some more Côtes-du-Rhône. His hand was shaking. The neck of the bottle was tapping on the rim of the glass. He grabbed me by the shoulders.

'Do you know why he was arrested, Michel?'

'How could I know?'

'Stop it, Leonid Mikhaïlovitch!' Igor cried. 'There's no point!'

'He was accused of selling drugs on the black market.'

He took a small brown flask from his pocket and put it on the counter.

'Do you know why I take ten drops of this stuff morning and night?'

I shook my head.

'Because it stinks! It stinks everywhere. Dimitri felt sorry for me. He wanted to help me. That's whiy he was arrested. I'll tell you something and don't you forget it: the only friends who don't let you down are those who are dead.'

He drained his glass, put the flask back in his pocket, tossed a note on the counter and then walked towards the door.

'Where are you going?' Igor asked.

'I'm off to work.'

Igor smiled at me sadly.

'He's a real bore once he gets started. There's nothing one can do. He can't stop himself harping on about it. Well what do you know: Leonid has left without finishing the bottle.'

He poured out the rest of the wine equally. We clinked glasses.

'Here's to us.'

'Igor, when you talk with your double-barrelled names, it's as if we were in a Dostoevsky novel.'

'In Russia, you don't call someone *Monsieur* or *Madame*. In order to show your respect or friendship, you use the patronymic, never the surname. Gregorios would tell you that "patronymic" comes from "father". You take your father's first name and you add *ovitch* for men and *ovna* for women. If I ever meet Khrushchev, which is unlikely, I would never say Monsieur Khrushchev, but Nikita Sergeievitch, because his father's name was Sergei. My father's name was Emile. My official Russian name is Igor

Emilievitch Markish. You were talking about Dostoevsky. His father's name was Mikhail. His full name in Russian is Fyodor Mikhaïlovitch Dostoevsky. What's your father's first name?'

'Paul.'

'In Russia, you'd be called: Mikhaïl Pavlovitch Marini.'

'That's far classier.'

3

In Fotorama's window, there were photographs of the bridges of Paris at night. My own photos had disappeared. Even though I tried to peer through the glass, I could not spot them on the walls. Sacha was in conversation with a young couple who were choosing photographs from among the dozens scattered over the counter. I waited until he was alone and I went in. His face looked drawn and weary.

'Hello, Sacha. I wanted to know if you'd sold any other photos.'

'At the moment, we're not selling anything.'

'Don't you think that if they were in the window they could be seen better?'

'I can't leave the same photos there. After a while people get used to them. I change them every month. Don't worry, Michel, I've kept a good space for you.'

On the back wall, my five photographs, enlarged into 20 x 30 glossy prints, were placed in a row alongside twenty or so others. In the wooden display cases, there were hundreds of photos waiting for a collector to discover them.

'The boss displays them for love of the art. Photography isn't appreciated in Paris and a photographer finds it hard to make a living. Without first communions and weddings, we'd have to close down.'

'I left some photos at your place.'

'I asked you to bring me some fine photos and you've just given me stuff from your bottom drawer.'

'I haven't any others.'

'Take some. Get to work.'

'I've got a second-rate camera and no money to buy another one. And anyway, I don't want to. I don't want to do anything.'

'What's the matter, Michel? Do you have a problem?'

'If there was just one, it would be wonderful. Everything feels pointless.'

'Come with me, I've got a lot on my plate. We had a big wedding at Saint-Sulpice. Twelve photos in leather albums for their two hundred and twenty guests. They want quality and they don't care what it costs. They don't make families like that any more.'

He put up a sign on the front door saying: 'We're working for you. Press the bell for a long time and be patient'. I followed him into the back of the shop, into a darkroom where he printed the photos with an enormous enlarger that he controlled with precise movements. He inserted a negative into the slide-changer, placed a sheet of paper beneath a feeder, adjusted the blades, fine-tuned the lens with a focusing wheel, opened the diaphragm for fifteen seconds and repeated the operation.

I told him about the business with Nicolas and about Leonid's reaction. He was absorbed in what he was doing. I didn't know whether he was listening to me.

'It's not Nicolas's fault,' he said eventually, without looking away from his worktop. 'You're the one who's to blame.'

'How can you say something like that? It's nothing to do with me!'

'You reckon that Nicolas behaved like a little shit.'

'I do.'

'If he had thought of you as his friend, he wouldn't have reacted like that. So he wasn't your friend. The blame really does lie with you for accepting just anyone as your friend. You've got to know how to distinguish between real friends and false friends. With friends, we often indulge in wishful thinking. You've been a bit thoughtless in your choice. Leonid, on the other hand, has reasons for blaming himself. He knows or suspects the truth.'

'What do you mean?'

'I believe Dimitri Rovine is dead.'

'Igor said that he had been freed and must have gone back to his job as a doctor.'

'Igor's a real friend to Leonid. He cheers him up as best he can. It was a rotten time. They shot people for the slightest thing. Dimitri was probably shot a few days after his arrest. It happened frequently.'

'Leonid seemed to be being genuine.'

'Pretending to hope means not being a total bastard. Deep down, he knows the truth. The KGB didn't announce the executions for two reasons: first, they were sticklers for etiquette. Only a court could sentence someone to death. So they killed and they kept quiet, because then no one could blame them for anything. But very soon, they realized there was a problem with those who were still alive. They had to be prevented from rallying round relatives who had been arrested, had to be prevented from causing problems. Stating that someone had been sentenced to forced labour by implementation of Article 58 meant: he is alive, even though you might never hear of him again. The relatives preserved some minute hope. That was the important thing, being able to cling to the tiniest hope. So they killed two birds with one stone: they got rid of whomever they wanted and their families stopped pestering them.'

He went on with his work, extracting the prints like a robot.

'If they had told the truth, their families would have resigned themselves.'

'For political police, that's of no consequence. Leonid is right to feel bad. The mistake Dimitri made was not a very important one. Buying and selling on the black market was less serious than being an opponent of the regime. Leonid knew Stalin and the people's commissars. He was a Hero of the Soviet Union. Had he asked for this favour, it's likely that Dimitri would have been released. He let his best friend down, a guy who really did save his life.'

'And what would you have done in his position?'

'Leonid was right. He got away. He's the one who's alive.'

'I haven't asked you, Sacha, what's your patronymic?'

In the half-light, I saw him shrugging his shoulders.

'It's such a long time ago since I heard it that I've forgotten it. In France, it's useless.'

Sacha looked at his delicate white hands. Beneath the feeble orange lamp, he turned them one way and then the other. He wiped his forehead with the back of his sleeve and sighed deeply.

'These society weddings are really tedious. They're deadly boring. You wonder what she sees in him. They're hideous, aren't they?'

I looked at the faded image projected onto the paper. It was the moment they said yes in the town hall.

'They don't suit one another.'

'He's a banker.'

'If you like, I'll take you to the Cinémathèque. They're showing *The Music Room*.'

'I'd happily have seen it again, but I can't. I've a pile of work to do. Preparing the developing baths, doing the drying. I'll be up all night.'

'It's in Bengali with English subtitles.'

'It's an excellent thing to do and it fills several hours of lessons.'

'I'm going to wait. They're showing it again next week. I don't like going to the cinema on my own.'

'You've got no excuse for missing this film. Let me know what you think of it. I don't want to influence you. You can take me another time. And I promise you that if an American happens to come into this shop, I'll force him to buy your photos.'

I went on my own. It was a very beautiful film even if I didn't understand all of it. And it was when I was coming out that... That's how meetings happen. All because of a fancy, flashy wedding. If Sacha had said yes, if his professional conscience had not exceeded his love of cinema, he would have come with me, and nothing would have happened. He had work to do. That changed everything.

4

This country had a population of forty-eight million. To simplify the calculation, let's say that there were as many women as there were men. There was thus a one in twenty-four million chance that I would meet her. I was more likely to win the jackpot in the World War I Veterans lottery than to bump into her again. She had been there right in front of me. We had spoken to one another. We had been close, and I had allowed her to vanish. When I had asked Igor for his opinion, he had explained to me that he was not an authority on meeting people and he advised me to ask Leonid, who was an expert.

'You really are an idiot. I didn't think you were so silly.'

'He's young,' Igor pleaded.

'In my day, it was very different,' Leonid went on. 'This new generation is depressing. It's hard enough when you know their surname, their first name, what they like and where they live. Next time, you'll know better.'

'I want to find her again.'

'But didn't I speak to you about Milène? What lesson did you draw from that?'

'That you were unlucky.'

'I'm speaking about a moral, as in a La Fontaine fable.'

'That you shouldn't dream, or confuse your illusions with reality?'

'That's better. I'll tell you one thing that you must never forget. Life is like the Russian mountains,' Leonid declared in a moralistic tone. 'You descend very quickly, you remain at the bottom for a long time, and you find it very hard to climb up again.'

He wanted to order another bottle, but Igor dissuaded him, asserting that Côtes-du-Rhône had a bad influence on Russian philosophy. We played a game of baby-foot. They won, but when it's two against one and both of them are cheating, it's not a game.

'I count on your discretion.'

'What do you take us for?'

The Club was the last place to keep a secret. What one of them knew, the others would soon discover. Confidential matters, whispered in someone's ear, and not to be disclosed under any circumstances, were passed on with the promise that they would never be mentioned: 'You know me. I'm the soul of discretion.' They were revealed under the same conditions and they all swore that they would not be repeated to anybody. 'Otherwise, you can't trust a friend any longer.'

On the very next day, as soon as I arrived, I found myself at the centre of a heated discussion. For Werner, this was an understandable distraction, especially after seeing *Le Salon de musique*. Tomasz maintained that it would not have happened to him, the Poles being renowned for their quick-wittedness. Gregorios reckoned it was normal to pursue someone of the opposite sex, from the Greek *hétéros*, which means 'other' and that it would wear off after marriage, from the Greek *gamos*, which leads either to monogamy or polygamy. The advice rained down and I didn't know where to put myself.

'It may well be that the girl forgot you after a couple of seconds,' Imré reckoned.

'If she didn't ask you your name, it means she wasn't interested.'

'Nowadays, girls have two or three boyfriends.'

'Or else she's a pain in the neck, and you would regret having got to know her,' Pavel concluded.

I found myself honoured with the unexpected compassion of Big Ears whom we had not seen for ages.

'There are many men, such as you and me, whom women can see through. Don't be disheartened.'

'Thank you, Monsieur Lognon.'

'I'll tell you one thing, my boy, I find a woman who reads as she's walking a bit suspect.'

They discussed whether I was stupid, clumsy, shy, or whether it was all a result of my lack of experience. I could tell the verdict they had reached from their expressions, from their smiles of sympathy, from their uncustomary kindness, and from the way they patted me on the shoulder to cheer me up.

'I'd like to ask you something else.'

Of course, Michel. We're here to help you.'

'What sign of the zodiac are you?'

The world was obviously divided into two sides. Those who believed in the zodiac, even slightly, and those who took the former for idiots. It was hard to make up your mind. In spite of the conflicting views that were aired, three principles emerged: everybody knew his own star sign, including those who thought it was rubbish. Each also knew the signs of those closest to them and what their main characteristics were. None of the opponents was able to explain why he read his horoscope in the newspaper when he came across it. The reply 'out of curiosity' made the believers laugh.

'I don't rush to read the small ads for properties or the stock exchange rates. They don't interest me. So one wonders why you waste your time reading what you call "crap",' said Imré, who was Capricorn, to Vladimir, who was Taurus and fiercely hostile.

The third thing to note was that it aroused endless debate, which got bogged down in illogical and contradictory statements.

'You see,' explained Leonid, who was Sagittarius and did not believe, 'Milène was Taurus with Cancer in the ascendant. It could never have worked between us.'

'Even though astrology comes from the Greek *astron*, which means "star", and *logos*, which signifies "knowledge", those who believe in this nonsense are right-wing arseholes and those who don't are genuine socialists!' declared Gregorios in a peremptory manner.

All ten of them shouted: 'Hold on, I disagree!'

I left them squabbling away. I don't know where they drew the energy and strength from to battle so tirelessly for the final word as if their lives depended on it. They exhausted me. I left, with my doubts and my misgivings. The likelihood that I would bump into her again was almost nil. She may merely have been passing through Paris, in which case I hadn't the remotest beginnings of a chance of seeing her again. I looked up.

The moon was mocking me. It was a proof that everything was decreed beforehand and that we were moving onward down the endless tunnel of our fate. I was crushed by the overwhelming weight of my destiny.

5

They say that it is through adversity that we discover our true friends. It didn't take me long to decide. Everyone at the Balto had made fun of me, apart from Gregorios, who had no sense of humour. I therefore began my enquiry into predestination with him.

'Why do Greek stories always end in bloodshed?' I asked him. 'Could Orestes or Oedipus avoid their destiny? Did they have a hope of escaping from it?'

'Your question is of no interest. Remember that in Greek tragedy, the gods are powerless and unable to change the lives of humans. No one can evade his destiny: neither gods, nor men. We know the end from the beginning. There's neither mystery, nor suspense. If the heroes don't die, there is no further tragedy. If Clytemnestra forgives Agamemnon, if Orestes doesn't kill his mother, if they forgive one another, then you have just invented redemption and Christianity. Had Freud been born earlier, Oedipus would have enjoyed a peaceful retirement. He would have said: it's my father and my mother who are to blame. He was not aware of this excuse and he gouged his eyes out. Jocasta didn't know about it either and she hanged herself.'

'What about you, you don't believe in horoscopes and yet everything is pre-ordained?'

'Horoscopes are for mugs. Our room for manoeuvre is tiny. We are determined by our social background and our intellectual abilities. I spend my life establishing the fact that it's impossible to educate a majority of idiots. You can't force the hand of fate.'

The only one who helped me was Sacha. He had understood just how serious it was and took it to heart.

'Let's go back to the beginning, Michel. If we haven't found the solution, it's because we've addressed the problem incorrectly. Forget the emotional side. Imagine that a detective were in your position. He's looking for this young woman. He'll make use of the few objective facts at his disposal. Facts, nothing but facts. No verdict based on opinion or interpretation. There can only be a yes or no answer to every question.'

'All right.'

'We know that she likes American literature, reads *Le Matin des magiciens* and believes in horoscopes.'

'We don't have any other clues, I agree.'

'You spoke to one another for an hour: what about?'

'I don't remember a thing. We laughed at one point.'

'Did you laugh together or did you make her laugh?'

I shrugged my shoulders feebly.

'I don't see what I could have said that was funny.'

He closed his eyes and considered the matter.

'I'm going to give you my conclusion. You do have a chance of seeing her again. A young woman who reads in the street is not passing through. She's a student. She lives in the neighbourhood. Nobody walks around reading in an area they don't know. There's a strong likelihood that you'll find her again one day. The best way would be to wait at a strategic place, on the corner of rue Soufflot and boulevard Saint-Michel, say, and not move, day or night. Sooner or later, she'll come by. Unfortunately, it's impossible to pick the precise point. According to your description, she's not a flirt, she doesn't frequent the fashionable shops, or the hairdressing salons: have a look in the bookshops, hang around the Sorbonne and place Contrescarpe.'

Sacha had cheered me up. I did search for her, everywhere it was possible to do so. I waited outside the lycées and colleges of the area. I paced up and down boulevard Saint-Michel and the narrow surrounding streets and looked in at the countless cafés, bistros, bars and brasseries of the neighbourhood. I searched the shops and bookstores, in the record dealers, in the public gardens, on the park benches. Nothing. I reported back to Sacha on the pointlessness of my searches. He encouraged me not to give up: 'Nobody told you it would happen quickly. If you give up, you'll have no chance of succeeding. I've had an idea that may be more effective. When you don't succeed on one path, take the opposite direction.'

'I'm sorry, Sacha, that's not very clear.'

'A problem has an entrance and an exit. One can start from the beginning or from the end. We'd started from the premise that you needed to find her. We've never examined the opposite hypothesis.'

'Which one?'

'She's looking for you too. She bumps into the one nutcase in Paris who reads as he walks. And you made her laugh. If I were her, I'd want to see you again. In that case, what can she do? The same thing as you. She'll start from the few facts she has in her possession in order to find you. Perhaps if we manage to join the two searches together, it will be quicker.'

I was astonished by his intelligence. I realized what a good friend I had, someone capable of treating my problem as if it were his own.

'She knows that you go to the Cinémathèque and that you borrow books from the library. You should restrict your search to those two places.'

'I also told her that I was Libra.'

'That's of no interest.'

'Have I asked you what sign you are?'

'Are you joking?'

'It's an important part of our conversation.'

'It sounds like a joke.'

Sacha was the exception that proved the rule. I never found out what sign he was. From that day on, I spent my time within a five-hundred-metre triangle extending from Henri-IV, to the library of the town hall in the fifth arrondissement, to the Cinémathèque in rue d'Ulm.

''What does she look like?'

I tried to describe her. The jeans, the sneakers, the curly hair – they were all important, otherwise he could not imagine her. But it's impossible to describe an image. Words were useless. She didn't look like anyone we knew who might serve as a reference. I set about drawing her profile. But my artistic development had ended at nursery school – I had made no progress since then, and drew as though I were holding a broomstick. I was incapable of creating a likeness of her, but I set about trying. I took a soft lead pencil and a piece of charcoal. I drew a few shadowy sketches.

As far as I was concerned, it looked like her face. Allowing for a certain amount of imagination. I showed the profile to Christiane at the library: 'Have you seen this young woman?'

'She looks like a mare with its mane flying in the breeze,' she observed.

'It's a young girl with curly hair.'

'There's no shortage of young girls with curly hair in the library.'

I looked around the room. There were several of them sitting around the large table.

'Michel, you should take up drawing lessons.'

'It's too late. What star sign are you, Christiane?'

'Capricorn, with Scorpio in the ascendant.'

'And your husband?'

'He's Capricorn too.'

'Do you have to belong to the same sign in order to get on well?'

'It can't do any harm. Are you interested in horoscopes now?'

'Just for information. I'm doing a survey. By the way, I looked for *Le Matin des magiciens* and couldn't find it.'

'I don't know why not, it was filed under Pauwels. Do you really want to read that?'

'Isn't it any good?'

'It's a con. Are you keen on horoscopes, do you want to read *Le Matin*, you're not going to tell me you believe in aliens, are you?'

I spent long sessions at the Cinémathèque, testing the absolute limits of what was possible. I had a few scholarly duties, as excessive as they were pointless, that required my presence on the school bench. I watched countless films, some that were extraordinary, some that were deadly dull, and others that were pre-war trash. I selflessly endured an uncut Dreyer and an Ozu, a retrospective of silent Mexican comedy films and, more happily, a tribute to Louise Brooks and another to Fritz Lang. I sat at the back of the cinema always in the same place near the entrance, so as not to miss her if she came in. I became a regular. They welcomed me and started asking me for my opinion. That's how I came to meet William Delèze. He was an assistant director, and had worked with a director whose anti-colonialist film had never been released because it had been blocked by monopolies and insidious capitalism. Since then, he had not assisted anyone and spent his time having discussions, hanging around and having fun. Every time I went, he was there. He was tall, with a huge mop of hair which he wore in a spiky style, and there were infuriated moans whenever he sat down in the auditorium. In the end, he sat in the back row. The first time, he sat down in my seat, but he moved to another without making a fuss. Those seats were ours. The first to arrive kept the other's seat for them. William took notes in the dark in a large spiral exercise book, writing pages and pages in an illegible hand. When the lights came on again, he had difficulty reading what he had written. His lines overlapped or went off at a zig-zag. Occasionally, he fell behind and would lean over and whisper in my ear: 'What did she say?' or 'What was his reply?' or 'He didn't switch off the light when he went out, did he?' or 'Did you notice: there's no continuity between the two close-ups, it's awful.' At the end, he would go and stretch his legs in the foyer. As he went out, he would say either: 'Great film', or 'The next one will be better'. During the film, the comments would come thick and fast. Occasionally, he would change his mind. 'Actually it's crap' or 'On second thoughts, it's a film that makes you think'. I didn't want to strike up a conversation or get to know him. After seeing *Tokyo Story*, he asked me: 'Can't you speak?'

'No,' I replied.

We didn't talk to one another for a long time. Not until we watched *Written on the Wind* by Douglas Sirk, which put me in a good mood; before the next film, I approached him: 'Not bad, eh?'

'Are you crazy about films, too?'

'Not especially. I'm looking for a young woman. According to a friend who knows about such matters, she'll show up here sooner or later. I'm waiting.'

He looked at me with raised eyebrows. I didn't feel like giving him any details. I plucked up the courage and showed him my profile.

'Does this drawing mean anything to you?'

He moved the sheet in every direction and turned it to the light. He hesitated.

'Is it Bette Davis?'

I had to tell him my story quickly, as the auditorium was beginning to fill up.

'It's a great story,' he said. 'I'm looking for a subject for a script so that I can make my first film. It's a good beginning. Tell me what happens next.'

The interval was over and the credits of *Vera Cruz* were just beginning.

'If you happen to come across her…'

'What shall I say to her?'

Someone called out 'Silence!' and someone else said 'Shut up!' I sat down. I tried to think of what he should say to her. I couldn't find the words. William was engrossed in the film. He was right to be. It was a fine western.

I continued to pace up and down the triangle. I extended the boundaries of my search area by a hundred metres, but to no avail. Months went by. The only person I came across every day was William, who asked me what was happening and who did not seem very pleased because it meant his script was held up.

'Why don't you invent a story?'

'Cinema should reflect reality. It's time you made progress. Supposing you met another woman? A bit of action would do no harm. And if you're on your own, the dialogue's not going to be easy.'

'What sign are you?'

'I'm Taurus. But I've a big problem. My mother can't remember the time I was born. Can you imagine? It's impossible to know what my ascendant is. What about you?'

'I'm Libra. I don't know yet whether I believe in it or not. I'm waiting to find out.'

'Are you coming to the Cinémathèque? They're showing *Les Enfants du paradis* next, in the uncut version.'

'I'd rather go to the far end of rue Soufflot.'

I had an unpleasant sense of déjà vu. And yet this had never happened to me. And then, I remembered: *Les Nuits blanches*. I had so loved that book. The frozen romantic dreamer who meets a suicidal stranger, harbours all sorts of illusions about her, roams around a deserted St Petersburg concocting dreams and comes crashing down when confronted with pitiless reality. What was different was the certainty I felt. I could not have deluded myself. I was not a dreamer. I waited. At the main intersection outside the Luxembourg, during the afternoon, thousands of people walked by. I set myself impossible aims: the eleventh person to emerge from rue Monsieur-le-Prince or the eighth to come out of the métro or the thirteenth to get off the 38 bus, would be her. Really stupid challenges. She may have taken another road twenty metres away, or perhaps she lived in another country. On two or three occasions, I did a double-take. A shape, a shock of hair. And what if she had changed her hairstyle, would I recognize her? I felt unsure about the shape of her face. Supposing it slowly became blurred? Or disappeared? I wondered at times whether I had not been dreaming, whether I really had met her, or if it wasn't just my imagination or the hero of *Les Nuits blanches* who had come to make fun of me. I might as well be looking for a grain of sand in the desert. I gave myself one last achievable challenge: 'If she's not here in five minutes' time, I'm pushing off.'

I went back and joined William. I arrived as the lights were dimming. He had kept my seat.

The following evening, while we were having dinner, accompanied by the droning hiss of the television, the telephone rang. Juliette rushed over, as usual, and took the call. She looked surprised.

'It's for Michel.'

'Who is it?' my mother asked.

'I don't know. A gentleman. He wants to speak to Michel.'

My mother frowned. I took the receiver.

'Michel, it's Sacha. I hope I'm not disturbing you?'

'Not in the least.'

'I read some information in the newspaper that may be of interest to you. Bergier and Pauwels, the authors of *Le Matin*, are giving a talk for their magazine *Planète*. So I thought...'

'You're right. Where's it happening?'

'At the Odéon theatre.'

'When?'

'Right now.'

I believe I heard someone say: 'Michel, where are you going?' as I slammed the door.

6

I ran just to be on the safe side. It was a race against the gods. Or with them. I would soon find out. There were hundreds of people emerging from the Odéon theatre and gathering in the square outside. Cars were being turned back by the police. If she were there, I would never find her in this crush. A murmur rose from among the crowd. There was something mysterious in the air. People were beaming with pleasure. I walked up the steps of the theatre. I searched for her among this amorphous mass. Suddenly, I noticed the mime artist Deburau in front of the doorway. If this wasn't an omen, then fate was having fun throwing pebbles in our path to help us find our way. Tall and willowy, with an angular face and delicate movements, he was shaking countless numbers of hands. I joined the group surrounding him. He was talking animatedly. He stopped, turned round for a moment, stared at me with his dark eyes and smiled warmly. As though he knew me.

'I saw you yesterday. At the Cinémathèque.'

'In what film?'

'At a certain moment, Garance says to you: "You're talking like a child. It's in books that people love each other like that, and in dreams. But in life!" and you reply—'

'"Dreams, life, they're the same thing, or else it's not worth living. And anyway, what do you expect life to do for me? It's not life I love, it's you!"'

'I loved that film.'

'Me too.'

'You haven't changed.'

'Twenty years have passed. Thank you.'

I suddenly felt a slight pressure on my left shoulder. Deburau turned away. I turned round. She was there. In front of me. Her hand raised. She was looking at me with an amused expression.

'What are you doing here?'

'Er...'

'It's incredible that we should meet here.'

'It must have been meant to happen.'

'You'd have to think so.'

'There's a huge crowd here.'

'It's always like that at the *Planète* lectures. I didn't know you were interested.'

'I'm interested in everything.'

'Wasn't it fantastic?'

'What?'

'Bergier's lecture.'

'Yes, it was extraordinary.'

'Look, they inscribed it for me.'

She handed me a copy of *Le Matin*. I opened it. Written in violet ink on the flyleaf it read: 'For Camille, who has brought the Morning of the Magicians to pass'

'It's a lovely inscription.'

'They explain so many mysteries. They're geniuses. Have you read it?'

'I've had a lot of work. I'll get it from the library tomorrow. We can talk about it.'

'Do you know Barrault?'

'Not really.'

'I've often thought about you.'

'Have you really? So have I.'

'I went to the Cinémathèque several times.'

'I saw masses of films, I can tell you. Why didn't you come in?'

'I looked in the foyer. I didn't see you. I knew we'd see each other again. My name's Camille.'

'It's a very pretty name. Mine's Michel.'

We shook hands like two old friends.

'Did you come on your own?'

'I was going to come with a Russian friend. He had something that cropped up at the last moment. What about you?'

'I was with my brother. I spotted you and he vanished. I'm in my final year at Fénelon.'

'And I'm at Henri-IV.'

'I've a brother who's at Henri-IV. First year. And three others at Charlemagne.'

'You're a large family.'

'I also have a younger sister.'

The theatre had emptied. The crowd had congregated on the square outside. The discussions continued. Nobody wanted to leave.

'I don't know where he could have gone.'

'I'll walk back with you, if you like.'

'He's my elder brother. I'll be in trouble if I go home without him.'

'It doesn't matter. He'll find his way.'

'It's my father. If we don't come home together, he'll kick up a fuss.'

I didn't dare pry.

'If he discovers that we came to this lecture, he'll kick up a hell of a fuss. He loathes Bergier, Pauwels and *Le Matin*.'

'He's a scientist through and through.'

'That's another matter. We're rather an odd family.'

'We're going to have a lot to talk about.'

She stood on tip-toes searching for her brother. She waved. A ruddy-faced young man appeared.

'What the hell are you up to? Where were you?'

'Gérard, this is a friend from the Cinémathèque. Michel, this is my brother, Gérard Toledano. He's also doing his *bac*.'

I held out my hand and put on my best choirboy smile.

'Michel Marini. Glad to meet you.'

He frowned as he looked at me. He crushed my hand.

'Camille: we've got to get a move on! You've wasted my time with all your nonsense. How can you believe in this rubbish? We'd have been better off going to the cinema! What are we going to tell Papa?'

'The truth.'

'*Tchié faul lou koi?*' he said, asking her whether she was completely nuts in a pied noir drawl that was intensely familiar to me, and would have

492

delighted the Delaunays from Algeria. He disappeared into the crowd. Camille followed him. She turned round.

'Tomorrow, I get out at five.'

Stories need to continue. I don't know whether it's because of or thanks to anyone that it happened. Whether the stars have anything to do with it, whether it's chance, or our free will, or our desire, or whether someone, somewhere, is enjoying himself pulling strings and getting tangled up in them. In actual fact, I didn't mind whether there was an explanation or not. I was happy. I strolled around among the crowd. Six months later, I wondered whether I had been right to persist in my search for her. I should have listened to the wise counsel of the members of the Club and not tried to force the hand of destiny. I would have preserved the memory of our encounter on the pavement of rue d'Ulm, and she would have remained one of those beautiful girls who pass by and elude your grasp.

7

I had only one chance and and I didn't have the instruction manual, or anybody at hand to answer the basic questions: what should I do? What should I say? What will she think of me? At five o'clock the following afternoon, I waited by the crossing on rue Suger, in a doorway. Hundred of girls of all ages were coming out of the Lycée Fénelon. I had never seen so many of them together. At Henri-IV, they said every year that the school was going to become mixed, but nothing happened. I turned into rue de l'Eperon. I could feel thousands of girls' eyes lingering on me and staring at me. I pretended to be lost and rescued myself by making a half-turn towards boulevard Saint-Germain. The stream of schoolgirls dispersed. I spotted her standing in front of the door of the lycée looking from right to left. When she turned her head in my direction, I disappeared behind the corner of the building. She was going to think I was stupid: I had nothing to talk to her about. I didn't dare move. When she drew level with me, then I would appear. She took her time coming. I took a quick look. She was walking away in the opposite direction. I shot off. I ran round the block of houses to my right at full speed three times, going through the cours du Commerce passageway and up rue Saint-André-des-Arts. I looked for her and couldn't see her. I heard her voice behind me: 'Michel!'

She had stopped in front of a shop window. I was out of breath.

'I was late coming out.'

'I'm glad to see you.'

I didn't really know what to say to her. She spoke before I did: 'Aren't you hungry? My afternoon snack is sacred.'

She bought a pain aux raisins in the bakery on rue de Buci. She wanted me to have one. They were the best in the neighbourhood, apparently. She finished it in three mouthfuls. Then we went to the Bistrot du Marché, on the corner of rue de Seine. We sat down in the café and ordered two coffees. She leant over and pointed out something to me. I leant forward across the table.

'Did you see who's at the bar?'

'I wasn't paying attention.'

I turned round. I glanced across at the dozen or so people there.

'With the velvet jacket and the roll-neck jumper, that's Antoine Blondin,' she whispered.

'I don't know him.'

'I thought you were a specialist in French literature.'

'I didn't say that. I'm interested in Russian literature.'

'And Greek.'

'I know Kazantzakis. That's all. I've not read anything by Blondin. Is he any good?'

'Didn't you see *Un singe en hiver*, last year?'

'I don't go to the movies much, apart from the Cinémathèque. And I've a friend who's a projectionist in rue Champollion. I wait for the films to be shown at his cinema.'

'What did you like best yesterday?'

It was an unfortunate question. I should have thought about it beforehand and had a vague reply ready. I put on my solemn expression.

'I've not read *Le Matin* yet. I came with the Russian friend I told you about. He's the one who's an expert. What interests him is... the... magicians, I believe.'

'Alchemy, you mean.'

'Yes. It's his job. He prints photos. But you seem to be fascinated by it?'

'You have to read *Le Matin* and *Planète* magazines, otherwise, we won't be able to talk about it.'

'I read very quickly. By next week, I will have done.'

'You have to spend time taking it all in.'

'Don't worry, I read a four hundred page novel in two days. Afterwards, it's etched in my memory. And what about the *bac*, how's it all going?'

'It's a taboo subject.'

'Oh right. And why's that?'

'Life's not just about the *bac*, is it? From morning till night, it's the one and only topic of conversation. I hate people of my own age. They're not very bright and they're narrow-minded. They think of nothing but their parents or their dreary little studies. You get the feeling that if the door opened, they would be blown away by the breeze.'

'We're the same age.'

'With you, it's different.'

'It's true, the *bac* is not one of my obsessions.'

'For me, it's vital to have it.'

She saw that I didn't dare question her.

'It's absolutely essential to avoid family problems. It's complicated. What about you?'

'Ever since I moved up to the A-stream, everything's fine. We won't talk about it, I promise you. What are you reading at the moment?'

From her coat pocket, she pulled out a book with a crumpled cover and dog-eared corners. She handed it to me.

'*On the Road*. Jack Kerouac. I don't know it.'

'I don't believe it!'

'I haven't even heard of it.'

'You should read it straight away. He's the Rimbaud of today.'

She opened the book at random and read a passage that had been underlined as naturally as though she were reading it in French: 'But then they danced down the streets like dingledodies, and I shambled after as I've been doing all my life after people who interest me, because the only people for me are the mad ones, the ones who are mad to live, mad to talk, mad to be saved, desirous of everything at the same time, the ones who never yawn or say a commonplace thing, but burn, burn, burn like fabulous yellow roman candles exploding like spiders across the stars and in the middle you see the blue centerlight pop and everybody goes "Awww!"'

She closed the book. She was silent, a far-away look in her eyes.

'It's very beautiful. I like it a lot. Are you… are you American?'

'My mother's Irish. She teaches English. She came to Paris to study and she met my father.'

'You're lucky. You'll get top marks in the *bac*... I won't mention it again.'

It was her bedside book. She spoke about it with great enthusiasm. You only had to hear her talk about it. It was a manifesto for a new world, another way of living, beyond conventions, prejudices, materialism and the pursuit of money. We created useless and artificial needs for ourselves from which we were unable to free ourselves without great difficulty. We had to take action before becoming trapped.

'You've convinced me. Shall I start with *Le Matin* or *On the Road*?'

'Kerouac can wait. He's not easy to read. It's more a state of mind. *Le Matin* is a priority.'

'I'll have a go. Which American author would you advise me to begin with?'

'Why not Hemingway? He's his spiritual father.'

'It's sad that he committed suicide.'

'You must be joking! He was murdered!'

'Who by?'

'The FBI.'

'Are you sure?'

'We don't know who the murderer was exactly. It may have been the CIA.'

'No one's ever told me that!'

'That's normal. It's a conspiracy of silence. He had to be done away with.'

'Why would they have done that?'

'He got in their way. After his death, the press weren't allowed access to his medical files.'

'That's scandalous, if it's true!'

'People talked about it for a while and then moved to something else. Most people aren't interested. They won. Who killed Kennedy? And Oswald? And the others? Hemingway wrote a book about Cuba that was unfavourable to his government. He used to live there. That manuscript has disappeared!'

She seemed so convinced that I didn't push the matter further.

'Michel, there's something important I need to say to you.'

'I'm listening.'

'I don't know what your intentions are, but there's not going to be any funny business between us.'

'I don't follow you.'

'You and me – we'll just be friends. I just wanted to tell you now, in case you had other ideas, so that there would be no misunderstanding. Things must be transparent. I can't stand lies.'

'I just enjoy being with you.'

'So do I.'

'Did you read that in your horoscope?'

'No. By the way, you must let me have the time and day you were born. I have a girlfriend who will work out our birth charts.'

'I don't know what time I was born.'

'Ask your mother.'

'I don't want to know what my future holds. It's you I want to know.'

She looked put out by my persistence. She dropped a lump of sugar into her coffee.

'I want us to be friends. Just friends. Nothing else. Do you agree?'

'I don't imagine I can say no, can I?... May I ask you a slightly delicate question?'

'You can always try.'

'Are you pied noirs?'

'We were repatriated in 1962.'

'I realized when I heard your brother. How come you don't have the accent?'

'Because I don't want to. May I ask you something important?'

'Go on.'

'I want you to promise me not to read while you walk any more.'

'I will if you promise me the same thing.'

It was the first promise we made to one another. The last too. It may have saved our lives.

8

Fotorama was closed. There was a notice on the door: 'We're working for you. Press the bell for a long time and be patient.' I rang the bell for five minutes. Sacha appeared, dressed in a white jacket. Spotting me through the window, he grimaced.

'Michel, I've got an incredible amount of work to do. You're disturbing me!' he groaned through the half-open door.

'Please, Sacha. It's serious.'

'Are you ill?'

'I need your advice. It's important.'

'I've three hundred photos to print by this evening. Come back another day.'

'Please, Sacha, it's to do with the FBI ... or the CIA.'

He frowned and glared at me with cat-like eyes. He glanced to left and right down rue Saint-Sulpice.

'Why do you think I should be able to help you with this?'

'I said to myself: Sacha, he'll have an idea. If you know nothing about it, I'll go to the Club. There's bound to be someone there who'll be able to help me.'

With a jerk of his head, he motioned me to come in. He did so grudgingly. He locked the door and put back the notice. I followed him into the laboratory at the back of the shop. He drew the curtain, switched off the light and, in the orange-tinted darkness, went on with printing photographs on the enlarger.

'I'm listening.'

I told him about my conversation with Camille and what she had told me about Hemingway's death. Sacha didn't answer me. He went on working, moving his hands with precise motions. He inserted the sheets three at a time into the developing tray. He used tweezers to separate them. He watched for the image to appear. After two minutes, he transferred the sheets into the stop bath then, with another pair of tweezers, into the fixing tank. After another ten seconds or so, he dipped them into the washing tray and started again.

'My dear Michel, if you don't know the reason for an assassination attempt, for an accidental or inexplicable death, for an unexpected riot or for a good half the lousy tricks committed on this earth, tell yourself that it's the work of the FBI or the CIA.'

'Surely it's not possible – even of 50 per cent of them!'

'Let's not quibble. There are good years and bad years. Don't worry, the other half is the KGB. With that poor Hemingway, however, I'm afraid he blew his own brains out. Even though they might have wanted to. For once, they're innocent.'

'So why does she say that?'

Sacha took out the sheets from the water, shook them and hung them from taut wires with clothes-pegs.

'It's a logical and reassuring explanation for events that are incomprehensible and worrying. It's like our own disbelief when confronted with death. We find it hard to accept every time. The fact that a death might not be due to natural causes is comforting. And we can say whatever we like, in a knowing way, without fear of being contradicted. Plots and conspiracies are more exciting than reality. Bergier and Pauwels have made their money from it. She gets carried away, it's her age.'

'Thank you, Sacha. I'm going to let you get on with your work.'

'What's bothering you, Michel?'

'I've bored you enough with my stories.'

'Don't take offence. After all, there's nothing to be ashamed of about liking *Le Matin des magiciens*. She wants to dream and to escape from the humdrum.'

'You're right. Her favourite author is Arthur Rimbaud.'

'Michel, think about everything she has told you. What she likes is not Rimbaud, it's the poet. It's not poetry, it's the rebel. It's escape. Be idealistic and rebellious and she will look at you in a different light. It's quite common among young women who daydream. Make the most of it: later on, they change. One day they want children, a house, a husband, holidays by the sea and household appliances. That's what kills poetry.'

'What can I do? I've never written any poetry. Sure, I'm a bit of a rebel, but it's not very obvious.'

'I'm going to think about it. You try too.'

9

That's how vocations are born. I'm convinced that Rimbaud's biographers are mistaken about the roots of his genius. Perhaps he had a secret. A girl from Charleville high society whom he encountered during Sunday mass at Saint-Rémi, to whom he was unable to speak and whom he wanted to impress by letting her see his poems, hidden in a missal. Perhaps this silly little goose shrugged her shoulders and crumpled into a ball the page covered in his neat, slanting handwriting. I struggled away at clumsy alexandrines. Poetry is complicated. You think that it comes while you're gazing at the moon, beside the roar of the ocean, with your nose in the air, in a spontaneous way — a sort of torrent that sweeps over the turmoil of the words and changes them into allegories and feelings. But it's so unnatural. You have to slave away like a carpenter with a plane on a piece of wood. Having sweated and suffered until dawn, you produce four feeble lines.

I found myself sitting on the bench at the Balto writing pages and pages. Pages and pages is metaphorical, for I felt completely uninspired. I spent hours staring at a blank page on which I had written 'Poem No. 1'. I had the first two lines. They began:

> Today is a beautiful day
> The sun shines and the lights play…

I hesitated: … *play*… *play*… Apart from the rhyme, which I thought was pretty, I wondered what the sun could do next. I thought that there might be some fleeting clouds in the sky and a slight wind. I stopped. It sounded like the weather forecast. I gave up on the clouds and the breeze. The skies were empty. Rimbaud could sleep in peace.

The Balto was not a suitable place for poetic creativity. I was disturbed by friends who came and shook me by the hand and asked me how I was feeling today and whether I was ready for a game of baby-foot or chess. I adopted the attitude of someone who was being disturbed while doing important work.

'It's kind of you, but not today.'

I was also confronted with the permanent spectacle of Pavel Cibulka, who suffered from logorrhoea and who took up three tables with his monumental opus. He had spent his afternoons at the Balto ever since I first started coming to the Club. In the evenings he was a nightwatchman at a large hotel, where his refined manners and polyglot talents were appreciated. He had been labouring over this vast work for several years. In spite of the vicissitudes and vagaries of fate, he carried on with his mission to general indifference.

'It's the common lot of exceptional people who have within them that which is beyond them, but which they must complete and which will assure their fame for ever in the history of the human species,' he explained to me one day when I asked him whether it was worthwhile going to so much trouble for such poor rewards. 'With your parochial mentality, Kafka would have spent his time playing billiards instead of working and Van Gogh would have been an ironmonger.'

Three years previously, he told me, Kessel, wearing a gloomy expression, had returned the manuscript to him, tied up with string.

'I told you, Pavel. No publisher these days will agree to read a book that is handwritten, especially one that is so bulky. You should type it out.'

'It's a considerable amount of work. I'm not a typist — I type with two fingers. It would take me ages.'

'You could start work on it again. You've still got the Remington I gave you.'

'The ribbon's playing up. It only writes in red.'

'You must buy another one.'

Kessel put his hand in his coat and took out his wallet.

'Thank you, Jef. At the moment I can afford to buy myself two or three typewriter ribbons.'

Over three years, Pavel transcribed the pages one by one. He used the little finger of his left hand and the middle finger of his right hand. The pages were densely written. He pressed on doggedly. Every page written in his diplomat's handwriting produced a sheet and a half in Garamond type. In its entirety, the work amounted to two thousand one hundred and thirty-four pages, not including the contents, or the index, or the bibliographical references, which amounted to one hundred pages.

'That's it. I've finished.'

Pavel heaved a sigh of relief and gazed at the mountain of manuscript pages that lay piled up in front of him. He contemplated his life's work, which was going to make his name all over the world. We took his word for it. *The Treaty of Brest-Litovsk: Diplomacy and Revolution* had been published in Czech after the war and translated into Russian. Pavel had been fortunate to have had access to secret and unknown archives when he did his internship at the Czech embassy in Moscow, and British and American academics quoted his book as the definitive source on this subject. At that point, it was a slab of one thousand, six hundred and eighty-seven crammed pages. But later Pavel had gone back to his text, which he considered incomplete, and had expanded it to include aspects that he had suppressed so as not to upset the Soviets.

Pavel reminded us just how critical this treaty was: more important than that of Versailles, Vienna, or indeed any other in the history of the planet. Kessel and Sartre had tried it on some publishers in Paris. Between them, they knew them all. But their recommendation proved to be insufficient. The responses were polite and courteous. Some were friendly. The publishing world recognized the importance of the work and its exceptional documentation, but their interest always waned eventually. Igor maintained that a historical work was not publishable if it was over a thousand pages.

'Especially on a subject for which the entire world couldn't give a damn,' Tomasz pointed out when Pavel was not there.

After superhuman efforts, endless dilemmas, pangs of conscience, regrets and years of constant work, Pavel had cut it drastically. There were now only one thousand two hundred and thirty-two pages that could not be reduced. 'It's not possible to make it any shorter. I've taken out the technical details, the legal facts, the reports and the diplomatic telegrams. I've retained the historical and social context, the basic political and military issues. I'm down to the skeleton. Any further, and it becomes an historical operetta. They either take it or leave it.'

They left it. They advised him to publish it first in English. If it went down well in the United States, there would be no further problem. Pavel set about translating it into English. He was still waiting for a reply from a young publisher to whom Kessel had given the manuscript, but you sensed that he no longer had the heart for it. But when we felt bored, or the conversation lagged, we only had to ask him how things were going and the machine would start up again. He was unstoppable.

'Are you any further forward?' I asked him.

'Wouldn't you like to read it and give me your opinion?'

I hesitated to confess to him that I had to tackle *Le Matin des magiciens*, fourteen issues of *Planète* and *On the Road*.

'Listen, Pavel. I have to prepare for the *bac*. It's a lot of work. I'll read it during the holidays.'

'What are you doing just now? Are you working for your *bac*?'

'It's different... I'm writing an essay on poetry.'

'A talk?'

'That's right.'

'In your final year, you have the First World War and the Russian revolution on the syllabus.'

'It's so huge.'

'All you have to do is suggest a talk on the Treaty of Brest-Litovsk.'

He pushed the slab of one thousand, two hundred and something pages towards me.

'That will help you revise. You'll have to be careful, Michel, this is the only copy I've got.'

'Imagine if I were to lose it, if there were a fire at home or a flood. You'd never forgive me. I'll read it here. I promise you.'

Pavel was over the moon. At last, his talent had been recognized. The young publisher had written to him. His work had attracted his attention. He wished to meet him as soon as possible to discuss matters with him. Pavel had just telephoned from the Balto. An unusually pleasant secretary had made an appointment with him for that same day. Such a speedy meeting was unheard of. We were happy for him. He bought a bottle of sparkling wine to celebrate the occasion. He was given masses of advice: to be firm about the terms and not show that he was waiting for this outcome like the arrival of the messiah.

I had given up wondering what the sun did and was planning to embark on another subject, such as the springtime with its dipping swallows or the blazing summer with its golden wheat and its red poppies, when I saw Pavel coming back, with a distraught expression on his face. He looked as though he were sleepwalking. He threw himself down on the bench, which creaked beneath his weight.

'Would you like a beer, Pavel?'

'I'd love one.'

I passed the order to Jacky. Pavel remained prostrate. I didn't dare question him about the disaster that was written all over his face. Jacky placed the beers on the table. Pavel drank his half in one gulp and, since he was thirsty, he downed my shandy. He gave a small burp.

'Didn't he like it?'

'On the contrary. He was engrossed by it and he congratulated me. He'd never read a work of this magnitude.'

'Where's the problem?'

'The 1914 war. What sells is the Algerian war.'

'Why did he send you that letter?'

'Because of Roman Stachkov.'

'Who's he?'

'If you'd read my book, you'd know.'

'Pavel, please.'

'It takes place in late November 1917. A grim period. At the beginning of the month, the Bolsheviks have succeeded in their takeover bid and have overthrown Kerensky's government. They're holding on to power by a thread. For the revolution to succeed, they're obliged to sign a peace treaty with the Germans, whatever price they may have to pay. Trotsky is in charge. He asks for talks to begin. For the Germans, it's an opportunity

506

to bring the troops that are bogged down on the Russian front back home so that they can be redeployed on the western front – crucial reinforcements necessary for them to win the war. The negotiations are due to open at Brest-Litovsk, where the German headquarters are based. The Russian delegation, led by Kamenev, consists of a symbolic cross section of soldiers, women and members of the proletariat. At the railway station, as they are about to leave, Kamenev realizes that there are no peasants, even though they represent 80 per cent of the Russian population. Since the Bolshevik government wants to give the impression that the entire population is behind it, they set off in search of a peasant. In deserted and snowbound Petrograd, they come across an elderly, bearded peasant, with straggly hair and dubious-looking clothing, who is in the process of eating a smoked herring with his greasy fingers. They drag him into the delegation as the representative of the revolutionary peasantry. Roman Stachkov, that's his name, stands out at the diplomats' banquets because of his country-bumpkin manners, his exuberance and his misplaced cheerfulness. He's not used to champagne and food in abundance. He eats with his fingers, wipes his mouth with the tablecloth, thumps the dreaded General Max von Hoffman on the shoulder and cheers on the impassive Prince Ernst von Hohenlohe when he stuffs the silver cutlery inside his military uniform. To begin with, the Germans believe he is a top-level fraudster, using Machiavellian machinations to extract secrets from them. They take two months to realize that he's just a wild fellow from a village. The funniest thing is that he extorts money from Kamenev by threatening to leave. His utter ignorance of what was at stake in the war did not prevent him from going down in history as one of the negotiators of this treaty. He wants me to write his story.'

'He's right. It would make an amazing book.'

'Do you reckon?'

'If you wrote this book, you could publish the other one afterwards.'

'Do you really think so?'

'I'm sure of it. What did you say to him?'

'To go fuck himself!'

10

We would see each other after lessons. To begin with, whoever came out first would go and collect the other. She avoided the area around Henri-IV in case she ran into her brother. She had advised me not to speak to him under any circumstances and not to be taken in by his friendly manner, which concealed dreadful hypocrisy. As for me, I kept my distance from the Fénélon so as to avoid the sidelong glances and the sniggering. We met halfway, at the Viennese cake shop on rue de l'Ecole-de-Médecine. We had a *café crème* and talked for two hours in front of an apple strudel. When the weather was nice, we wandered up and down boulevard Saint-Germain or beside the river. For reasons unknown, she refused to give me her phone number, but I got hold of it through directory enquiries. When I suggested ringing her, she begged me never to call her at home. It was complicated, she said. I didn't ask why. When Camille stated: 'It's complicated', you had to accept it and not ask any questions, just accept that there was an insurmountable and inexplicable obstacle. I thought that her parents must be stern, with old-fashioned morals. I imagined an Irish mother, strict and purit-anical, a stickler for principles; it's a slightly old-fashioned notion, but then the Victorian novel would not have existed had the education of young girls not been a problem. I was still bogged down in my naivety and my illusions.

When she could, that is to say when she was on her own, she would ring me at home. As usual, Juliette rushed to answer the phone, so it wasn't long before they got to know one another. Sometimes she talked more to Juliette than she did to me. Occasionally, Camille would cut short the conversation suddenly: 'I must go now!' and hang up. I had to endure daily interrogations from Juliette, who wanted to know what she was like, what we did, where we went. Since I evaded these questions, she asked Camille. She wanted to meet her. I opposed the suggestion vehemently.

Apart from the evenings, it was complicated for us to see one another. Thursdays were difficult: there was always a brother hanging about and no way around this. Saturdays were very complicated. Sundays were impossible. Based on various crosschecks, deductions and suppositions, as well as the authoritative opinions of Leonid and Sacha, she came from a happy, close and intrusive family. The great inconvenience of united families is that the presence of all of them is required as proof of collective happiness.

One afternoon, we were walking side by side along rue Bonaparte when she dived between two cars, disappearing behind them in a flash. I noticed three young men walking past us. I recognized her elder brother whom I had met at the *Planète* conference. The youngest one stared at me with a questioning look. I seemed to have seen him before at Henri-IV. They went on their way, chatting. Camille reappeared, looking agitated.

'Did they see me?'

'I don't think so.'

'Did they see you?'

'What's the problem?'

'If they see us together, there'll be one hell of a fuss.'

I was unsettled by this attitude, but it didn't bother Sacha: 'You shouldn't worry. Has she told you she doesn't want to see you again?'

'No.'

'Well, you're still alive. You'll have to sort it out. Relationships between men and women are destined to be complicated. Show me your efforts.'

I took a sheet of paper out of my pocket and gave it to him. He read it in three seconds.

'Is that what you call a poem?'

'I did warn you.'

'You had no talent for drawing either. Your future in the arts seems to me to be in jeopardy.'

'And what if I borrowed the words of a great poet?'

'If she recognizes it, she may not be very pleased and you would look like an idiot. I've something better to suggest.'

This was how Sacha developed the strategy of the poems. He suggested that he should provide me with some, which I could recite to Camille. I wouldn't even have to lie and say that I was the author. The less I talked about them, the better it would be. Let her imagination roam. Give no explanation. An artist doesn't have to justify himself.

'If, by any chance, she asks you an awkward question, don't answer. Smile. And if you can, take her hand and squeeze it tightly while looking straight into her eyes. Make the most of your smile, Michel.'

On the back of an envelope, he wrote a poem very quickly, without thinking, or looking up. It flowed from his hand like water from a fountain. He handed me the dozen scribbled lines. I had to learn them by heart – he refused to leave them with me.

'If, in addition to not writing poems, you have no memory, then tough on you. You'll leave here once you know the poem. Don't rely on me to check it through. We're not doing a recitation exam.'

'I'm frightened of forgetting it.'

'Think of her and you won't forget it. If you're incapable of doing that, then you don't deserve her. I'm only making one condition: you must not alter a comma. I trust you. If she likes it, I'll give you others.'

'I could learn several of them all at once.'

'A poet who produces too much is suspect. Poetry requires time. It can't be churned out. A writer can get up in the morning and say to himself: I'm going to write fifty lines, or five hundred or a thousand words. If a poet says that, he's an impostor. It's like diamonds. When you gather them by the bucketful, they're worthless: they're like bits of coal.'

I hadn't contemplated for an instant asking for time to consider it, or refusing, or seeing whether I liked the poems. He was rescuing me, so obviously, I accepted. I didn't ask a single question. I was frightened he might withdraw his offer and forget about me. Or that she might meet a poet, a real one.

A customer came into the shop. While Sacha served him, I read the poem. I was astonished by its clarity. I read it again. I recited it to myself with my eyes closed. I could see Camille. I was smiling, her hand in mine.

'Is it all right?' Sacha asked.

'It's a very beautiful poem.'

Sacha smiled. He took the envelope, tore it up and threw the pieces into the waste-paper basket.

'Thank you for what you're doing, Sacha.'

As I walked across the Luxembourg, a doubt occurred to me. Supposing I forgot it? Shouldn't I keep a copy of it for safety's sake? I took out a sheet of paper to write down the poem. I hadn't promised not to do this. Then I thought of Sacha and recited it to myself again until I knew it was imprinted on my brain.

11

It was during this period that I adopted the style that would be mine for years to come: a slovenly look, shirt pulled out of baggy corduroy trousers, black gym shoes and that tousled hair that I miss so much today. I had to put up with my mother's comments: 'Did you wash today? I don't often hear you taking a shower. What's this mop of hair? You're going to the hairdresser's!'

In her presence, I kept up appearances and avoided confrontation, but before setting foot on the pavement I would ruffle my hair and make my clothes look dishevelled, taking on the appearance once more of someone who has just got out of bed – at least as far as the lycée, where Sherlock was standing guard.

'Where do you think you are, Marini? This isn't the circus. Does Monsieur like to think of himself as a Beatle, perhaps? May I remind you that gym shoes are intended for sport and that the *bac* includes an oral examination. What is this get-up?'

You had to be smart and use your imagination and wits in order to circumvent the edict of 'nice and short above the ears'. I wasn't the only one. The epidemic had affected other pupils. We got together. We started to resist. We felt as though we were living inside a pressure-cooker and that they were preventing us from breathing. It was heating up, but the lid held firm. It was like an endless bout of arm-wrestling. We were gaining ground and each advance was a small victory, each defeat strengthened our determination. We knew we were going to win. We were the young ones, and every day there were more of us. They would kick the bucket eventually.

'I've got a present for you.'

Camille stared at me in surprise.

'What is it?'

I had been wondering where the most appropriate place might be. I couldn't see myself playing the poet in front of a cup of hot chocolate in the noisy back room of the Viennese patisserie, where people were pressed up against one another. I hesitated between the riverbank and place Fürstenberg. I should have thought about it. I hadn't planned anything. But our footsteps led us there. To the Médicis fountain. Like a magnet. We were beside the pond. I held my breath and… my mind went blank. Nothing came. My head felt as light and empty as a ping-pong ball. I made desperate efforts to remember this damned poem that had flown away. Perhaps I didn't deserve it. This gave me the idea for the title of a poem: 'Plea for a vanished poem'. All I had to do was write it. Perhaps I was making progress. She noticed my tense expression.

'What's the matter, Michel?'

I looked her straight in the eyes. My lips were trembling:

> … Sheer glimmers and rekindled smiles
> The watchtowers of our hearts endlessly extend
> Over the ruined temples, the muffled words,
> The doubtful returns and the timid desires
> Our bleeding, sleep-filled shadows
> And the howls stifled
> By belated memories
> The expressions embellished by uncertainty
> The diverging paths all awry
> The pale gleams, the interrupted beats,
> Our breathing heavier than a mountain…

She looked at me in astonishment, her mouth half-open, her hand on the balustrade. A light breeze ruffled her hair.

'It's marvellous, Michel.'

'Yes.'

'Is it yours?'

For once I was prepared. I put my hand on hers. I smiled, my thoughts lost in the magic fountain. We stayed there until closing time.

That is how my career as a poet began. It wasn't a glorious beginning, but I had succeeded in avoiding the worst: not pretending to be anyone other than who I was. Let he who has always told the truth, who has never said yes when he thought no and has never covered up a shred of his incompetence, his ignorance or his arrogance throw the first stone. Likewise those who smiled when they didn't feel like doing so or who appeared interested when they couldn't care less about what they were being told. I'm the first to regret my behaviour. But did I have any choice? I didn't like the deliberate ambiguity, but I told myself that the important thing was the poetry and the fact that emotions were genuinely felt and shared. I made other vague attempts, but I had a leaden weight at the end of my pen and my scribbles ended up in the waste-paper basket. Should we accept our limitations as inevitable? We fight with the weapons we have and the dream justifies the means.

'Really, did she like it?'

'She loved it. And I'm not just saying that to please you.'

'I'm very glad, Michel. You can't know what this means to me. They're poems from another era. I had a slight doubt. I wondered whether she would appreciate them.'

Sacha broke off from developing photographs and hung up the most recent ones so that they could dry.

'We must go and celebrate this.'

We walked over to a small cubbyhole which was used as a kitchen area. He picked up a bottle of pastis and poured out two large glasses.

'That's a lot for me.'

'My dear Michel, all poets drink. The more they drink the better they write.'

'Do you think so? Is it obligatory?'

'The poets I like drank a lot. Or they suffered. If there's no pain or if your head's not spinning a little, the poetry is dull. The best ones suffered agonies and drank too much. There are few exceptions to this rule.'

We drank to poets and to poetry. I had never seen him so cheerful and jolly.

'I'd really like another.'

'I did warn you, Michel. In small doses. Each poem must give the impression of having been a struggle. You're not giving her a pair of shoes. A bit of mystery.'

He picked up an envelope, turned it round and, as he did the first time, wrote a poem in a minute, without difficulty, or hesitation, or alteration. It was impossible for him to be composing it on the spot. How many did he have in his memory? He held out the envelope to me.

'I'm going to learn it by heart.'

At home, after dinner, I experimented with Sacha's theory. I poured myself a whisky. My father loved drinking some on Saturday evenings. It made him merry. But this concoction had a medicinal taste and burnt my throat. I wanted to finish the glass, but I didn't manage to. I threw half of it down the sink. My stomach was on fire. I sat in front of a blank page and waited. My head was spinning and I wanted to be sick. It was wonderful: I felt the confusion of drunkenness; I suffered; I felt rotten for much of the night. But Sacha must have had more precise recommendations in mind because it did not produce the promised results. Inspiration did not come. I was expecting to see the pen run over the page and fill it with magical verses. It remained glued to my hand, while the other hand clutched my stomach. I can personally vouch for the fact that whisky is ineffective and was of no use to me for poetry. The mystery of creation must lie elsewhere.

The Pont des Arts at dusk. The lamps were switched on. For a long while, we had been contemplating the Pont-Neuf clinging to the tip of the Île de la Cité, the top of the towers of Notre-Dame, the smooth perspective of the plane trees over the silvery water, the silent barges. We were beyond the city there, in a miraculous and sheltered space. It was the perfect moment.

> What has become of the birds of our souls?
> Flown away into the long plain
> With their pitiless cries
> And their madness like a spinning-top

Frantic are the reasons for our love
Yellow and red the eyes
From the healing of our hatred
The silent birch trees
I speak once more to the night
To the fleeting mist
Eternity is a single day…

She looked at me with a strange intensity. There was clarity, a kind of excitement. I was expecting her to cross-question me, but she said nothing. She took my hand and squeezed it. We didn't speak. We had no need.

This is what's known as a snare. Once you have inserted a finger, the hand, the arm, then the whole body goes through. There's no way of retreating, of pulling back. To begin with, you don't think about it. Later, you realize that you're a prisoner. Recognizing your mistake, saying 'I deceived you', is easy. But admitting 'I am merely an illusion. I have no virtues; there is nothing remarkable or original about me' is impossible. It is to deny your very self. So, you say nothing. You persevere. It was at quarter to seven that evening that I understood what a vicious circle meant.

12

We went to the Cinémathèque for a change. In memory of our falling flat on our faces, we observed a few moments' silence, heads bowed towards the pavement. The first one to laugh had lost and would pay for the tickets. I paid. It was raining. We took shelter in the cinema without checking the programme. There were few people there. The lights went out. The credits went up. It took me a few minutes to realize that I knew the star of the film. Tibor Balazs had gone completely out of my mind. He had lost his wrinkles, as well as a few kilos, and he looked ten years younger. The man known as the Hungarian Marlon Brando played the part of a heroic and resolute freedom fighter who blew up a train, cut the throat of a Gestapo officer, sacrificed himself to save the members of his network, refused to confess when he was tortured and ended up by being shot after he had let out the heartrending cry: 'Long live free Hungary!' The censors had allowed it through.

I told Camille how I had come to know him, and about his escape and return to his own country. She thought he was handsome and had 'an animal-like virility'. The cinema is the art of lying and illusion. I didn't tell her about Imré, about their impossible love affair, or about the chicken. Stars have a right to boundless esteem in women's hearts.

'One day, if you like, we could go to the Club, and I'll introduce you to my friends.'

'I find chess boring.'

As we left the Cinémathèque, we came across William Delèze. His woolly sheep's hair was dripping wet. He shook himself. I didn't manage to avoid the expression of his delight at seeing me again, which took the form of a great slap on the back.

'You vanished. Where have you been? I can't keep your place for you any more.'

'Camille, this is William. He's a friend from the movies.'

'Do you make films?'

He couldn't resist. The urge to talk about them was stronger than the desire to see one. We went and had a coffee in the café next door.

'Michel told me about how you met. It started off well and after that I thought it dragged a bit. It needed new developments. People were going to get bored in my film. I had a better idea. It starts the same, but then he bumps into another girl whom he confuses with the first one. She's Dutch. They set off together and they're going to discover the world on bicycles. I wrote the script in a month. It's called *Summer Promises*. Everyone who reads it adores it. I'm waiting for a reply from the people who provide producers with loans against future takings. I'm quite hopeful. My future producer is pals with one of the members of the committee. We're waiting for an answer from Jean-Claude Brialy. He's not able to shoot a movie and read at the same time. I'm going to try and be an assistant on his next film. I'll be able to talk to him about it. Hang on, here's the script, you must tell me what you think of it. It's the seventh version.'

He put down a 150-page manuscript on the table in front of Camille. On several occasions, I had asked him to give me a script to read, to see how it was done. I leafed through it. Sometimes, in between two passages of dialogue, they got off their bicycles but continued to chat as they walked on side by side. His idea, which was revolutionary, consisted in shooting just one long, single, shot without cutting or continuity, and in real time. It was a genuine technical innovation.

Once William started, there was no stopping him. He knew everything about French cinema, the actors, the producers, the directors. He gave us masses of fascinating detail which you couldn't read in the press. You would never have thought it was so complicated to create a film. It was the story of our cinema as it was happening. He took Camille's hand and gazed into her eyes.

'You're much prettier in real life.'

'How do you know?' she asked.

'Michel drew an identikit picture. He gave you a funny-looking head.'

I aimed a kick at him under the table. I missed.

'Did you do a drawing of me?'

'It was just an idea. So as to find you,' I mumbled.

'I'd love to see it.'

'It wasn't really you. I tore it up.'

'You haven't missed anything,' William went on. 'It was rather cubist.'

This time, I did not miss.

'It's a pity,' Camille said. 'I should have loved to see it.'

To relieve the tension, William started giving an imitation of a fly dive-bombing. It buzzed around in circles, which he followed with his head, and he managed to trap it in mid-air. But as soon as he opened his fist, it escaped and the whole thing began all over again. Camille burst out laughing.

'Can you ride a bike?' he asked her.

'Yes.'

'Would you like to be in my film? You'd be wonderful.'

'I haven't the time. I'm studying for my *bac*.'

'Afterwards. This summer. It's a marvellous part.'

'It won't be possible.'

'I'll leave you my phone number. Read the script. Ring me whenever you like and we'll talk about it.'

He got to his feet and picked up his newspapers.

'By the way, Michel, I went to see your photos at Saint-Sulpice. They're not at all bad.'

'Did you like them?'

'For a beginner, you manage pretty well. Your friend, the photographer, he couldn't develop a few films for me, could he?'

'You only have to ask him.'

'I find him expensive.'

'I haven't had to pay him. He reimburses himself through the sales.'

He was in a hurry to leave and forgot to pay for his drinks.

'Do you take photos?'

'I try.'

'You didn't tell me. Can we see them?'

'If you really want to.'

'Was your friend William trying to chat me up?'

'You mustn't take any notice. He can't stop himself.'

Through the window of Fotorama, I could see the manager of the shop laying out rolls of film on the shelves. On display in the right-hand window were black and white photographs of a stormy sea-front, with particles of foam spraying up against the jetty and passers-by bent against the force of the wind.

'Are they your photos?' Camille asked.

'Mine are inside. They were displayed in the window for a month. They sold several of them.'

I pushed open the door and we went in. When he saw me, the owner gave a big smile as though he were pleased to see me. He came over to us.

'How are you... ?'

He searched for my name and couldn't recall it.

'May I show my photos to my friend?'

'That's what they're there for. Did you want to see Sacha?'

'He doesn't work on Thursdays.'

'At the moment, he works every day. We had a nice order from the Ministry for Cultural Affairs. The first prints of Chagall's ceiling. Sacha, your favourite photographer is here,' he shouted through the door.

We went into the display room. Camille stood in the middle of the room and spun round. Her gaze swept over the photographs hanging on the wall. She paused at the right-hand corner.

'They're yours.'

It wasn't a question. She walked towards the five photographs of the Médicis fountain. She studied them carefully.

'They're wonderful, Michel.'

'Do you think so?'

'Really. Only you could have taken these photos. If I had the money, I'd buy them.'

'There's no point, Mademoiselle.'

Sacha appeared, wearing his grey overall. He had the drawn features and bloodshot eyes of a man who hasn't slept.

'I've got a spare set. I'm giving them to you.'

'I feel embarrassed.'

'Don't you like these photos?'

'They're magnificent.'

'We'll take advantage of the photographer's presence. He's going to sign them. Do you agree, Michel?'

He didn't wait for my answer. He went behind the desk and pulled a white envelope out of a drawer. He brought out the five prints and spread them on the counter. I wrote 'For Camille' and signed each of them in the white border.

'Take great care of them. In twenty or thirty years' time, they'll be worth a fortune.'

'That wouldn't surprise me,' she replied. 'You know, Michel is a real artist. He's also written some wonderful poems.'

'You didn't tell me about them,' he exclaimed with a half-smile. 'I'd really like to read them one day.'

'That's not possible,' she went on. 'Michel refuses to write them down. He recites them to me.'

'He's right. It's much better when one listens.'

He put the signed photographs in the envelope and handed it to Camille.

'With the firm's compliments.'

'Thank you very much. I'm very touched by the present. Michel told me that you were interested in *Le Matin des magiciens*.'

'He told you that?'

I didn't know where to put myself. I gestured to him and shook my head.

'I've never read anything like it!' he said.

'Nor have I. But Michel still hasn't read it.'

'I told you, Camille, I read things that are useful for the *bac*. During the holidays, I'll have time.'

'Tell him it's fascinating.'

'What's interesting about this book,' Sacha explained, 'even when you don't agree with them, is their non-conformism, the way they put the cat among the pigeons.'

'Ah, you see!'

'We're not going to take up any more of your time,' I interrupted. 'You have work to do.'

'Michel, Camille would make a lovely subject to photograph. What are you waiting for?'

'She doesn't like having her photo taken.'

'Camille, may I call you Camille?'

'Of course.'

'Suggest a swap to him. A photograph of you in return for a poem by him. You wouldn't be losing out, would you?'

'I don't know whether he'd want to.'

'Michel, do you agree to this deal?'

If she had not been there, I think I would have kissed him.

That was how I came to take my first photos of Camille. To begin with, she wanted me to write down the poems. I transcribed them all without changing a line. But I didn't have an unlimited number and the moment soon came when I had no more to offer in exchange. Sacha supplied me with them sparingly and he developed the photos of Camille. He printed them in large format, with a strong, grainy contrast. He refused to let me pay for them. One day, when I was telling him that it embarrassed me to accept his poems and to be incapable of writing any, he replied that the poems belonged to those who liked them and that he was happy because he knew why he was giving them to me and this was what they should be used for.

Camille thought that I took too many photos and did not write enough poems. I explained to her that it took time and that a poem was worth several photos.

> … Death believes she has killed me
> But my body does not exist
> I am within three notes of music
> A half-starved smile
> A weary memory
> And paths on the horizon

Forgotten by this freakish wind
I am in these immutable lines
Anchored in memories
Murmured and hidden
Resumed and transported
My torments like farandoles…

'Michel, it's marvellous.'
    'I know.'
    'Your poems are sad.'
    'For this poem, I want a photograph. Just one.'

13

In the current circumstances, with the bailiff's affidavit drawn up
following Mr Marini's departure from the marital home, the latest
attestations emanating from your employees and your relatives
seem to me to be sufficient to obtain a favourable decision from
the court. At the present moment, the opposing solicitor has not
communicated a single exhibit to the proceedings. The absence of
testimony in favour of your husband will be a determining factor in
obtaining a divorce on the grounds that the blame lies exclusively
with him. It is of the utmost importance that we should arrive at the
hearing with our evidence…

The letter had been sent by Maître Fournier, the family lawyer. I
came across it while sorting through the post on the concierges'
doormat. I was expecting a detention from Henri-IV for having smoked
inside school, and had spotted his logo. It was not the first time he had
written to our home. I don't know why I took the letter that particular
morning, and opened it. Because of the silence perhaps. For months, we
had been living in a muted atmosphere, as if there were no problem. My
mother answered me quite naturally and in a voice that was as collected
and persuasive as her smile: 'Nothing's going on, my darling. Everything's
fine. Don't worry.'

My father telephoned on Sunday evenings. Juliette and I spoke to him
in turn, while my mother sat in the armchair with her nose buried in
Paris-Match.

'How are things at school?'

'Fine.'

'I'm glad.'

'How about you?'

'Business is tough. You have to have your wits about you.'

To begin with, we used to ask what the weather was like in Bar-le-Duc, and he replied either: 'It's damned cold', or else 'It's filthy weather.' The conversations were short and ended with 'Take care, darling. See you next week.'

He came on flying visits to Paris to see suppliers. He came on the first train and went back on the last to avoid paying for a hotel. He used to arrange to meet me in a café and would arrive an hour late. On one occasion, we missed one another, each of us sitting in a different café on place de la République. Afterwards I would accompany him on the métro to Gare de l'Est. For a long time he had hopes that it was not all over and that there was a slim chance of keeping the family together. When a couple is not getting on, the best solution, apparently, is to separate in order to take stock of things.

'It's like the weather, do you see? You let the storm pass, and afterwards the sky is blue.'

Given the result, this can't have been the right method.

One day, a strange and unpleasant feeling came over me. He had arrived, out of breath, moaning about the dreadful traffic, the stink of exhaust fumes and the filthy streets.

'It's sheer madness. I wonder how I put up with this city for so many years. I can't breathe any more.'

I looked at him as though he were a stranger.

When I read the letter, my heart skipped a beat. I almost went back upstairs to tell my mother what I thought of her attitude. I would have to warn my father about the plot that was being hatched against him, so that he could do something and defend himself. I managed to get through to him at his shop: 'There's a problem, Papa. We have to see each other urgently.'

'Tell me what it's about.'

'I can't speak on the phone. It's very serious.'

'Have you done something foolish?'

'It's not me. It's to do with Mama.'

He said he would find a way of coming to Paris. He would take the opportunity to see a new supplier in Boulogne. We met in a packed brasserie opposite Gare de l'Est. He arrived with a pile of catalogues from Italian lighting dealers. He gave me one so that I could see the quality for myself. He had arranged to represent them in Lorraine.

'What do you think of them?'

'I don't know much about lights.'

'They're twenty years ahead of us. I'm going to make a killing with these. Not a word to your mother, whatever you do. Do you smoke these days?'

'I've done so for a while, Papa.'

'I'll have one.'

I gave him my pack of Gauloises and the book of matches.

'So, what's going on?'

I handed him the letter from the lawyer. He read it without batting an eyelid.

'When I think of all the money I gave this bastard.'

'They haven't won yet. Are you going to defend yourself?'

He shrugged his shoulders and reflected for a moment.

'I'd need to make up false witness statements. I'm not like that. I can't imagine asking people I haven't seen for years to say nasty things about your mother.'

'That's what she's doing.'

'It's my fault, Michel. I left the marital home. After that, it was a mess. We had a lovely family and then it all collapsed. I thought that we were going through a difficult patch, the kind that happens in every family. When I realized, it was too late.'

'Was it because of Franck?'

'The truth is that we weren't from the same background. It's something you can't put right. Some manage to. We didn't know how.'

'You could share the blame.'

'How? She has ten people to testify against me and the bailiff's affidavit. We'd be tearing each other apart for no reason. Are you able to keep a secret?'

'You're not going to start all that again.'

'I could have made things awkward for your mother socially. But we came to an understanding.'

'What understanding?'

'We decided to leave you both out of all this business. I want your word of honour.'

There was no way out. I promised.

'We agreed that I should take the entire blame and won't provide any further information to the proceedings. I'll retain parental authority along with her. She'll have custody and I'll have every other weekend when I can, and half of the holidays. She'll get a small maintenance allowance for both of you and will pay me financial compensation for the business.'

'How is that possible? You've deserted us just for money!'

'Michel, don't talk such crap! We'd have been at each other's throats otherwise and I don't have the means!'

'You had no right! You should have fought for yourself!'

'That's the way life is, my boy, and that's the way it's always been.'

'In the end, you came out of it quite well.'

I got to my feet. I picked up my fags. I walked away. I came back.

'Tell me where Franck is.'

'You don't need to know.'

I left the letter from the lawyer on the table in the front hall. My mother was surprised. I told her that I had opened it by mistake. On Sunday evening, when my father phoned, Juliette answered and spoke to him for five minutes. She wanted to pass him over to me and held out the phone.

'Just tell him that I'm not here.'

He couldn't not have heard. My mother looked up from *Paris-Match*. She said nothing, smiled and went on reading. On the other Sundays, I refused to speak to him. This went on for a long time. It's still how things are between us to this day.

I never spoke to Camille about my family, nor did I tell her about Franck and Cécile, their disappearance, the family breakdown and my father's exile in a distant province, though I thought of them every day. They say that time heals wounds. If you are going to wipe out of your memory those who have gone away you ought not to love them too

527

much. My predominant emotion was anger, and that urge to cry out that suffocates you because you are holding it back and because you are powerless. A sort of hatred had taken root in me. For whatever reason, Camille refused to talk about her family. We were all square. We shared the peace of orphans.

14

I thought I'd get away with it, but I had overrated my powers. I held out to the very limits of what was possible. But there comes a point beyond which no man can go. Our will is ineffectual in the face of the laws that govern the world. My fate was sealed somewhere in the remotest corner of the universe, near the galaxy of Andromeda, between Orion and Aldebaran. Camille wanted to draw up my astral chart and needed the exact time of my birth. I thought this request was ridiculous, but I couldn't tell her so to her face. She believed in astrology utterly and she was very touchy about such matters. I came up with the excuse that pain had caused my mother to lose all memory of my birth, that she was alone, in a deserted hospital, abandoned by her family and her husband.

'You were born in the Port-Royal hospital, right in the centre of Paris!'

Because of the break-up, the matter was not resolved. Divorce, as is well known, harms the memory. Without the exact time, it was impossible to establish the map of the sky at the moment of my birth, so no horoscope, no lunar node, no chart of the Houses nor associated signs. I thought I would be rid of her ridiculous questions.

My relationship with my mother improved spectacularly from one day to the next. We discovered an equilibrium. I observed three rules, a sort of legal minimum: I had to look after my appearance, achieve average marks at school and be present at family meals, especially Sunday lunch with the entire Delaunay family, at Grandfather Philippe's home. In return, she would not bother me about anything else. It was after attending the course 'Negotiate successfully using win-win solutions' that this unexpected change occurred. My father should have gone with her to these training courses that he made such fun of. It might perhaps have avoided the present Berezina disaster. One evening, during dinner, I got an unpleasant surprise.

'By the way, Camille telephoned,' said my mother as she passed me the grated carrots.

'Oh, really?'

'She's a nice girl. Do bring her home, if you want to, I'd be delighted to meet her.'

'I left her ten minutes ago. Why did she ring?'

'She wanted to know the time of your birth.'

'What did you tell her?'

'Five thirty in the afternoon precisely. I didn't understand what she was talking about. There were no problems with the birth. With your sister, it was ghastly. Girls do more harm to their mothers. I'd like her to draw up my astral chart. I was born on 28 January at ten past four in the morning.'

'And what about me, what time was I born?' asked Juliette.

Camille may have had a few faults, but she did not bear grudges. She was not angry with me for lying, for she was excited that she would soon have my birth chart. A friend of her mother's ran a fortune telling service in a flat overlooking Montsouris park. She was going to compare our horoscopes and we would then be able to decide on our future.

'Don't you believe in it? I'm going to convince you.'

'Camille, we can't foresee what's going to happen. It would be too easy.'

'There are people who know, who are initiated and who can guide us.'

'Personally, I'd prefer not to know.'

A few days later, she informed me that there was an unexpected hitch that was preventing my chart from being set up. Materializing suddenly out of space after a journey of millions of kilometres, Holmes's comet had just appeared between the constellations of Cancer and Taurus, a tiny, brilliant splash with a fan-like tail, and as long as it remained visible, certain lives would be drastically affected because of it.

'She says it's the comet of people who love one another and find each other again because of it.'

'Camille, you can't really believe in this nonsense?'

'She says that you are going to be affected.'

'We haven't lost one another. Can your friend, the seer, not tell us if we're going to pass our *bac*?'

530

'She determines the trajectories. Not the episodes along the way. Soon, you'll have proof.'

She displayed not the slightest doubt or hesitation. Her enthusiasm swept away my certainties. Cartesian folk are boring. Her fantasy was beautiful.

We very rarely saw each other on Sundays. She had family commitments that she could not get out of. When I asked her why, she replied: 'Don't ask me why! If I could, we'd see each other. I can't.'

I spent my Sunday afternoons at the Club. Some new faces were appearing, from the USSR, from the Baltic countries, from Yugoslavia and Romania, with their rolling accents, their pre-war clothes, their features furrowed by mistrust and anxiety. The carry-on about papers and files was beginning all over again; the need for proof that you were a fugitive and that you had escaped urgently and in a great hurry so as to avoid arrest and imprisonment. The older ones took care of these people, gave them shelter and put them in touch with the suppliers of authentic-looking false documents. These were expensive and they had to moonlight in restaurants and building sites to pay for them. Several of them had used an emigration network to go to Canada, which was more welcoming than France. On Sundays the Club was crowded. The Club room was no longer large enough and, gradually, the adjoining restaurant had been colonized. The obligatory rule of speaking French had been forgotten, and almost every language could be heard. Maybe it was because they had spoken in hushed voices for so long, but they certainly let their hair down now. There was just as much of a din as there was in the rest of the Balto, and those who wanted peace and quiet sighed as they remembered the good old days, when the members of the Club could be counted on the fingers of two hands.

'Given the good will of our providers, there's no risk of a lack of customers,' Igor insisted. 'We're doomed to increase.'

Sacha dropped by occasionally. I observed him carefully. Aware of their hostility, he enjoyed provoking them. He appeared noiselessly. People looked up and there he was, watching us, rather like Big Ears. The others controlled themselves, tried to look contemptuous and ignore him.

You looked up again, and he had gone, without anyone having heard him leave. I took care to keep up appearances and to display indifference towards him. He insisted that I did so and he did not want me to intervene or become involved.

I had made serious progress at chess and was becoming a sought-after player.

'Being a good player is a relative notion,' explained Leonid, who agreed to play a game only when no one else was available. 'The new lot are really useless.'

I was following an endless revenge match between Imré and Pavel. The former was making the most of the absence of a clock to win by wearing his opponent down. Igor appeared, in a state of high excitement.

'My friends, you'll never guess who I've been talking to for a couple of hours.'

From his animated behaviour, we concluded that it was a well-known name. We guessed at pop singers or film stars, television presenters, politicians and famous sports personalities. We listed half of Paris without success.

'Is he French?' Gregorios asked.

'No. He hailed me on boulevard Malesherbes. I said to myself: Igor, this is your lucky day. I watched in my rearview mirror. I couldn't believe my eyes. Him in my taxi! I waited for a few moments and then I took the plunge. I spoke to him in Russian.'

'Was it Gromyko, incognito?' Pavel suggested.

'He's a living god!'

Then we all said 'Nureyev' at the same time.

'To begin with, I didn't want to come out with commonplace remarks such as: I'm one of your great admirers, which he must hear twenty times a day. He was slightly on his guard. I mentioned *La Bayadère*, which we saw in 1961 with Leonid and Vladimir. He remembered that magical evening and the crowd on its feet clapping and yelling bravos as though they would never stop. He sensed just how moved I had been. He opened his heart. I dropped him at the Opéra, by the artists' entrance. He was in a hurry and yet he continued talking and laughing. He's the handsomest man in the world and the greatest artist. We stayed in the car. We remembered the Kirov and Leningrad. He had tears in his eyes. He was late. I didn't charge him the fare. He invited me to follow him inside where he was appearing with the Royal Ballet. I watched part of the rehearsal. It was extraordinary. The others stop in order to watch him. It's as if an angel has come down to earth. When I left, he came over to thank me. Can you imagine? Him! Saying thank you to me! For having reminded him of home.'

'What a wonderful coincidence,' Imré said.

The word made me prick up my ears. It was clearly preordained. I wondered whether I ought to mention Holmes's comet, but I didn't have time.

'My friends,' Igor continued, 'today is a very special day. Rudolf Nureyev is going to join us!'

This produced a chorus of exclamations, astonishment and incredulity.

'In the taxi, I told him about the Club. He asked me masses of questions. He shook my hand and asked me for the address. He's coming this evening, after the rehearsal.'

There was a hubbub of panic and consternation. The members rushed about in every direction, put their coats back on, did up their shirt collars, adjusted their ties, brushed the cigarette ash and specks of dandruff from their clothing, and combed their hair in the mirrors. They queued to go for a pee and wash their hands.

'We can't greet him in this mess!' Vladimir pointed out.

They cleared the tables, wiped them with dishcloths, emptied the ashtrays, put away the crates that lay around, dusted the benches and swept. Madeleine directed procedures and she took the opportunity to have the windows cleaned by Goran and Danilo, two of the newcomers. All of a sudden, Igor noticed Sacha, who was polishing the bar with a white duster. He hurried over.

'What the hell are you doing here?'

'I'm making my contribution to—'

Igor didn't allow him the time to finish his sentence. He jostled him and grabbed him by the lapels of his coat. They were the same height, but Sacha was slimmer. He could have stood up for himself, but he offered no resistance. Igor shoved him outside forcefully.

'That's the last time! I've warned you!'

Sacha walked away without replying. Igor came back inside. He was furious.

'What are you waiting for? Get to work!'

The Balto looked like a brand new café. Tomasz borrowed an Instamatic and a new roll of film from a pinball player who lived upstairs. We all went outside. It was a sunny day. We formed a welcoming committee on the pavement on the corner of boulevard Raspail and place Denfert-Rochereau. We kept an eye on the taxis, but they passed by without stopping. We waited quite happily. After a while, some went back inside to have a rest and a drink.

'What time is he meant to be coming?'

'They're running late,' Igor explained.

Vladimir displayed his decisiveness. He got hold of the phone number of the Opéra's administration office from directory enquiries. We all gathered around him. But on this Sunday in May, there was no reply. Hopes of Nureyev's anticipated arrival turned as flat as a cold soufflé. The members left one by one. Nobody made any unpleasant comments. Tomasz returned the camera. We were left with the members of the original group.

'Maybe he's forgotten,' Pavel said.

'Or else he couldn't find a taxi,' added Gregorios. 'That can happen on Sundays.'

'Or he was tired and went home to bed,' Imré suggested.

Madeleine joined us.

'In my view, he's not going to come now. It's kind of you to have tidied up, in any case. Drinks are on the house.'

I stayed with Igor, who was not giving up hope: 'Something unexpected must have happened. Rehearsals can take ages. He'll turn up.'

We had not found ourselves together in a long time

'How are the studies going?'

'They seem to be all right.'

'And your girlfriend?'

'We can't see each other on Sundays. She stays with her family.'

'Put yourself in her parents' position. They work during the week. If they don't make the most of their children on Sundays, they'll never ever see them.'

'How long will it go on? She's not going to spend her life with them.'

'You young people, you're all the same.'

'May I ask you something? Why are you like that with Sacha?'

'It's ancient history. Don't involve yourself. He doesn't deserve the slightest attention... Shall we still wait for him or not?'

'Supposing he arrives and there's no one here to greet him, what would he think?'

'You're right. We'll wait for him. Artists turn up when it suits them. He spoke to me as he would to a friend. He won't forget me. Do you know what his dream is?'

'No.'

'Do you promise not to talk to anyone about it? It's a secret he's entrusted to me. He wants to put on Prokofiev's *Romeo and Juliet*. Can you imagine? It's the most beautiful opera in the world. Do you know it?'

'I'm not very well up in opera. My father adores Verdi and *Rigoletto*.'

'Then he'll love it. Ask your parents to buy the record for you. 'The Knights' Dance' is my favourite bit. You listen to it and you're transported to heaven. Do you know why Prokofiev is the Russians' favourite composer?'

'Because he's talented.'

'Not just that.'

'He's composed great operas and beautiful music.'

'That wouldn't have been enough.'

'He's kind and generous.'

'They're not virtues in our country.'

'I give up, Igor.'

'Prokofiev is adored in Russia because he killed Stalin.'

'What?'

'On 5 March 1953, they woke Stalin up to tell him about Prokofiev's death. The news devastated this man who had murdered millions of people, particularly since he had traumatized him, treated him badly and had humiliated him. For the first time in his life, Stalin felt remorse. He had a stroke and died that same day. Because of Prokofiev.'

'I didn't know that.'

'Michel, it's a joke people tell in Moscow. I feel sure that if Prokofiev had thought his death would rid us of Stalin, he would happily have committed suicide.'

We stayed by the boulevard Raspail entrance. We were sitting on the bench, waiting. It was still sunny. The others went home, waving at us, telling us that he wouldn't come and that we'd take root there. Dusk began to fall. We resigned ourselves. We smoked one last cigarette. We spotted Leonid walking along, with a crazed look in his eyes, each of his hands swathed in bandages.

'Hey there, comrade, here we are!' Igor called out. 'What's happened?'

Leonid took a moment to recover from his stupor.

'Did you have an accident?'

'I'm thirsty.'

We followed him inside. He appeared to be about to faint. His face was contorted and he started to sniffle. With his clumsy, swollen hands he took the small bottle from his pocket, opened it and breathed in several times through each nostril. He ordered a 102, added a few centimetres of water, knocked it back in one gulp and ordered three more from Jacky.

'I'll have a 51,' I added.

'You'll never guess what's happened to me,' he said, his voice quivering. 'I saw her again.'

'Who was that?'

'Milène.'

15

'I like working on Sundays,' Leonid began. 'People are relaxed and the tips are better. I'd picked up a couple of Spaniards at the Ritz. They wanted the grand tour. An entire day. Malmaison, Auvers-sur-Oise and Versailles. A damn good fare. At porte Maillot, in order to avoid a motorcycle, I pull out and get stuck on the pavement. In the ten years I've been driving taxis, it's the first time I've burst a tyre. The very nice Spanish guy says to me: "Doesn't matter, we'll change the wheel and set off again." Believe it or not, I never managed to take the wheel off. The nuts were really tightly screwed on. I strained like crazy. The Spaniard, who was strong as an ox, tried with all his might. Impossible. It was as if it was soldered on. They took another taxi. I struggled away with the fucking jack. After an hour, I managed to get it off. I was dripping with sweat. The palms of my hands were bleeding. I was grazed and covered in grease. The chemists are closed on Sundays. I'm going home, I said to myself, this is a bad day. A woman with a large suitcase comes up and asks me to take her to Orly. I tell her that I don't want to go there. She was leaving for New York. She asks me to drop her at the Invalides air terminal so that she can take the shuttle. Better than nothing. I had a bit of vodka left. I disinfect my cuts with it. The woman was screaming. It seemed as if it hurt her more than me. I put a handkerchief around each hand and I drove like that. I carried the woman's case to the Air France counter. She gave me a good tip and told me to go to the hospital to be vaccinated against tetanus. I was about to leave when someone called out my first name. A shiver came over me. I turned round. There she was. In front of me. She hadn't changed. She still looks like that American actress who is so beautiful. What's her name, Igor? You know, the one in the film?'

'Deborah Kerr.'

'The same eyes. The same hair. A queen. In my mind, it was as though we had left one another that morning. I don't know how long we stood there face to face.

'"How are you, Milène?"

'"Fine."

'"You seem to be in good shape."

'"So do you."

'"You're still just as beautiful."

'"Don't go by appearances. The wrinkles are on the inside."

'"Don't you work at Orly any longer?"

'"I was transferred here. It's five minutes away from the flat. I walk here."

'"Since when?"

'"Almost five years."

'"That's incredible. I didn't want to accept a fare to Orly in case I bumped into you. I've come here dozens of times and I've never ever seen you."

'"We must have just missed one another."

'"I must go. The taxi's badly parked. I'm going to get a fine."

'"Are you a taxi driver?"

'"Yes."

'"Are you happy?"

'"I can't complain. Well. See you. Now, I'll have to avoid the Invalides."

'I walked away. I was happy. Coming across her was a gift I hadn't dared hope for. I couldn't ask for more. "Leonid…", I heard. I turned around.

'"I'm glad to have seen you again."

'"So am I."

'"I've often wondered what had become of you."

'"As you can see, not much. I've still got the watch you gave me."

'"So have I…what's the matter with your hands?"

'The handkerchiefs were red. Blood was pouring everywhere. She arranged for a colleague to take over from her and took me to the air terminal's infirmary. She took out some cotton wool and hydrogen peroxide from the first aid box. She cleaned the wounds. I observed the busy and meticulous way she looked after me. It was bliss. I wasn't in pain. She smelled of that very mild scent. I forget what it's called.

'"How did you do this?"'

'"I had a problem with… the car."'

'She put on these bandages for me. We went to the cafeteria at the air terminal. There weren't many people there. We had coffee. We talked, about what I don't know — just as we used to do. Sometimes we were silent. We looked at one another. It's difficult to piece together bits of time you didn't spend together.

'"Aren't you going to have problems at work?"'

'"On Sundays it's quiet. What about your car?"'

'"I couldn't care less!"'

'"Did you never try to see me again?"'

'"Milène, I'd made a promise. To that guy."'

'"You're the only man I've ever known who keeps his promises."'

'"One can't just have faults. I've thought about you every day."'

'"I've often said to myself: Leonid must have got himself a job as a pilot. Perhaps he's in that plane, up there, in the sky. He's happy. I was sure of that."'

'"It's true that if I'd been told I'd end up as a taxi driver, I would never have believed it."'

'"Shall we see each other again?"'

'"I don't know. What about my promise?"'

'"Are you with someone?"'

'"I'm free as a bird. And you?"'

'"Why do you think I'm working on Sundays? Let's have dinner together, if you like."'

'"On one condition. That I pay."'

'And that's it. We're meeting tomorrow evening. I'm going to pick her up outside where she lives at eight o'clock. Life is beginning again.'

'I'm happy for you,' Igor said.

'I'm like a kid who's feeling nervous about his first date. What do you reckon, Michel?'

'You'll be able to take fares to Orly again.'

Igor bought a bottle of sparkling wine to celebrate this miraculous meeting.

'It's not a miracle. It's because of the comet.'

'That's a load of crap!' Igor exclaimed. 'It's luck.'

'This time, it may be different,' said Leonid. 'I was careful. I said nothing against the Rosenbergs.'

'Leonid, they were innocent!' I proclaimed.

'As far as I'm concerned, they were guilty! But from now on I'm keeping my trap shut.'

'You're right,' Igor concluded. 'It's the secret of happiness.'

We were in the midst of discussing fate, the turmoil of our feelings, the influence stars have on taxi drivers, and the mystery of our lives, when a courier entered. He had an envelope in his hand, with the proof that Igor had not been bragging. To make amends, Rudolf Nureyev was offering him two seats for *Swan Lake* with Margot Fonteyn, a gala evening at the Opéra de Paris for the unveiling of Chagall's ceiling, in the presence of the artist, of Mongénéral, of Malraux and *le Tout-Paris*. Igor was over the moon. Leonid did not drop any hints. Igor understood. With a heavy heart, he gave him the two tickets. Leonid invited Milène. He told her that Nureyev had sent him two invitations. She was impressed. She accepted with pleasure. Leonid had to hire a dinner jacket and buy himself a pair of shiny leather evening shoes. He did not regret it.

16

As I left the Balto, I said to myself that if this was the day for encounters, I would meet Cécile again. I'd have liked her to know Camille. I rang home to say what I was doing. My mother asked me not to come back too late. I called by at quai des Grands-Augustins. I hadn't been there for months: I had given up going there. The concierge was not around. There was no post in the letterbox. I walked up the three floors without putting on the lights. I rang the doorbell for a long time. No one answered. I was convinced that our lives would start again from where they had broken off, as though nothing had happened. I heard a noise. I waited, but no one opened the door. The key to her apartment was on my keyring. If she'd wanted to, she would have asked me to return it to her, but she had left it with me. I went in. It was dark inside the flat. Glimmers of light shone through the open shutters. I switched on all the lights. There was the same disarray, with even more dust. In the kitchen, the fridge was empty and had been unplugged. Cécile's bedroom. Pierre's. Everything was motionless. I went back into the drawing room. Nothing had been moved since my previous visit. My attention was drawn to a cardboard box on the table. A photographic frame was propped up on top of it against a pile of paperbacks. It hadn't been there last time. One of my photographs of the Médicis fountain stood prominently on top of the box. One of the five bought at Fotorama. I stood rooted to the spot in front of a close-up of Acis and Galatea. There could be no doubt. To set my mind at rest, I turned the frame over. On the reverse was the Fotorama stamp. The mystery collector was Cécile. No one could have bought these photographs other than her. Why had she left one of them as proof? To show that she had been there and to send me a friendly greeting? To tell me, I haven't forgotten you and I loved your photos, or something else? She knew that I would be coming. She had left the photo propped up against the books, on top of the box in the middle of the table, so as to be certain that I would not miss them. Perhaps she had left a note for me? I leafed through the books, rummaged through the drawers, went through the piles of documents, newspapers and magazines. I took no precautions. I signalled my arrival like a policeman signing a search warrant. In the waste-paper basket, there were shreds of burnt paper and scraps of charred postcards. I emptied them onto the carpet, but couldn't find anything amongst them.

Pierre's possessions were inside the cardboard box: a bundle of letters from his lovers, several of which had not been opened, his wallet containing an address book and a few banknotes, and inside a flap with a shiny clasp were some coins; a page torn from a spiral notepad, folded in eight, with the recipe for a Molotov cocktail, and, jumbled together, some photographs, his army record, his student cards, some exercise books filled with notes and pasted-in press cuttings, his Algerian notebooks, his letters and Cécile's replies, the first six chapters of her thesis on Aragon, and a dozen or so photographs of her that I had taken in the Luxembourg, with an elastic band around them. I knew her. This was no coincidence. It was deliberately staged. I sat down and lit a cigarette. I tried to decode the message she was sending me. And then, I understood. She was leaving everything to me, letting me have it, giving it to me. It was a present to make up for her silence and her disappearance. Or an exchange. She was telling me that with these photos of the fountain, I had come back to her, and that she was keeping the others as evidence of our pact. I took the box along with its contents. I left the books on the table and, propped up against them, once I had signed it, the picture of the fountain so that she would know that I had called by and that we would see each other again one day. Whenever she decided we should.

Who remembered Pierre nowadays? What remained of him? Of his huge smile, his impassioned ideas, his determination to change the world by killing all the bastards? Did the frail hearts he had conquered still think of the man who rejected them so that they would not become too attached to him? He lay, forgotten, in some provincial cemetery. In my arms I was carrying a box weighing four or five kilos, his life's work, rather like a blackboard rubbed out in a hurry. All of a sudden, I heard his voice: 'Hey, little bugger!'

It was definitely him. I turned around. I knew there would be no one there, just anonymous passers-by and my battered memory. I put down the box on a car bonnet.

'You really have become a little bugger! Is that what I taught you? Go on like that and you'll become a little shit like the others. Don't pretend you don't understand. Look at yourself in the mirror and you'll want to be sick. You're not allowed to change like this. Not you. Otherwise, I shall have been of no use at all.'

I didn't need to ask him any questions. I knew. There are some dangerous words in the French language. For example: *méprise*, which means an error or a mistake. A *méprise* is amusing. It's comic. Except when it changes and becomes the verb *mépriser*: to scorn or despise. Pierre was right. I could not lie to Camille any longer and let her think I was a poet and an artist when I was merely an imposter. I had made up my mind to tell her the truth. I would live a life of transparency with her and not a lie, neither error nor scorn. I phoned Camille. It was late. A man with a strong pied noir accent answered.

'Good evening, I'd like to speak to Camille. It's important.'

There was a groan and a long silence. Down the phone, I heard: 'Camille, there's someone who wants to talk to you.'

I recognized Camille's voice in the background, asking who it was.

'I don't know. This is not the time for phone calls, my girl.'

'Hello?'

'It's me. I'm ringing you because…'

'You're crazy! Do you know what time it is?'

'We must see each other tomorrow.'

'Tomorrow's Monday. I've classes until six o'clock. I can't.'

'It's very important, Camille. I'll wait for you.'

She hung up. It was a weight off my shoulders. I went home with Pierre's box. I left it in a corner of my bedroom. On it, I wrote in large letters: 'Do not open'.

I waited by the fountain. It was half past six. From the Lycée Fénelon to the Luxembourg takes less than ten minutes, without hurrying. She would not come. She must have had a problem or she had not appreciated my late phone call and was annoyed with me. We might never see each other again. My heart was thumping, I had a lump in my throat and my shoulders sagged. I was gazing at Polyphemus with his raised arm and that restrained motion that broke the perspective. At that very moment, I felt a strange sensation. A sort of cleaving in two, and an unaccustomed lightness, as though there were another person inside me. It took me completely by surprise. I would never have believed that this would ever happen to me. I took out a scrap of paper. I held my breath. I shuddered and out it came. In a burst. Without me pausing for a moment to ask myself what I was doing, I wrote eight verses. At speed. Like Sacha. I didn't have time to read them again. I looked up, my pen in the air. Camille was standing there.

'I'm sorry. I was kept back by the philosophy teacher.'

I handed her the sheet of paper. She took it and read it.

> Supreme in a marble palace
> Gazing at the darkened chandeliers and the flaming candles
> I wish only to ponder myself and my extended shadow
> In the captive towers buried passion
> Suddenly explodes and takes possession of my soul
> As an intoxicated bird flies into its tree
> I search for you, I lose you and my sadness flees
> I wait for you, distraught, by the foot of the fountain.

'Michel, it's very beautiful.'

'Do you think so?'

'I love it. It's not as sad as the others.'

I stood up. I took her in my arms. She closed her eyes. I kissed her. She didn't protest. On the contrary, she clasped me to her tightly. We remained there, intertwined, each of us overwhelmed by the other.

'Why did you ring yesterday evening?'

I hesitated. Should I reveal the truth? It is quite clear that women love poets. I looked into her eyes and I smiled. In the end, I said nothing.

17

The countdown had begun. Thirty days to the *bac*. I wasn't bothered. I had not the slightest anxiety or doubt as to the outcome. Ever since I had moved to the literature stream, I had become good at maths. If I had had a teacher like Peretti beforehand, with his unique teaching methods, everything would have been different. He never made fun of anyone. He wasn't sarcastic, contemptuous, arrogant or irritating. When we had not understood something, we dared tell him so. He began again with a smile. He didn't mind. On the contrary, he liked it. He wasn't in a hurry. Camille, on the other hand, was worried sick. I tried to reason with her: 'Did your clairvoyant say you were going to get through?'

'Yes.'

'If she says so, there's no need to worry. You'll pass. And if you don't, what will happen? Nothing. You'll repeat the year. You won't be the first. It's not a disaster.'

'My father would be furious with me.'

'This pressure you're under is ridiculous. He should be doing the opposite and putting you at your ease. I'm going to give him a piece of my mind.'

'Don't, whatever you do! Please recite a poem for me.'

'Right now I'd better be getting on with revising, don't you think? She smiled and nodded. I was exhausted. What sort of poet doesn't write poems? I thought I had got myself out of trouble, but every time I took up a pen and a sheet of paper, nothing happened – no outpouring. However much I tried to force myself, to shake my head, close my eyes, go for intensive sessions by the fountain and summon up my emotions, I remained dull and unproductive. I had almost come to the conclusion that my creativity was limited to this one poem. Once again, I was obliged to resort to Sacha's compositions, even though Camille found them gloomy and melancholy. I drifted around between '*la méprise*' and '*le mépris*', between contempt and misunderstanding. I loathed myself for lying to her and deceiving her. After one last, useless attempt, I decided to come clean with her. Whatever the price might be.

We met as we did every evening at the Viennese patisserie in rue de l'Ecole de Médecine. I ordered two hot chocolates.

'Camille, I've something important to say to you.'

'So have I. I must talk to you.'

'All right. Would you like me to begin?'

'What I have to say to you is vitally important.'

I wondered what could be more serious than my lies. Her clairvoyant must have told her about the arrival of another comet.

'I'm listening.'

She didn't speak. Her eyes were cast down. She looked as though she had a weight on her mind and didn't know how to get rid of it. I began to feel anxious.

'I haven't told you the truth, Michel.'

She stopped. I dug my fingers into the bench. I was prepared for the worst. I would never have believed it possible. It had to be faced. There was somebody else.

'I've got two bits of bad news.'

'Why don't we go outside. It's hot.'

We made our way towards the Seine. We walked along the riverbank and sat down on a bench. She must have been searching for the appropriate words, rather like a doctor who tells you that you're going to die soon, that it's sad and you need to be brave.

'I didn't mention it because I didn't think it would become an issue between us…. I'm Jewish.'

'That's not bad news.'

'It is in my family.'

'I don't understand.'

'Things are not possible between us, Michel.'

'Because you're Jewish? I couldn't care less. We're not very religious at home.'

'In our home, it's the opposite.'

'We're not in the Middle Ages any longer.'

'You don't know my family.'

'We get along well together. We're taking the *bac*. You're the first girl I've met who means something to me. You're not obliged to talk to your parents about it. We can wait and see how it works out.'

'We won't see a thing, Michel. In July, we're leaving France.'

'What?'

'We're emigrating to Israel.'

'I don't believe it.'

'They don't like it here. My father says that our place is over there. They're waiting for us to pass our *bac*. It's really bad news. That's why I just wanted us to be friends.'

'You're not obliged to go there. They can't force you.'

'I'm a minor, Michel.'

'You've got family here. You can say you have to do your studies in France. You can live at one of your uncle's homes. You can go and see your parents during the holidays.'

'The whole family is leaving together. The tickets are booked.'

'What if you failed your *bac*? Nobody is sure of passing. That way, you'd be here for another year.'

'I want to pass for my parents' sake. It's a dream they've had for a long time. Before I knew you, I was happy to go there. A new land at last, where everything is possible. Living in a kibbutz: doing away with property, social classes, salaries, removing the children from the family dwelling, working for the community, taking decisions together. You should understand.'

'They're bloody stupid ideas! They'll never work!'

'It's best we don't see one another any more, Michel.'

'What?'

'It would be best for us to stop. I don't want… I don't want to…'

'You should have said you were leaving right away! We could have broken up immediately!'

'I wanted us to be friends, nothing more.'

'I couldn't give a damn about your friendship! I believed in us.'

'I didn't want there to be any complications between us. It's your fault.'

'Oh really? And what did I do? Eh? Can you tell me that?'

'I hadn't anticipated that I would meet a poet.'

She started to gasp for breath and began crying. She stood up. She ran away. I tried to order my thoughts. Everything was in turmoil inside my head. She had got it wrong. It was a misunderstanding, a mistake, an error. I felt washed out. I stood up and I yelled: 'I'm not a poet! Do you understand? I'm not a poet!'

She was a long way off. She couldn't have heard.

I began talking to myself. Kicking out at invisible enemies. I cursed the Jews, the kibbutz dwellers, socialism, comets, poets and women. I wanted to scream. A pleasure boat crammed full of tourists went by. They were taking photographs. I yelled insults at them. They didn't understand. They laughed and waved. I swore to myself that I would change and that I would never be trapped again.

It was the last day of fine weather. A depression emanating from the Arctic took us back into winter. The sky was dark. The rain poured down. This weather suited me perfectly.

18

It all came back to me. Pins and needles all over the body. Lungs gasping for air. I found Pierre's old shorts and his PUC rugby shirt. I went back to the Luxembourg and it wasn't in order to swoon in front of that wretched fountain. I started to run again. For the first few days, I hitched on to a group of firemen who were doing their training. I found it hard to keep up, but I made it a point of honour to match them stride for stride. And then I left them all behind me. I completed the circuits at a steady pace, and as soon as I saw one of the firemen, I accelerated to overtake him. What with the rain, the muddy track looked like a swimming pool. I loved the drumming sound, this thud of footsteps on the drenched earth. I kept smashing my previous record. I no longer counted the circuits. I would run for two hours without pausing, stopping at closing time or at the point of exhaustion, when my pulse was thumping in my temples at top speed, and my legs were starting to wobble.

I went home soaked to the skin. I replied in onomatopoeic grunts. I took a boiling hot shower and shut myself in my bedroom. Juliette would sometimes come and sit on my bed. She talked about this and that and she didn't ask a single question about Camille. But I never stopped thinking of her. It's not easy to reason with oneself. You can't control your own brain. More than once, I wanted to go along to the Lycée Fénelon to set eyes on her, to talk. But I decided against it. It would be pointless. You can't change the way things are or force the hand of fate. When it became unbearable, I accelerated until I was out of breath. There's an actual moment when your mind eventually gives up and leaves you in peace. Can you have a heart attack aged seventeen? The more I exerted myself, the more I thought of her. I wept for her as I ran. There was no need to hide away. No one can tell the difference between tears and raindrops. How many circuits did I need to do in order to forget?

*

I was bent double. My lungs were bursting. I had a stitch in my side, and I was panting and spitting, trying to get my breath back. It was drizzling. Anyone would think it was November, rather than June. I was by the deserted tennis courts. I straightened up. There she was. In front of me.

'What are you doing there?'

'I was looking for you.'

'What's happened?'

'Listen… ever since the other day… I've… I…'

Her clothes and her hair were dripping wet, she looked strained and her eyes were red. Her lower lip was quivering.

'Michel, I can't bear it any longer.'

'Things aren't too good with me either, let me tell you.'

'Michel… let's run away.'

I didn't understand what she meant. I opened my mouth to say 'What?' but no sound emerged.

'Let's leave immediately. Both of us.'

'Where would we go?'

'Doesn't matter. Far away.'

'Where are you thinking of?'

'To a country where no one will find us, where no one will look for us.'

'A country like that doesn't exist.'

'To India. America. To the end of the world.'

'Do you mean: go away for ever?'

'Yes. That's right. We'll never come back.'

'I don't know what to say.'

'We'll always be together. Don't you want to?'

'Of course I do.'

'Then let's go.'

'Camille, it's not possible. There's the *bac*. Next week.'

'It'll be too late. I won't be able to. I won't have the guts. We have to go now.'

'People do that in dreams. Not in reality.'

'If you love me, Michel, take me away. Don't let me go there.'

'Running away on a sudden impulse is not a good idea.'

'Let's go to your grandfather's house, in Italy. You told me he was—'

'We're minors. We'd be stopped at the border! We don't have enough money to buy tickets.'

'We can try hitch-hiking. Some people go round the world like that.'

'Let's take the *bac*. That's the important thing, for you and for me. Afterwards, we'll find a solution, in our own time.'

'So, it's not possible?'

'I don't think so.'

She nodded several times, as though to let the notion sink in. I wanted to take her hand. She withdrew it.

'You mustn't—'

'I was joking, Michel. It was just to see what you said.'

'I'm going to see you home.'

She shook her head and walked away.

'Camille, we'll think about it.'

They say that good fortune only knocks once and that when she knocks you have to seize her. Afterwards, it's too late. She's gone elsewhere and won't come back. Only amnesiacs have no regrets. I've thought about this scene a million times. Each time, I've come to the same conclusion: I was a complete idiot. A coward. A man with no ambition. I belonged to the category of those who stood on the quayside and watched the ships depart. You need courage to go away. What had she thought of me? Where would we be now if I had said yes? In which African country? In Aden? In Pondicherry? In the Marquesas? In deepest Montana? It is in the heat of adventure that a rebel's strength is measured.

I needed to talk to Sacha, to ask his advice and get him to make me feel better. At Fotorama, the owner told me that he was ill. A bad bout of flu. What with this lousy weather, it was hardly surprising. I went to his place. I hadn't been back there for almost a year. I had forgotten that the service staircase was so filthy, with its crumbling steps, its blistered walls and its dangling electric wires. On the top floor, one out of every two light bulbs was missing. I no longer knew which his door was. I assumed it was the one with no name. I knocked a few times. I heard his voice inside: 'What is it?'

'It's me, Sacha. It's Michel.'

After a minute, the door was unbolted. In the crack, I could glimpse Sacha's eye.

'Are you alone?'

'Yes.'

He opened the door. He was wearing nothing but a blue woollen dressing gown. He looked like death warmed up, his hair was dishevelled and he had a week's growth of beard. He glanced left and right down the corridor.

'What do you want?'

'I came to see how you were getting on.'

'You're the only person in Paris who remembers my existence. Would you like to come in?'

He stood back. I walked into the servant's room. He shut the door and bolted it. He was shaken by a fit of coughing. The ashtray was full of cigarette butts. A standard lamp cast a pale glimmer and a book in Russian lay on the small table beside the unmade bed. There were patches of damp on the walls.

'It's freezing cold!'

'That's why I caught this lousy cold. The landlord doesn't want to switch on the heating in June.'

'You should have a little radiator.'

'Yes, I should.'

'I think there's one at home. I'll go and get it for you.'

'It's not worth the trouble. The bad weather won't last. Would you do something for me, Michel?'

'Of course, Sacha.'

'It would be good if you could get some medicine for me. I haven't the strength to go downstairs. Something for bronchitis and a cough. Something strong.'

'I'll ring your doctor.'

'I don't have one! Ask the man at the chemist's in place Monge, the one with a brush cut and an English scarf. Tell him it's for me; he knows me. Thanks to me, you'll meet an unusual person. A chemist who gives credit!'

'Would you like me to do some shopping? I could call in at the grocer's shop. I think you've got thinner. You must get your strength back.'

'I'm not very hungry. It's kind of you, Michel. Really.'

Given the condition he was in, I didn't want to bother him with my problems. I called by at home. They had switched on the central heating in our apartment. We had an oil-filled electric radiator lying around in a cupboard, which was never used. I was careful. Nobody noticed me taking it out of the flat. I pushed it down the street on its wheels. The chemist on the square gave me a bag of medicines and wrote the dosage on the packets. He jotted down the total in a notebook. I bought apples, some ham and some gruyère cheese at the grocery shop. I had a hard time taking the radiator up to the seventh floor. We plugged it in. The temperature rose rapidly. The feeling of being inside an ice box vanished.

'It's going to use a lot of electricity,' I told him.

'Don't worry about that.'

He told me he had made a minute hole in the electricity meter, no bigger than the head of a needle. Through it, he had threaded an unfolded paperclip that blocked the motion of the serrated wheel.

'My neighbour showed me how. They all do it upstairs. In Russia, we would never have dared. It's fraud. It's not the same here. We remove the paperclip a week before the official from Electricité de France is due so the meter works a bit. Apparently the man knows, but he doesn't say anything. Tell me, have you taken some good photos of Camille?'

'At the moment we're getting ready for the *bac*. You should take your medicine and you must stop smoking.'

'That's what I forgot to ask you for. Some cigarettes.'

The next day, the central heating in our building broke down. The temperature dropped to fourteen degrees. The oil-filled radiator had disappeared from the cupboard.

'It can't just have vanished into thin air!' my mother exclaimed suspiciously.

'It was there last week. I'm sure of it,' Maria protested.

'I find that strange.'

'I swear to you, Madame.'

'Michel, did you touch the radiator?'

'What do you expect me to do with it?' I objected, with obvious sincerity.

The puzzle of the vanishing radiator preoccupied us for weeks. My mother showed the family the cupboard where it was supposed to be kept. We searched for it everywhere. We asked the neighbours and the concierge. She suspected my father of having sneaked in and taken it away to the chilly part of the countryside where he lived. There are mysteries that give rise to incomprehension and fuel discussions and controversies such as the abominable snowman, the Loch Ness monster, or flying saucers. But there are no such things as mysteries. Simply liars, two-faced bastards and idiots.

'I'd like a bit of warmth!' I moaned. 'It's incredible how freezing it is in this place. Anyone would think we were in Siberia. It's impossible to work. Don't be surprised if I fail my *bac*!'

19

I woke up in the middle of the night. It was obvious: I had to board the ship. Slip anchor. Turn my gaze from the disappearing coastline. Confront the unknown seas and sail past the headland. My decision was made. I would go away with her. I would accompany her. Nobody could prevent me doing so. A few technical details remained to be resolved. I wondered whether I should do this before or after the *bac*. I hesitated. The boil had to be lanced, we couldn't prevaricate any longer. I knew from Camille that her father came back from work early. It wasn't going to be easy to get my way; to impose myself come what may; to apply pressure and stand firm until I had what I wanted. I skipped the last lesson and went to ring his doorbell, determined to use the experience I had gained at chess to enforce my will. A man of about fifty, with a pleasant expression and an athletic build, answered the door. I recognized him from his gloomy voice.

'Hello, Monsieur Toledano, I'm Michel Marini.'

'Hello, Michel, how are you?'

I was surprised by this warm welcome, the outstretched hand and open smile.

'Camille's not here.'

I didn't know he knew.

'It's you I've come to see.'

'Very well, come in.'

I went inside the flat. Cardboard boxes were piled up in the hallway, labelled so that they could be distinguished one from the other. He was in the process of packing one in the dining room.

'Leaving shortly?'

'These boxes are going ahead of us. Some coffee?'

'No thank you, Monsieur. I don't feel like any.'

He looked at me and waited. He poured himself a large cup.

'You should. It warms you up in this rotten weather. What is it, my lad?'

He had noticed I was finding it difficult to speak.

'Come and sit down. We'll be quiet here. Would you like some biscuits? My wife made them.'

We sat round the table. He opened a tin filled with biscuits.

'Help yourself. You'll never have eaten any like these.'

I took two, out of politeness.

'They're delicious.'

'You'll have noticed there are some with orange peel. It's my mother's recipe – authentically Constantine.'

There comes a moment when you have to take the plunge. Even if the water is freezing or you don't know how to swim. Before the ship sinks.

'Monsieur Toledano, I'm leaving with you.'

He stopped munching his biscuit and put down his cup. He looked neither surprised nor angry.

'With us, to Israel?'

'Yes.'

'Would you like to come on holiday?'

'No. For ever.'

'Because of Camille?'

'Yes.'

'And what does she think of this?'

'She said goodbye to me, and told me it was over.'

'She's right. It's not possible between the two of you.'

'Why?'

'Because you're not Jewish.'

'For me, it's not a problem. I couldn't care less about religion. I'm not a believer.'

'You're a nice boy, Michel. I like poets.'

'How do you know?'

'My daughter tells me everything. I, too, loved poetry when I was young. Apollinaire especially. Do you know Apollinaire?'

'Not very well.'

He searched his memory.

'I no longer remember. It was a long time ago.'

He closed his eyes…

> … And how I love your rustling o season, how I love
> The tumbling fruits that no one picks
> The wind and the forest weeping
> All their autumn tears leaf by leaf…

'It was somewhere there inside,' he said mischievously, pointing to his temple. 'When you think about it, it's amazing what we have in our heads. I've nothing against you. But I'd prefer my daughter to marry a Jew. It's better.'

'Why?'

'For the children! Have you thought about children?'

'Not yet.'

'That's the problem. Would you like it if your children went to the synagogue?'

'Perhaps my children won't go anywhere.'

'You can do what you want with your children. My daughter's children won't go to church. Peace means being among your own kind. Jews with Jews, Catholics with Catholics.'

'Why go away? You could be Jewish in France.'

'If I were Chinese, I'd live in China. That would be normal, wouldn't it?'

'Yes.'

'I'm a Jew, I'm going to Israel. It's not complicated. You're French. You live in France. You're Catholic, you've got nothing to do with Israel. This doesn't prevent you and Camille being friends. But you don't belong together. I'm glad that my daughter won't be seeing you any more. It would not have had a happy ending.'

'I don't think Camille is glad to be leaving.'

'I'm not forcing anybody. My children are free. If she had said that she wanted to stay, I would have left her with my brother in Montreuil. She wants to go to Israel because that is her country and because her family is making *aliyah*. We're as close as the fingers on one hand. And tell me, your parents, do they agree? Have they given their consent for you to leave the country?'

'No.'

'In any case, I don't want you around. You're young, Michel, make the most of life. There's no lack of girls, but you leave mine alone, all right? I'm not kicking you out, but I've got to finish packing two boxes. Here, have some biscuits. And keep going with the poems, you've got talent, I can tell you.'

I found myself on the pavement with a parcel of biscuits in my hand. Old man Toledano was very good at getting you where he wanted. I had said 'Thank you, Monsieur' as I left. I was not equipped to do battle with a man who recited poetry with a Bab el-Oued accent and offered you coffee and biscuits. In order to argue with the slightest chance of success, one needed great skill in dialectics. Twenty or thirty years of the Communist party. The real one. On the other side of the Wall.

Two hours later I pushed open the door of the Balto. Vladimir was distributing unsold food: four roast chickens that he was cutting into pieces, some chicken vol-au-vents, meat pies, tarts, cheese pastries, eggs in aspic, brawn, hocks of ham and mortadella. Everyone was striking bargains and going away with enough for two or three meals.

'Is there anything you want, Michel?'

'No thank you, Vladimir.'

'I've got some rice pudding.'

'I'm not hungry.'

'Shall we have a game?' Igor asked me.

'I don't feel like it.'

'What's the matter?'

'A small problem. I'd like your advice.'

It was a very obvious mistake. In my defence, it has to be said that I was a novice in these matters. I should have thought before I spoke about it. Seeking Igor's opinion in public also meant getting those of Leonid, Vladimir, Pavel, Imré, Tomasz, Gregorios... There was no question of dealing with sensitive matters in private. They were there to help, were they not? We were sitting on both sides of the restaurant bench. Leonid ordered two bottles of sparkling wine, and I told them my story. Not in its entirety: just the most recent episodes. They listened to me as they sipped the wine and sampled the biscuits. At the end, they looked thoughtful.

'These biscuits are very good,' Gregorios said. 'In our country, we don't make them like this.'

'Jacky, bring us another,' Igor called out.

'What's the difficulty?' asked Pavel.

'I've explained to you. Her father doesn't like me because I'm Catholic.'

'He's right,' he replied.

'That's discrimination!'

'He has the right to want his daughter to marry a Jew.'

'I know what she's like. She's being tricked by her family.'

'He's not forcing her to follow him. It's true that they belong over there.'

'Pavel, are you Jewish?'

'Of course. I haven't believed in God for donkey's years, but I'm Jewish to my fingertips.'

'Why don't you go there, to Israel?'

'The United States is where I want to go. You know, Slansky was sentenced to death because he was Jewish. Like most of those who were hanged with him.'

'I'm talking to you about a father who's preventing me from seeing his daughter because I'm not Jewish!'

'It's normal that he should not want you. It's the reverse that would be abnormal,' Vladimir maintained.

'If he agrees to that, he's no longer Jewish,' Igor intervened.

'Are you going to join in too?'

'Where have you been? Have you just landed from Mars? Who do you think we all are? Communists on the run? Enemies of the people? In this club, we're all Jews!'

'I'm not!' Gregorios shouted. 'I'm an atheist. I was originally baptised Orthodox. I go to church to keep my wife happy.'

'I'm not much of a believer,' Leonid said.

'You see, we conform to the original percentage,' Igor continued. 'Two out of every ten.'

'I didn't know we were in a club of sanctimonious bigots here!'

'Don't forget, Michel, that although very few Jews were revolutionaries, the majority of revolutionaries were Jewish. This has been forgotten, but in 1921, there were seventeen of them, out of Lenin's twenty-two People's Commissars. Stalin drew attention to the fact, even though we no longer knew what being Jewish meant. We no longer practised. We never set foot in a synagogue. It was an aspect of our lives that was unimportant. We became Jews again in spite of ourselves.'

'I don't see the connection with me and Camille. You have a boy of my age and a younger daughter, if I remember correctly?'

'She was two years old when I left. She's fourteen now.'

'If your daughter or your son told you they wanted to marry a Catholic, would it bother you?'

'I'll never see my children again. I don't even know whether they're alive. For a long time, I didn't feel involved. They were a legacy of a world that no longer existed and deserved to be destroyed. I was anti-religious. Our memories have been jolted on either side. I knew doctors who were murdered, not because they were believers, but because they were born Jewish. I can understand your girlfriend's father. You don't know what he's lived through.'

'You haven't answered my question. Would it be a problem for you with your daughter, nowadays?'

'A bit. More so in the case of my son. Because of the children.'

'Have you forgotten your grand principles? It's the opposite of what you've always maintained!'

'Perhaps I've changed or grown older.'

'We'd be better off going to live in Israel,' Vladimir said. 'We could work there in peace.'

'I think so too,' Igor carried on. 'At least I'd be allowed to practise my profession there.'

'I thought that religion was the opium of the people.'

'Being Zionist doesn't mean being religious,' Tomasz announced.

'You're nothing but a bunch of... of...'

Words bounced around on the tip of my tongue. None came out.

They stared at me, surprised at my aggression.

'You mustn't get annoyed, Michel,' said Leonid. 'We were just chatting.'

I felt like screaming. Something had just snapped between us. I no longer felt part of their group. They had excluded me. I had come needing to be cheered up a little and I had gone away feeling downcast. How could I have been so blind and stupid as not to notice anything? I loathed them. I made up my mind to leave this club and never set foot there again. Whoever said that revolutionaries end up as oppressors or heretics was not mistaken. He had forgotten that some of them become religious bigots.

On the day before the *bac*, I went to the movies. Apparently, it's the best way of relaxing. For weeks, Werner had been inviting me to come and see the film of the century according to Igor and Leonid, who spoke about it with tremors in their voices. Werner found me a seat in the cinema. There weren't many people. *The Cranes are Flying* was a shock. Not just because of the perfect harmony between the lyricism and the emotions that whirl us away, but mainly because of the story, which was so simple and so human. I recognized my own parents' story, separated as they were by war, though in their case they found each other again.

The *bac* was a formality. We had been trained like cattle at an agricultural show. It was as though our teachers knew the questions beforehand. There then began that lethargic, unsettled period of waiting for the results without knowing whether to be anxious or relieved. I didn't know whether I should phone her or try to see her. I decided it was best not to show my impatience. I ran my circuits of the Luxembourg at a mad pace. It's not easy to rid oneself of an *idée fixe*. I still had a slim hope that Camille might fail her *bac*. If she didn't want us to be apart, she knew what she had to do. The choice lay in her hands: her parents or me. My fate would be settled in twelve days' time. The prisoner sentenced to death, facing the firing squad, can retain one hope and tell himself, just as I did: for the time being, everything's all right.

20

I had banned myself from the Club, but not from the Balto. I returned to my old habits and caught up with my old pals. They, at least, did not split hairs, nor did they give a damn about History. They behaved as though nothing had existed before they did; they lived in the present, they did not expect to change the world, but to enjoy it, and they did not hang around privately cursing people. Their discussions were about girls on Saturday evenings, football on Sundays, and rock'n'roll every day of the week. It was a great breath of fresh air. I played with Samy, who was still just as lethal. I took genuine pleasure ignoring the greetings of Club members. I pretended not to hear them saying hello and 'How are you, Michel?' They had already forgotten the previous week's argument. They could yell and curse one another, yet ten minutes later they were joking and offering to buy drinks. But I could not rid myself of these bitter feelings. I did not have the strength just to shrug my shoulders and smile as though they had not discarded me like a stranger. Friendship is worth nothing if it is not stronger than our convictions. If it were me, I would have stood up for them against the entire world. I was less annoyed with Camille's father than with Igor and his hopeless principles. He walked over to the baby-foot table. I kept my eyes stubbornly on the players.

'Have you time for a game?'

'Igor, can't you see I'm playing?' I replied without looking up.

'We can talk about it, if you like.'

'I don't need your help. You'd be better off looking after your own children!'

'What you say is disgusting.'

He walked away towards the door of the Club. My cheeks were burning. I took it out on my opponents. Samy and I won about ten games. We were unbeaten. We were exhausted and dripping with sweat. We ended up at the bar, and old father Marcusot poured us two shandies. Samy and

Jacky were ranting and raving about Stade de Reims' baffling game plan. I listened to them absent-mindedly.

'How do you explain that, Michel?'

'It's one hell of a problem.'

'Or else, they're being bribed.'

'Who by?'

'Who knows?'

Our companion, a builder, was convinced that it was Real Madrid's fault. He launched into a heated discussion with old father Marcusot, who was in the process of preparing his celebrated croque-monsieurs. He disagreed: 'The Stade de Reims lot are actually useless! They were given another thrashing by Racing.'

This technical level was beyond me. I picked up the copy of *France-Soir* that was lying around and read the comic strips. I made the mistake of glancing at my horoscope. I was not entering a period of good fortune. Had I been born the previous day, all would have been happiness and bliss. I was doomed just by a single day. Old father Marcusot offered us some Aubrac sausage made by one of his cousins. We tasted it. It was excellent. He cut up some slices and poured himself a glass of claret. They started telling jokes. A sort of competition with laughter as the only reward.

'And do you know this one?' said Samy's pal. 'A priest is ambling along in the African bush when he comes face to face with a ferocious lion. "Dear God, vouchsafe that this lion may have a Christian thought," implores the priest. "Dear God, give your blessing to this meal!" says the lion.'

We burst out laughing at the same time. The laughter grew hysterical. We had tears in our eyes. I no longer remember precisely what happened. I was bent double. Someone was leaning over me. I heard cries. When I recovered, old father Marcusot was clutching the lower part of his neck with his left hand and holding his chest with his right. His jaws were clenched and he was gasping for breath. Within a few seconds, his face had turned red. His head was shaking. He collapsed. Behind the bar, Jacky tried to lift him, but he was slim, and old Marcusot must have weighed at least a hundred kilos. He was unable to hold him up. Emerging from the kitchen, Madeleine began to panic. Old Marcusot was spluttering.

We rushed over to help him, crowding into the narrow space behind the bar. Samy held him under the arms and dragged him into the main room, knocking into those who were clustered all around. It was turmoil. Old father Marcusot was groaning. His chest was heaving.

'Go and fetch the doctor from the block of flats!' Madeleine shouted to Jacky. Old Marcusot was suffocating. Samy tried to open his shirt collar, but he couldn't manage it because of Marcusot's bow tie. He took a kitchen knife and sliced through it. I raced to the Club where the usual calm prevailed.

'Igor, quick!' I yelled. 'Old father Marcusot has had a heart attack!'

Igor rushed over with Leonid. He knelt down beside Marcusot, who was moaning in fits and starts. He took his pulse by pressing two fingers to the middle of his neck.

'Call the emergency services!' said Leonid. 'Hurry! And shut up!'

Leonid pushed the group of onlookers aside unceremoniously. Madeleine, who was squatting beside her husband, held his hand.

'Don't worry,' she said.

Igor began to massage his heart. He pumped his chest vigorously, both hands over the plexus. He paused for a moment and started again. Strong, regular thrusts that sank deep into his chest. Old Marcusot shuddered twice. Igor tilted his head backwards, pressed his nostrils together and, holding his chin, gave him mouth-to-mouth resuscitation. Huddled against one another, we formed an oval around his body. Leonid, his arms spread wide, provided a counterbalance. They looked frightened and distressed. I felt sure that Igor was going to save him. He blew air into his lungs. Old father Marcusot's chest barely heaved. For about ten minutes, Igor took turns applying thoracic compression and mouth-to-mouth resuscitation. We could hear him blowing. He was pumping him vigorously. He checked his pulse at the carotid once more, bent over him, and pressed his ear and then his cheek against his mouth. Old Marcusot did not react. Igor drew himself upright and shook his head helplessly.

'I think it's all over.'

Madeleine was stroking old Marcusot's face. She bent over him and clasped him to her.

'Albert, it'll be all right. The emergency service is on its way. They'll look after you.'

'There's nothing more that can be done for him, Madeleine.'

'I don't believe it, Igor! Where's the doctor?'

'He didn't suffer, you know. He wasn't aware of anything.'

She stared at her husband's face, reached out her hand and, shaking as she did so, closed his eyes. Igor and Leonid helped her to her feet. She fell into Igor's and Leonid's arms and began to weep.

Certain customers took advantage of the confusion and left without paying. That's the way it is in Paris cafés: as soon as the owner takes his eyes off his cash, it disappears as quickly as his friends do.

The Balto was closed on Wednesday, the day of Albert Marcusot's funeral in his hometown of Saint-Flour. He was the shrewdest man I've ever met. He ate and drank too much, smoked his daily pack of yellow Gitanes, and no one could ever remember him doing any exercise apart from a game of pinball. He worked like a Trojan all his life because he loved his job. When he was happy, he tapped his large belly and exclaimed: 'That's where the dosh is. And no one's going to take it from me!' He was right. He took it with him.

21

Thursday 2 July was a foul day. The results of the *bac* were announced. I didn't even go and look at them. A friend told me that I had been given a 'satisfactory' pass. Any normal human being would have been over the moon, and would have gone and had fun at the student ball. But I couldn't give a damn. I had had no news of Camille for a fortnight. No phone call, no letter, no meeting. I had been expecting her to show up after the exams. We could have spent this time together. Instead every day took us a little further away from one another. I ran round the Luxembourg until I was out of breath. In the afternoons, I went to the Lycée Fénelon. It was deserted. The lists of those who had passed and failed were pinned up on the noticeboards. She had passed 'with merit'. She had made her choice. Judging by my expression that evening, my mother thought at first that I had failed. She opened a bottle of champagne to celebrate the occasion, but I refused to clink glasses. I was clearly a killjoy. She asked me what I wanted to do next year.

'Gym teacher.'

'You! Are you joking?'

'I've never been so serious in my life.'

It continued to rain. How long can you go on running before you're forced to stop? The firemen tried to keep up. As soon as I accelerated, I left them standing. How about being a fireman? Do you need a diploma? I decided I would go and ask them. It would be better than teaching sport to a lot of softies. As I passed the statue of Delacroix, I spotted her. Camille was leaning against a tree. Because of the rain, we went and took cover beneath the park keepers' mushroom-shaped shelter.

'I called your home. Juliette told me you would be here. You're drenched.'

'I like running in the rain.'

'She told me you wanted to be a gym teacher. Is that a joke?'

'I've changed my mind. Now I've decided to be a fireman.'

'Are you mad?'

'Didn't you know that it's what every boy dreams of doing? The big red truck that really does go nee-naw. Why should you be interested in my future?'

'You passed. You must be pleased?'

'If you start talking to Juliette, you'll never get away.'

'I went by Henri-IV. I saw the results. I'm happy for you… My brother failed his *bac*.'

All of a sudden, the man condemned to death and facing the firing squad opens his eyes. I understood what Dostoevsky must have felt when he was told that he was reprieved. He surely did as I did. He took several deep breaths. It's wonderful to breathe. We don't think about it enough. I was dripping with sweat. What a lovely day it is today. How beautiful she is.

'So will he be forced to do it again?'

'In Israel. We're leaving tomorrow.'

The shot had been fired. I shuddered. How long would it take for me to feel it? Why wasn't I dead?

'Damn it all, Camille! Why won't you stay?'

'I can't, Michel.'

'Your father told me that if you'd wanted to, you could have gone to stay with your uncle in Montreuil.'

'Did he tell you that?'

'I promise you.'

'His brother's in a kibbutz on the Jordanian border.'

'Was he making fun of me?'

'What did you think of my mother's biscuits?'

I collapsed onto the bench.

'You shouldn't have come, Camille. You should have let me go on running.'

She sat down beside me. She took my hand. She gazed at me with a strange expression.

'Michel, I love you. I love only you. I think of you day and night. Every moment. It's unbearable. I can't go on. I want to live with you, stay with you, never ever leave you.'

'So do I.'

'I feel so close to you, do you understand?'

'Why haven't you been in touch with me during these two weeks? I felt terrible.'

'I wrote you two letters a day.'

'I never received anything.'

'I didn't send them.'

'Why have you come back?'

'I couldn't help it.'

'Camille, don't go. We'll find a solution.'

'I can't, Michel. I'm sixteen. I must obey my parents. I couldn't do that to them. I'm trapped.'

'I'm ready to go with you.'

'It's not possible. My parents wouldn't want it.'

'Let's go away together then. Doesn't matter where. You suggested that to me. Do you remember? I know a place where we can go. No one will find us.'

'Michel, listen to me. Do you love me?'

'How can you ask me that question? Do you really doubt it?'

'You'll wait for me and I'll wait for you.'

'How long will that last?'

'I don't know. A long time. It's a hurdle we'll have to overcome.'

'It's torture.'

'If we manage it, we'll feel stronger. Nothing will be able to separate us again. We'll be together for life. And after all, it's not the end of the world. Perhaps we'll manage to see each other during the holidays. Do you agree?'

'Is there a choice?'

'I swear that I'll wait for you.'

'Me too. I'll wait for you.'

She smiled at me, picked up the bag that lay at her feet and took out a book, which she handed to me.

'I'm giving it to you.'

It was her copy of *Le Matin des magiciens*, inscribed by Bergier and Pauwels.

'It's my most precious possession. Think of me as you read it.'

'I will, I promise. It will never leave me. I've got nothing to give you.'

'It doesn't matter. Will you write to me?'

'Every day. Wait.'

I took out my wallet. I pulled out a sheet of paper folded in eight. I gave it to her. She unfolded it carefully and found my rapidly drawn sketch of her.

'I knew you hadn't torn it up.'

'It doesn't look much like you.'

'I like it a lot.'

We sat there in silence. We wanted this moment to go on for ever. We stood up. Her eyes were red. I took her in my arms and I clasped her to me with all my strength. She gave me a long kiss on the lips. My body thrilled from head to foot. I closed my eyes. When I opened them again, she was gone. It was pouring with rain.

22

Madeleine Marcusot was back by Monday. She couldn't bear the Auvergne. Since her children had left the drinks trade and the Balto was too big a business for a woman on her own, she had decided to sell it to the son of a cousin. They were in the process of preparing the papers and the loans with the brewery agent. She introduced us to Patrick Bonnet. He was young and looked no more than thirty. From now on, he was the owner. He was full of ideas for enlarging the terrace, expanding the restaurant business in the evening and improving its reputation. He was going to change the pinball machines and would leave the baby-foot tables as they were. A lick of paint would do no harm. He offered drinks all round to celebrate his arrival. We raised our glasses in Albert's memory. Madeleine would help him initially. In October, she would be taking over a small restaurant in Levallois. She would be near her daughter.

I was awaiting my turn at the baby-foot table when Sacha arrived. I had been round to his place three times to see whether he needed anything. His cheeks were hollow. He had grey circles under his eyes and two weeks' growth of beard.

'What are you doing outside? You'll never get better with this lousy weather.'

'I'd run out of cigarettes.'

'They're bad for you, Sacha. You must stop smoking.'

'Michel, you're very kind, but you're a bit of a pain in the arse.'

He went to buy two packs of Gauloises at the tobacco counter. Madeleine was in the kitchen preparing the dish of the day. She spotted him and went over to him. They embraced.

'I'm sorry, Madeleine, I couldn't come before now.'

'It doesn't matter, Sacha. You look tired. You shouldn't have gone to the trouble.'

'I wanted to offer my condolences. To tell you just how upset I was by Albert's death. You know how fond I was of him.'

'He liked you very much too.'

'He was a friend. A fine person. It was so sudden.'

'I'm annoyed with myself, you know. He was too fat. There was no way of putting him on a diet. I should have been more forceful.'

'It's not your fault. He was happy.'

Suddenly, behind us, we heard a roar: 'What the hell are you doing here?' We turned round. Igor was red with fury.

'I warned you: I didn't want you bloody well setting foot here again!'

'I came to see Madeleine.'

'You're forbidden to stay in this café!'

'Fuck off!'

Igor hurled himself at him. He had lost control. He gave Sacha a colossal slap in the face that caused him to spin round ninety degrees. He grabbed him by the neck and dragged him outside, onto avenue Denfert-Rochereau. He began pummelling him with blows to the body and the head. We were dumbstruck. We watched Igor beating him up through the window. Sacha offered no resistance. He didn't try to protect himself. He fell to his knees. Igor seized him by the lapels of his coat and hammered his face with furious blows. Sacha's face was bleeding, but he didn't defend himself. I went outside and hurled myself at Igor. I grabbed him by the back. He was bigger and stronger than me and he was struggling, but I clung onto his arms and he was forced to let Sacha go. Sacha collapsed with his face to the ground. Igor went on kicking him violently in the ribs.

'Stop it! You're crazy!'

I managed to heave him a couple of yards away and hold him off. Nobody came to help me. Igor was yelling that he wanted to kill him. He pushed me away. I punched him in the stomach with all my strength. He wasn't expecting it. He looked at me in stunned amazement, his mouth gasping for air. He drew back, clutching his belly. I knelt down beside Sacha, who was unconscious and bleeding from the face. I heard loud voices. Madeleine was preventing Igor from entering the Balto: 'Get out of my place!' she cried. 'Did you hear? Outside!'

She turned to Patrick Bonnet: 'I make it a condition of sale that this brute never sets foot here again!'

'I don't ever want to see you again!' he said to Igor, shaking his finger at him. 'Or you won't know what's hit you!'

Igor walked off in the direction of place Denfert-Rochereau. Sacha let out a feeble moan. I wiped his bloodied forehead with my handkerchief. Madeleine and Jacky came over and joined me.

'We must ring the emergency services,' Madeleine said.

'No,' wailed Sacha with a groan.

He stood up with difficulty. His eyes were staring, his face was swollen, one eye was closed, his nose was crooked, and one of his lips was split. He was bleeding everywhere.

'Take me to the hospital next door. Quickly!'

He put his arm on my shoulder and we inched forward. At times, he faltered. I struggled to hold him upright. He was limping and clutching his ribs. They were the toughest three hundred metres of my life. People passing by stared at us in terror. They stepped aside from us as though we had the plague. He was breathing with difficulty. Drops of blood fell on the ground and I was spattered with it just as much as he was. At Port-Royal, he collapsed. A policeman who was guiding the traffic helped me and, each of us holding one arm, we dragged him to the casualty department of Cochin Hospital. The policeman left. Two male nurses laid him out on a stretcher.

'What happened to you?' the elder of them asked.

'I fell down the stairs,' Sacha murmured.

The nurse made a face.

'I'm going to alert the duty houseman. He won't be long.'

He disappeared. I stayed with Sacha. He opened his eyes. He beckoned to me with his hand to come closer.

'Michel, you mustn't say anything. You found me in the street. You don't know me.'

'As you wish, Sacha.'

'It's better. I want them to look after me, but not to operate on me.'

'We must wait for the doctor. Let's see what he decides.'

A doctor arrived. He stared at me and frowned. He palpated Sacha's body. He couldn't help crying out in pain. He examined his face carefully. His fingers ran over every inch of skin with the delicacy of a blind man.

'I don't want to be operated on!'

'We're going to X-ray you, Monsieur, don't worry. It's not painful.'

A nurse pushed the trolley. Sacha disappeared behind a swing door. I sat down. There was the same procession of battered and blood-streaked bodies as last time, dumped here like parcels by well-meaning policemen or firemen, and the same smell of fear clung to these people living on borrowed time. Four years later, here I was again in the casualty department where I had waited after Cécile's attempted suicide. Where was she at this moment? Did she ever think of me? I would have so liked her to be with me, to be holding my hand. Would we see each other again one day? Perhaps it was this doctor who had attended to her at the time. Camille would have told me that my being here once more was a sign, and that it was written in the stars somewhere. If she had been there, I would have cried out that there is no such thing as predestination. It was just that I lived in this damned neighbourhood and I was unlucky with my friends. I began to blubber like a kid, like a bloody fool. The only advantage of being in this human pigsty was that nobody gave a damn, no one even noticed.

Sacha was brought back after less than an hour. He was dressed in green pyjamas and wrapped in a grey blanket. They put him in the corridor and we had to stand aside to allow the constant stream of other stretchers to go past.

'What did they tell you?'

'You're to turn over and not move.'

His face had been cleansed with arnica. He tried to sit up. He grimaced in pain. The slightest movement caused him to cry out. He breathed with difficulty in small breaths. His voice came from deep inside his throat: 'I have to go, Michel. You'll help me.'

'Sacha, you can't leave like this.'

'They're not allowed to keep me against my will.'

'You're not able to walk. What will you do?'

'I don't want to stay here. I want to leave.'

He gripped me by the arm and pulled me towards him with unexpected strength. He tried to raise himself, but had to give up because of the pain. His jaw was clenched. A stretcher-bearer pushed the trolley into a room where the doctor was waiting for us. He was examining the X-rays that were spread out on a bright screen in front of him.

'You have a fracture of the nasal septum at the point of the frontal sinus and the ethmoid. We're going to have to operate.'

'I don't want you to.'

'There are splinters of bone. A clot will form. You'll be in a lot of pain. You'll find it increasingly difficult to breathe because you have no nasal ventilation. Your turbinate bones are crushed. You risk an infection. We can operate on you immediately. Under anaesthetic, you won't feel a thing. It's not a major operation, but it's vital. In three days' time, you'll be out. You also have two broken ribs.'

'Can you put my nose back in place and nothing else?'

'That will be enough for today. As for the rest, we'll see later on. Are you ready?'

'You're not going to touch anything else?'

'I promise. What's your name?'

'Gauthier. François Gauthier.'

The doctor jotted down the name.

'Where do you live, Monsieur Gauthier?'

'In Bagneux. Avenue Gambetta. Number 10.'

He wrote down Sacha's false address on the entry certificate.

'I've got no other papers. He beat me up so he could rob me.'

'Don't worry. We're here to look after you. The anaesthetist will come to see you.'

He left with the X-rays. Sacha's eyes were closed as though he were asleep. He opened them. A tear rolled down his cheek.

'He's stubborn, this doc.'

'It's for your own good, Sacha.'

'My name is François Gauthier. And you don't know me.'

'You're a stranger whom I picked up in the street, and you were beaten up by a thug who stole your wallet.'

'It's the truth.'

'You must relax. As he told you, it's a very minor operation.'

'You'll be pleased, Michel, I'm going to have to stop smoking. Do one thing for me. I can't move my arm. In the right-hand pocket of my coat, there's a flap. Hand me the contents.'

I did as he asked. I pulled out a one hundred franc note, folded in four. He took it with his good left hand and unfolded it.

'Take this, Michel.'

'What are you doing, Sacha?'

'I'm not giving you anything. You're to keep it for me safely. You'll give it back to me when we see each other again. It's a tradition at home. It's to make sure the person who's being operated on comes to collect it. If you think I'm leaving my cash to you, you're quite wrong.'

'I'll give it back to you tomorrow.'

'I should hope so. I've got a good reason to recover now.'

He smiled with difficulty. I took his hand. It was frozen.

'Get some rest, Sacha.'

He closed his eyes. After a while, I felt the pressure slacken in his now warm hand. He had fallen asleep. A man in a white coat came in. They were going to examine him. He took Sacha away without waking him. I slipped the hundred-franc note into my wallet.

It was still raining when I emerged from the hospital. I went back to the Balto to give Madeleine the news. The café was abuzz with excitement. Patrick Bonnet had locked the door of the Club, sealed it off with an enormous chain, and had stuck up a notice: 'Permanent closure of these premises. Gambling forbidden. All drinks are to be consumed in the main room and orders must be renewed by the hour.' Leonid, Vladimir, Pavel, Imré, Tomasz and Gregorios tried to make him change his mind, but the owner remained adamant.

'He didn't have to hit him. I don't want any trouble with the police.'

'He was right! The only thing I regret is not having done it myself!' Leonid declared.

'We should have got rid of him earlier. He's been making fun of us for years!' Vladimir added.

'This is a café and restaurant for normal people. I don't want any maniacs. The chess club is finished! And if Igor comes back, I'll call the cops!'

'If there's not going to be a Club any more and if Igor is no longer allowed in, we'll go somewhere else!' said Pavel.

'Fine!'

They all trooped out together, with their heads held high. We really did think that Patrick Bonnet had shut down the Club because of Igor and Sacha's brawl. Later on, Jacky told me that it had been decided to close it at the time the sale was being negotiated in Saint-Flour. By doing so, he hoped to improve the café's reputation and its profitability. No one was angry with Igor. He had founded the Club and it was because of him that it was closed down. Interpreters date the official end of the Club, and of its period of renown, which some people still speak of with emotion and regret in their voices, to that Monday 6 July. As if to say: those were the good old days. The members searched for a friendly café in the neighbourhood, but didn't find one. When times got better they moved near to the orangery in the Jardin du Luxembourg. They became accustomed to playing there in summer or winter alike. They came from countries that had polar temperatures, so it didn't bother them if they spent hours sitting outside in the open air. Apparently, it's invigorating for both mind and body. Some of them still play there.

23

I woke up at three o'clock in the morning with a tight pain in my chest. There wasn't a sound. Outside, it was raining. It was a rotten July. I wondered how Sacha was and whether the operation on his nose had gone well. I would go and visit him tomorrow. In my mind's eye I saw Igor hitting him in fury, and him not defending himself. Why did they all hate him? What was the secret binding them that they would not disclose under any circumstances? Why did he pretend his name was François Gauthier? What did he have to hide? I suddenly realized that I only knew his first name. I had no idea what his surname was. Was he the son of a famous and fearsome person? Or one of those war criminals, whom police forces hunt for all over the world but who eventually manages to assume a new identity and vanish? Or maybe there was no explanation and it was merely a whim on his part. Even though other members of the Club made no secret of their names, he took care to conceal his own. I decided to get to the bottom of it and call by at his place to get an answer. His name must be there, somewhere.

In the morning, I went to his room in rue Monge. Behind the glass in the concierge's lodge was a list by floor of the residents of the building. On the seventh, there were some ten names. No Sacha, no Gauthier, nor anything that sounded Russian or Slav. I walked up the service stairs and arrived at the top floor. There was no name on his door. It was half-open and the lock had been broken, probably with a crowbar, which had shattered the wood of the door frame. The room had been burgled. It had been turned over from top to bottom. The mattress and the pillow had been slit open, and there were feathers everywhere. The wardrobe had been emptied, clothes lay in heaps. The two shelves had been torn down. The books were strewn around. His crockery was on the floor. I didn't know whether I should go to the police or tell Sacha in hospital. I heard a noise. A young woman was leaving her room. I had bumped into her the previous week when

I was bringing him some food. I showed her the damage.

'This happened last night, but I heard nothing.'

'I've come to get some things for Sacha. He's in hospital,' I asserted confidently.

'It's not serious, I hope?'

'He'll be out in three or four days.'

'He's not been lucky. It's the fourth or fifth time he's been burgled. Last year, they stole my iron. The concierge doesn't keep an eye on anything.'

'Do you know how Sacha's surname is spelt?'

'I've no idea. I've always called him by his first name.'

I picked up a plastic bag that was lying around and put some underwear in it.

'I'm going to tidy the room and put on a new bolt,' she said.

When I went downstairs again, there was a light on in the lodge. I knocked on the window. The concierge appeared.

'What is it?' she asked, opening her door.

'Do you recognize me? I'm Sacha's friend. I came to get some clothes for him. He's in hospital for a few days. His room was burgled last night.'

'Again! There's nothing to steal in those attic rooms. In my day, burglars didn't steal from the poor.'

'Do you have the exact spelling of his name?'

'He didn't tell me what his surname was.'

'What name was on his post?'

'I've worked in this building for seven years and he's never received a single letter.'

'And the electricity?'

'The meter is still in the owner's name.'

'What about paying his rent?'

'He brings me his rent in cash every three months. And he pays for the electricity as well.'

'Don't you give him a receipt?'

'We don't do that here. When he's a little behind, we don't harass him.'

'How did he get this room?'

'It was before I arrived. I think it was a friend of his who helped him.'

'Sacha doesn't have any friends.'

'The caretaker before me told me that he was someone well known. I don't remember who. Why are you asking me all these questions?'

'Don't you find it strange that this man has no name and that his was the only room to be burgled?'

'I'm not the police. As long as he pays his rent, and doesn't make any noise or mess, it's none of my business.'

I tried my luck with the chemist on place Monge, the eccentric guy with the brush haircut and the English scarf. I already knew what his answer would be.

'Sacha? I don't know. That's what I've always called him. How is he? Is he aware of my little bill?'

I went back to the Cochin, resolved to obtain an answer from the man who did not exist. He was going to explain to me clearly and precisely the reasons why the members of the Club hated him. This time, he wasn't going to get out of it either with an evasive smile, or a sidestep. I was determined that no one was going to take me for a ride any more.

At the hospital reception desk, I addressed the official behind her glass panel.

'Can you tell me which hospital building Monsieur François Gauthier is in?'

She stared at me, picked up her telephone and spoke briefly to someone.

'You may sit down. Someone will be coming.'

'I just want the number of his room so I can visit him.'

'You'll have to wait. You can't go there on your own.'

I sat down in the waiting room. After ten minutes, the doctor who had sounded Sacha's chest the previous day appeared. He asked me to follow him. Instead of going inside the hospital, we went into a room close to the reception area. A portly woman was sitting behind a desk. She did not introduce herself.

'In what capacity do you wish to see Monsieur François Gauthier?' the woman asked me.

'He had an operation on his nose. I wanted to find out how he was getting on.'

'Do you know him?'

There was a deliberate slowness about the way she expressed herself. She weighed each one of her words.

'Has something happened to him?'

'Be kind enough to answer my question. What is your relationship to him?'

'Yesterday, he was lying semi-unconscious on the pavement. He had been beaten up and robbed. He was bleeding. I brought him here.'

'You didn't know Monsieur Gauthier beforehand?'

'No.'

'Why are you interested in him?'

'I feel sorry for the poor man. Is that forbidden? I live in the neighbourhood and I was calling by to find out how he is. Has something gone wrong? Is he dead?'

'He's disappeared,' said the doctor.

'I don't believe it! What's happened?'

'The operation went perfectly. He woke up. Everything was fine. We put him in a room with another patient. I went to see him at the end of my shift. We chatted. He thanked me. He had supper. The nurse passed by three times during the night. He was asleep. By five o'clock in the morning, he had left the hospital. Vanished.'

'It's not difficult to get out of here. There's no supervision.'

'It's a hospital, not a prison.'

'We were obliged to inform the police about his disappearance,' said the woman. 'It's the law. The problem is that there's no Gauthier at the address he gave us. Can you give us your name and address? In case the police want to question you...'

'I gave her my identity card. She jotted down my contact details in her file.

'I'm not going to tell them anything else, you know.'

She gave me back my card. I got to my feet and left, accompanied by the doctor.

'Without betraying the medical oath,' he continued, 'I can assure you that this man needs looking after following his operation. There are various medicines he must take. He has a temporary splint and some stitches. There's a risk of infection. If you see him, tell him to call in so that he can be treated. We won't ask him anything. We also have the results of his blood tests and there's a problem. He must seek advice. It's urgent.'

From the way he spoke to me, I sensed that he did not believe my story. I was probably unconvincing. In any case, there was nothing they could prove. François Gauthier did not exist.

I went to the Balto, but not a single member of the Club was present and the new people did not know him. I questioned Jacky and Madeleine half-heartedly.

'Sacha?' said Jacky. 'I couldn't care less what his name is. That one, he's Samy. The other boozer at the bar, he's Jean. And you, you're Michel. Do you want to know my name?'

'Sacha?' said Madeleine. 'He's Sacha. He's Russian. With a Russian surname, I imagine. We called the others by their first name, too. They've all got names that are tough to pronounce.'

I told them about his disappearance and how important it was that he should be looked after. They promised to speak to him if they saw him. To set my mind at rest, I ended my search at Fotorama. His boss had not seen him for a fortnight.

'He's an exceptional laboratory assistant. In a career of thirty years, I've never seen someone more gifted. Since he's been here, the turnover has risen. I should very much have liked to put him on a salary and have his situation sorted out. He was the one who didn't want that. Why? I don't know. His surname?... Strangely enough, I never asked him.'

I didn't know how to explain his disappearance. He must have gone to some quiet place to recover and get some peace. He would come back when he wanted to. It was just like him to appear and disappear in an unpredictable manner, when it was least expected. He would not let me down. Sooner or later, I'd hear from him.

We had been talking for a while about spending a fortnight at Bar-le-Duc, but my father still didn't have a flat big enough to accommodate both of us. As a reward for my *bac* results, I was allowed to choose my own holiday.

'What would make you happy, Michel?' my mother asked me. 'England? Spain? Greece?'

'I'd love to go to Israel.'

'What an extraordinary idea! Why?'

'I want to know about life on a kibbutz. It must be thrilling to meet people who make tomatoes grow in the desert. There aren't many pioneers around nowadays.'

'Isn't it dangerous?'

I could sense that this was taking an awkward turn. I knew how to convince her.

'I should also like to go to Nazareth and to Bethlehem. I'd love to visit the holy places.'

Maurice made enquiries and discovered that it was expensive. It wasn't the right time given that business wasn't going too well. Eventually, in August, we would go back to Perros-Guirec.

24

Patrick Bonnet did not hang about. He was teeming with ideas. He spent his time redesigning the plans with the architect, looking for the perfect solution. In the latest version, he separated the bar and the restaurant and gave them their own entrances, enlarged the café and bar area by getting rid of the present kitchen, reclaimed the Club premises and converted them into a kitchen open on both sides. He also renewed the benches and decorated the restaurant like a brasserie, like his cousin's at the Bastille. He was pleased with himself and asked us our opinion. Madeleine did not show overwhelming enthusiasm. She was going to have to give up her territory before she had intended.

'If you demolish everything, it's going to cost you a lot.'

'We'll do one hundred sittings a night.'

'Only the regulars dine here. People prefer to go to Montparnasse. We do well at lunchtime.'

'The clientèle exist, we'll go and find them. You'll be able to take holidays.'

He stood drinks all round for Madeleine's farewell party. At the same time, we celebrated the start of the building works. The Balto would close in August for the first time and everything would be finished by the time everyone returned from holiday in September. The workmen arrived the following day. Samy and I gave them a hand dismantling the old benches and loading them into the lorry. The foreman wasn't able to open the Club door. The small key didn't fit the lock. I tried, but it was jammed. He went to look for Patrick, who banged on the key with a screwdriver handle without success.

'They must have forced it. Too bad about the lock.'

He picked up a pair of pliers, applied them to the screw and, with a swivelling movement, freed it from the door. He went in, switched on the light and let out a yell. We followed him inside. Sacha was hanging in the middle of the room. His body, suspended at the end of a short rope, had begun to revolve on its own. His feet were barely thirty centimetres from the ground. We thought he was still alive and rushed over to take him down, but he was as stiff as a piece of wood. I heard Patrick's voice shouting to call the police. Sacha's face was grey, almost black. His open eyes were staring at the ceiling. His neck looked huge. He had a splint on his nose and his jaw was twisted. An overturned chair lay by his feet. Within a few moments, the room had filled with workmen and customers, all of them panicking and shouting. Jacky put his hand on my shoulder. I took hold of Sacha's legs and lifted him. I stood back. His body slumped down a few inches. I couldn't stop staring at his hands and his clenched fingers. Samy made everyone leave the room. I stayed there with Patrick and Jacky.

'Who is this guy?' Patrick asked.

'The one who was beaten up the other day,' Jacky replied.

'Why did he do this here? It lands us in the shit as far as the refurbishments are concerned.'

I had tears in my eyes. I didn't know whether from anger or sorrow. I kept on saying to myself: I don't believe it! Sacha, please. Not that. Stop fooling around! A police siren grew louder and louder until it became unbearable. Sacha, why? We would have sorted things out. There's always a solution. Why didn't you say anything to me? Didn't you trust me? Wasn't I your friend? Why? Bloody hell, Sacha, why did you do this? Then some policemen made us leave the room.

Sacha's death was like something out of a thriller . Nobody knew how he had entered the Club, when both keys to the room, the one for the door and the one for the padlock, were on the chain that never left Patrick Bonnet's belt. Who had opened the door? Who had closed it? Since the keys used were not in the room, where were they? The police were unable to cast any light on the puzzle. They interrogated us, but nobody had seen or heard anything. They discovered a shoelace behind the stacked stools, but we didn't know whether it belonged to Sacha or to someone else, or whether it had been there for years. According to one police officer, Sacha had picked the lock with a piece of wire or a hairpin (although none was found) and had locked it again by tying the shoelace to the half-opened door. Apparently, it's one of the devices burglars use. We all tried it, but it was impossible. They also found a bent nail on the pavement on boulevard Raspail, close to the window. He could have used this nail to pick the main lock, and then locked the one inside, thrown the key out of the window and hanged himself. We tried this too, but no one managed to do it, not even Samy, who had mixed with bad company in his youth. No one thought this scenario, worthy of a third-rate thriller, credible. The logical explanation was that someone had helped Sacha to die or had killed him, and had then left, closing the lock and the padlock from the outside. But this hypothesis was discounted.

'The mystery of the hanged man at Denfert-Rochereau'. That is how *France-Soir* announced the case the following day at the bottom of page five: a man known only by his first name, which they were unsure about, and who lived a secret life. The following day, there was no further mention of it. It was forgotten, like a receding wave that washes away all traces from the shore. His death remained unexplained. Many thought he had been murdered by the KGB or another secret service. The police were incapable of deciding whether the bruises on his face and body dated back to his brawl with Igor or were inflicted just before his death. Perhaps he had had a fight with someone else? He had a scar on the back of his skull. Had he fallen while escaping from Cochin Hospital? Or had he been beaten up before he hanged himself? It was established that his death had occurred two days ago and had coincided with his disappearance from the hospital. His medical file established that he had no other injuries. The police classified the case as unresolved. As though they did not wish to discover the truth. I was convinced, and I was not the only one, that he had been got rid of by people from whom he had always been fleeing. When they took his body down, they laid him on the tables. A policeman closed his eyes. The key that he carried with him and which he was never without had vanished. This seemed to me proof that his death had been faked to look like suicide in order to rob him and steal whatever he kept in his hiding place. But I couldn't talk about any of that.

Three days later, I received an envelope wrapped in brown paper and reinforced with sticking tape. I recognized Sacha's handwriting. Inside, rolled up in a sheet of white paper, was the key he kept on his cord. There was no note or signature. On the flap, a red fingerprint was visible. Probably blood. The postmark was illegible and it was impossible to determine, even with a magnifying glass, the date on which it had been posted. If it was Sacha who had posted it, as one assumed from the bloodstain, the package would have arrived the next day or two days afterwards at the latest. Why had it taken five days to travel one kilometre? I put the question to the postman, but he had no answer.

That evening, I waited until everyone was asleep and left the flat at about eleven o'clock. I went to rue Monge. The building was completely quiet. I made no noise. Like a cat, I walked across the courtyard and up the backstairs in the dark, using the banisters to guide me. On the top floor, I went into the toilets, closed the door behind me and switched on the light. I clambered up the wall, supporting myself on the window-ledge, as Sacha had shown me. I took the key and slid it into the lock of the manhole cover behind the standpipe. The heavy metal panel toppled over. I put my hand inside the cavity and started to empty it. I was surprised by the amount it contained. A bulky loose-leaf ledger full of old photographs, cardboard files held together with a strap, three large exercise books written in Cyrillic characters and two dozen notebooks of various sizes; a short book by Hemingway, a Leica reflex camera and a small suitcase containing lenses, and a thick white envelope addressed 'For the attention of Michel Marini'. I made sure that there was nothing left inside before replacing the panel. I used a vegetable crate that was lying around in the courtyard to carry everything and I left the building. I went back home and, in my bedroom, I started to delve into Sacha's treasures. I opened the letter. There were twenty or so pages written on both sides in careful handwriting…

Michel,
When you read this letter, I shall have found peace at last…

LENINGRAD 1952

1

The lighted candles of the two candelabras placed on the mantelpiece were reflected in the drawing room mirror. Irina glanced for a moment at her wrinkled features and her white hair and, feeling tired, let out a sigh. This was a very special evening. She had laid out the embroidered, Hungarian-stitch tablecloth, the Baccarat crystal glasses and the Limoges porcelain dishes bought for her by her husband before the Revolution. In the middle of the fully-extended table she had placed the huge gilded and beaten bronze dish acquired at the souk in Istanbul in the days when you could travel there by taking the train from Odessa. Fifteen places had been laid. Each guest would have two glasses, even the children who didn't drink wine. In another era, she would have placed cut flowers in a third glass, but it had been ages since there were any florists in this frozen, ice-bound city. She had cut flowers out of coloured paper and made garlands and spiralling bouquets from them. They looked as though they were real. In the cupboards she had found forgotten objects, bought to be looked at, that had become useless and dangerous. She wondered whether there was any point in going to so much trouble, in taking so many risks. But she couldn't be blamed for anything. She had done what had to be done. With her sister, her sister-in-law and her cousins, she had prepared the matzo crackers, even though this was forbidden nowadays. It was not the first time that a woman had to defy this edict. It was simply not possible to celebrate the flight from Egypt without these flat biscuits that you did not allow to rise in the oven. This year once again, she had had to use age-old ingenuity to procure the flour, the chickens, the herbs, the cucumber, the celery, the black radishes and the knuckle of veal. They had prepared the broth with kneidels, the stuffed carp and the entire feast taking precautions worthy of the secret service. None of the neighbours had seen, heard or smelt anything. She remembered what Emile, her husband, had said before he

589

had disappeared, during the siege, when they celebrated their last Passover together, with only stale bread and hard-boiled eggs to eat: 'During the Inquisition, the Marranos of Seville had adopted the somewhat suicidal custom of preparing sumptuous Seders. Whereas they should have been discreet, merged into anonymity and disappeared. They would say, "May this Seder be the most beautiful of our lives, since it may be the last we observe together."' Ever since, she had made it a point of honour to celebrate it according to the rules.

Valentina, her sister, who had difficulty moving, put a log in the grate and stoked the fire. Vera, her cousin, lay a plate with herbs on the table. Anyone would think they were in an old people's home. The war and the purges had meant that there were only old people left to look after the children, who chased one another round the flat and hid beneath the table and behind the armchairs, laughing uproariously.

'Quietly, children, you're making too much noise. Don't run around. We'll attract the neighbours' attention.'

Irina pricked up her ears. She had heard the familiar sound of the key in the lock. Igor came in with Nadejda. She walked over to them, but the two children overtook her in the corridor. Little Ludmila hurled herself at Igor, who picked her up, threw her in the air, caught her and then did it again. Piotr snuggled in Nadejda's arms.

'How are you, my darling?'

'We've done some drawings, Mama.'

'Have they been good?' Nadejda asked.

'As they always are.'

'It's nice in your home,' Igor said to Irina as he kissed her on the forehead. 'There was a strike on the underground. We walked for two hours. There's never been so much snow at this time of year.'

'Come and warm yourselves.'

'Irina Viktorovna,' said Nadejda, as she too embraced her mother-in-law, 'I've left you all the work. I'm sorry.'

'It doesn't matter. We've got the time. Everything's ready.'

Irina went over to Igor who was warming his hands by the chimney.

'Sacha's coming to dinner with Anna.'

'What? You didn't tell me.'

'He rang up two days ago to ask how I was. I couldn't do other than suggest that he joined us.'

'It's unbelievable! He never comes. How could you have invited him?'

'I was convinced he'd refuse. He accepted.'

'He'll ruin our celebration.'

'Igor, he has an important job. You must be diplomatic.'

'He didn't move a finger for Lev. And what did he do for Boris?'

'He's not the one who decides. He's like us. He does what he can.'

Igor uncorked a bottle of Crimean wine and placed it next to a silver beaker. He looked at his watch slightly impatiently.

'We're not going to wait all night for them. Why don't we begin?'

'With this foul weather, there must be problems,' Irina explained. 'The canals are frozen over again.'

The doorbell rang. The children sat stock-still and did not say a word. With an automatic gesture, Nadejda pushed her plaited hair up from her neck, walked somewhat anxiously over to Igor and put her hand on his shoulder. Ludmila rushed over to Igor's legs. He took her in his arms.

'It's nothing, my darling. Nadia, will you answer the door?'

She walked to the end of the corridor and opened the door, which was concealed behind thick brown material.

'Welcome,' she said to Sacha and Anna, as she kissed them.

'The underground stopped running. We had to walk through the snow,' said Anna.

'And the children?'

'We left them at home. My sister's looking after them.'

Nadejda helped her take off her soaked shawl and parka. Anna, who was pregnant, had difficulty turning round in the narrow corridor. Irina joined them.

'How are you getting on, Anna Anatolievna?'

'As well as possible. My legs hurt. We've walked for too long.'

'With a wind like this, you're bound to have a girl,' Irina remarked. 'Come and rest.'

Nadejda and Anna moved away. Irina took Sacha's black leather coat

591

and his blue cap with its red headband, dripping with wet snow. He kissed her on the cheek and smiled at her.

'It's nice here. Outside, you'd think it was December. How are you?'

'I'm glad to see you. It's good that you've come. Oh, your hands are frozen.'

'Is everyone there?'

'We were only waiting for you.'

Sacha did not hurry as he entered the dining room. He embraced Valentina, Vera and the children. He spread out his hands over the fire in the hearth. Igor came up to him.

'You could have changed! Fancy coming to a Seder in uniform!'

'I've come from the Ministry. You could at least say hello!'

Sacha removed his khaki tunic and handed it to Igor.

'Be careful with it. I hope your hands are clean. There mustn't be any stain or crease on it.'

Igor took the jacket. Sacha held on to it and drew Igor towards him. 'I need to speak to you in private,' he whispered in his ear. 'It's important.'

Nadejda passed them a plate with cream cheese cake cut into squares. Igor walked away and placed the jacket on a chair.

'I don't know how you manage to make such a light cheesecake. Anna, you should take the recipe.'

'The hardest thing is finding some cheese,' replied Nadejda.

'How can we change this country when there are people who are constantly moaning? You're not the worst off,' said Sacha.

'Have you heard me complain? Last week, I worked seventy-five hours at the hospital. Igor worked longer. In appalling conditions. We're not paid any more. We don't ask for money. This is the first evening we've spent together for a month. When people say they can't find anything to eat, they're not being anti-Communist, it's just that no one understands what's going on. There's nothing to buy anywhere. You queue for hours for nothing. Before the Revolution, people could buy cheese for themselves. Nowadays, even if you have the money, there's none left. We're weary, Sacha.'

'There are problems of supply, the government is addressing them. We'll succeed.'

'Supposing we all sit down?' Irina suggested. 'The children are getting rowdy.'

Assisted by Piotr and Ludmila, Nadejda brought in the three matzos, each of them covered with an embroidered napkin, and placed them on the tray beside a platter containing hard-boiled eggs, dishes laden with sticks of celery, black radishes, some dark-coloured apple purée, the knuckle of veal with the grilled meat and a bowl of water to which she added salt. Once they had all sat down, there were three empty places.

'How many are we this evening?' asked Sacha, as he counted the number of chairs.

'There are two who are absent,' Igor explained.

'I thought one only kept one place for the poor man.'

'Last year, Boris and Lev were with us.'

'They are where they should be,' Sacha replied. 'If they haven't anything to feel guilty about, they'll be set free.'

'Shall we say the prayer?' Irina intervened.

'These two places must be removed.'

'But Sacha, they're for Boris and Lev!' Irina insisted. 'It's the tradition for those who are absent. So that they will come back and be with us again. Where they are, they're forbidden to celebrate Seder.'

'Is your head made of stone or are you stupid? We're not allowed to gather together this evening! These medieval practices are forbidden! These matzos are forbidden! And what's more, you're showing solidarity with counter-revolutionaries!'

'Can you tell us why they in particular have been arrested?' asked Igor. 'A paediatrician and a music teacher! What abominable crimes have they committed? And the hundreds of others who disappear at the drop of a hat?'

'Do you think I've come to risk my own and my wife's necks to take lessons from a gang of retrograde fanatics?'

'Why do you insult us, Sacha? I know what you do at the Ministry and you have nothing to be proud of.'

'I work for my country and for the triumph of the Revolution!'

'Please, let us say the prayer, my children,' said Irina in a quavering voice.

'Remove these two places, mother.'

'You've gone crazy!'

'Boris has confessed. He's been sentenced!'

'I don't believe it! He's a doctor!' Igor cried. 'He's done nothing apart from his job.'

'He's guilty. And so is Lev!'

'Get out of my house immediately!' Irina yelled as she rose to her feet. 'I'm ashamed to have a son like you! Get out! I don't ever want to see you again! Both of you, out!'

Sacha stood up. He nodded to Anna who walked over to him. He helped her on with her parka and the shawl that went on top of it. He put on his own overcoat and left without a glance. They heard the door close.

'Let us recite the Haggadah, my children,' said Irina. 'And let us pray for our family.'

2

The Tarnovsky Hospital did not have a good reputation. Not just because it forced the prostitutes to be treated for venereal diseases in the grim building and because the militia brought the tramps, the senile old men and drunks they picked up in the streets of Leningrad to its night dispensary, but also because they had built a vast morgue there capable of accommodating for five or six months the corpses of those who could not be buried because of the frozen ground. It's true that it was not a pleasant place, what with its wooden huts from the 1930s, which were draughty and heated by a stove whose pipe ran the length of the tiled roof and only managed to maintain a temperature of fifteen degrees. People spoke very disparagingly about it, but there were no more deaths there than in the city's other hospitals. There was a recently constructed three-storey concrete building, nicknamed the Palace, which, from the outside, looked like a prison because of the bars over the windows. It accommodated those dignitaries or their families who benefited from preferential treatment and were given private rooms, central heating and different food from the rest of the hospital. Whereas the other buildings were arranged according to their area of speciality, this one was for general practice and treated eminent party members. Working there procured considerable advantages, among them benefiting from the abundant good meals. Igor Markish had begun to train there as a heart specialist. The war had prevented him from acquiring his degree, but he had been appointed to the hospital because there were very few medical specialists.

The arrest of Professor Etinguer had spread consternation among the nursing staff. Four men in MVD uniform had stopped him for questioning as he left the operating theatre and had carted him off without giving him time to change his clothes. For a week, his family had no news of him. Larissa Gorchkov, the director of the hospital, was not easily deterred. She telephoned the Ministry for an explanation. She received the worst sort of response: 'Jacob Etinguer is not known in this department.'

A delegation of doctors went to call on a district secretary of the party whose life Erlinguer had saved following a severe heart attack. They were stunned when they learnt that the professor had been arrested on accusation of murder, several patients having died in his care. However much they swore that these were natural deaths, some of them dating back three or four years, they were told the professor had just confessed. The matter was in the hands of the Public Prosecutor. Detailed articles in *Pravda* explained that a diabolical plot hatched by doctors had just been uncovered. Several dozen doctors, all of them Jews, had been arrested. They were accused, with supporting evidence, of having disposed of a number of executives and of planning to get rid of comrade Stalin himself. A major trial was in preparation. Over two entire pages, *Pravda* printed the indignant reactions of foreign dignitaries and sister parties all over the world who applauded the arrest of this group of Zionist criminals.

Igor was taking a break and drinking a cup of hot tea when he was informed that a woman was calling him on the telephone very urgently. He went down to the ground floor. The nurse on the admissions desk handed him the receiver.

'Yes, hello.'

'Are you Igor Markish?' a faint, sharp, nasal voice asked.

'What do you want?'

'I'm advising you that you are about to be arrested.'

'What? What are you saying?'

'Tomorrow. At the hospital.'

'Why?'

'You're a doctor, a Jew and a colleague of Professor Etinguer's.'

'I've done nothing.'

'Neither have the others. They have been arrested. They will be sentenced and shot. The unlucky ones will be sent to Siberia.'

'Why are you warning me?'

'It doesn't matter. You have a slight head start. Take special care. Escape via Lake Ladoga.'

'I can't abandon my wife and my children.'

'Will you be any help to them once you've been shot?'

'Who are you?'

'It's not important.'

'How am I to know it's not a trap?'

'The MVD doesn't need a ruse or an excuse to arrest you. If you stay, you're nothing but an idiot! Think of your family!'

The call ended. Igor's face was distraught. He was trembling. The nurse came over to him.

'Is there anything wrong, Doctor Markish? May I help you?'

'I'm going to be arrested!'

Igor collapsed on a chair and held his head in his hands.

In the telephone box on Vitebsk station, Sacha relaxed the pressure of his left hand, which was squeezing his nostrils. He took out the small spoon he had placed at the back of his mouth, unwound the scarf that he had wrapped round the receiver, and replaced the phone. He breathed in several times and remained lost in thought for a moment. He took out his handkerchief and wiped the handset. He readjusted his uniform and left the public call box. He glanced around the concourse. He loathed this Art Nouveau style, these floral volutes, the exaggeratedly intricate gilt lighting, the cold colours of the frescoes. He pretended to admire the over-embellished décor and the Eiffel-style glass roof and he gave it a complete panoramic tour. Nothing unusual claimed his attention. Outside, the storm grew more intense.

At the same moment, Igor left the main hospital building. He was wearing only his white coat and he shivered at finding himself out in the open again. Heavy flakes of snow were falling. He walked through the hospital in search of his wife. Nadejda was employed as a midwife in the maternity unit. She was in the labour ward. Igor paused at the door for a few moments. A woman's cries came from inside. He waited for almost an hour, unsure about what attitude he should adopt. Nadejda was surprised to find him there.

'Are you not well, Igor? You're very pale.'

'I need to speak to you, Nadia.'

Despite the cold, he dragged her outside. They sheltered beneath a porch roof. Igor told her about the telephone conversation he had just had.

'Do you think it's serious?'

'What do you mean? That they're playing a joke on me?'

'I feel so confused that... You didn't recognize this person?'

'I don't know whether it was a man or a woman. Perhaps it was a patient I've been looking after and who is warning me out of gratitude.'

'What are you going to do?'

'If I stay, they'll arrest me. I must get out!'

'I'm leaving with you, Igor.'

'And the children?'

'They have their grandmother. She'll look after them.'

'If we both escape, they'll be put in an orphanage. Do you know what that means?'

'Let's leave with them.'

'Nadia, we won't get through with the children. It's minus thirty at night in the Gulf of Karelia. They wouldn't survive. A man on his own might manage it. Together, it's bound to fail.'

'Are you going to abandon me?'

'Suggest any other solution to me. If I succeed in getting to Finland, we can bide our time. See how things work out.'

'We know what will happen. I want to come with you.'

'You can't do that to the children, Nadia. Think of them. If you're there, they'll understand why I left. If we leave together, we're abandoning them. They can't lose their mother at this age.'

'I beg you, Igor, don't leave me. I would die. I need you so much.'

She threw herself against him. He hugged her. They remained like this for a long time. Tears were streaming down Nadia's face.

'You must go back to your department, Nadia. As though nothing has happened. I'm going home. I'll take some clothes, some dry biscuits, some dried herring and I'll leave straight away. This evening, you'll tell the neighbours that I haven't come back. You'll be anxious. Tomorrow, when they don't find me here, they'll come and look for me at our home. You'll have to disassociate yourself and show your disapproval, otherwise you'll lose your job. Don't hesitate to denounce me to the local committee. If you don't hear from me within three months, open divorce proceedings.'

'Don't ask me to do that. I wouldn't be capable.'

'You must be strong, Nadia. Think of yourself. Think of the children. They're the most important.'

'I don't care about the children! Igor, I implore you!' she murmured.

He grabbed her vigorously by her forearms and, in his despair, he shook her.

'You must promise me you'll do it! I'm going so that you can be safe. Tomorrow, Ivan, the male nurse who works in my department, will deliver a message to my mother. He lives five minutes away from her. Afterwards, try not to see her or help her again. You must sever the links. And with all my family. It's the only way to extricate yourself. It won't be easy. I would never have believed it could end up like this. The only thing I can say to you is that I've never loved anyone other than you. You know this, my love, you're the only woman in my life. There will never be anyone else. And I swear to you that if I survive, we'll see each other again one day.'

There are moments in a life that no man imagines he will have to suffer, such as making the woman he loves weep, brutally pushing her away, having to extricate himself when she is clinging to him, and not turning round when he hears her screaming and collapsing on the snow. Her cries and her tears tore him apart and froze inside him. Those are what he hears throughout his sleepless nights.

3

It was a vast, anonymous, three-storey block in the northern suburbs of Leningrad, ten minutes from the Devyatkino métro station. On a metal panel on the wall at the entrance read two lines: 'Municipal Department – entry forbidden'. It had been rebuilt at the end of the war. No one would think of entering it or asking what went on there. Young people could be seen going in and leaving. They didn't have the usual gaiety and exuberance of students who shout and call out to one another at college doors. These were silent and discreet. It was an administrative building to judge by the red flag that hung at the end of a mast. For reasons unknown, a white band split the flag outside into two halves, which was why the place was nicknamed 'the Red Banner', since it resembled the decoration of the same name. You entered through triple security doors. The interior was as austere as a Benedictine monastery and was partitioned like a prison. There were metal gates everywhere. Officials dressed in the uniform of the Ministry of Internal Affairs stood behind reinforced concrete sentry boxes. They checked the passes against their huge ledgers, and opened and closed the iron gates on arrival and departure by means of electric buttons, which they activated after twice carrying out inspections. Some people, though not many, were astonished on arrival by this wealth of precautions and pointed out to the wardens that they came past morning and evening and that it was pointless checking their authorizations every time. The wardens said nothing. Perhaps they were deaf or dumb? The students came to understand that the very first rule was silence. Delays sometimes meant that students' names were not mentioned on documents. The official made a phone call to someone who either authorized entry or did not. You quickly adapted to this rule. It meant time was wasted, but it guaranteed absolute security. Time was of no importance here. Security, on the other hand, was their profession. You entered classrooms according to the same procedure. The teacher entered by a different door to the one the students used, activated from inside, which implied that there was a system of internal corridors which doubled the amount of access routes.

The day began with one hour of gym. The lessons started at seven in the morning and ended at midday, with a fifteen-minute break at ten o'clock. The students took their meals in a dining hall situated in the basement. The lessons, which were often practical exercises, started again at one o'clock and ended at seven in the evening. After dinner, there was another hour of physical activity. On Sundays the students were allowed to revise. In this place, the principles that governed the rest of the country did not apply. The staff was huge. The means were limitless. They were in an institute run by the Ministry of Internal Affairs. There were two others, one in Moscow and one in Kiev. The Leningrad institute was the only one to include on its study programme such important subjects as propaganda, disinformation and manipulation. These were regulated by the Ministry's celebrated second division, which concerned itself with internal enemies. To be entitled to this teaching, you had to have passed highly selective exams during the first two years. This was the reason why the Red Banner had its reputation for excellence. Only the best students were given access to the best professors, who were not teachers, but experienced practitioners, some of whom carried out their principal activity in the south and west wings of the building. The top students in each year were entitled to express where they would like to be posted. With a little luck or a lot of connections, they would join the third or fourth bureau of this second division. The Propaganda department was considered the most prestigious. This meant that they never left the building. They entered and left by another door and would work under the authority of their professors until the day they replaced them.

Eight soldiers in uniform, and five men and three women between the ages of twenty and thirty were waiting for the photomontage class to begin. The door at the back opened, and Commandant Sacha Markish entered. Well disciplined, the students got to their feet, stood to attention and saluted. At the back of the room, a Staff-Sergeant operated a slide projector, showing slides which corresponded to the point Sacha, on the podium, had reached in his talk. With a wooden stick, Sacha indicated the details that should be taken note of.

'... Your work will consist in eliminating the enemies of the people from all photographs in which they appear: class or group photos, family reunions or banquets. We're not interested in individual photographs. They are destroyed. The person who has been sentenced must vanish completely. Not the slightest trace of his existence must remain. In order to falsify a photo, you can splice two images from the negatives and make them into one before enlarging them on the positive. It's a delicate operation that requires negatives having the same exposure and the same contrast. You have to create a game of hide-and-seek to make up the two images. On the first negative, you colour in the person whom you wish to remove, on the second: you do the reverse. You expose the positive with the two negatives one after the other; since the coloured portions have no effect on the negative, the two collated parts will be brought together. In this way you remove from the photo the person who shouldn't be there. The film used should have a coarser texture than the original. It will conceal the fine grain and the image will be clearer. In certain cases, I will teach you how to use sulphite solutions; it's simpler. Frequently, we don't have the negatives. The easiest way is to work on the developed photograph. With a sharp scalpel, you make an incision, meticulously following the contours of the person or face to be got rid of. In order to stop yourself shaking, you can place your hand on a pencil laid sideways. With the help of a tube of glue, you superimpose the cut-outs. You just need to put a little paint or ink on the joined up bits and background for the illusion to be complete. Before sticking it down, colour the cut-out paper thoroughly. If the person needs to be placed against a grey or black setting, you should paint the background with an identical colour, otherwise you will have a white edge that will be detectable. For a good job and to hide imperfections, use the airbrush. A compressor squirts a light drop of ink through a spray gun operated by a compressed air cylinder whose flow you control. The paint should be thinned as much as possible and the pressure must be as low as possible. Once again, you

602

have to go from the palest to the darkest colour and not hesitate to use a mask. The finer the spray, the better the result. This enables you to obtain impressions of aging, staining, shadows, light effects or movement. It is recommended that you apply several layers and shade them off. You can also spray the person or object on the photo directly, but you need practice. You will obtain slightly ethereal and unreal effects. We shall see how this can be significant in some cases. It is recommended you wear a mask and glasses to avoid spray projected by the solvents. The finishing-off near the borders and joins must be done by hand and with a brush. It is vital that this retouched photograph be converted into a negative. There is a twofold benefit: this will enable it to be reproduced ad infinitum, and it will prove its existence. If you have done everything meticulously and skilfully, no one can prove the negative is false. Why?...'

Sacha questioned his students. His gaze went from one to another. They were struck dumb and searched for the answer. They looked down and consulted their notes without finding the solution.

'Why?... You haven't understood a thing, you bunch of idiots! Because a negative is always true! It's what has been exposed over it that has been adjusted. Thanks to your contribution, questions as to its veracity will not be asked. What is true is what you see! Now, you must ask yourself about the usefulness of this photo, its political significance. What message do you wish to get over? If it's a matter of sticking on a double chin, or a roll of flesh, or a wrinkle, the work must be invisible, like that of the retouchers in Hollywood. You can replace hair that has disappeared with age, make grey hair dark, you can wipe out the ravages of time. It is not acceptable for unflattering photos of our leaders to appear in the newspapers. Retouching a lined, pockmarked or puffy face, removing spots or getting rid of scars, requires experience. They must be credible and reassuring. The subject must not look younger, he must simply age more slowly than us. Ideally, one adds a smile or a glint in the eye. Our department has been blamed for producing conspicuous, even crude retouches. It's a technical and practical application of historical materialism. I have often been asked to restore photos that have been touched up perfectly and to make the retouching blatant. We could have done it artistically, like genuine forgers, and no one would have seen a thing. But it's about sending out a clear message: this is what happens to traitors! They disappear. They are eradicated. As though they had never existed. Those photos that are faked crudely are intentional. It encourages friends and relatives to follow the right example, to demonstrate their affection for the revolution by mutilating photos of traitors themselves, by removing them from family albums and from drawing room frames. How many thousands of women have erased their arrested husbands or brothers? How many sons have expunged their fathers for ever? All that remains of them are shadows, holes, voids, hacked out by a razor. At best, a hand, a shoulder, a boot: not much. In this way they prove what side they are on and their lives are safe. Otherwise, how can one forgive them for having married an enemy of the people? How can one trust the son of a scoundrel? Those who forget to tidy up must disappear. Keeping photographs of an enemy is a proof of guilt. In our schools, children are taught by their teachers to use scissors to cut out criminals who have not yet been removed from schoolbooks. When one is young, one understands better, and the new generations will be more efficient. In the end, the only photos that will remain of those who have disappeared will be those that we have taken full-face and profile. The moment they are placed under arrest, we do a clear-out. We retrieve photographs, letters, exercise books, notebooks, pieces of identity and we burn everything in the boilers at the ministry. Not a single trace of our enemies must remain. We can't be satisfied with killing them. Their names must be obliterated. No one will remember them. They shall have lost and we shall have won. It's the ultimate sanction. Their books are removed from the libraries. Their thoughts no longer exist. Neither must we forget to remove the books of enemies who fought against them. Had Trotsky not existed, the anti-Trotskyites would have no reason to survive.'

4

When Colonel Yakonov put down the phone, his hand was shaking and he was sweating. You didn't receive a threatening call at night from your minister without having palpitations. How could this business have got back to Moscow without his having been informed of it by his department? He was certain of only one thing. It was not an accident. This did not happen in the Ministry of Internal Affairs, or in the Ministry for State Security any more than it did in the time of the NKVD troikas or the State Political Directorate, and neither would it happen in any future ministry should he live long enough to see it. You did not spend a thirty-year career in Soviet security departments, living through the turnarounds, party lines and alliances, purges and coteries, without mastering the basic rules of survival. He would deal with this malfunctioning later. It was time for the right decision. He had a few moments in which to make it. His life depended on it. When Abakumov, who only received his orders from the Little Father of the Peoples in person, took the trouble to speak to you for twenty minutes on the phone, giving you details that you were supposed to know, you might be regarded as an imbecile or an incompetent, which was not in itself a handicap if you wished to survive in this administration. When he employed this icy, sepulchral tone and ended the conversation with an ambiguous: 'I give you forty-eight hours to rectify this matter', it was a bad sign. You didn't need to have studied at length to know that the countdown had begun. He picked up his phone.

'It's Yakonov. Is Commandant Markish in the building or has he left the department?'

'One moment, Colonel, I'll check… Commandant Markish is at his post.'

He hung up. He felt ill at ease. Yakonov was an instinctive man. He sensed and he knew. He had no degrees. He had risen through the ranks and had climbed to the top. This sixth sense was his strength. He owed his rise to it as well as his escape from the numerous traps into which his superiors and colleagues had fallen. He had known Sacha Markish for a long time. They were not friends. You didn't have any when you worked at the MVD or the MGB. Only old acquaintances, fellow-survivors. There were not many officials of this rank who had over twenty-five years' length of service. Markish was a conscientious and honest officer. Yakonov would have staked his life on his being innocent and not having done anything wrong, and it was a waste of time investigating him. You could count on the fingers of one hand the number of those who worked until ten o'clock at night without being obliged to do so. But he wasn't being asked for his opinion. They required a result. Too bad for him. Markish would not be the first or the last to be reprimanded for nothing. Did he have a choice? It was his neck or that of the head of the photomontage department of the fourth bureau of the second division of the ministry. He had to play his cards close to his chest. Markish was too experienced to allow himself to be caught in the usual traps. He grabbed hold of the Aeroflot file, which would give him an excuse to justify his arrival and would allay any suspicion. He summoned two sergeants from the security department and ordered them to accompany him. They could be useful for the arrest. Yakonov could not risk any mistake.

In the photographic laboratory, lit by a faint yellow light bulb, Sacha, who was wearing a grey apron, was bent over a group photograph. About fifteen men and women in white coats were spread out over three steps in front of a wooden building. It looked like a gathering of doctors and nurses. It might have been the Tarnovsky Hospital on a fine June day. With their hands in their pockets, they were smiling and relaxed. Some of them had cigarettes at their lips, others had their arms round their neighbours' shoulder. Igor Markish appeared on the second step, third from the left, with a stethoscope round his neck, a cigarette in his right hand, which he was holding up, as if he had just removed it from his mouth, and his left hand on Nadejda's shoulder, who was also smiling, her hair blowing in the breeze. Sacha put a magnifying glass to his right eye. Igor's face appeared, enlarged. He picked up a scalpel and checked the tip, which he stuck into the collar of Igor's coat. He drew it along the neck, cutting out the face. The incision was so fine it was invisible. The blade slid down the coat as far as the step and was then turned in the opposite direction. He lifted up the photograph and pressed on the cut-out part, which dropped out. Igor's silhouette lay on the board. Sacha opened a shoebox. He put his hand inside and brought out dozens of cut-out faces. He chose five, which he positioned behind the photograph, in place of Igor's face. He grimaced slightly. He brought out other faces and tried again. None of them was suitable. He put the cut-out faces back in the box. He placed the photograph on a marble plate and, with the scalpel, cut it widthways. He set about cropping the two sides without Igor. He scraped and he brushed, removed an overlapping foot, and aligned the two sections. With a fine brush, he pieced them together, adjusted them until everything fitted, and he breathed over the glue. He took a slightly thicker brush, which he dipped into a pot of white paint. He covered the splicing with a steady stroke. With another brush, which he inserted into a tube of black paint, he set about reconstructing the wooden step and the side of the door that featured in the background. When he stood up straight, the two parts of the photograph were joined together. The door was at the right distance. The step was replaced. Nadejda had her hand on another doctor's shoulder. He placed the reconstructed photo on an upright easel and switched on several lights, which he arranged to create a cross-effect. He regulated the speed and distance on a box Rolleiflex and took several pictures. He took hold of the photograph. He picked up a cardboard folder and slipped the two prints inside: the original and the retouched version. He opened an enormous black register and, following on from the last name, he wrote in Cyrillic characters over ten columns on both pages. He closed the register which he put back in its place in the filing area where dozens of metal shelves about three metres high, open on both sides, stored the thousands of grey cardboard folders with straps around them, each with its label on the edge. He was about to file Igor's dossier away when he heard knocking at the door.

'Who is it?' he asked.

'It's me, Yakonov.'

He unlocked the door. Yakonov came in on his own, a folder under his arm.

'You seem surprised, Sacha Emilievitch?'

'You don't often come here, Anton Nikolaïeveitch. Especially at such an hour. What's going on?'

'Can't you guess?'

'About what?'

'It's your brother.'

'Igor?'

Yakonov nodded, without replying.

'What's happened to him?'

'Don't you know?'

'We're not on good terms, as you know.'

'He managed to escape before his arrest.'

'I didn't know. I'm not in touch with my family any more.'

'Really?'

'We haven't seen one another for years. Once, we bumped into each other by chance, at the reopening of the Kirov. We hardly exchanged three words. He's never forgiven me for standing up for my country and belonging to the NKVD.'

'He's escaped! He's disappeared! Do you realize what that means?'

'I'm not responsible for my brother. I parted company from him a long time ago.'

'He received a phone call warning him of his arrest.'

'I had no idea he was going to be arrested. How would I have known? You know very well that a decision like this is not up to our department. And even if I had heard about it, I would have had no reason, no interest, no desire to warn him. You know my loyalty, Anton Nikolaïevitch.'

'The nurse who took the call wasn't able to tell us whether it was a man or a woman. She had the impression it was a woman.'

'Ah, you see.'

'You could have found a woman to make the call.'

'Who would pass on a message like this?'

'Your wife.'

608

'My wife is six months pregnant. Do you think I'd let her run such a risk? You'd have to be crazy! They can get themselves arrested, him and his lot, for all I care.'

'At the moment he received this call, you were out of the building. You could have distorted your voice.'

'You know me. If I had made this call, I would have arranged to have an alibi.'

'There's a doubt. And in our country, a doubt is a certainty.'

'You know who I am. You know what I've done. I was recruited in 1927 and I've given a thousand proofs of loyalty to the regime.'

'One more is required, Sacha Emilievitch.'

'What more can I do?'

'Give evidence at the Doctors and Nurses trial.'

'I'm not a doctor. What would I testify to?'

'To your brother's guilt and that of others charged. To the fact that these doctors were plotting against the regime and were preparing to get rid of several important people who trusted them with their treatment. Their leader was preparing to poison our First Secretary in person. You could say that you overheard conversations, that you carried out your own investigation and that you informed your superiors of the result of your enquiries.'

'I see no objection. I've told you that we had broken off all relationships. That means that this man is no longer my brother. One has no right to betray one's country.'

'You would be ready to testify? At the trial? In Moscow?'

'Of course, Anton Nikolaïevitch. It's the duty of each one of us to expose traitors.'

'Are you quite sure?'

'As you've often said: we are soldiers, we fight and we obey orders.'

'I'm going to refer this back to the top level. Abakumov thought you wouldn't agree. I'll call him tomorrow morning. He'll be pleased. This decision will make life easier for us. There wasn't much evidence in the folder. I'm relieved that you're taking things this way. It's a weight off my shoulders.'

'Does the fact that I'm a commandant in the Ministry of Internal Affairs not risk making my testimony less convincing in the eyes of the judges?'

'The important thing is that you're his brother and that you'll give evidence spontaneously, without constraints. We'll discuss it again tomorrow. Ah, I forgot: the Aeroflot file has come back. There were some omissions.'

Sacha took the bound folder and looked carefully at a note attached to it.

'I see, the folder was dealt with by the second branch. This incident will not occur again. I'll deal with it immediately.'

'Another day won't make a difference.'

'I must correct the department's error. I'll adjust it right away.'

'Ah, if only everyone had your professional conscientiousness, Sacha Emilievitch, things would be better in this country,' said Yakonov as he left the laboratory.

For reasons impossible to fathom, following some rigging or unfortunate confusion, or a series of human errors or incompetence, the winner of the 1948 Aeroflot staff chess tournament always featured in a photograph in which competitors were shown wearing their pilots or stewards uniforms, or in their civilian clothes. This individual should have disappeared from the group portrait several years ago. He was standing in the front row. The president of the company was awarding him the winner's cup. The appended note, which came from the director of internal security in the Ministry of Civil Aviation, provided no information about the offence committed or the verdict. It stated that the declared winner was the person who came second. It was logical that the original winner should be made to disappear on ideological grounds. It was a complicated job. If he had had the time, Sacha would have cut out the silhouette of this Leonid Krivoshein and shifted a row of twenty or so people from left to right. But he hadn't a minute to spare. He made do with cutting out a square containing the man's face. He groped around in the shoebox for some anonymous person to replace him. He couldn't find any face that fitted. He smiled, took out his wallet and pulled his party card out. He removed his passport-sized photograph in which he was shown full-face, wearing his MVD cap, and he stuck it down in place of the face that had been removed. He added a few dabs of black paint with his brush. It belonged to a different period and was not touched up, but it would not be the first or the last time a photograph had been tampered with so as to be not what it seemed. He sealed the note with the department's red rubber stamp, signed it and scribbled down: 'Photo: the head of department of the fourth bureau', and placed the folder in the 'Return to sender' pigeon-hole. He took off his grey apron. From a drawer, he picked out a couple of dozen notebooks and exercise books. He placed them in a bag which he stuck on his shoulder and put on his officer's uniform jacket and his overcoat. No one could see that he had concealed something beneath his coat. He put on his cap, switched off the light and left the laboratory for ever.

For reasons equally incomprehensible, this photograph continued on its journey. It was printed in the Aeroflot catalogue, which was distributed for the 1952 tournament. Nobody asked a single question about this officer with the impenetrable expression who was holding the 1948 cup. Sacha wanted to leave a memento before his departure. For him, it was a reckless little joke, a derisory wink. He could never have imagined that this photograph would pursue him all his life and would earn him Leonid's unremitting hatred.

PARIS, JULY 1964

I didn't want to leave without rectifying my error. Give Leonid the photograph, the real one, which is his to keep. Tell him that I'm not angry with him. I understand. In his place, I would have acted as he did. I would not have forgiven. I was not on the right side.

I interrupted my reading of Sacha's letter. In the envelope there was a group photograph of the Aeroflot 1948 tournament, with Leonid receiving his cup. It was impossible to know whether it was the original or a touched-up version. Running my finger over it, back and front, there was no trace of cutting or glueing.

As I made my way along the endless and deserted corridors, I didn't know whether I would succeed in getting out of the Red Banner. I had extricated myself by agreeing to testify, but it was a stopgap. I had no doubt as to what would happen. There were only two hypotheses and I would be the loser in either case. Not giving evidence proved that I was aware of the plot. The brother is guilty because he is the brother. Giving evidence meant knowing about the plot and recognizing my guilt. I knew only too well how they reasoned to have the slightest illusion about my future. They make no distinction between the innocent and the guilty. After the trial, I would be of no further use to them and they would get rid of me. Witnesses are awkward and do not have the right to a court hearing. A bullet is enough. Had I been in Yakonov's shoes, I would not have taken the risk. I would have had myself arrested and transferred to Moscow. The iron gates opened. I found myself outside in the freezing night. You only get one chance, Michel. Seize the moment, don't think, just get on with it. I went back home. I didn't go up to my flat. I had fitted out a hiding place in the cellar of a neighbour who had been arrested. I collected what I had left there. Along with what I had just brought out of the Red Banner, I had a sufficient amount of evidence and I had rescued anything that could be used. I put everything in a bag and I left.

I didn't say goodbye to my wife. Anna Anatolievna was asleep. What was the point of waking her up to tell her that her husband was abandoning her? She was six months pregnant. She had dreadful pains in her back and her legs and she was confined to bed. I slipped a note under the door to bid her farewell. Don't judge me, Michel. Don't think: he behaved like an absolute bastard; he should have talked to her and explained. You may be correct in thinking that now, but had you lived in Leningrad in those grim years, you would know that there was no other solution. I warned her that she would have problems on my account and should get a divorce as soon as possible. In our country, it takes ten minutes to get married and five minutes to get divorced. The priority was to spare the children. I wrote to them with the usual platitudes one comes out with in such cases: that I was obliged to go abroad, that I was thinking of them, that they had to be brave to overcome this ordeal and that I would never forget them. Can a child understand when his father explains that he won't ever see him again? One day, you will have children and you will realize what it can mean for a man to go away without kissing them, without clasping them one last time in his arms. I escaped like a thief. I thought that leaving quickly would make the separation less painful. On the spur of the moment, I was strong. The grief caught up with me later, when I was safe. It was anguish. I've never had any news of them. I don't know whether she divorced, whether she's alive or was shot, whether she had a boy or a girl. The wall has descended again. Each in his graveyard, but alive.

Finland is seventy kilometres from Leningrad. Igor and I knew this region of Karelia from having wandered around it in our youth. Before the revolution, our father had a dacha on the shores of Lake Ladoga. We used to go fishing there in the summer. There is no other place on earth where the light is as beautiful as it is on this lake in June when the sun disappears over the horizon and night has not yet fallen. For years, we roamed the paths, the forests and the thousands of lakes between Ladoga and the Gulf of Finland. At that time, this region had not been annexed. The border existed only on maps. That April, there was a metre of snow and polar temperatures. The shortest route goes through Vyborg, but they kept a close watch on it. I opted for the tracks to the north, which I knew better. By day, I slept in abandoned fortifications. On the first four nights, I followed a path that overlooked the frozen lake. Before Priozersk, I veered off through the woods. The border guards don't come out at night. I was in a good position to observe the patrol rounds and the control points. A week later, I got through into Finland. I think Igor followed the same route.

I had myself invited by my mother to the Seder not out of conviction, nor to give her pleasure (I despise these superstitions), but to warn Igor that he was definitely on the list of Jewish doctors and was going to be arrested. They threw me out before I was able to warn him. I was forced to phone him. I've never told Igor that it was I who saved him. I'm convinced it has never occurred to him. Anyway, it wouldn't have removed the resentment he feels towards me. I should have liked him to forgive me, not because I had saved his life, but because I was his brother and he loved me. But I didn't want to get involved in this haggling. I've waited twelve years for his forgiveness, and I've realized it won't ever come. I'm not angry with him. I, and I alone, am to blame. I've committed so many crimes and I've been party to so many others that I deserve no mercy. It's right to pay for one's mistakes. In any case, I didn't have long to live. I didn't want to look after myself and, for what I have, there's no cure.

For years, I was a loyal servant, convinced that we were right, that we had to fight and destroy our enemies. It was them or us. When there's a war, you don't ask questions, you obey. You fight. Each soldier has his job to do. We were creating a revolution. We were changing the world and its rotten organization. We were going to have done with exploitation and the exploiters. It was normal that there should be resistance, that our enemies should use every means to prevent History being fulfilled and that we should use our weapons to destroy them. You are forced to kill when you can no longer discuss, or negotiate, or compromise, or accept. There's no alternative. The victor is the one who survives. The hatred that was directed against us was commensurate with the hope aroused by the international working class. An endless furore. All we did was to defend ourselves and retaliate. The capitalists of the entire world had risen up to eliminate us. They feared for themselves and their money. The First World War did not stop in 1918. It began that very year when our country was attacked by those who wished to crush the revolution. They stirred up a civil war. They lost. But they continued by manipulating our enemies from within. They had to be slaughtered. We killed the aristocrats, the cadets, the social-democrats, the Mensheviks, the bankers, the industrialists, the landowners, the bourgeoisie, the priests, those who clung to their privileges, as well as the countless others who opposed us. We still believed. And then we were told that there were enemies of the people among us. We did away with them. Trotsky and his gang. The Cossacks. The kulaks. The engineers. And others as well. The more of them we shot, the more sprang up. They had to be removed from our ranks. Their crimes filled us with loathing. But there was no end to it.

As for me, I erased. To begin with, it didn't bother me making Lenin's paunch disappear, his muddy shoes, his creased and torn trousers, his stained shirts, Stalin's American cigarettes and his spare tyre, the bags under his eyes, his pallid, disdainful manner, the emblems of the bourgeoisie: tie, waistcoat, watch, paintings, gramophone. After that, we had to erase the comrades of the early days: Kamenev, Zinoviev, Bukharin, Radek, Tukhachevsky, Lenin's sister and thousands of others who were less famous, and even Gorky, the icon of the entire people. Little by little, we realized what was going on. We couldn't say anything. We were frightened. Those who showed surprise disappeared immediately. We continued. When they arrested someone, they made a clean sweep. They filled sacks and boxes: books, letters, papers, and these fed the boilers. They burnt everything. When they arrested artists, they burnt their paintings and their drawings. Writers' manuscripts disappeared, their drafts, their notes and notebooks. When they arrested Mandelstam and sent him to Siberia where he died soon afterwards,

I asked myself: what can they blame a poet for? In what way can he be harmful? Why were his poems destroyed? None of them remain. They were marvellous. What would our world be without the painters and the poets? They shot hundreds of artists, writers, playwrights and poets. They were not counter-revolutionaries. Their only crime was to be Jewish, or Catholic, or Polish, or Ukrainian, or Baltic, or peasants. I didn't know how to resist. How do you fight against the fire that destroys poems? I came up with just one solution: learn them by heart. I learned them by heart. There, they could not be found, removed, erased. When the sacks of confiscated goods arrived, I stole a few notebooks from the flames. I implanted them in my memory. I repeated them to myself every night. I learnt later that others did the same. Wives rescued the work of their husbands who had disappeared by memorizing their poems. As long as you were alive, you had a hope of saving them.

The passages I gave you and which you recited to Camille: I didn't write them. They are the work of poets who were murdered. I have passed them on to you. Here, I had the time. I transcribed them one by one in these notebooks. I haven't altered a word of them. The only limitation was my memory. I would never have believed I was able to learn so many. There are hundreds of them. Not a line is by me. I've never known how to write poems. When I could, I jotted down the name of the poet. In many cases, I didn't know who the author was. I rescued the poem, but not the poet. They will remain anonymous. Perhaps researchers or academics will manage to piece together this appalling puzzle and attribute them to their rightful author. I know I can trust you. I have chosen you because you belong to a generation that has been spared the horrors we have lived through. We didn't know how to avoid any of them. We have all committed them. Nothing can redeem us. You will know what needs to be done to preserve the memory of those who deserve to be rescued from oblivion. It is only memory that is beautiful. The rest is dust and wind.

And let no one come and tell you: 'I didn't know'. At fairgrounds, there is a large wheel which the man in charge spins. You bet on a number and you win a prize. 'The more you bet, the more you win' he calls out at passers-by so as to entice them. For years and years, just one thing terrified us: that the wheel would stop on us. It stopped on your next door neighbour. Phew, we said. Once again, it's not me. There's no reason I should be picked out. I'm innocent. He's guilty. No one knew of what. If he had been arrested, then he must be guilty. While they were still breathing, no one paid these victims, these martyrs, the least attention and they mattered less than the leaves on a tree. Those who could do something raised not a little finger to help them. Now that they're dead, we don't stop talking about them, asking ourselves why we bother more about the dead than the living. Perhaps because they rouse us from our slumber and demand justice. A long time ago, Gorky wrote to Romain Rolland: 'No single "betrayed people" exists in the twentieth century.' To declare: 'We didn't know' is a comforting collective lie. The Russians, like the Germans, the French, the Japanese, the Turks and the others knew what was happening in their countries. No one was fooled. The arrests, the expulsions, the acts of violence, the tortures, the deportations, the executions, the propaganda, the faked photographs. Anyone who protested disappeared. So, we kept quiet. Igor, Leonid, Vladimir, Imré, Pavel, I, myself and the other: none of us knew anything. One day, the wheel stopped on us. We were lucky enough to be able to get out. We're no more innocent than the torturers from whom we escaped. I acknowledge my errors and I am more racked with guilt than Lady Macbeth. At least when you are shot, you are considered a hero and you end up being honoured with your name on a marble plaque. Once a year, they come and lay a wreath or a small bunch of roses or carnations in your memory. It gives pleasure to those who bring the flowers. In my case, I acted out of conviction. You'd really have to be a complete imbecile, wouldn't you? I erased my brother! I erased my friends! I erased innocent people! It's as if I had erased myself.

I don't want any prayer at my burial. I don't mind what they do with me. Don't concern yourself. It's of no importance if I end up in the common grave. Apart from you, perhaps, no one's going to come and put flowers on my tomb. Take care of yourself, Michel, there have been six burglaries in my attic room. Don't forget the first lesson they inculcate KGB apprentices with. There is no such thing as chance. I find it hard to end this letter. I've still got so much to say. On the point of departure, I wonder whether it would not be better to stay so that I can give evidence. I think I'll stop here.

I bequeath to you the little I possess. There are three books in my bedroom that need to be returned to the library. I leave you my belongings, my Leica and the lenses, my books, my records, my archives, my photographs, my books of poems. You will find three large black ledgers written in Cyrillic characters: the endless list of those I have erased, and a folder containing black and white photographs. Before and after. They are all I was able to rescue. Do with them what you will. My savings amount to 1,583 francs. They are in a brown envelope. Pay the landlady for this month, and the electricity account, and the bills I've run up at the grocer's in rue Monge, the baker's shop around the corner and the chemist on the square. Lay a bunch of daisies on my grave and keep the rest. Do me one last favour: buy Prokofiev's *Romeo and Juliet* and think of me as you listen to it. And take some fine photos. Real ones.

2

It was a rotten summer. A July that was more like November. It rained and we froze.

Igor was not at home. I didn't want to leave a note in his letterbox. I called on Werner in rue Champollion. He was the only one, along with Igor, whom I could trust. He was sitting on the steps of his projection room, sheltering from the rain and smoking a cigarette. He seemed pleased to see me. He was showing *America America* and he invited me in, but I didn't feel like going to the cinema. I told him everything.

'Nasty business,' he murmured. 'You're right to tell me about it.'

Werner and Igor took care of everything. It was all settled in three days. From what I understood, Daniel Mahaut stepped in to smooth over the difficulties. The members of the Club banded together to pay for a funeral at Montparnasse cemetery. They might have done better to have offered him their handshakes sooner. But apparently, it's not possible to forgive. Each of them remained caught in his own trap. It functioned very well.

When I woke up, on the morning of the funeral, the rain was still bucketing down. Do they postpone funerals because of downpours? Each crossroads reminded me of a heated discussion, each café of another time in my life. Camille, Cécile, Pierre and Franck resurfaced in my mind, like those disjointed puppets that come to life with jerky movements, those restless dreams which could be nightmares or joys. Things should have lasted for ever between us, for dozens of years, and resulted in affairs and break-ups, entire lifetimes and children. Instead everything had disappeared like a flash in the pan. Even though I was unsure of his whereabouts, I knew that Franck was in a safe place and that sooner or later my father would tell me where he was hiding. As for Cécile, our story could not just stop there. Then I remembered what both Igor and Sacha, each in their separate way, had kept on saying to me: 'You're alive, don't complain, everything is possible for you.'

We gathered at the funeral parlour on boulevard Edgar-Quinet. All the members of the Club were there for Sacha's burial in the Jewish section. The old-timers and the newcomers. Madeleine came with Jacky and Samy, as well as a few customers. There were also Sacha's neighbours, the concierge, the shopkeepers from rue Monge, the owner of Fotorama and some other people whom I'd not met. I wasn't sure how they had known about it. Even Lognon was there, standing slightly apart as usual. We didn't know whether Big Ears was there on duty or whether he had come because eventually, in spite of himself and in spite of us, he had become a member of this club. They all looked upset. Sacha would never have believed that there would be so many people at his funeral. When it comes to death, people patch up their quarrels because they know that in this respect, they are all equal. Each of us sheltered from the rain as best he could. There was a forest of umbrellas, but they weren't much use. The gusts of wind blew them inside out. The gutters were swollen with raging waters that flooded onto the pavement. We were dripping wet and we squelched about in puddles and mud. The sky was black and we could hear the rumble of thunder. With Igor and Werner at the front, and Imré and Vladimir behind, the coffin was lifted out of the hearse on outstretched arms and placed on the ground. The undertaker's men attached ropes to the handles and lowered it into the grave, which was filled with water. Sacha's coffin disappeared into a muddy morass. Igor came and stood opposite the drowned grave. The wind blew his skullcap off. Werner stood over him with an enormous umbrella. Igor took out a small booklet from his pocket and began to recite a passage in a strange language, stumbling over the words. From all sides, the other members of the Club came and stood in a line and accompanied him.

'It's the Kaddish. The prayer of the dead,' Gregorios whispered to me.

They proceeded in a solemn, slow, staccato tone, stressing each syllable, without bothering about the rain that was drenching them. It was Sacha's atonement. The forgetting of the past, the hatreds and the misdeeds. It was the assurance that they were reunited and that nothing would ever separate them again. They ended simultaneously, took three steps backwards and bowed. Igor was weeping. Still protected by Werner's umbrella, he stood on his own in front of the grave to receive our condolences. Everybody stood in single file, shook hands, embraced him and uttered a kind word. I was the last to go past. I didn't embrace him. We stood looking at one another for a few seconds. I had tears in my eyes. I handed him a bag. Inside it were the three ledgers written in Cyrillic characters and the folder of photographs. He flicked through it. He smiled at me sadly, ran his hand through my hair, and murmured a 'Thank you' that I can still hear. It was the last time that I saw them all together.

After Sacha's burial, the weather turned fine and summer began.

You shall leave everything you love most dearly:
this is the arrow that the bow of exile
shoots first. You are to know the bitter taste
of others' bread, how salt it is, and know
how hard a path it is for one who goes
descending and ascending others' stairs.

DANTE
Paradiso, Canto XVII*

* From *The Divine Comedy of Dante Alighieri: Paradiso*, translated by Allen Mandelbaum